WIDOW

BOOK 3

BLENDED

WIDOW

Copyright ©2014 Erica Chilson

Wicked Reads
PO Box 29
Nelson, PA 16940

www.ericachilson.com/wicked-reads

Printed in the United States of America
First Printing, 2017
ISBN-13: 978-0-9979899-3-9
ISBN-10: 0-9979899-3-9

Titles by Erica Chilson

Mistress and Master of Restraint

Restraint
Unleashed
Dexter
Dalton
Queen Omnibus*
Jaded*
Queened*
Checkmate*
King
Faithless
The Hunter
Integrated

-Coming Soon-
Hero

BLENDED

Good Girl
Wildly Wedded Wife
Widow
Wanton
Warped

RUSTY KNOB

Rusty Knob
Tarnished
Stainless
Polished

Dedication

To all those who have lost their significant others. To my cousin, Wynn, who lost his wife while I was writing this journey.

In memoriam

Sueann Chilson– you will live forever within your daughters.

Clover Webster and Malcolm Mason are trying to overcome insurmountable odds: Lifelong secrets plaguing both families. The failed, bitter romance between their eldest born. The ghosts of their deceased spouses. Most importantly, the addiction that taints everything it touches. Will Malcolm and Clover be able to forge an unbreakable bond in order to traverse this landmine of a blended family?

Widow is book #3 in the Blended Series, the sequel to Good Girl. Not suitable for younger readers: 18 +. Contemporary romance involving sensual, erotic themes. Prepare for a roller coaster ride of emotions: devastating loss, the mourning of death, the renewal of hope, the awakening of love, the unexpected humor of watching one's loved ones fall down, get back up, and dust themselves off. Blended is the chaotic calamity of everyday life.

PROLOGUE

The phone call that started it all

Top Cop: *I'm so glad you answered.*

Lucky Clover: *I called you, remember?*

Top Cop: *Nah, I'm pretty sure I'm the one who dialed the phone.*

Lucky Clover: *Certifiable lunatic. The reason why I called... I need help with Auggie.*

Top Cop: *Color me surprised but equally flattered that you came to me first.*

Lucky Clover: *I didn't. I went to Robin first, but he was no help. Willow is starting at Revamped on Monday, and I worry over the way Auggie looks at her.*

Top Cop: *And just how does Augustus look at your illegitimate daughter?*

Lucky Clover: *Forget I called, and forget my number while you're at it.*

Top Cop: *I'm just teasing you. I only mentioned Willow as your daughter because I love reminding you how I know your deepest secrets. As for your brother, Robin's a jealous little bitch, which is why he's no help.*

Lucky Clover: *You can't just say shit like that without explaining.*

Top Cop: *Yet another thing I love, how you never swear around anyone yet you always do with me. I remember when you were a dirty girly, Silly Rabbit. Don't censor yourself on my account.*

Lucky Clover: *Malcolm, dammit! Just cut the shit. How do I get Auggie to back the hell off my underage daughter? And what the hell did you mean about Robin being jealous?*

Top Cop: *So direct. So blunt. No fun. I hope you can hear me sighing from your end of the line, because it's loud and exhausted sounding on my end.*

Lucky Clover: *I'm going to castrate you with the items on my desk. Right now, all I see is a ballpoint pen, a letter opener, and the ancient stapler. Your choice.*

Top Cop: *I'll go with the letter opener, thank you. I have enough kids, I guess. Did you hear that sigh? Auggie is complicated, and I agree that placing Willow in his care is a horrific idea. With that being said, even I have no idea how to change it. As long as Willow is underage, Auggie will behave because he knows I will arrest him. My favorite thing to do is to arrest child predators. Willow is safe for the next five months. You and I can find a go-around when the time comes.*

Lucky Clover: *You'll help me?*

Top Cop: *Wow! The vulnerable note in your voice really turns me on, Clover. I'm not kidding. Such a strong woman asking for my help.*

Lucky Clover: *I'm reaching for the pen and the stapler, and I'm about to walk down to the Batcave and make a eunuch out of you.*

Top Cop: *Good God, woman! Stop the dirty talk before I get so hard I hump the edge of my desk. The criminals would see it as a weakness. I'd pay to see you stomp down to the basement. I always figured it scared you, like the rest of your kind on the upper floors.*

Lucky Clover: *And just what is my kind?*

Top Cop: *Office workers– administrators. None of you will set foot into my lair.*

Lucky Clover: *Because you're a perverted motherfucker, and you'd probably lock me in a jail cell and terrorize me. Wait! Stop distracting me. Are you gonna help me or not?*

Top Cop: *Silly Rabbit, of course I'll help. I have two grown boys who find your pot-headed, comic-reading, cuss-spewing, child-sized daughter intoxicating.*

Lucky Clover: *Wow, way to compliment one's daughter to her face. So which are we talking about? Your man-whore son or the pot-headed son?*

Top Cop: *Wow, way to compliment one's sons to his face. I think your daughter is a miniature Sam and Clover. She's perfect. So don't make fun of my sons, since they are your first line of defense against Augustus Kline, the predator. Little Willow has always had a massive crush on my man-whore son, and contrary to Kieren's reputation, he's the best kid in the world. As for the* *pot-headed boy, he just got back from the academy, a full-fledged police officer.*

Lucky Clover: *Congratulations on Devon. I bet you can't wait until he's hanging out in the basement with you.*

Top Cop: *As it just so happens, Dev's down here right now, scrubbing all the toilets. The drunk tank's toilet is always the nastiest.*

Lucky Clover: *That's an evil laugh ya got there, Chief Mason. I'm impressed.*

Top Cop: *Why, thank you. My ego just inflated. My advice on your problem. Don't go to Robin– he's Auggie's little bitch first, and your brother second. I'll start sending the boys to Revamped, but it all depends if they can get past the watch dog at the door.*

Lucky Clover: *Watch dog? Huh?*

Top Cop: *Augustus Kline. While he loves my sons as if they were his nephews, I fear his intentions when it comes to Willow. So it will be up to chance if either of the boys makes it inside the store to see your daughter.*

Lucky Clover: *Now, I'm more worried than ever.*

Top Cop: *Shhh… it's okay. It's going to be okay. Willow is safe until her birthday, and after, Auggie won't hurt her. Between Robin, Isis, and the boys, Auggie is going to have a difficult time molding Willow into his dream girl.*

Lucky Clover: *What is this dream girl?*

Top Cop: *Young. Innocent. Impressionable. Moldable and malleable into his ideal of the perfect, subservient woman. Auggie is playing by John Mason rules. Just be thankful he's also playing by the laws of the land as well. Because my mother was only fifteen when my father married her. Lisa, Auggie's mom, was only 18 when Dad dragged her and a three-year-old Auggie home.*

Lucky Clover: *Are you like that, too?*

Top Cop: *Hell, no. And don't sound so petrified. Auggie's known Willow since she was shitting in her drawers. No matter how much he lusts for Willow, she'll forever be that toddler in his eyes. Nothing will overcome that. As for me, I have kids. I wouldn't want to marry one, too. I'd rather have a fully grown woman who can help my ass, not cause me to raise her with my teenagers. My dad was a special breed, and Auggie is using Dad as an excuse to avoid the inevitable.*

Lucky Clover: *And what's that?*

Top Cop: *Being happy. If Auggie would just get over what happened four years ago, and get out of the way of his own life, he and his partners could be very happy.*

Lucky Clover: *Are you speaking in code? I feel like we aren't speaking the same language.*

Top Cop: *No, but you're blind. I wonder if your daughters are as perceptive as you are, Silly Rabbit.*

Lucky Clover: *Sarcasm isn't appreciated. I don't like being made fun of, nor do I appreciate you distracting me from the topic.*

Top Cop: *You're a smart cookie.*

Lucky Clover: *Malcolm?*

Top Cop: *Yes, Lucky Clover?*

Lucky Clover: *Explain! Dammit!*

Top Cop: *Explain what?*

Lucky Clover: *Are you drunk?*

Top Cop: *Nope, nary a drop to drink. I'd hate to have my own men arrest me for public intoxication while sitting in a police station. What would the Mayor think? Tsk. Tsk. I'll let you go. Thank you for answering when I called.*

Lucky Clover: *I called YOU!*

Top Cop: *I will call again. Please answer or I will be forced to start rumors about your wanton ways that will spread like wildfire throughout the entire Courthouse. Imagine the fallout.*

Lucky Clover: *You wouldn't! Don't you dare! I will get my stapler handy. Stop laughing, you lunatic.*

Top Cop: *Be on the lookout for my next communications, Silly Rabbit. I don't like being ignored. You've been warned.*

Lucky Clover: *I don't associate with blackmailers. HEY! You hung up. Bastard.*

CHAPTER ONE

The Widow

As I stand at the front window in my living room, my eyes refuse to blink until they burn. I wait with my son as he waits for his ride to school and I wait for my pesky secret admirer. Feeling disregarded and anxious, this is the only time I can corner my child into spending quality time with me.

"Did you study for your algebra exam?" I ask Seth for the tenth time as he continues to ignore me. His frenetic texting is driving me insane. Seth communicates with Willow on an incessant basis, all the while ignoring me. I love that they are as thick as thieves, but the little shits are up to something. I'm sick to death of being frozen out.

I hate how my son doesn't give me the time of day. I'd ask other moms of teenagers if this is par for the course, but I'm not friends with any. I have no idea if it's normal or not for your children to act like you were put upon this earth just to feed, clothe, and shelter their entitled behinds. They do not see me as a living, breathing human being, who has feelings that can, and always do, get hurt.

"Uh-huh," Seth mumbles while his fingers tap lightning-quick on his cellphone. I'm not even sure Seth heard me until he replies. "I'll ace it... I always do." He rolls his eyes at me like I've lost my ever-loving mind. My son is obsessed with math and science, so he can't figure out why I'd worry that he wouldn't study for algebra. "Why do you keep looking out the window?"

Seth only sounds mildly curious because he's trying to catch me in a lie. He knows damned well I can't honestly answer that question. If I lie, I prove him right about my horrible mother status. If I tell the truth, it ruins a year's worth of effort I've put into Malcolm Mason. Who do you lie to? The little prick, or the big pain in the ass? One I expect to hurt, use, and disrespect me; the other should never want to harm their mother in any fashion.

So I lie, because Seth should respect me by not trying to trap me in the first place. I am the adult. Seth is the child. I will never allow him to dictate how I should live my life.

"I'm just waiting for Kieren to pick you up," I deny poorly. I fight my natural instinct to look away from the front window out of a sick sense of guilt. I loathe being in a '*damned if you do, damned if you don't*' situation. Since this is a constant state of being for me, I should be used to the stress of it by now. Sadly, I am not.

My box of baked goods is still there– my version of a rabbit snare. But I'm pretty sure I'm the defenseless bunny in this scenario. Two dozen sour cream donuts, a cherry danish, a chocolate layer cake, and four dozen sugar cookies rest on my porch. My not-so secret admirer sent me two sets of demands last night: one set from him, and one set from one or more of the scheming children. I yawn hugely as I think about how late I had to stay up to accommodate the requests. I curse within my mind at how quickly these demands are draining my dwindling bank account. Sometimes– at all times –I wish I had some help... with everything.

"Sure, you are," Seth grumbles, sounding dubious, "waiting on Ren." Seth dismisses me with his cold indifference more so than his words. "Twin!" he shouts. Voice husky, smoky–already reaching the cadence of his dead father's voice at the tender age of fourteen. Seth has also perfected the mien of his father: unresponsive, unemotional. Just as Sam always was, Seth is indifferent to me when the world receives his affectionate warmth and attention. Impatience finally leaking through, he shouts at his sister again. "Ren will be here any minute. Gitcha ass down here."

"Don't be vulgar," I chastise, and receive another disrespectful eye roll in response. I try my best to teach my family not to be heathens, how to behave in public, and how not to embarrass oneself. But it's an uphill battle.

My parents are pot-headed tree-huggers, who are a foot away from a retirement home if they don't behave. Rob is a sneaky, snarky, smutty bastard. Somehow my amazing aunt and uncle reared an adulteress with the self-esteem of dog shit. Willow acts like a pissed off drunken pirate, and is teaching Violet the same stilted vocabulary and dirty fighting style. My sweet, caring little guy has turned into the world's biggest prick, but only to me. Everyone else gets the chipmunk-cheeked, good kid.

Is it really too much to ask for them to act civilized?

"Ass-lapper. Shitdick. Sonofabitch. Motherfucker. Cunt-sniffer. Twat-tickler. Cockgobbler. Carpet-muncher. Cumdumpster." Seth succinctly utters, baiting me– challenging me. His brown eyes glow with a bitterness I cannot fathom. I ignore his litany, knowing if I say a word, this will go on forever and a day.

"Pole-shiner. Spawn-breeder. Leg-spreader. Thundercunt–"

Yes, it most certainly is too much to ask for civilized, respectful behavior. Seth needs a father to kick his ass for the disrespect. If Sam were alive today, the pair of them would most likely gang up on me. No doubt they would celebrate Seth's behavior as independence, not as the disgusting display that it is. Sam wouldn't have dared to speak to his mother in this fashion. Margaret 'Peggy' Webster would have had Sam's nuts mounted above the mantel.

I've been in a *'lose-lose'* situation since I was sixteen. The boy is bigger than me now, and he really doesn't care if he upsets me or not. I'm just the person who gives Seth whatever he wants, whenever he wants it.

No respect.

No consequences.

It's not like I can hit Seth, and there is nothing to take away. Other than forcing Seth to spend time with me, which would be a dual-punishment in his current antagonistic mood, I have no recourse for this abhorrent behavior. I would be the bad guy since Seth doesn't behave as such around anyone else. Only when we are alone does the prick break the surface. If I grounded him from anything other than sustenance, sleep, homework, chores, and hygiene, I'd look like the world's biggest bitch of a mother. Another *'lose-lose'*, *'damned if you do, damned if you don't'* situation that is inescapable.

I fear there is no love for me on Seth's part as well.

I'm invisible. Just as Sam wanted. I can almost feel my dead husband gloating from Hell.

"Way to be derogatory to women in every single one of your curses, you heathen," I grumble, playing off the hurt as if it doesn't affect me. I give a dramatic eye roll of my own, refusing to take my child's bait. "I can drive you to school. It's on my way to work," I offer helpfully, wanting a few minutes with my kids where they can't get away from me, trapped in a moving car where they're forced to talk to me.

It didn't take me long to figure out why my kids were hanging around the Masons, especially with my secret admirer stalking me. Since the Mason kids have entered our orbit, I've had no one-on-one time with my children. Our cooking lessons are the only quality time we spend together, and the Mason kids are the ones who act appreciative and happy to be around me. The earth turning on its axis, Violet is being polite while Seth is turning into the world's largest prick. The drastic change makes my brain hurt just thinking about it.

"I'm ready," Violet chirps happily, bouncing into the room. Happy is not in my daughter's vocabulary. Something is up. My self-conscious need for perfection has led Violet to act like a stick is firmly lodged far up her ass. A stick she inherited from me.

Exasperated, Seth releases an impatient sigh. "It's just easier, Mom. Ren is already taking Rae and West to school. We were on the way," Seth supplies logically as he grabs for his messenger bag.

Feeling lonely, I'll try anything for a few extra minutes of my children's time. "I–"

"You have enough to do, don't worry about us getting to school," Violet says sweetly, and my suspicions rise. I narrow my eyes, but something out of the corner of my eye catches my attention, or a lack of something. My secret admirer managed to take the huge box of baked goods off of my porch without me noticing. How the hell does he do it? How the hell do his minions do it undetected? Minions who pull up to the curb in Kieren Mason's piece of shit pickup truck. No doubt their breakfast will include donuts, chocolate cake, danish, and sugar cookies.

"Fuck," I hiss in awe, receiving identical looks of disbelief from Seth and Violet. I never swear out loud, but I swear worse than Willow inside my own mind. "Um… nothing. Have a great day at school today," I say brightly.

"Yeah," Seth mutters, knowing I'm full of shit. "Later," is his emotionless goodbye, and Violet mumbles the same. It hurts my heart that my children won't touch me out of affection– ever. I haven't had a hug in years, just as Sam wanted it.

I watch my children engage the Masons, hugging and giggling as they pile into Kieren's beat-up pickup truck. With delighted eagerness, Willow envelops Seth so they can all fit into the cab. My twins act like kids around their friends and big sister, chatting animatedly and smiling.

The ease, the connection, which they have with the Masons, hurts more than their lack of hugs. Do my children truly see me as a food source and money distributor, and little else? Do my children think I'm that terrible of a person, one they can't be themselves around? I get sullen and dick, while the world gets sunny and affectionate… and Willow, it's a good day if I can get her to grunt in my direction. Usually it's a bad day, where she screams a string of expletive words that makes me feel small and worthless and guilty.

Failure thrumming in my veins, I grab my keys. I make my way to my parents' house to begin my daily routine. Wake and feed the kids, call the Spook House and make sure Willow is still breathing, check in on my parents for the same reason and make sure they won't harm themselves while I'm at work. Then I work a ten-hour day, only to come home to take care of all the things that people count on their mate to lessen the burden.

I am not a singular person with emotions and needs. I was placed on this earth for the sole purpose of taking care of my children and parents. I am male and female. I am husband and wife. I am mother and father. I am daughter, sister, and parent. I am a walking banker, maid, chef, handyman, servant, nurse, therapist, and teacher… and I do it all alone.

I am the Widow.

CHAPTER TWO

The Widow

Since my birth, my life has been filled with responsibility. When I was six years old, Robin was born. My mother always had her head in the clouds while my father worked day and night to keep a roof over our heads and food in our bellies. I love my parents more than life itself, but even as a child, I knew it would be my role to keep everyone breathing.

I'm probably the only person in recent history who had to strive for perfection in order to rebel against their family. The Prynnes thrive on chaos and disorder– defiance and destruction. Drink, smoke, get high, talk back to your elders: they see it as an act of independence, of finding oneself. You must make a stand for your beliefs. Pacifism in the extreme. If your ass lands in jail over the rebellion, the more respect my parents will bestow upon you. Tenets of Dave and Mary Prynne: civil disobedience, law breaking, and spitting in the face of the '*man*'. My father wouldn't pay his taxes if it wasn't for the paper trail. But he'd give the shirt off his back to someone in true need while my mother opened her arms to lend them comfort.

I understand why my parents think as they do. But I cannot respect their stance after thirty-five years of coming in last to every single one of their whims, and not one of them was ever fruitful. Picketing outside of City Hall because a new business was erected, a business that added fifty new jobs to our community, helped no one. All the while Dave and Mary shouted their stance, their eight-year-old daughter was at home taking care of her two-year-old baby brother (illegal and unsafe, but nothing legal is ever worth it in the eyes of my parents).

Their frivolity never brought about true change. All it did was build a wall of resentment over the burden that was placed on my shoulders since birth. That picketed business is still going strong twenty-seven years later, now employing several hundred Fairport residents and sustaining hundreds more.

Pushing your responsibilities to the wayside in order to protest an imagined injustice just makes you irresponsible. Take care of your own shit first, and then, and only then, do you help others. My parents bore me and Robin, so our welfare should have come first and foremost to everyone's but their own.

I am conservative for survival, yet rebellious in nature. I fight my true self every moment of the day. I hunger to run free, enjoy the sweet release of acting without consequence. But it's not a pleasure I can afford. My family's survival balances on my fierce control. If I let go, our lives could collapse– the domino effect.

I am the parent. The voice of reason. The one who takes responsibility when everything falls to shit because Dave and Mary join a new cause. I've never had the pleasure of doing what I want at the expense of others. My parents' selfishness is hidden by the façade of charity, while my selflessness is overshadowed by my bitter resentment.

Never lighting on one core belief, how much do you believe in a cause if any ol' cause will do? That isn't conviction– it's being lost and looking for a place to belong. Their independence, rebellion, just shows a lack of direction, a mindlessness that changes nothing and seals them into dependence. They are just another sheep hiding behind their big mouths as they challenge the wolf.

I was born to be the wolf. A person who knows what they want, is willing to do whatever it takes to obtain it and keep it, and will never be distracted from her true course, even if it's not the path she longs to take.

My words to Willow echo in my mind. Words I said to snap her out of the sheep mentality. My daughter needs to find her own path, take it, and never compromise. Willow needs to have the life I was denied.

"You have the freedom to be who you should be, not some man's ego boost, not your children's lifeline, not your parents' keeper. You have the freedom to work anywhere you dream, date whomever you wish, experience anything you desire. I'm locked in now, Willow. T. R. A. P. P. E. D."

"You don't like being a mother?"

"Being a mother is who I was meant to be, Willow. I don't regret a second of being a mother. My point is, that until you become a mother or take over the responsibilities of your family, you're free. You have no debt: financial, familial, or emotional."

"Willow," I say sharply to gain her attention. "Don't shit on the freedom I'm giving you."

I've been entrapped since birth. I've never known a time where I didn't pay the debt my parents accrued, and it's suffocating. Just once, I want to come first in someone's life, even in my own. I want the liberty to fall and know someone will catch me before I land.

I hate walking into my parents' house every morning. It wasn't as petrifying when Willow still lived here. I knew she'd catch them in the act before they caused bodily harm. Since Willow moved to the Spook House, I've had to check on them constantly or I'd worry myself into an early grave. One of my biggest fears is walking into the house to find one, or both of them, sprawled on the floor dead. Dead from a circumstance I could have mitigated, had I caught it in time.

Such as the situation I walk in on right now.

Exasperated, "C'mon, Mom," I mutter in disgust as I enter her kitchen. As usual, I find my mother lost inside her own head, completely oblivious to the alarm she elicits in me. The gas flame from the burner licks inches above the stovetop, without a pan or kettle to dampen the hazard. Panic overcomes me as the twang of natural gas ruffles my nose.

I charge across the kitchen floor to fix the situation before it turns into a disaster of epic proportions. "You have the burner on. You're going to burn the house down one of these days, and the rest of the block with it." Sighing deeply, I twist the stove knob until the gas flame extinguishes. "Your grandchildren could be injured," I scold in a voice gone tight with control. "Or me. Lord knows how you'd all function without me doing your jobs."

Ridicule flows right over Mom's head. "Do you want some tea?" Mary Prynne asks brightly, as if she is one of the Sun's rays. Mom flashes me a smile that would melt the coldest of hearts, but it does nothing to improve my mood. I don't find her forgetfulness and irresponsibility cute. Cute is not the word that should ever describe a sixty-eight-year-old mother and grandmother. At least not the description I could swallow.

After thirty-five years of being a stifling, controlling bitch, I love my mother enough not to enable her behavior– her life and the lives of others are at stake.

Mom hops up from her seat at the country-style breakfast table. She makes a fast move to the tea kettle. I could've sworn I tossed the kettle last time I found her trying to make '*tea*'. Mom always does all the steps, but she never completes any task. Don't ask how many times I've walked into the kitchen and found the tap water running in the sink, Mom nowhere in sight. She always forgets what she's doing, distracted by a new task. Like now, she's doing a crossword puzzle instead of making '*tea*', where she forgot to put the kettle on the burner, after she lit it.

"Mother," I say in warning as I yank the tea kettle from her grasp, noting there isn't even any water in it. "I bought you the water cooler, remember?"

Confused, Mom bites her lower lip. The movement is young, innocent– cute. Blonde hair gone gray, vibrant blue eyes still youthful, my mother's childlike personality has kept her heartbreakingly beautiful. "But I didn't want iced tea," she grumbles, sounding like a petulant child. "It's breakfast. I wanted hot tea."

For the billionth time, as I do with everything I show my parents, I pull her toward the water cooler for instructional purposes. "Gray is room temperature. Blue is cold water. Red is **HOT** water. Just put your teabag in your mug, and then put it right here," I say with the patience of a saint, demonstrating the act. "Like magic, instant tea, and the house stays intact."

"There is no way that can boil water," my mother says in disbelief, and a moment later her fingertip is disappearing inside her cup. With a startled cry, I yank the teacup away from her, sloshing it on my blouse in the process. "You're right," Mom slurs from around sucking her burnt fingertip.

"We can't keep going on like this, Mom," I warn, scared to death on how to proceed. I'm not sure if it's the fifty years of smoking weed, her naturally immature, irresponsible personality, or early onset Alzheimer's. I fear for my own future. A future where my children leave the nest to experience lives of their own, where I end up back with my parents, parenting as I have since I was a child. Not one day of my life has been my own, and the day I move back in with my parents is the day any hope of ever truly living is gone. I exist so others may be free.

"Oh, for fuck's sake, Clover," Mom growls at me, sounding just like Violet when she's angry. The women in my family swear worse than the males. "I've been making tea for seventy years."

"Huh?" I grunt, thoroughly impressed. "I wonder if Grandma knew you were making tea way before you were a twinkle in Grandpa's eye, considering you're only sixty-eight." I drop the argument before it starts. It's not like we haven't had it for years on end. The woman could argue the color of the sky above and the grass below. When Mom knows she's wrong, she tunes me out.

"I'm not addled. I've been doing Sudoku, ya know?" Mom fingers the nearly finished book of logic puzzles that are resting next to her partially filled in crossword. "Strengthens the mind. I saw it on The Doctors."

"It only counts if they are correct. Just filling in the squares with any ol' number doesn't make it right," I grumble underneath my breath. "Never mind. Where's Dad?"

"Making Mr. Dobson's cabinetry, out in the garage," she says guilelessly, as if this isn't disastrous news.

"Christ," I hiss, bolting toward the backdoor. "I can't leave you guys alone for a second. Dad will cut a finger off... or a goddamned hand."

"Clover," my mother sighs out my name. Now she's as exasperated with me as I am with her. "Your father has been making cabinets for over sixty years."

"Yeah," I drawl out. "Somehow I doubt he was using a jointer at age ten, but at least you didn't date him to pre-womb carpentry like you did with your tea steeping."

"Well, Dave was," Mom says defiantly. Defiance is the one trait we all possess, and we all look just alike when it flashes across our faces. "The Prynnes come from a long line of carpenters.... All the way back to Jesus Christ, I suspect."

"Oh. My. God." I shake my head, at a complete and total loss. "I'm going to be late for work. I'd tell you not to burn the house down in my absence, but our almighty ancestor can keep watch over you," I say sarcastically.

I grab the tea kettle on my way out.

Panting with fury, I rush from the house, tea kettle clasped to my chest. I leave my father to his crafting. With Dad, I know he's competent enough to perform his tasks. The man still puts in a sixty-hour work week, leading Prynne Renovations in Sam's absence. Sometimes my fears make me coddle my parents as if they were small children. I know I suffocate them as much as their lack of responsibility always suffocated me.

My parents aren't without responsibility. Five years ago, my father's short-lived retirement ended when Sam passed. Dave

Prynne stepped back into his old shoes and kept his business afloat.

Living on a limited income of barely above minimum wage with a small stipend from Sam's social security, I scarcely make ends meet. I only let go of my pride when one of the kids need something I can't provide. Prynne Renovations fed me as a child, housed, fed, and clothed my oldest child from birth, provided my husband's salary that put a roof over our heads and food in our cupboards, and now gives my children the creature comforts I couldn't provide otherwise. I live the life of a working widow of two teenagers. My pride chokes me with the knowledge that I couldn't pay Willow's way, and now I can't pay the twins' way either.

My true nature peeks out from behind my façade of perfection as I throw a mini-temper tantrum out on the sidewalk between our side-by-side homes. Sometimes a girl just has to vent.

I breathe out, "Fuuuck..." Stalking to the edge of the sidewalk, I lift the lid on the garbage can, and then smash the tea kettle onto a cardboard pizza box. A grotesque scent wafts up, smelling of onion peels, rotten fish, and sauerkraut. Close to retching, I string together a litany of curses that would even make Seth-the-profane blush.

I shut the lid with force, praying that this time the tea kettle stays where I placed it. Trash collectors will be by in the next half hour, and the tea kettle will make its way to the landfill. That is, if Mary Prynne doesn't dumpster-dive in the meantime. I wouldn't put it past Mom. She's probably watching me from the kitchen window, waiting for me to drive off to work, ready to commit an act of defiance– thieving her property back. She'll most likely try to make tea, without washing the kettle first, or putting water in it, or making sure the stove burner actually lights. Then she will blow the entire block sky-high, or at the very least, contract an infection from the filth.

Entering panic-mode, I contemplate being late for work. I could sit in my car, waiting for the trash collectors, just to be certain no foul play will befall my mother.

"What'd that tea kettle ever do to you?" comes a voice thick with judgment, causing the fine hairs on the nape of my neck to rise in alarm.

"Mrs. Dobson," I say with a smile as I turn to face the woman whose occupation is gossip and going to church– she makes it an art form by combining the two activities. Feeling anxious under the fifty-something-year-old woman's hawk-like gaze, I rub my palms on my skirt. I hastily rumble out a reply without taking a breath. "They don't make tea kettles like they used to. The bottom was rusting on the inside. Metal isn't a good additive to Earl Gray." I give a little laugh at my inane joke, and Mrs. Dobson doesn't join me. She just stares at me like I've grown a second head, and it's speaking in tongues.

"Are you here to check out Dad's progress on your new cabinets? How exciting," I say with false enthusiasm.

I've acted my way through life, no sense in showing how I really feel now. The world would burn to ash if I let my true emotions out to play. Mrs. Dobson has made my life a living hell, trying to ferret out the truth of Willow's birth (which she damn well knows, but wants the world to know too). The woman would be ash before anyone else. Strike that. She would be a close second after my mother-in-law, Margaret Webster. Yes, the women are the best of friends, and their houses mirror my parents' and mine across the street. There is nowhere to go to escape their scrutinizing gaze. They spend their lives on their porches, investigating every breath I take.

Welcome to the Clover Webster show!

"Your father is an incredible man, skilled, just as your brother is," Mrs. Dobson says from between her tightly drawn, thin lips. The backhanded compliment isn't lost on me. Yes, my father is a striking man, a man who only gets better looking with age, and Robin is following in his handsome footsteps. But that isn't what Mrs. Dobson meant. She loves to rub it in that she finds me failing, that Rob is the perfect son. A perfect son just because he was born and has done nothing to earn that respect, while the daughter lives and breathes for her family.

When it comes to women like Pat Dobson and Margaret "Peggy" Webster, I could tear my still-beating heart from my chest and hand it to them, and it would never be good enough because I don't have a dick. Daughters were born to serve, while sons were born to be worshiped. Any woman who has the balls to nab a man with this type of mother should be sainted. There is a sick obsession, possession, territorialism with women like this, as if you are stealing their '*man*' out from under them. I, on the other hand, will praise the girl who captures my son's interests and takes the budding prick off my hands. My husband was born from Peggy, raised by Peggy, and treated me with the same disdain as Peggy.

Fuck you very much, Peggy.

I raise my head and glimpse the woman sitting on her porch, watching us. I give a little wave and a secretive smile, and the expression that flashes over Peggy's face screams that my negative thoughts were transparent.

"Don't let Mr. Dobson hear ya saying that about my dad," I tease, burying the bitter resentment into the center of my chest, where my cold heart lies. I feign ignorance of Mrs. Dobson's insults, because it always rubs her the wrong way. She is defeated because she can't say outright that she finds me as worthless as dog shit. It's a delicate game we ladies play. A game my dead husband taught me well. A game I may never win, but one I will survive.

"You should pay closer attention to your children, Clover. Willow is gallivanting around Fairport, no doubt bedding both older Mason brothers. The twins are glued to the youngest Masons, being influenced negatively. Robin has been shacking up with that nightclub hussy for nearly a decade. It's a woman's place to make their family behave. Peggy is beside herself, fearing for her grandchildren…"

I stop listening to Mrs. Dobson as she lectures me on the role a woman should play in her family's lives. Every word is thickly laced with judgment and skewed with Peggy's perception.

I bite my tongue against the '*fuck you*' that threatens to erupt. Instead I say, "The Masons are a good family. Those kids are well-behaved, hard-working, and delightful. Malcolm and Devon are police officers for heaven's sake, and Kieren is one of the most responsible men I've ever met, even at only nineteen." I sound defensive, volatile. The real Clover is threatening to erupt.

"Police officer or not, Devon Mason is a philandering drug user. I know with Mary's '*hobby*', you don't find drugs an issue, and since Devon bedded both Willow and Essie, he's keeping it in the Prynne family. But Peggy is scared over the way this could influence her grandchildren."

"Then Peggy can take it up with me herself," I snarl. "Her grandchildren are *my* children," I stress fiercely, leaning toward the older woman. She's not intimidated in the least by my size, anger, or glare. Mrs. Dobson and my mother-in-law have been tag-teaming me since I was sixteen years old.

"Clover," Pat gears up to tear me a new asshole, but I'm saved from whatever hate-filled words the woman was going to spew and my resulting vicious reaction. A song sings from the cellphone hidden in the pocket of my linen jacket. *Hey Brother* by *Avicii*, signals that Robin needs my attention.

"Have a nice day, Mrs. Dobson," I say in dismissal as I fish my cell phone from my jacket and walk toward the driver side of my car. Pat's pissed off sputtering over how rude cellphones are makes me grin.

"Ya lazy fuck," I say in greeting as I slide into the driver's seat of my fifteen-year-old *Honda*. I don't shield myself around Robin. There's no hiding from the man you've practically raised. Robin knows my strengths, weaknesses, and faults. He's been there when I succeeded and when I failed miserably. I don't have to feign perfection around the kid who watched me fall to my ass time and time again. Never asking Rob for a hand up, he would grin down at me while I struggled to stand– metaphorically and physically speaking.

Exhausted, I close my eyes and whisper the truth that I haven't wanted to voice out loud. "We need to do something about Mom before she burns the neighborhood down, and by burn, I'm not talking about getting high with the Brogowski sisters."

Robin's laughter vibrates my eardrum, causing me to shiver from the happy sound. "Ah, Clover, you're so pleasant first thing in the morning. I am *not* lazy." I can practically hear him pouting.

"You've never worked a day in your life, pissy pants," I tease but there is an underlying resentment. "Not once did you find your way to a job site. Every one of us has shoveled debris into the dump truck but you. Now you sleep all day or paint, and then follow Cruella around all night. That's not working, little brother."

"You don't pay my bills, so why do you care?" Robin bites out, pissed. I have a way with getting underneath people's skin, like a disease they can't fight off. I'm not well liked because I tend to cause people to see their own failings.

"I don't care as long as you're healthy and happy and well taken care of. But I do give a shit about the fact that you have more than enough free time to do absolutely nothing, yet you never take care of your parents." I sigh, resting the crown of my head against the back of my car seat.

I can feel Mrs. Dobson's and Peggy's eyes burning a hole through me from their position on my mother-in-law's porch. I start the ignition, and then drive down the road, only to pull over two blocks later. Mustn't drive while talking on the cellphone.

"Clover? You still there?" Robin's voice trills from the phone clutched against my ear.

"Yeah," I whisper out. "I can't do this anymore, Robin. It's draining me dry. Mom is getting worse because Willow isn't in the house with her. Violet is acting strange now that she knows the truth. Seth has turned into a misogynistic prick overnight. The crones are on my ass more so than ever. My bills are due but my bank account is empty. My secret admirer is making me cook and bake until two in the morning with his demands. He's goading Mayor Ross into firing me, and you know he'll do it, too. I need my job so I can afford to raise my kids and pay for my ridiculously high grocery bills, thanks to the astronomical amount of baking supplies I need. I just…" I take a deep breath.

"Clover," Robin says my name softly. "I've always been here for you, but you never take my help. I'm your little brother, remember? You told me that you were supposed to slay my dragons, not the other way around. I offered you a lot of money after Sam's death and you slapped me."

"This isn't about money, Rob," I breathe out in despair because no one understands. "I need… I need some support, some help. I need a breather. I need five minutes to myself."

"I will do my part, but you are creating your own drama, causing everything else to feel more desperate. Just swallow your pride and tell Willow the truth, Clover. Violet already knows. Essie is asking around, has been for years. The only one who is in denial, and it has to be subconscious because she's not a fool, is Willow. Your kids would help you with anything if they didn't feel like you were lying to them. Word of advice: your son hates your guts right now because he knows the truth about Willow."

"How?" my voice breaks as tears roll slowly down my cheeks. I'm going to be late to work, just when I need the money more than ever. I brush the tears away with the cuff of my sleeve, feeling more alone than ever.

"Seth is like a valve. If Willow or Violet knows anything, it flows directly into Seth. Do you honestly think Violet wouldn't tell him? Seriously, Clover?"

Frightened, I ask, "Then why doesn't Willow know?"

"Seth is a valve, remember? He collects the information and shuts the flow down. He talks to me, Clover. Seth talks to me," Rob admits softly, fearing it will break my heart. "Violet told him immediately. Seth is hurt because you told Violet and not him. He's angry that you have kept this from them for fourteen years. I know why you have, and I understand it and agree with you. But to Seth, Willow is his world. Until Willow knows the truth, Seth is going to freeze your ass out, and Willow's reaction will influence Seth's behavior. You better hope your daughter can get over this or you'll lose your son, too."

"Great," I mutter hopelessly. "It's Willow. She's going to murder me. If Seth turns into Sam on my ass, I don't think I can survive the fallout. Violet will follow their lead, and..." I can't even voice the horrific thoughts that inundate me.

"Kids are resilient. They'll get over it– eventually." After a heavy pause, Rob continues speaking. "I don't know what was going on in your marriage, but that's the first time I've ever heard you say something that was tinged with anger against Sam. I thought you'd want Seth to be more like his father. Sam was a good guy." Rob sounds so hurt and confused that I just play it off.

"I don't know what I was thinking," I mutter. "Sam was kind, caring, the world's best dad and son. He was faithful, spiritual, and honorable."... *"to everyone but me,"* I think to myself.

No one ever speaks ill of the dead. The truth is always hidden by grief. We sanctify them as if they were never human. All human beings have faults, none are perfect creatures. Sam was perfect, inside and out, in life and in death. The man could walk on water if you asked any person who came in direct contact with him, and even those who never met him. But the man I knew in private was not the man he projected. Was the real Sam the one everyone knew? Or was the flawed Sam, the one only I knew, and always behind closed doors, the real Sam? Quick to laugh and lend a helping hand, he drew the masses in like moths to flame. Yet he wouldn't even spit on me if I was dehydrated. Even years later, I wonder if Sam was just a snake charmer only I could see. Or was there something about me that he hated so much that I turned him into someone I despised?

"Clover?" Lost in thought, my brother tries to draw me back to the present.

"It's time," I mutter. "Give me a few weeks and I will tell Willow the truth. I've been trying for the past few months. The truth just chokes me until I can barely speak."

The truth is, how do you tell the entire truth when it's tied to something you vowed never to speak? To tell Willow why I gave her up for adoption is to tell my children their father was a worthless sonofabitch who loathed me. I can't burden my children with the knowledge that their parents hated one another. My children were made up of two halves of the whole, where their parents hated their other half. I would never want my children to be ashamed of who and what they are, nor do I want them to fear that I don't love them, even the parts that remind me of their father.

Never.

I've spun an alternate reality in the saga of Sampson and Clover Webster, just so I could drag one foot in front of the other and survive. A story where we were fated, soul mates. A story of a perfect life with two kids, a family business, a home of our own, and true happiness. The American Dream. A story everyone believes but me. Two can keep a secret if one of them is dead...

Reality: my husband charmed me, lured me in and trapped me, and burned me when I finally saw through his ruse. A life where I could protest and scream, *"No, Sam is a false prophet,"* and no one would ever believe me.

"How's Cruella?" I ask to change the subject.

"Clover," Robin draws out, exasperated. "Between you and your oldest spawn– Willow calls Isis Elvira. What is it about you guys and the evil female nicknames? Isis is the epitome of her namesake," he says in a voice filled with reverence.

"Jesus," I hiss, surprised. "You've got it bad, little brother." I snort, thankful that I'll never do the love bullshit again. Love is for masochists. I don't like pain so I'll avoid it at all costs. "So when is the wedding? Time to stop being lazy and learn what it's really like. How much fun it is to wash someone's clothing, do their dishes, cook their food, pay their bills, raise their kids, put up with all their bullshit, and listen to their lame stories, all the while you want to stab yourself with a fork."

"Very funny." Robin releases a humorless laugh. "Since when are you a commitment-phobe? I thought it was just grief keeping you away from the opposite sex."

"I'm not scared of commitment," I answer honestly. "Didn't you just hear that list? That's the short list, too. It gets worse...

much, much worse. I'm not avoiding commitment. That is a lot of work, and I don't have the time for it. No orgasm is worth all that drama– no way, no how. Marriage sounds like you're splitting your workload in half, when in reality you are gaining another set of problems. It's even more fun when your other half shirks their responsibilities because he has to work... like you don't work. Like being a housewife, mother, daughter, sister, and employee is just sitting on your ass, so you should have the time and desire to wait on your husband. A man wants you to put his needs first, while you both put yours dead last."

"You sound bitter," Robin says, sounding surprised. "I thought you loved your life?"

"I have less work to do now that I'm alone than I did when Sam was alive. That should be example enough of how much marriage fucking sucks. Either way, it all fell to me. I'm never going down that road again. As I said a few minutes ago, I'm at my breaking point. What is there to love about my life? I have no life. I never have."

"Seriously, are you all right?"

"No," I snap out. "I don't want money to mask the problems because it's the easy way out for you. I want some fucking help. Check in on our parents twice a day for me, or at least call the house. During your heart-to-hearts, tell your nephew to stop acting like a prick. Tell Seth that no matter what, he shouldn't treat his mother like shit, especially when she is working her ass off to feed and house the selfish little bastard. Spend some time with Violet– she thinks you don't like her. Tell Papa Bear and his cubs to stop emptying my cupboards before they are bare–"

"Papa Bear?" Robin pipes in, ignoring every word of my tirade before that. "You figured it out?" He sounds giddy while I'm pouring my heart out, begging him for some relief.

"No comment," I bite out. "Can you do that?"

"Do what?"

"ROBIN!" I scream shrilly in the confines of my car, stinging my eardrums.

"I'm fucking with ya, Clover," he says absently, like he's thinking of something else or only half-listening to me. I hear the murmur of a female voice in the background, probably Cruella/Elvira. "Okay. How's he holding up?" Pause. "Yeah, don't worry, Ice. I'll fix it."

Red washes over my vision. My brother won't help me after twenty-eight years of licking his ass clean, but he's playing knight in shining armor for Isis Mason. Long seconds later, where I sit and seethe, I realize I'm behaving like Mrs. Dobson and my mother-in-law. Jealousy. Fury. My brother is making a life with a woman, giving her his all, giving her the life my husband failed to give me, while taking his help away from me. That is how those mothers feel. Their husbands treated them like crap, and their only help was from their son. Here comes this piece of ass, who sucks all the attention away from you, and it causes hatred to bloom. Too bad in my case, Sam didn't ever shower me with help and attention while he continued to give his mother his all. Still, I can empathize, creepy or not. It doesn't change anything. I still want to tear Robin's nutsack from his lazy body.

"I have some bad news, Clover. It's why I called in the first place, but I wasn't sure how to approach it. Isis is getting impatient with me, knowing that you can help."

"Great," I drawl, furious. "Sure, why not? I'll help your little woman out. I've got nothing better to do. After all, I live a life of leisure."

"I'd say sarcasm doesn't become you, but you invented it, after all," Robin counters. "One of the cubs' true colors finally exploded. The last time anyone saw Devon was last night. He was high out of his mind on some strong shit. He was yanking food out of the refrigerator, and since it wasn't what he was craving, he would smash the container on their kitchen floor."

"Malcolm should have detained Devon and had him arrested," I say, sounding bitter. Mrs. Dobson was correct. Devon was exposing my children to unacceptable shit. I'm a horrible parent.

"Malcolm was at work. Ren had to subdue Dev, which led to an argument where Devon ran off and didn't come back. So, as you can see, I haven't been lying on my ass, drawing pretty pictures of unicorns and puppy dog tails. I've been trying to keep Auggie and Isis from losing their shit. Malcolm is beside himself but in family management mode. Ren is distraught, unmanageable, refusing any help while he searches for his brother because he thinks it's his fault. The kids are just pretending it's an ordinary day, going to school and hanging out with the twins."

"I get it," I gasp out. "My problems aren't important." I mean it. No sarcasm to be heard.

I do feel a healthy dose of heartache, both for the Mason family, and the fact that whatever I'm going through gets reduced to nothing. Because, somewhere, someone, is having a breakdown of their own. Just like when my team won first place in all of New England for Mathletes but my parents didn't show because they had to protest the fair treatment of turkeys in the processing plant. They still ate turkey every Thanksgiving and Christmas and on their deli sandwiches, so what good was any of that? They gave me life, but couldn't support my endeavors. We could never celebrate my achievements because it would hurt the feelings of the children who didn't place first, rendering all my hard work to dust. No kid likes a tree planted in their honor for their tenth birthday. Just like no grown woman likes to hear, *"I'm sorry, Clover. I know you are stressed out, but so is everyone else."*

I am not a selfish human being. On the list of who comes first, I place myself dead last. A vital part of me who sees anyone in pain immediately jumps to their rescue. While my parents worry about the problems of the world, and Robin obsesses over anything Mason, I am left to pick up the pieces. Now I find myself wanting to rail against my brother, scream about how when I told him our mother almost burnt the house down around herself, he was more worried about a family who has rallied together and is supporting themselves, how my children have ran to offer their aid as well. No one is in eminent danger, not like they are at the Prynne house.

"What can I do?" flows from my mouth without thought, because I am my parents' daughter. The desire to help is too powerful. "Ask Isis if she wants me to take the kids for a few days while they figure out how to proceed with Devon. It's the end of the school year, finals are coming up. They have to keep to their routines."

"After what just happened, Ren isn't going to let the kids out of sight." Feminine laughter flows from the other end of the phone, and in a heartbeat I understand why Robin is so taken with Isis. The woman bleeds sexuality.

"My bad," Rob laughs out. "There is a two hour time period where Ren runs off to parts unknown every night." Rob's warm laughter flows through the phone. "Unknown to anyone but me, that is. Isis will stay with the kids while Ren searches for Devon and gets his nightly Willow fix. So all's good at the Mason house. Malcolm contacted a residential rehab facility in Arizona. A substance abuse program that deals with past traumas that caused PTSD, where the victims took to drugs, alcohol, and destructive behavior as their cure. When they finally catch Devon, he will be there for at least sixty days." Sobering up, Rob rocks my world. "He needs you, Clover. He needs you."

CHAPTER THREE

The Widower

"I won't be home very early tonight, Kieren. Sorry about that," I mumble, sounding exhausted. I won't be working tonight. Chief Mason will not be the one going from lowlife to lowlife, interrogating (beating) the whereabouts of my eldest son from their sniveling mouths. Malcolm Mason, Devon's father, will be the one laying down the law.

I gaze around our breakfast table to my struggling children, struggling to maintain their emotional calm, and I see my father gazing back at me from their cold, dark blue eyes.

The John Mason rules for dealing with unfortunate events: Pretend until it becomes reality. Don't dwell on the past, because it only exacerbates the problem. Be proactive and move on. When shit happens out of your control, don't blame yourself or feel shame. Fix it, move on, and get even. Law is subjective, and justice is too blind at times. Man law overrules governmental law. It is your right as a man to protect your family. If you commit a crime during your vengeance, your brothers in blue will clean it up. Almost thirty-nine years I've followed these rules, and they are a comfort in times of need.

My eyes light on the only empty seat at our table, a seat that has been filled for almost twenty-one years by Devon's ass, until this morning. Pain lances deep within my chest. Unbidden, my gaze uncovers what bleach cannot hide. My kitchen is spotless, scrubbed clean by my two youngest children in the wee hours of the morning while Kieren and I searched futilely for Devon. What can't be cleaned away is the rips in the vinyl tile. Gashes Devon created when he smashed Lucky Clover's glassware because they didn't contain heroin. The shards of glass left a permanent reminder of Devon's drug rampage.

I'm failing them… my family.

"It's all right, Dad." Kieren shrugs off all the responsibilities I put on his shoulders. Since long before my wife killed herself,

Kieren and Devon have been my wife and support system. The pressure combined with the painful memories is why there is an empty seat at our table. My son, Devon, is spiraling down to beyond rock bottom because he cannot cope, and it's entirely my fault.

"I have a shit-load of paperwork and reports to file. I'd rather be here for you kids, but I have to clear some of this away so I have free time once school's out." I lamely offer my excuse, and not one of them buys it. Identical expressions of "*liar!*" scream from my three youngest children's eyes. They all know what I'll be doing until Devon is found. It's what we'll all be doing, searching.

"It's *fine*," Kieren stresses as he begins to clear away the breakfast he made me and his siblings.

I stare at my son's side profile, and see a grown Mason male. Ren's jaw is exactly like mine, like my father's– clenched. I think to myself, "*NO! Goddamn it, NO! It is not all right.*" I refuse to be like my father, where he'd bellow and rage. But I am like my father in another way, aren't I? My father left me with the responsibility of my baby sister, Isis. Just as I'm doing to Kieren, making him take care of house and home… Weston and Raven.

When Kieren graduated high school, Devon was already at the police academy and I had to work to put a roof over our heads. Without being asked, my son threw away his own happiness to take care of ours. Kieren had a full ride to State on a football scholarship, but he threw it away to be a grease monkey so he could be close to home. It's why I never let Kieren get away with shit. Most parents would have kissed Kieren's ass, but not me. I rode Kieren hard, all the while thinking Devon was perfectly fine.

I'm a fucking failure.

"Don't," Kieren barks at me as he stacks the cereal bowls, knowing exactly where my head is at. "Get your book bags," he says to Weston and Raven. "Your lunches are on the kitchen island. Meet me in the truck in five minutes."

I stare at my hands, waiting for Kieren to light into me. I deserve it. I sigh, wishing our lives would've turned out differently, especially for my eldest sons. Kieren should be taking finals for his freshman year at college, worrying about getting piss-roaring drunk and how many chicks he could bag at this weekend's frat party. Instead, he's playing happy homemaker, raising my kids, cooking my meals, paying my bills, and working a minimum waged job.

… But then again, Devon should be getting into the squad car with me to ride to the station, where we would protect and serve our community. But Devon is on the run because Ren told him about his future at rehab in Arizona.

Failure. Fucking. Failure.

My father was a ruthless, cold bastard who failed Isis. Camille failed us all. I failed us all. Devon failed Kieren by leaving him to take care of Weston and Raven. What a legacy I've created.

"Knock it the fuck off," Kieren hisses, and he never raises his voice at me. Kieren will scoff or make fun of me. But usually he's gentle, understanding and giving. I've never had a father/son relationship with Devon and Kieren. I grew up right alongside them. That's what happens when you become a father at seventeen. My sons earned the right to be called men when they survived the attack and its aftermath.

I raise my eyes to the boy who was fashioned in the image of our relatives. All of my children are a mix of my family. Devon is the spitting image of his mother, but with my coloring: on the small side, light blue eyes and dark curls. Kieren is built like my father and me: HUGE, but Ren has his mother's blond hair. Raven is all Isis. If my sister weren't still breathing, I'd swear that my only daughter was her aunt's reincarnation. I've never seen anyone as heart-stoppingly beautiful as the women in my family. But it doesn't make me proud, it terrifies the hell out of me. Weston will look just like Kieren when he grows up, but his hair is a shade or two darker.

"I'm so fucking sorry," I mumble to the reason I still breathe. Only six people mean anything to me, and I've failed them all. I've stared longingly at my service pistol, wanting to taste its barrel. But I can't do to them what Camille did to us all. That dumb cunt used my service pistol to end her pathetic existence. Every day I get to carry a reminder of how much I've ruined my family.

"I said," Kieren bites out, "to knock it the fuck off. I'm sick of this attitude you walk around with." Pointing at me, Ren swirls his finger in the air, like he can point out my visible failings and erase them. "We were doing good until Devon's fuck up. He's going to be twenty-one soon. Devon's a man, and he wouldn't be running from rehab if he took responsibility for his own actions. You walking around, blaming yourself, is total bullshit!"

Standing, I clutch the backrest of my chair, trying to hold my emotions in check. "He's my son." I wince when my voice dips down to a whine.

"And he's *my* brother," Kieren counters, pounding his chest with his words. "We were supposed to take care of each other, have each other's back. But Devon is a selfish asshole. That ain't got a thing to do with you, Dad. It's just who Devon is. Isis, Auggie, Dev, and I are adults. Rae's sixteen and West is closing in on fifteen. All ya gotta do is blink and they will already be out of high school. It's time for you to move on and get a life."

'*Play pretend until it is reality*' glows from Kieren's eyes. He's done venting and expressing his emotions. He wants to forget and be proactive, so I follow suit.

"I'm working on it," I say with a secret smile, and Kieren laughs like a man. That satisfied rumble that only a real man can make. I've been waiting for Devon to join our ranks: Augustus and me. But Kieren's beat Devon to it.

"I'll have Rae text Princess to occupy Clover so you can get your loot. That is if Willow doesn't beat you to it. The girl has been hoarding the sweets for our TV time." Kieren chuckles heartily. "I'll see you at lunch. And I don't give a shit about how much "*work*" you have to do, be home by seven-thirty or I'm sending out a posse. We're having spaghetti."

"All right, I'll be home by seven. See ya later, son," I say while clasping my son's shoulder. I grab my belt on the way by, hooking it into place. I never leave the house without pulling on my Chief Mason persona.

Raven and Weston are waiting for me at the front door for our goodbyes. "Be a good girl," I murmur against my baby girl's velvety soft forehead.

"I will, Daddy. Not too much is going on at school," Raven says sweetly. But I trust her as much as I trust Devon. Zilch. An angelic smile from Raven? Yeah right, lest she forgets who raised Isis? I know all of my daughter's tricks before she even thinks of them, because her aunt already pulled the bullshit a decade before.

"Um-hmm..." I murmur while smiling against Raven's forehead, endlessly entertained by my baby girl. She hugs me tightly when she feels my lips curl up into a smirk. Giggling, she calls me Daddy again and tries to extract herself from my embrace.

I don't even have to ask, Weston automatically gives me a hug from behind before charging out to Kieren's truck. Weston is a good boy. I don't have to remind him to behave.

But I thought Devon was a good boy, too, now didn't I? I wasn't completely blind to his faults. I've always known Devon had issues. I just thought he had them in hand. So far so good with Weston and Raven: Rae can be a little bitch, closed off, acting just like Isis. She is a young woman who was raised to put herself first and never compromise, just as my father taught me to raise her. Weston can be devious and playful, but no issues are cropping up from our shared nightmare. West bears watching for other reasons that will tilt our world on its axis.

I slide into my Government-Issue vehicle. My heart still stings over the fact that my first born isn't with me while we ride to work. After six months of this routine, it feels foreign to be driving solo. I hum along with the radio, trying to fill the void. On autopilot, I drive in the opposite direction of the Courthouse. I have some treats to pick up.

I always said I'd never be like my dad when it came to women, and I meant it. My father was an alpha male. Chief John Mason was a fair man, but he was unemotional. He liked to call me a pansy-assed girl because I'm over-emotional. I cry, which is unacceptable in a man. I respected my father and all he stood for, because he did all that he could do to keep us alive. He taught us to be good human beings, and to be self-reliant. Dad worked hard, and he found even harder women to take care of Isis and me. I swore I'd never do that.

… But as I park down the street from Clover Webster's home, I wonder if I'm doing just that. Not in a million years would I call Clover a whore, like the women Dad brought home to us. Stalking the woman seems wrong. But fuck if it isn't the highlight of my day. A highlight I need right now.

Clover has grown into a good, respectable woman, just as I knew she was destined to become. I was sixteen when I met a twelve-year-old Clover. She was a tiny little thing: blonde, blue-eyed, the epitome of angelic with the foul mouth of a sailor. With the confidence of a miniature general, or as I later discovered, a maternal instinct that rivals all others, I watched as Clover berated Rob, Isis, and Auggie for fighting. Never having seen a girl behave like that, I fell hard.

I left the girl alone because she was still a child. Waiting for Clover to grow up was out of the question. Less than two years later I found myself in a situation that required a woman. My father had a fatal heart attack, leaving me responsible for Isis, Lisa, and Auggie. I needed a woman, a woman like Dad would choose.

Camille Jamison.

Two years after my marriage to Camille, my sister-in-law Ginny dragged a woman-child into my home, startling the shit out of me. Clover was quiet, with a sarcastic curl to her lips, where you just knew she was thinking naughty thoughts about you. I wanted her even though I could never have her. John Mason's man rules prohibited me from even thinking of Clover in a less than honorable way. But after hearing my best friend screwing the sixteen-year-old girl in my baby sister's bedroom, I beat the living shit out of Sam. That day changed so many lives: Sam, Clover, Devon, an unborn Kieren, and a freshly conceived Willow.

Our lives have finally come full circle. Now is my chance with Clover, and I'm not going to stop trying until the day I die.

Almost a year ago, I began speaking to Clover again. Auggie was preying on her daughter. Rob and Isis were trying to decide between my sons as a way to keep *their* Auggie away from Willow. I just wanted my sons and Willow to allow nature to take its course without our interference, and no one would listen to me.

Jealousy: Auggie was jealous over my sons, and Rob and Isis were jealous over Auggie's interest in Willow.

Hands tied, I called Clover, and the two of us started a tenuous relationship that was built solely on our children's welfare. Hands tied tighter than mine, all Clover could do was issue a warning, and then sit idly by while Auggie and Devon murdered her daughter's trust.

Clover and I text a few times a day because voice communications are too intimate. Our conversations never venture outside of parenting.

Top Cop: *Raven is impossible to live with. Is it hormones?*

Mayor's Slave: *Did you remember to feed her? Teenage girls are like wild animals. Food, water, entertainment. If those are covered, it's hormones. Seth is being a prick. Is this a phase?*

Top Cop: *No, not a phase. It's called being a man. Is it normal for teenage girls to lock themselves in their bedrooms for forty-eight hours at a clip?*

Mayor's Slave: *Yes, as long as you hear her moving around in there, she's still alive. Is Willow playing around with Auggie? If so, make him stop before I shoot him in the junk.*

Top Cop: *Your illegitimate daughter has moved onto my son. I'd like grandchildren, so leave his testicles alone.*

Mayor's Slave: *You have two other sons and a daughter. Masons breed like bunnies. I'm positive you'll have a litter of grandkids. Keep your Mason DNA away from my kids.*

Top Cop: *Looking forward to being a granddaddy, Grandmamma.* ☺ *Shouldn't Rae eat more than just popcorn and diet soda?*

Mayor's Slave: *She's a teenaged girl. Be happy she eats. Is it still legal to whip your son as long as the switch is no thicker than your pinkie? I read that somewhere. Because Seth's visiting YouPorn, PornHub, & XNXX Stories, and I need to know if it's legal to beat him for it. Is he a porn addict?*

Top Cop: *Seth's a man. We love porn. Get over it.*

Mayor's Slave: *I threw up in my mouth a little bit just now.*

Top Cop: *Haven't you been nauseous since their birth? I know I have been. Am I a bad father if I want to cuff my daughter in the mouth for being a smartass?*

Mayor's Slave: *I'm not above beating the shit out of my daughters. Send Rae my way. Willow, Violet, and I can smack some respect into her bratty mouth. I'll send Seth to your sons for a thorough beating.*

Top Cop: *Um… how do I react to this: I caught Weston plucking his eyebrows?*

Mayor's Slave: *Please tell me Weston had a unibrow? If he starts putting on makeup, then I'd get worried. I once caught Seth counting his armpit hairs. Not that counting to six was difficult. Are men obsessed with hair?*

Top Cop: *The hairier we are, the more manly we think we are. The question is: why the fuck would Weston want LESS hair?*

Mayor's Slave: *Your spawn is dead! DEAD! Forget Augustus, I'm coming after Devon's nuts first. One nut for each of my girls: Willow & Essie!*

Top Cop: *WHAT? SHIT! Sorry?!?!?* ☹

Top Cop: *Clover?*

Top Cop: *Widow? Why did you have Rob send me an MP3 of crickets chirping?*

Top Cop: *Lucky Clover? Come back, damn it! Need advice.*

Top Cop: *You've done it now, woman! I will not be IGNORED!*

Clover didn't speak to me for nearly two weeks after Devon cheated on Willow with Essie. That alone pissed me off more than Devon's drug addiction. His shit was bleeding over into my future.

Refusing to be ignored, my alter-ego Papa Bear blackmailed Lucky Clover into giving me attention. I began texting and emailing Lucky Clover a few hundred times per day, and those conversations were XXX, involving making children, not raising them.

Papa Bear: *What are you wearing?*

Lucky Clover: *Stalker, you're looking at me as I sit at my desk! I. Can. See. You. Texting. Me!*

Papa Bear: *Who? Me? I don't know what you're talking about.*

Lucky Clover: *I can literally see you texting me, dumbass. You must have sucked as an undercover cop. No wonder you're stuck in this Podunk town. Some TOP COP you are.*

Papa Bear: *nope, drawing a blank. No idea what you're talking about. Pop a button on your blouse for me, won't you?*

Lucky Clover: *you just gestured at me when you sent the text, really?*

Papa Bear: *wasn't me...*

Lucky Clover: *Fuck. You.*

Papa Bear: *Yes, please!*

Lucky Clover: *You know what I mean, asshole.*

Papa Bear: *I could see your panties if you'd just move your leg a little more to the left.*

Lucky Clover: *Leave me alone. You're going to get me fired.*

Papa Bear: *Ah! I almost had you. Your foot twitched! ☺ Did my email make my baker hungry?*

Lucky Clover: *STOP! MOLESTING! THE! BAKED! GOODS!*

Papa Bear: *You SHOUT a lot. Ya know that? I bet you're a screamer in the sack. Well, you turn me on to the point that I had to fuck a hole in your donuts. I just couldn't help myself.*

Lucky Clover: *You sent a picture of yourself eating the donut afterward, you sick fuck!*

Papa Bear: *Cream filled.*

Lucky Clover: *Not when I baked it, it wasn't. Gross.*

Papa Bear: *C'mon, watching me eat my own spunk turned you on, admit it? You're a kinky little slut, eh? I bet it made your panties wet. I watched you wiggle in your seat. Made me bust a nut in my pants, it did.*

Lucky Clover: *Do you eat all of your body fluids?*

Papa Bear: *Nope, but I do fling my shit like a monkey. We are genetically cousins, ya know?*

Lucky Clover: *Go fuck yourself.*

Papa Bear: *Love, I'm hung, but not that hung.*

Lucky Clover: *Fine, forget your Vienna Sausage-sized dick. I want you to shove your nutsack up your ass and sit on it.*

Papa Bear: *ah, now she wants to talk dirty to me. What is it with you and men's balls? You're always de-manning everyone. I'm gonna start calling you the "Emasculator".*

Lucky Clover: *mmm... baby, you make me so hot I want to emasculate you in the most painful way possible, and then shove it up your ass.*

Papa Bear: *You also have a sick fascination with sticking stuff up people's asses. Why don't you demonstrate it for me? With your tongue. Do you think your tongue is strong enough to shove my balls up my ass? I bet it is. Open up. Is your tongue forked like everyone says it is? Your words are quite cutting.*

Lucky Clover: *Go away. I have to take a call... as you already know since you are standing ten feet from me, laughing!*

The day our children got together and asked me to woo Clover blew my mind. Here the little shits thought they were being geniuses, and I'd been stalking Clover for months. With the green light, I went from concerned father to prospective husband. I began the secret admirer game, and it actually took Clover a few weeks to figure out it was me. Clover told me to stop terrorizing her, but I thought it would bring us closer together to play the game on the kids instead. Plus, I have a wicked sweet tooth.

I rub my belly as a smile stretches across my face. I exit my vehicle, dreaming of molesting some more baked goods, and then texting the evidence to Lucky Clover. Her outraged reactions are always worth it. She acts like an innocent virgin when I send her shots of the Playroom, but I can see the artery in her throat throbbing with excitement as she stares at her computer screen. I always stand across the hall from her office and watch her open my emails. It's the highlight of my day.

I ghost down the street toward my prize. A bouncy ponytail catches my eye, causing me to growl. "Girl," I hiss. "Gitcha skinny ass right back here!" I run headlong toward the bane of my sons' existences, and if all goes well, my future stepdaughter, and undoubtedly, my future daughter-in-law.

Willow jogs up to me, sarcastic smirk plastered on her pixy-like face, with my box of baked goods clutched to her chest. "Seth said Clover was guarding the front window. So I had him distract her with profanity while I grabbed the goodies," the tiny thing gasps out breathlessly. "Here's your cut."

I grudgingly take my two dozen sour cream donuts, feeling utter disbelief. I stare at my loot, and then at Willow's, and then at Willow herself. Eyes flicking back and forth, over and over, causing Willow to fidget restlessly. Unimpressed with my ration, I scowl the girl down.

"Where's the cherry danish? All I asked for was the donuts for the guys and the pastry for my breakfast." Tipping my chin in the direction of the cardboard box overflowing with sweet smelling treats, I ask, "Whatcha got in your box there, girly?"

"I don't know what you're talking about," Willow lies poorly. She thinks she's no longer transparent, but it's laughable. Willow never has to tell us what she's thinking because it's written across her face like a ticker tape on a newsfeed.

Turning into a schoolyard bully, I warn, "Girl, don't make push you down and steal my treats like it's your milk money. I can smell the cream cheese icing..." I sniff the air. "Is that chocolate I smell?"

"Here's your danish," Willow says as she flops a box on top of my donuts. Willow flashes me a brilliant grin, and then takes off at breakneck speeds toward an ancient piece of shit *Ford F-150*. I momentarily get distracted because my children are helping Willow steal my treats. Pouting, I marvel over the fact that Willow can run like a gazelle.

Brain finally registering that decadent scent, "Hey, that's Clover's seven deadly sins chocolate cake, isn't it?" I run toward Kieren's truck as it idles at the curb. My son laughs at me through the windshield, looking beyond entertained that I'm fighting his girlfriend over her mother's baked goods.

Tossing my youngest son my treats, Willow spills into the passenger seat, slamming the door shut on me just as I reach the truck. My traitorous baby girl is gobbling up a sugar cookie while Weston gazes down in awe at a box like it's his long-lost best friend. Worshipping the cake, I presume.

Looking slightly naughty and a whole lot evil, Willow yells out the window, taunting me. "Clover was mine first. I'll always get dibs on her food."

Growling as a pink tongue sticks out at me in victory, I barely restrain myself from wrenching the passenger side door open. "You'll get a fat ass," I warn caustically.

Eyes glittering with delight, Ren shouts back, "God, I hope so, Dad!"

All Willow does is laugh at me as they drive away, only to park a block down, directly in front of the Webster household.

The loneliness suffocates me as two adorable kids skip out to the truck, laughing and hugging, packing into the truck's crew cab like a happy family. Ren drives away toward the high school, driving right by me. Every kid waves, flashing me sugar cookies and shit-eating grins.

I envision Devon magically appearing before me, and together we abduct Clover from her house, and the three of us join the rest of our family packed inside Kieren's truck, and we drive off into the sunset.

John Mason was right. I'm too damned emotional for my own good.

Standing alone on the street, reality crashes back into me.

I am the Widower.

CHAPTER FOUR

The Widower

Phony. Fake. My family smiles at me from the photograph I've stared at day-in-and-day-out for the past four years. It was taken when times were better. Were times ever better?

No.

Weston is missing a front tooth, and now he is growing like a mighty oak tree– the kid is going to tower over me when he's a grown man. Raven looks like a little girl, and now she's a stunning sixteen-year-old recluse, who never leaves her bedroom. Devon is smiling, eyes clear and shining, not the drug addict on the run that he is today. Kieren has a smile playing along his lips, like he has a secret you don't want to know. When I left him earlier, Ren was still wearing that smile– some things never change. Isis looks as beautiful and naughty as she did a few minutes ago when she was harassing me. I look the same, too.

Miserable.

The only thing that drags my attention from the family portrait that sits atop my desk is knowing *she* is here, directly above me in Mayor Ross's office. I can feel Clover through four floors of wood, steel, and concrete. What started in the past had blossomed into parents commiserating, but our children's enthusiasm to be a blended family has turned this into an obsession for me. It's the only highlight of my day. I know to the marrow of my bones that Clover Webster is my salvation, as I am hers. I know her better than she even realizes. I hunger to remove her layers of protection and find the real Clover beneath.

I just want all of us to finally experience true happiness. Is that too much to ask?

I quickly text Clover via my *Top Cop* cellphone. Yes, I use two separate phones to harass the woman, using her work-issued cellphone and her personal cellphone as a leash to keep her connected to me at all times. *Top Cop* is for innocent interactions. *Papa Bear* is for intimate interactions. But, lately, neither one of us can distinguish between the two types of contact. Like our family, it's been blending together for weeks.

Top Cop: *You outdid yourself on the danish. I may have to have it for breakfast for the rest of my life.*

I snort at Clover's instantaneous reply. For someone who protests so much, she always hits me right back.

Mayor's Slave: *You'll have a heart attack, old man. Ya better lay off the sweets.*

Top Cop: *I could lay off the sweets, but it would make more work for you in the long run. I know you can make a mean lasagna. Maybe I will request that for my dinner once a week.*

I smile ruefully as I type the words. Clover is a self-possessed, reserved lady. I've known Clover since she was an awkward twelve-year-old girl who was a helluva lot smaller than Willow. It was back in the day when Clover's eyes would get a naughty glint. I don't know what took that gleam out of her eye, since it diminished long before Sam's death. But I relish the thought of being the one who brings it back. Surprisingly, Clover is playful with our little game of secret admirer.

Mayor's Slave: *Hmm… if I didn't think my children were somehow getting their hands on my baked goods, I'd lace your acquisitions with laxatives. Plus, I'd hate to have half of the Courthouse out sick with diarrhea. Who would protect Fairport? I'm not an idiot. I see my donuts walking around in our coworkers' greedy little fingers.*

Top Cop: *Well, I always knew you were a genius. About that lasagna, you'd save my personal chef a lot of trouble making spaghetti this evening by making us a big ol' gooey pan of Italian goodness. Plus, Ren sucks at Italian. All he does is boil noodles and dump luke-warm sauce over top.*

Mayor's Slave: *First: I'm not Italian… and I'm pretty sure your ancestors originated from the same area as mine. How about some Shepherd's pie… or haggis?*

Top Cop: *Ugh! Well, I do love Shepherd's pie… but I want tomato goodness for supper. You can make that Shepherd's pie for tomorrow night if you wish. I like a bit of cheddar cheese melted on top and extra Worcestershire sauce in the meat.*

Mayor's Slave: *Jesus, you are a demanding bastard. I'm not making you anything for dinner.*

Top Cop: *Umm…hmm… seeing is believing. Clover, do you remember what happened last time you denied me? You don't want me to go there again, do you? What are you having for dinner this evening, my sweet?*

Minutes tick by without any reply. Just as I stand to take my cellphone into the bathroom to snap Clover a cock-shot punishment text, I get an alert tone. I bark a laugh when I open Clover's text message.

Mayor's Slave: *Lasagna.*

"What so funny?" Colin, my second in command and one of my closest friends, asks me as he wanders by my desk.

"Ah, just talking Shepherd's pie and haggis with Ross's personal assistant," I say with a proud grin.

"Oh, Lord," Colin moans, sounding like a highlander from *Braveheart*. "Save me some if Clover makes it. It's been years since I had some food from home." The longing in the man's voice makes me want to text Clover back and tell her to make us some food for our homesick friend.

"Tomorrow night, come on over for dinner. I can guarantee we'll be eating the best food you've had in years," I say arrogantly, voice filled with pride, and all the pride is in Clover.

"Ross was reaming Clover's ass out this morning for that last batch of pictures you sent. I'm not posing for the next set. My freckles were obvious," Colin grumbles, looking freaked out.

"I'll put a sepia filter over the picture," I offer as a solution, not wanting to stop my amateur photography. "Besides, Mrs. Ross would be sorely disappointed if the photos stopped." I start chuckling and can't stop.

"You're such a dick." Colin rumbles a laugh as he walks past my corner of the office to check on the drunk tank.

Not much goes on in our tiny town. Most of our calls are little old ladies bitching for some reason or another, and drunks sobering up in the holding cell. We do have a big problem with drugs in the area, but I don't want to think about that… and so I do. Isn't that how it always goes? The one thing you don't want to think about always dominates your thoughts.

Meth and heroin are running rampant. I used to arrest the bastards because it was the law, now I feel a personal duty to eradicate them from Fairport. The two drug pushers cooling their heels in a cell already learned that Chief Mason doesn't fuck around. When I asked if they've sold to my son or know where the hell he is, they sang like canaries underneath my questioning fists.

Since we arrested some major suppliers in the area and shut down seven meth labs, the pickings are slim. I'm at a loss on who to question next, but happy they aren't on the streets contributing to Devon's spiral into Hell. Devon should've been standing next to me, receiving a commendation from the state for his dedication on cleaning up Fairport's streets, not contributing to the problem.

If it wasn't for the respect the community has for me, because there have been three generations of Masons who have protected and served their denizens, Devon would have been arrested, regardless of what I tried to do. Everyone knows what my boy has been up to. There are no secrets in Fairport. If I can't find my son and put him on a plane to rehab in the next few days, our citizens are going to tar and feather him when they get their hands on him. At this point, it's either rehab or jail for Officer Devon Mason.

Devon. Just the thought of my eldest son has the paper in my hand shaking. I quickly put it down and smooth it out. I hadn't meant to crinkle the report in my tight fist.

Devon. Right now our family is mourning the loss of him as if he died, while he is somewhere getting high. A high that isn't meant to be pleasurable because he's punishing himself. I feel helpless because I can't do anything for him. Devon has to do it for himself. As a parent, this hopelessness is the worst feeling in the world.

I blink back the tears that threaten to spill from my eyes. Mind-bending boredom is on today's agenda, and it won't overpower these destructive thoughts. I can't bother Clover any more today without risking her charging down here and beating my ass. But… that does seem to hold promise.

A yellow scrap of paper catches my eye. "McGregor," I shout, and Colin appears a second later.

"You rang," Colin says, flashing his pearly whites.

"Did you see who brought this down?" I ask, hiding the quiver of fear that runs through my voice. But after ten years of being by my side, Colin notices it.

"No," he says, rapidly shaking his head. "Why? Probably one of the dispatchers. Opal, maybe? What is it?"

"Well, Sherlock. It's a clue," I murmur while waving the report, trying to lighten my worry with humor.

"I'm flattered. I thought I'd be Watson in this scenario," Colin teases.

07:05 am: Tina Kline and Devon Mason were seen at the No-Name Diner, acting erratically. 5 calls were placed to 911.

08:43 am: 3 calls were placed to 911, disturbance at Fairport Area Elementary School playground. Tina Kline, Taryn Elsberry, Tommy Braxton, and Devon Mason were listed as the suspects. Fled before caller was finished with the call. Suspects fled on foot to destinations unknown, presumably to a private residence.

Mal, let me know if you want me to dispatch an officer to search their homes. I already called Tommy's and Taryn's parents, and spoke face-to-face with Auggie and Kieren. I'll try to track them the best I can. I'm sorry that I can't be any more help than this.

-Opal.

Fisting the report, I imagine it's my first born's throat in my grasp. "I'm sick of feeling helpless. There is absolutely nothing I can do. While I feel comforted with the knowledge that the cocksucker still breathes, I don't know what he's up to right this fucking second. That ass rounded up all the rehab-bound deviants, did you notice that?" I tilt my head to look at Colin, and he nods his head in assent. "One last bender before forced sobriety? Those names Opal sent us, those are the kids who were slated to go to rehab with Devon come Monday morning."

Coming to sit on the edge of my desk, Colin asks, "How did Dev know that?"

"That's just it, I have no idea," I mutter, baffled. "Tina's always rehab bound, nothing new there. I've had Patrick Weathersby on speed-dial, just waiting for Tina to fuck up again so he can push through the order that she's too incompetent to take care of herself. Tommy was arrested for possession last week, and the only way I let him off is if he signed up to go to rehab. The administrator for the Sedona Center told me that Taryn was scheduled at the same time as Devon and Tommy. The man was pleased that he didn't have to make multiple flights across the country, and asked why my town was a breeding ground for so many drug addicts."

"Asshole," Colin grumbles beneath his breath.

"Very," I agree. "But if he can get these kids clean, he can be the world's biggest dick for all I care." My fist finds itself pounding the top of my desk out of sheer frustration. "Ahhh...." I half scream. "I can't take this shit any longer. I feel like my head's going to fucking burst if I don't do something. Sitting in this office where Devon should be... it's pure torture. I'm scared

I'm going to kill the next asshole who comes through processing."

CHAPTER FIVE

The Widow

Lasagna?

Shepherd's pie?

My cupboards are nearly bare as it is, and my bank account is bone dry. I'm not about to ask Dad for some cash to feed the Masons. I know it's not all Malcolm. After a year of contact, we've found a common ground. He likes to taunt me, push my limits, but he doesn't like to tax me. The donuts and savory foods are all Malcolm, but the rest of the dessert orders… The kids, and I'm not sure how they pull that off.

I called Malcolm just after Willow started working at Revamped. Rob was ignoring my protests, so I went to the *Top Cop* instead. If anyone could make Augustus Kline behave, it was Malcolm Mason. We've only had one phone conversation, both of us finding it too intimate. After that, the text messaging started: one or two per week. If I needed advice on Seth, or if Malcolm needed advice on Raven, we asked the other. Being a widow is difficult, but being a single parent of the opposite-sexed child is even harder. I found comfort in Malcolm's unflinching honesty, and he found it in return.

We were companionable, respectful, so when the smutty, demanding text messages started pouring in from '*Papa Bear*', I didn't think for an instant that they were from Malcolm. It was more like, someone who knew I was communicating with Malcolm, was fucking with me. The texts were crass, derogatory– borderline humiliating. All I knew was, whoever was sending them wasn't trying to '*date*' me or get into my bed.

I know who I am and how the outside world perceives me. Perfect: mother, daughter, sister, and wife. An unattractive stick in the mud woman. I'm a widow with two teenagers, who is hiding her oldest daughter by calling her little sister. I'm not a date-able woman. I'm the type of woman men make fun of for being controlling, a nag, and a bitch– a cold fish. And all of that couldn't be further from the truth.

I knew the nasty emails and texts were to put me in my place, knock Mrs. Perfection down a couple dozen pegs. For a nanosecond, I feared it was my mother-in-law trying to demean me.

… And then a few weeks later, the secret admirer deliveries started. It was sweet– the gifts. My only communication with this person was through the notes delivered with the packages. At first I enjoyed the '*me*' time, being in the kitchen, baking. I actually thought it was Malcolm trying to be nice to me, make me feel wanted and useful. But then I realized it was probably just another way to get inside my head and warp it.

The truth was revealed one evening when I was exhausted, bogged down with a billion tasks, and I couldn't meet the demands. The sweet secret admirer turned into the demented, tyrannical, life-ruining Papa Bear– merging my smut texter and secret admirer into one.

Ignoring my secret admirer, I decided to go to sleep instead of baking his cookies. Five minutes after the requested delivery time, the texts started from '*Papa Bear*'. The secret admirer had never sent a text before, always sending cute notes that had a tinge of innuendo. But *Papa Bear* was a notorious texter, sometimes hundreds in several hours. Every thirty seconds I received a text, each one progressively worse than the last.

Two hours later, I found myself baking chocolate chip cookies until well past my bedtime. I received a '*thank you, don't disappoint me again*' text thirty seconds after I put the warm cookies on my porch. Of course I ran outside to check it out, and sure as shit, the cookies were gone.

Lesson learned: this wasn't a woman. Only a man is that impatient, refusing to be ignored. Men are like toddlers screaming, "*Mom. Momma. MAA! MOTHER!*" when you don't give them what they want, when they want it. Papa Bear taught me to do as he requested, that whatever small task he wanted wasn't worth the fallout from ignoring him.

I'd breathed a sigh of relief, the texts stopped as soon as he had his cookies. I had made the lunatic happy. But I was wrong, so very wrong. I went into work the next morning without a lick of sleep. The texts may have stopped, but my work email was filled to the brim with perverted images of sexual practices I didn't understand– my work email that my boss monitors. The message was loud and clear: disobey a request and you'll regret it. Thank goodness my boss is Fairport's seventy-six-year-old Mayor, who is completely senile. I somehow convinced Mayor Ross the images of people engaged in sexual activities were artistic expression.

Exhausted, nerves rubbed raw, I refused to be bullied. I was being stalked and I wouldn't live that way. What if this person harmed my children? The rest of the day I played detective. I used the mayor's pull to have the cell number the texts were sent from traced. Of course I had to ask Malcolm to do this for me, convinced he wasn't malicious enough to pull this horrific thing on me. After all, our children were friends, and two of them were dating. Our siblings have been best friends since kindergarten, and in love with each other just as long. Malcolm was my dead husband's best friend– he had been with us at the end. We were practically family, so I trusted him. As expected, Chief Mason promptly sent me a report, stating it was a disposable cell, virtually a dead-end.

It was up to me to solve the mystery of Papa Bear, my bullying secret admirer. I called the number countless times from my home, work, and cell phone, and no one ever answered. I tried a new tactic, I sent a smutty message. *"I want your honey stick deep inside my jar."* Oh, yeah, whoever the hell it was loved innuendo, and their favorite innuendo was Clover honey related. Don't get me started on the shit they come up with about lucky charms and rainbows– magically delicious!

The following week, I scanned the dirty images for hints as to who this perverted secret admirer could possibly be. Each picture was a new experience for me. The only man who had ever touched me was my late husband, Sam. I'd thought our passions ran hot when we first met, but those pictures proved just how innocent I truly was.

I wanted to ask my best friend, Ginny, but I didn't think a lesbian could help me with penile-related information. I almost asked my brother, because I know he's into some weird stuff with Auggie and Isis. Fairport is a small town, and most rumors are based on fact. Going it alone, I took my search to the internet, and it was eye-opening. One minute into my search, I was mortified and strangely aroused, not to mention the color of a ripe tomato.

There was one common denominator with the photos– my secret admirer. I printed the pictures and used a magnifying glass to study them. Up until I figured out the truth, all pictures were taken in a way that you never saw more than a curve of a hip or the angle of his penis. The most graphic was a video he texted me– a video of hands caressing Papa Bear's writhing naked form. Male and female hands stroking the cock he was so proud of, stroking him until he found release. I wasn't sure what he was getting out of torturing me, but he was most definitely getting *off* on it, that's for sure.

Papa Bear got careless and started tripping up. I was devastated. I felt violated the day I figured out Papa Bear the smut texter, demanding secret admirer, was Malcolm Mason. I felt eyes on me as I opened an email attachment. It was an image of a cock piercing one of my donuts– meant to be mocking or playful, I wasn't sure. I rolled my eyes up from my computer monitor, only to connect with Malcolm's cold blue stare. I'm not sure if he was tired of his sick game or what. Malcolm was typing on his cell phone while holding my gaze, and less than a second later I received a text message.

Papa Bear: *Do you like what you see?*

I ran off to the bathroom, humiliated, distraught, and cried for the first time in years. I haven't been able to shut off the waterworks since. Malcolm never apologized, and he never stopped, either. I knew better than to ignore him, but I tried a few times just to be sure. I've come close to being fired because of the pornographic images, and Mayor Ross knows who they are from. What do you do when your stalker is the Chief of Police and your boss is the Mayor? You relent, that's what. You just deal with it and hope and pray he gets bored.

I felt alone, just as I did when Sam was alive. Trapped. Stuck. A man whom everyone loves and respects was treating me poorly. Just as I couldn't say, "*Sam's being mean to me,*" and have people believe it. I couldn't say, "*Chief Mason is taunting me.*" I would be told to loosen up and get over myself, because Clover Webster isn't the type of woman a man would ever pursue. She's the type men tend to avoid and humiliate in private.

Admitting defeat, I answer every text and meet every demand as quickly as possible. In the past few weeks, Malcolm has changed. He's less derogatory and more playful. He's behaving like the Top Cop I found comforting, even when the communications are from Papa Bear. He still plays the game, refusing to admit that he's Papa Bear and my not-so secret admirer. But when he and I text each other as parents, he says he's just playing along to fuck with the kids. Malcolm Mason is an honorable, respectful man. But color me skittish after Sampson Webster.

Malcolm still refuses to tell me what he actually wants, and that terrifies me.

I hunch over at my desk, head lowered so the office spies don't overhear. "I yield," I breathe into my cellphone, calling Malcolm for the second time in my entire life.

"Clover?" Malcolm breathes back, the sound runs up my spine and sparks. "I…" he huffs a laugh as if he's uncomfortable. The creak of his office chair is unmistakable as he shifts in his seat. "You're calling me?"

"I yield," I repeat. "You win. I'm not sure what the object of your twisted game is, but I give up."

CHAPTER SIX

The Widower

"Huh?" I lean back in my chair and pop my feet up on my desk. Warmth blossoms in my chest over something so small– Clover reached out to me. I'm the one who always initiates and she begrudgingly answers. "Wait. What?" I mutter when what she said finally clicks. "What's wrong?"

"I can't make your lasagna tonight," Clover barely breathes, sounding scared, and it confuses the hell out of me. "It takes a long time to prep and bake. Plus, I'd have to go shopping first. It wouldn't be ready until at least ten tonight, and then I'd have to fill the dessert order," spills rapidly, jumbling up into one continuous word, as if Clover has to get the words out before she loses her nerve. "I know tomorrow is Saturday, but I have a lot of work to do. It's cooking lesson day for the kids. I just… can't make your dinner tonight. I'll beg if I have to, anything to make sure you don't make Mayor Ross angry. I need this job, Malcolm," she pleads.

"I was only teasing you, Lucky. I didn't expect you to cook my dinner," I admit with all sincerity, and silently add "*yet*".

"How can you say that after all the texts and emails?" Clover demands, and hastily adds, "And don't you fucking dare say it wasn't you."

Clover is seething, and for some inexplicable reason I find it entertaining and arousing. My cock swells in my pants, giving me a warning throb of need. I wonder if Clover is as passionate in bed as she is in war. Dropping my boots from the edge of my desk to the floor, I lean forward so none of my underlings can hear me– cops are worse than teenage girls when it comes to gossip.

"We both know it's me," I whisper, barely a breath of a sound. "You have no issue with tearing into me. I thought you were just playing back. Trust me– Ross thinks it's funny, and his wife would miss the pictures. I'm just teasing you."

"It's malicious," hisses from the other end of the phone.

"Malicious? Sending you pictures because you arouse me is not malicious," I hiss right back, louder than I expected.

I gain the interest of Colin, who just shakes his head at me, the Brogowski sisters, addicted shoplifters and the first link in Fairport's gossip chain, Matt the public intoxicator, and Nina, the dispatcher on duty, also as big of a gossip whore as an actual whore. We're very lax around here. All of our criminals are habitual offenders, and they just hang out down here with me and my guys knowing we will find them either way.

"You're a goddamned liar," Clover snarls, startling me.

"Do you kiss your children with that dirty mouth?" I sound angry, but I secretly love how I can force the prim and proper Clover Webster to behave like the Clover Prynne from years gone by. "I think we need to start over, Lucky. Something is getting lost in translation, and now I'm confused. I thought we were having fun."

"Fun?" Clover breathes into the phone, trying to be quiet. No doubt she's drawing the attention of half of Fairport's County Courthouse. Everyone has been waiting for one of us to snap.

"I'm exhausted, Malcolm. I want to ask you how you're doing with everything going on with Devon, but I have to wade through all this stalker bullshit: your humiliating texts and emails, and your food demands that are draining me dry. I want the real Malcolm, the one who wants to talk about our kids and doesn't find it entertaining to make me feel demeaned."

"I'll give you Top Cop in a second. But first, tell me how I'm humiliating you. Demeaned? What the fuck, Clover?"

"I don't want to talk about it," Clover closes herself off to me, and it boils my blood.

"Fine," I bite out, hating it when she ignores me. "I don't understand women. I'm just playing schoolyard games with you."

"You mean bullying me?"

"No," I bark. "I mean pulling your ponytail and pushing you down." "...*so I can see your panties*," I silently add.

"Yes, and then steal my lunch money. Point at me. Laugh at me because I'm a shrimp. I spent kindergarten through third grade getting beat up. By fourth grade, I was fighting back. By sixth grade, I decided the hell with it. I faded to invisible and just did my schoolwork. School was an experiment in torture techniques for me. I don't want to relive the traumatizing experience at thirty-five."

"Ah," I sigh, finally getting it. "You think I'm terrorizing you, not flirting with you?"

"What? This is not flirting!" Clover shouts, forgetting about the listening ears around us. "Are you fucking insane?"

"Clinical, pathological, criminal: whatever flavor of insane you want to call me, Lucky." I huff a humorless laugh, wanting to kick my own ass. Clover is not like other women. I have no idea how to fix this. "I didn't think it was possible for another person on the planet to be as daft as Willow, but I'm talking to one."

"Now you're insulting me! Fuck you!"

The buzz of a dead phone line taunts me, screaming with its silence that I didn't handle that well at all.

CHAPTER SEVEN

The Widow

Panting furiously, I stare down at my office phone as it screams at me like an accusation. There is no escape.

RING... RING... RING...

Papa Bear: *Answer the phone.*

Top Cop: *Answer the phone.*

RING... RING... RING...

"You've got to be fucking kidding me," I mutter in awe as three phones ring simultaneously. My personal and work cellphones and the office phone on my desk. All lighting up with three separate numbers– Malcolm's numbers.

RING... RING... RING...

Papa Bear: *I will NOT be ignored. Answer the goddamned phone before I leave the Bat Cave and make you answer it.*

Hand shaking as I hold my cellphone in my palm, I contemplate answering it. "No," I say with conviction. "I said I was done with this game and I meant it."

As if hearing me, silence descends. Breath wheezing in and out, I fear Malcolm is charging up from the basement to beat the shit out of me. Lord knows what kind of images Malcolm will send Mayor Ross after this.

The phone vibrates in my hand, causing me to jump several inches out of my seat.

Top Cop: *I warned you not to ignore me.*

Ring... Ring... Ring... Ring... Ring...

"So Clover?" Rhonda, who collects more secrets than taxes, leans against the wall. Ready to add to her collection, no doubt. "What's this about? You dating?"

"Do I look like some cheap piece of ass Malcolm Mason would want?" I ask defensively. I feel homely when Rhonda nods her head, agreeing with me. Winging it, "We're having a disagreement over the kids. It's common knowledge his ass of a son cheated on my sister with our cousin."

Looking disappointed, the forty-year-old brunette pouts. "Oh, that makes sense. Your life is like a Jerry Springer episode."

"You don't know the half of it," I mutter underneath my breath. I'll need Maury Povich after I tell Willow the truth.

Mayor Ross exits his office, half-blind eyes shining with mirth. "I'm supposed to physically make you answer the phone. I'd do what Chief Mason says, if I were you, Clover. Mrs. Ross would be sad if I missed Friday night at the Playroom."

Playroom?

I don't want to know what my boss would consider a playroom. I also have no idea what Mrs. Ross's first name is, because the mayor always calls his wife Mrs. Ross, along with everyone else. Then again, I only know the mayor's first name because I'm his assistant. But I highly doubt Mrs. Ross shouts Dwight in the throes of passion. I bet they scream out Mayor and Mrs. Ross... somewhere in a place called the Playroom.

"Answer the phone when it rings," is my final warning. Mayor Ross points at Rhonda, his way of telling her to leave me alone, and then goes back into his office to take his afternoon nap.

I slump forward against my desk, mind reeling. "AH!" I shout, freaked out when my cellphone vibrates beneath my cheek. I press the talk button but stay silent, waiting for Malcolm to terrorize me some more.

"I thought I could handle Devon's bullshit, but I was wrong," flows hesitantly from the other side. "Earlier today, I almost killed a kid who was hauled in for possession. I wanted him to tell me where my son was. The poor kid pissed his pants before I even laid a hand on him. I felt like a monster."

Swallowing a dozen times... if Malcolm can pretend the last few minutes didn't happen, I guess I will, too. "Odds are, the kid has never came into contact with Devon. It's like saying all thieves know one another."

"That's what Colin said after I beat the hell out of my desk for just sitting there being lazy." Malcolm laughs humorlessly, drawing tears to my eyes. "That was a joke, by the way. No desks were harmed by me today. Uh, relatively unharmed, that is."

"How's the hand?" spills before I can stop it. The mother: healer, fixer, boo-boo kisser rises to the surface before I can stop it. "You must have one of those squeezey ice pack things with the magical stuff inside."

"Let me guess, you've taken one apart before?" Malcolm sounds calmer than usual, as that intimate quality slides into his voice. It's as comforting as it is unnerving.

"Not me, but Seth has. One of the many times Violet and Willow had a cat fight. I can't remember which one was hurt. They were always equal in strength, but Willow was craftier," I ramble on. Getting embarrassed, I mumble, "Overshare, much?"

"Clover?" Malcolm whispers into the phone. "I'm sorry for whatever I did or said. I'm out of practice with women–"

Feeling uncomfortable with his apology, I quickly mutter, "Somehow I doubt that."

"It's true," Malcolm sounds sincere. "I have three sons. Then there are Auggie and Robin. Let's face it, Isis may be a girly girl when it comes to most shit, but she is all guy in her brain. Raven is the only little lady in my life, and I'm her daddy. I hang around with men all day. Men and hardened criminals, so I sometimes come off as too rash."

I bust out laughing, and the sound echoes against my desk. Idiot that I am, is leaning on my desk, ear pressed to the cellphone, hiding my face behind the veil of my hair. I can feel the eyes of my coworkers on me. "Hardened criminals? Yeah, it's terrifying down there, with your card games, pizza deliveries, donut-eating, and shit-story swapping. I'm guessing the bathroom is disgusting with all that shit-flinging."

"Ah, we're all just monkeys down here," Malcolm sounds embarrassed and surprised that I remembered how he teased me about shit-flinging. "I didn't say it wasn't fun down here, just that we aren't very sensitive. It'd kill the badass atmosphere in the Bat Cave if we were talking feelings and giving each other Hallmarks after a bad day."

"And not only are you having a bad day, you're having a bad week. I'm sorry, I'm fresh out of Hallmark cards, but I can lend an ear if your badass reputation can stand it."

"Bad week?" Malcolm's voice is tight with suppressed emotions. "I'm trying to channel my father for sanity's sake, and remember all of his sage advice. It's something along the lines of, '*Shit happens. Deal with it. It's not your fault, so don't dwell in it.*' Can you please tell me that my son's behavior isn't my fault?"

Malcolm sounds so much like a little boy that my heart literally stops beating inside my chest. When it restarts, it hurts so much that tears sting my eyes. I try to put myself in Malcolm's shoes, and the thought alone makes me want to throw up.

"It's all your fault," I deadpan. "Everything that anyone ever does wrong is your fault, Malcolm. You should probably just get up from your desk, walk into a jail cell, lock yourself in, and flush the key down the toilet. Let's face it, you're the world's worst father."

"Clover?" Malcolm whispers, and it flows down my spine with a billion sparks of warning. "You're the worst pep-talker ever. You know that, right?"

"If you want me to hold your hand and tell you everything is going to be fine, I can't do that. If you want me to feed into your guilt and tell you what you've done wrong, I can't do that either. If you want me to tell you the truth, then that I can do."

"This I've got to hear," Malcolm murmurs back. For once, I wish we were face-to-face. I don't want to have these conversations via text message or email, or over the phone while we sit at our desks, whispering so no one will overhear. I want to sit down at a table with a cup of coffee and have an adult conversation about adult situations. I want to feel like a woman, not just a mother, daughter, or sister.

"I had to let Willow mess up her life. She was a teacup-sized stoner. I sat back while she moved out of my parents' house so she could go screw her boss, and then your son, and probably your other son. Let's face it, my daughter is a fuck-up. You know how she was created, so it's no wonder that she's… warped. But I love Willow anyway. I love the way my past and hers has shaped her. Willow wasn't a mistake, and I wouldn't change her for anything. She's perfectly flawed. Ask me why I didn't stop Willow from making those mistakes?"

"Why?" Malcolm breathes.

"Free will and regret. I wanted my daughter to grow up, and I didn't want her to regret her life like I regret mine. I know that sounds odd, like I should have stepped in to stop her mistakes. It's not regret over our poor choices that I'm talking about. It's regret over not making the mistakes in the first place. Not living life because all you do is what's expected of you. Living in fear, never taking a chance because it's safer that way. That doesn't make memories, Malcolm. That doesn't teach you anything. It just makes you bitter. In an odd way, Devon is living his life and shaping his future right now."

"What if Devon doesn't have a future?" comes so faintly I'm not sure I heard Malcolm correctly.

"Where Devon is isn't important. What he's doing is. He ran away because Kieren told him about rehab, didn't he? I heard through dispatch that Devon's rounded up the rehab kids. Do you know why?"

Voice shaking, Malcolm's fear bleeds through. "So they could run away?"

"Devon's a drug addict, but Officer Devon Mason is deeply rooted inside him. I bet they're somewhere getting fucked up–the bender to beat all benders. Devon made sure when he's ready to be found, they will all be found together. Do you know why?"

"No. I don't have a fucking clue what my son is up to or why. It's killing me."

"This isn't false hope, Malcolm. I know your son. Hell, even after hurting Willow and Essie, I still love the little bastard. Stop looking for Devon because he didn't go anywhere. He's right here. Deep down I know Devon's doing this because he knows he needs help, and he wants to help his friends, too. Just think outside your grief, and you'll see your son beneath."

"What if he overdoses?" Malcolm's voice cracks, and I have to swallow back the sob that threatens to escape my throat. If someone were to give me this advice about Seth, I wouldn't take it. But Devon isn't my son, so I'm not so clouded by grief that I can't see reason.

"Devon is a drug addict. I know overdoses happen constantly. But the odds of an overdose happening today aren't any higher than they were three days ago or last month. I know that doesn't sound comforting because you were ignorant then. But for Devon, this is just an ordinary day of drug using."

"How do you know that, Clover? How do you know Dev hasn't taken so many drugs that he's not already dead?"

"I don't. Maybe if I say it enough, you'll hear it. Freaking out isn't going to change anything. Devon was a drug addict months ago, and he survived. He's still a drug addict today. You will find Devon when he wants to be found. You have hope because it's no coincidence that he rounded up his rehab buddies. These are kids that have never had contact before. There is a five year age gap between them. They wouldn't have even gone to school together. The part of Devon that is a police officer is ensuring that they all get help. Have faith, Malcolm."

"I don't know what to do," Malcolm utters hopelessly.

"What would John Mason do?"

Malcolm barks a humorless laugh. "Punch me hard enough to make me land on my ass, and then call me a dumbass."

"You're being snarky, right?"

"Sadly, I am not. That was a position I found myself in at least once a day for the first seventeen years of my life. I should have done that to my sons, and then I wouldn't be living in hell right this second."

"That explains a lot," I mutter, shocked that Malcolm just admitted he thinks he was too soft on his kids. "So one of your kids messed up. When Willow was fucking up, I just made sure it didn't bleed over onto Seth and Violet. That's what you need to do. Sad truth: whether Devon runs away, hits rock bottom, falls victim to addiction, or gets his act together and stays clean, you'll still be Kieren, Raven, and Weston's father. No matter what happens, they will still need you. If you fall apart, it's like telling them they don't matter– like Devon was more important than them."

"Thank you," Malcolm breathes into the phone. "I needed to hear that. I wish their mother would've been more like you: smart, resilient, rational. A man needs a kick to the nuts sometimes or he becomes deaf to everything but the negative track playing out in his mind."

"Don't thank me, Malcolm. For some reason, I have faith you would never forget your other children. You would've been more involved, fearing they would follow their brother's path… and trust me, I'm just phoning it in. I don't have a clue what I'm doing most of the time. I'm just making it up as I go along."

"You give me too much credit, and yourself too little. If you won't take the thank you for the advice, then take it from the shady bastards you saved tonight. I was about to go on a town-wide manhunt, beating the life out of anyone I came across who might have known my son's whereabouts. Now I'm going to go home early, eat crappy spaghetti, and watch a movie with my kids."

"Malcolm?"

"Yeah, Lucky Clover?"

"Don't text me like before. Ya know, as Papa Bear. From now on, if you want to talk, just call me and we will talk."

"No promises. I like terrorizing you with my flirtatious ways."

"Lord, save me."

CHAPTER EIGHT

The Widow

I lean back, palms on my thighs, enjoying the warmth of the morning sun on my face. For early May, there is still a crispness in the air– moisture that keeps the eighty degree weather at bay. Lately, my only '*me*' time is when I'm doing household chores. My children disappear as soon a dust rag, broom, toilet brush, or a rake materializes.

Elbows deep in the front flowerbeds, unearthing the budding dahlia bulbs, I find my center. I'm not even irritated that Seth is inside the house, ignoring me. I placated him with pancakes and sausage. The trick to fending off the prick inside my son is through food. I wonder if this is true for all males. No, it didn't work on Sam.

The silence from my usually chatty son isn't as odd as the clinginess from my usually frigid daughter. I feel like an inmate on death row. It's time to tell Willow the truth, because the twins aren't allowing me to ignore it any longer.

"Just once, I'd love to see you get dirty," comes from behind me, startling the shit out of me.

"Robin Basil Prynne!" I shout. "I almost peed my pants– how's that for dirty? Walk heavier next time." Unbidden, my hands fly up to make sure my hair is still smoothed back in its French Twist, causing Rob to laugh at me. I smile up at my baby brother as his warm brown eyes smile back down at me.

"Really? Your hair is fine. Geez." Crouching down beside me, Robin starts tossing the pulled weeds into the refuse bucket. "I'm being serious. It's creepy how you manage to keep clean while you're pulling weeds. And who the hell pulls weeds at nine in the morning?"

Frustrated, I slump to the ground. "I'm in the front yard," I say as my answer for the perfect guise. "Look across the street. Don't you feel their eyes judging you?"

"Peggy's a piece of work, isn't she?" Robin says to me as he looks over his shoulder at my mother-in-law and Mrs. Dobson. "Do they always sit on the porch?"

"Yeah, even in the dead of winter," I mutter, disgusted. "The bitch even keeps a journal of what she considers my unsavory actions. The one time the twins were dropped off after curfew, she called CPS on my ass. Lana Baxter, the county case worker, nearly choked when I said the kids were dropped off by Officer Devon and Willow after the school's science fair. Bullshit. Last night, Peggy accosted me as I got home from work. She threatened to take me to court over the kids if I didn't spruce up my lawn. Something about how her grandchildren shouldn't live in squalor. Even had the nerve to say I was disturbing her son's eternal rest with my lazy behavior."

"W-o-w," Robin drawls out, clearly impressed with my mother-in-law's lunacy. "Sam was like that, wasn't he? I would've never guessed it, but some things are finally clicking into place." Rob touches my hair in example, tucking a stray strand back into place.

I turn my head away so my brother can't see my expression. I have the most expressive face, and Willow inherited it from me. "I don't want to talk about it," I murmur as I begin weeding again. "Just know that Peggy's insults aren't original in nature."

"So… Malcolm slept well last night," Rob says to unnerve me.

"Yeah, that's probably a good thing," I mutter with a shrug. *What the hell?* "Why are you telling me this?" Since I refuse to look at my brother, I don't know what facial expression he is making. But for some reason, I just know he's laughing at my transparency.

Ignoring my question, Rob asks conversationally, "What's on your agenda today?"

"Well," I sigh, sitting back on my heels. "After this very glamorous job of weeding the flower beds for my mother-in-law's entertainment, I have to work the weekly budget, and then I have to teach the kids how to cook this afternoon. If Seth and Violet have plans tonight, then Ginny and I are splitting a bottle of wine and watching eighties movies. Fun, exciting, is the life of a widow." I roll my eyes at my dramatics.

"Well, that sounds kinda nice, actually," Rob says with all sincerity. "Reason I'm here, I'm visiting with our parents all day.

I thought that would give you a break… and since I was coming here anyway, someone wanted me to deliver something to you."

I freeze like a rabbit in a snare. Scared shitless. Refusing to so much as even breathe. What could HE possible want from me? I thought our phone conversation absolved me from ignoring his texts and calls. I can't imagine what horrific thing Robin is delivering to me for Papa Bear.

"Relax." Robin laughs, a deep chuckle that is comforting. "I'm nosy, so I read the attached note. I had to drop it off before the kids saw it. Malcolm doesn't think it's time for them to know you guys are talking."

"Oh," I sigh, surprised. "Well, what is it? Where is it?"

"On your kitchen table, sis." Rob flows fluidly to his feet, and then reaches his hand down to draw me to stand beside him. "How about I finish your weeding while you investigate Malcolm's offering? Huh? Would that be helpful? Ma and Dad are still at the hardware store, so I have nothing else to do but wait."

"That's so sweet." I draw Robbie into a hug, surprising us both. I whisper into his ear, "but you can't help. That would be worse than if I didn't weed the beds in the first place. I would go from lazy to helpless. The day Dad replaced the broken porch spindle, Peggy ran over here and said I was a spoiled brat who had to have her daddy do everything for her… and she said it in front of our entire family. I was humiliated. Just know I appreciate the sentiment, Robin, but I have to do it on my own."

"Now, the question is: why do you put up with Peggy's shit?" Robbie draws away from our hug, holding me out at arm's length, looking deep into my eyes like the answer is written there. "Why? That's not the Clover I remember when I was growing up. My sister was messy. She'd play in the dirt with us, and then kick my ass while calling me a shithead. The sister I remember was fierce– a lot like her daughters."

Blushing, feeling guilt and shame, the words just spill off my tongue. "That girl was smothered the day she had to decide on the well-being of that daughter you're so fond of, and then she had to deceive everyone every day thereafter. That's the why of it: Peggy holds it over my head. Do this or that, say this or that, go here or there, because if I don't, she will tell my daughter the truth."

"Don't give that bitch the power. Take it back by telling Willow the truth."

"I will," I say sheepishly. "I'm just not ready yet."

"Why not?" Robbie huffs out as if the conclusion of eighteen years of lying is just that simple.

I stare into my brother's eyes and profess the God's honest truth. "Because Willow isn't ready yet. As with all things, they come first."

"Ah, you might be right on that. If Willow was ready, she'd have figured it out when you tested the waters by telling her about your illegitimate kid."

"Exactly," I mutter, stepping away from my brother.

"Well, Peggy's gonna kick the can soon, right?" Rob asks, teasing yet sounding serious.

"No such luck, brother. Peggy is only fifty-seven. She's a baby compared to our parents. I have a good thirty years left of her pleasantries."

"No," Rob orders firmly. "You have exactly the amount of time until you tell Willow the truth. After that, fuck Peggy. Fuck 'em all. I want my sister back," comes fiercely between clenched teeth as he stares over my shoulder to the porch across the street. Calming down, he orders, "Now, go inside and check out your goody box before it spoils. I'll be out here doing your weeding, and I might even trim the bushes while I'm at it."

"Robbie," I sigh, exasperated that he doesn't understand the dynamics I have with Peggy.

"No." Rob points at my front door, and then shoves me up the steps. "Go delve in your treasure box before my nephew gets to snooping and finds your note. It's not a '*Papa Bear*' note," he warns. "Go!"

In the center of my kitchen table is a wooden crate overflowing with food. I peer into the box, speechless. Not knowing how long the food has been left out, I quickly sort the contents into pantry, refrigerator, and freezer items. Potatoes... onions... carrots... and by the time I find beef and lamb, I know exactly what Malcolm wants me to cook: Shepherd's pie. I huff a laugh when I find the huge bottle of Worcestershire sauce and Malcolm's additive of shredded cheddar cheese.

"What the?" I murmur as I slide the lid off of a gift box that was hidden beneath a pound package of salted butter. "Huh?"

A bottle of red wine, lavender bubble bath, a linen-scented candle, and a little girl's pink journal– the kind with a small lockable latch. The tiny key is safely resting in its lock. Unsure what these objects are meant for, I grab the typed and signed note that was taped to the top of the gift box. Rob read this note, which means he searched the contents of this box to find it, and then re-taped it. Snoopy bastard.

Lucky Clover,

I'm writing this in the early morning hours, after debating how to fix what I broke. So I'm going to go with honesty. I believe you are the type of female that appreciates honesty over flattery as a form of apology.

First: I want to apologize for our past correspondences. You found insult where none was meant. I meant them to be teasing, playful, flirtatious. Looking back, I can see why you would see them as domineering. No one will ever call me a softy, so I don't realize I'm being difficult until it's too late. I make no excuses for my behavior, nor will I ever change who I am. This is me– take me as I am. But I know when I've fucked up. So my most sincerest of apologies on being an ass.

Second: From now on, you and I will communicate as Malcolm and Clover, with the exception of the occasional 'Papa Bear' request to keep the kids on their toes. While I'm ready to see you in person, to no longer hide what I hope is a budding friendship, I don't think the kids are ready. They would expect more out of us, and we aren't there yet. I refuse to make my intentions clear over an email, text message, note, phone call, or a smoke signal. I want us to sit down and talk so there will be no misunderstanding or miscommunications. Put everything on the table, where we either digest it or toss it in the trash.

Third: Thank you for the advice over Devon. I actually slept last night for the first time in a long time. Thank you for entertaining and educating my children as well. I know the kids act like they don't give a shit, but they truly do enjoy your cooking lessons. While you and I haven't had our talk, those kids know exactly what they want to happen. Not to freak you out, but my children are learning you. No matter if you and I have a future together, our children always will. Regardless, we are family. So thank you for giving my children the mothering they are starved to feel. Thank you for lessening the guilt I feel over being a single parent. I could have gone out and remarried as soon as Camille died, but I didn't want my children growing up as Isis and I had. It's not a regret I have, yet it doesn't lessen the guilt. What does absolve me is you: you speaking to me as a woman would, speaking to my children as a mother should. Thank you.

Fourth: This box of groceries is not a demand. I don't want to make another request. After I looked back, I realized how the past suggestions seemed like demands. This offering is merely a suggestion for your cooking lesson with side benefits. Colin McGregor is missing his grandmother's cooking, and here is this amazing cook of a similar heritage teaching a cooking lesson today. If you would, please teach the kids how to make Shepherd's pie, and allow them to bring it home so I may feed my friend a home-cooked meal.

Fifth: Your children are more than welcome to join mine at my dinner table this evening. It feels selfish of me to send you a box of groceries, request you make a meal, invite your children to eat with us, and then deny you the pleasure. I want you at my table, but it would confuse our children if that happened before we had our face-to-face conversation. A bonus of being denied my company, you can have an evening without your children. I know how relaxing those can be, and far and few between.

Sixth: the small box is for your evening alone. The journal has two keys: one for you and one for me. I want you to write your regrets down. As you said, not the regrets over the past mistakes you've made, but the regrets over not doing the reckless things that ultimately teach us who we are. If you think it, write it down. Every few weeks or so, I will personally make sure you experience something from your list. Even if it takes the rest of my days, you will never regret again.

Lucky number Seven: I actually don't have anything for seven. I'm not the superstitious sort. But when writing to an Irish woman named Clover, you tend to become slightly superstitious. So, seven: it pains me to say, that yes, I am a softy. I'm overly dramatic, emotional, clingy, and cuddly, to the point that my family groans when I walk into the room. I'm disgustingly romantic, formal, and traditional. My father saw this in me and tried to stop it, only to starve me to the point that I could never get enough attention, affection, and intimacy with my nearest and dearest. I'm only telling you this to prepare you for our face-to-face. You'll have to steel yourself against my affections. You've been warned.

–Malcolm.

"What's that?" Seth asks, sneaking up behind me, trying to peer over my shoulder.

Nearly jumping out of my skin, I clutch Malcolm's letter to my chest like it's a secret I don't dare share. "Just a recipe," I lie flawlessly after nearly two decades of practice. "I didn't have time to get to the store this morning, so I sent Rob with a list. I was just double-checking to make sure he didn't forget anything."

"We're cooking with wine?" Seth asks, not buying my bullshit. He picks the wine bottle up in his hand, eyeing it like it's poison. "We're cooking with wine?" His eyebrows meet his hairline as he gives me the most patronizing glare I've ever witnessed. "Wine with *Willow*? While Devon is on the run?"

Anger simmering beneath the surface, I don't lie, even though the bottle of wine in question is not the same bottle in his hand. "The wine is for me. I invited Ginny over for a girls' night."

I want to kick my own ass for falling into old patterns. I don't have to explain myself to my *son*. If I want to drain the bottle of wine like it's water, that's my business. Seth is standing in *my* kitchen questioning *me*. This will never happen again. It's gone on far too long, and the older Seth gets the worse it's going to become. I am Seth's mother, not his bitch.

Fingering my new journal, my son transforms into his father before my very eyes. Nausea twists my stomach. Seth gives me a pointed look, and then leaves the kitchen as if nothing just transpired between us.

I take a deep breath, unable to deal with this kind of attitude any longer. I'm unsure how to change the course we are on. If my son continues on this path, either he will torment me until death or transfer this bitter hatred onto some unsuspecting, innocent girl.

For the first sixteen years of my life, love and respect were absolute. There was no payment, and nothing you could ever do would take the love away. With my parents, my aunt and uncle, Robin and Essie, it is still absolute. My world changed with Sam, and then Peggy, and now Seth.

It's a feeling that can't be explained. The words are cordial, without implied threat. The expression on Seth's face is pleasant, that of a boy growing into a young man. Anyone who witnessed our encounter would see us as having a conversation between mother and son, and this is exactly how it was with Sam.

From the age of sixteen to thirty, I lived in a constant state of emotional chaos. Sam never raised his voice nor his hand in anger. He had other ways to control me other than the physical.

I would get into a routine, feel comfortable, and then I would get a tingling sensation in the back of my skull. Some call it intuition. Willow calls it spidey-sense. But I would just know. I'd make sure everything was perfect before Sam got home, not that it wasn't perfect every day. The house would be spotless. The food would be gourmet. The kids would be well-behaved and thriving in school. My appearance would be flawless. I never nagged, never complained, never questioned, and never asked for anything.

Sam would enter the house, and the feeling would intensify to the point that I couldn't breathe. The kids couldn't feel it as they hugged and kissed and chatted with their father. We would sit down to dinner, and Sam would say something as innocuous as, *"The chicken is seasoned well, but a bit dry, don't you think?"* or *"Is the microwave moved a few inches to the left? What do you think, kids? Is your mom slacking in her duties?"* Sam would flash his charismatic smile and laugh as if he was teasing, but it was no joke.

That's how it would begin, followed by comment after comment until I was reduced to nothing. If it was a task I performed, performed the same way as last time, it was torn to shreds.

The small things: *"Why are my socks folded wrong?"* *"If you were smart, you'd stop hanging my shirts up like this. The shoulders are getting stretched out from the hanger."* *"The shampoo was two inches from where it should be on the shelf. I got soap in my eyes trying to locate it with my eyes closed. Are you trying to blind me?"* *"The peanut butter was spread too thin on my sandwich, and too thick last time. "How many times do I have to repeat this? You mow from left to right, not up and down. My mother doesn't like how it looks"* *"Can't you do a damn thing right? Are you retarded?"*

The big things: *"Mommy doesn't love us, does she? If she did, she wouldn't be home late from work and we wouldn't be hungry. Empty bellies means Mom is a terrible mother."* *"Doesn't Mom have a funny laugh? We shouldn't make Mom laugh anymore, should we, kids?"* *"Dave and Mary, you guys are the sweetest folks I've ever met. It's too bad Clover didn't take after either one of you."* *"Seth, you know how when you do wrong, you get put into timeout. Well, Mommy didn't do as she was told. Her time out is no hugs for the next two weeks." "Rob, you're a lucky fuck, getting all the talent in the family." "Don't be rude, Clover. Mom bought you the self-help book on how to be a better wife because she cares about you, and wants me to be happy."*

The soul destroying things: *"If you moan during sex, I won't touch you again for three months." "You stupid cunt, I lost my hard-on because you came." "Don't breathe. I hate the way you breathe." "Your ass is too fat and your thighs are too thin. You look ridiculous, like a mix between a lolly pop and a stick figure." "Don't move. I swear to God, if you move I will never touch you again." "Just lie on your side until I'm finished. Is that too much to ask?" "Don't turn the light on or I'll get turned off looking at you." "Never mind. Just looking at you, hearing you, smelling you, makes me fucking sick." "I'll be at Ida's. Her cunt wasn't stretched out by three kids, and she doesn't just lie there like an ice queen. She actually moans and gets off." "Clover, I'm pretty sure you're broken sexually."*

Deep down in my soul I knew I wasn't at fault, that there was nothing I could do that would make Sam love or respect me. I also knew that I didn't do anything to deserve the maltreatment. In the grand scheme of things, who gives a fuck if the toaster was placed in the cupboard with the cord facing in versus out? No matter how big or small, I was tormented, while others could do no wrong. Sam just hated me because he could. He hated me because I wasn't who he wanted me to be. I couldn't be anyone other than myself, no matter how hard I strived.

I realize this now, five years after Sam's death, and I still haven't come to terms with it. I can't wrap my mind around abuse that wasn't visible to the naked eye. If Sam had hit me, it would have been obvious. I could have pointed at the bruise while screaming, *"See this? Do you see this? You did this! I'm not the liar!"*

When a person emotionally abuses you, your mind is twisted until you doubt everything about yourself, even why you feel the way you do. You start to feel insane, as if you can't make your own decisions, because no matter what, you are wrong. You live in a constant state of doubt. You try and try and try to do as you're told, do it perfectly, because their pride in you is all that matters.

There was no pride. No love. No praise. It took a long time, but this I finally came to terms with: nothing was ever good enough because it wasn't about me. The insanity was always about Sam, and whatever insecurities and doubts he held inside. I was the one who was reduced to nothing so he could feel like the almighty god standing on my back while my face was pressed into the mud. I will be damned if I allow my only son to grow up and act like his father, not to me and not to his future wife.

This ends now.

"Seth David Webster!" I scream at the top of my lungs, refusing to behave like I did as a wife. I will *not* keep quiet. I *will* speak my mind. I have emotions, and I have a right to feel those emotions. I have a right to be treated with respect in my own home.

Slowly walking into the kitchen from the living room, cellphone clutched in her hand. "Mom?" Violet's voice breaks, scared by the look in my eye.

"Where's your brother. I need to speak with him *now*. If Seth's not in this room in the next ten seconds, he's grounded until school starts next year." Breath rasping in and out, I start shoving food into the refrigerator with little care.

"What'd I do wrong?" Seth plays innocent. It takes everything in me to see my son clearly, to not transfer my emotions about the past over his father onto him. I almost stop myself, until I see the faint antagonistic curl to his lips.

"This is my house. I work every day to pay to keep a roof over our heads. The food in your gut: I bought, prepared, and served you. The boxers covering your ass: I bought, washed, folded, and put into your dresser drawers. The television you were just watching: I bought, lugged into this house, and installed. The bed you are sleeping in: I bought, assembled, and made. The toilet you shit in: bought and scrubbed by me. And I do all these things out of love and responsibility. You are my son, under my roof, and you will not disrespect me to my face. I can see through your act, Seth. I don't give a fuck if no one else does."

"You said fuck," Seth says like he's not getting verbally smacked. My sweet baby boy, the one with the chipmunk cheeks and big chocolate brown eyes, turns into a self-righteous prick before my very eyes, like he's possessed with his dead father's spirit. "That's a bad word, Mom, remember?"

"Seth," Violet warns for me. Voice strong and unforgiving, causing me to wonder what has been going on between my twins. "Don't do this. Mom's being serious."

"I know, you know, I know, what you're doing. You're so young, you don't even realize the ramifications to your actions. So I will leave you with this: we make mistakes. I made a mistake I'm still paying for– a mistake that has enriched our lives exponentially. And it sickens me that you are forcing me to call her a mistake," I practically sob out.

"Just say it out loud, Mother," Seth challenges me.

"Willow," I breathe out. "You're treating me like a dog because of Willow. I am your mother. I am Violet's mother. I am Willow's mother. You love your sisters more than anyone on this earth. I. Am. Their. Mother," I slowly stress, pounding my chest with every word.

"That's not good enough, *Mom*," Seth twists my name nastily. "Just because you can spread your legs and get knocked up, doesn't make you a mother."

"Oh, my God, Seth." Palm covering her mouth, horrified, Violet gasps out, "No."

"You may think it's okay to disrespect your own mother, but it's not okay to disrespect theirs. Look at your sister," I demand, pointing at a silently crying Violet. "You are treating her mother like shit. She is a part of me. I am a part of her. Just as I am a part of you. To hate me, is to hate yourself, is to hate your sisters. So think about that the next time you want to act like a little prick because you don't understand adult situations that happened four years before you were born. Think about making the same decision in eighteen months when you turn sixteen… and then we will fucking talk like adults."

"You don't get it," Seth snarls in my face, going chin-to-chin with me like a cherub-faced bully.

"No, you don't fucking get it!" I shout, throwing my hands up in the air, so frustrated I'm choking on my words. "You're fourteen years old. You haven't even lived long enough to know what the fuck is going on. I have shoes older than you."

"Way to disrespect your son, Mom." Seth is either being ironic or hypocritical, and I don't think he knows which.

"Do you want me to treat you as nastily as you treat me? Do you think you can take it?" I threaten.

"Yeah," he sneers.

"Spread my legs, huh?" I say, feeling sick to my stomach. "All I did was spread my legs? I didn't create life from my own, carry it for almost ten months, deliver it, and then feed the child from my own body for another year? Two children at the same time. No man can ever do any of that," I mutter arrogantly. "Now, would you say all your father did was rut on me, then? If you're going to be nasty about it, reducing something amazing to something dirty, then it involves *both* your parents."

Seth is rendered speechless, so I continue on, since I'm a worthless whore. "I didn't raise Robbie and Willow and Violet and you, all the while keeping an eye on your grandparents? None of that happened? I've never went a day since I was sixteen years old without holding a paying job. So after all that, I should just lie down and die because my teenage son is pissed at me. I'm a worthless bitch because he doesn't like a choice I made when I was a child. What gives you the right to dictate my fucking life, Seth?"

"Because I'm your son!" Seth screams, true emotions finally breaking through. The vein in his forehead bulges, his eyes gloss over with unshed tears. I feel horrible that I had to get into a battle of wills with my son so he would finally just let it out… let it go.

"As the man of the house, perhaps you should go out and get a job and pay your due. You don't even mow the lawn or take out the trash. I've been doing this the wrong way, treating you like a prince because you were a good kid and your father demanded that you be treated that way."

"I am a good kid," Seth bites out. His hands curl into fists at his sides, betraying his frustration. "I don't do a thing wrong."

"Good kid? Except when you treat our mother like shit, bad-mouth her behind her back, and act like a douchebag when we're home alone," Violet comes to my defense. "I keep telling you I understand, Seth. I'm in the same situation as you. But you're being an asshole. Be angry all ya want, but don't make me feel bad because I love our mother. Don't make me pick a side, because it won't be yours."

"It should be Willow's," Seth snarls.

I slump to the nearest seat, my legs no longer holding me. Numb, I watch my children continue the fight I've already lost.

"I *am* taking Willow's side. This is between Mom and Willow, and it's none of our business. Willow has treated me like shit since I was born, and you never took *my* side. You were my twin, thinking she was your aunt, and you left me to deal with it on my own. I forgave Willow, and Willow forgave me. But I don't know if I can forgive you for always loving Willow more than the rest of us."

"I–" Seth gasps out but is interrupted.

"Our mother is the best mom in the world, and here you are treating her like trash because she got pregnant at sixteen. I don't know what I would've done if I was in the same situation. We're not guys, Seth. We can't just screw a chick and walk away. We're left with the kid. You make me sick, Seth. Grow up."

"Don't." I say to stop the oncoming fight. My voice is thready, barely audible, but the kids hear me anyway. "When you grow up, you'll understand why Violet and I are angry with you, and why Willow will be angry with you as well. You're acting like a man." I laugh humorlessly.

"What is that supposed to mean?" Seth sounds confused but no longer angry, like Violet's admission drained his frustration away.

"Like a big baby," Violet teases. "You're always right. You think you can tell us what to do because you're the *man*," she twists the word, sounding like a raging feminist. "And we're just girls. Unless you're Willow, Seth treats you like shit," Violet spits, sounding insanely jealous.

"This is the honest to God's truth: I refuse to raise my son to go from his mother to his wife, never growing up, always having the emotional maturity of a teenager. You'll be ignorant, and your wife will be miserable if she has to raise you along with your kids. It will be insufferable."

Before Seth can say a word, Violet interprets for me. "Mom means, you'll go from one woman washing your dirty underwear and serving you food, to another. I'm never getting married, because you're all little boys who think all you have to do is go to work and you're done after you punch your timecard."

I laugh like an escaped lunatic from an asylum. I scrub my hands over my face, at a complete and total loss. "Violet, are you secretly married to some douchebag, and you didn't tell me about it?"

Blushing, looking sheepish, Violet grumbles, "Too many talk shows, I guess."

I stand up and do the one thing I haven't done in months, I yank my son's hand and pull him into a hug. "I love you. You are a good kid. You are loyal and honest. I respect that you are angry with me, but I won't kiss your feet because of it. It's my job as the parent to raise you into a functioning adult. I won't allow you to disrespect me because I'm a woman and by chance you were born a boy."

"I'm mad at you," Seth whispers in my ear, arms tightening around me. "I think I hate you right now."

"That's your right," I say stiffly, moving to pull away from our hug. "But it doesn't change the fact that I love you unconditionally."

"God, I pity the woman you marry!" Violet shouts as she charges from the room.

"What your sister was *trying* to say: women want a partner, not another father. Be the type of man who is a husband to his wife, not another son."

"I don't understand," Seth whispers. "How can you be the father and the son?"

"Because the wife's father was raised just like all the other men before him: from mother to wife, without learning to do anything on his own except for his job. It's why you see divorced men eating frozen dinners and living in squalor for a few years until they learn. They were ignorant to cooking and cleaning because it's woman's work. I won't stunt you, not only as a man but as a human being. You will treat all women with respect, no matter who they are. There is no such thing as women's work. It's just a necessary evil if you want to eat edible food, have clean clothes, and sleep in clean sheets. That toilet upstairs doesn't give a shit if it's a man or woman holding the toilet brush. You're going to learn this stuff before you leave my home."

"Or what?" Seth challenges me.

"Or what? Then next four years of your life are going to suck. Then, if you manage to get a wife, I'll tell her how you really are, or Violet will. But none of that will matter," I threaten.

Curious to why my tone went from flat to amused, Seth asks, "Why's that?"

"Because Violet and I will call your favorite person, and we will tell her how you are acting toward women in general, and then she will come over here and kick your ass. But worse, Willow will be as disappointed in you as I am." Taking a deep breath, I blurt out, "I made a mistake. It's not the end of the world. Nobody died. You can be mad at me, you can hate me, but you will respect me. Now, go. I need to be alone."

CHAPTER NINE

The Widower

"What's up with that kid?" I mutter more to myself than to Ren. We're sitting on the back steps watching everyone play Ladder Ball.

Belly full of Clover's most excellent Shepherd's pie, we all spilled out in to the yard for some not-so friendly competition. Striving for a bit of normalcy, we all made a point not to mention the drugged-up runaway, and we're actually having a fun time. Willow and Colin have ganged up on Violet and Rae, while Weston and Seth wait to challenge the winner.

"I suck at this game. The playing field isn't large enough. I'm sure that's why," Ren mumbles, cheeks pinking from embarrassment.

"Yeah," I draw out. "That's exactly why you had your ass handed to you." I smirk to myself, doing my damnedest not to laugh outright at my boy. "Make sure when you get your own place that your backyard is the size of a football field."

Pouting, Ren keeps rambling on, "Willow shouldn't have told me I couldn't be her partner anymore."

"You threw the bola into the neighbor's yard. You were nowhere near the target." I chuckle to myself. My athletically inclined son found a sport he sucks at, and now his girlfriend told him he couldn't play anymore. Which means I can't play because she stole my partner. "You're so going to be out here practicing when no one is looking, I just know it."

Not hearing a word I'm saying, "Willow wasn't complaining last night. No, she wasn't. Lose one game of Ladder Ball and she calls me clumsy." Grumbling to himself, while we watch Willow do a victory dance. The girl makes me smile– she's such a dipshit. "I wasn't clumsy when she was getting off on me, now was I?"

"Excuse me?" Eyes bugging out of my head, I turn to my son as he keeps rambling on about things I should never know. "Since when did this happen?"

Startled, Ren blinks a few times. "Was I saying that out loud?"

"Yes." I clear my throat. "Yes, you most certainly were," I say slowly. I lean in to my son and ask, "Did you have sex with Willow?"

"Not yet," Ren sounds disappointed. "She's skittish but horny. The combination is killing me."

"What did I tell you about patience? Just make sure she knows you want her, and she will come to you when she's ready."

"I never thought I'd be in a place where I could be in a relationship, let alone with Willow. Not after the date rapist I made myself out to be at Rush, or after all the heinous shit *he-who-shall-remain-nameless* pulled. Jesus, I never thought I'd be… awkward," Ren twists with disgust, pulling a face. "An awkward Mason? What the fuck?"

"Who knew?" I laugh out, feeling damned awkward when it comes to Clover. "Ren, listen to me," I order to draw my son's attention back to our conversation.

Such a fool in love, Ren watches Willow like she is the center of his universe, all the while going on and on about his awkwardness. The boy never shuts up about Willow. A hollow ache forms in my chest because I've never felt that compelled by another person before. I wonder if it's like watching your children sleep. No, that always elicited fear. Unless… Ren does looks scared shitless, invigorated or not.

"Ren, focus." I snort when the kid blinks at me, words dying on his lips. "My God, you're horned up. Knock it off."

"Two nights in a row of dry humping may get us off… but if I don't have sex with her soon, I'm going to die!" Ren shudders. He sounds so overly dramatic that I tilt my head back and release a laugh.

"Idiot, don't gloat," I chastise. "I haven't had sex in eight years. I wouldn't complain over some grinding."

Burning me for my beliefs, "Well, that's what happens when you only believe in sex within a marriage."

"And what's that exactly? You think I'm crazy for thinking that sex should be between partners? You shouldn't fuck someone when the risk is too high for disease and kids. Sex is to connect a couple while making children. It's not something to be taken lightly. So what do I get besides respect for my future wife and my body? What do I get?"

Ren cackles at me, shoving me in the shoulder. "The world's largest set of blue balls."

"Dick," I mutter, but he doesn't hear me over his cackling.

Settling down, "Now, the patience has worked. Willow trusts me, wants to hang out with me, and now she wants me." Ren puffs his chest out like a proud peacock. "I could finally relax if she'd just have sex with me. You said girls like Willow see that as a commitment, right?"

"Yeah, just don't fuck it up by pressuring her."

"So, if Willow gives in, I get to keep her. Like, keep her forever?" Ren has never looked more like a kid than he does now, while asking me advice on how to get his girlfriend to screw him. I'm sure this is a bad parent moment for me. But, Lord help me, I'm going to tell him how to hunt, catch, and keep the girl. I know Ren is excited over the physical, but he sees it as a way to trap Willow into a real relationship.

My baby boy has grown into a Mason man. Never prouder.

"Kid, I've only had sex with your mother. I'm winging this shit. But so far, Dad's advice has held true. Dad's theory was that if you made a woman happy by taking care of her needs, then once she's in your bed, she will stay there."

Fevered, Ren looks slightly high on Willow. "So what do you suggest? What can I do to move this grinding into sweating and moaning?"

"You know nothing of women." I sigh, and then huff a laugh at how ridiculous the kid is being. Ren is vibrating as he watches his girlfriend toss a bola at the Ladder Ball frame. With a shriek, Willow scores, hopping up and down. Ren's smile splits his face in half.

"Neither do you, old man," Ren says to me, eyes never leaving Willow as she instructs Colin on a better throwing technique. "Eight years? It's been eight years? Your massages can't be that good."

"Shut up," I spit, but there is no anger behind the words. "You need more than just a quick, meaningless fuck. Good sex is more complicated than technique. Intimacy, trust, and a foundation of connection are more important than knowing how to wrench an orgasm out of a person. If the Playroom has taught me one thing, it's that women will shut themselves off if they don't trust you. To make love to another person is to lay them bare before you, and I don't just mean nudity. It's why my massages are enough for me for now. It's impossible to experience this with a random stranger."

"I know that feeling more than you could imagine," Ren mutters, sounding sick to his stomach. "If I could change how I screwed every girl in high school, I would. I get it. The last two nights with Willow, it's like she was taking what she wanted from me, and that made it better than the dozens of past encounters combined. I'll be patient, and I can wait, because I don't want to lose what this could turn into."

"Already planning on marrying her, aren't you?" I think back to myself at Ren's age, already married, Devon already born. It wasn't a love match. I married out of necessity. I rushed to make a family for Isis and myself, and to give Auggie a better female role model than Lisa. I failed miserably. I will never regret my children, but I do regret taking Camille as my wife. I wish I would've had what Ren is building with Willow. Maybe if Camille had had that type of love for her husband, she would have used the strength in our love to survive instead of killing herself.

Lost in thought, Ren pops a, "Yup," startling me. "Always planned on marrying Willow. I would say to myself, '*Willow's going to be my wife one day.*' And I've never doubted it for a second." Fists clenching on his thighs, knuckles turning white, he struggles to contain his anger. "It's a miracle Auggie and Devon still breathe."

Automatically my arm slides around Ren's shoulders, drawing him into a half-hug, draining the anger from my son and simultaneously comforting me. "I had nothing to do with that, son. I need you to know that. I wanted Willow to choose for herself. Isis and Rob were jealous over Auggie's interest in the girl, so they shoved your brother at her."

"I know," he whispers tightly. "They should have pushed *me* at Willow, but then we wouldn't be where we are right now. So I can't murder them, I guess."

Feeling horrible for what my sister and her man did to my boy, I decide to help Ren out. "Okay, let me think for a minute, kid."

"Take your time. Don't rush, or you'll fuck up my chances," Ren warns. His attention is immediately taken by Willow.

Competitive in the extreme, the girl is taunting Raven for wearing a huge sun hat. My baby girl might as well be allergic to the sun by the way she burns. Thank goodness growing up with three brothers toughened Rae up. She taunts Willow back by scoring a point for her team while shouting, *"Take that, ya bony bitch."* Sure a fight will break out, I move to intervene. But Willow laughs it off, flips my daughter the bird, and then plays cheerleader when Colin scores a point.

I lean in closer, whispering conspiratorially in Kieren's ear so no one can overhear. "Here is what you do… go about it how you've been doing it because she's comfortable with that. But make it sexier. I don't know. Tell Willow you want to dry hump with some clothes off, clothing that won't get in the way later. Tell her you're not ready to have sex, because you're scared of how intense your feelings are for her. Tell her that you can't kiss her without taking her. Let Willow see how insane she makes you."

"Christ," Ren hisses out of appreciation.

"Don't push. Make Willow insane. Bring her to the brink, and then pull back. Tell her you have to stop, because you can't go any further without having sex. Wait a heartbeat, and then ask her if she wants to continue. Give her the choice– the power. Willow will feel in control."

Arching an eyebrow like Auggie– he no doubt picked that annoying trait up from Willow –Ren asks, "And then she's mine?"

"And then she's yours."

"Forever?"

"Yeah, forever." I take a deep breath and give my son the best advice he will ever receive. "Don't tell Willow you love her before, during, or after sex– same goes with a fight. She won't believe you. It's a ploy weak men use to get a girl to put out on a date or shut up during a fight. It's bullshit. Tell Willow you love her while she looks like hell, sick or something. Maybe when she's doing something goofy, like teasing you for hitting the side of the house with the bola."

Eager, Ren moves closer to me, hungry for more information. The kid's got it bad. "More."

"Swallow any and all pride you possess when it comes to your wife and children. A happy family is more important, no matter the circumstances. There will be days you will hate each other. Just remember that she's allowed to feel how she feels. You're not her father, and she's a grown woman. For the love of all that is holy, never, ever, tell her what to do. Unless she is going to harm herself, let her do what she wants, and then comfort her when she fucks up. Don't only *tell* Willow how you feel, *show* her every damned day, and you will live a long, happy life." I yank my son into a hug, squeezing the hell out of him because he is healthy, happy, and in my arms. "You chose a good one, son.

Content just sitting on our back steps while allowing his dad to cuddle him, Ren sounds hopeful. "You think so?"

"Yeah, I do. You're a good man, Kieren, and Willow's loyal and a little bit crazy. You'll take care of each other, drive each other insane, and you'll never be bored."

Kieren laughs out, "That's for sure–"

Movement in my peripheral has me on my feet in a heartbeat. Kieren joins me as we watch in stunned silence as Weston shoves his palms into Seth's chest and pushes the smaller boy to the ground.

Ass planting, Seth shouts, "What the fuck is your malfunction, West?"

"What's your malfunction, *Seth*?" Weston twists out nastily. Weston has never laid a hand on anyone, not even to wrestle with his brothers. Weston always knew he would be large when he became a man, so he has always tried to keep his temper in check. Something major is happening. "If you're going to be a dick, do it to someone your own size, asshole."

Lunging to his feet, Seth charges Weston, flinging them both to the grass. With a grunt, my son's large body thuds the ground beneath our feet. Curses flying, gangly arms and legs flailing in a blur, the boys beat the ever-loving hell out of each other.

"Stop!" Willow shouts, rushing to stop the boys while the rest of us just look on in awe. Kieren and I make our way over slowly, not wanting to interfere. But Willow has never left well-enough alone. The girl is going to get an accidental punch.

"Spanky," Ren calls out, trying to prevent a banged up Willow. He grabs for her arm, but she flings him off. "Let them fight it out, Willow," Ren says, sounding reasonable. "It's how men do it."

"Idiot! No one hurts my family," Willow says in a shaky voice as she reaches down to yank Seth away from a panting Weston. Willow is protecting– emasculating –the poor kid.

"Tell that to Seth!" Weston shouts at Willow, furious. "I get that you think it's okay to be nasty to your own family. But I'm sick to death of listening to Seth talk trash about Clover and Violet."

"You don't understand!" Seth screams, struggling to get out of Willow's tight hold and back to fighting with Weston.

"I don't give a shit," West snarls. "You're being nasty about the woman I want as my mother, you dick."

"Trust me, she sucks as a mother," Seth grumbles beneath his breath, earning himself a swift kick to the shin from Willow, followed by a punch to the back of the head. Seth falls to the ground, but not because he's hurt. Seth's shocked that Willow clobbered him.

My usually calm boy is radiating fury as he bends over the fallen kid. At fourteen, he's a big guy, built to work hard and play even harder sports. But Weston's size doesn't scare Seth, because he knows my son is a big softy just like his father. Only family brings the bear out of us.

"You have the balls to say this to me when I don't have a goddamned mother!" Weston screams, spit flying, inches from Seth's face. "I'd even take Auggie's cokehead mother over no one! Fuck you, Seth." Straightening to stand tall, Weston glares down at his friend and warns, "If you talk trash about your own mother, maybe she would rather have me as a son!"

"I'm willing to make a trade," Violet agrees coldly. "Either Seth leaves the house or I do!"

"Violet," Willow points at the furious girl. "Bathroom. You and I have to talk. Weston, you're right. Seth needs someone his own size. If we're going to be a family, then you've earned the right to defend Clover and Violet. Kick Seth's ass, but don't break him."

"Holy fuck," Ren whispers near my ear. "Willow must be *really* pissed. That's Seth she just pushed from the nest."

"As the future mother of your offspring," I whisper back, "You better be fucking scared, boy."

"Why?" Ren ask, confused.

"They're scrappers. Violence is in their DNA. Willow will be beating the crap out of your kids for sport," I say with a hearty laugh. I step away from Ren just as Willow drags Violet by me, to the bathroom I presume. "Okay, let's get this out. What's up?"

I stare down at Seth as he sits on the ground. The boy looks more like his father than ever. Sam was a cute little bastard, charismatic– could resell you your own children. But his eyes would shine when he was angry, and then you better get out of his way. Seth's eyes look like this now, but sad, too.

"Everyone out of the yard but me and the boys," I order. "Ren, serve that delicious pie Clover sent over, will ya?"

"Okay, Dad," Ren says, ushering his confused sister and an amused Colin into the house.

I crouch down and yank the kid into a hug. Boys aren't difficult to figure out. They're like wild animals lashing out in pain or fear. My guess, Seth is experiencing a bit of both. The first sob is silent but it radiates from his tiny chest. Hands balled into fists, Seth makes to push me away but he only pulls me closer.

"It's okay to cry," I murmur as Seth struggles not to. "I do it all the time, and don't let Weston fool ya. He cries in my arms just as you are now. I've got a clue on what's going on," I begin as I rock the kid back and forth while sitting on the ground in my backyard. I pat a foot or two away from me for Weston to plant his ass next to us.

"I think you have a secret and it's suffocating you. All of your life you told your secrets to one person, but this time you can't because it's about them. So instead of telling your mother why this is really bothering you, you turn into an asshole. You start fights with her, and in turn, she fights back. So both of you are hurt and alone. How am I doing so far?"

"Good," Seth chokes out. "She deserves it, though."

"I won't debate with you over what your mother does or doesn't deserve. I was there, kid. Your mother was a little girl, smaller than Willow by about two inches and twenty pounds. She didn't have a Seth and Violet, or a Dev and Ren. Your mom didn't have an Auggie. She didn't even have your Uncle Rob because she was busy raising him. You see, Clover was a child, alone, with a huge decision to make, and she made it the only way she could. I respect Clover for that, as should you."

"Lying is wrong," the right-fighter grumbles out. Seth's breath warms the side of my neck as he holds onto me for dear life.

"Not always. Life isn't black and white. You feel betrayed, thinking your mother betrayed you when it was something that occurred four years before you were born. You need to tell your mother that the silence is what's really killing you. You feel like you're lying to Willow every time you look at her. You feel alone, because the only people you can talk to about this are the same ones you're pissed at, and the one you always talk to about everything is the one you can't. Did I put it into words for you, words you can tell your mother?"

"Yes," Seth sobs out, finally releasing the pressure of months of pent up frustration, anger, and guilt.

"Your mother is going to tell Willow very soon. So instead of adding to the stress, which makes it all worse, be the man in your family. Be the one who keeps the peace, keeps the family whole. You should be the kind of son to the mother you want. If you want a happy, loving, and loyal mother, then be the son to one. If you want an unhappy, cold, and bitter mother, then be a prick of a son."

"God–" Seth shudders in my arms. "I can't take it."

"You don't have to, buddy. I know how hard it is to talk to the people you're angry with. So, if you want to talk to a guy, talk to me or Robin. If you want to talk to a woman, say the fuck with pride, and talk to your mother. But the one thing you never do, don't fight with your brother."

"I don't have a brother," Seth grumbles, pulling away from me. Cheeks wet from tears, eyes bloodshot, face red from a flood of emotions, Seth looks calmer than he has in weeks.

"Yes, you do. Blood or not, Weston is your brother. Don't ever fight with him again," I warn in a calm voice. "I know from experience that it takes a lot to piss West off. I've never seen him pissed a day in his life. So you crossed a line."

"I'm sorry," Seth murmurs weakly, sounding ashamed.

"Willow is your sister, and she loves you. But she's a woman, and in a different time in her life. Right now, Weston is who you need– the one you tell your secrets. Just know, Weston will always have your back. He won't just understand because he's a guy, too. He'll understand because he's next to you, going through the shit, right alongside you."

I stand, yanking the kid up with me. I reach over and tug my boy to his feet, too. Both of the boys look guilty, sheepish– miserable. "Shake hands, and walk it off. I want you guys to *literally* walk it off," I say pointedly. "Those walks you take with Willow now belong to Weston. If you want to be a man, you'll stop making Willow mother you. Support her, love her, but never belong to her. Got it?"

"Yes, sir," Seth says firmly. A moment later he walks across the lawn with a slight limp. He turns around when Weston doesn't follow him. I wave my son off, forcing him to join his brother on their very first walk– a walk Auggie and I have taken a thousand times. The first one is always the hardest.

The ability to swallow your pride is what makes you a real man.

They don't shake hands or hug it out. Weston simply pats Seth on the back as he walks by.

I pull my cellphone from my pocket as soon as the boys walk out of sight. I sit on the back steps, listening to the rest of the kids and Colin clatter around the kitchen. I type her number into my phone from memory, and call the woman who started it all.

CHAPTER TEN

The Widow

The door in the back of my mind is rattling again. No matter how strongly I chain that bitch shut, the memories try to burst forth. It's why the tears are flowing freely down my cheeks. I had to open the door wide in order to shove today's miseries inside. Fragments of past heartaches flicker in a montage of torment.

My cold, ice-queen bravado is my shield. It's the only thing that keeps the memories from flooding my mind and overtaking me. I've dealt with them as they happened by detaching myself from the reality of my life. It's getting more difficult to keep the door chained shut.

Today's revelations leave me feeling curiously numb– numbed to everything but pain. I can't even pull one thread of thought and unravel it. I guess this means I'm not actually dealing with it. A vital part of me feels like it's dying. Seeing my son in such pain, and knowing I am the sole reason for it, kills me.

I understand why Seth feels as he does, but I can't allow him to speak to me in such a way, to treat me in that manner. It would set a precedent for the future, not only in how he treats his own mother, but how he would treat his sisters, his wife– his daughters. I can't allow my son to treat women with disrespect just because I feel guilty and think I deserve it. To treat me like shit means it will be easier for Seth to do the same to anyone in the future.

I'm Seth's mother.

I can't imagine treating my mother with the same level of bitter hatred that Seth has shown me. My mother is far from perfect, but all I want to do is love and support her. The thought of Mary Prynne not on this earth makes me feel empty, alone, frightened. That is how I want my children to see me. I don't care if I make a difference in the world at large, not how my parents want to. The only footprint I want to leave is the one in my children's hearts and souls.

I try to relax in the only way I know how. I lie in my bathtub, praying for guidance and hoping for a reprieve from the stress. The warm water isn't melting the bad day away as usual. My usual escape from reality lies discarded to the floor– the romance novel was frustrating me with its saccharine storyline. Even my imagination land has to be filled with realistic situations or I get annoyed.

My happy place is no longer happy. The hot bath, steamy read, and the bottle of wine do nothing for my disposition. Every emotion seems heightened– the aggravating ones that is.

It's moments like these that I wish my life was a bit more extravagant. At an inch over five-foot and a hundred and fifteen pounds, my bathtub should feel huge. Instead, the eight inches of water barely covers my chest and belly, and my feet are propped up on the edge of the four-foot-long bathtub. I shouldn't bitch, I guess. It could be worse. I could only have a shower stall.

My dinky bathroom is where I go to center myself. It's the only place I can go and find some inner-peace without interruption. Usually the nightlight is my candlelight, the whirr of the exhaust fan is my soothing music, and a *Capri Sun* is my faux fine wine. But since Malcolm gifted me with the bubble bath foaming the water around me, the fresh-scented candle flickering in the darkness, and the wine filling the glass clutched in my hand, I can pretend I moved up from dirt poor to simply poor.

This evening's music slices through my nirvana. I blindly reach over to my cellphone, where it rests on the closed toilet seat lid. I press it to my ear without looking at the caller's name. With my kids out of the house, I'm too anxious not to answer immediately.

"Hello," voice breaking with anxiety.

"What are you wearing?" Comes warmly from the other end of the phone.

The stress of the day dissolves in a heartbeat, laughter bubbling up my throat. "You don't want to know. Trust me," I say with a smile.

"Oh," Malcolm draws out. "I beg to differ. I was hoping to catch you wearing my bubble bath, and I believe I caught you at the right time. Clover? Oh, Lucky Clover?" he sings, causing me to smile wider. "Are you in the bathtub? I hear water sloshing. You better be wearing nothing but my bubble bath in your water," he purrs, actually purrs the words.

Feeling embarrassed and confused, I mutter, "No comment."

Delighted laughter fills my ear, a deep man laugh that has me moaning before I can stop myself. The laughter dries up and an echo of the sound I made vibrates against my ear, only sounding masculine and slightly feral.

"Clover," Malcolm breathes. "You little minx. Now I understand what my son meant when he said he felt like he was dying. Christ."

"Huh?" I grunt out. "I don't want to know which son is talking about my oldest daughter. Creepy." An uncomfortable laugh slips out before I can stop it.

"Mmm... is there room in your tub for two?" Voice thick with suggestion, Malcolm teases me.

"HA! Yeah, right. There is barely enough space in here for me. I can't imagine two people in this bathtub. Hell, I doubt your thigh would fit in here."

"Lucky," Malcolm breathes the nickname he gave me. "Have you been fantasizing about my thigh? Mmm... I like the thought of that. Do you like my thigh?" The cadence of his voice flows over me like honey.

"My God, you're relentless in your taunting," I mutter, feeling a mix of anger, disappointment, and bitterness. "Malcolm, we both know you're just playing me. I'm just not sure why."

"Playing?" He sounds surprised. "My dear, we need to have that face-to-face sooner rather than later. I'm not playing you. Teasing, being playful, yes. But I mean everything I say. So... is there room in your bathtub for our future watersports?"

Not believing a word out of his honeyed-mouth, I huff a laugh anyway. "So sure of yourself. Malcolm, you are truly a Mason. But I assure you, this bathtub was made as a joke. My thigh barely fits in it." My foot taps the floor, subconsciously testing out my theory.

"Back to my well-formed thigh again, are we? You have a thing for male body parts: thighs, asses, and nutsacks. Well, how about the bathroom upstairs. Is that made for two?"

"Most certainly made for two. It's a jack-and-jill three-quarter bath." I roll my eyes at this ridiculous conversation. I lean forward, and drain the contents of my wine glass– the buzz going straight to my head.

"N-i-c-e," he draws out. "But I'm not a real-estate agent. I haven't a clue what any of that mumbo-jumbo meant, so I'll pretend it's sexual."

"Dumbass." I chuckle, and then hiccup because of my wine. "The bathroom is made for two because Seth and Violet share it. It's in between their bedrooms. It's also only a shower, toilet, and sink. My house is the size of a postage stamp. Actually, I'm pretty sure there is more space on a stamp."

"Why'd you buy that house if it was so small?" Malcolm's curiosity forms a lump in my throat.

"Sam bought it while I was still at college. He wanted to be closer to Willow. By the time I left college to move home, Sam was next door and Peggy was across the street. Let's just say there was no escaping my past and moving on." Realizing I overshared, I cover my face in embarrassment. "Sorry, forget I said a word of that."

"That must have felt like an impossible situation for you." Malcolm's words are soft and filled with understanding. The intimacy of this conversation scares me as much as it loosens my tongue.

"I made my bed, so to speak. When I came home from college, I was already pregnant with the twins. Trapped is a better definition. I did what was required of me," I utter flatly.

"I may be old, but I remember that era very well." Malcolm's humorless laugh forms a ball of ache in my chest. "Hard times, and we were young and dumb. Some of us younger than others..." he trails off.

"Yeah, I was married and pregnant with the twins by the time I was nineteen. I never got my degree, and I ended up living ten feet from the house I grew up in. I really traveled," I mutter sarcastically.

"I was born in this house– literally born here. Every good and bad thing that has ever happened to me happened in this house. I'm moving," he abruptly announces.

Malcolm's revelation startles me. "What?" I gasp out as I sit up in the tub, sloshing water over the side to flood the linoleum.

"After everything, I didn't think it would be a good idea for Devon to return here after rehab. That is if I can locate the pain in the ass in the first place," flows snidely. "I'd rather move than not have my son with me. This house is a reminder, so I fear that it reminds the rest of the kids as well."

"I'm sorry, Malcolm. Are you sure you need to move?"

"Yeah, I don't want to be here anymore," he mumbles like a lost little boy. "You can repaint and replace furniture, but the memories themselves are imprinted in the structure of the house. You mentioned escape. There is no escaping it. Before Devon, I thought the best therapy was to look your demons in the eye every day and know you're strong enough to conquer them. It never occurred to me that perhaps my children weren't strong enough."

"I don't know what you're talking about, Malcolm. But I can tell by your tone of voice that it haunts you. I get it—I would kill to have a fresh start," I say, and for the first time ever, I realize I truly need it. "I'd love to take my life back, own it for once. I'd love to sit on my porch, reading a book and drinking a glass of wine, and not have eyes not-so silently judging me from across the street. I want to feel comfortable in my home, like I own the house, not like it owns me."

"Clover," Malcolm says abruptly, interrupting my rambling. "You and I need to talk, sooner rather than later. I have a proposition that will benefit all of us."

Voice quivering, I mutter, "What?"

"Not now," Malcolm says gruffly. "Face-to-face." Pausing for a heartbeat, where I try to think of a reply, he speaks for me. "I called for a reason. Seth got into a fight a few minutes ago."

"What?" I half-shout, bolting up in the bathtub, more water spilling onto the floor. The tub will be empty at this rate. "What is wrong with that kid?"

"Don't worry." Malcolm ties to soothe me with his calm voice. "I handled it. Seth picked a fight with Weston because he felt safe doing so, and Weston snapped. It makes me wonder how long Seth has been bottling this up, because it takes a lot to upset West."

Slumping back into the bathtub in defeat, I whisper, "What happened?"

"Seth finally let it out. Weston and I sat with him while he cried. Clover," Malcolm breathes, as if he's worried what he has to say will upset me. "He's frustrated and lashing out. Willow is his favorite person in the world, and he's keeping a secret about her, a secret he'd normally share with her. It's isolated him because the only people he could talk to are the ones he's pissed at. So I told Seth to stop seeking Willow out, and no matter what it is, talk to Weston. I made the kids take a walk together. They aren't back yet, so either they killed one another or they're working it out."

"I've tried to tell Willow on at least a dozen occasions. The last time Violet interrupted. It was on the tip of my tongue. I need you to know that I'm not being selfish. This isn't about me. I wait for the best time for Willow, and then it's never the right time."

"You need to tell Seth that, make him understand. He's going to be pissed at you for a long time. But if you tell him you're waiting for Willow, he'll probably back off some."

"I *am* waiting for Willow," I protest. "The last time, she was going through all this stuff with Auggie and Devon, trying to get her shit together. She had just started college, and was dealing with her own addictions. Now Seth is pressuring me so it's easier on him, and I know he should never have felt pressured in the first place. That is my fault. But... Devon," I whisper, knowing Malcolm will understand why now isn't a good time for any of us to reveal life-changing secrets.

"You need to sit your youngest children down, and tell them why you did what you did. You need to explain that you will tell Willow when things calm down, but now isn't a good time because we are all going through something. Then you need to tell Seth that you understand why he is upset, but you all have to put your hurt feelings aside and be strong for Willow. Just tell Seth everything is in Willow's best interests, and the kid will comply."

"You're scary manipulative, you know that, right?" I mutter in awe.

"I only use it for good, never evil. I promise," Malcolm vows. "I'm the chief of police of a shit-slinging town called Fairport, and the father of four kids. I also lived through Isis and Auggie's bullshit. Manipulation is a survival instinct at this point. If I need something, I know how to get people to give it. It's what I do. It's one of the requirements of my job. It's why Devon was able to manipulate and fool so many of us."

"That doesn't make you a bad man," I quickly say, because Malcolm doesn't sound proud of his manipulative powers. "I can't tell them everything, but I will try to explain why we're in this shit-storm now."

"Why can't you tell them everything?" Malcolm asks, sounding relieved that I didn't want to dissect his less than honorable personality traits.

"Some things children shouldn't know about their parents. I'm more willing to have Seth hate me for life than to have my children hate their father in his death. I won't ruin Sam's memory for them. Sam was the best father, son, and friend on the planet. But he wasn't the greatest of husbands. I take ownership of that, but it's no one's business but my own."

"Shit," hisses from the other side of the phone. "I'm not the only one with baggage? Christ, you're going to make this impossible for me. Aren't you?"

"What?" I mutter, confused. "Shit," I shout, bolting up, almost dropping my cellphone into the bathwater. "Someone is ringing the doorbell!"

"It's all right," Malcolm says, rumbling a laugh. "They have a key."

"Excuse me?" I squeak out, fumbling for a towel.

"Your kids are spending the night. I'm going to throw a tarp down in the middle of the living room floor, and tear open a few boxes of cereal. That ought to tide them over until morning, right? They're just an ornerier version of dogs."

"Malcolm Mason!"

"Good God, Lucky Clover," Malcolm purrs in a deep voice, "hearing you chastise me just about made me blow a load in my pants. I love a bossy woman."

"Are you insane?" I force out tightly, neck muscles straining as I slip around my bathtub. "Who is walking through my house? It could be a psycho, and you're laughing!" I struggle to find purchase as I grab for a towel and not drop my phone, body sliding around in the bathtub.

"Relax." Malcolm laughs long and hard. "Seth and Weston have each other. Everyone has someone. So I sent over more wine with your personal outlet. Bitch and complain, let it all out, and then in the morning talk to your kids."

"Malcolm!" I shout again, causing him to moan as if in ecstasy. "You freak!"

"You better get out of the bathtub. You might get attacked by your visitor. I hear she has a thing for the ladies." I swear the man giggles.

"Oh, thank God," I murmur a prayer as I slump back into the bathwater, knowing exactly who's in my house.

"Have a good night, Clover. Don't be too naughty," Malcolm says in parting just as the bathroom door opens, revealing my best friend.

"Girl, we have got to talk," Ginny says, grin splitting her face. She's haloed in the light of the hallway. Arching a perfectly manicured blonde eyebrow, "My brother-in-law, really?"

"This isn't what it looks like," I mutter guiltily as I push 'end' on my cellphone. "We weren't… we weren't having phone sex," I stammer out, blushing. "Honest. Seth got into a fight with your youngest nephew."

"I believe you," Ginny says, amusement thick in her voice, smile spread across her face. "Protest all ya want, but your chest has that ruddy flush woman get when they're aroused." She waggles her eyebrows, smirking at me. Voice dipping low and seductive, "And I would know."

"It's the hot bath water!" I protest as I climb out of the bathtub, not caring that Ginny is devouring me with her eyes. When you lived with someone for two years back in college, when they held your hand while giving birth to three children, when they helped you through abuse only they knew existed, when you supported them while they mourned the losses of their sister and best friend, you tend to forget they have the hots for you. Best friend trumps lust: a lesson Sam, Ginny, and I have dealt with for almost twenty years.

"Here," voice husky, Ginny passes me my robe. "Put this on before I do something only you will regret."

Giggling, either from stress or relief, I tug on my robe. "You make that threat so often, it no longer has any punch. You're also the only person who has ever taken an interest in me. If only I liked girls," I muse. "My life would be so much simpler."

"If only I liked guys," Ginny replies, turning somber. "Our lives would have been simpler. You would have lived a totally different existence."

"Don't go there," I warn, but there is no bite to my words. It's a conversation Ginny has wanted to have for nineteen years— one no longer necessary to be voiced as of five years ago. I change the subject as I tidy up my bathroom: draining the tub, blowing out the candle, wiping up the floor. "It's a Saturday night. No hot date?"

Helping me clean up, Ginny steals my empty wine glass and bottle, tilting them both upside down, impressed with my thirst. She bends down to finger my romance novel with interest.

"Hmm… what is up with you and bodice rippers? I've never understood it. You project the perfect image of a stuffy woman who could crack walnuts with her puss muscles, yet you secretly harbor a romantic side for brawny heroes."

"Shut up," I bark as I grab my well-worn paperback out of Ginny's greedy little fingers. "You know why I'm the way I am. You remember me when I would fly off the handle. When I was messy and awkward. Quit trying to dredge up the past, or you'll have to leave," I warn, charging toward my bedroom.

"Clover," Ginny sighs out, following me closely behind. "How can you move on if you don't deal with it? I've waited and waited for you to return to the girl I fell in love with, and she's just as stubborn as before. Let. It. Go."

"Maybe this isn't an act," I defend. "Maybe this is really me." I tug on a pair of yoga pants and a tank top over top of my bra and panties– all a gift from Ginny at one time or another. I was hoping the gesture would shut her up.

"No one loved Sam as much as us, so I understand how his ghost lingers." Yanking me by the wrist, Ginny forces me to look into her hazel eyes, eyes that are filled with endless pools of sadness. "I love you, and I want you to be happy. My brother-in-law has never pursued a woman in his life, not even my sister. I need to know you guys won't hurt each other. I need to know you've both let go of the past so you can move on into the future."

"Ginny," I say her name, unsure what I truly want to say. "Malcolm said you were bringing more wine? I haven't been drunk since junior year in college." My face twists up in pain, and Ginny's face mirrors my own.

"Yeah, and that worked out so well for the both of us." Releasing my wrist as well as a humorless laugh, Ginny gestures to the kitchen. "The wine awaits."

Walking away from my friend, I say over my shoulder, "Dumbest mistake of my life. But then again, I've only made two mistakes, and both times were with Sam. Mistakes? Fuck no. They are my children."

"Just promise me that you won't call Malcolm after you're piss-roaring drunk. You know how you get when tipsy– you repopulate the earth," Ginny deadpans.

"Bitch," I hiss out, but I'm smiling. "Each time, it's progressively worse. I'd probably have triplets." My eyes widen in delight. "Oh, I love you," I draw out as I gaze at the box of wine sitting in the center of my kitchen table. "I don't even have to struggle with the bottle opener. Glasses," I sing.

"Shit," Ginny breathes, shaking her head back and forth, "You're already lit."

"Let's see," I murmur as I tap the box. "My daughter is cavorting with not one, but two, Masons. As we've already established, Prynnes are good breeding stock. And as you well know from your sister's perpetual state of pregnancy, the Masons breed like bunnies. So I want to sew Willow's cervix shut as an added precaution."

"I think you better stitch your own," Ginny taunts me. "You're only thirty-five. You've got a long ways to go before menopause."

"No worries, my love. Top Cop/Papa Bear/Malcolm is only playing with me for some reason. No mashing of sex parts necessary."

"You're delusional." Ginny rolls her eyes as I fill two wine glasses to the brim. "My brother-in-law is stalking you, and you know it. But keep on pretending I'm not speaking. I can hear you going 'la... la... la... laaa... la-la,' in your mind."

"Am not!" I deny poorly. "We're just commiserating parents of kids who love each other– both in the platonic and not-so platonic sense of the word. He gives me son advice, and I give him daughter advice."

"Malcolm is stalking you, using the kids as his in. He's running a long game on your ass. I'm not saying he doesn't like you, or want you, or need you. Boy/Malcolm started dating my sister on a Tuesday night, and was married to her by Sunday afternoon. They were parents nine months later. Man/Malcolm has been in contact with you for nearly a year, several times a day, both parental chatter and sexual banter. He's learned from his past mistakes, and he's got you locked in his sights."

"Malcolm was friends with Sam. He's just checking up on his friend's family because Sam can't," I mutter, feeling devastated for some reason.

"Checking up on Sam's wife and kids doesn't involve asking you what you're wearing or sending you hundreds of nudies of his cock." Ginny shudders in revulsion. "Flaccid, hard, mid-eruption, and post-orgasm… pastries included."

I swallow half a dozen times as every one of those images does a slideshow in my mind. "Malcolm's just taunting me," I offer lamely.

"Wake. Up. Clover!" Ginny half-shouts, frustrated with me. "Malcolm Mason doesn't date. He marries. The man has never been on a date in his life. He doesn't interact with women who aren't related to him or work with him. Yet he's been talking to you constantly. I don't know about you, Clover. But I call that a relationship."

"We're not dating." I ignore Ginny because her words scare me shitless. "Where was I?" I shift around in my chair until I'm cross-legged. I sip my wine, find it tasty, and then drain the glass dry. "Oh, yes. Why I felt compelled to get shit-faced. Well, I figure we both need it since your nephew is on the run. My son hates my guts: Seth called me a stupid cunt last week– to my face –and today he said all I did was spread my legs to become a mother."

"No," Ginny's voice quivers, tears erupting from her eyes. "You must have seen Sam right then. You didn't go postal, did you?"

Hand shaking, I refill my glass. "No worries," I say around a huge swallow of wine. "I've struck both Willow and Violet, but I've never laid a hand in anger against my son. Maybe I should have," I muse. "I wouldn't be a good mother if I didn't do everything in my power to ensure that my son doesn't grow up to be a misogynistic prick."

"Seth won't," Ginny tries to reassure me. "He's half of you."

"And Sam only despised one person on this planet– the person who is half of all three of his children. How fucked up is that?" I say pointedly, staring Ginny down. "Even after everything Sam put me through, I never hated him. Seeing Sam in Seth, the good and the bad, that's killing me. So it's not a stretch of the imagination that Sam's son would grow up to hate the woman Sam hated. Just as long as Seth doesn't hate himself for being a part of me, or hate every other female besides me, I'm good. I'll sacrifice myself. After all, that's why I was born. Right?"

"Clover–"

I cut off the sympathy routine that all best friends are known for, because I refuse to be pitied. "So, I'm gonna take a page from my illegitimate daughter's playbook and get fucked up tonight. I'm sure Mom would offer me some Mary Jane, but that's too hardcore for a cold fish like me. Plus, the asthma kind of puts the kibosh on everything smoke-related. Mom once tried to get me to make pot brownies, saying I needed to relax a little."

"Clover, you're losing it," Ginny warns, sounding frightened. She's not even drinking her wine.

"Why no date tonight?" I look my best friend over– the one person who's loved me unconditionally as a woman. Ginny's always wanted me. I've known it since the day I met her. When Ginny asked me for my number after class, I misunderstood it as friendship or school study buddies. I had just turned sixteen, still in high school but taking college courses. I was the epitome of naïve. Ginny had to explain to me that she wanted to go on a date, not do homework. I'd never met a lesbian before, so I just blushed, and we've been best friends ever since.

Looking me dead in the eyes, Ginny shows her frustration. "This is Fairport, not Boston. There aren't exactly lesbians crawling out of the woodwork."

"Yeah, they're still in their closets." I give a giggle, followed by a hiccup. I lean forward and refill my glass, all the while Ginny eyes me patiently.

Ginny is soft, pretty, with big dimpled cheeks and huge hazel eyes. A sandy blonde wave of hair falls to her hips. Camille and Ginny were both gorgeous girls. It's no wonder Malcolm chose Camille as his wife. I can see my best friend's features reflected in all four of the Mason kids, especially Kieren with his fair coloring.

I blurt out what I'm thinking, "You're gorgeous. If I liked girl parts, I'd marry your ass."

"God," Ginny groans. "Don't be a cunt tease."

"Seriously? I don't understand why you'd want me. Why anyone would want me," I mumble, never having wrapped my mind around that one. "You're curvy, and I'm–" I gesture at my slim body. "–not."

"Yeah." Ginny takes a sip of wine, skews her face up in distaste, and pushes the glass toward me. "Cheap shit." She shudders. "Malcolm has piss-poor taste in wine. Men and women alike, like the size of you. I'm lucky to squeeze into a size eighteen on a non-bloated day. Fairport + fat = horny, lonely, and bored."

"Idiots. Women are just as big of idiots as men. Skinny doesn't mean good in bed. Sam made sure at every turn that I knew how horrible I was in bed. Something tells me he preferred his women big and beautiful." Hating the wistful quality in my voice, I tip back Ginny's glass and drain her wine.

"Sam only thought he was in love with me. We both knew him better than anyone. I was the one he couldn't have, so he became obsessed. I'm sorry," Ginny whispers.

"Nothing will ever ruin our friendship," I vow. "Jealousy could have killed us, but I didn't allow it."

"It helped that you were the one I wanted," Ginny mutters. "But that fucked you in the end, didn't it? If anything, jealousy ruined Sam. No, selfishness and arrogance ruined Sam. Never having heard no until me ruined Sam."

"Hell," I groan, wine hurting my belly more than making me drunk. Inhibitions lowered, we have the conversation nineteen years in the making. "I know," I finally admit. "He told me."

Ginny's voice breaks. "Told you what?"

"I know Sam only targeted me at Malcolm's graduation party because he wanted to make you mad. He didn't even see me as a person. He saw me as a way to punish you. Sam fucked me in his version of a tantrum. Willow was Sam's tantrum," I utter in a dead voice.

"Oh, no, sweetie. No," Ginny gasps out, reaching for my hand but I pull away. Ginny's not saying no to me because I'm wrong. She's saying no because she wished I didn't know the truth.

"Let's finally get this out on the table," I utter emotionlessly. "Sam wanted you." I point at Ginny. "As a lesbian, you couldn't want him back in the way he needed." I point at myself. "You wanted me. But since I was straight, I couldn't want you back. Sam couldn't have you, so he trapped me to punish you. He was a selfish man/child who threw a fit when he didn't get what he wanted, because he always got what he wanted. I figured it out while I was pregnant with Willow. But he told me on our wedding night."

"Jesus," Ginny hisses. "I never wanted you to know. After Sam messed around with you at Malcolm's party, I didn't speak to him for four months. I thought Sam learned his lesson until he followed us to college–"

"And the rest they say is history," I murmur, feeling nauseous.

Angry, Ginny pounds the tabletop. "It's not history, because you're still living it. You need to deal with it so you can move on and finally be happy. You deserve it."

"But why should I get to be happy when Sam's dead?" I admit for the first time. "Sam never got what he wanted. You'll never get what you want. Why should I ever get a damned thing that I want after what I did to Willow?"

Leaning across the table, Ginny grabs my hand. "Our friendship has withstood Sam's selfishness, his abuse, his lies and manipulations. It will withstand my lust," she vows. "I love you as a human being. I think you are a beautiful person inside and out. I think you've paid for Sam's unrequited obsession long enough, don't you?"

"No," I mutter honestly. "I don't."

"None of this was your fault. Your dead husband targeted you because you were my best friend. It was jealousy times two. Sam was my best friend, my world, until you came into my life. No matter who I befriended, Sam would have hated them. It didn't matter that I was attracted to women. Sam was so conceited that he thought he could conquer my sexuality. His anger was worse because I fell in love with you. I tried to hide it so Sam wouldn't take it out on you."

"I know," I cry out, clutching Ginny's hand tightly in mine. "Not once have I ever blamed you. Not. Once."

"I know," Ginny says, leaning back against her chair's backrest. "I wish you would, though. But you're too good of a person to blame anyone but yourself, and you're the only person innocent in this equation. You don't even really blame Sam. Let's face it, he was far from perfect."

"Sam was a good person. He was the perfect father, son, and friend," I mutter robotically.

"Keep repeating that until you believe it, Clover," Ginny calls me on my bullshit. "I know who Sam was, and I know he didn't have a selfless bone in his body. Sam could tear your beating heart from your chest, and not only would you buy it back, you'd thank him for it. Was Sam charismatic, engaging, and intoxicating? Yes. When Sam spoke did he make you feel like the center of his universe? Yes. Did I love him like a brother? Yes. Just because I loved Sam, it didn't make him perfect. Just because Sam died, it didn't make him a saint. Sam was…"

"Sam," I whisper. I wipe my cheeks with the back of my hand, not realizing I had even been crying.

Smiling weakly at me, Ginny says, "Exactly. So move on. It doesn't have to be with Malcolm. Just move on. Know that I love you, but I haven't been *in* love with you in years, and I will love again. Sam did love– he loved himself and his children, and he did love you no matter how shitty he was at showing it. Now Sam is gone, so you need to move on and forget the past. Don't let it drag you down in baggage. You *will* finally love someone."

"I don't know if I can. Sam always said I was broken." I slump forward against the top of the table, defeated and emotionally exhausted.

"Sam was the broken one. He was broken since birth. Our parents were childhood friends, and I knew him since we were shitting in our diapers together. I was the perfect ideal that he could never achieve. I was just a fantasy. Sam didn't want me. Sam didn't love me more than as a sister. But after years of hearing our parents gush about how we'd marry and make babies, after years of always pleasing Margaret Webster, Sam failed. Sam never failed at anything. Sam never knew what he actually wanted. Sam loved you, Clover. He truly did. He was just too fucking blinded by himself to see anything he hadn't envisioned at age ten."

"In some sick and twisted place in my cold, dead heart, I loved Sam, too," I murmur while scrubbing my palms across my face, collecting the falling tears. My eyes slowly focus, bringing my worst fear to life. Horror dawning, Ginny looks over her shoulder and cries out in panic.

Voice quivering, I blurt out, "What are you doing home? I thought you were having a sleepover at the Mason's. How much of that did you hear? Please, God, make sure they didn't hear too much," I pray, not to our Heavenly Father, but to my twins as they stand in the entryway to the kitchen from the living room, expressions of disbelief and pain marring their young faces.

"I-I-I wanted to talk to you," Seth stammers, voice shaking, fists clenched at his side. He's never looked more like Sam than he does right this second. "I wanted to apologize, and tell you why I was upset. So we left the sleepover to come home… We-we-we," he stammers some more, overwrought. "We heard everything."

"Look at me," I demand of my children. A pair of warm, chocolate brown eyes, the exact replica of Sam's, and a pair of hauntingly blue eyes the shade of mine, latch on and won't look away. "Sam was just an ordinary man– a human being who made mistakes. No matter what you tell yourself in the quiet hours, it was not about you. He loved you more than life itself. Never forget it. Learn from your father's mistakes and become better people because of them. That was his legacy to you."

"How?" Violet struggles to find words, face crumpled in betrayal. "Why?" she sobs out, sounding more like a child than ever.

I stand quickly from my chair, unsure what to do now. My children are frozen like baby rabbits awaiting slaughter. "Ginny, thanks for coming over," I say in obvious dismissal. Her look of utter disbelief has me saying, "Really. Truly. I never wanted them to know this. I tried to hide it from them. But you are right. I need to move on– we all do. I'm alive, and while I won't defame Sam, I won't sanctify him anymore, either. I need to respect my children with the truth because I'm the only one they have left."

"I can help you talk to them." The pleading quality in Ginny's voice has tears springing to my eyes, and that's why I need her to leave. Ginny is my comfort object, and right now, I need to be strong.

"I think, I think it's best if we do this alone, just me and the twins. I'll call you soon."

"You better," Ginny says as stands to leave. She presses a kiss on my cheek on her way by. When she goes to hug Violet, my daughter shrinks away. Hurt, Ginny doesn't even try to touch Seth.

Still frozen in the entryway, my children look shell-shocked. "How much was all?" I ask Violet, the most responsive of the pair.

"Since you explained why you feared Seth was turning into a misogynistic prick. You used that term earlier today, so Seth and I had to Google it," Violet rambles, visibly shaking.

"I-I-I–" I stutter. "I don't know what to say," I admit, feeling like the worst parent who has ever lived. "Come with me," I order, hand automatically going out to clutch their thin wrists. I draw my children to my side, and then tug them from the kitchen toward my bedroom. I crawl on my bed, pulling the twins with me.

"I know we need to talk, but I'm going to be selfish for a minute and take what I need. I need to hold my babies." Voice breaking on a sob, I draw my children up against my sides as we lie on my bed. It takes no less than a second before my twins are crying as they did the last time I held them– the night their father died. This night– Sam dies for them again. Their perception of their father has been tarnished, tainted. No matter how true or not, no child should ever know the dark depths of their parents' souls.

Whether it's minutes or hours, I hold my children to my chest, squeezing them against me. My mouth wanders from subject to subject, some important, others not. By the time I am finished, the sobs have dwindled to sniffles, and all eyes have dried. I tell my children what I loved about their father, and I mean every word I say. I tell my children every single memory of Sam's interactions with them, from their first breath to Sam's final breath.

Sam may have never truly loved me, but he loved his children more than life itself.

CHAPTER ELEVEN

The Widower

The last thing I remember was lying on my bed, giving the kids some privacy as I caught up on the shows I DVRed for the week. The kids shouting at one another as they played *Farkle* in the living room was keeping me from dozing off while I watched *Alaskan State Troopers*. The remote impression on the side of my face says I dozed off anyway.

Scrubbing my face with the back of my hand, hating the pasty taste in my mouth, I roll to sit up. I bark a sharp laugh at what's playing on the TV: *Chopped*. Somehow in my sleep, as I dreamed of her, I subconsciously turned the TV to *The Food Network*. I instantly think of my little cook, and I want to reach out and touch her.

I want Clover Webster in my bed– always. Only I want her name to be Clover Mason– always.

Unable to stop myself, I stretch over to grab my cellphone off of my nightstand, startled to realize it's exactly midnight.

Top Cop: *How was your Ginny time? Did you get tipsy? Hope you had a good time.*

Disappointment pounds into my chest when Clover doesn't text me right back. Usually her reply is instantaneous. But maybe she's sleeping. It was a horrible day for all of us.

Top Cop: *Lucky Clover, you sleeping?*

Either I'm gearing up for a heart attack or the primal male inside of me is giving me a warning. A gut-wrenching tightness twists my stomach as my instincts flare. I decide the best course of action is to check on the kids– make sure lungs still breathe and hearts still beat.

Weston and Rae sit side-by-side on the sofa, enthralled by some IQ-lowering reality program with screaming females and straight males trying their damnedest to appear like chicks. "Why's this trash on?" Suddenly realizing something, "Where the hell are the rest of the kids?"

Shit, Clover is going to kill me. I lost all three of her children, one of mine is already missing, and the responsible one is also gone now. What. The. Fuck?

"Answer. The. Question." I demand of my youngest kids as they blink out of the mind-draining show.

"Wreck & Ruin," Rae mutters, eyes never leaving the television as a woman screams about her boyfriend cheating on her with her *other* boyfriend. As a man who frequents the Playroom, a man who is okay with my sister loving two men, even I find this show perverse.

"Turn that trash off. Watch The History Channel for a change," I growl, grabbing for the remote, but it's glued to Weston's palm somehow. The brat won't relinquish it. West tugs hard enough that my hand snaps back. "What the…" I trail off as I stare down at my desperate looking son. Hands held out, I mutter like I'm talking down a criminal, "Okay? You can keep it."

I swear I can hear the phrase, "*it's mine*," echoing in my youngest son's mind. "*Well, the remote should belong in a man's hand,*" I think to myself with a shrug.

"It's midnight on a Saturday night, and your brother is missing. Telling me the rest of you are at the shop isn't going to cut it."

"Probably not at the shop anymore," Weston says, tucking the remote behind his back for safe keeping. "Willow had to study for an exam with Lang, so Kieren was going to work on some dude's rusted-out exhaust."

"Nah, that was earlier," Raven mutters. "They said something about–" Rae makes air quotes with her tiny fingertips, "*TV Time.*" Smirking like she has a secret, "But I doubt that, 'cuz they both blushed." My daughter giggles like a full-grown woman and I decide I'm going to surf *Amazon* for chastity belts the first chance I get.

"Well, that explains the adults who are missing," I say in annoyance. "But I only give a shit about the ones who aren't sitting on the couch next to you. You know, the minors? Clover will cut my nuts off if one of my guys accidentally arrests the twins for breaking Fairport's curfew," I warn.

"They left with Willow and Ren," Raven supplies. She leans into her brother and whispers, "this is recorded, right? I want to know what happens."

I stand in front of the TV, demanding answers. I cross my arms over my chest, trying to look threatening, even though I've never laid an angry hand on my children. I've cuddled them to death. "Why?" I demand with false sternness.

"Seth said he wanted to talk to Clover," Weston answers, and I can tell by the way the flickering on the wall has stopped that he somehow managed to pause the trashy reality show with the remote still tucked behind his back.

"Do I need to stage an intervention for you guys next?" I mutter more to myself. "I'm embarrassed at just the thought that I was once a teenager. I must have looked like an idiot. It's no wonder my dad beat my ass." I stare down at my kids who never met their grandfather, and I'm thankful because he would have beat them unconscious tonight. "So, how long ago was this, and why didn't you tell me?"

"About two hours ago," Rae readily answers. "We tried to tell you, but you were snoring. We could hear you all the way in here. Figured you were exhausted." Rae looks like she was trying to give me a break, and it melts my heart. Too bad I should know where all of the kids are at every given second because none of them can take care of themselves. Obviously, I've dropped the ball, or my son wouldn't be on the run from rehab.

Deep in parental-mode, I ask the questions that usually earn me a '*Daddy!*' "Did they text you when they made it home safely?"

"No," The kids answer together. "We tried to text them," Weston continues, with Rae adding, "A lot. No one responds."

"Radio silence," Weston murmurs. "I even tried to call them– the house phone, too. I figured they were fighting again, and I didn't think it was any of my business." Hating conflict, Weston's fingers seek the solace of his hair. With a stiff yank, his frustration is momentarily released, leaving behind a blond haystack on his head.

"Cowboy up," I call as I grab my keys and head for the door. "I've felt off about this since I woke up."

Two minutes later, we're parking in front of the pitch-black Webster residence. After twenty years on the force, I can sense them inside the house. I spend the next few minutes looking for their hide-a-key with a smug smirk on my face.

"Why are you smiling?" Weston asks quizzically while wearing a faint smile that lingers on his lips. West and Rae are pacing a foot behind me, holding hands. I have a feeling the Masons are the only family on the planet who seeks comfort from one another instead of freaking out and lashing out. This makes it easy to spot when my family is upset.

"It's alright, kids," I placate them, having no idea what's upset the Websters, but somehow knowing something did. "What a woman. I know there is a spare around here," I murmur more to myself than to my children as I search every nook and cranny on Clover's porch. "You don't have kids and family who need in your home without a spare key lying around. Clover's crafty," I say with adoration as I hop over the porch railing.

The Websters and Prynnes live in sardine can homes. Small Cape Cod houses, which are so closely packed together, it only takes three strides before I'm at the Prynne's front porch. I take the steps three at a time, and trespass like a two-bit criminal. I dig around Clover's folks' porch, looking in the usual locations. The Prynnes are just asking for a robbery. I take their house key, which was rolling out the welcome mat for would-be thieves, from beneath their welcome mat, and then relocate it to their porch light.

Bingo!

Clover hid her key in her parents' jelly-jar-style porch light. Smart woman.

I plug the key into Clover's door, and it creaks open in welcome. "Sit in the living room while I check on everyone," I murmur as I click on a side lamp.

It's strange being in Clover's home. It brings back the few times I visited Sam on his last days. Everyone was always over at the Prynne's house. Clover even avoided me, giving me time alone with my ailing friend. Not allowing the children to witness their father's death, everyone was forced to stay at Dave and Mary's house during Sam's final hours. I was here with Clover when Sam died. She never cried, and that somehow made it worse. I didn't cry either. It was like we were in a standoff. As long as neither one of us cried, we would keep it together. I lasted until I made it to my car. I wonder how long Clover lasted.

That horrific day was the last time I stepped foot inside this house. I wonder if Clover and the twins feel like this house holds too many painful memories, just as mine does for my family. I wish I could say I can't fathom how Clover feels when she sleeps in the room her husband died in, but that isn't the case. Sam died of pancreatic cancer while lying in their bed. Camille died of a self-inflicted gunshot wound to the head near the foot of our bed. To say I know and understand Clover on a level no one else could, is an understatement in the extreme.

Walking blindly, my feet carry me to Clover's bedroom as if I've walked this path a billion times before, not a handful of times more than five years ago. Clover's door is shut, without any noise coming from behind it. I reach out to grip the knob, slightly anxious over Clover's reaction when I invade her very personal space. With a deep breath, I twist the knob, opening the door.

My breath catches in my lungs. A lump the size of a *Buick* forms in my throat as I choke on tears that threaten my sanity. Clover is in the center of her bed with her children latched onto her like a lifeline. The twins are wrapped around each other while Clover holds them both. It's as if they are trying to seep back into their mother, like when they were in the womb. Not sleeping, fully aware, they gaze up at me with hollow, wounded eyes– empty. Mother and twins gaze at me without a lick of shock at seeing me materialize in the bedroom doorway. It was like they were silently calling out to us for comfort.

"Hey." Clover's voice is rough and I pray it's from disuse. "How'd you get in?" she asks as I stand speechless in the doorway to her bedroom.

"I give you bonus points on the spare key. Very original. But I get paid to outthink the criminals. Took me but a minute," I try to tease and sound smug, but I fall flat on my ass. Not one tilted lip from the bunch of them. "You watch '*It takes a Thief*', don't you?"

"They always steal the remote," Clover replies, not sounding lighthearted in the least. "And leave the TV."

"Then they drive by your house later on and switch your channels," I add with a humorless laugh.

"Garage door openers, too," Seth murmurs.

"What happened?" I ask, because I can't *not* ask. It's like they're practically begging me to yank it out of them.

"Is she really your sister-in-law?" Violet sounds lost, pained. Apparently I'm enemy number one because someone related to me spurned her somehow. Classic Violet. I can handle it since her personality is similar to my sister's.

"I only have the one… What did Ginny do?" I don't reply to Violet. I look at Clover as I ask the question. I hate the bluish-black circles beneath her eyes, as if she hasn't slept in days.

"Did you love your wife?" Violet asks, speaking like an English teacher– not a single cuss word. Something bad went down.

"With my entire being," I truthfully answer, barely smothering the emotions that always twist my voice. "I miss Camille every day, and I always will."

"Was she prettier than Ginny?" Seth asks, sounding curious, not judgmental.

"No," I say slowly, unsure where this is leading. "Ginny is Ginny. Camille was Camille. They were sisters, different in a lot of ways and similar in others, and I loved them both. But marriage doesn't work like that, kids. You marry the one who makes your heart beat faster. It has nothing to do with pretty. Real love doesn't give a shit," I speak the truth.

The words out of Seth's mouth startle me. "Did you pick Camille because Ginny only likes girls? Was your wife your second choice?"

"What?" I half-shout in shock. "Why would you ask such a thing?"

"That's enough," Clover warns as she disentangles herself from her children. "Don't be disrespectful of Mrs. Webster's memory." A split-second later she tacks on, "Or your father's."

Confused, needing to speak to Clover alone, I lightly announce, "I brought reinforcements. Why don't you kids go raid the kitchen? I'm sure you'd rather talk to your cohorts."

"Mom needs us," Seth says as he sits up. His brown eyes have lost their boy shine.

Jesus, what the hell happened now?

"Seth, your mom will always need you. I'm not taking her away. But right now, I think I can help. Just as you needed to talk to Weston this afternoon, your mom needs to talk to me. Go blow off some steam. It's not good to wallow in your pain. It's best to move forward like nothing happened." I look Seth head-on and say, "Trust me."

"Go," Clover whispers hoarsely to Seth, somehow sensing Seth is the one in charge of the pair of twins. "Malcolm's right. I wish… I wish I could take back what you heard," Clover murmurs wistfully. "But since I can't, I want you to forget you ever heard it. You, Violet, and Willow were your father's world. Nothing will ever change that."

"Why don't you guys camp out in the living room tonight? Eat until you puke and watch television until your eyes bug-out. Go on now… I'll take care of your mom," I coax.

Violet flashes me a '*you better make this better*' scowl. The little bitch is going to be a ball-cracker. A thrilled smile splits my lips. "No fear, girly, it's a man's job to take care of his woman." I'd expected Violet to get riled up, but for some reason my goading comment made her relax. Odd girl, that one.

"I can't talk about what happened," Clover declares as she crawls off the bed. "I need a few minutes to process it. I knew this would happen one day. I just hoped I'd be dead first."

The pain in Clover's voice kills me. My fingers ache to comfort her, to take comfort from her. I lean against the doorframe and try to pretend I'm not watching Clover, but it's fruitless. Clover has to feel my eyes devouring her as she paces her tiny bedroom. Wearing nothing but a pair of tight yoga pants and a thin t-shirt, my cock tries to punch a hole through my jeans to get at her. Clover's ass is worthy of a spotlight on *Girls in Yoga Pants.* A sigh escapes me as my eyes stalk her pacing form around the room.

"I need to warn you," I announce in a stiff voice, fingers curling into fists against the insane need threatening to overpower me. "I have a touching problem."

Stopping dead in her tracks, facing away from me, Clover squeaks out, "Excuse me? What did you say?" A giggle slips past her lips, causing me to smirk. I don't have to wait longer than a heartbeat before she burns me good. "Touching yourself? I heard boys go blind from that."

"HA-HA!" I mock-laugh. "I don't want to get into specifics of why, but I have a touching problem. It's a coping mechanism, actually. If I'm anxious or happy or sad or aroused, or if the other person is anxious or happy or sad or aroused, I have to touch them. I don't go more than a few minutes without holding a hand or patting a back. This is why I waited so long to see you face-to-face. It was safer texting you while watching from across your office."

"Why me, though?" Clover sounds so confused that the need to touch her overcomes me.

"I don't molest anyone. It's not entirely sexual," I say softly as I place my hand at the small of her back. Just that slight touch relaxes me, but it has Clover's muscles stiffening up, almost flinching.

"Who do you touch?" Clover breathes out, thankfully not moving away from me.

"It started with Isis. I was so starved for human connection that the day Isis was born I decided she belonged to me. Since we had no mother, and Dad said all little girls needed a mother, he allowed me to coddle Isis. Then Auggie, but that was when my father wasn't looking– but Dad knew. Nothing gross, just holding them. I liked it when they were sad or hurt, so I could comfort them. I wanted to be that person for them. I'd get pissed when they comforted each other," I admit with a sad laugh. "After my father died, I went out of control. I used Camille to satisfy me."

Stilling beneath my hand, "That's why you have so many kids?" Clover asks hesitantly.

Closing my eyes, need ripples throughout my system. I knew it would be hard to be around Clover and not touch her– consume her. I waited a torturous year as proof that I could control myself. My hand slides up from the small of Clover's back to the nape of her neck. She is taut beneath my touch, so I find my fingers squeezing and releasing in a rhythmic massage to calm her.

"No," I answer, trying not to chuckle. "I feel absolutely no shame for my needs. I love sex, but touching for me is about trust and intimacy. I like it when people come to me for comfort, like I'm the only person who can fix it. So sex… sex is the ultimate, and that is part of why I have four kids, I guess… and other reasons," I reluctantly admit, not wanting to voice how the thought of reproduction during sex gets me off. Duplicating oneself, and the lifetime of care that follows, is what separates a man from a boy. If Camille still lived, no doubt we would have several more children. But I can't tell Clover yet. I don't want to frighten her off.

"Do you have sex with a lot of people?" Clover is hesitant to ask, I can hear it in her voice. After all the text messages I've sent her, she knows I'm a randy sonofabitch. When Camille was healthy, we could go several times a day without issue.

"I don't believe in sex outside of marriage." Clover shudders in surprise, and it draws my eyes to the nape of her neck. My spine ripples with the need to place a soft kiss on that delicate spot. And suck. Bite. Leave my mark.

"Really?" Clover sounds skeptical to say the least. "Really, Malcolm?" She flips around, stunning me. My hand falls from her body, feeling empty and cold. I clench my hand against the need to reach out and touch her once more. "I've seen the pictures of hands stroking you. A guy *and* a girl."

Amazed at Clover's quick to anger, I blurt out as if guilty, "I've only had sex with Camille, and I've saved myself for my future wife. No wife should have to worry that her husband will compare her to past lovers, that he may have a disease, or has illegitimate children running around. I respect my body as much as I respect my wife's, and I hope she does too. Sex is about reproduction. I don't believe in contraception. If I have sex, it's with a purpose. All other touch is just intimacy."

Stalking away from me, Clover bites out, "So you're okay with being intimate with a shit-load of people, then? Let me guess, your future wife will be a virgin? Good luck with that, Malcolm, unless you're hunting at the junior high."

Sarcastic and caustic in the extreme, Clover's reaction causes my dick to throb with the need to prove that I want her above all others. A smile stretches my lips, and I'm so thankful that Clover doesn't witness it. She is vibrating with anger. The potent energy is wafting around her. If Clover is upset, it's because she's jealous of this unnamed woman I keep referring to as my future wife. I swallow a laugh– Clover is jealous of herself.

"I touch my children, my sister and brother, my close friends, and sometimes your brother if my family isn't around. The touch is about comfort, nothing perverted. I have two friends who I touch in a sexual manner, and those are the images I sent to you. Even that isn't about lust or sex. It starts out as platonic and turns to the need of release. All three of us are without a partner, and we're lonely," I breathe out.

Hearing the pain in my voice and empathizing with it, "I'm sorry," Clover says just as quietly as I had spoken.

"I'm not ashamed over it, nor am I gay or bi or whatever. I just like connecting with them. I have no desire to touch a stranger for any reason." I make an air clearing motion, tired of this conversation when more important things need to be discussed. "I will explain this in greater detail later. I thought we'd have our talk now. Then, maybe after, you'll be comfortable enough to explain what happened before I showed up."

Flipping around, Clover pins me with her pale blue stare. "You don't have sex with them?"

"I've penetrated no one but Camille," I answer honestly. "I've had a lot, and I mean a LOT, of touching. In the past seven years, I've been celibate."

"Oh," Clover breathes out, finally satisfied. She leans forward and bundles up her long blonde hair into her fingers, twisting a hair tie around and around until she creates a perfect ponytail. I smile because Clover and Willow's hair would be identical if it wasn't for their shades of brown and blonde. Both wearing it long, when in a ponytail, they look like young girls.

I ache to comb my fingers through Clover's hair. I quickly blink the lust away. "May we talk? You mentioned how you'd like to sit at the kitchen table and talk over coffee? I bet your kids DVRed that insane show West and Rae were watching earlier. I doubt they'd notice if an atomic bomb dropped behind the sofa if we park them in front of the TV."

"I'm so fucking sorry," Clover rushes to say, the cussing pirate finally making an appearance. "It's none of my business who you touch or why. I just needed to know why you wanted to touch me. I'm a fucking mess," she admits, no doubt for the first time ever.

Spilling before I can stop it, "I'm proud that you trust me enough to be a fucking wreck around me. Let's get that coffee, hmm?" Without asking for permission, because I gave Clover ample warning, I reach over and take her hand.

I just hope Clover realizes I'm never letting it go.

CHAPTER TWELVE

The Widow

Unsure how I feel about Malcolm standing in my kitchen while our children sit on the sofa like siblings, I do the one thing that is guaranteed comfort: baking. I muse over Malcolm's '*touching*' revelation as I pull ingredients from the pantry.

In a way, I understand Malcolm. We all have these coping mechanisms we use in order to survive. For me: it's a long bath with a good book and a glass of wine, or cooking and baking for my family. Even when Sam was being hard on me, I'd fall into house cleaning or cooking for comfort. I believe Sam recognized it for what it was, because he left me alone while I performed the comforting tasks. For Willow: it used to be pot and hard liquor, and now she uses work as a way to relieve the anxiety and feel useful. Poor Devon fell into the drug trap instead of finding a healthy outlet.

As long as Malcolm isn't fucking the populous, I guess hugging and cuddling isn't a bad way to relieve anxiety. But then again, it's none of my business if he's screwing all of Fairport. So why does that thought make me feel queasy and sad?

"What are you making?" Malcolm's deep voice breaks into my internal struggles.

"Donuts," I reply automatically. My hands are shaking as badly as my voice quivers. "They will be good for Sunday breakfast. I still have to dream up something for Sunday dinner. I think I'll go easy on myself and use the CrockPot." I vigorously zest up the rind of a navel orange to add to the batter. It's a secret ingredient that Malcolm keeps asking about.

"Clover, you don't have to do that," Malcolm mumbles in his deep, rumbly voice. Whether on the phone or now in person, Malcolm's soothing voice calms my nerves.

"Have a seat at the dinette," I order politely, finding it unnerving how Malcolm is in my personal space. "The coffee is almost ready. The batter has to sit for a while for the ingredients to marry. We'll talk in a moment."

Malcolm's palm meets the back of my neck again, squeezing tenderly, before he takes a seat at the table. Unnerved, and not in a bad way. My body is still reeling from the feel of Malcolm's skin against mine. He was so warm. I shudder from just the memory. How long has it been? Six... no, seven years. Sam passed away almost six years ago, but it was months of caretaking without simple affection. Before that, affection was dealt out as payment by Sam. He only touched me when he felt I deserved it. I don't even want to contemplate how long it's been since I've had sex.

Touch is such a foreign concept to me now, to the point that I almost have a panic attack the minute I feel the pressure, warmth, the flutter of breath on my skin. Sam used to withhold affection when he was angry with me, and he was always angry. My children sought him out for cuddles. I've tried, really tried to touch them, but they always make a noise in the back of their throats and run away. I thought it was something I'd passed down to them, a fear of touch. But Seth readily seeks out Willow's affections. I fear Violet is as skittish as I am.

The first time in years that I felt the heat of another body and arms embracing me, was when Willow came to me after Auggie broke her heart. Until tonight, I've never had another man touch me or hold my hand. The intensity of my body's reaction frightened me, but nowhere near as badly as the need that erupted: an urge to be touched and the need to reciprocate in kind. Malcolm had said his problem started because he was starved for human connection. I'm beyond starved. I've went so long that I'm now emaciated. I fear once touched, I'll either hate it or need it to survive.

Earlier, just as I was seeping into Malcolm's warmth, relaxing into the idea that he would touch me without question, he told me he was only touching me because he touches everyone. It meant nothing to Malcolm when it meant so very much to me. I've seen the pictures. I hear Malcolm loud and clear. Any warmth between us will be a means to an end. If I deny him, Malcolm will get his needs met elsewhere.

Doing what I do best, I ignore my emotions. They aren't important anyway. "Since the kids took all the salty snacks into the living room," I place a platter of assorted cookies and tarts, and a carafe of coffee in front of Malcolm. I pour two cups and take one for myself. "I know you have a wicked sweet tooth, so I'm sure this will be fine."

"Thanks," Malcolm murmurs softly, suddenly looking unsure and bashful. A bashful Malcolm is a sight to behold. I haven't had a man at my table in years, yet I've never had a man such as Malcolm at my table. Huge, black-haired, with eyes as blue and deep as endless pools of water, Malcolm commands all attention, sucking all the light from around him until he radiates power like the sun. I was beyond shocked to see Malcolm in person when he showed up earlier tonight. Distressed as I was, my knees had weakened and my heart had thumped into hyper-drive.

Until this past year, Malcolm and I had an easy truce. Never speaking nor truly acknowledging the other, but we maintained a respectful silence. Our friends and family were intertwined: his sister with my brother, and his sister-in-law is my best friend. Always knowing what the other was doing through the grapevine. It wasn't until our children befriended one another that we broke the communication barrier.

Commanding and demanding, Malcolm has never been anything but honest with me. I find comfort in his presence when others find him intimidating. I, of all people, know how size doesn't indicate a person's ability to be nasty. For me, Malcolm's size screams protection, not assault. I was slightly sad and confused when Malcolm avoided me after we lost Sam. No doubt I disgusted him by my past behavior.

"Umm..." I swallow half a dozen times. "What did you want to talk about?"

Reaching over, Malcolm squeezes my hand. "Just don't freak out on me, okay?" His hand retreats as quickly as it came.

"I'll try not to." My voice quivers, betraying how nervous I truly am. No one would ever call me flighty or irrational. After years of pretend, I have the emotional stability of titanium.

Malcolm wraps his hands around his coffee cup, as if the heat is fortifying him. He looks down, but then rolls his deep blue eyes up, capturing me in his gaze. "I promise I will do this in a more romantic fashion later, but we can't afford any misconceptions or misunderstandings between us. Okay?"

"Okay, I guess," I stammer. "I don't know what you're talking about, Malcolm."

"Clover Webster," Malcolm says my name in a voice gone serious. "You *will* be my wife, and the quicker we come to an agreement, the better for everyone."

"What?" I gasp out, shocked, speechless. My heart beats into overdrive, pounding the inside of my chest. My mouth dries out like a desert at high noon. My hands shake so badly that my coffee mug clatters against the tabletop. The gush of my blood flowing through my veins fills my ears, but the sound is shadowed by a clacking noise– the sound of my chair legs vibrating against the floor as my body involuntarily quakes. Gasping for breath, Malcolm holds my gaze, centering me as if he reached out to physically touch me.

Unfathomable.

"You said you wouldn't freak out," Malcolm tries to hold me to my word, knowing challenge will snap me out of a panic attack quicker than reassurance.

Taking a deep, fortifying breath, I still my body. I gulp out, "I'm good."

A lie.

Malcolm shakes his head at me, seeing right through me. The corners of his sinful lips slightly curve in amusement. "You and I, we need each other."

"How so?" I try for nonchalance and fail miserably. I roll my eyes at my piss poor attempt to seem unaffected, swallow the huge lump forming in my throat, and try again. "How do we need one another?"

We both turn businesslike, devoid of emotion, as if sitting at the negotiating table. I'm not gullible, naïve, or innocent. I'm a thirty-five-year-old widowed mother of three. I have no delusions anymore. To discuss this with emotion would murder us as surely as the pain we felt when our spouses abandoned us.

Forever alone.

I close my eyes, tamping down the volatile mix of pain, survivor's guilt, loneliness, regret, and the sense that I'm betraying Sam's memory by holding this conversation. I don't have to look at Malcolm to know this is as difficult for him as it is me, more difficult even.

I stopped crying the day I learned I was pregnant at sixteen. I didn't cry when I left my first born with my parents and hid away at college. I didn't cry after I was drunk date raped, and never voiced my secret to a living soul, not even to the man who did it. I didn't cry three weeks later when the test turned pink, or when I returned home just as Sam had planned. I didn't cry as I stood numbly beside Sam as our minister declared us husband and wife, eternally locking me into an endless pit of despair. I didn't cry when that same man twisted my children to resent me as he mentally, emotionally, and verbally abused me. I didn't cry when I learned the truth of my reality: my past, present, and future. I didn't cry as I sat next to my husband in the doctor's office when we were told to prepare for the worst. I didn't cry in the months leading up to Sam's death.

I've never shed a tear over my husband's passing, and not because I didn't care, not because I didn't love to the bottom of my heart. I cared *too* much. I loved *too* much. To release the pain in the form of tears meant I'd never stop. I couldn't drain myself dry. I had to be strong for those who counted on me.

Six months ago. It was an inconsequential moment. Malcolm was teasing me while we chatted about something stupid one of the boys had said. I practically hung up on him because I broke. I bawled, sobbed for hours, missing Sam. Missing the Sam I should have had. That moment of nothingness was something I was meant to share with the father of my children— a moment we'd never share. I broke because I finally experienced the feeling I've always associated with a husband— a feeling I hadn't felt with Sam but with Malcolm, and I was stricken with guilt.

I've been crying ever since. Crying for no reason and every reason. Crying because a fist is constricting my heart. I've been on the horizon of change for the past six months, and now I understand why, and I don't know how to process it. I don't know if I can live through it.

The guilt.

Voicing the exact reason I broke, Malcolm begins our journey into Hell. "We've been co-parenting for the past year. We make a good team. We get along. We complement one another. We've fucked up a lot this past year, too. So imagine how well we could parent if we were all in one house. Imagine how the kids would like to have two parents. Seth and Weston are still young enough that they need a mother to teach them how to treat a woman, and they need me to teach them how to be a man. My baby girl has never had a mother— never had a sister. Our children need us to be their parents. Our children need us to be husband and wife. I need you to be my wife as much as you need me to be your husband."

Scared. Shaking. Disbelieving what I'm hearing. "Why me?" I whisper into my cup. I take a sip, never taking my eyes from the dark liquid.

"Camille and I married for the right reason, but it was all wrong. I know all too well about responsibility. I was a dipshit kid who fell for a beautiful blonde. I wasn't ready for marriage at seventeen. The night my father died was the only night I've ever royally fucked up. Grief blinding me, I had a one-night stand with a girl who had a crush on me all through high school."

"Wow," I breathe out, shaking my head in commiseration. "I know all about those. My one-night stand turned into marriage too."

Voice thick, Malcolm says, "Yeah, I know." He clears his throat– several times. "I was there, remember?"

Blushing fiercely, I hide my face in my hands. "Oh. My. God. You all could hear."

Malcolm flashes a sinful smile in answer, blue eyes sparking with naughtiness. "You bet your ass I did. I had a front row seat."

"What?" I squeak out, mortified.

"I stood in the hallway, making sure I was the only one who knew what was happening in my sister's bedroom." Sobering, Malcolm picks up the conversation where he left off before I interrupted him. "After my father's funeral, I had to become emancipated to keep Isis. I was seventeen, not a legal adult. There was a house, a little kid, and a mistress and her son to think about. Getting married was an express pass to keeping my father's vision alive. My father would have killed me if he knew I'd slept with Camille. John Mason believed that if you slept with a woman, you kept her for life– or at least until another man could take care of her."

"Are you f'n serious?" I gasp out. My inner-feminist rears her angry head.

"Wife, mistress, sister, daughter, niece, granddaughter. If your shared blood runs through her veins, or if your children were grown within her, or if you've been inside her, John Mason's rule was that you were to take care of her until her husband could, and even after as well. They are your responsibility for life. Needless to say, after taking care of the women in my life, I refused to have a quick fuck."

"No shit," I mutter bluntly. "I don't blame you. I envision a line of women following you around like baby ducks… or parasites."

Malcolm barks a laugh. "Clover," he chastises. "I'm trying to tell you my past in explanation as to why I want you to be my wife. So don't make me laugh my ass off, or I'll lose my train of thought."

"Sorry," I mutter, having forgotten why we were talking in the first place. Or I was being blissfully ignorant because it's creeping me out. "I just don't get it. Why burden yourself?"

"That's the point," Malcolm says, sounding defensive. "They are not a burden. I *love* them," he stresses. "That is why you don't touch someone you don't love."

"I…I-I-I," I flounder as I try to understand Malcolm's view on women. I just can't fathom why he doesn't see them as a burden.

Shrugging, refusing to explain color to the blind, he continues on with our conversation. "I was unaware of Camille's mental health until it was too late. Shortly after we were married, Camille was pregnant, so we had to consult a doctor on her medication. I was sitting in the doctor's office when I found out Camille was manic depressive. They call it Bipolar now."

Malcolm's silence settles around us. Unable to reply to his revelation, I sit and wait. I want to ask if Camille's condition made it difficult to be her husband, but that seems like a ridiculously insensitive question to ask. Earlier when Violet asked Malcolm if he loved his wife, I could hear the sincerity in his words, as well as the pain, longing, and guilt.

"After we got married, I needed a way to support my growing family. I had a house to maintain, a little girl to care for, Lisa and Auggie to support, and a pregnant wife with a mental illness. I needed something to hold onto, to keep me grounded. Walter, my father's second in command— the man who was Fairport's Chief of Police until this past January when I took his position— became my mentor and pushed me to the academy so I could continue on the Mason tradition of civil service."

Overwrought, I give Malcolm privacy as he tries to get his emotions in check. I pretend I don't hear him crying softly. It kills me not to reach out and comfort him. But after a lifetime of Robin and Seth, I know a man needs to feel like a man. They cry in secret to maintain their pride.

Instead, I listen to the kids chatting in the other room, laughing and teasing, as they shout obscenities at the television. I'm most likely a horrible mother, but I allow them to say words that would make most people's hair curl. The children are happy together, and in this moment, I know I'd do anything to keep it that way.

"When I visited during holiday break, we made another baby. You remember my graduation party," Malcolm says wryly, winking. "Devon was a toddler and Camille was carrying Kieren. No positions were available in Fairport, so I had to petition the academy to find me a position. With my aptitude, blue lineage, and my size and age, it wasn't long before I went undercover in Boston. My need for my wife was all-consuming after going long months without her. When I'd come home, we would make more children."

Not meaning to interrupt, "I'm impressed," I mutter in awe. Malcolm is so unlike Sam that it renders me speechless. Not that one is good and the other bad, just the complete and total opposite of the other. It's unfathomable how they were good friends. But then again, Ginny and I have nothing in common. It's what makes our friendship so rewarding.

Reading my mind from earlier, "Did I love my wife?" Malcolm breathes so quietly I barely hear the words. His voice cracks from either pain or guilt. "Yes, I loved Camille. She was the mother of my children. But I never got to know her, truly know her. By the time I came home from trying to better our future, I had four kids, and the woman I knew as Camille didn't exist. Her undertreated mental illness was slowly dissolving the woman I knew. By the time I came up with a way to save her... I was too fucking late."

Malcolm is so abrupt that I'm shocked speechless. He never looks up from his coffee, either. Neither of us has the nerve to look at the other as Malcolm pours out his past. I startle as I realize how Malcolm is laying it all on the table: regret, guilt, love, motivations, his past, present, and future. Malcolm is not taunting me or teasing. He is not playing me. Malcolm Mason means to make me his wife.

I draw in a deep, shuddering breath and hold it, fearing if I release it, my own truths will spill to the table in the form of voiced secrets.

"I'll sound like a real bastard, but I have to say I would've done things differently if I knew the course our lives would've taken. The system of love and marriage is flawed. It's why it's so easy to divorce if you don't have any rules of morality to live by. A boy can't know what he'll want when he's a man, just as a girl can't know what she'll want when she's a woman. Camille was the girl I wanted when I was a boy. The man I became recognizes you as what I want in a wife, mother, and a woman."

"I can respect that," I readily admit. "It's why I want my children to be prepared before they marry."

"I know I sound harsh, cold, removing the romanticism as I look at marriage and child-rearing in a calculating light. The momentous decision of marriage shouldn't be made in lust. A husband and wife create children. If you can't stand your partner, beware, because I can guarantee that which you hate will manifest within your children. Evolution has sucked our instincts out and replaced them with foolishness. Lasting love can only grow from respect, trust, communication, friendship, partnership, and a similar core-belief system. Outside of that, all you have is good chemistry and an infatuation that burns brightly and fades quickly.

"I... damn..." stammering, staggered in the enormity of Malcolm's speech. I have no idea how to reply to his marital sales pitch. Malcolm is, in fact, trying to sell me— sell me him.

I can't even fathom why I understand what Malcolm's trying to describe. Why I agree with everything he's said. A small part of me is shriveling— the part that has always wanted a man to want her for being her. The part that has never felt that all-consuming lust. Just once, I want to burn brightly, even if it fades quickly. But the larger part of me knows that will never happen, and it's thrilled that a man exists who would be proud to call me his wife.

I'm dumbstruck that a man such as Malcolm Mason would be proud to call me his wife. Is he addled? Doesn't he know I was a horrific wife, and an even worse mother? The man knows I've lied to Willow for almost nineteen years. Surely he has lost his ever-loving mind.

"I know," Malcolm answers my unspoken thoughts, getting them all wrong. "I could blame myself on how our lives turned out, and remove all the blame from Camille because of her mental illness."

"Malcolm, no," I gasp, reaching out to grab his hand on instinct alone. He flips his palm over and entwines our fingers, squeezing gently. Warm, intoxicating, our body heat mingles at our palms to radiate up my arm. "You can't blame yourself. Ginny and I have spoken of her sister's illness at length. It was hereditary. Their mother was Bipolar, and she lived a happy, healthy life."

"Until the car crash that took both of the Jamison parents," Malcolm utters lifelessly. "Also why Camille was so eager to marry me. Ginny could take care of herself, while Camille was never able."

"Doesn't make either a better person than the other," I defend my friend and her sister. "You said it yourself, how your father believed in taking care of the females in your life. I know you didn't see Camille as a burden." I omit the *"or you wouldn't have made four children with the woman."* Anyone with eyes can see the love Malcolm has for his wife, and the guilt and pain, too.

Malcolm laughs faintly, the unhappy sound coils in my chest and tears my heart out. "I'm my father's son. I even tried to take care of Ginny, but the girl wouldn't let me." Smiling blindingly, respect for Ginny shines from Malcolm's eyes.

"Ginny's my rock," I admit with pride, smiling because I can't help myself. "If you had given her a dime, she probably would've spent it on me. The woman is always buying me the shit I deny myself," I mutter beneath my breath, hoping to God Malcolm didn't hear me.

Malcolm can play pretend even better than I can, because I know he heard me yet he gives me the privacy to keep my pride intact. Refusing to be led off course, he continues on as if I'd never spoken. "The most important lesson I learned was that you choose a wife or husband for the right reasons. Lust and love aren't the right reasons. Love dies and lust is just chemistry. I will never regret my children, but I will forever regret all of my other choices– Camille being the largest one."

I sink into the sound of Malcolm's voice, allowing him to go on and on with his sales pitch when he's mostly won me over. No matter what he's saying, it sounds feasible with his confident cadence. It's no wonder he's the Chief of Police. Absentmindedly, I take a bite out of an almond crescent. I fear Malcolm will stop speaking, but at the same time, I wish he'd say no more. It's comforting that I'm not the only fuck-up at this table made for two.

"I picked a wife because we had sex when I was wallowing in misery. My older-self wants to beat the living shit out of my younger-self. Since I can't do that, I'll make sure my kids never make any of my mistakes. The woman I should've chosen would've been a good mother and wife. I wasn't the perfect husband, but I was always faithful. I put my kids first. My absence was because I needed to do the work when I was young, when the kids were young, so I could provide for them and be with them afterward."

I end Malcolm's rambling by spewing my own verbal vomit. "To a point, I can understand most of what you said. I made my girls get the shot as soon as they menstruated so they'd never repeat my mistakes. Sex is a choice, but not always. Sometimes you said yes the first time, so they believe you have no right to say no the next time." I startle, suck in a sharp breath, and hiss it out. "I didn't say that out loud," I murmur in denial, and go on to cover up my mistake. "I don't want my girls to feel trapped, or to make a guy feel trapped. Mistakes happen, and it shouldn't have to ruin your life. Girls shouldn't be made to feel like bad girls because they had sex, and they shouldn't have to live with a lifetime of consequences, either."

"I don't believe in birth control," Malcolm admits, stunning me.

I mutter, "It's not called protection for no reason. It's not to protect the guy from a lifetime of child support. It's to protect the girl from being used, abused, victimized, and tossed in the garbage. Every female should have a choice of what goes into her body, especially when the man doesn't give her the choice."

My eyes roll up and connect with Malcolm's, frightened to see condemnation shining down at me. He gives me a reassuring look filled with potent understanding. He begins hesitantly, "I may not believe in contraception for *me* or *my* wife, but I can understand why you would. I won't judge you, and I believe it's your choice and your daughters' choices. I won't murder Rae if she uses birth control, but I'd rather she didn't. Just please educate our daughters," Malcolm begs, and the desperation brings tears to my eyes. "I did the best I could with Isis, but her words of advice will just be mine parroted back at Raven."

"Okay," I agree. "But before I do, we'll have to talk about your beliefs. I don't want to overstep my bounds."

Piercing me, showing me how confident he is with his decision, Malcolm utters the words meant to comfort as much as frighten. "Before we marry, you and I will know where we stand on every single detail of everything. I'm not fucking this up like I did in the past," he vows.

In a state of shock, my mind glosses over the '*before we marry*'. "Then you should know I'm a perpetual fuck-up," I say without a hint of sarcasm. "I need to be honest with you, Malcolm. My perfect persona is just that, total bullshit. I don't know what I'm doing any more now than I did back then. I'm just winging it."

"Clover, I know exactly who you are. I came to you fully enlightened," he says in all seriousness.

"That scares the shit out of me," I grumble, "wondering where you got your information."

Malcolm laughs, a deep, warm sound that fills my heart and pools deep in my stomach. I could be mistaken, but I'm positive he whisperers, "*silly rabbit*," beneath his breath. "I got the info from you, Clover. I'm an observer. I pay attention. We've been speaking for almost a year. I used that time to get to know you, to learn you."

"Oh," I huff out. "See, there is a vital error in your plan. I don't lie, but I don't always tell all there is to know."

Leaning forward across the table, hands within touching distance, Malcolm lures me with his persuasive voice. "Then tell me something I don't know. Tell me something you have to hide." I shiver from the intensity of his words and the way his blue eyes glow with silent command.

Usually I balk at authority. But for some inexplicable reason, I like the way Malcolm makes me feel. Malcolm asks for what he wants, he expects to get it, he's honest about why he wants it, and I want to give it to him. I know Malcolm won't be irrational. You know from start to finish what is expected of you. I find a perverse sense of comfort in that.

Cause and effect, that is Malcolm Mason.

"Well, I... I gave Willow to my parents for a billion little reasons, and none of them were about me. The major one was so I wouldn't do to Sam what you just described. I didn't want to be Sam's burden. I wanted Sam to love me for me, not for the baby growing in my belly. He would just end up resenting me and the child, and I couldn't have that. I wanted my child's father to love her."

"Clover," Malcolm's tone is a warning. "I knew Sam better than that. Nothing would have made him love his children any less."

My, "*and nothing could make Sam love me*," goes unvoiced. "I didn't know any better. I was sixteen, as old as Raven is now.

How the hell was I supposed to know what a grown man would think? A grown man I'd never even held a conversation with."

"Point taken," Malcolm concedes. "Sam received the '*John Mason: what it means to be a man*' speech after I heard you guys screwing in my sister's bedroom."

"Now I understand why," I whisper, another layer of sadness washing over me. "When Sam found out about Willow, he asked me to marry him. But I didn't think Sam should have a life sentence because we had sex for a few minutes. I wasn't capable of being a wife and mother at sixteen. I thought I was doing all the right things for the right reasons because *I* had fucked up, and only *I* should have to pay the price. But I fucked up again three years later. Trusting when I shouldn't– still a fucking kid myself. History repeated itself, only I couldn't give two more kids away. Responsibility screamed that I get married and suck it up… so I did. I don't regret it, but I want better for my children's futures."

I fold my arms on the table and collapse on top of them. "Ahhh… Fate is such a bitch. Another one-night stand, only this time I was drunk– the first and the last time I was drunk. Blackout, lie there like an idiot drunk," I admit for the first time.

I flush bright red, and then pale to a gray-green as I'm sucked into the past. The mortifying memory of lying beneath Sam, completely limp– paralyzed with shock and alcohol as Sam used my body over and over. Hovering over me, inside me, Sam kept repeating it was my fault. I should have married him. I should have come home when he asked a billion times. He couldn't be near Willow without me being the connection. He kept snarling how he'd look like a pervert stalking a child who no one knew was related to him. Sam became vicious when he spoke of his mother needing access to Willow. Sam would make me marry him so he could at least be Willow's brother-in-law. As he used my body for hours, he promised he'd force me to come home… Promise kept, I came home.

It was all my fault.

I blink out of the memory, horrified. I twist the past into a swallowable fantasy. "I should have known better, but Sam could sell you the panties off your own crotch. Ginny likes to tease me, saying I'm the most fertile woman on the planet. What were the odds?"

Smiling ruefully, Malcolm just shakes his head back and forth, back and forth. No doubt he's calling me an idiot in his mind. "That right there," he says pointedly, "is why I don't have sex. Birth control fails. Condoms break. All sex should be looked at with the intent to procreate. A quick fuck with a random stranger, where you have no emotional connection whatsoever, so even the sex sucks... BAM! Their DNA is now intermingling with yours inside your child. No. Fucking. Way."

It *was* sex with the intent to procreate. It wasn't a matter of what are the odds. Whether I was sixteen or nineteen, I was a dumb girl either way. I've never voiced my true thoughts on the events, not that anyone would've ever believed me. I doubt Ginny even would. To this day, I waver between date rape and consent, never settling on an answer because it hurts so much to remember. The pain wasn't only from when Sam betrayed my trust by using my body– it was the devastating words he spoke and the motivations for creating life, all as a way to get what he wanted, when he wanted it. No one knows, and no one will *ever* know. It is not the legacy I want my children to live. Every child should believe they were created from love.

Sam made an excuse to visit Ginny and me for almost six weeks, saying he needed to get away and wanted to reconnect with his childhood friend and the mother of his *child*. Sweet, understanding, Sam helped me study. He helped cook and clean and do the shopping. He was supportive and kind and caring, showing me what it would be like to be his wife. He asked me to marry him no less than fifty times over that six week period. I didn't realize at the time that no one told Sam no. Ever. While I was saying no, he was ensuring a yes. I hadn't realized Sam was patiently stalking me, waiting, calculating my cycle.

If only I had said yes. My life may have been different, but the twins wouldn't be here now.

One evening, Sam convinced Ginny to go out to a party. He wanted to hang out with me alone. Sam and I sat on the sofa while he told me funny stories. I remember laughing, having a few beers, and truly loving Sam. I fell for him– hard –and that's what makes it hurt so badly. I wanted to be Sam's wife. I wanted to be the mother of Sam's children. I wanted a future with the man who was making me laugh– the sweet, compassionate man whom everyone loved. I wanted that future when I grew up more, because I wasn't ready yet. It was a no for now, but it was a yes to the future.

It's like I blinked, and then I was being taken on the sofa, and later in my room... until morning. I didn't say no, but I couldn't exactly say yes, either. I take responsibility for my own stupidity… and that is the history of how my twins were conceived. The twins were created as a trap, as a way for Sam to have full-access to Willow. Stubborn as I was, Sam knew of the agonizing pain and guilt I felt over Willow, to the point that I couldn't even hold my child without being physically ill. Sam knew I'd never go through that torture again, and he was right.

Malcolm chuckles softly, musing how his '*rules*' of sexual engagement offer more protection than contraceptives. He doesn't realize what happened, and I'm too humiliated to ever say the words out loud. So as he smugly laughs, the knife twists deeper, just as it did every single time anyone took Sam's side over mine.

Angry with myself, I turn defensive in my failings. I allow the Clover I used to be to erupt, and end up saying way too much. "Yeah, well," I twist with a nasty attitude, sounding just like my daughters. "There *is* an f'n way to prevent pregnancy without condoms and birth control and abstinence. Sam learned my cycle. He never touched me for a week every month, and not once did he ever–" I close my eyes and mutter the mortifying word, "ejaculate inside me. Sam used to say, '*I'm not making any more kids with the cold-hearted bitch who would just throw them away.*' Shit," I moan, feeling sick to my stomach. "I shouldn't have told you that. I was an awful wife– a pestilence –and I'm an even worse mother."

Smacking his palm on the table loudly, causing me to jump, Malcolm demands my undivided attention. "I will hear none of that, Clover," Malcolm reprimands me. I glance up to meet his stormy blue eyes. Surprising gentleness and understanding lurk in their depths, rendering me brainless.

"I-I-I don't know how I can truly feel this way," I muse, confused. "But it's the truth. I loved Sam. I *really* loved him. I wanted him to be proud to be my husband and me his wife. I wanted Sam to be proud that I was the mother of his children. But once you give away a man's first born, can he really love you or be proud of you after that?" I ask hypothetically, because the only answer is no. No, he can never love you. "It wasn't an easy marriage. Sam was the best father on the planet. But he could be very cold, and I'm sure I was the cause because I was the only one affected. Sam never touched me, with anger or affection, and my children followed suit." I shrug like it's not a big deal, like my heart isn't torn to shreds and bleeding me dry.

"Clover," Malcolm says in a way that makes my heart speed. He reaches across the table for my hand, but I snatch it away. I can't have Malcolm's pity or his touch. I deserve neither. I expect Malcolm to look rejected, but he smiles at me patiently and tucks his hands around his coffee mug.

"I'm trying my damnedest not to speak ill of the dead, especially about the father of my children to his lifelong friend. I can't have you resenting me over something I say," I admit why I can't be fully honest with Malcolm about my life as a wife. "Sam really is who I would have chosen– eventually. If I hadn't fucked up, if I had been perfect enough, if I was a different person, we might have been good for each other. But our problems were of my own making. I just look at it as my punishment that I will endure for the rest of my life."

I can't look at Malcolm. The cop in Malcolm makes him too perceptive. I can't have him see through my perfect façade. I glance down and notice one of my pink-polished nails is chipped. I quickly tuck it under to my palm, hiding the imperfection.

"I didn't realize," Malcolm admits sadly. I see movement in my periphery. His fingers unwrap from his mug, hesitate, and then return to his mug. "It's why we need to do this. I can't allow our mistakes to ruin our children. Camille and I were flawed. You and Sam were flawed. I don't want those flaws to leak over to stain our children."

"Me, either. Sam would roll over in his grave if he could see the shit I've turned our lives into," I grumble in shame. I've tried and tried, and it was never good enough– never enough to earn Sam's favor. He'd offer me a small taste, and then pull away as soon as I got comfortable.

"Ah! Now that makes so much more sense," Malcolm drawls out, causing me to flinch. "You never know what's going on inside anyone's marriage. Half the time you don't even know what's going on in your own. I was married for fourteen years, and I never knew what was up from down." He barks a humorless laugh at our mutual plight.

"I spent my tenth wedding anniversary alone," I murmur lifelessly. "It was like Sam was judging me from the grave. Screaming that I wasted three years of our lives studying for a degree I'd never possess." Snapping out of it, I hiss, "Shit! Why do I keep telling you this shit?" I flick the cookie I pretended to eat earlier and pound it with the side of my fist. It crumbles into a million imperfect pieces. Instantly, I regret how I allowed my emotions to get the better of me.

"Clover," Malcolm drawls, trying to gain my attention. I glance up in hope that he'll continue speaking. "You're telling me because you trust me and know I'll understand. I knew Sam better than anyone. I'm also someone who's been exactly where you've been and is living with the irreversible consequences."

Annoyed by Malcolm's unflinching compassion, I lash out because I'm uncomfortable and scared. I try to stop the immature words from spewing, but it's like the girl I used to be wants out of her cage. She wants to roam free, and she wants to do it with Malcolm.

Irrationality spills from my mouth like verbal vomit, and there is nothing I can do to stop it. "Did you come over here so we could chat like hens over coffee? Do you want me to say that I never expected in my wildest imaginings that I'd be a widow a week before my twenty-ninth birthday? This is my lot in life, Malcolm. Here you sit, telling me how we are so alike, saying you want to be my husband, all the while making my life more difficult by actively trying to get me fired. Ross will eventually fire me if you keep sending nudies. You realize this, right? I'm a woman with no discernible skills. What kind of job do you think I will get if I lose the one I have? How would I feed my kids?"

Smirking at me, looking all proud, Malcolm gives me the complete and total opposite reaction of the horrified one Sam would have given me. I would have been lectured to within an inch of my life on the ways a wife should behave toward her husband. Peggy would have sent me articles and self-help books on etiquette. Yet here Malcolm sits, enjoying my outburst, reveling in it actually. Unfathomable. I expected Malcolm to be angry, not what is staring me in the face. Malcolm's deep blue eyes sparkle with an unknown emotion. Arousal?

Smiling wider at my confusion, Malcolm's voice is thick with… lust? "I could bullshit you, lie to you, romance you and seduce you. I could lay on the charm, but it would annoy you and you'd see right through it. You're the kind of woman who likes truth, like a blunt-force trauma to the skull." Malcolm laughs heartily. I clench my toes against their need to curl, even as my fists curl with the need to strike out to stop that decadent sound.

"In other words, a bitch," I murmur bluntly, not offended in the least. I am what I am. I hear my kids and family call me a cold-hearted bitch behind my back. Hell, Willow has screamed it in my face more times than I can count.

I see it, the change in Malcolm. When I was calm, he was calm. When I was in pain, he was in pain. Now that I'm fired up, he's fired up. My fire is from repressed anger, while his is from repressed lust. It's no wonder I'm comfortable around this man, because he gives back exactly what you give and gives exactly what you give back.

Equal.

Balanced.

Halves of a partnership.

Terrified, I realize that somehow my aggression is amping up Malcolm's sexual frustration. Malcolm is vibrating a carnal energy that is borderline frightening. His nostrils flare. His eyes are wild. His chest rises and falls in rapid succession. His fingers are curled around his coffee mug until his knuckles turn white.

This time, Malcolm spews the verbal vomit, and yet again, it's a comfort that I'm not the only freak and fuck-up at this table made for two.

"I like a bitch. I like messy and chaotic, too. I want you unraveled and writhing beneath me." Malcolm rumbles a sound that can only be described as a growl as he eyes me like succulent prey. "Don't forget, I was married to crazy. I can take anything you can give, and give it back two fold," he warns ominously. "I don't want perfect Clover. I want the perfectly flawed Clover I remember as a kid. You were dirty, and I wanted you back then. You made me feel like a pervert." Malcolm flashes me a blindingly devious smile. A hank of hair falls into his face and he brushes it away. "I felt like a jealous pervert as I beat the hell out of Sam for touching you."

"What?" I whisper, unsure if I heard Malcolm correctly.

Ignoring me, because I know he heard me, Malcolm continues on with his filibuster of 'what the fuck'. "I plan on making you filthy, and I won't say 'I plan on making you filthy by the time I'm finished with you', because I'll never be finished with you. Expect to be dirtied several times a day until death do us part. I won't be pulling out like a pussy, either. I made it for you, so you're going to take it, and you're going to like it. And I'm going to get off on the thought of my kid in your gut."

Stunned, speechless, I just sit at my kitchen table with my mouth gaping wide open. I stare at a panting Malcolm, and he stares back at me with blue eyes filled with a hunger so deep it leaves me– wet. A sensation I haven't felt since I was a teenager. I can actually feel moisture wicking from other parts of my body to well between my thighs.

Looking off kilter with his face tipped to the side, staring me down, Malcolm says in an eerily calm voice, "I had this all planned out with bullet points. But I think I'm just gonna wing it from here on out."

"Wing what?" My voice cracks under the strain of Malcolm's abrupt transformation. I wet my throat with a swallow of coffee, because everything on me should be wet if a man's going to talk to me in this manner. Unfamiliar with this sensation, I go on the attack. "I wasn't aware that pornographic images sent to the mayor of our town was in need of bullet points. I wasn't aware that declaring your intent to procreate inside *my* womb was in need of bullet points. We already have seven mouths to feed between the pair of us. Are you fucking insane?"

Am I insane? Because right now, I can't think of an argument against Malcolm's abhorrent behavior. I delicately sniff my coffee. Did he drug me?

At least Malcolm has the decency to blush. "My favorite activity is sex. Sex I haven't had in seven years. My ultimate favorite activity is coming inside another human being. I've only done so in my wife. My dick misses pussy, and it's hungry for yours. I miss the thrill of wondering if I'm manly enough to impregnate my wife. I thought you got the picture– literally. I know Ross understood the underlying meaning of my cum-covered cock in your inbox. I. Need. To. Cum. Inside. You."

Eyes bugging out of my skull, "F-U-C-K," I breathe, shocked senseless. The pulsing between my thighs is in agreement with the defrosting organ in my chest, but my mind is a jumbled up mess of '*What. The. Fuck?*'

"Okay," Malcolm mutters more to himself than to me as he calms down. "Clearly, I'm doing this wrong. We've went off course with this conversation. My *need* is getting the better of me. I promise I'll explain the mayor/fire thing later," Malcolm willingly admits that he is, in fact, trying to get my ass fired. "But first, I will lay out why you and I should get married, and the sooner the better, for sanity's sake. Sooner, as in, like, yesterday."

"What?" I shout, flabbergasted. I freeze, listening to make sure the kids are still watching smut reality TV for teenagers. When I hear them arguing over the cast of characters, I hiss at Malcolm, "You're fucking kidding me, right? First you admit to trying to get me fired, and then spring a proposal on my ass?"

"Not the reaction I was going for." Malcolm laughs shamelessly while running his fingers through his thick, black hair. Instead of a hero, Malcolm is flawlessly pulling off the rogue look of a villain.

After years of sharing a life with the poster child of the perfect husband and father, Malcolm's cool confidence with being a fucked-up mess is a breath of fresh air. Odd but welcoming. Malcolm reminds me of a marshal from an old western movie: justice-seeking, loyal, flawed, and real. A man.

In his darkest hours, Sampson Webster reminded me of Ted Bundy: everything perfect, right down to the hair, eyes, height and weight, especially the smile from lips speaking the words you wanted to hear, but were never the truth.

Thrown by the cacophony of my thoughts, words just spew on their own. "Well, that was by far the worst proposal I've ever had, and since I had to buy my own engagement ring last time, that's saying something," I mutter quickly, wondering why those words flew out of my mouth.

Dumbfounded, Malcolm just stares at me with his mouth hanging open. "You bought your own engagement ring? Seriously?"

Turning sarcastic because the memories threaten to overpower me again, "Color you shocked, but yes. I bought it as a reminder of why I had to get married, and it gave me the strength to go through with it. It wasn't much of a ring, but it was Willow's birthstone," I admit, getting choked up. "For all the proposing Sam did, not once did he present a ring. Actually, my mother bought our wedding bands." I remember how everyone wanted a shotgun wedding, fearing I'd bolt before the ink was dry on the license, and then leave them with three illegitimate kids to raise.

Malcolm shakes his head back and forth, as if he thinks the movement will erase my words. "Okay, I thought you'd appreciate the logical sentiment of a blunt proposal." Malcolm blushes and looks away. "Yeah, that was pretty shitty to spring it on you like that, wasn't it?"

I close my eyes and mutter the real reason I'm so upset with Malcolm. "I know what you're proposing would be more like a business arrangement." Drawing a phrase from the bodice rippers I shamefully read, "We wouldn't be a '*love match*'. But yeah... that was really shitty, Malcolm."

Malcolm slaps his palm on table to gain my attention, and I snap my eyes open to meet his. "I'm not proposing a business arrangement," Malcolm growls. His blue eyes glow darkly in the bright of my kitchen. They take on a sinister appearance– nearly black.

Flustered and filled with guilt, I quickly ramble, "I was a horrible wife, Malcolm. You'd be better off staying single than marrying me." I look at the remnants of my smashed cookie scattered across the surface of the tabletop, refusing to return Malcolm's penetrating stare.

I swear Malcolm murmurs the word '*landmines*', or at least that's what I read from the movement of his lips. I narrow my eyes, trying to reason out what that word would have to do with anything.

"Bullet points, it is. I'll start with the obvious: our kids. First: they chose us. My kids picked you as their new mom and yours picked me as their new dad. Not knowing that I had been courting you for the past year, Willow brought it up to Devon, and they separately asked the rest of the kids. I think at their age, they should get a say in who will be in their lives forever."

The foreign feeling of my heart melting terrifies me, causing me to hold on to the *bitch* of *coldhearted bitch* by the skin of my teeth. "All right, let's go get hitched," I say sarcastically as I move to stand up.

"Sit your ass down, Clover," Malcolm hisses. His hand latches out and encircles my wrist. With a tug, I'm firmly planted back in my seat at the dinette table. A zing of pleasure arcs down my spine and takes root between my thighs at the forceful way Malcolm manhandled me.

What in the hell is wrong with me?

"I'll start with what my kids need. They've never had a mom. Their mom never baked them a birthday cake, let alone a nightly meal. No encouraging words. No cuddles in bed with a bedtime story. No kissed boo-boos. They soothed each other, and now they are too old for any of that. But they still need a mother," Malcolm pleads, "especially Raven."

Another chunk of ice melts and turns to feelings of warmth, causing my hand to reach out and take Malcolm's. His fingers wrap around mine in an instant. "I... oh," my voice breaks, rendering me incapable of speaking without crying out. I've been so emotional lately that the tears are already threatening to erupt.

Choking on his own words, Malcolm grits out, "My oldest boys had to mother their own mother, and then she killed herself. I've had to ask too much of Devon and Kieren to sustain Raven and Weston's childhoods. This led to Devon's downfall, and Kieren is miserable even though he hides it well. My oldest boys acted as my wife and the mother to their siblings. Kieren cooked the meals while Devon cleaned and made sure the homework was completed. They did that so I could work and have the energy to give them what kids need from a dad. Frankly, I don't know how you do it, Clover. Work all day, take care of your home and family, and still find time to nurture. If I had to do the household shit, I wouldn't have the time to give a hug let alone hold a conversation."

I allow myself to be vulnerable, because Malcolm and I seem to feed off on how the other is feeling. He's being honest and vulnerable, so I must be too. "It's not without difficulty," I admit out loud for the first time. "I struggle every day, and I think I've failed in the nurture department."

"Not like I've failed in the parenting department. Right now, Devon is shacked up somewhere, higher than a kite, doing Lord knows what, while on the run from rehab for Christ's sake. All three of us work our asses off and it's never enough, and I don't mean monetarily. I mean keeping our shit together. Devon and Kieren should be building their own lives, finding their own wives, buying homes, working their careers, and creating the next generation of Masons. They shouldn't be living *my* life, while acting like *my* wife, as they raise *my* kids and tackle *my* housework."

Malcolm gets up from the table and starts pacing my kitchen. The emotions wafting from him are suffocating me, so I can only imagine how he must be feeling at this very moment. As he paces, he continually tugs at his hair while mumbling '*John Mason's rules on being a man*'.

I don't know what to think. But I do have an idea on how Malcolm feels: set adrift, completely alone and desperate, guilty–

a failure. On paper, what Malcolm is proposing makes perfect sense: a partnership where both parties bring something needed and equally important to the table, where they are honest and responsible. You can't map out love, and I can't live in a loveless marriage. It was too stressful last time, choking on my own failings while continually disappointing the one person who I wanted approval from the most. But would it be loveless when we love our children more than anything?

Malcolm comes to a stop right beside me. He squats down to my height until we are face-to-face. The earnestness of his emotions is written across his features. "So, my kids need a mom. The only female I can turn to is Isis, and let's face it, that is a nightmare to imagine. The only girl advice Isis knows is the shit she asked *me*. It would be no different than if I was speaking to Rae myself. There are things a girl just can't ask her daddy, things I should never know. The boys need a mom to ask about girls. They need a feminine touch."

I swallow, wetting my throat so I can get the words out. "I agree with everything you are saying. Most of the time I just feel like an older version of my younger self. I don't know a damned thing. So when I need to help my kids, I'm at a loss."

Malcolm closes his eyes and draws in a deep breath, "I know," he says solemnly, but not about me, about himself. "Your kids need a dad, especially Seth. I talk a big game about being a man, but that is about how I believe I should behave, and it has no bearing on how I perceive women. Seth has strong misogynistic views, and I have a sick feeling I know where that is coming from."

"I can't repeat what started my fight with Seth this morning." I glance at the clock on the microwave, noting that it's almost one in the morning. "I mean yesterday morning."

"I believe I know the particular phrase you're refusing to speak. Violet confides in Weston, especially the things she can't get through her brother's skull. Let's just say Weston was defending your honor when he pushed Seth to the ground."

"No," I breathe out, horrified, bowing my head in my hands. "I don't want the kids fighting."

"No worries, Clover," Malcolm reassures as his heavy palm lands on the center of my back, and begins a circular pattern of soothing comfort. "I had it covered. That's why you need me–

that's why I need you. That's why we will make one hell of a team."

I turn my head so I can meet Malcolm's eyes. "Can I… do I have to give you a decision right now?" I ask hesitantly.

"No," Malcolm says, shaking his head no while wearing a shit-eating grin. "I would be concerned if you gave me a yes right away, and very, very sad if you told me no without mulling it over. We will go slowly, get to know each other better. Do some test runs with the kids."

"I'm scared," I whisper, the sound barely audible. A tremor starts in my hands, continues to my arms, and travels down my spine to the rest of my body. My teeth begin to chatter as I hug myself. Malcolm curves over my back, warming the frigidness that has nothing to do with cold and everything to do with being petrified.

"I know," Malcolm whispers back. "Me too. Clover, I've been contemplating this for over a year, and the primary emotion I've felt was guilt. But I have to think positively right now as I deal with Devon. I have to be proactive in helping my family. I'm doing all I can do: trying to locate Devon to get him into treatment, trying to blend our families for the strength, safety, and comfort, and looking for a new home. I have exactly the amount of time Devon is in rehab to get my shit together, because Devon will need stability when he returns."

Overcome with sadness, completely bereft, I mumble, "I'm so sorry," and I don't even know about what. I just know I'm sorry.

"There is no one to blame. We just drew the short straw in life. I could wallow in remorse, believing that I ruined all four of my children. I could wonder if there was something I could've done differently and my wife would still be alive today. But instead of dwelling in the past, I choose to make a healthy change for my present and future instead. It may or may not be the correct fix, but we won't know unless we try."

"So what, we get married for the kids? The kids are almost adults. What do we do when they find a life of their own? Move on?" Frustration infuses my tone, but the fear is the loudest. I can't be used again. I voice the one thing I never felt Sam realized, "Malcolm, I'm a human being."

"Do you honestly think I'm that type of man?" Malcolm says stiffly as if I insulted him, but his comforting touch remains. If anything, he curls around me more. Only touching me with the palm of his hand, his chest a scant inch from my back. Malcolm uses his presence and his calm voice to reassure me.

"How should I know? We're strangers who know each other. That is my point. We know each other's children, we know each other as parents, but we don't *know* each other," I stress. "What kind of marriage would that be? It's one that is destined to end in four or five years when the kids finally grow up and get lives of their own."

"Clover, I told you the selfless reasons first. Now, I'll tell you the selfish ones." Malcolm grabs my shoulders, spins me around, gets more into my personal space if that's humanly possible, and then captures my undivided attention.

Gripping my shoulders, lightly shaking, "I *need*," Malcolm stresses with an intensity that borderlines on insanity. "I *need* a wife. I'm so goddamned lonely. I want to come home to a warm, clean, inviting home, that's filled with my kids. I want to hear laughter. I want to smell good food that feeds the soul. I want a companion to listen to my problems and tells me hers. I want someone in my bed to warm me when I can't sleep, who eagerly accepts my body. You ask what happens when the kids grow up: weddings, grandkids, life. I want someone to share those milestones with. I need someone who understands me. I don't care if we fight, as long as we fight each other."

A flood– a flood from my melting heart pours out my eyes. Unable to hold back any longer, not the tears or the words, I sob an unvoiced truth for the first time. "I'm so goddamned lonely," I repeat Malcolm's words right back to him. Stunned at my passionate outburst, he just stares at me. "No one gets it. I can be sitting with my friends or family, with my kids, but feel completely alone, more alone than when I'm all by myself. So alone that it physically aches. I'm scared, Malcolm. No, petrified. I'm petrified that I can never be what you want me to be."

Stated simply, "I want you to be you, Clover. I want to get to know the *real* you. This won't work if either of us plays pretend."

"What if it doesn't work? What if one of us decides that getting married is the worst decision ever?"

"Whether or not you agree to marry me, we'll still be connected for the rest of our lives. So we better get used to each other now. Are you blind? Ren is so in love with Willow that he's already naming their future children. I'm not shitting you. You and I will be family someday. We can either wait for our kids to connect us, or we can connect ourselves. But regardless, we will be in each other's lives for the rest of our lives. Either way, we're grandparents," he promises. "It will be up to you whether or not we're husband and wife while we hold those babies."

Out of nowhere, tears begin again. It all sounds so right, logical, the perfect life. Is it selfish of us or selfless? But… I'm a selfish, cold-hearted bitch. Sam taught me that.

"No, Clover, no," Malcolm demands softly. "No more tears. I can't handle when a woman cries. You're perfect for me because you're so strong. Will them away, now," Malcolm murmurs and wipes my tears away.

I sniffle and do as Malcolm says. I will my tears to stop. "That's what you want, but what do I get out of it. I can't live for someone else. I already did that with Sam."

"I'm a highly perceptive man," Malcolm murmurs arrogantly, but grins to humble his words. "I've been trying to get you fired because you hate your job. We want the same things, Clover. We have the same core belief system, the same values, and complementary needs. I need a wife and mother for my children, and you want to be a wife and mother. Stay home, raise our family, and keep our house. There is nothing wrong with wanting that kind of life. Your passion is food– so cook. Cook for us or for the community."

"I… I couldn't do that," I stammer out.

"And just why not?" Malcolm challenges me, smiling as if he knew I'd respond as I did. "Now, I'm a simple man. My passions lie in being a hero, even though I thoroughly suck at it," he adds wryly. "I'm thankful that I get to do a job I love. Clover, I want that for you. I want you to be happy. I want you to finally find your passion instead of just surviving."

"I have," I deny poorly, being stubborn.

Dramatically sniffing the air, Malcolm teases, "I smell bullshit. We could be really good together, Clover. Our kids would be well taken care of and well loved, and we'd both be happy doing what we're good at. Only thing I ever wanted was a wife who put her children above herself. The only thing you've ever wanted was a husband who put his wife equal with his children."

I gasp in shock. "I… Sam wasn't like that," I defend weakly.

"There's that smell again, and it mysteriously smells like a woman bullshitting me," Malcolm growls, annoyed that I'm not being open and honest with him. "I'm perceptive, remember?" He taps his temple. "I caught on with all your little tells. Sam was a good man. I will speak no ill will of him, but he didn't treat you well. You are still grieving. You are overcome with guilt. There is a profound sadness that I've tried to decipher this past year. I've pushed you in order to take note of what upset you, so I could figure it out. I knew you weren't ready to tell me the truth."

"I can't," I whisper. "Don't make me."

Ever-patient and understanding, "I won't, and you don't have to tell me. But someday you will trust me enough to talk to me, or at least talk to someone about it. You've been a font of information since we began our negotiations. It's what I do for a living, seeing what lies beneath the words left unsaid. Would you like to know what I've discovered so far?"

Filled with indecision, I just close my eyes and nod my head.

Eyes narrowing until fine lines appear at the corners, Malcolm sighs heavily as if the weight of the world is bearing down on his shoulders. "Okay, here goes: You were a sixteen-year-old girl, who was under my care while in my home, and I failed you. Sam was a twenty-one-year-old grown man who stalked a girl to the bathroom and took her innocence. You couldn't consent, Clover, whether you wanted Sam or not. I threatened to arrest him for statutory rape after you left my house. Instead I beat the shit out of Sam and lectured him while he bled. He and I didn't see eye-to-eye for a very long time after that. Actually, not until Sam righted the wrong by marrying you. When I replace you with Isis or Rae or Willow or Violet, I would have killed Sam. Your parents should have pressed charges."

"Malcolm," I protest, unsure what I'm actually protesting. Maybe I'm just surprised that someone saw the event from my perspective for once, instead of being blinded by Sam's charismatic manner,

"Listen," he warns me not to interrupt. "I know you blame yourself over Willow, and the guilt is eating you alive. But know this: at any time Sam could have said '*no, I want my kid. I want to raise my kid.*' Sam could have legally had Willow in less than a second after she was born. But he didn't. Instead, Sam followed you around and took the future you were trying to build for yourself by knocking you up again."

I hide my head in my hands, unable to look at Malcolm any longer. He sees the truth, but instead of taking Sam's side, he's taking mine. I don't want Malcolm to view his dead childhood friend in a poor light. Sam's not here to defend himself, so I do.

"Sam made mistakes, but so did I," I whisper gravely, voice sounding empty.

"Listen to me," Malcolm shakes me lightly. "Hear me out. You were still a kid when you got pregnant with the twins, but Sam was an even older adult than he was when you conceived Willow. He was almost twenty-five and you were a young college student. Sam kept asking you to marry him and you kept saying no because you wanted to finish your schooling first. Isn't that why?"

"Yes," I reply immediately, and the rest of the words spill like water, relieved to be voiced. "Every time Sam asked, I told him no. But I also told him why. I wanted to finish college, get a job, and then I'd marry him. I wasn't ready yet. I didn't feel like I would make a good wife and mother. I didn't want Sam to see me fail. I failed, and he witnessed it, and he never let me forget it."

"I'm a man, so I know exactly how Sam was feeling right then. Fear. Bent pride. He saw the future he envisioned slipping away, so he got desperate. Sam knew that if you accomplished your goals, you wouldn't need him anymore and you'd move on. Sam probably thought you'd find an intellectual man, and he was insecure about being a carpenter."

"God, Sam had no reason to be insecure. He had no reason to fear a goddamned thing. I wasn't going anywhere. I wasn't moving away from him. I was trying to move toward him by growing up and getting smarter."

Cold, calculating, Malcolm slowly speaks in a menacing voice. "Clover, you can put Sam on a pedestal because he's gone. But if he wasn't dead, I'd kick his ass right now."

"Malcolm, don't," I poorly attempt to defend my dead husband.

"You slipped up a few times during our talk. I'm a trained police officer– a twenty-two-year veteran and the Chief of Police. Don't think I didn't figure out how Sam convinced you to marry him," Malcolm states emotionlessly. "Don't think Sam didn't already confess everything to me. It didn't make Sam a bad person, just someone who would do whatever it took to get what he wanted. You don't have to admit it out loud, but I think you need to come to terms with it so you can heal. I hadn't realized I'd have so many emotional landmines to tiptoe around."

Emotionally exhausted, I breathe, "Landmines, oh." Malcolm had mouthed the word earlier. I wasn't losing my mind. "Sorry."

"No reason to be sorry," Malcolm reassures me. All of the sudden, a wicked smile twists his lips. "Darlin', you're gonna have some fun traversing my landmines. It's not one or two. I've got a motherfucking field of 'em."

"I... I don't know how to reply to that," I stammer out. "Where do we go from here?"

Shrugging, Malcolm says, "We wing it, just as we do everything else."

"That's for damned sure," I mutter in agreement. "We don't know each other," I state the obvious, but I smile anyway.

Malcolm pulls me toward him, until my forehead rests against his lips. I shiver from the light contact. "Yes, we do," he murmurs confidently against my skin, and then he kisses my forehead. "You won't have one single regret when it comes to us," he vows. "We'll have a lifetime to get to know each other. It'll be a fun journey," Malcolm says cockily.

"Hell," I groan. "We're gonna crash and burn."

CHAPTER THIRTEEN

The Widower

Jesus, watching Clover fry donuts shouldn't give me an erection, but fuck if it doesn't. The smell alone is putting a slow-building fire in my belly. If I didn't already know that Clover would kick my ass for it, I'd run off to the bathroom and snap her a new photo. It would take everything in me not to print the image and slap it on the fridge– all proud like.

The instant Clover agreed to be my wife– at least that's how I perceived it –she flew from her chair and insisted on making the donuts. It's been a quiet twenty minutes, where I've sprawled at Clover's table and eyed her beneath my heavy-lidded stare. Watching her make icing is the worst– reminding me of the many times I've cream-filled her donuts and captured the Kodak moment. I've been hard since I stepped foot into this house. The smell of food will always remind me of Clover from now on.

The kids are so quiet that one would think them asleep. But from my vantage point in the kitchen, I can see the top of Weston's blond head as he towers over the rest of the kids. I know he's awake, watching a movie on low. The way his head keeps moving, it appears he's chatting with someone every once and a while. I'd ask Clover if the kids should go to bed, since it's nearing two a.m., but I'm not sure if she'd kick me out of her house afterward. I make the kids take one for the team. Thankful tomorrow is Sunday, so being sleepy won't be an issue. I need to spend more time with Clover– it's a compulsion I can't deny. If I have tired kids, so be it.

I'm just content watching Clover.

"How are we doing this?" Clover asks sheepishly, cutting into my sexual tension like a hot knife. God, I want to rub the glazing all over her body and lick it back off.

I give a slow blink when I feel Clover's gaze on me. "Malcolm, are you still with me?" She smirks.

"Uh… yeah…" I chuckle and rub the back of my neck. Don't get too close, girl. I'm a hairsbreadth away from pressing you into the countertop, and you're still too skittish to enjoy it.

"Are you sure? I've been talking to you for a few minutes, but all you've been doing is staring at me in a haze." Clover swallows so loudly I hear it across the kitchen. The movement is fascinating. I want to start at her neck and work my way… *Malcolm!* I scream at myself, *Behave!*

"How come all of your donuts don't have holes?" I ask an idiotic question.

I give one quick glance in the direction of the children, find them not paying attention to us in the kitchen, and then I risk bodily harm by approaching Clover from behind. I hover near her back as she presses hot and steamy donuts into gooey chocolate glazing. She gives the doughy goodness a practiced swirl, coating the top perfectly, and then places it on a cooling rack. Mmm… I'm salivating.

"I made you the cake donuts in the beginning." I can actually hear the woman swallow. Silently wishing I could watch her throat work, I turn to the side for a better viewing angle. "But once I made you yeast-risen donuts, you've requested them ever since."

Impressed with Clover's skills, never thinking anyone could just make these yummy snacks in their own kitchen, I begin rambling like an idiot. "I loved the blueberry and chocolate ones. The boys like the sour cream ones, and the girls like those pink ones– I think they were cherry. So the cake ones have a hole? Those are denser. These ones, I like their pillowy texture," I answer, sliding a step closer, getting into Clover's personal space. "I like the way it feels on my tongue, between my teeth," I murmur in a husky voice. "The way it feels soft and caressing on other parts of my anatomy.

Clover's sharp intake of breath is all the invitation I need. I press against her back, my hard cock nestling in the curve of her spine. "Would you like a donut?" She asks hesitantly, thickly, no doubt trying to ignore my pounding arousal beating against her back. "You've never had them when warm."

Was that an invitation?

Was Clover's voice breathy?

I slide my hands around Clover's hips, spooning her closer. When she doesn't tear my nuts off, I settle my palms, fingers splayed across her soft belly. Shuddering from the warmth of holding Clover for the first time, combined with the intoxicating smell of the donuts, I am in heaven. I rest my chin on her shoulder, catching the scent of her skin, and for the first time I realize Clover is emitting the drugging scent. She smells warm, sweet, and fattening, like sugar cookies and butter. Home. Clover smells like what I always envisioned a wife, mother, and grandmother should smell like.

I whisper into Clover's ear, causing her to tremble in my arms. "Hold up a donut and give me a bite," I ask her to feed me from her hand. I open my mouth, patiently waiting. Clover is unsure, I can feel it in the rigidness of her spine, the way her muscles tense, and the short puffs of breath she takes. From here on out, I have to treat Clover as a wounded animal: Patiently coaxing. Unfaltering consistency. Pushing boundaries. Unconditional trust.

I wait, with my mouth wide open, and after a few seconds, Clover turns her face to the side to look at me. Her cheek caresses my forehead, causing my body to go insane. A sound is torn from Clover's throat, a cross between a gasp and a mew. The sound speaks volumes. Clover knows how she affects me. She can feel how my body continues to swell and throb as it readies for her, and it petrifies her.

"Shhh…" I whisper in a coaxing tone, trying to reassure her. "I'm not going to molest you," I promise, but quickly add on, "unless you want me to, that is. I can't help that he likes you. So let's just give me a taste of your sweets. Lucky, please," I beg in a pleading tone.

Clover unleashes an uncomfortable laugh, short and sardonic. "You have a wicked sweet tooth, Chief Mason," she taunts.

"You have no idea," I agree, secretly laughing because she smells like every decadent dessert that could possibly make my mouth water. "Gimme a bite, Clover," I beg, knowing she's now teasing me by holding out, no longer scared.

I expect Clover to smash the pastry into my mouth, but she surprises me by tearing off a bite-sized piece and gingerly placing it on my tongue. My eyes slide shut in bliss, the flavors exploding on my taste buds.

I've been sustained my entire lifetime by shitty convenience food: processed food, frozen dinners, the No-Name Diner and the bakery, and now Kieren's mediocre attempts at feeding us nutritiously. I never had a mother, I never had a wife, and I never had a knack for the chemistry of food.

"Gawd," I groan. Becoming desperate, clingy, I turn Clover in my arms until we are face-to-face, our bodies still arched together. Insanity, this level of want. In my mind's eye, I see my dad's fists clenching, preparing to stop my '*girly*' emotions from rising. But if I want Clover to be real with me, I have to be real with her. Not above begging, I do just that. "I'll do whatever you want, Clover. Ya gotta marry my ass. I *need* you."

Eyes tracking across my features, Clover looks spooked. Scared, she still holds her ground, not giving into me. "Just let me get comfortable with the idea, okay?" Clover gives me the answer I expected– the *right* answer.

"Fuck," I hiss out at myself. "I'm not trying to pressure you. I just now realized why I want this so badly, and selfishly it doesn't have a goddamned thing to do with our kids. It's all about me. I never had a woman in my life, not really. John Mason's rules taught me how to be a man, and what a real man needed in a woman. I never found what I was looking for before you. Lord knows, I'm looking at what I want, and I want what I see."

"I think you're blind," Clover says self-deprecatingly. Blinking guileless blue eyes at me, Clover shifts in my arms. "But in case you aren't, what do you see?"

I smile, thrilled to see that Clover does have womanly emotions: insecurity and the need to be complimented. "I see a woman who puts her family, her children, and her husband before herself. It isn't out of selflessness, it's because of who she is. I see a woman who would be happy to take care of a home, and would find great reward in a woman's traditional roles. I see a woman who would complement me perfectly. But beneath the surface, I see a woman who needs to be set free– freedom to be herself and know she's still loved."

Turning her face away from me, Clover hisses, "Stop it!"

"No," I mutter patiently. "I'm going to push you now," I warn a split second before my mouth feathers across Clover's– a fleeting touch. Using my entire body, I press Clover into the countertop until she's trapped. She doesn't fight me, nor does she freeze, so I take that as a welcoming sign. Slightly rigid, I can feel her fright, but I push anyway.

"You said you'd see if this would work," I remind Clover, challenging her. "I wasn't just talking about the division of labor, our parental strategies, or whether or not we will end up killing the other. I told you of my issue with touch, how I need to touch. Well, my need to be touched is worse. So touch me, Clover," I plead. "I don't want a marriage of convenience. I want a real marriage. Let's see if there is passion waiting to be set free."

Blinking in surprise, Clover's lashes entice me. "You want me... you want me to touch you?" she stammers, confused. Her arms lie limply at her sides, but her fists are clenched against her own need.

"Yes," I breathe, just as confused that Clover has missed the billion ways I've told her this over the past year. I know Willow isn't very perceptive, but perhaps her mother isn't as well. I go for broke, being blunt. "Touch me. Touch me anywhere, anyhow. I don't care if you make me hurt, because the ache of needing your touch is worse than anything else."

"Wha... what-why?" Clover stutters, but her hands slowly rise to rest on my bare forearms. A tremor rolls down my spine to explode in my groin at the first contact.

"No more talking," I demand, patience dissolving in an instant.

I don't kiss Clover, because I want her lips to seek mine. I bury my face against the side of her neck and inhale her honeyed scent. Using my entire body, I touch her without hands, pressing and releasing, rolling my body along hers.

The most surprising revelation of my life, Clover is rendered passive. She relaxes, turns boneless, and presses back against me. A mewing sound from Clover's throat unleashes my hands. They rove her back, fingers starved, and follow along the curse of her round ass.

Yoga pants + the world's finest ass = Malcolm Mason's erotic destruction.

"Christ," I breathe out in wonder. My palms grip the firm globes of her ass and squeeze perfect handfuls of flesh. Pulling Clover into my body, pressing my hard-on against her soft belly, I greedily feed my hunger.

Passive + hesitant = intoxicating.

Clover leans back against the counter while I molest her with my hands. Her eyes are heavy-lidded as she stares at me through the fringe of her lashes. Lips pouting, swelling with arousal, Clover looks relaxed with an edge of fright. No doubt scared over my intensity, or her own.

"We're going to be amazing together, in all areas," I vow, but it sounds more like a warning of our impending sexual implosion. Years of being without have taken their toll. When we finally unleash our lusts, the world will burn to the ground around us.

With me in the driver's seat, Clover follows my lead. Wherever I touch, she touches on me. Our eyes connect, both awed, as Clover's tiny fingers clench on my ass, testing us both. My eyes slip shut, my neck arching, as her touch seeps into me. Every movement of mine is mirrored in her hands. Testing her bravery, my fingers slide downward, over the swell of her ass, and sneak into the warm heat between her thighs.

I slump forward, forehead resting against hers, when I feel how damp and hot her pants are. I can almost feel steam rising from between her legs, and I'm the one who made her aroused. Shuddering, jerking beneath my insistent touch, Clover bites her lip like she's trying to be quiet.

"Be real with me," I growl out in a gravelly deep voice, not sounding like myself at all.

Reassured, trusting me, the dirty girl I remember when I was a young man erupts– the brave girl who screwed a man she barely knew in my little sister's bedroom. No, not screwed Sam– she fucked the living hell out of the man. I remember how Sam was wrecked for weeks after. Clover isn't going to wreck me for weeks, she's going to wreck me for the rest of my life– a thought I welcome.

With the most sensual noise I've ever heard– sweet, sultry, orgasmic in the extreme –Clover's hips buck into my hand. She's as starved for me as I'm starved for her… and then she touches me back.

"Fuck," Clover hisses for me when her tiny fist grips the bulge in my jeans. Hand shaking, petrified but horny as all hell, my Lucky Clover is the bravest person I've ever met. Grinding the palm of her hand into my bulge, she feeds my need.

Flying high, "Fuck it," I parrot her. I shift my face until we're aligned. Breath mingling, hot puffs of air scalding my lips, Clover wordlessly begs for it. Her fingers tighten on my cock as anticipation intensifies the need.

I finally kiss her, and goddamn it, she kisses me back.

It's a dirty kiss, filled with tongues and lips and teeth and spit and grunting noises of animalistic urges. Clover rides my palm as I ride hers, grinding into oblivion. The sweet sting of pain from tiny, blunt teeth scoring my bottom lip has me moments away from climax. One palm is terrorizing my cock, with her other roaming every inch she can reach. Wild. Unbridled. The woman who calls herself cold-blooded is hotter than anything I've ever encountered.

Without finesse, both of my hands are gripping and prodding, pulling her ass cheeks apart to get closer to her internal fire. My fingers probe, undeterred by the fabric of her yoga pants. I press inside of her as far as I can manage, hungering to be *inside* her. Perfectly in sync, Clover sucks my tongue into her mouth. I shudder in bliss at the relief from finally being *inside* her.

"Harrumph," a throat clearing sound has me freezing in surprise. It takes Clover another few seconds to realize we're no longer alone. I use my body to shield her from sight. Not one inch of the woman is visible behind my larger frame. Clover hides her face against my chest, her hands twisting in my shirt.

"Shh... it's okay," I say, trying hard not to laugh or cry or scream or orgasm.

Holy. Fuck.

I'm in flames. Burning to death for this woman.

"Dad," Weston calls out when I don't acknowledge him. "I... I thought I should warn you. The other kids want snacks. I... I could hear everything you've said, but they couldn't. I knew what you were up to."

"Christ," I voice, eyes bugging out of my skull. I turn my face to glance over my shoulder at my very uncomfortable son. Weston is a boy housed in a man's body. The kid stares at his shoes while gnawing at his bottom lip.

Clover loses it. At first I think she's crying, but then the sound clears, turning into embarrassed laughter. "I'm sorry," she coughs out. "Only cooking in the kitchen from now on. Oh. My. God. I'm going to go hide now."

Mortified, Clover extracts herself from my arms. I scowl, hating how cold and lonely I instantly feel. The slip of a woman tries to make herself invisible as she crosses the kitchen, having to walk by Weston to flee the room. No doubt her destination is the bathroom.

"Clover?" Weston stops her escape short.

Mind in control of my body, I smother the lust as I turn to my son and soon-to-be wife.

"Yes?" Clover responds. I choke on a laugh. The woman's flesh is bright red, a mixture of arousal and embarrassment. I want to shout, "*I did that!*" while doing a touchdown dance.

"I…" Weston's gaze remains on his shoes. "I just wanted to let you to know that I'll be proud to call you Mom when you're ready."

I step forward before Clover even has time to react, but I'm too late. The woman's fragile hand flies up to cover her mouth as a sob escapes. Her eyes leak tears like she's drowning. A pained sound flows from her throat as she brushes by my son, headed toward the bathroom or her bedroom, but not before she half hugs my son on her way by.

"What'd I say wrong?" Weston's blue eyes are tinged with red, as if he wants to cry because he made Clover cry.

I tug West into my side, careful not to fully embrace him since I'm still amped up. "Remember when you tried to hug Violet the first time?" I ask, wearing the largest grin. Anyone else would have seen Clover's reaction and thought rejection, but not me. My son just bought me an express-pass to marital bliss.

"Yeah," the huge kid sounds confused. "V. thought I was putting the moves on her. She tried to punch me in the junk, so my hug ended up giving her a bruised wrist. When I tried to help her, she kicked me in the shin."

"Remember how I told you we don't see a hug as anything because we are always touching, so it means a lot more to Violet. Poor Violet almost cried the first time Rae was nice to her. Remember?"

"Yeah, I guess so," West mumbles, still confused on how this has anything to do with Clover's reaction.

"See, it meant a lot to Violet that you guys wanted her around, so she was sensitive about it. Well, it's the same way with Clover. She didn't run away because you hurt her feelings. She ran because it meant so much to her."

Finally getting it, my kid's eyes clear to crystal blue. "Should one of us go check on her? See if she's okay?"

"No, Clover will be out after she composes herself. Women have their own pride they contend with. A lot has happened in the past few days. If a woman needs comfort, comfort her. If she needs space, give it to her. Now, don't ever forget that, son," I caution.

West smirks at me, like I've lost my ever-loving mind. "Dad," he uses my own patient tone on me. "You do realize I'll never have a use for your '*women advice*', right?"

I return Weston's look with an amused one of my own. "You have an over-emotional aunt and a big sister, or did you forget? If all works out, you'll have a new mother, sisters, and a grandmother. Plus, Essie and her mother. The Prynnes have a lot of ladies, and my advice will make it easier to breathe around them."

"Point taken," West says as an invasion of partially awake teenagers ramble into the kitchen. Seth's hair is sticking straight up, and drool is dried on his chubby cheek. Violet is wide awake, clearly Weston wasn't the only eavesdropper, judging by the fact that she's sizing my ass up for her mother. My baby bird is scrubbing at her eyes with her little fists, trying to recover from her nap.

"Hungry? You're always hungry after a nap," I tease Rae as she sniffs the air like a bloodhound. Her eyes clear the instant the scent of fresh-baked donuts hits her nostrils.

Playing hero, I save the baked goods. "No donuts!" I warn. "That's our breakfast."

"It *is* morning," Seth stresses while picking up a donut, only to have it drop back to the cooling rack. Bewildered, Seth stares at the fingers braceleting his wrist.

"Dick," Weston says, still angry with Seth. "You're gonna have to start listening or you'll be getting your ass kicked a lot."

"You said Malcolm has never laid a hand on anyone," Seth challenges, not meeting my eyes because they're fused to the donut he covets.

"Yeah, Dad says we fight our own battles. Don't doubt he hasn't hit Auggie. If you don't listen to Dad, it's up to me to keep you in line. Just as it was Dev and Ren's responsibility to keep me in line, and Aunt Isis's with Raven. I might be younger than you, asshole, but I'm a lot bigger."

I just lean back against the counter, crossing my arms over my chest. Amusement and pride war inside me while my son schools Seth on what it means to be a brother. The kid's lucky. I didn't have a peer when I was growing up. Isis was to be coddled, and Auggie was too young to be my equal until later in life. If I didn't listen, a gigantic man named Dad beat the ever-loving hell out of me.

"Knock it off." Surprisingly, Violet orders Seth, not Weston, to behave. "Don't even pretend you don't get it. You know Mom left it to me and Willow to punish you. Mom wouldn't hit you, but we would. After pissing Weston off earlier, I think I'd behave if I were you. You'll have all of us after your ass, like a pissed off gang of Mom supporters."

"Suck up," Seth mumbles out of the side of his mouth at his twin, but he listens to her anyway.

Conflict forgotten, the kids start foraging in the pantry. "How many times did you guys eat today? Five? Six?"

Cookie halfway up to his mouth, Seth flashes me a grin. "More like eight. I'm a growing boy."

Rae scoffs, "You'll need a hundred meals a day, and even then you'll be lucky to hit five and a half feet, squirt."

Clover materializes out of thin air. "We're taking a walk," Clover declares, while toeing on her *Skechers*. Thankfully her reappearance stops the impending fight before it starts. I forgot how volatile teenagers can be.

Baiting little bastards.

"I know it's late, but I just feel so restless. There is no way in hell I could go to sleep, even if I tried." Out of breath, eyes glittering with an unknown emotion, Clover looks like she needs to run free.

"Good deal," I agree. I glance over at the four idiots attacking the kitchen. They look like rabid raccoons foraging in the garbage cans at a campground. Which to choose… which to choose… I nibble on my lip as I decide who should be in charge. It has to be one of the boys, because the girls emotionally fly off the handle if you so much as even blink. Weston is the youngest, but the most mature.

Ah, shit!

"We're going for a walk," I shout to stall their gluttony. "If the shit hits the fan, call us."

Raven blinks up at me with a brownie crammed into her piehole. She grins evilly with a chocolate-kissed mouth. "You d-bags have to listen to me," she chortles.

"Fucking eerie," I mumble underneath my breath. I'm going to axe all the time Raven spends with her Auntie Isis. "I'm in charge," I say to stop the shit-storm that's brewing. "I said call *me* if you have a problem." I stare them all down until they look to the floor in acquiescence.

I feel a set of eyes on me, and since the idiots are looking anywhere but at me, it has to be Clover. I meet her awe-filled gaze. She's looking at me like I'm her hero, and if that doesn't make me feel like a man, I don't know what would. I stand up straighter, with my shoulders back and my chest puffed to max capacity. I even jack my pant leg up for good measure.

"Don't break anything, burn the house down, or kill each other," I warn as I walk away. A few snickers inform me I forgot a few somethings. I quickly look over my shoulder and notice Seth's hand cocked backward and filled with cake. "Don't make a mess or you'll lick it up," I threaten. "Oh! Don't commit any crimes. I'd hate to have to arrest your asses." I smile like I look forward to slipping the cuffs around their tiny, juvenile wrists.

"Um…" Clover stammers. "What your dad said… and yeah… behave."

My heart stops beating for a fraction of a second, and then it explodes into action. Clover said '*your dad*' to all of the kids.

Freudian slip?

God, I hope not.

CHAPTER FOURTEEN

The Widow

"We work really well as a team," Malcolm murmurs into the night.

The silence is divine. The crickets shut off their mating call as we walk forward, only to start cranking it out again as soon as we pass. Other than the parting tide of crickets and the occasional dog barking in the distance, the night is calm. Malcolm continually tries to coax me to chat as we head toward the river, needing the reassurance of our conversation that I'm comfortable around him.

"I'm not ignoring you," I assure Malcolm. "I'm trying to formulate my thoughts into words."

"Okay," Malcolm murmurs softly. His hand keeps flexing toward me, and then retreats. I take a fortifying breath and reach for Malcolm's hand. I don't do this for him, or for me– I do it for *us*. Malcolm needs the connection of touch, and right now, I need the comfort of his warmth. Malcolm's large palm engulfs my hand, fingers tightening around mine. A shudder rolls through him as if he's a bird settling its feathers. He doesn't try to engage me in conversation again because he is content with this small gesture of affection.

Seeing Malcolm's hand flex toward me every few minutes, and how he keeps himself in check because he fears I'll panic, drives home the point that Malcolm isn't Sam… and that is a very, very good thing. Everything Malcolm does is the opposite of how Sam would react. It's as unexpected as it is delightful. If there were any similarities between the two men, I couldn't do this, because it would be a reminder of all that I lost, and all that I've been through. Just as I'm sure Malcolm appreciates how Camille and I differ.

"I think we could work well together once we iron out a few things," I admit as we get near the rocky path that leads to the river. The river is where I've always gone to be introspective, to contemplate the best course of action I need to take within my life. For some odd reason, I'm perfectly comfortable with Malcolm joining my sacred place, just as my children had a few years ago.

Malcolm doesn't respond to my comment, but I can feel his satisfaction wafting around us like a lover's caress. It makes me smile.

"I want you to know I'm truly considering your offer. I also don't want to lead you on. I can't say yes right away because this is a major decision. I could go with my gut, I could go with my heart, but I've learned from my mistakes. So I'm going to go with my head first."

"And I expect no different," Malcolm murmurs softly, followed by a gentle squeeze of my fingers. "That's why I suggested a trial run, where we get to know one another better. We talk it out. We have to show the other that we mean what we say. I always follow through."

"Tell me the truth, Malcolm. This isn't a trial run for you, is it?" I can't see Malcolm offering me this solution if he wasn't one hundred percent positive that it would succeed. "You're doing this for me, aren't you? You were fine with either reaction. If I would've said yes, you would've tried to marry me by Monday." An uncomfortable laugh slips past my lips, sounding borderline insane.

"Yes," Malcolm admits, not sounding the least bit ashamed. "If you had said yes, we would've used our life together to get to know one another, grow to love each other. I already care for you, Clover. I want you to be happy. I love your children as if they were my own. Real good kids. But I knew you wouldn't give in easily– it's not who you are. So I plan to endear myself to you. I'll make you realize that blending our families will make it easier on all of us, not harder. I want you to trust me."

"I don't trust easily," I admit, and for the first time I feel badly about that fact. I want to trust Malcolm. I need to trust Malcolm. But after the life I've led, it's not without great difficulty.

"Nothing worth a damn is ever easy," Malcolm says with a smile thick in his voice. "And I think you and your children are more than worth it."

I suck in a sharp gasp of air, unused to hearing anything that borders on praise. Unsure what to feel, verbal vomit flows from my lips. "I've had a bad day... but fuck, it got worse. I don't know if it was a good thing or bad thing that the kids overheard. If they hadn't, we wouldn't have been drawn closer together. But now, they're in pain. It's selfish of me, but I'm glad they finally see me. See me as a human being with thoughts and feelings, not just someone who gave birth to them, someone they use to survive."

I shake my head a couple of dozen times, disbelieving I just said all that. My ponytail whips me in the cheek, clearing my mind even more. "Did I just say all that, really?" Malcolm tips his chin in answer, trying to hide the smile curling his lips. "Shit," I blurt out with feeling.

"I know this is hard for you to talk about," Malcolm begins hesitantly, ever-patient. "But I have no idea what happened tonight, so our conversation will be one-sided until you explain."

I use my environment to center myself so I can put my thoughts into words. The lapping of the water on the shore is a lullaby from the heavens. The moonlight casting its glow on the water is a spotlight from God. The atmosphere of standing on the riverbank, overlooking the rippling water is soothing. It lulls me into opening up to another human being for the first time in my life– truly allowing them to gaze at the heart of my soul.

"I was a wild child," I admit with a wry grin. "Willow's got nothing on her momma. My parents loved it. I was their first born, spoiled, and I had six years before Robin was born. They coddled their tiny child within an inch of her life."

"I bet you were a cute little brat," Malcolm says, causing me to blush. You can hear the love he has for kids when he speaks. It humbles me to hear the reverent yet amused quality in his voice.

"Yeah, I was. But I couldn't relate to anyone and I didn't make friends easily. When I started school, it was like an entirely different world, where I was bullied for my size and my smart mouth."

Feigning surprise, "Who? You? A smart mouth?" Dark blue eyes sparking with humorous intent, Malcolm smirks at me. "If I didn't know any better, I'd think you were trying to push me away with your flaws." Malcolm laughs silently. If it was anyone else laughing at me, I'd be offended. But I can tell Malcolm is teasing me. After all, he raised Isis into the woman she is, so he must love chaos.

"Ya gotta know what you're getting yourself into," I reply.

"I already know, Clover," Malcolm says in all seriousness.

"Yeah, well, my sarcastic and slightly caustic attitude has pushed all those away who could see past my stunted body. I was a smart kid, so teachers gave me attention and praise, and I fed off of it. After that, I decided I wouldn't be the wild child, like I could just change my personality. I became the girl with the perfect grades. It was utter bullshit, playing pretend. I strived for excellence and I don't know why. It never made me happy. I was taking college courses at fifteen and graduating high school at sixteen."

"That's admirable, Clover. It's not a bad thing to be smart," Malcolm tries to compliment me while reassuring me.

"Sure, I don't discount the knowledge I learned, but it wasn't me. My dream wasn't to be in an academic career. I just wanted a small town life, I guess. I wanted to be near my family. I only went to college to rebel against Mom and Dad's, and even Rob's, rebellion."

"I can see why you'd do that. Being normal when dealing with eccentric would stand out. But truly, don't discount your education because you never got a degree. You put in three years. It's three years more than most of us will ever get, and you did the work yourself."

"I know." I sigh, and finally admit the heart of the problem. "I was lonely, and I wanted friends. But I was never myself, so how could I get friends to like the real me if I was pretending? Ginny was the first girl who drew me in. She wanted to get to know me for me, and she liked what she saw. I'd just turned sixteen when I showed up at your party, and I'd hoped Sam saw me, liked me. Understood me. But he didn't. Sam thought I was a goodie-two-shoes, just like everybody else."

"I didn't," Malcolm says gruffly as he stands next to me on the riverbank. "I can spot a naughty girl at fifty-yards."

"Oh, on that I have little doubt," I drawl out. Malcolm chuckles in reply– a happy, warm sound that curls my toes inside my sneakers. "Every day was an exercise in restraining my true nature. It made me feel a semblance of power when I had none. I think it's how an anorexic must feel. You feel powerful even as you destroy yourself from the inside out."

"Clover," Malcolm murmurs near my ear. "There is power in letting someone else care for you."

I acknowledge what Malcolm said with a nod of my head. "I'm not ready for that yet. I've never had a choice in anything, so now that you've given me one, I'm going to take it seriously."

"I know," he whispers.

"I lost my mind at your party. I couldn't think straight. I'd gotten into a fight that morning with Mom, and I just had to do something stupid. So when I met Sam, there was no hiding the girl I used to be. We were ravenous. If it hadn't been for the obvious signs, I'm sure he would have assumed I was experienced. There was something magnetic about it," I say in a dreamy tone, almost re-experiencing the sex. Without thought, the words flow, "It was the best sex I've ever had because I was finally… free."

Malcolm unobtrusively coughs into his hand, and I fear I've made him uncomfortable. He gazes at me from the corner of his eye, pretending to look at the water. The moon shines on his cheeks, revealing a faint blush. Ah, not that kind of uncomfortable. Malcolm whispers 'sorry' underneath his breath and squeezes my suddenly clammy hand.

"Reality came crashing down when I found out I was pregnant. Yet again, I rebelled by doing the one thing that wasn't expected: I ran away to school with Ginny, and Sam followed her but found a very pregnant me instead."

"Truth be told," Malcolm says hesitantly, as if navigating the landmines he mentioned earlier. "Sam followed Ginny, looking for you. He wanted to see you again, after he healed up from the beating, that is."

"Huh?" I huff out, confused. "That's not what Sam told us."

"I should warn you– men are creatures of pride, and it gets in their path of true happiness. I should also warn you– I'm completely shameless and pride-free. I want to be happy, and I won't get in my own way. My point is that Sam probably lied to you ladies to save face."

"That doesn't sound like the Sam I knew. He was brutally honest with me," I mutter to myself. "What you probably don't know about my past, the final semester of my junior year was concluded, and I had a job on campus so I wouldn't have to go home for the summer. Even on holidays, I avoided coming home to Fairport. Between Sam pressuring me and my family pressing my child in my arms… all it took was one look at Willow and I'd be trapped. I wouldn't be able to leave. Ginny would yank my ass back to school for my own good."

"Oh, God," Malcolm sighs out. "I can't imagine. It was hard for me to go back to Boston after coming home for a few months at a time, but I knew they would be there when I got back. My children knew I was their father, loved me, waited for me, talked with me on the phone... I just can't imagine," he repeats, somehow understanding the torture I felt when I left Willow.

I draw in a large gulp of air and expel it in a rush. "I've never told this to anybody, not even to Ginny," I warn.

As if whispered on the wind, "Okay," falls from Malcolm's lips.

"When Sam found out I wasn't coming home, he visited Ginny and me. He stayed for six weeks over the summer. Which was odd, because it was the height of the season for Prynne Renovations. Sam got what he wanted from me, and then he left the next morning. It was a few weeks away from the start of my senior year of college. I was nineteen, pregnant, and my life, as I knew it, was over."

"Oh, Clover," Malcolm wretchedly groans, but I continue on.

"I did what was required of the perfect girl. I walked numbly in the direction my feet took me, while my mind was screaming madly, begging me to flee in the opposite direction... or maybe it was my heart. The wedding was planned by Peggy and my mom, and I felt no emotion over it– not one single feeling. I knew it was the responsible thing to do, but it never felt right. The day before the wedding, I found out I was having twins. I was excited about the twins, and I was thrilled that I was home with Willow. I. Love. My. Kids," I fiercely profess.

"I've never doubted that for an instant," Malcolm vows.

"I'm glad someone doesn't doubt me," I utter, hopelessly. "I was so very alone. My husband turned out to be the opposite of who I thought he was, and I didn't feel I could talk to Ginny because they'd been friends since diapers. I needed a mother, but mine was flaky and raising Robin and Willow. I... I had no one. So I drew into myself and worked on the perfect. Perfectly clean home, perfectly behaved kids, the perfect façade from the outward perspective. But I was dying inside. Sam was cruel."

"You can do this, Clover. I think you will feel better once you've released the words out into the universe," Malcolm encourages me.

The way Malcolm holds his body informs me that he has an inkling of where I'm headed. The strength and warmth of his hand wrapped around mine steels my nerves and forces the words to flow from my throat.

"Cruel. If I thought about it, I'd see it clearly. But Sam was a master manipulator. Sam loved his children, and he was an incredible father. Everyone built Sam up on a pedestal, and there wasn't a single person who would believe me if I told them my reality. Sam turned my children against me. If I held them, Sam would take them from my arms. If I tried to comfort Sam or the kids, he'd bat my hand away. Sam was to be the center of our universe. I can't," I gasp out, feeling frustrated and angry at the same time. "No matter what I say, no one will believe me."

Malcolm's fingers fall from mine as I pace the shoreline in order to get the words out. Malcolm silently ghosts behind me as I anxiously wander. The destructive sound of pebbles crunching beneath my feet seems to intensify the anger I'm feeling. It's like nearly two decades' worth of oppression is clamoring to get out. I hope Malcolm realizes this is a sign that I trust him. If not, he's going to change his mind on me as a prospective wife.

"Try me," Malcolm says, ever-patient. With the mood I'm in, his compassion snaps something in me, unleashes a flood I've tried to hold back. A culmination of nineteen years of pure, unadulterated frustration boils my blood and releases out my mouth in the form of a silent scream. The vein in my forehead pulses as my blood pressure rises. I have to release it or suffocate.

Too much shit has been happening: my children hating me, the anvil hanging over my head, forcing me to tell Willow the truth, Essie and Willow fighting, Devon's addiction, the pressure from friends, family, and my boss, and lastly, Malcolm. Malcolm is trying to hand me everything I've ever longed to have but knew I'd never receive, because I didn't deserve it.

The tenuous thread, which has been unraveling for months, finally snaps.

Insane with anger, I flip around, seething, looking like a lunatic. "You don't get it!" I shout, not giving a damn who hears. Alone on the riverbank, it's safe for me to explode. "Everyone saw a saint." My arms fly wildly, frustration filling every movement.

"Clover, look at me!" Malcolm demands, grabbing my chin. He wills me with his eyes to calm down and get a grip. "I get it.

I really do. Sam wasn't just my childhood friend. He was more of a brother to me. You have to look at it from a man's perspective. Sam was scared."

"Scared of what? Being scared doesn't make you hate a person. It doesn't make you treat them like shit, to abuse them!" I shout, sick of never defending myself and always defending Sam.

Calm in the face of my anger, Malcolm makes sure he has my undivided attention by squeezing my chin with his fingertips, just this side of bruising. "You can lie to yourself, but you can never lie to your best friend. Ginny is who you go to when you need to confess your sins, is she not? Do you honestly think I don't know all of your secrets?"

Voice gravelly from suppressed screams, I force out, "There is no way you possibly could."

"I know your secrets from Sam's perspective. There are two sides to everything, whether it be a conversation or an event in your lives. Sam came to me with his side of it, just as I'm sure you went to Ginny."

"I couldn't go to Ginny," I cry out, real tears forming in my eyes to spill down my cheeks. "I couldn't do that to her. Ginny loved Sam like a brother. I loved Sam enough not to ruin how people perceived him."

"Good and bad," Malcolm murmurs. Grip never leaving my chin, a fingertip juts out to stroke a tear off my cheek. "Bad, because you needed someone to talk to. Good, because I'm finally seeing some true emotion in you. Before this very minute, the only time the real Clover has erupted in the past twenty years was when we were sucking tongue in your kitchen."

With a sharp jerk of my head, I try to yank away from Malcolm's grip, but he's too strong, too determined to keep me open– raw.

"I was starting to wonder if you ever loved Sam. So much hurt, so much hate, so much passion, means so much love," Malcolm chants in perfect meter. "You and Sam were too much alike in that regard. When you hate yourself, you lash out at the ones who love you the most, because it's safe. Sam loved you more than life itself."

The cadence of Malcolm's voice, so lulling and trustworthy, the intensity of his dark blue stare, so compelling and honest, and the firm grip on my chin, has me blurting out the words I promised never to speak out loud.

"Bullshit. Love? Loving me so much Sam felt safe enough to harm me?" I mutter in disbelief. "Sam had you brainwashed just like all the others. He wished I was Ginny– my total fucking opposite. I love Ginny, so I understand why Sam would want her. But since she couldn't want him back, he chose me as his second choice. How flattering, building a life, creating children, with your second fucking choice." Bitter resentment, most directed inward, warps my voice.

"Sam was a fucking idiot," Malcolm murmurs as his fingers drop away from my chin. He takes a step back from me, like he's worried he will harm me if I'm within arm's reach. "But so were you. So *are* you– a fucking idiot, that is."

Sputtering, speechless, all I can do is stare at Malcolm in the pre-dawn light. "What. The. Fuck?" I draw out slowly, wondering if I need my ears checked. "You just called me a fucking idiot. Really?"

"I'd like to tell you to grow up, but that was Sam's fault for falling in love with a child," Malcolm says calmly. "You need to stop being oblivious and get your head out of your ass. Sam was wrong across the board. But sometimes you need to put yourself in the other person's shoes to figure out why they're doing what they're doing."

"Great," I blurt out. "Just fucking great. I have to be a goddamned mind reader, now? That right there is why I promised myself I'd never remarry. It's too much stress. I shouldn't have to play games to get a straight fucking answer. I shouldn't have to play mind reader."

"Not all men are like me, Clover," Malcolm issues as a warning. "Some men don't even know what they want."

"Well, Sam knew what he wanted, and what he didn't want. He spent our entire marriage criticizing me for being a bad wife and mother. He cheated on me continuously because I was horrible in bed. Even on his death bed, he blamed me for Willow." I turn snide. "Sam seemed pretty locked in on what he did and didn't want, and told me so on an hourly basis."

"Oh, Clover," Malcolm sighs out. "Fuck, I don't want to be the one to tell you this. I don't know if it will help or hurt. I have a feeling it's going to kill you."

The pity and concern in Malcolm's voice freezes me. I can't speak for several long moments, and when I do, all I can get out is, "Tell me what?"

Dragging his fingers through his hair, Malcolm looks torn and tormented. "Yeah, those nights Sam said he was cheating? He was at my house, hating himself. Unless I grew a vagina and tits, Sam wasn't with a mistress," Malcolm says wryly. "The guy would've never been able to get it up for anyone but you, Clover. Are you blind?"

My world shifts beneath my feet. Light-headed, I reach out to Malcolm, gripping his forearm to stabilize myself. The river rocks suddenly feel like quicksand, sucking at my feet, trying to pull me down and swallow my pathetic existence. I think I'm going to be sick.

I trust Malcolm where I didn't trust Sam. Sam hurt me, yet Malcolm has no reason to help or hurt me. No motivation whatsoever at all. I don't want to believe him. If Malcolm is telling the truth, not only have I lived a lie since I was sixteen, I was betrayed on an even deeper level. To lie about betraying me, what was the payoff in that?

Voice breaking, I force out, "I only knew what Sam told me. No one lies about that kind of sick shit. Why wouldn't I believe it when my husband said he was going to go fuck his mistress because I was broken?"

"Oh, Clover," Malcolm sighs out again. His arm wraps around my shoulders, drawing me into his side as if he can't help himself. Thankful for the support, I slump into his embrace. It was either that or fall to my ass.

"You're very blank. You get that, right?" Malcolm's arm tightens around me, fearing I'll extract myself at his insult. "I know it's because of what Sam put you through. I don't blame you for it, but it fed into more of Sam's bullshit. Sam wanted you to kill him, not just impassively accept his bullshit. You were the first wife in history not to say or do a goddamned thing when her husband said he was cheating."

"So it's my fault?" Frustrated, exasperated, my voice rises several octaves. "Of course it is. Also my fault that I wasn't Ginny?"

"Silly Rabbit," Malcolm sounds just as exasperated with me as I am with him. "Welcome to the world of man: men do and say the worst shit to get attention, and usually it's to punish themselves. Sam was testing you in the sickest way possible, instead of just asking you how you felt. Your unresponsiveness made Sam think you didn't give two shits about him, and at the same time, you were numb because he was a complete and total prick toward you. So he would behave worse and worse to get a rise out of you for attention. It was a vicious cycle."

"Like a goddamned child, when I was supposedly married to a grown man," I snarl. "How was I supposed to know this? How? How do you hug the man who called you a worthless mother? How? I wanted to love Sam, but he ruined it. Always comparing me to Ginny."

"Sam loved Ginny as a sister. It's impossible to be attracted to someone you see as family. Male or not, our cocks shrivel up in the presence of one of our relatives. While Sam was disappointed because Peggy was upset over the fact that Ginny and Sam would never marry, he wasn't in love with Ginny. He was in love with you, even on his death bed."

Unable to deal with what Malcolm is telling me, I lash out. Just as Sam used to do– God help me. "You're lying!" I shout in his face.

"And you're in denial!" Malcolm shouts right back, fed up. "I doubt you've ever mourned Sam's passing. It's too painful, so you see the past viewed through a tainted lens. You see what you need to see in order to cope with the loss. If Sam hated you, it won't hurt as badly. It's easier to accept a brutal lie than a beautiful truth. You'd rather hate the selfish man Sam could be than miss the loving husband he truly was. Sam didn't betray you. He didn't leave you, Clover." Voice hitching, Malcolm speaks the words that seizes the oxygen in my lungs, "Sam died."

Shaking, an anxiety-filled quivering that starts at the tip of my toes and radiates throughout my entire body, my tumultuous emotions get the better of me. My palms seek out my ears to cover them, as if I'm a small child who can't deal with the pain-dealing words Malcolm is speaking. "I can't. I can't hear it!" I shout in denial.

"But you will," Malcolm threatens in a tight voice, "or we can't move on, and we both need to move the fuck on, Clover." Malcolm grips my chin again, gaining my undivided attention. Mind reeling as it is, heart breaking as it is, Malcolm still manages to stall my emotions until I can only focus on him.

"Sam saw you at my party and instantly wanted you. I recognized it immediately because it was how I looked at Camille. I will never lie to you, Clover. Lust, love, passion, hatred, insanity, fury, need and want, betrayal, and mourning:

I've felt it all for my wife. Just as you felt for Sam. Just as Sam felt for you. I know what I'm talking about."

Unfathomable, it hurts too much to contemplate. I can't even respond through the jarring anxiety-fueled shaking that inundates my entire body. I lean into Malcolm, unsure if he's mad at me, or simply telling me like it is, as I do with my own children. All I know is, I need Malcolm for support. I lean on him, and it makes him pleased.

"Here is the God's honest truth, and I think you and Ginny both need to hear it. Sam was jealous of Ginny, but not for the reasons you'd think. Sam was jealous over you, not because Ginny wanted you, but because he feared you would want Ginny back."

"I couldn't get any straighter. If Ginny couldn't change my orientation, no woman could," I mutter in a haze. "Sam had nothing to fear."

"Yeah, well, Sam was an insecure idiot hiding behind a charming persona. Sam wanted you, so he had you, and then he felt like a child predator because of it. Guilt changes a man. It makes them bitter and act irrationally. Sam turned jealous again when you sought Ginny for help instead of him when you made Willow together."

"I didn't want to be a burden," I whisper.

"A wife and children are never a burden to a real man," Malcolm grits out. "Guilt ate Sam alive. Guilt because he preyed upon a child and created a child. And then he was ashamed because he didn't have the balls to raise Willow by himself until you were ready. Sam loved Willow, but he wanted to parent with you. He was just too fucking stupid to tell you. Then Sam turned into a guilty, shame-filled, desperate man when he preyed upon you again. Sam loved you too much– obsessively so. Sometimes you fear something so much, you create it."

"You know," I mutter hopelessly, sounding listless. "I don't think I can live through anymore truth-telling, Malcolm."

"I'm not finished. This needs to be said out loud for once. You never have to tell me what happened, Clover, because Sam already did. I would have arrested Sam if you hadn't made him your husband. Sam's greatest flaw was pride. He felt weak, insecure, so he took it out on you. Every single time, Sam would come to me and spill his guts. I know every one of Sam's sins, and not a single one of them was loving Ginny, betraying you with other women, or not loving you. Sam was distraught over his maltreatment of you, yet he kept doing it anyway– hurting you to punish himself. Don't ever doubt this, Clover– it hurt Sam to hurt you."

All energy extinguished, I lean heavily into Malcolm. "And that makes it right?"

"No, it makes it that much more tragic." Malcolm squeezes me to his side, needing the comfort. "Sam told me all this shit, and I thought you saw through it. Never in a million years did I think you believed any of Sam's bullshit. I thought you guys loved each other so much that you'd see it as the lie it was. I thought you'd see the root of the problem, realizing it wasn't you, and you'd try to help Sam deal with his guilt. But after talking to you, teasing you, touching you, and your resulting reactions, I realized you believed every horrific word your husband ever spoke, and it killed a part of me. Just as it's killing me to tell you the truth you were too blind to acknowledge."

"Not blind," I barely breathe the words. "Lost. Confused. Agonized. You're right. It was easier to believe that Sam hated me. It made Sam's death feel more like a reprieve, instead of the soul-crushing pain. You're right about something else, too. I've been numb for so long that I can't cope with feeling anything. It scares me, Malcolm. I'm petrified, and I regret so very much now. I feel sick."

"Clover, Sam loved you so much. He never blamed you over Willow. He loved you, respected you. He was proud to be your husband and the father of your children. God, Sam praised the hell out of you to anyone who would listen. We all envied the bastard."

"I can't swallow that, Malcolm. Now I fear you're lying to me. None of this makes any sense." Confused, mind whirling, I don't know what to think or who to believe any more.

"Sam praised the hell out of you, and he had no reason to lie to me about you, Clover. None whatsoever. If Sam wanted to lie, he wouldn't have told me how badly he treated you. Everything Sam said or did to you, were the things he wanted to say and do to himself."

"I can't do this anymore. I can't listen anymore." I'd struggle to get away, but I don't have the energy to move, not sure if I'd stay on my feet. "No. No, I don't believe you. Sam didn't even like touching me. He said so."

"Bullshit. Lie to yourself all you want, but you can't lie to me. I know what you remember. How Sam would say things about lying still and not making a sound. He told me about that shit, too. That was the guilt and shame eating him alive. Sam was remembering how the twins were conceived."

"If… if Sam would've asked, I would have been with him," I whisper, horrified that Malcolm knows my secret. "Sam didn't have to take it."

"Christ," Malcolm mutters, sounding as exhausted as I feel. "I know you wouldn't have denied him, and so did Sam. He couldn't live with what he did to you. It haunted him, how he acted so selfishly, knowing if he would have waited your lives would have been different. But Sam was scared you'd move on."

"I wouldn't have," I repeat like a broken record. "I wanted a life with Sam, but I wanted to wait until I was older. I didn't see why it was so pressing when I was sixteen, seventeen, eighteen, or nineteen. Why couldn't Sam wait for me to grow the fuck up?"

"Because Sam was an insecure idiot, that's why." Malcolm makes a scoffing sound. "This probably won't be a comfort, but it needs to be said anyway. Those times during sex when Sam would get angry, he was angry with himself. He was remembering the past, and his own behavior sickened him. Sam hated how he broke you, scared you and hurt you, until you would just freeze in shame and terror during sex. When Sam said you were broken, he was leveling that against himself. He loved how uninhibited you could be during sex. Sam affectionately called you dirty girly to me."

I mutter lifelessly, "So it's my fault."

"No, it's not. Sam shouldered all the blame on that one. Don't lie to me by saying your sex life was awful. There were times you would let go, and those were the times Sam felt closest to you."

Anger fueling my emotionally and physically exhausted body, I shout, "NO! Even those times Sam would pull from my body and spill on the sheets, like he was sickened by me."

"Clover, there was nothing more Sam longed to do than to connect with you. But after how he–" Malcolm gulps in a large mouthful of air. "Raped you. He didn't want to violate you again. Sam knew no matter what you'd never say no, even if you hated what he was doing. You loved him too much, and in this, he loved you more."

"That makes absolutely no sense," I mutter in confusion.

"You have to look at everything with fresh eyes, and see it from Sam's position. Every single thought of him that plagues your mind, spin it until you see it from Sam's perspective. You will be surprised at how different his truth was compared to your own."

"So that just negates Sam abusing me? It's okay?"

"No, it's not. Sam raped you the first two times you had sex. It doesn't matter if you said yes or no. Both times you were incapable of consenting. Sam was mentally and emotionally abusive. He was manipulative. Sam was a loving and attentive father, but a shitty man. Flawed or not, I still loved Sam, and I'll miss him for the rest of my life. Flawed or not, Sam loved you, and someday you'll even believe it."

Unable to listen to this anymore, "Don't," I beg to halt Malcolm's words. Hating how pitiful my voice sounds, I flinch in revulsion.

"Clover, it's okay to love Sam. It's okay to admit that he loved you. It's okay to admit that you miss him— miss the future you had envisioned but never received. But it's *not* okay to feel so betrayed by Sam's passing that you taint the good memories with the bad. You can love Sam, miss him, hate him, need and want him, and still let him go. It's okay if you feel guilty for wanting all those things with me and more."

"How can you say this to me?" I whisper, feeling betrayed by Malcolm now.

"Because it's how I feel about Camille. On a daily basis I love, hate, and miss her. But I also need and want to either hug or kill her again. I know how you feel, Clover. Camille loved me, and she loved our children, but she loved her guilt and shame and pain more. Camille was my Sam, and I will miss her until the day I die. I will feel guilty for all eternity. But one thing I won't do is sanctify or crucify Camille for the life she led. I will remember Camille as a whole person— beautifully flawed."

Sounding like a lost child, I ask, "How do I let Sam go?"

"You don't get to pick how or when it happens. It will either be a major event or nothing at all, and then you'll just feel again. But I'll warn you in advance— it ain't gonna feel good, that's for damned sure. I thought I was dying. It was like being reborn."

"When did you let Camille go?"

"Seconds after I hung up after our first phone call a year ago. I found something worth fighting for, something worth giving up the past. I found someone who needed me as much as I needed them. I'm not replacing Camille with you, Clover. Camille let me go so I could be happy with you. There is no letting Sam go... Sam will let you go when you least expect it, and that's why it hurts so fucking much. If you think you feel abandoned now, you're wrong," Malcolm warns.

"I need you to promise me that all men aren't like how Sam was? I will admit that I haven't mourned him fully, but that isn't what's holding me back from giving you a yes. I can't live that life again, a life of constant worry over whether or not I'm failing. A life of '*damned if you do, damned if you don't*' was pure stress, and it was killing me inside and out. Are all men so critical? Are they as warped as Sam was?" I warily ask.

"Not all, but I've known a few," he gruffly says.

"Who? You?" My voice betrays my anxiety.

"No– never me," Malcolm shakes his head no. "I could never reduce a woman to that. All men have an ideal on what it means to be a man. Some men think perfect means they've matured. Men like my father thought it meant having your woman completely subservient to you. My definition of a man is taking care of my family, ensuring they are healthy and happy, and I won't let my injured pride get in the way of it."

"Someday I'd like to hear what your ideal is." I retake Malcolm's hand and gently squeeze it. "If... if I think it's appropriate, I want you to tell my son."

"You humble me, Clover" Malcolm says reverently. His eyes catch the moonlight– deep, dark, endless pools of midnight gaze back at me.

"Thank you," flows softly from my lips. "It will be a long while before I can process all you've told me tonight, perhaps not for a lifetime. But I can admit I haven't truly moved on yet. I've tried to move on a few times in the past. Men would ask me out and I would say yes, but a combination of fear and guilt would get to me. I'd rather be alone than live as I had with Sam. There was no... no evenness. No rhyme or reason to anything. I need structure, not feel like I'm living in an insane asylum devoid of rules."

"Clover, as I said, I loved Sam, but I knew him, too. I don't want you to think I'm blaming you. I just want you to see your part in your past so you can learn from it. No one should have to live in a constant state of doubt. *No one*," Malcolm stresses.

"I don't think the implications of Sam's death have hit me yet. I know that sounds stupid. It's been five years for Christ's sake. I've never admitted this before. I felt like such a bitch because I was sort of relieved when Sam died. I almost felt vindicated, like karma was kicking Sam's ass for being such a bastard to me. It took two years after Sam's death for Seth not to wince when I tried to touch him. The kids missed Sam so much and needed him, so I felt worthless as a human being for having such nasty, despicable thoughts."

Malcolm tilts his head back and barks a bitter, humorless laugh to the sky. "That is something I can relate to– wishing your spouse dead, and then feeling guilt when it finally happens. The roller coaster emotions after they are gone are dizzying. It's time to let go and move on. I *will* be here for you every step of the way, and I expect the same in return."

Groaning loudly, I shuffle around on my feet, trying to wake up. "God, I swear this was a Dr. Phil session in Hell." A manic giggle flows from my throat. "It's a good thing I brought you to the river, or half of Fairport would know our business."

"Indeed," Malcolm says with a grin. "Especially your spying neighbors."

"I can't think of Sam, or myself, or my past, or my fucked-upness. So it's your turn. Talk about yourself and tell me about your ideals on being a real man…"

CHAPTER FIFTEEN

The Widower

"Let's walk and talk," I murmur as I start walking down the riverbank. "We better make sure the kids are still in one piece." I cock my head to the side and listen to the night. "No sirens, so that's a good sign," I tease to pull Clover out of her funk.

I hadn't meant to tell Clover Sam's secrets, and I still withheld the majority of them. But Clover needed to hear the truth or she'd never move on from the past. I'm selfish enough to want a happy wife, but I'm selfless enough to want that woman to be Clover Webster, Sam Webster's trail of lies aside.

I want to reach over and take Clover's hand, but I fear she'll pull away from me. I don't want to push her, especially after what she's gone through tonight. I feel guilty because she was victimized by an important person in my life. I'm not responsible for Sam's actions. I just wish I would've checked up on Clover after Sam told me what he'd done. I really thought she saw through all of his destructive bullshit. I guess Sam and Clover really were good at pretend.

Jesus! It hurts me just thinking about it– it's either that or I'm having a heart attack. I can't fathom what this pain is doing to Clover and the kids. It's been difficult on all of us, losing a spouse and parent.

Clover's sharp, intelligent stare lands on my clenched fist. I relax my grip so she won't think too closely at what is making me feel violent. Clover's lingering gaze warms my hand and I realize that maybe she isn't confident enough to take what she wants. I hope I'm reading her cue properly.

"Me lady," I twist an accent to make Clover smile as I reach over to take her hand. Clover claps her hand into mine with a loud *crack*. I chuckle as I draw her near my side. "What does it mean to be a man: Chief Malcolm Mason edition," I drawl.

"Now, this I can't wait to hear." There's a smile in Clover's voice as she twines her fingers with mine. My chest swells to twice its size, because it has to contain my expanding heart. I'm such a big softy that such a small gesture of affection puts a lump in my throat.

"Most of this came from my dad. It's inborn, and I can't shut it off. It just feels right." I give a shrug. "Other rules are all mine, because when I saw what didn't work for my dad or what I didn't like, I tweaked them into something I could live with. I don't know," I mumble, feeling bashful all of the sudden.

My fingers rake my hair as I swallow my self-doubt. I lead Clover up the path from the shore to the rickety old bridge, which leads us back to town. This is the path that everyone who has ever lived in our town has taken since they could walk. It's the path you walk as you contemplate the direction you should take in life. I can tell by the intense expression on Clover's face that she's walked it many a time.

"Number one rule: a man should always take care of the women and children in his life. It doesn't matter if they are an infant or elderly. They are his responsibility. Their welfare, happiness, and well-being are in his hands and his alone."

"You sound like a caveman," Clover teases in a wary tone.

"My father taught me that a man should house, feed, and educate his people. John Mason thought respect was best drawn from fear. I changed this since the man couldn't keep a woman and his kids were miserable. I want respect because I've earned it. I think love and affection are at the core of a strong family. I will be a man when my family is living under a roof I provided, eating food I bought, and they're happy. It may sound caveman-ish, but I am closer to those long-denied instincts than most. I have to teach my boys to respect women, and I don't want my women to work."

The air around us heats with Clover's anger. Her fingers tighten around mine. I can practically feel her back bristling up. "Malcolm," she snarls at me. "I don't want that for my daughters and neither should you. They are worth more than that. They have a lot to offer this world."

"Hey," I say to quiet Clover's anger. "That's not what I meant. Ya gotta hear me out."

"Fine," Clover bites out. She kicks every rock that has the audacity to get into her path.

I chuckle, "Little bitch, you're closer to your instincts than most, too," I tease, and then get serious. "I would feel like a worthless shit if my girls had to work to survive because I couldn't give them what they needed. Isis works, but it's not about working for a living. Isis does what she loves. She's a creature of the night, running a club like Rush is her true calling. I take care of all of the needs that Isis can't meet, and I'll do it until your brother gets his head out of his ass. Actually, I'll always do it. Robin isn't the manly sort and that's okay… I want our girls to do what they love, not some dead-end job to put food in their bellies. It's my job to feed them," I growl deep from my chest.

"It doesn't seem fair. Why should the women feel like princesses and sit on their asses while the men do jobs they hate?" Clover pulls me to a stop and stands directly in front of me. She challenges me by holding my gaze and refusing to look away. It raises my need to make her submit and makes my cock pulse fiercely with excitement.

"What you said is bullshit," I grunt right in Clover's face. "First off, I raised them all. Isis is motivated. She doesn't sit on her ass and act like a princess. She works hard, and it's my pleasure to spoil her rotten. Raven's still a child. Eventually she'll find what she's good at. There is no ass-sitting in my house. And the men don't hate their jobs. My job lets me be a man. My personality is caveman-ish. I want to go out and hunt and bring home the kill to my family. It's in my nature. I can't do that, so I go out and hunt bad guys. The kill I bring home is my compensation from the town for protecting their asses. I get to be a protector, predator, and provider. Being a cop feeds every inborn instinct I have. I've raised my boys right. They do jobs they love."

Clover sputters a bit, unsure what to say. I have an idea of what she wants to say, but she's scared I'll punch her for saying it. I draw in a deep breath and infringe upon her personal space. I get right into Clover's face and snarl.

"I didn't fuck up Devon," I bark. "Fate intervened and messed the kid up. It was a test of our faith as men. We will overcome it as a family," I vow.

"I wasn't going to say anything about Devon," Clover breathes across my face.

"Shit," I hiss and take a step back. Clover's confused and hurt expression pierces me in the heart. "I'm being a prick. That's a sore subject for me. It's not my failure, but it makes me feel helpless."

"Malcolm," Clover says gently and takes my hand again. We start toward her home. I can see the porch light shining from two blocks away. "What do you want of me?" Clover says quietly, and the anguish in her voice jumpstarts my heart.

"I know that you'll have a lot to work through because of what you've lived through and what you've just found out. I will show you *my* worth. I will show you *your* worth, even if it takes a lifetime," I promise.

"It's not that I find you unworthy," Clover grumbles and rolls her eyes like I'm being ridiculous.

"Little Bitch," roughly pours from my throat. "You're pushing my buttons." My cock is trying to punch his way out of my pants to get at her. After the kitchen incident, where I was two seconds from blowing a load, and then her outburst on the shore, I'm barely keeping my shit together. If Clover rolls her eyes again, I'm taking her to the sidewalk.

Clover sheepishly gazes at me from the corner of her eye and says, "I just don't know what to expect."

"I'm a simple man. I want to go to work and provide for my family. I want you to keep the house I bought us and cook the food I provide. I want us to be happy and content. I want to laugh, talk, play, and sleep next to you. I want you to count on me... I just want to experience life with you. Can you do that with me, please," I plead.

Clover turns her head away from me and clears her throat, but not before I see the satisfied expression on her face. A blush tints her alabaster cheeks a beautiful pink. "It would be something I'm not accustomed to, but I'd... I think I'd like it. It would be freeing to be with someone who is brutally honest."

"I know what you need, Clover. You think I don't, but I do. You need consistency. You want to run a house and raise a family, but you need a firm husband. You need me," I growl and pound the center of my chest. "You've seen me with my kids. Devon... God, Devon fucked up, but I don't love him any less. Mistakes are forgiven and forgotten in my house. Affection isn't earned, but absolute. You need to know it's alright to be yourself and that I prefer you as her. I want you to have a voice in everything we do... You need to be free..."

Clover's tiny hand shakes in mine and it worries me that I've pushed her too far. I fear that she's crying. I can't handle a crying female. It trips every trigger in my mind. She clears her throat a few times, and I know my strong Clover is being emotional.

"We better check on the kids. I hear the television, but that isn't a guarantee," Clover murmurs after she pulls herself together.

A small porch, where Clover and I stand shoulder-to-shoulder without any breathing room, is the entrance to the Webster's residence. Clover's living room is the width of the house, which is pretty dang narrow. It's a tiny two-story with the living spaces on the ground floor, as well as Clover's bedroom. The upstairs is the twins' rooms and a Jack-and-Jill bath. The Cape Cod roofline makes the second floor much smaller than the first. Every room is claustrophobic, and I have no idea how three, let alone four, people fit into this house. The only advantage is that there is no place for four teenagers to hide.

My eyes rove around the dark living room, making sure everyone is accounted for while Clover checks on the condition of her destroyed kitchen. Raven's snores rise above the sound of the reality show droning on in the background. My beauty is lying on the sofa with her hand trailing to the floor. Her mouth is wide-open, sawing mighty logs. Violet's dainty feet are near Raven's head as she lies on the opposite end of the sofa. The princess doesn't make a peep as she sleeps soundly. Her small fist is curled under her chin, clasping her frilly purple blanket.

I locate the boys sprawled on the floor. Weston is the younger of the two, but he's a few inches taller and fifty pounds or so heavier than Seth. My son's large chest is being used as a comfy pillow for the chipmunk-cheeked teen. Seth's a cute little bastard, I'll give him that. Neither one of the boys has anything on Raven with the snoring– they barely make a breathing noise.

Movement catches my eye as Clover walks into the room, checking on everyone's respiration and removing half-eaten food that had fallen onto chests and laps. I stand frozen, near the doorway, unsure how to proceed. I know how I *want* to proceed, and it involves not leaving this house until the sun crests the horizon.

"It's probably better to leave them where they lie," Clover begins hesitantly. Her voice is more shy than quiet, as if it's nerves, not fear of waking the kids, that has rendered her soft spoken. "I'd drag them upstairs, but it's only a few hours before they have to be up for church."

I stare at my feet, and then roll my eyes up to gaze at Clover through my eyelashes. My voice comes out rougher, deeper, than usual. "So… um… You're not gonna make me drive home only to come back in three hours, are you? Or worse, make me sleep on the floor?"

With a deep breath, Clover says, "I don't know what you expect out of me."

"You said you'd do a trial run," I remind my skittish bride-to-be in the most earnest voice I can muster. If I'd pulled out the coaxing charm, Clover would see it as bullshit and kick me out of her home.

"So… once I let you in my bed, what happens next?" flows unemotionally back at me. Clover is keeping her emotions firmly in check, and I hate it.

"Sleep," I tell a half-truth. I expect to fall asleep, but I also expect to wake up like any other married guy: horny and wrapped around my woman. Clover runs cold in all things except sex, as was evident in the kitchen earlier. I thought she'd freak out, but she went passive, boneless, completely willing for anything. I never would have guessed that in a million years. I'm intrigued, and I can't wait to do it again.

Wringing her hands, "I'm scared," Clover whispers, voice warbling in fear.

"Don't be," I reassure her. "I'll be a good boy– a gentleman." But I expect her to be a dirty girly, so I'll behave as long as she does… and when she doesn't… "I'm an exhausted daddy," I appeal to Clover's mothering side.

"Oh, God!" Clover half-shouts, and then looks sheepishly at the sleeping children. "Sorry, I'm all about myself, as always. You must be worn out with everything going on. I bet you don't escape your worry over Devon, even when you're asleep."

"You'd be correct on that," I admit somberly. "I war between wanting to murder my first born by either strangling his drug addict neck or hugging him to death."

Clover makes a waving motion with her hand, beckoning me into the kitchen, where I slowly follow her into her bedroom. "Are you going to be able to fall asleep at all?" The concern in her voice humbles me. For a woman who appears so reserved and cold, Clover is one of the warmest souls I've ever met. My sister gets underestimated in this regard as well. Such a pity. Strong women aren't necessarily bitches, and if they are, maybe you should ask yourself what you did to make them that way.

Acting nonchalant, I enter Clover's bedroom, unsure how to proceed. I was in here earlier this evening, but it wasn't so stressful. I didn't think in a million years I'd be back in here hours later to sleep, among other things (I hope).

Standing in the small room, I take a good look around. Clover hasn't changed a thing in here since Sam was still alive. Nothing in almost six years. Clover's stuck as firmly in the past as I have been, more so even. Sad, the grown woman's bedroom is smaller than my children's bedrooms. My bed wouldn't even fit in here, let alone the rest of my shit. A full-sized bed for the petite woman, a single five drawer dresser, and one nightstand, and absolutely nothing else. Even I'm not that big of a masochist. Everything in my bedroom is post-Camille. Every furnishing is all mine, bought and chosen by me for me. Clover didn't even repaper the walls. It's still the same hideous 1970s avocado green from the last owner.

It's sad– tragic.

I answer Clover's question to take my mind off the fact that this woman hasn't lived a day of her life for herself, even the little things that make us feel good. "As soon as my head hits the pillow. I fall asleep easily, but wake just as easily. Par for the course with being a parent, I guess. We'd never get any sleep if we couldn't grab a few winks when they present themselves."

"So true," Clover murmurs, blushing a beautiful shade of pink. She closes her bedroom door and leans on it. "So… um… how we gonna do this? I haven't shared a bed in months, and that was with Willow. Before that, it's been years. And I've never shared my bed with any man other than Sam."

A cloud flashes over Clover's face. So expressive, it doesn't take a body language expert or a mind reader to know Clover is entering regret and guilt territory– a place I don't want her to visit.

"Well, I've slept with a lot of people." I try to get Clover to loosen up with my double entendre, but all I accomplish is her frown. "I'm practically an expert… in sleeping with other people. All relatives," I offer lamely. "We're an affectionate bunch. Auggie's a cover hog. For some reason, the more stunning the girls are in my family correlates to how loudly they snore. Weston sleeps like the dead, never twitching a finger. I used to make sure he was still breathing," I ramble on, feeling self-conscious– a feeling I barely ever experience.

"You guys are," Clover choses her words carefully while refusing to look at me, "Affectionate." She huffs a humorless laugh. "Total opposite of what I know, that's for sure."

"Well," I draw out, deciding I better get this moving along or we'll be standing here until it's time to be up for the day. "I'm going to sleep in my boxers." I don't ask permission, knowing she would balk at the idea. I simply tell Clover what I'm going to do. "I don't want to do my walk of shame in the morning with a wrinkled shirt."

"Oh, Christ," Clover gasps out for some reason. At first I think it's because I'm disrobing right in front of her: toeing my sneakers off, tugging my shirt over my head, and unbuckling my belt. But by the time I get to my zipper, Clover is avidly watching me, so I assume her 'oh, Christ' isn't in relation to my nakedness.

"What's the matter?" I ask as I stand before Clover in only a pair of navy polka-dot skivvies with my hands on my hips. Yes, I am posing for the woman.

"Walk of shame is the perfect phrase for it." Now she turns around, unable to look at me. But I caught the hot look in her eye. Mrs. Webster likes the look of Chief Mason. My ego gains a few inches of manliness because of it. Facing the door, Clover mutters, "The crones will torture me over this."

Confused, I mumble, "Crones?"

"Fuck it," Clover breathes out, like she's shoring up her nerve. She flips around to face me. "Already gonna be after my ass. Guess I'll dive right in and earn the lecture." My eyes bulge from my skull as Clover turns into the bravest woman I've ever encountered. She peels her yoga pants from her round behind right in front of me.

Voice thick and rough with a combination of shock and lust, I ramble, "I haven't the foggiest idea of what you're talking about." Knees weakened, black lace panties have my ass hitting the mattress. I haven't been this close to a woman in nearly eight years: the intimacy, the prospect of sex.

Clover takes her bra off locker-room-style: pulling the straps down over her arms and tugging the piece of black lace from her shirt sleeve. Standing before me, clad in a pair of panties and a t-shirt, Clover points to the bed. "Take either side. I've been sleeping in the center for years." Finally answering me about the crones, "Just be happy you don't know what I'm talking about. Don't worry, I can take the verbal tongue lashing. I'm a big girl."

I yank back the purple bedspread. I arch an eyebrow, mimicking Augustus Kline: *Purple?* I never pegged Clover as a girly-girl. "Who?" Tongue-tied, it takes several tries to get the words out. "Who are these crones, and why are they licking you?" I crawl in between the sheets– purple sheets.

Well, purple shouldn't come as that big of a surprise. Clover did name one of her daughters Violet, after all.

I prop a pillow beneath my shoulders, and snuggle down to get comfortable. My eyes track around the room, looking for something that is personal to Clover. The sight of my pink, little princess journal sitting on the nightstand makes me grin. But it's the well-worn, water-damaged paperback sitting on top of the journal that makes me huff a laugh. Clover reads smut while bathing and relaxing in bed. I knew this woman ran hotter than the sun.

"Who'd have thought–" words dying on my lips, I freeze in shock. My muscles lock up for Clover's self-preservation. The woman can't walk around the bed because the headboard and one side of the bed is pushed up against the corner of two walls. She can't get into bed on my side because I'm blocking the way. Instead, Clover crawls from the foot of the bed, ass and tits swaying like a pendulum. I groan while fisting the sheets.

In a state of utter shock, all I can do is watch as Clover slides between the sheets next to me. It's been almost eight years since I've experienced this simple intimacy. The Playroom has only whetted my appetite for a complete relationship. While it feeds my skin hunger, it leaves me feeling starve-gutted for the small things in life. Such as lying next to another human being who you feel an emotional connection.

Clover's unique cookie scent wafts up my nostrils as she settles down on the bed, tugging the covers up to her chin. Conservative in the extreme, or merely insecure, Clover manages to avoid touching me. It must be with great effort, seeing as I'm a very large male lying in a tiny bed.

An uncomfortable silence descends upon us, as if we're both waiting for the other to speak or act. Refusing to extend the discomfort, I reach over to the nightstand to click the lamp off. The darkness seems to relax Clover. While I can't see her, I can feel the tension bleed from her body.

"Did you suddenly forget who I am?" I ask, wondering why the woman is as stiff as a board next to me.

"No," she snorts out, sounding perplexed but amused. "Malcolm," she uses my name to prove her point. "Why?"

"I just thought I'd ask if you knew who I was, since you're not touching me, and you know how I crave it."

Flowing hesitantly in the dark from a small, quiet voice, "Do you want me to touch you?"

"Did you forget the kitchen?" I deadpan.

"I'm so embarrassed," she forces out, wiggling on the bed like she's being boiled alive. "I... I don't know why I got that way. I couldn't help myself. It's like my brain switched off and I acted on instinct. I made such an ass out of myself, assaulting you."

"Assaulting me?" I squeak, thrown for a loop. Reaching over, I search for Clover's hand but I find her bare thigh instead. She jolts beneath my touch but doesn't pull away. "We need to get this settled right now. I don't know the rules between you and Sam, nor do I wish to know them. Just as I'm sure you'd rather I didn't speak of Camille's and my intimacies." In a gruff voice, I order, "Just so we are clear, never forget who I am. Never guess what I do or don't want. Just ask me."

Clover tests the waters. "What do you want?"

"You," I simply answer. "I loved how you were with me in the kitchen. I love how everyone else gets this reserved woman. But in private, I get a wanton little thing who mews and rubs all over me like a cat. It makes me feel like a goddamned man who's won life's best lottery. My name should be Lucky Malcolm."

"You're insane," Clover scoffs, and I can almost hear her eyes rolling back in her head. Even though she sounds like she's brushing off my compliments, I know she's secretly smiling in the dark. "This thing with us wasn't a spur of the moment thing, was it? You've been planning this, but for how long?"

Shaking from the need to touch Clover, I refuse to torture myself any longer. I roll onto my side, facing Clover, and reach out to tug her into my arms. Passive, light as a feather, willing, Clover comes to me. She may act reluctant around me, but she's lying to herself. Clover eagerly cuddles up against me until she's the little spoon to my big spoon. My favorite position: round, firm, feminine ass pressed to my painfully rigid groin, small, handful-sized breasts resting beneath my forearm as it curls protectively around her chest, with the crown of her head tucked beneath my chin. I breathe in a deep sigh of contentment. I could lay like this forever.

"In truth, you were someone I've thought a lot about for a very long time. But it was a difficult situation. I wasn't sure if you were ready to move on. I wasn't sure if I was, either. I was scared over our kids getting along, especially with Ren and Devon's fascination with Willow. I knew eventually you'd tell Willow the truth, and there was a good possibility they would be thrust in the same household. So I was waiting for the three of them to become adults. But when you called me, I took it as an invitation to take what I wanted."

Clover releases an honest to God giggle. A trilling sound reverberates from her chest to warm my heart. I'd do anything to have her make that sound again, even though I have no clue what I did to earn this one.

"Oh, Malcolm…" Clover laughs, snuggling deeper against my chest, tiny ass rubbing me to the point that I have to fist my fingers or I'd attack the giggling woman. "You finally admitted that I was the one to call you first. Finally," she sings.

Smiling, I kiss the top of Clover's head. "I was planning on calling you that same day, for the same exact reason. As a man, I need to be the initiator. So I fudged the facts and tried to make you think I called first." I bark a sharp laugh. "Weston came to me the night before, saying he'd never wanted to beat up a girl before but he was debating it. Violet was this close," I squeeze Clover tightly, "to getting her ass handed to her."

"Weston's a big boy, but Violet plays dirty," Clover says in a voice filled with pride and amusement. "I think she could have taken him to the ground."

"Sadly," I admit, "I think you're right. But all's good now. I think Violet sees West as her younger brother. They've been getting along better now that Seth is acting like a prick."

"What were they fighting about? I can never get my kids to tell me a damned thing," Clover nearly snarls the words.

"Seth," I answer, and this time it's Clover's turn to bark a laugh. "Violet didn't want to share, and Weston wanted his buddy all to himself. Seth's recent behavior made them both angry, to the point that neither wanted him anymore. So now they are the friends."

"God, I've fucked my kids up," Clover sighs out, sounding on the edge of tears. "Seth's gonna stop taking it out on everyone else. He promised me last night while I was holding him on this very bed."

"Your use of '*last night*' is the reason why we better get some shut eye before the sun rises. I have no idea what's in store for us today. Eventually my wayward son will find his way home, and then my life will be turned upside down for a while. So we better get some sleep while we still can."

Clover's reply is to bend down to place a fluttering kiss to my forearm. Her lips are moist and warm, sending a lightning strike to my aching groin. Acting like a woman instead of a teasing girl, Clover ignores my pulsing cock as it beats against her ass. She sighs '*goodnight*'… how in the fuck do I fall asleep now?

My eyes slowly slip shut, preparing for sleep. But not before I wiggle my hips until my cock is happily wedged between black lace-covered ass cheeks. Finally, when all parts of me are content, I drift off to dreamland, a place that used to be better than my reality.

CHAPTER SIXTEEN

The Widower

I never want to wake. I want to live in this dream for the rest of my days. I'm too blissed out to open my eyes to read the expression on her face. As this is a dream of my own creation, I shape the experience into one of potent lust, need– hunger. The passion boils between us, so I have no need for a visual confirmation of the ecstasy that is surely broadcasting across her beautiful face.

A writhing, mewing, heavy-breathing handful of a woman is kissing me fiercely with tongue and teeth and lips… and biting fingertips. She nips sharply, bruising my lips, my jaw, my neck, in a heated display of wantonness. Searching hands lead to seeking fingertips, which clutch me closer, as if she wants to meld our flesh as one.

Acting without any conscious thought, my hands tear a swatch of thin lace from her hips, dissolving the annoying barrier with the power of my mind. Two perfect palmfuls of ass are revealed, which my hands devour hungrily. My fingertips delve in between her crevice, sliding south until they dip into the drenched silkiness of her aroused pussy. If only this were real, I'd be in heaven.

Envisioning a cloud of steamy perspiration filling the air, our bodies are slick with passion. I flip her over to her back, settling my body between her wide-spread thighs. She welcomes me home, as if she's been waiting an eternity for my arrival.

Lust-induced intoxication has my dream woman tugging impatiently at my boxers. As with my reality, there is a humorous undertone to the act. A frustrated growl reverberates against my lips as the woman tries and fails to tug my boxers past my thighs. Laughing while being helpful, all I do is think about my boxers lying on the floor– *POOF* –they are. My newly bared flesh is attracted to her scorching, saturated heat as if magnetized. We cry out in mutual shock, our spines bowing us together.

Demanding, she rolls her body along mine in a wave of pure pleasure, rubbing aroused parts in a motion that will prompt rapid release.

Shrouded in a foggy state, I suddenly blink my eyes and completely rouse. Disappointment slams into me when I realize my dream is over, never to be recaptured and experienced.

"Clover!" I shout as everything else ceases to exist except for the small hand wrapped around my naked and painfully erect cock. Pumping her hand up and down in an inexperienced, unsure manner, Clover milks pre-cum until I'm a slippery mess of pure need. "Fuck," I grunt out. "You better be awake, too. I'm not taking all the blame for this if you're half asleep."

Reality sharpens, and I find myself hovering over Clover, situated between her thighs, as she jacks me off, rubbing the head of my cock along her weeping pussy. "Maybe I'm still dreaming," I murmur in a thick voice while shaking my head back and forth to clear it. My eyes flick up to connect with Clover's lucid, blue gaze. "Maybe I'm not." I come to understand Clover is a carnal little creature who is starved for affection, intimacy, and sex, more so than I've ever been for touch.

"Malcolm?" Clover whispers my name, fright flashing over her features. Fright that I will push her away, call her names– reject her.

"Take whatever you want from me, and I'll give you twice as much in return," I vow. "But just know, if you slide me inside you, you're mine– I'm yours. It will be a yes to my proposal. So you better think with your head and heart, not your horny pussy."

"I'll try to behave." Clover sounds remorseful, guilty. But she flashes me a teasing, flirty grin that seizes the breath in my lungs. She smiles while flicking the head of my dick over her greedy little nubbin. This woman is going to give me a heart attack. "I'll avoid right here," she makes a pass over her drenched opening, and I almost lose my head and thrust forward like a young buck in the rut.

"If I come within three feet of your pussy, also a yes," I threaten. "You've been warned. You're the one in control– I'm just along for the ride, hoping you'll fuck up and make me yours. When, where, and how we have sex will be up to you."

Hand stilling, eye bugging out, Clover gasps out, "Always?"

"Silly Rabbit, only the first time. Once I have the go-ahead, it's rabbit season." A deep laugh is torn from my throat, but it immediately changes to a moan when she presses the head of my dick directly onto her clit and swirls. "Jesus Christ, Woman," I grunt. "Use me as your own personal masturbator all ya want, but don't torture me. Gimme a little squeeze while you're at it."

Eyebrows knitting together, Clover experimentally grips me, proving she's as inexperienced as I feared. Voice wavering with insecurity, "Like this?"

Leaning forward, I press my lips to the shell of her ear. "As long as you're touching me, it's the right way." I barely breathe the words, but she shudders beneath me.

Fists gripping the pillow beneath Clover's head, I fight the urge to molest every single inch of her trembling body. Toes curled into the sheets, I battle the need to thrust my cock as Clover toys with her core. Instinct screams that I must give Clover this power– the power she's never had. I could use her lust against her as Sam always had. I could have her writhing and screaming in ecstasy in less than thirty seconds. I could press into her and she wouldn't stop me. I need her to choose me, not because she's horny, but because she wants to spend her life with me. Clover has to have the choice, no matter how much she's torturing me– a sweet, painful source of torture that I'll forever cherish.

I can't touch. I can't thrust. I can only endure, experience this insanity with my eyes clenched shut against their urge to roll back into my skull from the simple pleasure of her silky pussy kissing my dick. There is one thing I can do. I lower my head for a kiss, while keeping my hips raised so Clover may use my cock any way she wishes.

The hungry little creature meets me halfway, raising her head to meet mine for a searing kiss filled with mashing lips and dueling tongues. Unable to keep the thrilled laugh at bay, I glorify in the contradiction that is Clover Webster: reserved, conservative, cold-hearted, stick-up-the-ass woman that she is publicly, but behind closed doors... Clover turns into a creature who would thrive in the Playroom: uninhibited while inexperienced, her body instinctively knows what to do to gain what it wants.

Lucky Malcolm.

"Thank you for trusting me this much," I whisper against her lips, feeling humbled and proud at the same moment. Clover whispers my name in reply, and I know she's made her choice. We rest our foreheads against one another, breath mingling, as she prepares to give us both what we, not only want, but what we so desperately need.

Remembering the ridiculous suggestion I gave Kieren, I doubt he's faring any better than I am as I bite my tongue against the need to drop a three word phrase. The admission isn't a manipulation, a way to get Clover to give in, it's how I feel in this very moment. Is the father stronger than the son?

At the threshold of no return, my mind blinks out and my over-emotional heart turns into an idiot. "Clover, I–"

"Jesus Christ, what in the Hell is going on in here?" yells from a man who's going to die in less than ten seconds.

I extract my very sad cock from Clover's strangling grip, and rest the poor fellow between our bodies. I then fling the comforter over my bare ass. I hope the '*comforter*' lives up to its name since Clover is trembling in shock beneath me. I fear it has more to do with what I was about to say and what she was about to do, more so than Robin '*I'm about to die*' Prynne standing at Clover's now open bedroom door.

"Go," I warn in a calm, quiet voice that belies the lust-fueled anger coursing through my veins.

"Holy shit!" Robin sounds amazed. "You're really going through with this, sis," he says to Clover, as if it's an everyday occurrence to walk in and find her having sex. But then again, Robin is one third of the perverted minds who created the Playroom, and his body has been used by the majority of its inhabitants.

Sounding mortified, Clover says stiffly, "Robin, if you loved me, you'd go."

Amazed, Rob mutters, "I've never seen Malcolm have sex before."

Turning on the Prynne charm, Clover's inner-pirate erupts. "Good God, I should hope you haven't! What the fuck is wrong with you? A normal person would've just turned tail and left without making themselves known. Thanks for ruining the moment, ya dick."

Laughing like a fucktard, Rob still doesn't make a move to leave. I could easily glance over my shoulder at him, but I fear if I look at him, I'll murder him where he stands. "I believe this is payback for the time I walked in and found Rob's head buried between my sister's thighs. I should add, Rob was only fourteen and a complete slut," I mutter dryly.

"You made me Scotchgard the sofa." Snickering like he's hilarious, "Payback. I was between your sister's thighs, and you're now between my sister's thighs. Even Stevens. Only difference, it was my face, not my dick."

"Only difference, I had to use the garden hose on you to cool you off, and my badge to keep your dick out of my sister until she was sixteen. So back the fuck off and get the fuck out before I release your sister to kick your ass for ruining our very nice wakeup call."

"Well, I came in here to make sure Clover wasn't sick. Not once in my life has she missed Sunday breakfast before church. Peggy was ready to break the door down."

"Oh, fucking kill me," Clover groans, trying to crawl out from beneath me. I drop all two hundred pounds of myself down onto Clover to keep her where I want her. A whoosh of air escapes her lungs as I render her immobile.

"In the kitchen last night, I was seconds away from getting off. Two minutes ago, I was less than a second from having sex for the first time in almost eight years. I'm so goddamned horny, I'll take you in front of Rob if he doesn't leave. If Peggy barges into this room, too, I hope she enjoys the show. Because I'm getting off before I get up off of you." Looking over my shoulder, I pin Robin in my furious stare. "Leave or watch another one of your relatives have sex. Your choice."

Blushing bright red, Robins jaw drops open. "I... I'll go make sure Violet and Seth's faces are clean, and shove 'em onto the sidewalk to their grandmothers. You have maybe," Rob thinks it over for a second too long, "Eight minutes to do what you're doing, plus redress. BYE!" he shouts, door closing behind his ass.

Sobered, no longer intoxicated with lust, Clover looks sheepish and confused. "Question, and then I will give you your breath back." I press down harder, hammering home the point that I want total honesty. "Were you going to slide me into you just before Rob barged in?"

Tiny fist tapping out on my hip, I rise up a bit to give Clover the ability to speak. Breathless, she gasps out, "Were you going to say what I think you were going to say?" Blue eyes filled with confusion stare up at me, so open and trusting.

My turn to feel awkward, I rise up onto my knees, and then flop over onto my back on the mattress. My fingers seek my hair and begin their anxious scratching– someday I will break myself of the annoying habit. I stare up at the ceiling, amazed that it's almost nine in the morning, stunned that I managed to sleep for almost four hours, wondering which one of us made the first move, and astonished that I almost had sex.

"So," I begin, sounding like a shy woman. "If I admit that I lost my head to my emotions, does that mean you were saying yes? Yes that you were going to have sex with me, knowing that yes is the same things as a yes to my proposal?"

"I know Robin was like an invading ice storm, but I hope you meant what you said to him. Because if you didn't, I'm going into the bathroom to rub one out before I face my mother-in-law. I already have a gut ache, my ovaries' version of blue balls, and I can't be around Peggy while frustrated. We don't have time for sex. But if you put me out of my misery, I'll admit the truth. Afterward," she tacks on, like I wouldn't jump at the chance of getting off with her.

"Silly Rabbit," I growl. Acting without thought, so Clover doesn't have a chance to avoid me. I yank her hard, until she's straddling my hips, drenched pussy resting on my hardening cock. In a deep, husky voice, I demand, "Get to riding, woman."

The corners of her arousal-reddened lips lifts into the sauciest smirk I've ever seen, and I know I'm in for one hell of a brutal ride. "Clover, you're gonna be the death of me," I mutter as I reach for the only piece of clothing on the pair of us– her t-shirt.

Fingers wrapping around my wrist, Clover stops me. "I'm operating on pure frustration. Unless I'm out of my mind with desire, I'm not comfortable showing you my bits in the bright of day. You give me a good orgasm, and next time, I might give you a show."

"You're in charge, boss," I say, grinning like a fool. Clover said 'next time', everything after that was just background noise. Next time, I will see those palmfuls of heaven and her honeypot. I shift around on the mattress until I'm comfortable. I fold my forearms behind my head, proving I'll behave. Out of my mind with curiosity, all I can do is wait.

Giggling, blushing, Clover covers her face with the palms of her hands. "This is so awkward." Her laughter turns to snorts. I have to bite my lip to stop myself from joining her. I know Lucky Clover– she'd take offense where none was meant. "Can I put a pillowcase over my face?"

"What?" I blurt out, laughter finally winning out. I close my eyes, and all the frustration, stress, and pain just melts away on a river of amusement. "Your face is too pretty to be a '*but 'er face*'. If you're embarrassed, lean down here and kiss me. We're running out of time. I give 'em five minutes before they're pounding on the door."

"I've never done this," Clover whispers like she's admitting a secret I didn't already know. All I can do is wait patiently for her to give me my kiss. Hesitant, Clover gives me what we both need.

The instant her soft lips brush mine, I spring into action. No longer cushioning the back of my skull, my arms seek out Clover. I wrap one hand around her ponytail, twisting the rope of hair around my fist. My other palm meets her ass with a loud smack. Within one breath to the next, we're getting the relief we so desperately need. Lifting up, I grind my pelvis against Clover's, showing her with my body instead of verbally instructing her. No one would ever call this dry humping. Judging by the wet slapping sounds, this is dirty grinding. The woman is like a sprinkler in ninety degree heat. Who in their right mind would ever call Clover frigid?

Erotic heat returning, Clover's a fast learner. Lips warring, hips rocking, hands groping, the woman has me from cool to scorched in less than thirty seconds. All I can do is arch my back and groan into her mouth. The feel of her wet heat gliding along my cock is too much to process. It will wreck me for a long time to come.

The sharp sting of fingernails digging into my shoulder focuses me one hundred percent on Clover: her needs, her wants, her pleasure and pain, and how I will do anything to give it all to her.

Raggedly panting into my mouth, Clover's moans spur me on. A rush of wetness saturates my cock, causing the honorable man in me to quiet her for propriety's sake. I perform a maneuver I haven't utilized since varsity wrestling. Hooking my calf around her leg, I reverse our positions until she's beneath me. My mouth covers Clover's, suffocating the scream of her release. Bucking uncontrollably beneath me, I suck her orgasm with my kiss.

The sensation of Clover's body heat rising to feverish level, combined with the wet pulsing between her thighs, has me toppling over the edge. Years of taking care of business in a house filled with listening ears, has my orgasm sound no more than labored panting. But no matter how quiet I may be, the climax rips through me with the power of a runaway freight train.

Neck straining, muscles twitching, eyes bulging from the force, I grunt as my cock does something it hasn't had the pleasure in almost eight years. I share my release by saturating Clover's cunt– my version of an engagement ring. Even as I groan, louder than I should, even as I thrash in ecstasy, the main thought in my head is how there is no escaping each other now– a thought I welcome with open arms.

Rolling over with a moan, pouting over the fact that the first true sexually intimate moment I've had in years is cut short by church of all things. Church? I hope Clover realizes I will take Sunday mornings as my personal time from here on out.

Still pouting, I mumble, "I'm a cuddler," as I roll to my feet so Clover can crawl out of bed. Woozy, slightly delirious from coming, I ass-plant back on the bed as soon as Clover wiggles by. I stare at my hands, feeling needy and girlish. John Mason would roll over in his grave if he knew his big manly Chief of Police son had the emotional signature of a woman.

"Hey," Clover sighs out, palm cupping my cheek. I nuzzle into her hand, smile springing to my lips over the affection she's giving me.

"You smell like me now," I murmur into the side of her hand, feeling extremely proud, probably more than I should. I kiss Clover's palm, longing to pull her back down on the bed with me forever. Clover moves away, leaving me feeling cold and empty.

I feel like such a goddamned girl right now. What is wrong with me? Clover whispers a word as she passes by. The word rings in my mind, echoing the entire time she gathers up her clothing and leaves the room, no doubt sneaking to the bathroom unnoticed– *my* stealthy silly Rabbit.

And Clover is mine now.

The word keeps pinging around my brain, stunning the shit out of me as I dress on autopilot. Still pinging, even as I stand out on the sidewalk, suffering stares from every Prynne in existence, except for Willow, who is no doubt still cuddled up snug as a bug with my son, if he's lucky. Looking like a fool, I pretend I'm not making a spectacle of myself, as my kids explain how I slept up in Seth's room while the boys took to the sofa.

Filthy, honorable liars.

All I can do is stare in awe as Clover walks down the front steps with her head held high, dressed in a conservative skirt and blouse with her hair knotted at the nape of her neck. The only indication that she was thoroughly debauched before church is the high blush on her cheeks. Clover greets everyone in her cold, precise manner, which has me chuckling beneath my breath and Rob laughing outright.

Frozen on the sidewalk, with my kids flanking me, I watch as the Prynnes and Websters load into several cars. Clover pats my kids on the back, and then acknowledges me by squeezing my hand on her way by.

Giving me no time to analyze the past few hours, my cellphone buzzes in my pocket. I pull it out, scared shitless it's something I don't want to hear.

Master Mechanic: *Where the fuck are you guys, Dad?*

Papa Bear: *& where were you to just now notice that the three of us are missing?*

Master Mechanic: *You don't want to know.*

Papa Bear: *I know where you were, and I bet I was doing exactly what you were doing.*

Master Mechanic: *Gross. I just threw up in my mouth… nice! Way to go, Dad! Except I didn't have sex, so… if you were doing what I was doing, BOO! Try harder next time. You'll get there, buddy!!!*

Papa Bear: *I always know when you've been around Willow. You turn into a sarcastic assmunch. We'll be home in five. I'll bring the donuts.*

Clover's word still pinging around in my mind, I turn into a fucking idiot. I hop on my heels while grabbing for my youngest kids' hands. "Guess what?"

"We don't have to guess." Raven sighs out dramatically, as if I'm boring her. "We heard long before Robbie stopped you."

"Yeah, because Rob was standing there listening with us. When he figured it went too far, he shooed us away from the door," Weston, the world's most honest kid– to a fault –says with a grin.

"Pervert," Rae mutters in disgust. "Auntie Isis needs her head examined."

My head kicks back, opening up my throat for the loudest laugh I've ever released. "I dare you to say that to her face, darling daughter. Now, guess what?"

"What?" They drone in unison, already bored with the conversation.

Overwhelmed with warring emotions, I finally acknowledge Clover's word– the one word that changed all of our lives. "She said yes."

CHAPTER SEVENTEEN

The Widow

Operating on autopilot for the majority of the day, I find myself sitting around the Prynne's Sunday dinner table, surrounded by my family. Everyone is accounted for except Willow, and as horrible as it is to think, I'm thankful she isn't here. I feel guilty enough when I think of Sam, to add Willow to the equation would cripple me. I fall into the perfectly unaffected role with great ease, responding to conversation as if I didn't know they were all wondering what happened last night and this morning with Malcolm Mason. Not one single family member has had the balls to ask me outright, so I don't feel the need to bring it up.

Aunt Ana and Uncle Will are chatting with my parents about their upcoming retirement move to Florida, with my father laughing about retiring at fifty, saying who can afford that. I feel badly for Dad, the loss of Sam meant at almost seventy, he's still working the job of a forty-year-old. Essie is pouting, commiserating with my twins about how her parents are abandoning her. Rob is in tease-mode, antagonizing everyone in Willow's stead… and Peggy, she's focused all of her attention on glaring me down from across the supper table.

This Sunday evening is no different than any of those before it, which is a comfort.

"I can't believe I said yes," I mumble underneath my breath. It's like I was suddenly dropped into a parallel universe, living the life of my counterpart but not remembering how I got where I am. I haven't had a moment's peace to contemplate the complete one-eighty my life has turned. I don't think I will ever resolve the feelings that erupted over Sam last night. Malcolm's revelation leaves me feeling guilty, ashamed, like I could have made our lives better but was too young, dumb, and numb to do anything about it.

Leaning in closer to me, my overly attentive brother asks, "Did you just say something?"

I don't know if Rob is trying to make up for walking in on Malcolm and me, or what? But the guy has been glued to me since we left the house. Out of everyone around me, Rob knows Malcolm the best, so it's like he's trying to get me acclimated to touching. Or maybe Rob finally realized I was never averse to touching in the first place, just that no one bothered to give me any affection. On the car ride to church, Rob put his arm around me. While in church, he held my hand, which he didn't relinquish until I was preparing dinner. Rob even helped cut up the salad and mash the potatoes. Now, as Sunday dinner is winding down, Rob is absentmindedly rubbing my back.

Peggy keeps eyeing me like Rob and I are going to start making out at the supper table. But that could just be the guilt rearing its ugly head, seeing as Peggy has been glaring at me since I stepped foot out of my house this morning.

"I have so much to process, to the point that I don't know where to begin," I answer honestly. "It's like I'm too numb to think." I turn to face my brother. "Thank you for interrupting. It was embarrassing and abrupt at the time, but that wasn't the time nor the place for what was about to happen."

"If that wasn't the place, I must be doing it wrong," Rob says snarkily. His amusement turns to concern. "It's gonna happen though, right?"

"Yeah," I sigh. "Just not in the house with our kids... and not in that bed."

Rob's face twists up in revulsion. "Ugh, gross. But you do realize that once you get married, the only way to do '*that*' is with them in the house. Unless you plan on celibacy until they fly from the nest. But what happens if they never leave?"

Mentally, emotionally, and physically exhausted, my responses are lifeless. "I know. It's just... it's just being in that house, doing what we were doing, it feels wrong somehow. Right, but wrong. If we are doing this—"

"There is no '*if*' about it. You're doing this," Rob interrupts. "If Malcolm went that far with you this morning, it's already a done deal."

"I know," I agree, believing it on a soul deep level, but it hasn't sunk in yet. "I mean, we have to go slow."

Looking and sounding confused, "Why?"

"Devon and Willow. We have to focus on them, and afterward we can focus on ourselves." Rob makes a funny noise in the back of his throat, but I hurry to speak before he interrupts me. "We're not being martyrs. It would be ridiculous to get married and go off into the sunset before we get our shit together. Dev has to get his ass on that plane to Arizona." I lean into Rob and whisper, because our conversation is collecting notice from the other dinner guests, as they turn silent to eavesdrop. "I have to tell Willow the truth. Malcolm and I have to finish what we started before moving on. There are things," I look at Peggy, "and people to prepare."

"Okay… okay. Okay. I get ya," Rob mutters in agreement. "Just don't take too long, or it will feel like living a double life."

"I get that," I agree, and I do. "Plus, Malcolm and I have to get to know how the other one operates. Phone calls, emails, and text messages aren't real life. I know him as a person, but I don't know him as…" I trail off, unable to say the word.

"Husband," Rob fills in. "Repeat after me: husband."

Glaring, I warn, "Don't push me, brother. I've had a hectic few days, and the crone is eyeballing me in a way that promises my night is ruined as well."

"Fuck her," Rob says so loudly the entire table turns silent. He pins Peggy in his piercing stare and directs right at her, "She'll either get over it, or she won't. It has no bearing on your life."

While pummeling Robin in the shoulder, I whisper fiercely, "I'm so dead now, jackass!" His only reply is to laugh at me like he's Eddie Haskell.

Baby brothers, forever a pain in the ass.

"Clover, may I speak with you in the kitchen, please," Peggy says in a tone that would rot your teeth.

The shit Malcolm said to me last night stuck. I let Sam treat me that way, so it's on me, and look where that got us. I was miserable. Sam was miserable. The kids were miserable. And all because we were pretending to be something we weren't. No more.

Refusing to be bullied in private any longer, I meet my mother-in-law's glare with one of my own. "It's time we got this out on the table," I say to Peggy in an emotionless voice. I'm mentally taxed, to the point I could sit through heavy gunfire without flinching.

"I will not have a private conversation with an audience," Peggy replies in a tight voice while standing from the table.

"And I will not have this conversation in private, so we're at an impasse, Peggy. This is my family– whatever you have to say to me, you can say in front of them. But then again, you want to tell me what you really feel, instead of the fake shit you spew when we're in public."

"How dare you?" Peggy says in mock-outrage.

"If I'm lying, then prove me wrong by sitting down at the table like a civilized woman and talk to me like the daughter I'm supposed to be. Sit down with *our* family and spill your differences.

"Fine," Peggy snarls, refusing to sit. "I don't believe my grandson. Not only am I angry that you had my grandson lie to my face, you spit on your own husband's grave by allowing another man into his house."

"First of all, you're right. Seth is your grandson. So you should know by now that no one tells him to do anything. I'm not admitting nor denying that Seth was lying. I'm saying I told him to do no such thing. Second of all," I point in the direction of my home, "That's *my* house now. My children's house. It hurts me to say this out loud, but Sam's gone, and he's not coming back."

Peggy flinches as if I struck her with an opened fist. Voice twisted with bitterness, she rests her palms on the tabletop as she speaks. "Clearly, since you were fornicating with a married man inside my dead son's home."

"Wrong on all accounts. I'm not married. Malcolm is not married. We are widowed. Our spouses left us, and they can never come back, no matter how much we may wish or beg or pray for it to happen," I bite out, hating how my voice breaks from suppressed tears.

Years later, the pain is still raw– an open wound that never quite heals yet slowly leaches your lifeblood away. I wished and prayed and begged God for help long before Sam died. I prayed for Sam's life, and then I began praying for Sam's release from the agony as cancer consumed his body from the inside. Only one prayer was answered, because Sam died hours after I got down on my knees and begged like I was the one dying.

Choking back a sob, I force out, "It's been almost eight years for the Masons and six years for us. Living life isn't the same thing as letting them go and leaving them behind. Sam will always be a part of me," I shout while pointing at my children. "You have no idea what goes on in our minds, Peggy, so don't presume anything. But I don't care if you were Sam's mother or my children's grandmother, it's none of your fucking business what *I* do in *my* house, in *my* bed, with *my* body, with whomever *I* choose."

Peggy's true colors erupt in a colorful show of malice. "You're still a spiteful, immature, little bitch, I see. You were never good enough for my son. You didn't deserve him. No matter how hard I tried, you wouldn't change yourself to suit his needs because you're a selfish, worthless excuse for a human being."

"Wow, way to paint me in a positive light," I mutter sarcastically, sickened. "You were always half of the problem, Peggy. You should have kept your nose out of *our* marriage. I get that you lost your own husband and Sam was your only child, so you felt he was your world. But it wasn't a matter of whether or not I was good enough. Sam chose me, it wasn't your choice to make, and he didn't even give me the choice."

"You should have told Sam no," Peggy shrieks. "You should have stopped tempting him with your body like a common whore."

"Margaret," my father warns in a gruff voice. "Check yourself."

"Peggy," I sigh, trying to stop a fight before it starts, but knowing we need to have this out or none of us will ever move on. "Sam and I went off course because I tried to be someone I wasn't, someone Sam didn't like. I wish I would have realized then what I know now. Sam wanted me as I was, not what I turned into."

"You're insane," Peggy spits out, transforming into the one person who truly frightens me. Sam had a scary side, and his mother is demonstrating it right now. "You're making absolutely no sense. My son was perfect. He loved you, and you were just a frigid bitch who got what she deserved."

"Thank you, Peggy, for telling all of us how you truly feel. But more importantly, for showing us how Sam got when he was upset. You've never been closer to your son than you are right now," I lifelessly mutter.

"You are always the instigator!" Peggy shouts. "Just as you're needling me right now to get a rise out of me, you did the same thing to Sam on a daily basis. You're a despicable human being."

"I don't care what you think of me anymore, Peggy. I kept the peace at first because I wanted you to like me, then I wanted you to love me, then I wanted you to be proud that I was your daughter. But that never happened. So then I just kept quiet out of respect for Sam and the twins. I put up with your syrupy shit in public and your bitter hatred in private because I loved my family. *MY* family: Sam, Violet, and Seth."

Blinded by her loss, I finally understand that Peggy transferred on to me all that bitter hatred she has at God for taking her beloved son away. It's easier to blame me than Sam or God Himself. Never wanting to be like that, I realize I need to move on, more so for my own sake than for my children's. In a few years, I could have turned into Peggy, looking at the women who join our family as someone who would be taking love and attention from me instead of adding more love to our family as a whole.

Anger nowhere near fizzled out, Peggy continues on her tirade of my failings. "You haven't loved Sam a day in your life, you cold-hearted bitch. If you did, you wouldn't have Chief Mason shacking up with you."

Drained, the words just roll off my tongue without forethought. "I loved your son: madly, insanely, loved your son. But it was in a twisted way. I will not sanctify Sam because he died. I know the agony he lived through, and ultimately died because of. I was by his side every day of our marriage until I buried him. Sam was a normal human being with faults, and I no longer blame him, or resent him, or hate him. I finally see Sam for who he was, and while he wasn't the best person, I still loved him in spite of it."

I look around to my silent family. Most pretend they aren't listening, all with tortured expressions on their faces. My mother is crying, dabbing her eyes with her napkin. My father is leaning back in his chair, looking at me with a level of respect I've never seen from him. Aunt Ana and Uncle Will are holding hands, and I know this because they are staring down at their entwined fingers. Essie is looking at me with a horrified expression, but she's doing her duty by tucking a twin under each of her arms. Seth and Violet actually look relieved, like the weight of the world is finally lifting off their shoulders because we no longer have to play pretend. But it's my brother who has me spewing the truth. Rob sits next to me, smiling with pride while tears glisten in his eyes. I'm not sure, but it looked like he mouthed to himself, "*My big sister's finally back.*"

"I won't sanctify Sam, nor will I vilify him. Here's the truth, the honest to God's truth. Sam and I started off wrong, and it spiraled out of control. We put on a good front for everyone but who did it help?"

"Stop!" Peggy shouts. "Don't do this. Not now. Don't smear my only son's name, especially in front of his children," she begs, and I almost give in.

"I can't do that, Peggy. Sam is gone, and he left us behind. My children need to know the bad so they don't emulate it. No matter the differences Sam and I had, he wouldn't want Seth behaving as he did. He knew of all people the toll his actions had on his conscience."

"He was faultless," Peggy vows in complete denial, because to admit Sam's faults, she'd have to face her own.

"Guilt was Sam's largest fault. His guilt caused him to warp how I saw myself. Sam changed me into a person I didn't recognize, a person he detested, and I allowed it."

Pain slices through my chest with such force that I fear my heart's going to explode. I didn't want to believe Malcolm last night when he explained how Sam felt. It didn't make any sense to my confused mind and hurt heart. But as I say the words, they ring so true that it murders a part of me. If I'd known, I could have fixed it. Yes, nothing would have helped Sam reach his thirty-fifth birthday, but he would have been happier all those years prior. For that, I carry my own set of guilt and shame.

"Sam fell in love with the girl I was, and I fell in love with the young man he was, but we both changed. I turned into this ball of numb insecurity while he turned into a bitter person, and those personalities fed off one another like cannibals. Sam hated me because he recognized that he created the tortured woman I became. Looking at me every day, meant Sam was facing his own guilt, and it destroyed our marriage and Sam as a man."

"Sam had nothing to be guilty over," Peggy cries out, but I can see the truth written across her face. She knew. She knew that the past was torturing her son, and she facilitated it to keep up appearances. If only she would have helped him. If only I would have helped him. We both ruined Sam by keeping quiet. It's why I refuse to step aside as my son exhibits the same destructive signs.

"He did, but it wasn't worth ruining his life over," I admit. "Cancer may have killed Sam, but guilt ate away at his soul. If the person who is sitting here today was the girl back then, our life together would have been drastically different. I would have known he wanted my forgiveness, and I would have gladly given it, and for that, I will be sorry for the rest of my life."

Heart heavy, I lean forward against the table with my head in my hands. Tears prickle my eyes but don't release– they never do when Sam is involved. I fear what will happen when the dam finally breaks.

"I could make excuses, shouting how I was only sixteen, but that would change nothing. The '*me*' I am now, would have never put up with Sam's shit. I would have respected myself. I would have required more out of, not only myself, but my husband as well. I would have gotten him professional help. While Sam was at fault for abusing me, I was just as culpable for allowing him to do it, and that is why our marriage was bitter and cold and destined for failure. But I didn't know any differently because I was a goddamned kid."

"Clover, honey," my mother says softly as she slides into Robin's vacated chair. She tries to pull me into her arms and comfort me, but I fear how emotional I'd get if I allowed it. What she reveals shocks me to my core. "I knew. I just didn't know how to fix it. I didn't know if you wanted it to be fixed. You were always so strong, even when you were a tiny baby. I'm so sorry."

Lying my forehead on the linen tablecloth, my only reply is a derisive snort. Unable to help herself, my mother rests her palm on the center of my back– a comforting touch I welcome.

There are only three people in this room I'm truly speaking to: my mother-in-law and my children. Knowing Violet and Seth are hanging onto every word, digesting it, I peer up at Peggy, making sure she's actually hearing me out.

"I could play the '*what if*' game. *If* Sam had lived, we would have been miserable together. Not just me, but him too. Hell, we were already miserable. The guilt ate any love and affection we shared. *What if* Sam would have let me grow the fuck up before he forced me to be his wife? Sadly, I think we would have worked out– we would have been happy. But Sam didn't wait, and Sam didn't live. There is no '*what if*' because death is the ultimate finality."

Anger deflated in the face of sorrow, "Sam might be dead," Peggy says as if saying he *is* dead would make it truth, "but that doesn't mean you forget about him. My Seth died when I was a young woman. I raised Sam all on my own. Why do you think you're so special to get a second chance?"

As if we're the only ones in the room, I answer her. "You're still a young woman. People every day find love at fifty-eight, and older and younger. Love doesn't have an age limit. And who's to say it has to be like that. Find a male companion for the activities and conversation Mrs. Dobson can't give you."

"I won't betray my husband," Peggy says with strong conviction.

"Your Seth is but a memory– there is nothing to betray. I can't live like you, Peggy. I give you accolades on martyrdom. But my heart didn't stop beating when I became a twenty-nine-year-old widow. So now, at thirty-five, I'm going to live the life of the living. The young man I remember, the one who fell in love with my child-self, I think… I think Sam would be happy that I've finally found my voice. And if there is a heaven above, I think he's finally at peace because I've come to terms with the past, and forgiven him."

I rise from my seat at the Prynne Sunday dinner table, the one night a week that is never without drama, and look for my brother. I spot Rob leaning against the wall, face wiped clean of all emotion. "Can you watch the kids, and make sure Mom and Dad take care of Peggy?"

Arms folding over his chest, remote, expressionless, Robbie demands, "Why?"

"I have to be alone. Like *really* alone. I have so much to think about, and I can't do it around any of you or anywhere near these houses. Too many memories haunting me, speaking to me as if they know what's right versus wrong. How am I to figure out what to do next when the ghosts are influencing me?"

"Okay, just text me when you get where you're going," Robbie says, and then tacks on, "Because I'll have to relay that, if you get me."

"Will do," I say in a rush as I bolt from the dining room, not even looking back at my children. My only thought is freedom.

CHAPTER EIGHTEEN

The Widow

Hand poised to knock, the door opens itself. A pair of arms are open and waiting, but they aren't nearly as welcoming as the grin I receive.

"Took ya long enough," Ginny says as she yanks me into her house. Enveloping me in a bear hug, Ginny squeezes me tightly while rocking me back and forth like a big baby. I want to cry from the pure comfort of the act. But mostly, because I have people I can count on, and Ginny's one of the best.

"Huh?" I grunt out when she squishes me too hard.

"I've been waiting on ya. You've been wandering around for hours." Ginny pulls me back at arm's length as her hazel eyes travel up and down my body, checking me over for maladies.

I step out of Ginny's embrace and further into her house. "How'd you know I was coming?" I look around, noting the living room has had a major upgrade. "New furniture? Didn't you just get the last sofa less than a year ago?"

Shrugging, like it's no big deal she pisses money down the toilet like it's water, "I don't have kids. I don't have pets. I don't have a girlfriend. Besides buying you presents– when you allow, that is– and buying Raven an unlimited supply of hair straightener, I have to spend my money somehow."

"Business that good, eh?" I mutter as I finger the new cashmere throw draped over the arm of the new leather sofa. "You need to be more careful. We're in a housing slump, crisis, whatever you call it. A downturned market. Hey!" I half-shout. "Don't do that! Don't distract me."

Laughing, "But you're so easily distracted. It's like '*oh, shiny!*' and then you lose track of what I didn't want to answer in the first place. Works every time."

Grinning, even though I don't want to, I mumble incoherently, "Wait, what was I asking?"

"If I had the hot tub uncovered and the wine uncorked, is what you were asking." Mouth split into a wide grin, Ginny walks backward out of the living room toward the French doors leading to her back patio. Beckoning me by wiggling her fingertips, "Follow me, Clover. I've got high quality Riesling chilling in a bucket, Florence and the Machine chanting their hollow-sounding angst on the surround sound, and your bikini resting on the edge of the hot tub."

"Are you sure we're not dating? This is pretty romantic, even by your standards. Why are you single again?" I tease as I follow like an obedient puppy. I toe my shoes off on my way. I'm a sucker for a big tub. "Oh! I remember now. How did you know I was coming? How did you know I'd need Ginny's famous cure-all?"

Ginny's backyard is as perfect as the outside and inside of her ranch house. Being a real-estate agent has its benefits. Ginny loves to buy houses for next to nothing, fix them up, and then resell them. House flipping, it's called. This house seems to have stuck with her, because she moved in and it's going on year three without her moving back out– a record. She just constantly upgrades the house to the point that it's now over market value– in Ginny's terms, unsellable. You would have to forcibly remove me from the property if it were mine. The backyard has a fucking kitchen, for Christ's sake. It's so private I have no issue stripping naked out here.

Distracted by the shiny objects again, "Can I move in with you? The kids are fourteen– they can take care of themselves. Better yet, you move in there with them, and fix the house up while you're at it."

Pointing, "Get in the tub, dirty girly," Ginny orders.

"Jesus Christ," I hiss out as I make quick work of the buttons on my blouse. "How the fuck did he know I'd be coming here? More importantly, why did he tell you that naughty nickname?"

Ginny doesn't even answer– the bitch. All she does is laugh while watching me strip. If it was anyone besides Ginny, I'd have ran off to the bathroom to change. Hell, I wouldn't be tying the tiny strings into a bow to make sure the small triangles cover the important bits. Everyone else would get the one-piece or the tankini. This morning, I wouldn't even let Malcolm see me shirtless, and I was sitting on his cock.

Best friends forever.

"Traitor," I accuse as I slide into the hot tub. "Talking to the enemy," I grumble. "Good God, this is fabulous," I cry out as hot water covers me up to my neck. My entire body sings in bliss, skin prickling with ecstasy. "I got the short end of the stick monetary wise. I should demand a higher wage. I could tell Ross it's for the kids, but I'll squirrel it away for a hot tub fund."

Handing me a glass of wine, "Me lady," Ginny acquires a fake accent, mysteriously sounding like Colin McGregor. "I see you're distracted again. So what took you three hours to get here? Malcolm had an APB out on you."

"He did not," is my automatic response, followed by, "No, he didn't, did he? Shit! He did. That's why you're talking like Colin. He didn't have Colin stalking me, did he?"

"You ran out of your parents' house four hours ago, leaving your pervert of a brother in charge of your kids. No doubt Robin was teaching Seth how to unhook a bra in under ten seconds. Malcolm had every right to be worried."

Drawing in a deep breath, "I… fuck it," I say with feeling. I tip the wine glass to my lips and drain the slightly sweet yet slightly dry liquid. The flavor bursts on my tongue, and then slides down my throat. "I just couldn't stay there anymore. I couldn't even be near that fucking street."

"Well, to answer all your earlier questions," Ginny says while refilling my wine glass. "Last glass, so you better savor it. Tomorrow is Monday and we've both got to work." Giving me a sheepish look, "Close your eyes."

"Ginny," I drawl out. "Just get into the tub. You just saw my naked ass. I can handle seeing you in a bathing suit."

"A woman has to have her pride, especially when dealing with a tiny size four and you're a size twenty." Sounding irrationally insecure, "Close your eyes."

"Fine," I sigh, sounding exhausted. "But I think you're being an idiot. I'd kill for your breasts. Mine are the size of oranges, and not those nice big Navel ones, either."

The sound of water splashing has my eyes peeling open. Ginny slides into the water, clad in a black bathing suit that showcases her décolletage while hiding the rest of her. "Trust me," Ginny says while shaking her head, laughing at herself in a self-deprecating sort of way. "You don't want my watermelon tits. I'd say they sag to my bellybutton, but that's if I could actually find it."

"You're beautiful. Your issues are all in your own head. I'm guessing you aren't dating because you're getting in your own way," I chastise.

"We're not here to talk about me, dirty girly," Ginny teases me to change the subject. "You tell me where you were for four hours, and I'll tell you how I knew to wait for you." When I don't reply immediately, she asks, "Deal?"

"Deal," I mutter begrudgingly. Embarrassed, I'm so thankful I can blame the hot water for my blush. "I basically wandered around, wondering what it would have been like to be a normal teenager. I played the '*what if*' game, even though I promised I wouldn't."

"*What if* what?" Ginny asks hesitantly.

"*What if* I was normal? *What if* I had went to football games and dances and clubs and groups and prom? *What if* I was normal-sized, and had a boyfriend in high school, or several? *What if* I had waited to graduate until I was eighteen?"

"It would have been a travesty, because you would've never met me, and that would have been very, very sad for me," Ginny whispers, looking on the verge of tears.

"No, a travesty for *me*," I stress. "I call you '*Ginny, my rock*'. I would be lost without you. So the '*what if*' game is not only counterproductive, it's destructive. If I changed one small thing, everything else I love would '*POOF*' into nothingness. So as I wandered around all the places teenagers go, places I've never experienced, I realized I don't have the power to change the past. But I do have the power to change the future. I can make sure my kids have that life, and there is no *if* about that."

"You're an amazing mother–"

"Ginny," I bite out between clenched teeth, "don't!"

Smirking, she does anyway. "It's true. You see yourself as this cold-hearted bitch because that's what Peggy always called you. The woman is just jealous because you took her baby away, when she should be thankful you gave her three grandkids– the bitter cunt. So you see yourself in this negative light, all the while we see someone different. But then you hold yourself apart from all of us, and we're not sure how to get close to you. That scowl of yours is rather intimidating."

"I don't want that," I admit, and now I sound on the verge of tears. "I'm usually scowling because I'm miserable, not because I don't want you guys around me."

"I know, and that's why I'm your best friend. You're lucky you have a strong, loving family that sees through your bullshit. But Violet and Seth, you're their mommy and you're unhappy. Kids just assume they're the cause. I know you think they don't cuddle with you because of what Sam did in the past, but it's because you're hard to get close to."

"Are you trying to kill me? Is it '*rip Clover Webster a new asshole day*' and I didn't know it? Don't ply me with alcohol and bubbling water, and then tell me I'm a good mother, but then tell me I'm a bad mother. Even I know I'm a daft, easily distracted bitch, but I'm not stupid."

"Clover," my name comes out of Ginny's mouth with an angry bite. "That's not what I meant, and you know it. If your best friend can't show you your flaws, who can? What I'm trying to say, if you want your kids to hug you, hug them first. If you want Willow to be nice to you, don't look at her like you're on your way to the executioner's chair. I know why you look that way, but she doesn't. So what's the girl to think? Let us in, Clover. We aren't going to hurt you like Sam did."

"I can't do this anymore, Ginny," I cry out, voice warbling from stress and unshed tears. "I came here to get away from my thoughts. I've been in an intense state of therapy for the past few days. I just walked around Fairport for the better part of four hours after getting into an exhausting screaming match with my mother-in-law in front of my family. I realize that no one is better for fault showing than a best friend, but sometimes a woman just wants her BFF to let her relax in the only hot tub she's ever been in. Okay?"

"Okay," Ginny mutters, looking guilty for pushing me. She leans over the side of the hot tub, stretching to reach for something. "Have some more wine."

"I shouldn't," I say as I eagerly thrust my glass in the direction of the wine bottle. Once replenished, I ask, "I told you the *where* and *why*, what's the *how*?"

"Oh, yeah," Ginny mumbles absentmindedly, like she forgot her end of the bargain. Yeah, right. Not only is Ginny prettier and curvier than me, she's smarter than me. Not once have I felt jealous. I'm just happy Ginny gives me the time of day. I'm a thirty-five-year-old woman who's only had one friend in her entire life. As sad as that is, I'm not going to ruin a twenty-year friendship over jealousy. It's easier to be proud to be called Ginny's friend.

Unconditionally, Ginny has always put me first. Her life has always changed when mine did. Ginny transferred from Fairport Community to State when I did. She came home with me when I found out I was pregnant with the twins. Ginny didn't get that coveted bachelor's degree, either. After her parents passed away in a car accident, she had to sell their home to pay for their final expenses. After seeing the exorbitant amount she'd have to pay the realtor, Ginny went back to Fairport Community and got her license to sell real-estate. Ginny sold her parents' home herself, and then started selling everyone else's. Somehow by following my destructive path, Ginny found what she was meant to do.

"So Rob called Malcolm because you were upset, worried you ran away. Malcolm told him you'd run to me, '*cuz all women run to their best friends,*'" Ginny impersonates Malcolm, causing me to huff out a laugh. "After an hour without you showing up, Malcolm posted an unofficial All-Points Bulletin. So I've been waiting for ya, chatting with Colin every time he checks in. A dispatcher reported you strolling this way– it's why I was at the door before you knocked."

"Are you fucking serious?" I gasp out.

"Yeah, dead serious. It's no big deal. They all work for Malcolm. It's not like he doesn't have eyes and ears on all the kids. Since Dev knows this, it's how he's managed to fly under the radar."

"Just thinking about Dev makes me what to throw up from the stress of it," I grumble. "I can't imagine how you must be feeling. I'm a selfish bitch. You want to talk about your nephew?"

"No, I'm sick of it," Ginny grits out, furious all the sudden. "If I can't fix it, I don't want to dwell in it. I'd rather talk about you– it's more interesting."

"Ha! Ha!" I mock-laugh. "Yeah, right."

Ginny smirks at me like I'm an idiot. "So Rob's back at the Spook House– something about spying on Willow and Ren for Malcolm. Your kids are camped out with my niece and nephew, supposedly studying for finals. Malcolm is on duty, so Isis is making sure the kids are actually studying. My guess–"

"They are," I snort out. "Everyone knows you don't fuck with Isis. She's scary. She even scared me when she was a little kid."

"She's scary to everyone, unless your name is Robin Prynne," Ginny taunts. "Or Raven Mason, Isis's little darling. The girl has us all wrapped around her little finger. Rae's a quiet sweetheart, though, so don't get nervous over mothering her."

Suddenly petrified, "Oh, God," I groan in misery. I quickly drain my wine glass, and then reach for Ginny's too. "My life is fucked. Playing phone tag with Malcolm was innocent enough. I could lie to myself while we did it. Getting off with him was hard to deny. But realizing that I'll be a cop's wife and the mother of seven kids… I need my head examined."

"Getting off? Come again?" Ginny's double entendre makes me giggle.

"Come again?" I mimic her. "That man is built for sex," I murmur in a dreamy voice. "You should have seen me last night and this morning. I was… not myself. My cooter was in control, and it had her sights set on Malcolm."

"Oh! My! God! You didn't just say COOTER!" Ginny shrieks as she splashes me with water. "No self-respecting woman calls her pussy a cooter. I'll take vagina over that any day. If you want a nickname for your snatch, you've come to the right place. Us lesbians are all about the coochie."

"Holy fuck, I'm so out of my league, it's not even funny." I draw in a deep breath of air and slip beneath the surface of the bubbling hot water. After walking for four hours straight, the only conclusion I came to was that I *was*, *am*, and *always will be*, a fuck-up.

Lungs burning, I try to stay beneath the surface for as long as humanly possible. "Clover," Ginny's shout comes muffled. A second later her fingers are tangling in my hair, yanking me to the surface. Sputtering while blinking chlorinated water from my eyes, I barely focus on Ginny bitching at me. "What is wrong with you? Do you have a fuckin' death wish? Your hair could have gotten caught in the filter!"

"I'm just so tired of it all," I finally admit. "Tired of trying to please everyone. Tired of trying to figure out what is right versus wrong. I'm tired of making judgment calls. It's too much responsibility. It's too much stress. I guess I understand Dev. I understand why he would rather check out when checking in is so much work."

No longer amused by my cooter usage, and no longer upset over my impromptu drowning, Ginny sounds as drained as I feel.

"Clover, tell Willow the truth and deal with the fallout. Over. Stress gone. I know Sam made you more stress than he alleviated, but Malcolm isn't Sam. Tell Malcolm what you need, and allow him to help you. Yeah, it's four teenagers and three adult children, but whether it's one or seven, it's the same shit, different day. So instead of doing it all on your own, share the burden."

"I can't unload all of my shit at Malcolm's feet," I declare as I slide from the hot tub. Between the stress, heat, and the wine, I'm about to pass out. I find my usual terrycloth bathing suit cover-up resting on the back of a chair, and tug it over my head.

"Why not? Malcolm will do the same with you. Unload your shit at his feet and let him unload his at yours, and shovel the shit together in half the time. When Violet has a problem, sit all the girls down. If Weston has a problem, Malcolm can sit all the boys down. Seven kids or not, that is two parents splitting the work with the kids learning from each other's mistakes. Don't overthink it, just fucking do it."

"Ginny?" I sigh, unsure what I truly want to say. I tug at the strings holding my bikini in place, allowing the wet fabric to fall to the patio floor. Hesitant to continue this conversation, I squeeze out my suit, and then drape it over the back of the nearest chair. "I'm just so tired," I admit.

"One last thing, and then I will let you pass out on my new sofa." Emotions overcoming her insecurities, Ginny steps out of the hot tub, allowing me to see her in a bathing suit. I know she's uncomfortable with her weight, but I'm uncomfortable with my own. '*Grass is always greener on the other side*' syndrome.

I cover my head with a towel, trying to block out whatever Ginny is going to say that I don't want to hear. I blindly walk back into the living room, starting to shiver from the massive temperature difference, or it could be from the panic attack that is brewing inside me.

Ginny pushes me to her sofa, woman-handling me like I'm a toddler. She drapes her brand new, fuzzy gray, cashmere throw over my shivering body. I roll up into a ball, moaning about the ridiculousness of the blanket and how much I'm going to steal it when she's not looking. My eyes slowly slip shut, preparing to block out anymore hard truths with sleep.

"Clover," Ginny whispers near my ear. "I'm never going to have kids. I'm never going to get married. I love you. I love your kids because I love you and I loved Sam. I love Malcolm, not only because he's my brother-in-law but because he is an amazing man. I love my nephews and niece. I can't think of two more deserving people to raise those kids I love."

Eyes snapping open, "What if I can't love him like he needs?"

"My sister was difficult to love, the mental illness saw to that. Sam was difficult to love, his faults saw to that. Malcolm is easy to love. It will be like breathing. You won't even realize you're in love with him until your air is gone."

Voice quivering, "That's what I'm scared of, Ginny. I'm not scared I can't come to love Malcolm. I already care for him too much. I'm frightened I'll fall in love with Malcolm and lose him. I can't handle it again. I haven't even gotten over losing Sam yet." Tugging the blanket beneath my chin, I admit the only thing that's been holding me back, "I barely survived losing Sam. I wouldn't survive losing Malcolm."

Stroking my hair softly, Ginny tries to comfort me. "I wish I could give you guarantees, girlfriend, but I can't. You and Malcolm have been through so much. If there is a God, He won't do this to you again. You guys will be one of those couples who tell each other they love one another while wrapped around each other in bed, and then together you will fall into eternal sleep. Allow that to be a comfort," is the last thing I hear as I drift off to sleep.

CHAPTER NINETEEN

The Widower

"Jesus, how much wine did you give her?" I shake my head at the passed out form known as Clover Webster. I've tried shaking her, poking her, growling in her ear– nothing. Curled up like a kitten around a ball of yarn, Clover won't rouse.

Hovering near my shoulder as I crouch down by the side of the sofa, "Four glasses," Ginny sheepishly provides. "I told her it was a two glass limit, but she drank my two glasses, too. She had a rough couple of days, and I'm a total pushover."

I poke the sole of Clover's pink foot, and she doesn't even react. I tweak her toes, one-by-one. Nothing. "Tomorrow is a work day, Gin. Ross won't appreciate a hung-over assistant. Mondays are always the worst after the buildup of emails and phone calls from the weekend. It's going to take Clover all week to play catch up."

"She won't be hung-over," Ginny assures me as she folds Clover's skirt and blouse and underthings, and then places them in a bag. "We were in the hot tub too long and the heat got to her. Malcolm, it's not like Clover's had it easy. She's been so stressed out I could see it radiating around her, and then she walked around for the better part of the evening. Clover's exhausted."

I close my eyes, scared of the answer. "Is Clover doubting us? Am I the reason she cracked at Sunday dinner? Am I stressing her ass out? I knew I shouldn't have pushed Clover by touching her. It was too soon."

Ginny's cheeks pink as she pretends to pack the same bag for the fourth time in the past two minutes. "We didn't really talk about that," is said in a way that means they did actually talk about '*that*'. "I wouldn't worry if I were you. Clover will need help with Willow. That's eating her alive."

"I will do whatever it takes," I vow. "Even if I have to handcuff the girl to her mother. Willow will come to terms with it– and fast." I palm Clover's cheek, and she snuggles into the touch. So I poke her in the foot again. Nothing. "Ah, she's a cuddly drunk, I see," I murmur, thoroughly amused.

"No one is good with change, Malcolm. But Clover is the worst. Not only does she have to change, she has to find herself. Clover's been in this state of stasis for so long that it's all she knows. Now that she's feeling something besides numb, she's petrified."

"I understand," and I do. "Well, it's bedtime for the kids sitting in the car, so I better get Momma Bear home." I lean forward, sliding one arm beneath Clover's knees and another beneath her shoulders.

I stand with Clover clasped to my chest. Cuddly drunk, Clover curls around me, murmuring my name in her sleep. The scent of her, the heavy feel of her in my arms, my name breathed from her lips, I grow a foot taller as a man.

"The neighbors are gonna talk," Ginny says, pacing me to the door. I open my hand, fingers extended for Ginny to place the grocery bag filled with Clover's clothing. "You're in your uniform, carrying a passed out woman to your police cruiser."

"It's the Chief Mobile," I say with great amusement. "I don't think I could have stuffed her into a squad car. I will say, though, it was hilarious to see the kids sitting in the back of the SUV behind the cage divide. Seth made a big show of yelling at me while weaving his fingers through the grates."

Laughing at me, not with me, "Oh, Lord. You're such a child."

"Violet freaked out when she realized there were no door handles and she was trapped as soon as I shut the door." I snicker into Clover's ear. "Your kids wanted to kill me. It was priceless. I took pictures for their Facebook profiles. Just wait until you see the expressions on their tiny, pissed off faces."

"Ah, Willow will love that!" Ginny grins at me when I nod my head in agreement.

"Open the door for me, will ya? My hands are full." I smirk the entire time, feeling the twins' glare as I wait for Ginny to open the passenger side door to my SUV.

"What'd you do to Mom?" Seth shrieks at me as soon as the door cracks open. Still gripping the cage, he rattles it to gain my attention. I want to tease Seth by telling him he looks like an adorable monkey, not a badass criminal. "Is she okay?"

"Why's Mom passed out?" Violet asks as she forcibly moves her brother out of the way so she can see into the front seat. "Seth just ruptured my eardrum and Mom didn't even flinch."

"She's just tired, and Ginny over-served her." I settle a sleeping Clover onto the seat and buckle her in. When I try to pry the blanket from her grasp, she yanks it back and wraps her arms around it. "Um... kinda attached to this blankie, aren't ya?"

"Clover can keep it. When I draped it over her, she was crooning its virtues." Ginny giggles. "She likes soft things." I raise an eyebrow at that but don't comment. I shut Clover and the kids into the car because I don't want them to hear what I have to say next.

I pull Ginny into a hug, and squeeze the shit out of her. Gravely, I whisper into her ear, "Thirty-two hours left." I give Ginny the Devon countdown. "Less than a day and a half to locate his ass. I'll let you know when we find him."

Ginny gives me a final squeeze before pulling away. "Have faith," is all she says in parting because she's so upset. I want to call Ginny back to comfort her, but I have two kids and their passed out mother in my car, with my kids and my sister back at my house, and I still have to get my ass back to work. My night is just beginning.

I hop into the driver's seat, and then pull away from the curb. It's a very short and silent drive to Clover's house. The kids are ignoring me in favor of concentrating on their mother. Violet's long, thin fingers are pushing through the grates, petting her mother's hair, and Seth is transfixed by the motion. Clover is curled around her blankie, not quite snoring but rasping out a wheezing sound.

Worried, "Does your mother have asthma or apnea?" I ask.

"Allergies and stuff like car exhaust or smoke bring out her asthma," Violet answers, and for some reason Seth finds something amusing.

"What?" I demand as I turn onto their street.

Still laughing, Seth answers, "Must have been hard for Mom being a Prynne with asthma." Violet's giggles join Seth's. "It's probably where she got that stick up her butt. She couldn't relax the Prynne way."

"I don't get it," I mumble, sounding like an idiot. "Whatever. We're home. Your grandmother is going to shit a brick when I carry your mother into the house."

"A ton of bricks," Seth adds when I open up the back door.

"A brick fucking factory," Violet says, giggling as she slides out to hop to the ground. She waves to some imaginary person across the street, but I have a feeling the action was witnessed by Peggy. I ought to hire the woman for surveillance.

Being helpful, Seth offers, "I'll grab Mom's stuff, and then unlock the front door." The kids stumble like drunks up the walk while dragging their backpacks behind them. My father would have dropped them to their asses for their behavior. But since I'm not my father, I just think they look like dumbasses.

"Upsy daisy," I sing to Clover. Half-awake, half-passed out, she tries to stand on her own two feet. But within one shaky step, I'm dragging her into my arms. "I've gotcha." She snuggles up against me and immediately falls asleep. "I could get used to this," I say with a smile as I stride up the sidewalk and onto the porch.

Seth and Violet turned all the lights on in the house: typical, non-electric-paying kids. They both stand by their mother's bed, acting like I'm going to molest Clover if they leave us alone. I reach for the edge of the blankets, but Seth's hand strikes out to stop me by circling my wrist.

"We'll get that," Seth says in his deep man-voice, which is at total odds with his boyish body.

Arms folded over her chest, Violet announces, "I'll put Mom's nightgown on her. Thanks for driving us home," she says in dismissal.

I reluctantly place Clover on her bed, missing her warmth in my arms immediately. "You guys do realize this woman will be my wife, right?"

"Right now she's just our mom," Seth states matter-of-fact, sounding confrontational. "None of what you were doing this morning until she's your wife. John Mason's rules of life, remember?"

Impressed that the kid has the balls to speak to me like this, I arch a brow and drawl out, "Oh, really, now?"

"Yeah," Violet grunts. "Isis was schooling us tonight."

"Shit," I hiss while strangling my baby sister in my head. "Fine," I growl. "Close your eyes– I'm giving your mom a goodnight kiss."

Retching and gagging sounds flow in unison as I lean down to give Clover a kiss. "Knock it off," I bark at the idiots. "That's the world's worst mood music."

I don't kiss Clover. I just nuzzle the side of her face with my cheek. Even half asleep, Clover reacts to my touch, pressing closer while making happy noises in the back of her throat. What I wouldn't give to crawl into bed with Clover and snuggle while we sleep. A tired and tipsy Clover is a completely different person than the one everyone else gets.

"I'll call you in the morning," I whisper in her ear. "Sweet dreams." I start to pull away, but Clover surprises me with a slow, lingering kiss. Disappointed that I have to stop, I lean away before she gets too carried away.

"Okay, put your mom to bed, and then I want you guys to wash up and hit the sack. No snacks. No smut reality TV. You have your first final tomorrow."

"Yes, Dad," the say in union, voices filled with sarcasm.

Pointing at my cheek while leaning down, "Kiss me goodnight, right here," I order Violet.

"No," Violet denies me, sounding grumpy. "Gross."

Still pointing at my cheek. "Seth?"

"I'm a boy," is Seth's immediate reply.

"Your cohorts kissed me goodbye," I remind them. I'm only teasing, but there is an edge of seriousness. I don't like how uptight they are about touch. I should be able to give my stepchildren a hug or kiss without them freaking out. Violet still flinches when one of us pats her on the back.

"They're your kids," Violet reminds me, as if I somehow forgot.

"And you're going to be my daughter very soon. So get used to kissing your new dad's cheek goodbye and goodnight. Same goes to you, Seth," I warn.

Growling, "Fine," Violet kisses my cheek, acting like I'm boiling her alive. But she's smiling when she pulls away.

"Night, kid," I say to Seth as I squeeze his shoulder on my way by.

"No fair!" Violet shouts.

"Didn't Isis tell you? Girls kiss their daddies goodnight, boys don't. Seth's a boy." I laugh the entire walk to the Chief Mobile, with Seth's cackle and Violet's giggle ringing in my ears.

CHAPTER TWENTY

The Widow

Still waiting for Devon to make his grand reappearance, Malcolm needs a distraction, and teasing me seems to be that distraction. "I see you read my text," Malcolm purrs through my cellphone, sending hot vibrations straight from my ears to the throb between my thighs.

"Hmm…" I give a purr of my own, causing him to release that panty-incinerating laugh. "It was nice, but a surprise. Couldn't get off this time, Malcolm?"

Moments before this unexpected call, I'd received a text. Thank God, it wasn't another email for Mrs. Ross to use tonight. It was different from all the previous ones. Malcolm loves to send me shots of himself mid-eruption. This time he was painfully hard. The moment I saw it, I wondered if a stiff breeze would've gotten him off. Malcolm accomplished one thing with his pornography, I'm painfully aroused now, too.

"I was saving my orgasm for my wife," Malcolm says cockily, causing my eyelids to flutter shut. I'm not used to a man teasing me. When Sam did, it was always followed up with an '*I gotcha!*' The '*I gotcha!*' was always meant to deeply wound.

"And here I thought you could always make more," snark flows easily from my smirking lips.

"You sound so much like Willow sometimes– it's scary." Malcolm rumbles a happy amused sound. "Come visit me."

"Speaking of scary, the basement is scary," I say with a shudder.

"It's my domain. All these big burly cops can protect your sweet little bod. Get your ass down here. You have five minutes before I start forwarding the entirety of my spank-bank to Mayor Ross." The phone goes dead in my hand.

"C'mon!" I shout, gaining the attention of anyone in earshot. "It'll take that long to walk down there." I rush so fast I have no time to think. I fly down the marble steps, praying this isn't a mistake of epic proportions. Either way, Malcolm has me by the balls: his spank-bank would definitely get me fired, so I might as well see what game he's got cooked up for lunch.

"Mrs. Webster?" calls one of my colleagues, and I nearly careen into the small man.

I don't have time for this shit!

"Can't now, Tony! My job is on the line." My breath comes out in puffs, winded from the jog down three floors. I need to exercise more. "Catch me later," I call out without looking back or stopping.

Hangover long forgotten, replaced by the adrenaline coursing through my veins. My feet create tap-tap sounds as I rush to my destination. The steel door looms ominously ahead. It opens with a hollow-sounding creak just as I reach it, causing my heart to beat in my throat.

"Clover," Colin McGregor says with a naughty smirk.

Malcolm's second in command is a feast of eye-candy. After one second of eye contact, I just gained ten pounds in my thighs and butt cheeks. Colin could star in his own Police Officer Calendar: he would be the months from January through December. Short, but not too short, with compact muscles that are obvious beneath his uniform. Only one word comes to mind when you look at the red-headed, green-eyes, freckle-faced cop: scrapper. Colin's Irish accent shoots lightning into my veins, and then it veers straight into my nether regions. Colin was the one who Malcolm always sent to Mayor Ross's office in his quest to avoid me at all costs.

"Colin," I say, holding my side as I try to regain my breath. I look away bashfully, blushing. Colin's flirted with me enough that I almost caved to his advances a few times. But I know it's harmless flirting– it's what Colin does. He always has a cute girl on his arm– once I saw him with two.

"Follow me," Colin offers cordially, extending his arm in invitation. Colin gives me a wink as he takes my elbow. He escorts me down a windowless, narrow hallway that's painted green– the shade reminds me of vomit. I don't like this part of the Courthouse. The basement is certified as a fallout shelter in cases of emergency, so it always feels oppressive, no matter the reason you're visiting. The walls seem to close in on us as we walk down the long corridor. The lack of windows makes it feel sinister– suffocating.

"You need to repaint," I say conversationally. My choice was either to speak or feel awkward in our silence. Usually it's easy to talk to Colin.

"Take that up with Ross. He wanted to use our town colors. I think it looks more like a leprechaun." He grins at me and stands next to the long wall. Colin is second generation Irish-American. He pulls a pose and does a little dance.

"Stop," I laugh and slap at his chest. "I will forever see you as a leprechaun now." A light bulb flashes in my mind. "No shit, Colin, you're the author of all that stupid lucky charms bullshit, aren't ya?"

"Guilty as charged." He sounds unrepentant. "Thanks for the grub on Saturday night, Clover. It was scrumptious." He makes a show of licking his chops.

"Anytime," I reply.

"I'll hold you to that, Lucky." Colin laughs as he points at the holding cell a few feet to our left. I sidestep wearily until I'm even with the cell. My sharp gasp ricochets throughout the long cavernous basement.

"Malcolm?" My heart is beating triple-time, reminiscent of a snare drum. Lower jaw hanging out with my toes, I stammer, "I… what?"

"You said perverts should be behind the bars, not holding the keys." Malcolm croons from his position inside the holding cell. A second later, Colin is placing a large key in my outstretched palm. I don't even acknowledge Colin because I'm all eyes for Malcolm.

The big, burly cop with unruly hair and wicked blue eyes is in a position that is only used for one reason. "This is the most inventive proposal I've ever heard of," I say in awe to the man kneeling on the other side of the thick iron bars. Malcolm reminds me of a caged lion, willing, but a sense of power radiates off him. Malcolm will not be kept caged for long.

"I'm a self-professed pervert, but I want to be your pervert. Let me out, Clover," Malcolm's deep voice drops an octave, a mix of pleading and manipulation. "You hold the key to my heart in your palm. You have a decision to make. If you turn the key there is no going back. It will be your yes," he purrs hypnotically. "Or you can leave me in here to rot for all eternity." His lips tilt up into a small grin and his eyes dart to the floor with surprising coyness.

Malcolm's entire demeanor is calling out to me to comply. His tone of voice lulls me, weakens my knees and bleeds my heart. His woodsy scent influences the way my brain processes thought, surrounding me in a fog of craving. I don't know what I crave. Malcolm? Now that I know I can have Malcolm, I crave him like no other. The way Malcolm's body language sways me: a strong man willingly kneeling before me, begging me to choose him. If Malcolm were to touch me, kiss me, I'd never be able to say no.

Malcolm placed himself on the other side of the bars, imprisoned himself, so he couldn't influence every last sense I have. Malcolm wants me to make a decision, but he wants it to be my decision. Malcolm's gifting me with freedom, and he wants me to free him with my choice.

My daughter hugged me before she went to school this morning. My son chatted with his sister at breakfast. I owe that to the man proposing a different kind of life to me. Malcolm isn't offering himself. He is offering me a new way of life, because the one I'm living has me barely treading water. At any moment, I could go under and drown. Malcolm is offering to be my life-preserver.

I reach forward without regret. The key slides easily into the lock. The turn of my wrist is a turning point in so many of our lives. The loud clank screams of finality– a path I take, with which I can never escape.

It's the first decision I've made that wasn't an escape from a desperate situation: not pregnancy or for survival. I chose Malcolm and he chose me, because we fit and our children need us to lead them. Mostly, it just feels right.

Malcolm's loud, relieved sigh makes me comfortable. Malcolm isn't as arrogant as he pretends to be. He has his own façade that I will tear down.

"I guess you're my pervert," I tease.

Malcolm stares up at me with glittering blue eyes that sparkle with mischief. He says Willow is like her momma. Well, Kieren got his playfulness from his dad. "Clover Prynne Webster, do me the honor of becoming my wife," Malcolm's strong words resonate around the hollow space. I smile when his voice cracks from nervousness. It makes Malcolm seem more real, genuine– it draws me into the moment. Instead of standing here, witnessing it from a self-imposed distance, as if looking down from the ceiling, as I've experienced every other pivotal event in my life, I live and breathe this moment.

"Crash and burn," I mutter underneath my breath as I extend my hand to my future-husband.

Malcolm stumbles to his feet on shaky legs and backs me up against the wall with his presence. The deafening clank of the cell door being locked breaks into our self-made bubble. The sound freezes me in a panic, an animal too frightened to move, let alone breathe.

"Colin's just giving us some alone time. He'll be down the hall to make sure we have privacy," Malcolm gasp breathlessly, nearly panting. "You still have the key in your hand," Malcolm says to reassure me as he gives my clenched hand a squeeze. "We can leave at any time… stay here with me for a few minutes," he begs, flashing me sad eyes, and pouts out his lower lip.

"Okay," I whimper, eyes glued to Malcolm's lush bottom lip. I can already imagine the taste of him on my tongue.

A dormant part of me awakens from Malcolm's nearness. I've kept her imprisoned my entire life. She's like my family: messy, chaotic– dirty. I locked her away to rebel against my family by being the perfect good girl. I could never let her back out because she was the girl Sam fell in love with. Glimpses of my true nature would make Sam angry and distant. I've maintained this façade for so long that I no longer know who or what I am. It's the person everyone expects to see, but never really sees clearly.

Malcolm's not touching me, but he's so close that the heat from his body warms me, seeps into my cold flesh. His manly scent invades my nostrils and floods into my system. Foggy-headed, he's a feast for my senses.

Fingers twine with mine and are drawn up to face-level. Malcolm holds my hand steady as he slowly slides a simple silver band onto my left ring finger with delightful finality. There is no going back now. There is a comfort in knowing there's no room for indecision. We're both people who think responsibility is first and foremost. This ring on my finger isn't a promise of what's to come with a loophole of escape. It's an agreement with which neither one of us will ever break.

Malcolm's devious blue eyes hold my gaze as he runs a fingertip around the band until the stone is front and center.

"It's beautiful," I gasp. Bursts of color create a glittering ball. All twelve months of the year are represented in the globe of birthstones. Hundreds of flecks of color catch the light to cast a glow onto Malcolm's elated face.

"It represents our family," Malcolm murmurs shyly. "I couldn't leave out our future grandkids, now could I? I didn't want this ring at the jewelers with every single birth. Hopefully, we'll have a kid for every month of the year. Don't want any of these gems to get jealous of the others," he teases gently in a humored tone, and then ducks his head in a boyish manner until we're eye-level.

"I don't know what to say, Malcolm," I stammer, voice breaking from intense emotions. "Thank you just doesn't seem like enough."

"You said yes, what more could I ever want?" Malcolm murmurs dreamily while staring at our joined hands.

"Malcolm," I call to gain his attention, needing to bring us back to reality. "We don't know each other, not really."

"*Yet,*" Malcolm enunciates as he catches my eyes. "We have a lifetime to learn one another. We'll never be bored."

"You can't love me," I admit with a cold flash of regret. "I don't feel that for you, either." My words say no, but my head is nodding yes.

"*Yet,*" Malcolm repeats with a flash of teeth from his wide grin. "What is love? Look how it destroys everyone. Usually couples think they're in love when it's actually just lust. Love takes time to grow– a lifetime. So, right now, I can do you one better: mutual respect and responsibility will bind us tighter than love ever could. I care for you. I want the best for you. I want you to be happy, and I know you feel those things for me, too. The love will grow from mutual trust and respect."

"I'm scared," I admit reluctantly.

"And I'm not," Malcolm says with a shrug, like it's no big deal to get married without saying the *I love yous* first. "You can be scared for the both of us, and I'll be confident for the both of us," Malcolm declares arrogantly while smirking.

"I..." but Malcolm cuts off my protests with a finger to my lips. My eyes flutter shut instantly from the contact.

"Is this too much?" Malcolm murmurs as he touches the inside of my elbow. "Is it too sensitive?"

Heavily-lidded, I reply in a drugged-like voice, "It feels nice."

Malcolm swirls a fingertip around in a circle, heightening my nerves and creating gooseflesh to bead on my eager skin. Malcolm speaks intimately, softly, into my ear. "You get panicky when someone gets into your space. I noticed if I let you come to me, you're fine. So I'll go slowly right now until you get used to my touch." He speaks quietly, almost as if he's afraid he'll spook me.

I want to scream that I don't feel that way around him, just everyone else. "How do you know?" Confusion helps me swim to the surface of his pleasure.

"Affection is an effective weapon. I know deprivation when I see it. I don't want to speak of Sam or my father when this is about you and me. But I know how it is, because it's what made me the way I am today. Someday I'll go into the details, but just know I can't go minutes without touching someone, even if I have to touch myself to satisfy the need. I just wanted you to know I understand." Malcolm gives a small self-deprecating grin at his plight.

"Slowly," he purrs, his breath flutters against the shell of my ear as his fingertips glide up and down my arms. "I love these three-quarter length sleeves. Your arms peeking out drive me crazy."

I melt against the wall, my system overloaded on Malcolm. My body is alight with sensation as my nerves soak in his attention. My brain struggles to reason between the pleasure and the panic as his fingertips skate over my deprived flesh.

After three swallows, I can finally speak. "How can you crave touch when it's so scary," I breathe, trying to understand the contradiction.

"At first, I couldn't take it. I would hold Isis to feed or change her, and it'd throw me into a tailspin. The sensations were too much. Just having someone too close would give me the sweats. A whisper near my ear made me want to run and hide. But a tiny baby needed me. Months I flinched when Isis would crawl to me, but I made myself take care of her. Eventually the panic receded, but the fear changed. I worried that I'd turn back into that animal-like kid. Touch keeps me centered."

"Oh, Malcolm," I breathe, feeling empathetic.

"I'm sorry, Clover. But I will touch you if you're in the same room with me. I understand, but I won't allow you to be deprived.

I can feel your hunger," Malcolm growls, stepping closer, pressing me into the wall. "I'll walk you through it slowly."

"I'm sorry," I say without a trace of pity. My voice is filled with relief. Malcolm understands how difficult a simple touch is– how I simultaneously panic and crave it.

"I'll show you that I'm an entirely different creature than Sam was. You'll never have to compare us, just as you can find comfort in knowing I will never compare you to Camille."

Malcolm's breath is ragged. His chest is rapidly surging and retreating. "Tell me when it's too much. It doesn't have to be sexual unless you want it to be." Malcolm's words filter into my lust-fogged ears. Hurt slams into me out of nowhere. I can't live a lifetime on repeat– the pain every rejected plea of affection bled from my soul.

"Oh, Clover," he chuckles sadly near my ear, arching his back to shrink to my smaller height. "You're like reading an open book. I'm giving you the power of choice–a choice you never had. The kitchen, your bed, I was following your lead, Silly Rabbit."

"I know," I grumble. "I feel like an idiot. It's like I couldn't think straight."

Laughing deeply from his chest, Malcolm drives all thought from my mind. "Prop your thigh on my hip. Invite me closer," he coaxes.

"I'm wearing a skirt." I sound timid, but the wanton woman is in control of me again. I clumsily slide my leg up to Malcolm's hip. A quiver rolls through my body– he's so warm and solid.

"A little further, bunny," Malcolm persuades. "Um-hmm... just like that," he purrs as he settles closer to me– pinning me to the wall with just the weight of his broad chest and strong thighs. He shifts his hips and I choke out a very unladylike grunt.

"Never fear that I don't want you, Clover. I keep sending you *'proof of arousal'* texts." He releases an amused chuckle that promises more texts in the near future. "I've been insane with want," he rumbles, and then nips my neck with his front teeth. "A real man wants his woman to eagerly take from him. Only a coward takes from a woman." Malcolm's warning growl reverberates down my spine like a tuning fork.

"Oh, fuck," I sigh. Falling limp, my head hits the cold, hard cement wall with an audible thump. "You're so warm. I forgot what it felt like to be surrounded and consumed." I shudder against him.

"Mmm… you smell like almonds and sugar. All those cookies you've baked have seeped into your pores. It's intoxicating." Malcolm runs the tip of his nose along the column of my neck, and then nuzzles my collarbone.

"You smell fantastic, too. Woodsy," I mumble in a haze. Like a fly captured in a web, I can't move. All I can do is experience. I'm no longer bound by self-made restraints where I separate myself instead of feel. The knowledge calms the panic that keeps trying to erupt.

"Too much?" Malcolm asks with a seductive curl to his voice. He dips his nose under the collar of my blouse, the rasp of his day-old stubble tickling me. When I don't stop Malcolm, his fingertips toy with the top few buttons.

"I think you're trying to drive me insane with need. Women who flash everything don't do anything for me. You cover yourself, and my mind goes into a frenzy, wondering what lies beneath. I want to unveil you to my gaze, one button," he pops the top button and I shudder in bliss. "At. A. Time," Malcolm murmurs as he methodically opens every single button, until he can spread my blouse apart.

"Beautiful," Malcolm moans. "My boys will be so pleased," he murmurs to himself.

"What?" I whisper in confusion, and Malcolm's answering laugh curls my toes and dampens my panties.

"Uh…" Malcolm mumbles and backs up a foot. His fingers seek his dark wavy hair. "You'll slap me." He snickers, turning uncomfortable.

"I won't," I say in a daze.

"Promise," Malcolm demands softly. I nod, and he continues, "You're a gorgeous woman, Clover. A tiny little thing, but your breasts are perfect."

"Not true," I murmur, still confused with what this has to do with the kids.

"Mmm-hmm," Malcolm moans. "They're small enough that you can get away without a bra, but big enough that if you do, your tits will jounce around and drive me insane. I want to watch you walk around braless in a silk blouse, the fabric teasing your nubs with every stride." His blue gaze hungrily devours my small bandeau lace bra.

"Outside your comfort zone time," Malcolm warns a split-second before his warm, wet mouth latches onto my nipple through the lacy fabric.

"Ahhh…" garbles out my throat as Malcolm's hot mouth works my sensitive nipple. My fingers wrap in his wavy hair and pull him away. My nipple screams out as his hot saliva turns ice cold in the air. "Wait– what was I going to slap you for?"

Malcolm rolls his eyes up to me and says, "Willow's tits will be nice and healthy in a few years." He blushes a gorgeous pink and descends to my breast again, pulling so hard that my hand has to go with him or yank his hair out at the roots.

"Ugh," I grunt in complaint, even as I think this feels too good to give a shit. "That comment better be about your idiot boys," I warn.

"Hell, yes… I want a woman. But I can appreciate that one day, Willow will make a man very happy. Just like her momma," Malcolm purrs salaciously. A devious smirk parts his lips a second before he bites my nipple. I yelp in shock as his teeth grip and pull. "You breastfed, that's scorching hot." He moans huskily from deep within his chest. "You don't have tiny nubs… nice big, suckable nipples." He groans, and then switches to the long-forgotten nipple.

My fingers tangle in Malcolm's hair to hold him tightly instead of pulling him away. I don't want the pleasure to end. I hope to God Malcolm doesn't give me what I crave only to punish me by taking it away. That is all I've ever known. A small taste to whet my appetite was always followed by a punishing rejection that left me feeling cold and empty.

My knees weaken as Malcolm attacks my chest, neck, and shoulders with his lips, teeth, and tongue. The rasp of his day-old whiskers enlivens my skin. The blunt edge of his teeth scrapes along the underside of my breasts, followed by the flat of his warm, moist tongue. The suction of his strong mouth pools moisture in my panties.

Malcolm is all man…

I wrap both legs around Malcolm's waist and groan like a wild animal as he grinds his *immortalized-by-photograph* flesh against the damp seat of my panties. I try to contain my true-self, but she won't behave. My fingers claw into Malcolm's shoulders, moans pouring from my throat. My legs quiver as they strain to hold onto Malcolm as he rocks rhythmically against me.

"Your panties are wet, aren't they, Clover?" he murmurs breathlessly, followed by a throaty grunt. "Admit it. Say, '*Malcolm, my panties are sopping wet.*' Say it," he coaxes.

"Malcolm," I gulp in disbelief. "I can't say that."

"Why? They're wet, aren't they?" Malcolm gives another moisture inducing suck in between every word he speaks, dampening my panties even more.

"You know they are," I cry out. I drop my legs from his waist and try to stand on wobbling knees. "I… I'm probably leaving a mark on your pants. Sorry," I whimper in shame. Malcolm will be so angry when he has to go back to work with my moisture staining his pants.

"Clover," Malcolm groans my name in frustration. "Say it."

"Why?" I ask, and I have to bite my lip against the litany of words that threatens to spill, most importantly, to stop myself from telling Malcolm just how saturated my panties really are. I've never been talked to like this. Sex was for Sam.

"Because I want to hear it," Malcolm growls around my nipple, and then he bites it hard, and then harder.

"Ugh! Jesus," I yelp when Malcolm keeps biting me harder and harder with every passing second that I don't comply. Each press of his teeth draws more moisture to pool between my thighs. "Malcolm, my panties are sopping wet. If you keep biting, I'll flood your slacks," I warn.

Malcolm laughs at the bitchy tone in my voice. "Crisis averted," he says as he pulls away. Malcolm sits on the long bench that runs the length of the holding cell. My eyes pop wide when he unbuttons his slacks and spreads them wide apart. Navy boxer briefs dominate my vision. The fabric is stretched tight against his arousal. My mouth waters when Malcolm starts to pulse and jerk behind the soft cotton of his underpants.

"If you keep looking at it like that, I'll misfire. I have a reputation to uphold. Imagine the paperwork I'd have to file for misfiring in the holding cell. Get over here," Malcolm demands.

"Too much," I squeak!

"Too much, what?" Malcolm leans back against the wall and juts up his lap in invitation.

"Sex," I gulp.

"We're not having sex. I'm a traditional man," he says, sounding serious.

"We almost had sex yesterday morning, remember? You were begging me for it!" Anger replaces my confusion. "I've seen the pictures, Malcolm. They were not traditional… *at all*," I say in utter disbelief. The majority of the photographs were only him, but a few involved more than one person. Several were of his naked torso with hands– many overlapping hands –touching him.

"Soon-to-be Mrs. Mason, I'm only saying I'm not having sex for the first time with you in a cell. There will be sex, plenty of sex. Now get over here and sit on my lap," Malcolm commands, patting said lap.

"What I took away from the images you sent me, is that it takes more than one person to satisfy you." I try to hide my hurt, at not only Malcolm's dishonesty, but his experience as well. I can't compete with that. I'm not sure I'll ever satisfy him.

"Satisfy *me*?" Malcolm stresses as he stares me down with his penetrating blue gaze. "It's not *your* job to satisfy *me*. It's *my* job to satisfy *you*." A loud growl fills the cell. Its intensity should leave me feeling chilled, but it burns me bright hot. "I sent the pictures to you for a reason. I want *you* to figure out which of them makes you hot, flips your switch. Write that shit down in the journal I bought you. We're learning each other here, Clover. Now c'mere," he orders.

I wander over on shaky legs that seem to move on Malcolm's command. I stare at him like a complex puzzle I can't solve. I can't figure out how to sit with him without touching the bench or having my skirt bunch up. Malcolm quickly takes my indecision away. Strong hands pull my skirt up to my waist to bare my panties to his sight.

"You wore these for me?" Malcolm sounds pleased. I shyly nod and look away. "Beautiful, Clover. I love lacy underthings. We can't have your panties getting even wetter, now can we?" Malcolm croons as his fingers hook into the side straps of my underwear and starts to shimmy them down my hips.

"Too much," I bark out in a panic. I'm overwhelmed, this is happening too fast. My body shivers, my breathing increases to near hyperventilating levels as I try to halt my panic attack.

"No sex," Malcolm promises. "I won't touch you here with my fingers. I just want to feel your hot slickness on my bare skin again. This isn't new territory for us, Clover." His deep, husky voice pushes the panic away and replaces it with fiery lust.

I swallow audibly, shaking, while Malcolm slides my underwear down my legs. My heel hooks on the fabric, but he expertly pulls them off. "For safe keeping," Malcolm murmurs as he tucks the ivory lace into his front shirt pocket, right behind his badge.

"Pretty curls," Malcolm murmurs as a fingertip swirls around the fluff of pubic hair on my mound. Malcolm's lips turn up into a devious smirk. "Beautiful, bare pussy lips. Why do you shave them?"

"It seems cleaner," I say shyly, shrugging like I'm not blushing cherry-red.

"Put a knee on each side of my hips," Malcolm coaxes. I awkwardly do as he bids while he shifts around beneath me. "There, now they aren't in the way anymore," he rumbles in relief.

"Malcolm," I shout in shock as his hot flesh meets my damp lips. I swear that the combination of his heat and my moisture causes steam to billow around us. "Is this safe?"

"Did you suddenly become a very bad girl when I wasn't looking?" Malcolm's dark eyebrows knit sinisterly.

"I…" swallows. "I've been a very good girl," I defend while licking my suddenly dry lips. "I was only with Sam… and well, you. The other morning was pushing it. Shouldn't we put a condom on? I know we're not having sex, but it's not safe," I protest.

"Well, I've been a very good boy, too." Malcolm smirks.

I roll my eyes at the bold-faced liar. "See earlier photos as example," flows sarcastically from my lips.

"I love that little bitch eye roll you pull," Malcolm purrs salaciously. "It turns me on like crazy." He presses into me, proving just how painfully turned-on he truly is. He groans in delight as our bodies slide slickly in my moisture. I bite my lip to contain a moan. "I'm always safe. The people who touch me are clean, and touch no one but us. Only once it got a bit crazy, but someone oversaw to make sure I was safe."

"What?" I breathe out, needing more information.

"Later," Malcolm says with a wink. "I told you– I'm a traditional man. I refuse to wear a condom with my wife… and I've only ever had sex with my wife. That's what I meant by being a good boy, handjobs notwithstanding."

"I'm not on birth control," comes out in a panic. The past slams into me, and it feels suspiciously like shame.

Malcolm's fingertips grip my chin to turn me until I'm looking right at him. "Clover," he brusquely grunts my name. "I'm a man. There will be no avoiding the middle of your cycle. You'll be lucky to get away with sex once or twice a day. I'm a voracious lover with a tactile fixation. If you have a slow libido, I'll seduce it to increase."

"I'm still fertile," I stammer and blush.

"Good God, I hope so," he drawls out. "Our kids may think we're ancient, but you're still a young woman." Malcolm groans and shifts his hips. "Feel my cock flexing like crazy. Spread your legs further apart. Let me between those silky lips of yours. Say, *Malcolm, I want your huge cock to come all over my hungry, eager pussy lips.*' Say it," he demands.

"Malcolm, I could get pregnant," I say instead– cooler heads prevail.

"If you do, it was fated to be. A man and woman's orgasms were created for procreation. It's half the thrill of sex. Say… it…" Malcolm enunciates slowly.

"I…" Malcolm grips my thighs and spreads me impossibly wide. I suck in a sharp gasp when my nether lips part in welcome to embrace his hot, firm length.

"*I* doesn't sound like the start of my name," Malcolm cautions. "Repeat the phrase or I'll make you say cock and pussy in front of Mayor Ross. No more unsexy vagina and penis out of these supple lips." Malcolm purrs as he outlines my lips with a gliding fingertip.

I roll my eyes at Malcolm in defiance, and he barks a husky laugh. The effect that deep, sensual sound has on me is obvious. My pussy spasms and quivers, squeezing my lips around his hard length in a delicious rhythm that has my nails biting into the strong flesh of his shoulders.

"We're going to have a happy life together, Clover. My mission in life is to laugh for you every single day," Malcolm wholeheartedly states in a teasing lilt.

"Oh, dear Lord," I pray. I drag in a deep breath and breathe out his damned phase, "Malcolm, I want your huge cock to come all over my hungry, eager pussy lips."

I hide my face against Malcolm's shoulder. I flush so hard that my skin tightens and prickles and feels hot to the touch. I can't believe our lower bodies are naked… and touching. I can't believe Malcolm just got me to say that I wanted him to come on me. Holy Hell, I've lost my ever-loving mind. It feels so good, though– freeing. The girl I used to be revels in the badness of speaking dirty.

"Music to my ears, bunny. As you wish," Malcolm croons. He grips my hips and pulls me down the hard, velvety length of him. The slow sensuous slide has me gasping for breath. "Your pussy is so wet, positively drenched. I've died and gone to heaven. It's been too long since I felt the pleasure of body fluids on my skin. The benefits are endless for us," he growls in my ear.

"I don't know if I'm ready for sex yet," I say to slow Malcolm down. He's a hairsbreadth from plunging deep into me. Hell, maybe I'm trying to slow myself down.

"Whether you are or not, on or before our wedding night, you'll find yourself impaled by this cock." Malcolm shifts his hips when he says cock. "It will be my right to take my wife. You can say no, but I won't listen."

"You're serious?" I huff in disbelief. Oh, God, please don't feel my body's reaction to the thought… please, don't!

"Hmm… Clover, do you have a fantasy you wish to share with your husband?" Malcolm purrs knowingly as my body betrays my thoughts by spasming.

"Nope, don't know what you're talking about," I clip out. "Where is this cum you promised my hungry, eager pussy lips?"

Malcolm directs a hearty laugh at me. My eyelids flutter shut and my lips part. "Touch me, Clover. Please," he begs shamelessly. "Move for me. Let me watch your tits sway as you take your pleasure from my body. Feed my hunger for your touch," he growls.

"You had me at '*Touch me, Clover*,' but the rest was a nice touch," flows snarkily, punctuated by a saucy grin.

"Little bitch," Malcolm growls under his breath.

I unleash the girl I've trapped since I was sixteen. The girl my daughter has fully embraced. I envy Willow's ability to be herself and seek what she wants. I want that for Willow and Violet, but I want it for myself, too.

Malcolm's warmth and scent drugs me into compliance. I do as he bids. My body seeks to fulfill its craving for affection and sexual gratification. My trembling legs wrap around his wide hips as my arms encircle his strong shoulders. Malcolm is a manly man, a traditional man who will always put me in my place. He'll shoulder the responsibilities of our family, and he'll make sure our needs are always met.

I give myself over to Malcolm– to his pleasure. Clutching, pressing him closer to me, I whimper because we aren't touching enough. I need more skin, more of his heat and scent.

I *need* him.

Smooth, hard, and pulsing, Malcolm's cock slides fluidly between my aching pussy lips. The bulbous head hits my clit with every rock of our hips. Malcolm's sawing breath in my ear doesn't incite panic, it causes fire to slowly build in my womb and radiate throughout my body. I shake, every muscle tremors from the pleasure I haven't felt in years, maybe never.

Early yesterday morning, I was lost in a state of lust mixed with exhaustion. Not fully aware, my actions in my bed were without consequence. This afternoon, I touch Malcolm with lucidity and intent, knowing there will be lifelong consequences: marriage. And I do so enthusiastically.

I dampen my pleasure by holding at bay the guttural noises that threaten to erupt from my throat. I can't release the sounds. It's shameful and embarrassing. Sam didn't like the sound. Why would any man? I bite my bottom lip and clench every muscle against the release that threatens to overcome me.

"Let loose," Malcolm groans gravelly in my ear. "I don't want perfect. I love messy and chaotic. Fucking scream if you have to– Colin will love hearing it. If it embarrasses you, then bite my shoulder. But don't you dare hold out on me, wife. I want you to unhinge, unleash that dirty girl inside of you who's dying to be set free."

Body locking up, "Malcolm," I whimper in shock as a wave of pleasure takes me by surprise.

"Let it go… please, just let it go. I ache from holding back. I need to come, Clover," Malcolm pleads, his cock erratically jerking beneath me.

"Ungh…" a garbled unintelligible word is torn from my throat. I release my muscles all at once. My entire being quakes as my nerves fire pleasure into my body in a large gush. My teeth tear into the soft flesh of Malcolm's neck. His skin tastes even better than his scent smells.

The first jet of Malcolm's scalding semen accompanies a grunt of pure pain– it spurs me to let go even further. "You're perfect for me, little bitch. I promise you'll never regret me,"

Malcolm mutters breathlessly as he falls lax to rest his back against the wall.

Every few seconds a spurt of warm dampness floods my already saturated, quivering flesh. Malcolm grins up at me lazily, with a drugged expression on his face.

"A few weeks from now, you'll be as starved for my flesh as I am for yours," Malcolm murmurs drowsily. "That was incredible. Look," he pulls the collar of his shirt to the side and I gasp.

"Oh, no," I cry in a panic as I witness the proof of what happens when I let my bad girl out. I ravaged Malcolm's neck. I try to pull his collar up to cover it.

"Tis nothing but a love bite," Malcolm slurs, "A mark of a job well done. I'll proudly wear it."

Malcolm's blue eyes glitter with barely suppressed elation. His mood is infectious. I let my bad girl out to play– my lips spread in a huge shit-eating grin, accompanied by a giggle. "Fuck, you're the incredible one." Proud, Malcolm laughs– laughs deep from his chest, a rumbling addictive sound that is music to my soul.

"Malcolm," a heavily accented voice echoes from down the corridor. "'*The Shit who refuses to join us*' approaches."

"Who?" I stand abruptly and look around, feeling criminal in this jail cell.

"Relax." Malcolm snickers. "It's just Ren." He leans forward to button my blouse.

"How do you know it's him?" I start on the top buttons as Malcolm languidly buttons the bottom.

"Every cop calls Kieren '*The Shit*.' They're put out that he won't join the force." Malcolm chuckles at their private joke. "Kieren's been showing up every few hours, bringing back info on the Devon search… so that's how I know for sure," Malcolm says as he zips his trousers.

"Oh," I mumble, at a loss of what to do now.

"We don't want you to lose any of this slippery goodness," Malcolm teases as he pulls my panties from his front pocket with a flourish. "No cleaning up except to go piddle. I gave this to you because I wanted you to have it," Malcolm croons as he pulls my panties up my thighs.

Malcolm pats my panty-covered mound and smiles. "Beautiful. I love knowing I'll be next to your skin until you shower, that you'll catch a whiff of me all day long." He smooths the wrinkles from my skirt, looking way too proud of himself.

I'd think about what's going on if my mind hadn't wandered off when I walked my ass down to Malcolm's lair.

"Dude, what the hell are you doing behind bars? I didn't come down here to chit-chat with Colin. I've got a lead." Kieren's annoyed voice filters in from the hall.

"You talk like a cop," Colin says with great appreciation. "You need to rethink your occupation, Ren."

"Shove it," Ren snarls, getting aggravated. "Dad? What the fuck? He won't let me through!"

"Kids," Malcolm rolls his eyes. "See, my dirty girl is wearing off on me already," he teases. "You might want to wait for Colin to escort you out, unless you want Kieren to taunt you endlessly."

"Ren would do that to me?" I ask, exasperated.

"It's Kieren we're talking about here, remember? Did his personality suddenly change when I wasn't looking? Why do you think he gets along so well with Willow? Plus, it would be best to keep us under wraps until Devon is dealt with."

Staring down at my new sparkler, "After I tell Willow..." I trail off, unable to elaborate.

"I'm coming in there, dammit! I don't want to be recruited," Kieren growls angrily. "Colin's worse than a Jehovah's Witness or a Time Share Devil."

"See ya in a few," Malcolm says as he grabs the key from where it fell to the floor. "I'll text you a few more times today," he threatens, and then disappears the second the key swivels in the lock.

"What in the hell were you doing in there?" Kieren accuses, his voice diminishing as he walks away. "You smell like good sex."

"Is there such a thing as bad sex?" Colin asks me from the cell door.

"Shit," I hiss. All the blood in my body collects in my cheeks, forming a furious blush. "What did I just do?" I murmur in awe as I stare at the glittering birthstones that are throwing splashes of refracted light around the cell. "Oh, yeah... there is such a thing as bad sex," I tell Colin as I join him in the hall. "It's the kind that makes you feel like shit: before, during, and after."

"Verdict?" Colin asks me.

"Huh?" I grunt in an unladylike fashion. Malcolm's wearing the perfect right off of me.

"Good or bad?" Colin notes my confused expression. "The sex?"

"Oh," I smirk, "Good… fan-fucking-tastic," I drawl. Then I silently add in my head, '*and we didn't even have sex*'… Imagine how it could be.

"Congrats!" Colin praises as he walks me upstairs.

"On the sex?" I arch an eyebrow and hold my smirk in. Colin looks at me sideways, like I'm bat-shit crazy.

"No," he grumbles, thoroughly confused. "On your impending marriage."

"No shit, Colin." I huff a teasing, throaty laugh. "I was just screwing with ya. Thanks."

I whisper to myself, "*Crash and burn.*"

CHAPTER TWENTY-ONE

The Widower

Leaning back in my desk chair with my arms crossed over my chest, I wonder when my chair will finally give out and plant me on my ass. "The past four days have been brutal," I whine to Colin, proving that grown men do in fact whine. They can also be clingy, needy, and over-emotional. But then again, that could just be me.

Contagious, Colin starts in on the whining, too. "And no donuts today, either." He's sitting on the edge of my desk, devouring a Honeybun, with a stack of vending machine food next to his thigh. I doubt the man knows you can buy boxes of this shit at the grocery store for under two bucks. I should tell him and save him a couple hundred bucks a month, but he keeps the vending company in business. Clover would make a killing if she'd start one of those bag lunch programs here at the Courthouse.

"Clover's just as strung out as the rest of us. She was sporting the hung-over, zombie look this morning. Even forgot to put on pantyhose."

"I'm sure she didn't tell you that." Colin winks at me, knowing damned well my eyes zeroed in on Clover's bare calves. "But Clover could have at least brought us in something from her cupboard, a stale cookie or something. I'm starving." Tearing into a package of fruit snacks like an enraged toddler, he gets frustrated and ends up piercing the package with my scissors. He just dumps the entire bag into his mouth and gets to chewing. We're both operating on caffeine, sugar, and fat today. After twenty-four hours on duty, neither of us are prepared to go home until Devon and his runaways are found.

"Well, I did get to eat the last donut last night. It was a bit stale, but it was made with love." I try to rub the goofy grin off of my face, but all I can see in my mind's eye is the moments *after* Clover made those donuts. "Just be thankful you didn't have the under-cooked pancakes from the No-Name at breakfast, lunch, brunch– whatever the fuck you call eating at ten in the morning. I finally gave in and got something to eat. This double-shift bullshit is killing me, not that I could have slept anyway."

"I feel ya on that. I had to have that sludge in the break room." Freckled face grimacing, "It's like drinking coffee flavored water out of a dirty jockstrap. I'd buy us a couple of Keurigs, but I doubt the K-Cups would be in our monthly budget. I'm about to hide a coffee machine under my desk."

"Then you know where I'll be," I say pointedly.

Sounding like Willow and Clover with an accent, the guy has to be joking, "Where?"

I bug my eyes out, a manly version of '*duh!*' "Your desk."

Chuckling, which means the idiot was being serious, "Oh, right. Sorry, I'm pretty dumb today. I even worked Saturday night after I left your place. It's now Monday afternoon and I've yet to go home. I showered with Matt the town drunk. What an experience, let me tell ya."

I'm thankful we didn't have any real emergencies over the past few days, or the whole department would have mucked it up. "Did you delouse Matt first? Better yet, did he give you a handy-jay for early release?"

"Goddamn you!" Colin shouts at me, pelting me with a Little Debbie oatmeal cookie. I grab the snack and take a big bite out of it, right through the cellophane wrapper. I chew up the cookie and spit the plastic out. "I had to wash the vomit off of him. It was," he shudders in disgust.

"I'm only taunting your ass." I hand Colin his cookie back as a peace offering. The guy has a bad reaction to handjobs outside of the Playroom, or it's just that he refuses to admit he likes handjobs *in* the Playroom. Colin and I usually go by Fight Club rules: no talking about the Playroom outside of the Playroom.

"Sooo…" Colin draws out, and I know he's going to retaliate for the handjob comment. "How was the lunch sex? Clover gave you two thumbs up with a fan-fucking-tastic."

"Did she really?" I add giddy to the list of things men aren't, but I am.

"Malcolm," Opal's worried voice flows across the cavernous space. I look up to see Opal and Nina barreling toward us at a fast clip. My heart ceases to beat, and then starts up double time.

The dispatchers are always glued at the hip. Opal is a registered nurse who volunteers all of her free time at dispatch in case she has to talk a 911 caller through an emergency, while

Nina is one of our fulltime dispatchers. The ladies always work in a pair.

Noticing I'm frozen in fear, Colin hisses, "Shit," as he slides off my desk. "It better be good news or I'm gutting you both."

"We found all of 'em. We wanted to tell you in person. Kieren called it in. Dev, Tina, Taryn, and Tommy are holed up in an abandoned house across from Rush. He found a dealer who had made a house-call last night. There's a couple of other idiots camped out with them. I already have a patrol out to pick up Gavin."

"Gavin was the dealer?" I grit out viciously. "I just had that fuck in here yesterday afternoon. I'm going to tear his nuts off."

Sighing, mimicking my nervous habit, Opal runs her fingers through her short blonde hair. "Gavin sold to Devon at the front door to the house. He could see the rest of them milling around the front room. But that's all he knew. He said they were all alive."

"I've got to get back to man the phones," Nina finally speaks. The woman has always been scared of me. Only a few years older than me, Nina was one of the women Dad turned to when Lisa lost interest in him and started running around on Dad. I was fifteen when I met Nina– she was kneeling before my father with his cock shoved in her mouth. I hated everything Nina stood for, and she knew it. Ten years later, I started working at the department, and I learned Nina worked here too. Dad got Nina the job as a '*thanks for the suck*', and it kept her in close sucking distance up until his death.

John Mason said there were two types of women. *Your* women: the women you marry and the women you raise to be another good man's faithful wife. Then there is the type of women you fuck. I don't agree with Dad, but Nina doesn't know that. So she never looks me in the eye, all the while she tries to get Auggie to see her in the former category. Auggie agrees with Dad. Since Auggie's mother was Dad's whore, he doesn't respect his mother Lisa or his sister Tina. Nina is the woman Auggie disrespectfully fucks while he puts my sister on an untouchable pedestal because she was John Mason's baby girl.

"Nina," I call out after her retreating form. She stops but doesn't turn around. Sounding exhausted, I shout out, "Thank you!" She nods her head, and begins moving again.

Grinning, "You've got your kid back," Opal says, while drawing me into a hug. I grip her tightly. I begin shaking involuntarily as adrenaline mixes with pure fear in my bloodstream.

"I'll call you with an update." Kissing Opal's cheek, I give her one last squeeze before pulling away. "Maybe you could drill it into Nina's thick skull that I'm not going to murder her."

Releasing a husky laugh, "You better blame Auggie for that shit. I can tell Nina 'til I'm blue in the face, but she still almost pisses her pants when you enter the room."

"Great," I sigh. Demeanor changing from friendly to authoritative, I clearly shout, "Cowboy up. We've got us some tweakers to wrangle."

I grab my belt off my desk and buckle it into place. After years of wear, it settles in a comfortable spot automatically. I dig around in my top drawer, locating all three of my cellphones. I start tucking them into their resting places, taking them just in case someone needs to contact me. My personal cell buzzes just as I'm shoving it into my shirt pocket.

Zombie Girl: *Found Dev. You need to check out these pics.*

I quickly download the attachment and nearly lose that bite of oatmeal cookie. Dev is passed out, naked and covered in filth. He's also covered by an equally naked Tina… and a fifteen-year-old Taryn. I'm glad Devon didn't die, but now I have to kill him myself.

Dialing my cell as I walk, my posse follows me. "Talk to me," I order Willow when she answers my call. "What?" I shout. "It's so staticky I can't hear you!"

"Wind! Not static. Wind. They stink to high heaven. Ren's about to toss Tina out the door. We're on our way to the Spook House. Dev and Tina are passed out but okay, I think. We're going to scrub them and sober them up. Rob and Isis are waiting on us. But there are a couple of kids still at the house."

"Okay, thank you!" I shout over the force of the wind. "I'll be there after I take care of a few things." I hang up without saying goodbye.

Just as I exit the basement stairs into the Courthouse's main vestibule, I turn to my group and start shouting out orders. "Take the van. Anyone who is lucid gets brought back here. Anyone who is semi-lucid gets taken into custody and transported to the hospital in a squad car. Call for a few busses. Anyone passed out gets transported to the hospital, but cuff their asses to the stretcher. Call Brad Cutler. We need his dogs– we've got to locate all traces of drugs in that house. A clean sweep makes it a clean bust. Anyone slated for rehab gets a pass. If they renege, their asses are ours. GO!"

Colin keeps pace with me while the rest of my officers run off to their tasks. "Call Reverend Braxton and Mrs. Elsberry after we get to the scene. Let them know their kids are still breathing. I'll push Tina's paperwork through so her stepdad can force her to stay in rehab this time. Fuck!" I shout to no one and nothing in particular.

"Malcolm," Clover's echoing voice has me drawing up short. I flip around to find Clover running down the marble staircase from the third floor. I stride over to her, cutting the distance in half. She collides with me forcefully, clasping my midsection with her arms.

"Is Devon alright?" Her voice warbles in fear as she shakes in my arms.

"Shh…" I whisper in her ear. My hands work circles into her back to soothe her. "Dev is going to wish he was never found. He's on the way to the Spook House with Willow, Ren, and Auggie. Tina is going with them. Rob and Isis are waiting on them. He's going to be fine," I lie to her and to myself. I have no clue if my son will ever come out of this the same person he was going in.

"The news went through the Courthouse like wildfire. I was so scared when I heard." My usually stoic wife-to-be is clinging to me in full view of half of the Courthouse's gossip crew. I allow us thirty seconds to forget about everything else but each other. "I'm going to be hard to get ahold of for the next day or so–"

"I understand, Malcolm. Do what you need to do. Don't worry about me. Just call me if you need any help with the kids– with anything. Especially if you need to talk about it." Clover makes a move to pull away so I can do what I need to do, but I don't let her.

I curl around Clover, shielding her from view of everyone. My lips seek hers, and I gasp into her mouth when she kisses me back passionately. When Clover makes up her mind about something, she goes all in. Her fingers seek my hair, and tug me closer. But before the kiss even begins, she's pulling away. It was all too brief and will never be enough.

I cup Clover's face in my hands, brushing her cheeks with my fingertips. I gaze down into her blue eyes and speak the truth. "I can't guarantee it will be okay, but I'll do my damnedest to make sure it is."

"I'll never doubt you. Get your shit straight, I'll be waiting." Clover arches up to reach my mouth, brushing a soft kiss over my lips. She pulls away with a smile. "Good luck." And before I have time to respond, she's running back up the stairs to the Mayor's office.

"Well, that answers that question," Colin mutters, sounding shocked. "I was worried for you."

I shake my head, trying to clear it of all things Clover related, not that it helps any. "Huh?" I grunt out as I head toward the main entrance.

Walking beside me, Colin replies. "I was worried about Clover being unresponsive to your advances. She always walks around with this air about her, like if you got within three feet of her, she'd kick your teeth in. But she's more affectionate than you are, which is fucking astonishing."

"I'm surprised myself. Clover flinched at first. But when she realized I needed to touch her, that I wanted to touch her, she melted into me. Now she's seeking me out. It was more than I hoped for."

"Well, keep those positive thoughts in your head today while we clean up Devon's mess. You're going to need them."

"I'm going to kill him," I warn, seething.

CHAPTER TWENTY-TWO

The Widower

"I just... I had to let her go. I couldn't go through it again," Auggie mutters hopelessly. With John Mason long dead and buried, I go from brother-figure to father-figure. The huge guy is resting his head in my lap, pretending not to sniffle.

I haven't even gone to see my son yet. It took over six hours to clean up the drug house Devon was camped out in. We found every drug known to man. The mushrooms scared the shit out of my cops. We didn't know if the kids were going to be violent, hallucinogenic, or passed out and docile. Lucky for us, they were dead to the world. Devon and Tina were spirited away by my family. That left Tommy and Taryn, and five unidentified idiots spanning teenager to forty.

Tommy Braxton's father was so sickened, he had me lock the kid in a holding cell until we make our way to the airport in the morning. Colin was torturing the boy by reading from the bible– the Reverend's idea. The Book of Revelation took on an amusing note with Colin's thick accent. Tommy was enjoying himself until the dry-heaves started. Reverend Braxton didn't appreciate Tommy's amusement, so he took up the reading in his practiced Baptist, raining Hellfire voice. Now Tommy is in a Hell of his own creation. I almost feel bad for the kid.

Mrs. Elsberry was annoyed when I told her I couldn't lock her minor daughter up with Tommy to share in the sermon. So I pretended I didn't help the kindly school teacher handcuff her fifteen-year-old daughter to a hospital bed. I wanted to assume Taryn's violent outbursts were drug-related, but Mrs. Elsberry said the girl became a demon at puberty, and that's why she wanted the jail cell preacher.

Fearing my own violent outburst, I'm in no rush to set eyes on my eldest child. I was hoping mindless tasks would calm me down. I went home to shower, check in with the kids, and pack Devon's bags. I even called the rehab facility, making sure the flights weren't delayed. Now I'm at the Spook House, listening to Auggie cry about his baby sister, how he put her on a bus but didn't say goodbye to her. Worse, as I hold Auggie, I can hear Willow weeping in the hallway, completely inconsolable, no matter what Robin tries to say to her.

Ren was so beside himself, the second I showed up here, he ran out. Rae had enough sense to text me to let me know Ren showed up at home, where he began destroying his and Devon's bedroom. Thank God, Weston is a huge boy– he stopped Ren from total annihilation. Not one of us is of sound mind at the moment. Every single one of us is throbbing like a sore tooth.

Isis is playing watch dog. Devon is so out of it, he doesn't even realize she's sitting in the room with him as he talks to himself.

The Spook House has turned into a goddamned insane asylum with the lunatics running the show.

"You did the right thing," I reassure Auggie for the billionth time over the past seven years of Tina's addiction spree. It's all Auggie has ever known. It's all Tina has ever known. My dad found Lisa and Auggie in a drug house similar to the one Devon was hiding out in for the past three days. Lisa was a drugged out teenager, and Auggie was a filthy, starving toddler. Dad was an imposing man, and even he couldn't keep Lisa clean.

The night my father died, Lisa told me she was pregnant with Tina, and she was high out of her mind. It was her way of keeping her bread buttered, since I took care of her until she moved on to another man. I've never told another soul, because no matter how hard I've pushed for a DNA test, I couldn't get one. But I've always wondered if Tina was my sister, even though Lisa denies it. The thought makes me want to puke for my sons' sakes, but I'll be finding out sooner rather than later.

Auggie tried for years to get his mother and sister help. But when Tina was a minor, Lisa would check them both out of the facilities. When Tina reached the age of majority, they just walked out after Auggie paid thousands of dollars to get them clean. Lisa met Patrick at her last treatment facility, and she got clean and stayed clean when they married. Only problem was, no one could keep Tina in treatment, no matter how badly we tried.

I made a deal with our local judge, waiting for Tina to commit a punishable crime. Earlier today, Patrick was made Tina's Guardian Ad Litem, placing her well-being under his care. The deal I have with Patrick was contingent on a DNA test. If

Tina couldn't sign herself out of rehab, Patrick would get that test for me. If Tina is my sister, I can bypass all that legal shit with Patrick and Lisa, and make sure Tina gets the care she needs. If it's negative, I won't throw up.

No one knows this but me.

"Tina's in safe hands. If the man who performed the miracle on your mother can't get Tina clean, no one can." I rock Auggie slightly, trying not to laugh over the parallels. I'm probably talking about my own sister, to her brother, while my own kid is detoxing a few doors down.

"Tina was such a beautiful child, so lively and smart." Sounding dreamy, like Auggie's caught in the past, "her white hair sparkled when she'd run around, giggling my name. I miss that." Auggie's voice warps, going from loving to demented. "Why'd Tina have to turn into Mom? Why'd she have to turn into a drug addict whore? There's no help for her now. There's no fixing her. Tina's tainted."

"Well," I sigh. "That's refreshing and soothing and hopeful. I think I'll go get the wailing teenager to sit with you if you're going to talk like that. You two can feed off each other's miseries while I try to fix this shit into something worth living."

I stand up from the sofa abruptly, causing Auggie's head to smash into the wooden frame. "Your sister never had a father. You are Tina's brother, but that wasn't good enough because girls need a dad. Let Patrick father Tina and see what happens. Just because she's shot up and screwed a bunch of guys, it doesn't make her tainted," I defend Tina's honor. There is no such thing as two types of women: good girls and whores. They are all human beings.

"No one worth anything will ever marry Tina," Auggie snarls, not looking like himself at all. Monstrous.

"Patrick married your mom, and he's an intelligent, strong, and caring man. Why can't Tina have that?"

"Something must be wrong with Patrick," is Auggie's answer.

At the end of my patience, "What's wrong with my sister then?" I bait Auggie.

"Nothing," Auggie squeaks out, confused.

"Then why is Isis with a whore of a man? You treat your body like a sewer plant. You treat my sister like she's untouchable while you taint yourself with countless used holes. Then you tried to take Willow and use her too."

"No!" Auggie shouts, getting pissed because he knows I'm right. "I wasn't going to use Willow like that. She's a good girl."

"No, you were just going to use Willow as the lifetime replacement for John Mason's baby girl and Willow's own uncle." Lashing out because I have to, "Get over yourself. Clean yourself up. Quit wallowing in your own shit. Quit blaming Tina for the shit life Lisa and you and me and Dad gave her. Let Tina heal in peace. Lastly, quit making your mother and your sister feel like trash. Maybe they'd stop acting like trash if the most important man in their lives treated them with the respect they deserve."

I turn to leave the room, pissed off that I'm now worked up before I witness what Devon did to himself. "Where are you going?" Auggie shouts at me as he lunges to his feet.

"I'm going to go tell your boyfriend to send in his replacement part. Maybe your security blanket can talk some sense into you, jackass! Then I'm going to go sit with your girlfriend, as we watch my son begin the detox process. Maybe by then you can get over yourself enough to help your loved ones through the shit they're going through, instead of acting like a spoiled little bitch."

Auggie grabs my hand, stopping me from leaving. "What did I say to piss you off? I've never pissed you off before."

"Lisa is someone's daughter– *your* mother," I stress. "Tina is someone's daughter– *your* sister. Every person on this planet means something to someone. I think of my daughter and my sister, and then I hear this hypocritical asshole saying bad shit about them, and I want to hurt someone. Now, I have to go see my son, who has fucked around and done drugs and lied and stole. Devon has committed the same egregious shit as Lisa and Tina, yet you respect him and not them. Once you figure out why I'm pissed, we'll revisit this conversation. Not all of John Mason's rules are sound. At some point, I'd hoped you'd start listening to me instead of a dead man."

"Mal-colm," Auggie draws out my name like he did when he was a little kid. "Wait. I'm sorry!"

Going out into the hallway, I say, "I'll send you Willow. You can comfort each other, because none of the rest of us have the energy to do it."

"She never came to see me," Devon says over and over again while rocking back and forth on Willow's bed. Scattered around him are the horrific reminders of what he's done. Dozens and dozens of crisp, detailed images from the past and this afternoon. Willow earned my undying devotion and respect by her tough love approach with Devon.

Images of Devon's spiral into hell: drugs, filth, garbage, and sickly-looking naked bodies covered in vomit and body fluids. Those were bad enough, but it's the happy pictures that have my son crying despondently. Images of all of us: Me, Isis, Auggie, Robin, Clover, Ginny, Kieren, Devon, Raven, Weston, Violet, Seth, Essie, and Willow. Some are group shots from the past few months of happier times. The surprising pictures are copies of Camille when the kids were babies and yearbook photos of Devon and Essie during high school.

Willow dealt the biggest guilt trip I've ever witnessed.

Isis is at the end of her rope after sitting in this room, guarding the door for almost seven hours. "Let me get this straight: you're upset that Willow said she'd come visit you, yet didn't? You, who broke every promise you've ever made, is upset that the girl was dishonest?"

"Yes," Devon shouts at us, looking unhinged. His blue eyes are as black as coal. His usually pink skin is a sickly gray. No longer able to hide behind sweatshirts, because he's refusing to dress in the clothing I brought him, his shrunken body is on display. Months of emaciating himself with drugs is obvious, along with the track marks on his inner elbows.

With a burst of energy I didn't think him capable, Dev lunges from the bed, picture gripped in his hand. He begins pacing around the room like a caged animal– a wild and out-of-control animal.

"Put some clothes on," Isis snarls at Dev when he walks in front of where we're sitting on the floor against the door, blocking his exit. "I'm sick of looking at your naked ass. It's making me sick."

Devon whips around and snaps his teeth at us. My gaze flicks to the image clutched in his hand– a photograph of Willow, Ren, and Devon, showing the three of them laughing together.

"What did you need to tell Willow? Maybe I can tell her for you," I try to negotiate with my son. His eyes narrow in suspicion, catching on immediately since we received the same exact training.

"It's private," Devon grumbles. Eyes wildly flicking around Willow's bedroom, something catches his attention. He stalks over to the girl's dresser. I huff in a sharp breath when he lifts a pair of silk boxers off the top of the dresser. Isis, noticing the tension in every muscle in Devon's body, reaches out to take my hand. "NOOOOOOOOOOOOOOO!" Devon bellows in rage, shredding the fabric in his hands as if it were made of tissue paper.

I'm easy to make emotional, but even the strongest among us starts to cry next to me as Devon goes insane with grief. Isis chokes every time she tries to draw breath. I don't move to comfort anyone in the room. It's too late for that.

Heavily panting with scraps of fabric clinging to his sweaty chest, "Well, I guess that settles that, now doesn't it?" Devon says to himself calmly. "Ren's boxers on Willow's dresser, smelling like both of them." Homicidal with rage, Dev whips around and pierces us with his glare. "Did Willow ever even want me?"

Devon and Isis are cut from the same cloth. Isis screams, "You cheated on Willow, you selfish sonofabitch! If you didn't want to share Willow with your brother, then you shouldn't have thrown her in the trash!"

Shouting back at his aunt, "I did it for Willow, you stupid cunt! I needed to get her the fuck away from me before I dragged her ass down with me. I didn't mean to cheat on her, no matter what I told her. That's why I need to talk to Willow, to tell her I didn't mean a goddamned thing I said that night. I! Didn't! Mean! It!"

"Then why did you fuck Tina? Taryn? Are you a child molester now? That girl is barely fifteen! She goes to school with Weston, for Christ's sake," Isis snaps. When she tries to rise to her feet, I yank her back down to me. Isis fights me like a wild animal. After a struggle, I have to grip Isis with my thighs, holding her on my lap.

"What?" Devon whispers, breathless. "No," he shakes his head in denial. "No. No, I wouldn't do that. Are you insane? I haven't touched anyone. I'm a drug addict. The only thing I give a shit about is getting high. We were naked because we got the sweats."

"And the semen?" Isis shrieks.

Smirking like an escapee from the Spook House lunatic asylum, Dev rasps shamelessly in a dreamy voice, "A pleasurable reaction to having the best high of my life."

I just close my eyes and sigh heavily. Some things you can't unsee or unhear or unlearn, and this is one of them. No father should ever see the junkie gazing out their son's eyes.

"I've only had sex with Willow and Essie. I'm a drug addict, not a moron." Dev has the audacity to look at us like we are the ones who are insane for thinking otherwise. "John Mason didn't leave any rules about drugs, but he left some very clear cut ones about sex. You don't fuck who you don't want to keep. If I was that into sex, I'd just become the cocksucking king like Auggie."

Some things are a trigger for Isis, and treating women without respect is one of them. "What? You a polygamist now? Willow *and* Essie? And you're pissed that Willow's dating your brother, actually dating him? Ren would never treat Willow the way you have. You don't deserve her."

"Isis, please don't incite him," I whisper into her ear, close to begging. "Dev isn't in there. Can't you see that? Your nephew isn't in this room with us."

"I left Willow for her own good, doesn't mean I don't love her. It means I love her that much. Why do you think I'm carrying this photo around?" Devon crouches down and retrieves the picture from where it fell to his feet when he went insane on Ren's boxers. "I love them both that much. Don't you get it?" Sounding like a lost little boy, Devon turns to us.

Isis relaxes, but I don't. I believe some of what Devon says is truth, but it's buried deeply. This is manipulation, pure and simple.

"I told Willow I never loved her. I told her I never wanted her. I told her she was just practice for a real woman," Devon admits, causing Isis to suck in a sharp breath, like hearing that physically assaulted her. "I need to tell Willow I was lying to protect her. I don't want her thinking that when it's not true."

"Devon?" I call out in a calm voice. "What good will that do? You'll only confuse Willow more. Do you want that? Do you want to hurt your brother? Willow and Ren are together now, like *together*," I stress. "Maybe after you get out of rehab, after everyone is feeling better, you can explain why you said what you said and why you did what you did."

Crestfallen, Devon breathes out, "But I love her. I want her." His voice is filled with pure pain.

"Son, listen to yourself. Everything you said is about you. If you really love Willow, you'll let her go. You'll let her figure out who she loves and who she wants. Don't do to Willow what Auggie was doing. Let Willow find out for herself."

"What if Willow falls in love with Ren while I'm away? If she doesn't know, it'll be easier for her to forget about me."

I want to tell my son the truth. Willow is better off without him. Right now, Devon is toxic to everyone, especially to himself. Willow doesn't need Devon warping her view of the truth, making her see things from his twisted perception. I love my children enough to want the best for them, even if it hurts them.

"Trust me," Isis says. "Willow doesn't have a snowball's chance in hell of forgetting about you. I don't think you realize how much our lives revolve around your well-being." Isis tugs at my arms until I relax my grip. She slides off my lap to sit next to me again.

The warped little fuck, known as Devon, loves the truth that Isis revealed. Devon puffs his boney chest out, and then rewards us by finally putting on some duds. I breathe a sigh of relief when his privates are fully covered by a pair of workout pants. I almost vomited when Devon got aroused during his '*I love drugs*' speech.

"I need to see Willow," Devon says after he's fully dressed in a pair of pants and a sweatshirt. "I'll promise to go to rehab if one of you will go get her for me." He smiles sweetly, looking like a serial killer.

"Sure, I'll go get her, just give me a second," Isis agrees as she rises.

"Are you insane?" I shout. "How can you not see through this bullshit?"

"I *said*, I'll be right back." Isis tosses me a look as she opens the bedroom door, a look I can't decipher.

"You need treatment," I say the second Isis shuts the door. "No manipulations. No negotiation. No lies. Nothing will stop your trip to rehab," I warn. "You can smile sweetly and tell us what you think we want to hear, but I'm not buying it."

"Don't you think I don't already fucking know that?" Dev snarls at me, sounding like a demon from a horror flick. "I'm going, and I'm going to hate it. There is still a part of me in here,"

Devon fists his chest. "That part of me wants to go. But the biggest part wants to run you over to get out that door, and once I was free, I'd go find some more drugs. Which part do you think is winning?"

Scared, I say as if I'm not, "I'm not going to answer that, Devon."

A knock on the door at my back startles the shit out of me. "I brought her, Devon," Isis says through the wooden barrier.

"I don't think that's wise, Isis," I warn, noticing the evil, calculating light shining in Devon's eyes. I don't know if Devon wants or loves Willow or not, but that larger, drug-craving side of him wants to ruin his brother just for the pain of it, and then drag Willow down with him. Misery loves company. I can see that much, and Devon knows I can see it, too.

"It's okay," Isis assures me, so I step away from the door. What happens next scares the shit out of me.

"I thought you went home," I mutter to Ren as he enters Willow's bedroom, followed by Auggie and Robin, with no Isis or Willow in sight.

"I came to check in with everyone," Ren says in a cold voice. "I'm glad I did." He turns to his brother. "You're going to rehab, no matter what." What started out matter-of-factly, ends up sounding like a menacing growl.

"You fucked her," Devon accuses, fists clenched at his sides, readying for attack.

"No," Ren says, not looking concerned at all. Confused, Devon looks at the remnants of Ren's boxer shorts confetti. Ren clears up the confusion, "Willow and I made love last night while you were too busy getting high with Auggie's sister and a bunch of high school kids."

My sons lunge at one another, and I learn that Robin and Auggie aren't here to protect us from Devon. They are here to stop me. Arms wrenched behind my back, Auggie breathes into my ear, "Mason rules, remember? Let Ren do what needs to be done."

"Auggie, you motherfucker," I snarl, struggling to get away from the huge guy. "Let go of me! They're going to kill one another!"

High out of his mind, filled with hatred and frustration, Devon goes after Ren, and Ren meets Devon halfway. They fall to the ground in a seething ball of flailing arms and legs. The sound of fists meeting flesh makes me sick to my stomach. These are my children beating each other to death, my first born.

"I'm going to be sick," I warn Auggie as my legs give out beneath me.

"Wait," Auggie cries out, catching me. "It's going to be okay. Just wait. Take a deep breath."

"I've got him," Ren shouts to someone while straddling his brother's chest. I blink a few times to clear what I'm seeing. Rob stalks across the floor. Sometimes happy, sometimes somber, the artist is always calm. But not this early morning. Robin kneels beside my fallen son, and spits directly into Devon's face.

"You are one sick sonofabitch," Rob sneers. "If you see Willow before your ass lands on that plane, you will keep your goddamned mouth shut about anything other than promising to stop taking drugs. You can tell Willow goodbye and that you love her. Not another goddamned word. Anything else, and you'll wish I would've killed you instead."

"Killed me?" Devon repeats Rob's words back to him. "Huh?" he grunts.

"This is for Willow," Rob warns a split second before his fist flies out to connect with my son's jaw. The crack is loud like a gunshot, reverberating in my ears. "This is for Essie," is said with another strike to the face. "And this is for calling Isis a cunt!" knocks my son unconscious.

I just watch in awe as Auggie holds me on my feet. At first I think Auggie is shaking from the adrenaline rush of watching Rob attack someone for the first time in his life, but then I realize Auggie is silently laughing.

"Well," Rob says as he stands from his crouch. "I feel better now. God," Rob groans as he rubs his bruised hand, "I feel so much better."

"Did you break your hand?" Ren asks as he slaps at his brother's cheeks, making sure Devon's TKOed.

"Yup, pretty sure I did," Rob replies immediately, sounding proud of himself.

"Seriously? You work with your hands, you dumbfuck," Auggie growls from behind me. He slowly releases his hold on my arms, making sure I don't fall to my knees. Auggie steps away, warning, "If we lose this newest commission because you had to pay the kid back…"

"Shut it, Aug," Rob fires off. "Dev will be easier to deal with now that he's passed out. The closer to departure time, the worse

Devon would have been with the manipulation. Malcolm, I'd handcuff him while he's passed out, if I were you. If Willow shows up at your house to say goodbye, uncuff him. Contrary to what we may think, the dumbass loves her, so Dev will behave around her. No matter what, that part of Devon will control the part that's been driving the crazy train."

"I'm not leaving them alone together," Ren warns. "Not after what I just heard this ass saying in here. I won't share– ever."

Grinning, a pair of handcuffs materialize from Auggie's back pocket. "How about some poetic justice," he says as he tosses Ren the cuffs. "Restrain Devon with his own set."

Emotionally, mentally, and physically exhausted, I ass-plant to the floor, and then close my eyes. "Kill me," I tell the owner of the small hands that tried to catch me. I pull my sister into my lap, hugging her, and then I start to cry... and then I start to laugh.

The newest inductee of the Spook House's lunatic asylum.

My eyes open slowly, taking in everything happening around me. Ren hoists Devon over his shoulder, just as Dev begins to wake. Devon starts spewing, "Let me down! I'm going to tear your dick and balls off. Let's see if you can fuck Willow without 'em."

Ren laughs out, "I'd like to see you try, bitch," and then he walks out the door with a struggling bundle heaped over his shoulder.

"I don't think it's broken," Auggie is mumbling to Robin, while nuzzling Rob's injured hand with his lips. "Nice right hook you've got there."

A groan is torn from my throat as I watch Auggie moon over Robin. "Those assholes belong to you? Are you fucking kidding me, Isis?"

"I was born into this family, do you really expect anything different? We're not normal," Isis says, but she sounds proud over the fact. "I'd tell you to let Clover in on that secret, but two of our idiots belong to her."

Idiot one's tonsils are being stroked by Auggie's tongue, while idiot two is crying her eyes out downstairs. Yeah, Clover will fit in just fine with the rest of the lunatics.

"Pull me to my feet," I order Isis. "I gotta get out of here before they start screwing. I've never seen it, and nor do I want to."

"It's a nice sight," Isis says, and she's not being sarcastic.

"Yeah, ya better go. You're the one driving Devon to the airport."

"Oh, joy," I turn sarcastic instead.

CHAPTER TWENTY-THREE

The Widow

Half-awake, half-asleep. I lie in bed, enjoying the last few vestiges of comfort before I'm thrust back into reality. Life hasn't exactly been easy lately, so I'll take the reprieve where I can get it. Plus, nothing is more entertaining than dreaming of Malcolm and his kid cereal fetish: Lucky Charms and Trix.

Silly Rabbit.

No longer able to delay the inevitable, my eyelids crack open on their own. "Ahhhhh!" I gasp roughly, heart stalling in my chest. A stunning black-haired harlot is inches from my face, staring intently into my eyes. "You're not here to kill me, are you?"

"No," Isis breathes creepily. "You need to get to the airport."

Shuffling backward toward the headboard to get farther away from Isis, I mutter, "Why?"

"Oh. My. God," Isis drawls out as she reaches to flick on my table lamp. "You really are Willow's mother. What's up with the Mason men loving daft pussy?"

I clutch my sheets to my chest, trying to reason out why the hell Isis is standing in the middle of my bedroom and how the fuck she got in here. But those questions don't spew from my lips. Instead, I sound like an idiot. "I'm not stupid. I'll have you know, my IQ is one hundred and twenty six."

"Wow, that high?" Isis pretends to be impressed by simultaneously insulting me. "Sucks to be you, doesn't it? Missed the genius mark by four lousy points. Maybe if Dave and Mary would've laid off the Mary Jane, you would've tipped over into Mensa territory."

And whoever says Willow is sarcastic obviously hasn't met Isis Mason. "Yeah, well, what's your IQ?"

Already bored with me, Isis flashes me a look like I'm shit on the bottom of her stiletto. "How the fuck should I know? And why the fuck should I care? I barely went to high school, let alone college."

"Didn't you want to learn?" I ask as I try to figure out how to get out of bed without Isis seeing my nightgown. Now I understand how Ginny feels around me sometimes. Lord knows, how Ginny feels around Isis.

Snooping in my dresser drawers, Isis replies with a snarky tone. "Learn about what? Art Appreciation? I can ask Robin or Auggie about that– real artists who work in art. Music Appreciation? Instead of asking some professor who never leaves his lectern, I can go ask Jackson Stone."

Fingering my panties with too much interest, "Drop that," I blurt out at Isis.

Ignoring me, Isis begins sorting through my intimates. "Carpe Diem they teach. I don't need some asshole telling me about life when I could just go live it. You know what they say: *those who can't, teach.*"

I spy my robe, so I inch closer to it, hoping to cover my ugly nightgown. "You seem very bitter about this subject, Isis. I enjoyed my studies."

Just as my fingers come in contact with my bathrobe, Isis yanks it away, throwing it to the floor like it's trash. "Yeah, well, those assholes took my money to hit on me."

"You *are* stunning," I say with great appreciation. Isis is perfect in all ways: silky black hair that softly waves. Dark blue eyes that intensify to black with deep emotion. Killer curves that cinch into an impossibly narrow waist.

"I can't help how I look any more than you can, Clover." Isis looks like she's about to cry, so I forget all about my ratty-old nightgown and move to comfort her. "So what if people like looking at me? Just because I've got nice tits and a perfect ass doesn't mean my head is empty. I was paying teachers to fill my empty head, not to get head."

Horrified, I mutter, "How old were you?"

"Seventeen," Isis says matter-of-factly as she picks out a pair of panties, a matching bra, and a pair of thigh-highs. All my best intimates.

"Oh, Isis," I cry out, reaching for her hand.

"No pity, bitch!" Isis snaps at me, avoiding my touch. "It wasn't one professor, either. It was four, and five high school teachers– one was a woman. Everywhere I go, all everyone sees is a piece of ass. It's annoying."

Being around Isis is like watching a movie or reading a really intriguing book. It's surreal. I never thought about how it would be to actually be Isis. We all either want to be her or be with her, not realizing how lonely it must be to actually be Isis. "What'd you do?"

Heading toward my closet, Isis says flippantly over her shoulder, "I bet you think I went to Auggie or Malcolm, don't you?"

"It's what I would have done if I were in your position." I clutch the undergarments Isis chose for me, confused as to why she's dressing me this morning. An ice blue demi-bra with matching panties. It's not as if Isis and I were ever close. She's as hard to get near as I am.

"Carpe Diem," Isis says with a flair for the dramatic. "I slit their tires, put lipstick on the collars of their jackets, and called their wives, telling them to get checked for the STD their husbands transmitted to me. I'm a motherfucking Mason. You don't fuck with this bitch."

"Wow! You're very scary when you want to be," I murmur in awe.

Peeking her head out of my closet, Isis says, "Get that disgusting cotton contraption off your body and toss it in the trash. My brother deserves better than that. I will say you have the most excellent taste in underthings, though."

"I… I didn't buy them." I mutter, hoping to God Isis can't hear, "Ginny gifted them to me."

"Malcolm won't like that…" heavy pause. "At all. It's like a fucking *Salvation Army* in your closet. Don't you have anything that isn't ten years out-of-date office drab?"

"Um… no," I grumble, completely offended. "And most of it did come from the *Salvation Army*. I'd rather the kids have up-to-date clothes. It's not like it's a popularity contest over at the Courthouse."

"You shittin' me?" Isis looks completely floored, her dark eyes bugging out of their sockets. "Rob needs his ass kicked something fierce. It's his job to take care of you since Dave is struggling as it is. The ass."

"Take care of me?" I growl beneath my breath. "Remember how you needed no help with your pervert teachers? Well, I will not be beholden to my baby brother."

"Clover," Isis drags out my name like I'm exhausting her. She tosses an acceptable blouse out of my closet, hitting me in the chest with it. "What kind of man lets his sister walk around like a fuckin' pauper when he's got more than enough to spread around? Rob's already floating Prynne Renovations."

"Great," I drawl out sarcastically. "So my parents and I are leeching off of Robin. Lovely."

"It's not like Rob's out anything. We're basically living off Auggie ourselves, while we do our own thing. I mean, we work for it, but the three of us are financially independent. Even after that, Malcolm shoves cash at me like I still need an allowance. I buy Rae shit with it."

"I'm fine on my own. You can spend Rob's money," I grumble. I try to figure out how to put my bra on without taking off my nightgown. Isis isn't going to leave so I can get dressed in peace. "About that," I turn inquisitive. "How come you've never married my brother? I know Rob's asked you a bunch of times."

Holding a skirt up to her hips, Isis checks to see if it's tight enough. "You're what? A size two? Four? Why is this an eight? It'd almost fit me. I need a distraction. While you're gone this morning, I'm emptying your fuckin' closet out."

"Please, don't," I'm not too proud to beg. "Why am I going to the airport, anyway?"

Ignoring me, Isis answers my earlier question. "Robin has asked me to marry him time and time again, but never formally. Never on bended knee with a ring or anything."

Isis yanks my nightgown over my head, and then rips it down the middle. The worn-out, paper-thin fabric tears easily. "Now, get dressed," she orders in a take-no-prisoner's voice.

"Is that what's holding you back? Robin isn't romantic enough?" I ask Isis uncomfortable questions since she's making me uncomfortable with her scrutinizing gaze staring at my palm-covered tits.

"No," Isis contemplates the question for a long moment while she watches me put on the bra, and then button up my best blouse. "Not really. Auggie."

Taken aback, my fingers still on the next to the last button. "You want to marry Auggie?"

Isis just shrugs like her admission isn't huge. Auggie and Isis get along like menstrual blood on white pants during junior high. "We've all talked about it. Whoever has the most to lose is the one who marries me, with the other signing papers for partnership rights. Robin and Auggie are talented, and they have a lot of money. I'm just a nightclub manager, so my earnings come straight from Auggie anyway. We have to do this right to protect our asses."

Sifting through all the excess bullshit, "Let me get this straight: you guys are all together, like you and Rob, and you and Auggie? They share you?"

Handing me my shortest, tightest skirt, Isis insults me again. "Daft. Share me? I share *them*," she stresses like I'm an idiot. "Me and Rob, me and Auggie, Rob and Auggie, and me, Rob, and Auggie. If doesn't matter what order you put the ingredients, it's still a sandwich."

"Jesus Christ, almighty!" I shout as I jump off my bed. "What?"

Isis palms the center of my chest, pushing my ass to the mattress. "Oh, simmer down. I don't find it weird because it's all I've ever known."

"What the fuck was up with my daughter?" I shout in outrage. "Auggie was fucking around with Willow while he was screwing you and Rob? Talk about keeping it in the fucking family, you perverted deviants!"

I cross the room in two strides, trying to get to the bathroom before I'm physically sick. Isis steps in my way, blocking my exit. "MOVE. IT!" I growl.

"Wait," Isis implores as she wraps her fingers around my upper arms. "Auggie's going through some shit, and Willow was a stumbling block."

"Stumbling block? What the fuck is that supposed to mean? The man who screws my brother was touching my daughter. Excuse me while I go get a tire iron. I have a dick to pulverize," I grit out fiercely.

"Auggie hadn't touched Rob in years. *After* Willow, Auggie reconnected with Robin." Her voice takes on a pleading note.

"Explain it to me, or else I go and destroy both men. I don't give a fuck if Robin is my brother or not, I'll take him down for harming my daughter."

All energy fleeing, Isis sags against me. "Just sit for a second, okay? I'll explain. I don't want anyone to know. Not even Malcolm knows, okay?"

Isis had me on '*not even Malcolm knows*.' I numbly walk across the room to sit at the foot of my bed. "Talk," I demand.

"We were going to get married," Isis admits as she paces in front of me, making sure I can't get out of my own bedroom. "Auggie and I. We had the marriage license and everything. I was pregnant."

In a fog of '*What the fuck*', I blurt out, "What? When? What happened?"

"Ectopic Pregnancy," Isis says without emotion. "I even lost a fallopian tube. It was four years ago, back when all was going good."

"Isis," I cry out, reaching for her hand. Yet again, she avoids touching me. "Whose baby was it?"

Refusing to look at me, Isis faces my bedroom door. "Auggie's. Rob was in New York for a showing at an art gallery. My cycle was off, and we weren't. Needless to say, Auggie didn't react well to the news." In a voice devoid of life, Isis breaths out, "Auggie blames me. He hasn't touched me since."

Isis flips around to face me so quickly that I gasp out in shock. "Auggie went a bit crazy after that. Saying a whore's son shouldn't breed. Auggie said he was tainted, and he tainted me. After that, he fucked anybody who would have him over the age of eighteen." Isis stresses, "Everyone *but* Rob and me."

"Willow?" I breathe out.

"Rob and I hated it. To say we were sick with grief would be an understatement. The day Auggie set his sights on Willow is the day he stopped fucking everything with a pulse. So we shut the hell up and dealt with it in any way we could. My nephews were who we used to stop the imminent disaster. Now those idiots are fighting over Willow like lions after a carcass."

I've seen that look in Isis's eyes before. I've seen it gazing out at me from my bathroom mirror since I was sixteen-years-old. Grief. "And you?"

"Discarded," Isis admits emotionlessly. "Rob's in Auggie's house, and most of the time in his bed. Neither one touches me. They say they don't want to hurt me again, like I'm spun of fucking glass or some shit. But–" Isis trails her hands along her body. "What good is it to look like I do, when the two bastards you want, don't want you back?"

I try to grab Isis's hand before she can get away, but Isis is quick like a snake. "Isis, c'mere. Please," I beg.

"I don't need pitied. It is what it is. I know they *want* me. Rob's stubborn, and Auggie is stuck on my dad's rules. All we can do is live the life we were dealt, right?" Isis bites her lip, like she's holding in something she wants to say. Instead she says, "Finish getting dressed, and wear your hair down. You're not a ninety-year-old librarian. Make yourself pretty for Malcolm, he'll need the distraction."

"What's going on?" I ask lamely.

"Malcolm's at the airport, waiting on Devon's flight. He's going to be a mess afterward. Malcolm will need you. So I'm driving your ass there, and you can drive him home. I'll go make sure your kids know to get themselves ready for school. Ren will take them."

Long minutes later, I'm still sitting at the foot of my bed, lost in thought. You never know what's going on someone else's lives. Stunning Isis is miserable, and I can't ignore it.

CHAPTER TWENTY-FOUR

The Widower

In order to survive, I must channel my father. John Mason was a cold yet fair man. Right now I need his strength to soldier forth. I know after the death of my mother, then my father, and then my wife, it took everything in me to put one foot in front of the other. Each step brought me farther from the pain and closer to normalcy. If you play pretend long enough, it becomes reality.

My family members were no longer living and breathing, able to interact with me, and the loss was debilitating. I did what had needed to be done, because I had people counting on me. I thought their deaths were the worst times I would ever live through, until the day when my own child broke.

Anyone who is a parent knows we don't know what the hell we're doing. Every year we get older, every new experience gains us wisdom, but every challenge that is thrown in our path is something we don't know how to overcome. There is no handbook. A list of rules doesn't magically appear in our minds when our child takes their first breath. In a way, I'm as unsure at almost forty as I was as a teenager. I'm no different in my mind, just a bit more world-weary and a lot less confident. The invincible feeling burns out the longer we live. The worse our experiences, the quicker the flame consumes the wick.

What would John Mason do? That is the eternal question Auggie, Isis, and I ask every time we reach something that is insurmountable. Answer: live as if nothing has happened. It's not denial. It's refusing to allow emotions to dictate your life. The only problem with this solution, I am a man with a great wealth of emotions.

For me, my sister and Auggie, and my eldest children, we are a team. I don't differentiate over our ages. I am almost thirty-nine, Auggie and Isis just aged another year older at twenty-nine, and my sons, Devon is weeks shy of his twenty-first birthday, and Kieren just turned nineteen. My father said you were an adult when you had responsibilities. So by all accounts, we are even. By the time I was seventeen, I was a husband with a pregnant wife, the guardian of my eight-year-old sister, the provider to my father's woman and her eight-year-old son, Auggie. I owned a home and was training to become a police officer. I was a boy living in a man's world, growing up alongside my own children.

Overwrought with emotions, to the point that I am physically shaking, I stare at my eldest son and wonder where I went wrong. At what point did I misstep. I provided Devon with the same code of ethics that has worked well for three generations of Masons, yet it backfired for my son. The code taught us how to deal with the stress when shit out of our control happened. Nothing can stop these occurrences. You just have to have the right tools to survive the fallout.

I provided the tools and tried to circumvent the catastrophes. I've tried everything I could imagine to help my children. Ignoring the problem exacerbated it. Addressing the problem only made my sons clam up and resent me. Years upon years of three sessions a week of family and personal therapy changed nothing. John Mason's *pretend normal until it is normal* worked the best for my children. I encouraged them, fed their talents and passions, was firm when boundaries were necessary and soft when need be. When a problem arose, I immediately had a plan of attack. I watched my children for any variant in their behavior that would be alarming, and I somehow missed all the telltale signs Devon was undoubtedly exhibiting.

My current plan of attack: the Sedona Healing, Health, and Well-being Residential Rehabilitation Treatment Center for Addiction. They specialize in healing all aspects of self: psychological, emotional, physiological, spiritual, while offering specialized care in re-entering everyday life upon exiting their treatment program. This isn't a sixty-day program– it's a forever lifestyle choice. The administrator claims the constant sunshine is something you couldn't ignore. It chases the darkness away so you can no longer hide in the shadows of your guilt, shame, and regret.

If rehab doesn't work, I'm not above shackling Devon in the basement and having his siblings bring him daily rations. I refuse to live a life like Auggie. Lisa and Tina spent the better part of their lives in rehab, draining Auggie's bank accounts as much as his soul.

The din of the airport barely registers as I imprint my son's visage into memory. I want to remember this moment for the rest of my life because Devon is incapable. Strung out, burnt out, wigging out– pick a term for how my son has destroyed himself. Gray skin limply covering emaciated flesh. Lifeless eyes staring into an abyss. Quivering, starved muscles protesting their lack of sustenance, either food or drug. This man-child is nothing but a shell of his former self– an empty husk. The Devon we all knew and loved is a ghost.

In my quest to feed, clothe, and house my children, I had to take the position of Fairport Chief of Police, taking valuable time from our family life. I didn't think it would put our futures at risk, especially since the very child who fucked up was the one who was shoved up my ass eighteen hours a day, with ten of those hours driving around in a squad car with either me or Colin McGregor, or sitting at the station with no less than five police officers at any given time. Proof that you can never underestimate the determination of an addict, and the very reason I'm purchasing the makings of a shackle when I drive by the nearest home improvement store.

All around us, happy families board planes to exciting destinations and businessmen travel to where the work is done. Here we sit, three desperate parents with expressions of horror on our faces as the SHHWRRTCFA administrator drones on about the benefits of their rehabilitation program. Not paying attention, I assume he's boasting about the sheer length of his program's name, because clearly the longer your title, the level of sobriety it requires to decipher the acronym rises. But no one is listening because we are too busy trying to figure out where we went wrong, how we broke our children.

It's like a sick joke: a Baptist minister, Fairport's Chief of Police, and an elementary school teacher walk into a bar, no doubt looking for their wayward children, only to discover they are camped out in drug den– together.

Our backgrounds just prove how drugs do not discriminate. No child is safe. No parent should be unaware. No matter how hard you try, drugs will infect your family, your schools, and your community like a cancer that can't be cured. The administrator says it's not our fault. Some people are genetically predisposed to become addicted. While one person can use recreationally for life and never become addicted, others will be addicted by the very first taste. Just as a drug's influence depends on the user, the addiction depends on its host.

Devon, Tommy, and Taryn sit here, unrepentant over their three-day bender. These three idiots, who are going off to rehab together like it's fucking summer camp in sunny Sedona, Arizona, for a fun-filled sixty days of relaxation.

Sitting in plastic chairs molded specifically to be torture devices of discomfort, the parents are on one side with their children on the other. The administrator paces in between us, spewing the virtues of clean living. We are all engaged in a silent battle of wills: desperate parents against our tweaking adult-children. The only difference in our sides of war: there is a wall of security standing behind the kids, making sure they don't make a run for it. The handcuffs weren't removed until security was put into place.

Mrs. Elsberry is the sobbing woman sitting next to me on my right. A gentle music teacher who has taught all of my children how to– musical stuff? I'm not entirely sure what goes on in her classroom, but I can only assume it wasn't teaching her fifteen-year-old daughter how to shoot up heroin. Across from the mother is the quietly plotting Taryn Elsberry. She is a bright child with hair the shade of a Manson follower– Chuck, not Marilyn. Yesterday I took one look at the girl who used to sell me Girl Scout cookies, and I wanted to send her off to federal prison. It takes a lot to frighten me after my stint as an undercover cop in Boston. The feral glow in her dead eyes is tainted with evil. Even the security guards are leery of this young woman. Out of the three addicts, Taryn is the only one who has two hands holding her firmly into her seat.

On my left is Tom Braxton, Fairport's minister, who is white-knuckling his tiny bible while trying to pray loud enough for his son to overhear. I'm not a Baptist, but eternal fire is universal in any religion. Tommy Braxton is suffering. The nineteen-year-old is nearly unconscious with his head drooped over his puke bucket. It's going to be a long flight for young Tommy and those sitting within smelling distance.

The combination of an hour of gospel from an angry, fiery pits of Hell minister, the administrator who hasn't stopped his sales pitch, and the stench and sound as another wave of nausea overpowers Tommy, Taryn finally snaps, and I want to join her. One hundred and forty pounds of drug-fueled child tries to free herself from the grasp of her captor. I lean forward, ready to take

Taryn to the floor if she breaks free. I'd take any distraction to exit my own personal hell, even if it meant restraining a pudgy, angry girl.

"You cunt!" Taryn shrieks, hazel eyes bugging out of her skull with fury. "I hate your fucking guts, *Mother*! How could you do this to me? You promised! YOU PROMISED!" is released from her tiny throat with enough force to break glass.

My hands cup my ears, stemming the sound. My control is about to slip. Instead of the child feeling betrayed for being shipped off to rehab, this parent wants to scream at their unresponsive child. I want to stand over my eldest son and roar, *"I gave you life, and you try to end it like your goddamned, worthless, coward of a mother. What the fuck is wrong with you? What did I do wrong? What. The. Fuck. Did. I. Do. Wrong?"*

Silence.

The radius around us in the busy airport is dead silent.

Dead silence. Yet my ears ring and my throat burns, because *I* wasn't silent. I find myself standing over my son, muscles tense, jaw and fists clenched, lungs heaving as I struggle to control myself.

"I'm sorry," I mutter out in shame. A sob builds when Devon doesn't even blink. My son never heard me rage against him. Never responded to his own father's howl of need. Defeated, I retake my seat, refusing to look at my son out of a mix of guilt and anger.

"Now I see why you're *Chief* Mason," Taryn says, looking like the Girl Scout, proving my theory that inside each of these addicts is the child we used to know and love. And then she goes and ruins my theory by saying, "You're pretty badass for an old dude."

Instead of helping my children, I've broken them. Devon became an Oscar-worthy performer in his quest of '*pretend normal until it is normal*.' Kieren resents us for the choices he made freely, because he took it upon himself that we were his responsibility. Raven is closed off, leery– a beautiful introvert who refuses to meet the world head-on. Weston is a good kid who is hiding a huge secret. All of them are broken, none of them are happy, but all of them are loved.

Where did I go wrong?

And how do I fix it?

How do I go back twenty-four hours, back to the time before the ground disappeared beneath my feet? Yesterday wasn't perfect. We were worried. We were ignorant. But now that I know the truth, I wish I could resurrect yesterday.

Like a light switch being thrown, Devon smiles a genuine smile, not that creepy evil smirk he's been wearing for hours. The curl starts slowly at the corners of Devon's lips, and then spreads into the brightest smile of his life... and then he starts to giggle like a young boy on Christmas morning.

"Devon?" I worry he's losing it. Maybe he did hear me screaming into his face after all. A hand settles on my shoulder, causing me to jump out of my skin. After a moment, I recognize the touch, and the ball of anger in the pit of my stomach relaxes.

I will survive Devon, no matter what happens.

I reach up to clasp her hand. Nearly choking on the sincerity, "Thank you for coming, Clover."

"Hiya, Mom. Did you come to see your new son off to rehab?" I expected sarcasm, or malice, but Devon sounds pleased, even though the words are off-putting.

"Devon," Clover replies calmly. "It's nice to see..." she pauses, at a loss. Her fingertips clench on my shoulder. "Answer me something: how much of this is real, and how much of this is an act? Do you blame the drugs for the things you say, or do you use the drugs as an excuse to say what you've never had the balls to say out loud?"

"Ah!" Devon's eyes spark in delight, happy to have someone who will spar with him instead of scream or negotiate. Either that, or Clover looks so much like Willow that Devon's just happy to see her. A few hours ago, Devon did the acting job of a lifetime for Willow's benefit. I'm curious to see which Devon he gives Clover.

"Both," Devon answers, sounding honest. But that doesn't mean jack-shit where Dev is concerned. Devon can lie straight to your face and you wouldn't know it. "Whether it's the lie or the truth, everything I say is to gain a reaction. I lied a lot this morning. If Dad, Ren, and Willow believed it, then they think the worst of me– never knew me. But if they didn't believe it, then they're naïve."

All Clover says in response to Devon's cryptic reply is, "Thank you."

Annoyed that Clover didn't give him more, "Why?"

"You just admitted that everything you do or say is with premeditation. So you understand all the pain you will cause. You're using drugs as an excuse to cause us all pain. I just wanted to know, that's all."

"No," Devon says, shaking his head. "I use drugs to be free."

"*No,*" Clover twists the word just as Devon had. "At first, you let the past own you. Now, you let the drugs own you. If you truly wanted to be free, you'd figure out who you are without a crutch. Being owned isn't very freeing, now is it?"

Jutting his chin out, Devon gets defensive. "How do you know?"

"I used the ghosts of my past to control me like you've been using drugs. It's all you know, so it's more comforting than the unknown. But sometimes, you just have to take a leap of faith. Like now, going off to rehab."

"This isn't by choice," Devon sneers, rubbing his bruised wrists in example. "Not much of a leap of faith, now is it?"

I can't see Clover, but by the way her arm moves, I can guarantee she shrugged. "You never know, that might change."

"I'm not going to promise I'll stop taking drugs," Devon snarls.

"I never asked you to. No one has. All we're asking is for you to *try.* Willow told me some of what you said to her a few weeks ago. The '*if you love me*' speech you said you'd never listen to. It's not about changing because you love them– your family. It's about changing because you love yourself enough to love them. This is all on you, Dev. Only you can fix this. Scary, isn't it? You have to go it alone."

All Devon does in response is nod his head, looking like he's going to wet himself: either by pissing his pants or crying. It's the first true reaction I've seen out of the kid since he smiled at Clover's arrival.

"I finally gave you a real mother. I hope I wasn't too late." I whisper the words when I realize why Devon is allowing Clover to speak to him in such a frank way, just as how Taryn gave me the respect I deserve after I exploded at Devon. Kids long for both parents, and they resent the one they have when they are missing the other. Taryn doesn't have a dad. Devon never had a mom. Tommy has a father, but he belongs to God.

Mind spinning a billion rotations a second, I realize Clover is frozen behind me and Devon's eyes are trained in her direction.

They seem to be communicating silently, and I have no idea what they are saying to one another.

"I'll promise to try, but I make no other promises," Devon finally says after a few tense moments.

"That's all we ask," Clover responds in an emotionless voice. No disappointment nor praise, only acknowledgement.

"I'm sorry to interrupt, but the flight is about to board, and we're first on. For obvious reasons," the administrator stresses. "Parents, say your goodbyes. But be forewarned: while these creatures may look like your children, until they're detoxed, they're not."

Frightened, I just sit in my chair, wondering if Devon will say goodbye to me. Tommy just hugs his puke bucket and follows after his security guard, never bothering to glance back at his father. Taryn hugs her mother, crying like she's dying, pulling everything out of her manipulation arsenal.

Frozen in a silent tableau, minutes pass as Mrs. Elsberry and Reverend Braxton leave, and the administrator stares at me out of curiosity. Neither Devon nor I make a move. Clover's the first to break.

"Well, I'm not a hugger, but..." I can hear the wry amusement in Clover's voice, but I can't see her yet since she's circling around the wall of seats. My breath catches in my lungs when Clover comes into view, and out of everything, that reaction affects my son. Devon hops up from his seat to meet Clover halfway. They embrace in an awkward hug. Both are speaking rapidly, as if they are operating on a time limit.

This time I don't jump when my shoulder is touched. I roll my eyes up to connect with Devon's. "Are you sure you want to hug me?" I ask, feeling guilty for whatever I did wrong to fuck up my first born.

"This is going to sound stupid," Devon begins, sounding reluctant to continue. "Out of everything, I'd regret not hugging you goodbye the most."

As if spring-released, I'm to my feet, yanking my son into my arms in a fraction of a second. It takes every ounce of emotional control I possess to keep myself together. I hate that we're in public, a place where I can't release my emotions as I feel them. Bottling up everything causes me to live outside of the moment, as if looking from high above. My son is in my arms, but he's not. I'm too numbed in my control to truly connect with Devon. It's surreal, and I hate it.

I say the words Devon needs to hear before I say the ones I need to say. "I love you. Nothing you will ever do or say will change that. Just as I will always be proud of you. You're my son, and that's the definition of unconditional. Don't worry about us. We'll be fine. We'll take care of each other. You just worry about yourself. Get healthy."

Not one for mushy, Devon just holds me tightly for a second more, and keeps it simple. "I expect you'll be hitched by the time I get back, so congrats. I already told Clover, '*Nice Rock.*' You did good."

"I'm definitely the one coming out on top of this bargain," I murmur, feeling the heat of a blush out of nowhere.

Devon pulls away and turns to walk away from me, leaving me feeling hollow and hopeless. He looks over his shoulder and says the only thing that could possibly comfort me, "I'll try, but no promises." If Devon has made promises, they would have been lies. So that '*try*' is the most honest thing Devon had the ability to say.

No goodbye. No excess conversation. After weeks of avoidance and days of worry while he was gone, I miss Devon so much my heart is aching. I missed him while he was beside me, how will I feel now that he's truly gone? Willow's wail of mourning echoes in my mind. '*I've got to be stronger than the woman-child*' I repeat to myself to get a grip.

Devon's '*try*' is the only thing that moves my feet as I exit the airport. It's Clover's hand holding mine, tugging me to short-term parking, but it's Devon's word of truth that propels me forward.

CHAPTER TWENTY-FIVE

The Widow

I'm left feeling utterly helpless, and I hate the sensation. Malcolm moved automatically through the airport, only saying how he couldn't go home, couldn't go to work, because the ghost of Devon was everywhere he looked. I could sympathize after living the past six years in that state. Devon is still alive, but even when Sam was sick and dying, his ghost haunted me.

Unable to drive in his numbed state, I did the only thing I could think of: I pulled into the Hilton near the airport and bought Malcolm a room to breakdown in. Now Malcolm is just sitting at the edge of the bed, head in his hands, not making a sound. A pitiful sight. The helpless feeling running through me is from watching such a strong man be rendered immobile by fear and heartache, and I don't have a fucking clue how to comfort Malcolm.

Fathers fix the problems.

Mothers comfort the ailing.

The father feels worthless because he thinks he created the problem, so therefore he cannot fix it. The mother feels helpless because how do you comfort the ailing when they, in essence, are causing their own discomfort?

Time to get real.

Crouching down by Malcolm's feet, I duck my head, trying to get into his line of sight. "Malcolm?" I call out softly, trying to gain his attention. "You've got this backward, Papa Bear. This is a very good thing, indeed."

Watery blue eyes filled with sorrow and guilt slowly become aware, but he doesn't speak. Knowing I have his undivided attention, I move forward. "Last week, even yesterday, Devon was in danger– a danger none of us could save him from. You hadn't slept well in weeks, petrified over Devon's condition, not knowing how to proceed."

Somebody's home, but they aren't answering me. I sigh deeply, and realize this is going to take a while, so I sit on the floor by Malcolm's feet. "This isn't only a good thing, it's an amazing thing. I know you're thinking of Auggie and Tina right now, that rehab changes nothing. But Devon isn't Tina." I tap Malcolm's knee with every word. "Devon. Is. A. Fucking. Mason... and a Mason never gives up."

Silent, Malcolm blinks his tear-thickened lashes, so I know he's at least listening to me. Doesn't mean he's digesting the words, though. "Devon is safe right now. He will be in a regimented program: eat, sleep, therapy, work— no drugs. Everything is centered on his safety and well-being. You can sleep easily now, Malcolm. Don't worry about Devon because he's the only one who can turn his life around. But there are things you must do, because when Devon gets home, your job as his parent starts again. You'll have no sleep. Your mind will forever be on Devon, and it will be this way until he can be trusted again— until he can trust himself again."

Appearing tortured, "You suck at pep talks," Malcolm breathes out, but he cracks a wan smile.

"John Mason's rules, but we're going to adapt them and throw the rest in the trash. We're operating on Malcolm Mason's rules from now on. You're going to get your head out of your ass and be proactive. There will be no living as if nothing ever happened. We're not going to ignore the issue, we're going to solve it. When Devon comes home, if he falls off the wagon, we're going to figure out why, and then make sure it never happens again. We'll do this over and over again until there are no reasons left for Dev to fall again. Got it?"

"Malcolm Mason's rules?" Malcolm murmurs, but otherwise he's dead to the world emotionally.

"Yes, Malcolm Mason's rules. You're the father now, Papa Bear. No more ghosts from the past influencing the future. So, step one: figure out how to proceed. The kids come first, so you've got until two o'clock to get your head on straight, because we have to be home for them. Then you will sit down and devise a plan of attack, so your life is in order for when Devon comes home. You have sixty days, that's it. You can wallow for that time period, or you can relax because Devon is safe while you're being proactive. Your choice, but don't be an idiot."

Light finally returning to his eyes, Malcolm says in a voice that is borderline whiney, "It's all I've been doing."

Not allowing him to wallow, "Good. What's the plan?" I rise to my knees, getting into Malcolm's personal space. If someone did that to me, it would cause me to flinch. But with Malcolm, he relaxes more.

"Well," Malcolm begins hesitantly, "I contacted Ginny. I can't move Devon back into that house for obvious reasons, and we all won't fit into it. So Ginny's looking for houses, but there aren't many to choose from that have as much space as we need."

"Shit," I hiss, dropping to fall to my ass on the floor. For the first time ever, I'm realizing how drastically my life is about to change. Malcolm's house hunt involves me. After years of going it alone, it didn't even dawn on me that Malcolm's plan of attack for Devon will involve me every step of the way. I have to move? I have to move away from my parents after thirty-five years of being hooked to them by an invisible umbilical cord? Can I do that? Do I want to do that?

Yes.

"Freaked out now, aren't you?" Malcolm says, face splitting into a satisfied grin. "I'm going to sound like a real bastard, but it makes me feel better knowing I'm not the only one freaking the fuck out right now. You had me for a minute with your General-quality morale speech."

"Nope, not freaking out," I lie. My voice dips down deeply, "and neither are you. We can't afford freak-outs, Malcolm."

"True," he says ruefully. "I'd ask for your input on the house, but there's only one in the area. I'm going to look at it as soon as Ginny sets up an appointment. I'm not too worried over the cost– everything seems to be about the same around here. Plus, it's not like I've ever had to pay a mortgage before. I look forward to having a home that wasn't gifted to me."

"Some gift," I huff out. "Your father also left you three dependents. I'm sure he would have rather survived his heart attack." I feel insensitive and awful as soon as the words exit my mouth, but for some reason they elicit an odd reaction out of Malcolm– he laughs, that deep man laugh that makes me tremble.

Malcolm rises to his feet, stepping over me in his quest to pace the room. "I'm not scared anymore, Clover. My head is on straight. You are my perfect counterbalance. As you've deduced, I'm over-emotional, pathetic at times, whiney, clingy, and needy. You're right. We will throw my father's rules away, because he's the one who made me what I am. He created what he feared most."

Sitting on the floor, all I can do is look up as Malcolm paces the hotel room. "What?" I mutter, confused at Malcolm's abrupt change.

"For the last year, I've been courting you to be my wife. So I've used that time to learn you, interrogate our children on your likes and dislikes, but you haven't been able to do so with me. You've said yes to being my wife, and you've seen me at my worst. I thought now would be a good time to explain the root of the problem since we're alone. Where there is no chance for someone to walk in and interrupt us."

"Like Rob the other morning," I mutter, blushing, still mortified.

Determined, Malcolm doesn't respond to my comment, nor does he stop his pacing. If anything, his pacing speed increases until I become dizzy watching him move. "John Mason was Fairport's Chief of Police too. He was an ornery bastard who demanded respect. I've lived my life by a code my father had drilled into me– with his fist. John Mason was the most consistent man ever born. Do *A*, expect *B*, without any doubt. I promised myself my children would never feel an angry hand from me, which broke John's code and made me even clingier."

"There is nothing wrong with wanting to love your children," I reassure Malcolm. It was odd for me at first, knowing he touched everyone, since I've always seen touch as one of the most intimate acts. But I see the connection Malcolm shares with his family, one wrought through positive touch, and I want it now too.

"Dad feared my emotions and their resulting reactions so much so that he made me feel ashamed, which made me crave it even more." Malcolm stops his pacing directly in front of me. His hand snakes out to wrap around my wrist. With a sharp yank, I find my ass situated on the mattress. "You're better than the floor, Clover."

Malcolm's words resonate within me, taking root. I didn't even realize the symbolism of me sitting on the floor while Malcolm towered over me. His actions prove how very much he longs to have an equal partner. I sit on the edge of the bed, while Malcolm rolls the desk chair over and sits. We are face-to-face, eye-level, and completely equal.

"Mom was fifteen when they married, and Dad was forty-five. As an adult five years younger than my father at that age, with a child of that age, I'm thoroughly sickened." Malcolm shakes his head, closing his eyes, and breathes, "It's criminal now, but not back then."

"Dad was so controlling over my welfare that I didn't even know my mom's name until *after* he died. *Penny* had me when she was fifteen. I don't remember her at all. I'm sure Penny held me and took care of me– loved me the best a child-mother could. So I understand how my children feel, because, I too, never had a mother. My first memories start at four years old."

Malcolm appears torn, so I do what is necessary. "You don't need to go on. I don't need to know, Malcolm. Nothing you will say will change my mind. I'm going to be your wife, so don't go on unless you need to." I reach out to take Malcolm's hand, and out of everything, that simple gesture pleases him the most.

"I have to say it. Even Isis doesn't know the half of this shit." Malcolm takes a huge breath, squeezes my hand, and then continues on with his past. "I was homeschooled because Dad didn't want anyone else to influence his first born while I was still impressionable. I was given books twice a day. He would school me, scold me, and feed me in the evenings. I never saw my mother as anything other than a caretaker. She wasn't allowed to coddle me, which meant all the attentive things a child needs to feel loved. Dad meant well, but it had adverse effects."

"Your father created what he feared most?" I mutter, confused. "Let me guess: real men don't cry, hug, or love. They work hard, and their word is law?" I speak the impression I'd gotten from the other times Malcolm spoke of his father. "To do those things meant you were what? Gay?"

"Gay was a mortal sin. Dad would have killed me if he thought that," Malcolm sputters. An odd expression crosses his face, but it vanishes before I can analyze it. "It makes me sick to say it. But he truly would have killed me, and that fucked Auggie up for life."

"Auggie?" I breathe out, eyebrows knitting together in confusion. "What?"

"Rob," Malcolm says pointedly. "Auggie's intimate relationship with Rob and Isis. Rob embraces being bisexual, while Auggie's always trying to pretend he isn't. Dad's rules impact us all."

"Isis told me about them this morning, but I didn't even give it a second thought. It didn't exactly come as a surprise," I say more to myself than to Malcolm.

"No, Dad wasn't afraid I would turn out gay. Dad said, '*gay didn't make a man a woman, it just meant they liked to suck cock.*' Dad had nothing against gay men– he just refused to have one as a son. No, Dad feared I'd turn out to be a woman. He said my mind was like a girl's, and that was intolerable."

"Because being a woman is…" I trail off, seething.

"Yeah, Dad loved his wife, his daughter, and Lisa, but he never respected them. Auggie's the same fucking way. There are only two women on this planet who he respects: Isis and Willow. Every other female is just Auggie's servant, and Willow almost fell into that category. You can thank Dad for leaving that legacy behind."

"Jesus," I hiss out in shock. "I don't know whether I want to throttle Auggie or hold him. Poor fucker."

"Yeah, so everything Dad feared he created. His '*spare the whip, spoil the child*' mentality, mixed with the absence of motherly affection, led me to the mindset he feared the most. I will admit, most of the time I think like a woman emotion-wise. I don't think there was anything Dad could have done about it, nor do I believe he made me this way. It's just my needy personality. I believe Dad exacerbated it, though. You're very controlled in that sense, that's why I said we balanced one another well."

"I'm emotional," I defend. "But most of the time I get overwhelmed and feel like I'm suffocating."

"I know," Malcolm says softly. "I'm hoping your control will rub off on me, and the ease in which I feel will rub off on you."

"It already is," I say with a snort. Proving my point, I lean forward to kiss the tip of Malcolm's nose. The man lights up like I just handed him the world. The sight makes me feel warm all over, especially on the inside.

"So my dad kept my mom away from me. I only heard her voice at night after I was told to go to bed. That was the time Dad spent with Mom. He loved her, never laid an angry hand on her or reprimanded her. Mom was a good woman in his eyes because she obeyed him in all things. He just didn't want her weakening me with her femininity. So this was my life until I was nine."

"Malcolm," I say gravely, but then a smirk pulls at my lips. "I hope you aren't expecting an obedient wife." I start giggling when Malcolm wrenches me forward, taking my lips in a searing but all too brief kiss.

"Good God, I hope not," Malcolm purrs against my lips. Pulling away, he sobers. "One night I heard sounds of agony, and then the siren of an ambulance. The lock to my room clicked open and my father was on the other side. Dad said, '*don't leave the house.*' He left my bedroom door open, which was a first. For a few days I was free to wander around the house without my father's shadow. I didn't know how long it would last. I remember being fascinated because the house was spotless and there were cooling cookies on the counter."

"Wait a minute," I stop Malcolm. "You never walked around your own house until that day?"

"No, my bedroom, the bathroom, the backyard, and the kitchen table were my domain, and only when I was escorted to those areas by one of my parents. Dad wanted to be the center of my universe until he was finished indoctrinating me to his way of life."

"Fuck," I breathe out, at a complete and total loss at what else to say. It's no wonder Malcolm is so clingy. Who wouldn't be after that?

"I had a day and a half or so alone. I fed myself, played in the yard, but otherwise kept to Dad's schedule. I was napping on the sofa when he came home. I remember being scared that he'd slap me for it. The only time I sat on the sofa was when family visited. But Dad wasn't angry, he just looked ragged."

"He wasn't angry? That doesn't make any sense," I mumble to myself.

"Dad was distraught, so he didn't give a fuck that I was taking a nap instead of practicing division. Dad brought me a surprise– a screeching bundle in his arms. '*I've got to get back to the hospital. Your momma's not doing so good,*" Malcolm mimics his father. "I was handed a squirming baby."

"What. The. Fuck," I mutter, shocked beyond belief.

"What: a baby girl. The fuck: what the fuck was I supposed to do with her?" Malcolm grumbles as if he's reliving the past. "I knew what to do with her because Dad had schooled me on taking care of what's mine. Hours upon hours of how to train your wife and rear your children. I knew where the baby went because I found her room earlier while I was wandering around. My mom had made a pretty pink room up for the baby, with all the necessary stuff to raise her. I remembered some of it as being mine. I bet my mom was excited to have a daughter she could raise without Dad taking her," he murmurs softly, affection thick in his voice.

"Isis," I breathe.

"Yes, Isis was my salvation and my ultimate responsibility. Dad came home a day or so later, looking and acting like a ghost. My mom had died from complications. Something about hemorrhaging," Malcolm says as if he isn't speaking of his own mother.

"Hey," I say to get Malcolm's attention. I lean forward to rest my forehead against his. "It's okay to miss your mother, even if you don't remember her. More so even."

"I *do* miss her," Malcolm admits. "Very much so. Mom was only twenty four years old," he breathes against the side of my face, sounding wistful. "I've tried really hard for Isis because I know my mom loved her a lot. I've never changed the wallpaper in that bedroom, telling Raven that her grandmother decorated it just for her and Isis."

I have to look away, choking on gut-wrenching emotions at the lost, mournful tone in Malcolm's voice. I'd do anything in this moment to comfort him, comfort all of them. I've been lucky. Even after the loss of Sam, I have so much to be thankful for.

"It's odd, speaking of my mother at all. I try never to think of her. Odder still, speaking of my mother as a grandmother when she's immortalized as a girl in my head. The woman I remember didn't look much older than Raven– *looked* exactly like Isis and Raven. I guess Mom will always be here with me."

"Always," I whisper to Malcolm.

"Yeah," Malcolm draws out as he runs his fingers through his hair. "Dad wouldn't touch Isis for a while because of it. He wasn't mean to her or anything, more like scared of her. He touched me enough when he was pissed. He didn't even name her. I was reading a lot of Mythology at the time and liked what Isis meant. Of course they're nothing alike," he deeply chuckles over the obvious difference.

"I don't know about that," I defend Isis. "I don't think Isis lets anyone really get to know her."

"You're right about that," Malcolm agrees emphatically. "Dad legally gave her the name Isis Penelope Mason. We were good for two years. I had to keep the house and take care of the wiggling, screaming ball of raven hair. I was told it was woman's work. But, by that time, Dad said I was strong from all he taught me so he didn't fear I'd turn out to be girly. Dad was highly ignorant," Malcolm says wryly. "A while later, Dad brought home a young woman. Amy was no older than Willow is now. Dad had a thing for saving young girls. My mom was orphaned. Amy was orphaned. Lisa was a runaway."

"A very warped hero," I grumble.

"Very," Malcolm stresses. "So Amy was the woman of the house, and I was sent to school while she raised Isis. Amy was only around for six months or so. Amy left, and a few weeks later Dad brought home Lisa and Auggie. Lisa was more of a mother to me than anyone. She was about eighteen at the time, with a huge toddler." Malcolm smiles fondly as he thinks of Auggie.

"Life was good. Lisa was a shitty mom, but she kept Dad busy. Isis and Auggie were the same age, so they played and fought together. I went to school, and Dad made me explain in great detail what went on so he could contradict their teachings. In the evenings, Dad taught Auggie and me what it meant to be a man. Auggie was more receptive than I was because he wasn't girly. Dad loved that Auggie was a huge fucking kid. He was my size when he was eight and I was seventeen. Auggie was the son Dad never had."

"Malcolm, I'm sure your father didn't really mean that," I say, hoping to God I'm right.

Somber, Malcolm nods his head in agreement. "My dad was proud of me. He'd be very proud that I walked in his footsteps. But that doesn't take away from the fact that Dad put up with Lisa just so he could have Auggie in his life. The man was the ultimate Alpha Male, and he put up with Lisa cheating on him, drinking and drugging, just so he could maintain his ties with Auggie. So when Dad died, I did the same. Auggie lived with me on and off until he finally got his own place. I'm the one who paid for the first three rehabs for Lisa, and the first for Tina. Auggie picked up the tab when he was financially able."

I reach up and caress Malcolm's cheek, marveling over how he sees his loyalty to his family, his affection and comfort, as a weakness when it's his greatest strength.

"I miss my father, and I wish he could see me now. I respected Dad, but we never bonded through love. John Mason was extreme in his mindset. I want my children's love, affection, and lastly, respect. Dad only wanted the respect.

"I'm sorry," and I truly am. Instead of using words, I speak Malcolm's language. I slide forward until I can reach him better. I rub my cheek against his neck, and then rest my face against his broad chest. Content to stay there forever.

"Dad was old and old-school. He was almost seventy and still working as a cop. Only a pine box could make him retire. Isis and Auggie were only eight when he died. I was underage by a few months, but being a respected cop's kids had some benefits. Dad's crew took me under their wing, and their wives helped out with Isis. I connected with Camille when her parents brought her and Ginny over to give their condolences– I was consoled by Camille in an odd way while everyone else was distracted by Auggie and Isis. We were married a few days later. It wasn't long before Lisa was pulling away to leave with Auggie. I thought Camille was perfect for me: daughter of a cop, so she'd understand the life. Just before my eighteenth birthday, I became a homeowner, the guardian of my sister, and a husband and soon-to-be father. … and the rest they say is history," Malcolm ends his painful story of the past.

"W-O-W!" Awed, my eyes are huge. "A bereavement fuck. Way to go Camille," I whisper slowly, impressed.

Malcolm chuckles deeply from his chest. "I'd like to think that had more to do with the fact that I was extremely handsy while bawling my fucking eyes out."

"No doubt," I say, equally impressed by him.

"Nowhere nearly as badass as your first time." Malcolm waggles his eyebrows. "Mine was in a bed– missionary style."

Years later, I can finally laugh about it. I tip my head back and laugh like an idiot. "God, I was shameless. I lost my virginity standing up for fuck's sake. I doubt many can boast that."

"You're an original, for sure," Malcolm says, giving me an appreciative look.

"What did Isis think of Camille? I don't see her sharing with other women well."

"Isis doesn't share, that's for sure." Malcolm flashes me a big grin. "Devon was born with black hair, so Isis called dibs. She wouldn't leave the kid alone. I was fine with it because Camille had postpartum depression and wouldn't touch Devon. Isis being maternal was interesting to say the least. Then Kieren was born with blond hair, and Isis wanted nothing to do with that.

Her narcissism demanded that her nephews look exactly like her."

"I can't see the maternal side, but I can definitely see Isis upset that her tiny minions weren't created in her image."

"We had a big motherfucking problem on our hands because Devon and Kieren were inseparable. Like the second Kieren was born, they were glued to one another. Isis was insanely jealous, so she made our lives a nightmare. She was only ten."

Malcolm gets this faraway look on his face, like he's reliving the past and enjoying the good memories. Lips tilted into a sad smile, eyes shining with unshed tears, it's like he wants to go back and experience it again, if only for a few moments.

"Years roll by. Camille was a ghost. She'd let me touch her and that's how the kids kept coming, but otherwise she was numb. Camille went to doctor after doctor, and they could never regulate her medication properly. Then Raven was born, named for the color of Isis's hair, by Isis," Malcolm says wryly. "My baby girl disappeared constantly, but it gave the boys and me a break. Then Weston was born blond. Even at fourteen, Isis wouldn't let that go. She ignored the boys and turned my baby girl into a miniature vixen."

"Rae may look like Isis, but she's nothing like her," I defend both girls, never wanting Raven to have to live up to preconceived notions of how she should behave. "Rae's her own person."

"That she is," Malcolm agrees. "My beautiful introvert," he says with affection. "At twenty, Isis moved out against my wishes. Auggie had bought Rush and she was gonna run it. Isis moved upstairs above the club with both the guys, and I found out they had created this place called the Playroom in the back of the club."

"Playroom?" I mutter, a light bulb flashing in my mind. "Ross keeps bringing that place up. What is it?"

"I'll explain later," Malcolm says in a way that makes it sound like he's not looking forward to that conversation. "It was a miracle, one night I had to work and Isis took both the little ones– they were seven and six."

Malcolm stands from his seat abruptly, only to sit right back down. Not only does he run his fingers through his hair, he scrubs at his face, too. Clearly uncomfortable, I go to stop him from going on, but he beats me to it by speaking.

"Earlier in the day, I'd been to the hospital, arranging for Camille to be committed for evaluation. It was a bad day, but it got worse. I'd walked in to find my wife unconscious and violated. My sons were tied to our kitchen chairs, desperately trying to get free– gnawing at the tape on each other's wrists. If I live to be a thousand years old, I will never forget it."

Malcolm chokes on his words, so I stop him. "You don't have to tell me if you're not ready. You don't ever have to tell me." We all know the official story, but I know what truly happened. It was a bad time for Malcolm, and Sam would visit him often– usually daily. In one of those rare moments when Sam and I actually acted like a real couple, Sam was suffering after his diagnosis and it all came to a head. He told me what had just happened to Malcolm's family in great detail, and then allowed me to comfort him afterward.

"I know you know, but I think I need to say it out loud. I guess I feel like I need to tell my wife what happened to my first wife, instead of her hearing about it from her husband." Malcolm stands up, clearly frustrated, and then sits right back down again. "Goddamn it, I'm not making a lick of sense."

"You don't have to make any sense, Malcolm," I say to reassure him. I reach out and take his hands in my own, fearful he'll yank all of his hair out. "I understand. Tell me what you need to say, and I will listen."

"Okay," comes out sounding as if he's a lost, little boy. "What's haunting me, why this is erupting to the surface, is that Devon had a look in his eye that night, and it's the same one he wears now from his addiction– petrified."

"I noticed the look, like a cornered animal ready to lash out at anyone, even those trying to help him. Please, go on," I say, not wanting to hear it but knowing Malcolm has to say it.

"Cop's intuition, maybe. I don't know. But I knew the men were still in the house by the way the boys were acting– frantic. Instead of panic, I felt calm, practical, in the moment. But afterward, I felt worthless. My mentally unbalanced wife was preyed upon with my sons in the house– this… this meant I didn't protect what was mine. Not only did I fail my family, I failed my father's code."

"Malcolm, no," I cry out.

"The men were there to hurt me in the worst way possible, by hurting my family. Without thought, I stalked three men in my house and killed them– a primordial instinct flared to life. I've never had reservations about it. I've never had a regretful thought on taking their lives. I killed them in cold blood, but it wasn't murder. We are human beings, but we are animals at our core. Protect and survive is a natural inborn instinct." A ferocity infuses Malcolm as he speaks, and I and see the moment doubt creeps in. "Do you think I'm a murderer?"

"No," I answer honestly. "I'm a mother, and I'd want someone to protect me and my children. The men were in your home with three vulnerable people under your protection. You didn't invite them in. When they walked into your house, even before the assault, they signed their own death warrants."

"Good," Malcolm says, satisfied with my reaction. "I called for an ambulance, and then called my Chief. I went out to the living room and untied my boys and made sure they weren't hurt. Then I shut them in their room and lied like a sonofabitch."

"You did whatever it took to survive, that is different than being a spineless liar," I utter impassionedly.

"Camille killed herself shortly after. We were all home. The selfish bitch just ended it. I never had a wife. I know all too well about how responsibility chokes the life out of you when you need a partner to shoulder the burden. I know about young girls marrying before they should. I will never allow our children to revisit our past by repeating our mistakes," he vows.

"Oh, Malcolm," I moan with great compassion and not a hint of pity. I palm his cheek, trying to empathize with him. I imagine a snap as our connection is firmly linked. Never have I ever felt closer to another human being. I'll do everything in my power to make sure nothing ever severs our bond. I'll forever show Malcolm the real me and hope he accepts it.

Smiling sadly, as if he knows the direction of my thoughts, Malcolm nuzzles into my hand and places a light kiss to my palm. Lips twisting into a wicked smirk, he gazes at me with blue eyes gone dark with lust. "And that brings us to the Playroom."

CHAPTER TWENTY-SIX

The Widower

"Playroom?" Clover asks, sounding so confused it makes me smile. She's going to kill me, surely.

Two people have been showcased in my thoughts over the past twenty-four hours, Clover and Devon, and for two very different reasons. I've been insanely worried about Devon, which ups my anxiety. When anxious, all I want to do is touch and be touched, and the person who stars in my wildest fantasies is sitting right before me. I want to forget about my son for a few stolen moments, and Clover is just the cure I'm looking for.

"Instead of telling you, I think I'll show you," I say in a deep voice as I rise from my seat. Unable to control myself, "I need you," I growl in Clover's direction, almost begging. I toe off my shoes, and then begin unbuttoning my shirt.

"What are you doing?" Clover's voice flutters. Her eyes closely track the movement of my fingers popping the buttons open on my shirt. Slowly revealing myself, I strip bare-assed naked for my future bride. "Why are you taking your clothes off?" I love the slight quiver in Clover's voice when I get to my belt buckle.

I tug my belt from my loops with a flourish and a toothy grin. "Speaking of emasculated, the conversation we just had did that to me. It's very difficult for me to talk about the past, but I wanted you to know. So now I need to power myself up, so to speak." When my fingers pull slowly at my zipper, Clover looks like she's going to jump out of her skin. "I've got to man up."

"By getting naked?" Clover scoots further onto the bed, actions belying her words. If she were truly scared, one would think she'd get *off* the bed, not get further onto it.

"Even while I was being boiled alive by Devon, when I saw what you were wearing, my breath caught in my throat. Your hair was down and your cleavage was showing... and you did that just for me," I murmur huskily.

"Isis made me," Clover croaks out, eye lighting on my fingertips as they skirt the edge of my waistband.

"Doesn't matter. You still showed up– for my son. For *me*. I need you," I growl. "I need to touch you, but what I really need is for you to touch me." My voice dips low with hunger. "Touch me, Clover," I beg as I tug at my boxers. "Touch me." I drop trou.

"Jesus Christ," Clover hisses as her eyes light on my cock, and she doesn't look away.

Never hornier, I grip my dick in my fist and give it a few quick pumps. "I've never been this stiff. Look at how hard I am," I say in a teasing manner. Clover doesn't want to look. I can tell she's trying to stop herself but failing miserably. "Fuck, I'm dripping like I'm about to come," I murmur in wonder just as a plop of pre-cum falls from the tip of my dick to splat on the floor.

"You... you... you stop mid-conversation to have sex?" Clover stutters out, still unable to look away.

"Are you mesmerized by my dick, bunny?" I tease as I walk closer to the bed, putting a little extra spring in my step to make my cock bounce. Clover freezes like a scared bunny rabbit in their prey's sights. My grin is huge and instantaneous. She tries to control herself, not realizing her quivering thighs are slowly opening and closing in invitation.

"Love the thigh-high stockings," I taunt, causing her legs to snap shut and a gasp to exit her gaping mouth. "No, I don't want to stop our conversation to have sex. I want to have sex *while* we have our conversation. Take your clothes off, Silly Rabbit," I demand, and even to my own ears, I take notice of the naughty note in my voice. "Here," I murmur as I crawl onto the bed, which Clover promptly jumps off, dashing to the opposite side of the room. "I'll get underneath the sheets so you don't have to look at my honeypot-seeking dick."

"But I like looking at it," Clover spews before she can stop herself. Blushing fiercely, "You know what I mean," she rambles, refusing to look away from me.

"I'm not going to attack you, not that you'd mind," I add as I settle the sheet over my hips so Clover can think straight. "I just want you to touch me while we talk. You like touching me, don't you?" I use manipulation as a tactic to get what I want. "I've had a hard few days, and I need a massage. You'll understand why this is important as I tell you about the Playroom. You want to know, don't you?"

Eyes narrowing, seeing through my transparent bullshit, "Yes, you know I do." Sounding suspicious, Clover walks closer to the bed. "I can touch you wherever I want?"

"Absolutely," I answer eagerly. "Anywhere. Anyhow. Pleasure. Pain. Just as long as you're touching me. My body is your playground," I respond in a teasing lilt. "Take your clothes off, and I promise I won't touch you back unless you want me to. I'll even leave the sheet covering me," I coax.

Wary, Clover unbuttons her blouse with shaky fingertips. I have a pang of doubt, fearing I'm pushing her too hard, but it only lasts for a split-second. Clover and I could go slow, very slow, but it would only prolong the inevitable. Why draw this out when we could be enjoying each other now? I've learned over the past few encounters, get Clover hot enough and her hunger overpowers her inhibitions. I just need to drill it into her how much I want her. Once Clover is confident, no longer bound by doubt and insecurity, she will flourish sexually.

A gasp is torn from my throat when she slips out of her blouse. The bra she's wearing displays her small breasts beautifully, plumping them up like ripe fruit swollen with juice. "Leave the bra on," I order, voice taking on a smoking tinge. "Gorgeous."

Wiggling to get her skirt over the flare of her hips, I nearly come undone at the sight. Clover's body is built for an ass-man. "Leave the stockings, too. Take the panties off."

Clover's unsure gaze flicks up to meet mine. I nod my head, silently egging her on to continue. She freezes for a moment before slowly slipping out of her panties. My cock jacks up at the sight of the little puff of hair on her mound and her bare pussy lips. I wonder what she'd do if I tried to taste her.

I shift around on the mattress, grabbing a pillow to shove behind my neck. In preparation for our *talk*, I smooth the sheet over my hips, and I snicker at the huge wet spot from where my pre-cum is dampening the sheets.

"Straddle me while we have our chat," I coax. "Your body is going to communicate with me instead of your mouth. If you don't like something I'm saying, you'll tense up and dry up. If you like what I'm saying, your body will moisten. If you l-o-v-e," I draw out in a husky voice, "Your body will spasm against mine. Understood?"

Petrified yet aroused, Clover knows she's not going to make it out of this hotel room without being thoroughly fucked. "I'm scared," Clover's standard go-to response when she wants to be reassured and pushed.

"I know," I say unsympathetically. "Do it anyway."

As I expected, Clover slowly creeps closer until her knees touch the edge of the bed. She stands near me, pleading with her eyes for me to take control since she's frozen in fear. Fear of rejection mixed with insecurity. With Clover, I have to be patient yet fast. There is no easing her into anything. Clover's a 'rip the Band-Aid off' kind of girl.

"You'll find out soon enough that I mean what I say and say what I mean, without exception– always. My father was a consistent man, and he beat the same quality into me. I get it, Clover. You're worried I'm going to pull the rug out from beneath your feet, so to speak."

Mouth opening to say something, she hesitates, and then repeats the action. Once in a while out of nowhere, I see a beaten down woman before me, and it makes me want to harm someone or something.

"Clover, you trust me," I make a statement, not ask a question.

"I'm..." Clover takes a deep breath and I can see her strength returning. "I never knew what was up from down, so call me leery because we haven't had time to develop a past enough for me to totally trust you."

"Go on faith," I say without a shadow of a doubt. "You trust me already, you're just letting the ghosts of the past influence you. It's why I told you my past, so we could overcome it together."

"Okay, so this is why I'm..." she chooses a word, "Cautious... and listen, I know I'm going to sound like a complainer, making a bigger deal out of this shit then there was, but it was accumulative. So now I don't know what's up from down."

"I won't think you're complaining, Clover. Please tell me so I may prove to you that I'm consistent." I'm at that stage where I'd agree to just about anything Clover wanted, as long as she sat on my dick. She's teased me for a year, after I went years without sex.

I'm dying.

I deserve a medal for having this conversation when I'm trying to have one about the Playroom, which will guarantee me sex.

"Sam would do shit like call me out in the middle of Sunday dinner. The day before he'd tell me not to make him lunch for work, and then he'd humiliate me in front of my family for forgetting to feed him. It was a game to him. So if I said, '*you told me not to pack your lunch.*' He'd smirk and say condescendingly, '*now why would I do that, Clover?*' Making it sound like I was insane and unreasonable. So the next time I'd make his lunch anyway, and then he'd say I was being wasteful. Sam systematically turned my family against me. They loved his innocent, good-natured bullshit lies, and I just looked like a cold-hearted, ungrateful bitch," she hisses and does that silent scream she uses whenever she talks about Sam.

"I can't imagine how frustrated that made you feel, Clover," I really can't, because right now I don't give a shit. I'll digest Clover's words later, because all I hear right now is **S E X**. My cock is chanting the word as it spreads a bigger cum-stain on the sheets.

My fantasy woman is standing next to the bed, one knee raised on the mattress, wearing nothing but a bra and stockings, and all I can smell is her ripe pussy... and now is the time she wants to talk about my dead best friend– her husband. I'm being an insensitive prick, but I'll make up for it later. I might think more like a woman than most men, but when I'm horny, I'm more alpha male than any before me.

S E X

Big brain checking back in, "Sam would take the car to the shop, and then blame me for not picking up the dry cleaning when I had no way to get it. He'd take apart a perfectly functional vacuum cleaner, saying he needed to clean it, and then he wouldn't put it back together. A day or so later when he needed an outlet, Sam would make fun of me in front of our children because the floors weren't swept. I know these events sound like nothing, and that's how he wanted it. But combined, it drove me into madness. It made me find ways to circumvent the obvious outcome. Sam would create impossible demands to see how I'd solve them, and then he'd blame me for failing. Sam would set me up for failure just to hurt me. Even to this day, sometimes I hate Sam's fucking guts," Clover seethes fiercely.

"That's my little bitch," I praise in a delighted voice, getting more turned on by Clover's anger-fueled passion. Then I get disgusted with myself, which strangely turns me on more. "Was Sam wrong?" I reach over to take Clover's hand, gently prodding her to climb onto the mattress beside me.

S E X

"Yes!" Clover's primordial growl has me groaning, cock kicking beneath the sheet. Clover's fingernails bite into the flesh of my forearm as I continue to slowly pull her to straddle my waist. Clover's anger is so hot it sucks the air from the room, and I have to stoke it hotter.

"Did Sam hurt you?" I coax Clover to go on, needing her to discharge all the pent-up anger and frustration she's internalized instead of releasing it. I want Clover to finally breathe without its constrictive oppression. That's what my big brain is thinking the entire time.

But my little brain has a different agenda. Clover is so involved with her emotions that she doesn't realize I've maneuvered her onto my lap. Finally. Clover's pussy burns me, even through the sheet. I bite back a moan when I realize her moisture is mixing with mine. I'm taking this fuck-sheet home with me as a souvenir.

S E X

"Yes, Sam may have never physically abused me, but he was a master at mentally, verbally, and emotionally abusing me. Slapping me would've meant he had to touch me, and I think that's the only reason he didn't. That, and the fact that if he had physically hurt me, my perfect façade would've crumbled when the real me exploded from my depths to kick his cowardly ass."

God, I'm an insensitive asshole. Somewhere in the back of my brain I'm filing away what Clover's saying so I can fix it later. Later... I'll give Clover every emotion, after I get...

S E X

"Good," I praise, somehow focusing on Clover instead of my hunger. "Feel this," I palm the small swell of her tummy. "Feel the fire in here and use it to banish those thoughts. Don't let Sam's abuse taint what's between us. I am not Sam. I will never be Sam. I don't react, act, talk, touch, fuck, or love like Sam," I chant, getting more forceful with each word as the lust beats out honorable husband. "You say you'll never judge me or belittle me. You are, Clover– *you are*," I stress. "If you allow Sam to taint your vision of me, you're allowing him to continue to abuse you. You'll allow Sam to abuse me because of it."

In the face of my blatant manipulation, Clover's fire recedes, replaced by confusion and remorse. "I'm sorry. I'll... I promise I'll try," she sniffles, and it punches me in the gut, all the way to my nuts. I blink back a few tears of my own. She's so brave and strong and beautiful, but she doesn't know it. I'll spend a lifetime reinforcing her strength and bravery and highlighting her beauty, because she's mine and I'm hers. It's what it means to be a real man.

Just *after* I get sex.

S E X

"That's all I can ask for, is that you'll try. Just don't close me out. We'll talk about it and work through it. Okay?" I reassuringly draw Clover closer to my chest and bury my face into the side of her neck. I ignore the potent pulse that waves through my cock when I get a hit of her cookie scent. The responding clench of her butt cheeks nearly has me flipping her ass over and pounding her into the mattress. I close my eyes and breathe deeply out of my nostrils, trying to settle the lust that's overpowering me.

"Okay, I'll try," Clover mumbles in the half-dark of the shadowy hotel room. Her fingertips flutter against my forearms, sending waves of delightful pleasure to lick along my nerves. It relaxes my craving for her heat, soothes the pounding in my cock. Just a small touch satisfies my skin hunger. On a baser level, Clover knew it would too, and that's why she did it.

Clover pulls from my arms, and I cry out in disappointment as I follow after her. Where her hot body was pressed against mine, it immediately cools from the loss. The disappointment is replaced with a slam of fierce lust as she finds her true self-confidence. I'm so dang proud of Clover that I want to weep with joy.

A finger pushes against my shoulder, eagerly complying, I lay flat on my back. Clover's self-satisfied smirk conflicts with the hesitant, light touch. She folds back the sheet, exposing my chest and stomach, until the sheet is barely covering my twitching cock. I'm so hard right now that I could jackhammer through the fabric to get to her.

"Ahhh... my little bitch." I groan when Clover slides back up my thighs to straddle my sheet-covered hips. "Oh, God! I can feel your heat… and your wet seeping through the fabric…" I moan in ecstasy, blissed out on sensation.

"You said I could touch you anywhere, anyhow," Clover says in a dreamy voice. She feeds my skin-hunger with her touch, and I begin to sympathize with my son. If this is what a hit of Devon's drug of choice feels like, I wouldn't give a fuck about stopping either. I'd rather die with Clover's touch than live without it.

My eyes flutter shut as my skin ignites into flame. Touch and affection always put me in a drug-like stupor, but this is *her* touch– the effects are a thousand times stronger. Clover isn't some friend who gives and receives. She is my future partner, and she is giving without a single thought of ever taking from me. She's taking care of me like no one ever has.

Out of nowhere, I begin to laugh, experiencing true happiness in the face of devastating loss. Clover's shocked gasp has me laughing deeper, which makes her pussy aggressively contract over the hard length of my cock. If the damp sheet wasn't between us, I'd be inside her, pounding vigorously into her cunt until she screamed her surrender.

"I love how my laugh has that effect on you," I purr and Clover's pussy goes wild on me. I have to close my eyes and steady my breathing before I can continue. "This is why I wanted to have this conversation this way. Neither one of us can hide from our body's reactions like we could with words."

"I want you," Clover whimpers, her hips swiveling in invitation. Her eyes beg me to take her–hard. My mouth simultaneously dries up and waters at the thought of Clover's tight, rose-tipped breasts swaying as she slowly rides me– our sexes mashing together.

"Don't," I grab Clover's hips, my words contradicting my actions as I roughly grind her into me, her heat over my hardness– over in over in mind-bending friction. Deliriously close to eruption, I stop the onslaught. "Behave," I teasingly scold. "I need to tell you about the Playroom. It's important."

Not only can I see Clover's blush, but I sense it. The swell of her breasts flushes an inviting pink. "Okay," she say bashfully as she rests her palms on my chest, playacting a good girl. Her thumbs are dangerously close to my nipples, causing my skin to pucker for her attention.

"Please, go on. I'd like to hear about this Playroom," Clover begs above me. Her pussy is constricting eagerly against my cock. Her muscles are gripping me hungrily, trying to draw me into her. Despite the fabric barrier, my cockhead is resting inside her quivering sex. She's so wet, the sheet is worthless. It's only keeping me from burying my cock to the hilt. My dick weeps and jerks as I imagine impaling Clover so sharply I tear the fabric, trying to spear her womb.

The origin of the Playroom is the only thing that stops me from fucking Clover from one heartbeat to the next. "The Playroom is Auggie, Isis, and Robin's insane creation. I think it was an outlet for their feelings. All three were young and confused. Isis was raised to be a wife. Auggie was raised to be all man. It conflicted with the fact that Isis was in love with two boys, who in turn were in love with each other. I think they couldn't handle the intense emotions so they created a place to express themselves. I didn't know about it until a while after, and then I used it for my own type of healing, and then I took my sons there after therapy wasn't helping."

Tiny brow knitted together, Clover looks so confused that I want to kiss her. "What is it? Or don't I want to know?"

"You probably don't want to know," I mutter, secretly smirking on the inside. Willow wasn't cut out for the Playroom, and neither were my boys. But I have a feeling Clover needs the freedom of the Playroom, even if it's just a taste.

"You don't have to explain." Clover leans forward and kisses my cheek. I jolt from the feel of her smooth lips on my skin. I'd rather pull her beneath me and forget all of this, but she's going to be my wife and she needs to understand why I tick the way I do.

"This is why I need you so badly," I admit reluctantly, cradling Clover's fine-boned face in my palms. I convey why our union is so important to my life and well-being. "My worth as a man hinges on how well I take care of my wife and children. The home and life I provide them. The love, respect, and affection I shower upon them. I needed the right wife for me. I created the right children for me. I need you, Clover," I beg. I'm not ashamed to admit that I *beg* her.

"I want that, too," she whispers, breath fluttering across my lips. "I need stability and the knowledge that I can be who I am without judgment." Clover casts her eyes down and away, and I know she's thinking of Sam. Good men don't necessarily make good husbands or fathers. Youth. This is why I know Clover and

I are a good match. The mistakes of our youth taught us what we need to know now.

I drop my hands to rest on Clover's thighs. I put as much distance as I can afford between us, because I don't want her thinking of Sam while I touch her, and I don't want to speak of Camille while we're physically connected. I will my cock to behave as my mind goes to places I'd rather not visit.

"I wouldn't date. The thought didn't appeal to me after the steady stream of women my father brought home. Wives were respected as a wife, and you didn't taint that union with whores. But if not married, you were either to be actively looking for a wife or employing a mistress. Lisa was Dad's mistress, and as such, he fucked whomever he pleased while they were together."

"And Lisa was okay with this?" Clover sound so flabbergasted that I have to laugh.

"Lisa was worse than Dad. It was disgusting and unhealthy. Dad was closing in on seventy, and Lisa was in her late twenties. She was knocked up with Tina when he died, and to this date, none of us know the paternity. But judging by the frequency my father was with Lisa, I suspect Tina isn't a Mason."

"That poor child," Clover cries out, proving how sympathetic she truly is, even though she thinks herself cold.

"Since I refused to date... The first time I went to the Playroom," I begin, and have to swallow back the suffocating need and craving for Clover's touch. A flash of the Playroom inundates me, where I see Clover in the space with me, and it amps up my tactile hunger. I speak to distance myself from the torturous heaven of having Clover's hands on my chest, of her fingers circling my nipples. I clench my eyes shut on the vision of her hungry mouth suckling eagerly at the swollen nubs.

Snapping out of the vision, I mutter, "Sorry. I went two years without any sexual contact. I couldn't even use my own hand. I was miserable and lonely for companionship. I felt like I did as a kid, waiting for my dad to give me attention. One night, I was curled up in my bed, and I'm not ashamed to admit, I was sobbing. My life was a living nightmare. The boys were... Kieren was a sexual deviant and Devon was a zombie. The little ones were becoming skittish. How could I raise four kids if I was broken?"

Warm fingertips tentatively touch my closed eyelids, fluttering kisses to my skin, giving me strength to continue. I'm thrust back into the past as I say the words, "I was kidnapped."

CHAPTER TWENTY-SEVEN

The Widower

Skin quivering, body shaking, I curl up into a ball in the center of my bed and cry into my comforter. Sobs threaten to overcome me, so I push my fist up against my mouth to stifle the noise. I can't wake the kids. I have to be the strong one. Drawing my knees to my chest, while lying on my side, I try to hug myself as I did as a kid.

Every night I'd try to self-soothe when I was growing up. Dad said I was a bad boy for wanting him to hug me. He never called me Malcolm– my name was little bastard. When I'd crawl into his lap and wrap my arms around his neck, he'd knock me to the ground. Then he'd beat me, swearing up a storm that I was trying to make him a pedophile. When I was really little, I remember doing the same thing with my mom, and she'd squeeze me back. But it was all too brief before I was settled on the floor, book in hand. Learning to read and write was more important than cuddle time.

The sobs get louder as I remember my dad patting me on the back– I lived for those times. Only one time in my life did my dad tell me he loved me: we were out in the yard, Dad was teaching Auggie and me how to disarm a criminal. Dad fisted his chest, cried out in agony, and then dropped to his knees in the yard. I tried to save him, but I didn't know how. Auggie wanted to save him, but he was too young.

Knowing he was dying, Dad called us both son, saying he loved us. I was jealous when Dad accepted Auggie's hug goodbye, and leery to give Dad a hug myself. Dad said Mason meant courage. Auggie got a hug, and he wasn't even a Mason. So I was courageous and hugged my father, and he hugged me back. After that day, I was never jealous of Auggie again, because I got something from Dad that Auggie never would: Dad told me he was proud of me and kissed my forehead just before he drew his last breath.

"Not this shit again," breaks into my self-imposed misery. "When are you going to stop calling out for that ornery sonofabitch?" Auggie yanks me from my bed, slapping me across the cheek. "Not once have you ever called out for Camille or Penny. It's always Daddy. Jesus, knock it the hell off."

Tear-filled, red-rimmed eyes roll up to glare at Auggie as he hovers over my bed. "Get out," I snarl, pointing at my bedroom door. "He was my fuckin' father!"

"You think I don't understand?" Auggie sounds incredulous, and pissed. "You think that bastard doesn't haunt my sleep? John Mason is more in my head than I am most days. But I don't find myself weeping in the fetal position every night. John Mason's ghost isn't strong enough to stop me from fucking Robin."

Borderline jealous and filled with bitter resentment, "You were Dad's favorite. He probably would have patted you on the back for getting a straight man to suck your dick."

"Well, then," Auggie's voice twists with wry amusement, "Consider my back well-patted, since I hold the most-sucked cock award in Fairport." Smirk disappearing, "Get over yourself. Dad wouldn't have gave a flying fuck about my over-sexed dick because I wasn't his son. So stop wallowing and acting like the little bastard he loved to call you."

"Just get the fuck out," I scream, not giving a damn if I wake my four kids. "I'm not only crying over Dad."

Furious, Auggie reaches out to grip my chin. I flinch, worried he's going to strike me like Dad used to do. We've fought, had some real knock-down, drag-out fights, but Auggie's never hit me when I wasn't ready for it. But he doesn't hit me now, either.

"You're reverting," Auggie whispers. "I remember how funny you acted. I was just a little kid, and it was even obvious to me. You'd go from clutching Isis like a security blanket to flinching when I tugged on your hand. You got better. You were fine for a long time. Now you're back to that shit again, and I'm sick and tired of it. We all are."

"Nothing's wrong," I poorly deny.

"Yeah?" Auggie murmurs, not buying it. "Then why did you fucking cry when Rae kissed your cheek yesterday?"

"You know I'm a basket case of emotions," I defend weakly.

"You don't date. Worse, you don't even associate with anyone who isn't related to you. You don't fuck. Hell, I bet you *don't even whack off. You shy away from your kids now, just like you used to do with Isis and me after Dad would pound you a good one for hugging us. John Mason isn't here anymore, so why the fuck are you starving yourself?"*

"I don't deserve it," I breathe, hoping to God Auggie didn't hear me. I don't deserve it because John Mason wouldn't be proud of the man I've become. It's why he's haunting me. What kind of brother allows their sister to work in a nightclub while shacking up with two men, fucking them both? What kind of husband watches their wife slowly kill herself years before she pulls the trigger on his own gun? What kind of father allows bad men to terrorize his eldest sons? Devon is a walking zombie, and Kieren is a fifteen-year-old slut. Raven is so introverted that she goes days without speaking to anyone. Weston is my father's worst nightmare.

I ruined my family, so I don't deserve it.

"I can't stand this shit, Malcolm," Auggie sighs out as he sits next to me on my bed. "Isis is sharing Rae's bed tonight, and I just threw West in with Ren and Dev. You think you're being quiet, but you're not. Dev had to call me at midnight to rush over here and take care of you. He's worried about you instead of sleeping as he should be."

"I'm sorry," I offer lamely. "I'll try to be quieter."

"Nope." Auggie reaches over and takes my hand in his. I flinch at first, but then I realize it feels good, too good. I feel ashamed instantly but Auggie won't let me pull away. "There won't be a next time for the kids' sakes. You're the best father, and I would know. John Mason was my father until I was eight years old. I had five years of my life with him. The thing is, someone else stepped up to the plate and took over. You've been my brother, my father, and my best friend since I was a fat toddler. Malcolm, twenty-one years is a long time."

"Christ," I mutter, getting teary-eyed again, and having no way to combat it. "I'm such a fucking mess. So weak."

"You're coming out with me tonight. Isis is going to stay with the kids, keep 'em safe and mindful. You know she's worse than Dad," he says with affection, causing me to smile sadly. "If you ever miss your folks, look at Ice. Penny's body and John's mind—fatal mix, that."

"No shit," I mutter in awe. "She'll be the scariest mother on the planet."

"Let's hope not," Auggie sounds wistful. "So you're coming with me, and you're doing as you're told. You're entering my private domain, where there are no ghosts of the past and my word is law. All you need to do is trust me. Okay?"

"Why do I feel like this isn't a good fucking idea? I know what kind of shit you're into, and I'm not a pervert. It's not just Dad talking– I don't want to fuck anyone who isn't my wife."

"It's not all or nothing, Malcolm. You just think it is." Auggie stands up, and then tugs me up next to him. "My rules: until you are one of us, you will remain blindfolded at all times– this is for the other members' anonymity. No one will do anything I don't want them to do, even if you want them to. You will do everything I want you to do, even if you don't want to."

Laughing for the first time in a long while, I think Auggie is joking. "Let me guess, because your word is law?"

Looking at me with green eyes gone serious, Auggie states firmly, "Exactly."

"Christ, you're fucking serious?" I tug my hand away, preparing to go back to bed. "Nah-uh. I don't think so. I'm going to sleep. I have to work in the morning."

Eyes narrowed, Auggie examines me. "I just said my word is law. I wasn't negotiating with you." Auggie pulls his hand back like he's preparing to strike, and I flinch out of habit. "This is your intervention, motherfucker." Fist flying toward my face, the last thing I hear as everything goes black, "Welcome to the Playroom!"

———

Coming to, my senses are heightened to code-red levels. Blinded, I reach out with my other senses, taking account of my body's condition: Heart beating out of my chest. Blood rushing in my veins. Mind spinning in circles. Jaw aching from a bruise. Breath sawing between my clenched teeth in a heavy, labored pant. Vision dulled to a shade of gray as I stare at a swath of cotton tied across my face.

All I can do is experience. No more numb. Nothing is numb. I'm alive.

With my sense of sight diminished, my sense of touch is elevated. I test my movement, only to find myself bound tightly to a table that feels suspiciously like one at the Chiropractor's office. I'm bound across my hips and chest, my arms and legs free. Not that I can move any part of my body at the moment.

No one speaks, but I know I'm not alone. Judging by the layers of breathing, I'd say I'm very much NOT alone. The dull thump-thump of bass informs me that I'm somewhere deep inside Rush. Since the music flows toward me, not beneath me, I know I'm not in Auggie, Isis, and Rob's loft.

Awareness floods into me in a heartbeat. Touch. My need. My hunger. My craving. Whatever you want to call my sick, shameful need to touch and be touched is being fed in the scariest way possible.

Hands.

Dozens of hands.

Touch me.

Everywhere.

"Shhh..." is breathed into my ear. "You're safe. Just trust me." Auggie tries to reassure me as the hands keep groping, squeezing, fondling, rubbing, and teasing me.

Everywhere.

"Who's touching me?" I beg, hating how my voice quivers. "Take this goddamned blindfold off me!"

"You're not a member of the Playroom yet. They are deciding right now. But judging on how much they're enjoying you... I'd say they will vote yes. A tight-bodied thirty-five-year-old male is a commodity around here."

Voice cracking, "Who's touching me?"

"Eh, trust me. You don't wanna know." Auggie releases an evil laugh that has me shivering.

"Yes, I do," I argue.

"Eh," Auggie repeats, his hair tickling the side of my face, so I know he's shaking his head back and forth as he speaks to me. "You really don't," is followed by a snort. "Just relax and enjoy. Don't they have soft hands? I've fucked each and every one of them in my own way."

"What? Like a perverted toll to your kingdom?" I snarl, never sounding more sarcastic in my entire life.

"Yes, actually," Auggie says without a hint of remorse. "If they want to play in my Playroom, they have to play by my rules. Rules state the price of admission."

Trying and failing to move, I snap, "I'm not paying or playing by your rules."

"Hmm..." Auggie purrs into my ear. Judging by his presence shadowing over me, he's sitting in a chair by my head, watching the others molest me. "If the person has a pretty mouth, the cost is head. If the person has a pretty dick, the cost is I give them head– especially if they're straight. Nothing's as orgasmic as a straight man begging for my mouth. If the pussy is pretty and willing, I fuck it. If it's not willing, I get head. Only three people in here have escaped my toll."

"Who?" Pops out of my mouth before I can stop it. Process of elimination would be nice. At least I know whoever Auggie mentions is most likely touching me.

"Well, you, for one. I love a thick cock as much as a tight pussy, but no matter how built you may be, the thought turns my stomach. So no toll from you. I'm allowing the others to collect in my stead. Feels nice, doesn't it?"

"You're fucking nuts!" I shout, startling the hands into stilling on my body.

"No, I'm being generous," Auggie says softly. His hair brushes the side of my face, a silent gesture made that has the hands roving again. "You need this, Malcolm. You're starving. Trust me to take good care of you. No sex. Not even if you ask for it. I won't break the vows you made for yourself. I love you too much to hurt you. So let go and trust me," he chants.

"This is all they're going to do?" I ask, and then add hastily, "Promise?"

"You might not want me to promise that, Mal. When you finally get horned up, you might want to get off. Since they are only rubbing the parts an ethical masseuse would touch, it would be mighty difficult to have a happy ending. So how about I say I won't let you penetrate anyone? Hmm? Is that fair enough? I'll even cuff you upside the head if you start begging for sex."

"You're an idiot," I grumble. "That ain't happening."

"You'd be amazed," Auggie says, sounding like he's lost in thought. "You'd be amazed what you're willing to do when in the height of ecstasy. So don't act too proud or confident, Mr. Mason, or you'll end up with a bruised head from the amount of times I'll have to bash you to shut up your begging."

My swallow is so audible, I swear it echoes. "What's this place for anyway?" I say, trying to take my mind off the hands roving around my body. It's starting to feel good, and since I'm buck-ass naked, everyone knows I'm responding in a way Auggie said I would.

I can tell the difference between the men and women as they touch me. The guys' hands are the best, not in a sexual manner.

They just seem to give a better massage– getting deep into the muscle tissue and forcing the tension to release. The girls are better at teasing– some veering too close to my swelling cock. The pair of hands rubbing my hips and inner thighs keeps flying out to swat the naughty girls' hands away.

"It's called the Playroom," Auggie answer me, sounding amused for some reason. "God, he keeps pouting. It's so cute."

"I'm not pouting," I grumble, confused. "Never in my life have I been called cute. Are you losing it, Auggie?"

"Not you. Our sad gatekeeper is pouting. Girls, behave," Auggie says in a sharp tone that has every hand freezing.

"King Augustus Kline, I presume," I say snidely, hating how Auggie has taken Dad's advice to the nth degree. No doubt everyone in this room is Auggie's whore. Playthings who he doesn't respect.

"I like that," Auggie says, pleased. "Continue," he orders the hands to resume, because I refuse to acknowledge that each set of hands is connected to a human being I most likely interact with in everyday life… and then my cock springs to life like a Victoria Secret's Angel just magically appeared.

I'm broken– fucked in the head.

I bite my lip against a moan as my cock starts to throb in time with Rush's bass thumping all around us. Whoever this gatekeeper is, he's enjoying himself immensely, getting closer and closer to my straining cock with every pass of his massaging fingertips. I've not once in my life thought of a man in a sexual manner. Even now, knowing the hands belong to a male, I don't see them as man-hands. I just feel them as something that will feed my hunger.

The more aroused I get, the more Auggie allows the upper-half of my body to be toyed with by the girls– God, I hope they are girls who are starting to use their mouths in place of their hands.

"Sweet Jesus," I shriek, nearly coming, as a pair of hot, wet lips begins suckling at my nipple… and then another mouth attaches itself to its mate. "Fuck," I shudder out, trembling from the tips of my toes to the top of my head as tongues begin licking me from my belly button to my neck, like hungry, helpful kittens giving me a tongue-bath.

"That one," Auggie murmurs dreamily, "is my favorite. What a mouth on her– Oh, don't pout for Christ's sake!" he

shouts at someone. "You're making me sound like I have Tourette's."

Auggie's annoyance is forgotten in the face of my pleasurable assault. My back arches up off of the table as far as my binds will allow. My eyes roll back inside my head in ecstasy. The pleasure is infinite, as if every nerve in my body is being stroked at once. As the hands get more fervent in their quest to touch me, I become more pliant, more willing to just lie back and experience.

Quivering, I succumb.

"More?" Auggie breathes into my ear.

Unable to answer, I just release a sluggish moan.

"I'm gonna come!" I shout in a ragged voice at the first touch– cock still ignored. Auggie's laugh rumbles near my ear as a woman begins to ride my hand, pressing my fingers deep inside her scalding hot pussy. A garbled noise is torn from my throat when a hand– man or woman, I don't fucking know, nor do I care– grips the base of my dick and squeezes until the need to release passes.

Man– definitely a man –the gatekeeper. Gatekeeper to my dick, is that what the title means? Because no one else has touched me in that vicinity.

The woman is tall, judging by where her hip is in relation to the height of the table I'm strapped down on. Her dress tickles my arm, my hand safely hidden beneath the fabric. She uses her own hand to guide me in the way she craves to be touched. She is gentle but sure, relaxing me further. I know without a shadow of a doubt that I know this woman, that I'm connected to her. I trust those in my life– I trust Auggie not to harm me intentionally. Whoever she is, I'm comfortable around her or else I'd be freaking out right now.

"Mmm... how's her pussy? Is she wet?" I just nod my head yes, causing Auggie to laugh harder. "Ah, interesting," he purrs. "Wet, you say? She chose riding your hand over letting me go down on her as her toll into the Playroom– stubborn bitch, this one. But I think she likes you, even if you do have a cock."

Auggie's words amp up the woman's movements, until she is grinding into my palm. Her pussy is as soft as silk, hair-free, and her clit is so swollen I fear it's been ages since she's been touched. I feel a sense of camaraderie with her instantly– she and I have both been without.

"Fuck me! She's really wet," I groan as her pussy juice sluices down my fingertips to my wrist. I marvel over the thought of touching a woman after so long– a woman I don't know and can't see with my own two eyes. It arouses me to the point I nearly pop again. I have no idea who is riding my hand, but she takes three of my fingers easily, eagerly. I imprint her moans into my mind, saving the information for later.

"Already begging for a swift fucking, are you?" Auggie is the definition of arrogant. *"Do I need to cuff you upside the head this early?"*

"It was a saying, assfuck!" I snarl, but it comes out distorted when the gatekeeper's rock-hard bulge decides it likes pressing into my calf. When he doesn't hump me like a dog, I relax.

"I think he was volunteering for the position of that particular nickname." Auggie growls, sounding pissed the fuck off. *"Back the hell up, or I rip it off!"*

Defiant, the gatekeeper presses into me harder, causing Auggie to sigh heavily. Not all of Auggie's minions are obedient. *"Asshole,"* Auggie mutters. When he doesn't get throttled, the gatekeeper relaxes against me and resumes his incredible massage skills, dipping a bit too close to my ass for comfort, though.

"If she comes, you get to keep her– eh... eh... eh..." Auggie stops me from protesting. *"Not for fucking. She'd rather go fist her own cunt for life than cockgobble. She likes ladies, so both of your virtues are safe. If you manage to get her off, the two of you can play handsy every once and a while. It's nonnegotiable,"* he orders, causing the woman to stop riding my hand.

Not wanting to lose out after going for so long, I blindly search for her. My hand comes into contact with her thigh. *"C'mere,"* I growl. *"I can feel how badly you need it. Let me give it to you. I don't need anything in return, honest."*

My fingertips skate up her smooth inner thigh, finding the heat of her wet core. I sink two fingers in to the knuckles, and then I pull them out and push them back in, in a rhythm she finds pleasurable. Wetter than before, her juice trickles down to my elbow.

"That feels good, doesn't it?" I murmur to the woman, loving how I'm taking care of her, that she's taking from me, making me feel like a real man for the first time in over three years. I'm so into it that I don't realize everyone has stopped

moving, hands frozen into place, as they all watch me touch the reluctant woman.

In less than thirty seconds, she comes for me. Full-bodied quivers roll through her as she bucks against my hand, crying out in a beautiful feminine voice that is music to my ears. The sound of her orgasm, combined with the sensation of her slickness on my fingers, has cum pouring out of me. I don't climax, but my cock doesn't care nonetheless as it shoots a small load up my chest.

"Christ, Malcolm," Auggie praises me, giving me a pat on the top of the head. "Color me surprised. You have mad skills with pussy. You made her weak-kneed. Poor woman just had to go lie down on the couch." He laughs a deep masculine sound, and unable to help myself, I join him.

Satisfied, I realize the gatekeeper is occupying himself by playing in the mess on my stomach and chest. Swirling his fingertips around like he's painting me a pretty picture. Skeeved out, I shudder, gaining Auggie's attention.

"Don't," Auggie sounds exasperated. Like a petulant child, the gatekeeper quickly gathers up my ejaculate like he's afraid Auggie's going to take it away from him– hoarding it. "Goddamn, you're a fucking idiot." Auggie sounds impressed, mystified, annoyed, and not at all surprised– all rolled into one. "I can't take you anywhere."

Shameless, the gatekeeper starts doodling on my thigh, using my cum as his medium. "Um…" uncomfortable, I'm at a loss for words.

"Just ignore him. He's like the village idiot: adorable, sexy as all hell, but a bit dim. I keep him around because he fucks like nobody's business."

Snorting, "You fuck the village idiot?"

"No, he fucks me," Auggie replies immediately, no teasing lilt in his voice. "Perfect-sized cock, also doesn't whine about how huge I am. Win-win, me and the village idiot." The doodling turns into the letters P R I C K. "Don't pout. You know it makes me horny, and I can't fuck with Malcolm around. My dick hasn't so much as made a twitch."

Auggie gets up from his seat next to my head, grumbling a litany of insults at the gatekeeper/village idiot. My stomach and thigh are wiped clean by something soft that feels like a t-shirt. "Resume," Auggie announces. "He just got a bit over-excited, *but he didn't orgasm. You, with the perfect suction– do your best."*

"Oh, fuck!" I grip whatever's closest to me: someone's hand– a smaller guy's –and a girl's tit. "Why is there a naked tit near my hand?" I shout, feeling awkward that naked people are touching me. I know Auggie is clothed, and the village idiot is most definitely wearing jeans, as was evident when he humped my leg a little bit. Even the girl I just fingered was dressed.

I can't see, but my body is so heightened it senses movement. A pair of lips descends to my cock, hot breath fluttering out to sear my flesh. Overwhelmed with a feeling of foreboding, I shake my head in a panic while screaming, "NO! Don't!"

"Fucking puritan," Auggie mutters in disappointment. "We can't even get you blown. No sex, he says. Saving myself for my future wife, he says. Won't even putt off in the bathroom, according to his spawn. Cries himself to sleep every fucking night. Doesn't appreciate the gift I'm giving him," Auggie rambles off, getting angrier by the second. "She could suck a bowling ball through a cocktail straw. Jesus, I think you'd rather play tic-tac-toe with dumbass than have the best set of lips sucking you off."

Someone draws an X on my thigh, marking their first move in tic-tac-toe, and I crack. I arch up off of the table, mad laughter spilling from my lips. I can't explain why I don't want that woman to suck me off, but my intuition was screaming that if I knew who she was, I'd hate myself because of it. As a cop, my intuition is my finest tool.

"Yeah, I'd rather play Hangman with Rob. He was pretty good at spelling out prick," I say dryly. "Auggie, c'mere."

"What?" Auggie breathes into my ear. "Is your fucking malfunction?"

Turning my head to the side, I search blindly in the dark for Auggie's ear. Frustrated, I reach up to yank Auggie's hair until he's where I need him. Not wanting to insult the woman, "I don't want her touching me," I whisper so softly only he can hear. "I don't know who she is, but no. I'll let anyone else touch me, but not her."

"Ah," Auggie says as if he was just enlightened, and not by me. "I didn't even think of that. It's why you're such a good cop." Auggie's unruly hair slips through my fingers as he stands up.

"Get out," is said in an emotionless voice– no censure, just command.

I feel horrible instantly when the woman makes a pitiful sound in the back of her throat. It's so quiet in here you could hear a pin drop– her bare feet make a pitter-patter noise as she runs from the room. I suspect she was the owner of the perfect tit that was hovering near my hand.

"I should have realized your tastes don't run in the same circles as John Mason's. Your nature is softer than that," Auggie says to himself, as if he's waiting for the woman to leave before he continues.

"Thanks for insulting me while I'm bound to a table, naked and molested," I say in a stiff voice.

"Not an insult," Auggie says in a way that makes me believe him. "Just an observation. So, since my personal cocksucker is gone, at your behest, you said anyone," he stresses. "Well, we have another stubborn fuck in here who refused to pay their toll. What do you say, Playroomers, do we make him pay?"

I freeze, shocked when more than twenty voices ring out– all resounding yeses... and Rob's lone no. "Shit," I hiss. "Why are you saying no?"

With the gatekeeper/village idiot's identity known, he's now comfortable to talk to me. "You don't want to know, so don't even ask," Rob drawls out. "When you find out who you just fingered, you're going to be wicked pissed. Actually, I'm surprised you're not kicking my ass for touching your dick. But I didn't think your pride could handle coming ten seconds into touching pussy."

"You have delicate girl hands," I tease, because even though Rob touched me, it did nothing for me other than feel nice. "It must be the artist in you."

"What's up with Auggie's paws then?" Rob grumbles, insulted.

"I dropped Auggie on his head a lot when he was a small child. He was so fucking huge, I could barely carry him around. I kept losing my grip and crackin' his noggin," I deadpan, causing everyone in the room to laugh, which freaks me the fuck out, because they all know who I am, and I bet I know all of them too.

I could be wrong, but I swear, Auggie breathes, "You'll regret saying that, Mal," near my ear. Straightening from his seat next to me, Auggie stands. "Well, the consensus is yes. I'm a bit of a bastard, born and made. When I want something and

I'm denied, I tend to get nasty. Malcolm said no to the cocksucking, said he'd take anyone else but Nina. I don't like hearing no," Auggie states the obvious while making an art form out of arrogance.

"No, shit?" I grumble. "It was Nina? No wonder I freaked the fuck out. Have you lost your goddamned mind, Auggie? Dad's whore is yours?"

Ignoring my jab, "Our newest member told me no last week. He wanted to join so he could watch, snoopy bastard that he is. But he wouldn't pay the toll, no matter what pleasant compromises I came up with. Wouldn't touch me, wouldn't let me touch him, and wouldn't fuck anyone. Straightest white boy I've ever came into contact with. Every hole is fused shut, except for his mouth– when he's swearing at me."

"Auggie, no," Rob orders. "Don't do this."

"It's the toll," Auggie says with twisted delight. "Mal can't see, but he can. So, if you want to stay in the Playroom, you've got to pay the toll. What do ya say, buddy?"

"Ugh!" Rob shouts, clearly frustrated. "Isn't it enough with who you had him finger? This is way worse."

Rob and Auggie hold a very private conversation as if they aren't standing in front of the ones they are discussing. "Truthfully, I think it's a great idea. If neither of them protests too much, I think the three of them could be... friendly from time to time. They are all so fucking skittish when it comes to sex. He won't fuck anyone either, and her dating pool is narrow to say the least."

"Two straight guys and a lesbian, and you think this is a good idea? None of them are attracted to one another. They are... ugh! This no saying names bullshit is for the birds," Rob grunts out.

"End of discussion," Auggie says tightly. "They're doing it."

"Doing what?" I ask, suspicious.

Auggie ignores me as he does everyone. "Resume your massaging, folks. Girls, you can use your mouths, but no sexual parts are involved. Village Idiot, clean off Malcolm's hands. I doubt you-know-who wants pussy juice tainting his precious cock," comes out snidely.

I try to enjoy the massage as I'm attacked by a dozen hands at once. Hands rubbing my feet, digging into the arch in a way that is pure bliss. Rob washing my hands in a practiced manner. Hands rubbing my calves and legs and thighs and hips. Big hands rubbing my shoulders and neck– Auggie's. I try to fall into the sensation of warm, wet tongues licking me between my bellybutton and neck. Sharp teeth pressing into my flesh and hot lips sucking hard. But my mind keeps rolling over possibilities.

Rob is very practical, more so than Auggie ever is. Auggie acts out of emotion, whereas Rob thinks about the consequences first. So if Rob is worried, I'm worried. "Rob?"

"Yeah?" He answers immediately.

"Is this person gross or something? Related to me? Has a disease?" I try to fish for answers. "A criminal?" earns me a dozen varying laughs.

"Nope," Rob readily replies. "Definitely not related. We're all clean. But he most certainly is since I doubt he's dipped his dick in many since he's saving himself for his wife," Rob stresses like he's giving me a huge clue. "And, he even makes the straight guys in the room curious to know what's beneath his clothes. They're envious. He's fucking hot, which is making Auggie pissed off because he doesn't get to have a taste. But then again, he and Auggie are working out some other issues."

"If you say another word, you won't be having sex for the next ten years," Auggie warns.

"And if I shut up now?" Rob inquires.

Auggie growls, "Then I won't beat you with my bare hands."

"We've never used condoms on a handy-jay before, why start now?"

"I... I didn't mean beat you off. Oh, fuck it," Auggie sounds flustered. "Goddamn you!"

Entertained more by Rob's antics than the hands stroking my flesh, "Why are you antagonizing Auggie?" No one antagonizes Auggie– ever.

Shameless, "Let's just say, Auggie loves a brat. We'll be lucky to be out of bed two days from now. He's going to be a fucking beast when we get upstairs. Isis is going to freak."

"No more," I beg. "I assume we're trying to turn me on here. Talking about the woman I've raised since her birth... fucking the pair of you lunatics, total boner deflator."

"It's Isis," is all Auggie mutters from beside me, sounding grumpy.

"What's that supposed to mean?" I mutter back.

"Auggie's pouting because Isis will be in charge," Rob says, *and I can practically hear him grinning– taunting Auggie. "If I pit them against one another, I could stretch it out for almost a week of nonstop sex."*

"Alright, my dick just inverted in shame," I grumble. *"Seriously, let me up. I'm so over this* 'lie here and get a half-assed massage with the biggest set of blue balls ever in recorded history.' *Unknot these ropes,"* I demand, hands fumbling to *release myself.*

"Everybody out!" Auggie shouts, and then adds on, "But you and you." Heavy pause where people start fleeing in terror, I assume. "And you, brat, go upstairs and call Isis home. Dev can watch the kids. Relay this message word-for-word: I've been a brat– punish me. GO!"

"About fucking time," Rob sounds too pleased with himself. "I thought I'd have to fuck him or at least suck his cock before I really pissed you off. You're getting too lenient, Auggie."

"Umm... what?" I stammer, thankful that it didn't come to that. I would have murdered everyone in this room if Robin had touched me like that, especially when it was just to get a rise out of Auggie.

"Don't ever get mixed up with a Prynne. Those bitches are insane," Auggie grumbles. "Clinically insane. Biggest bunch of pot-smoking martyr masochists. Fucking loveable bastards."

Sighing loudly, Auggie slumps next to me, placing his cheek against my shoulder. "Alright, here's how this is going to play out," he speaks to me and the two people who are standing to my left and right. "I'm going to leave the three of you to your own devices. It's freaking me out seeing Malcolm like this. I thought I was a pervert, but I guess I was wrong. I care about all three of you assholes, and you're not taking care of yourselves. We are human beings who need sustenance, and that isn't just food and water."

Auggie's words are sincere, heartfelt, causing me to tear up. I'm suddenly thankful for the blindfold's absorption. "Attention and affection." I try not to sniffle as I remember how it felt as a kid. I realize for the first time, I've been punishing myself just as Dad had.

"Exactly, Mal," Auggie praises me, sounding relieved that I'm finally getting with the program. "Umm... I'll call you Lady right now. Lady, I understand your need to only be with girls, but

there aren't many available to you. And the dates I send your way, you toss right back at me, saying they aren't to your impeccable standards. But you never tell me what those standards are..." Frustrated, "It's inconceivable."

Auggie reaches over to untie my binds. His hands work fast and sure. "I'll call you gentleman. Gentleman, your girl is still a child. A beautiful, broken child. I gave you my blessing, but she's tainted goods. If you want to wait for the rest of your life for her, you're a moron. She doesn't deserve you. I will bite my tongue, but I will not stay silent as you spiral down into misery."

Binds loosened from my chest and hips, I wiggle around on the table, getting the blood flowing. I flinch when the ropes hit the ground with a loud thump. I have no idea what Auggie is doing, but I can only assume he's letting me go.

"All three of you care for one another. All three of you are treading against impossible odds. Malcolm's waiting for a wife, but he's not even actively searching for one. Lady is looking for a girlfriend, but no matter who we set her up with, she brushes them off. Gentleman is waiting for an unrepairable girl to be repaired. So, if you guys refuse to play with anyone else, I suggest you play nicely together. I don't mean fucking. I don't mean be lovers, or whatnot. I know you guys won't be attracted to one another, so use your imaginations and get yourselves hot. All I'm saying: just give and take what you need to survive. Sustenance."

"Auggie," I reach out, trying to locate him.

"I'm done," Auggie declares, grabbing my wrist. "I've got my own problems to handle, Malcolm. I can't go running off to our house at all hours of the night to comfort you anymore. I also can't keep chasing his," he snarls, "woman down when all I want to do is murder her. I can't keep coddling our reluctant lesbian as she freaks out about touching other women. Hell, I've got to go throttle Rob in a minute. I've got my own shit that I don't share with anyone. So, you guys are on your own. Either come together as friends, or be fucking miserable."

Releasing my wrist, Auggie leaves me feeling cold and sad. Unsure if he was being sincere or the best manipulator, I give in. "Auggie," I call out to him, because I can feel his presence ebbing across the room. "Thank you."

"You're welcome," Auggie calls back to me. "It's good to be appreciated." Voice turning wry, "I'll still be on call for you guys' shit. Just give me a week, because it's gonna take me that long to get Rob back in line. Oh, and don't take the blindfold off

*until you guys are through– that's the only toll I require."
Auggie's evil laughter fades as a door slams shut in the distance.*

*"Umm... I take it I know you guys pretty well," I stammer,
beyond uncomfortable lying here naked and exposed. The only
reply I get is deft fingertips unknotting my blindfold.*

*... and then as my eyes blink in the light, "Eh, I'd say,"
comes from a heavily accented voice.*

CHAPTER TWENTY-EIGHT

The Widower

"Did you have sex with them?" Clover asks me, and I hate the betrayed expression on her face. I also hate that she doesn't ask who they were, like she's too frightened to know. Clover wants to get off of my lap, I can tell. Straddling my hips, sitting on my cock, I'm in the perfect position to judge her body language. No longer aroused, Clover is upset.

As she should be.

"No," I firmly stress. "Whether you were my future wife or someone else was, I didn't want my wife to have to go about Fairport, wondering if I'd fucked every person they see. That is the height of disrespect for all those involved."

"Just them? The two people in the photographs?" She's still not asking what I thought she would. She has the '*why*' and the '*how*', but she's refusing to ask the '*who*.'

"Yes, only them. We never kissed or anything. No sex, not even oral. We just used our hands. We'd massage until we were relaxed, and then it would turn sexual. We've done this for the past five years."

"When was the last time?" quickly flows from her pinched lips. "Wait!" Clover calls out, palms landing heavily on my chest. "Don't answer that. It's none of my business."

"None of your business?" I sound incredulous, eyebrows arching in surprise. "We would meet every Saturday night after Rush closed and the Playroom emptied out. We'd lock the door, and then spend around an hour or two letting the week's stresses melt away. Then we'd go about our lives as if we didn't erotically massage each other. We did it to survive."

Clover wants to scoff, and she's doing a damn mighty fine job holding it in. Her eyes narrow, her lips thin from the strain, but she controls herself. I don't want her controlled. I don't want her thinking things and holding them in, not letting *me* in.

Clover face is one of the most expressive I've ever seen. The thoughts practically scroll across it. *You don't need sex to survive, Malcolm. I've went without for almost six years, why are you any different?*

"I'm not ashamed, and I'm not going to make excuses. Nor do I feel as if I've betrayed you somehow. Until a few days ago, you didn't even know I wanted you like this," I buck my hips up, demonstrating how badly I want Clover. "Your insecurities blinded you to the truth. Did you want me to wait for you when I didn't even know if it would work out between us?"

"No," Clover utters tightly. "I don't think you owe me anything– no explanations, nothing–"

"Wait a minute," I interrupt Clover, but she takes the conversation back.

"Malcolm," she sighs my name, finally relaxing into me again. "I'm not judging you, so don't worry about me. Okay?"

"No, it's not okay," I grit out, hands reaching up to grip Clover's forearms. "You're thinking something destructive. I can tell. Don't shut me out like this. You have every right to feel whatever the fuck you feel."

"I'm fine," Clover throws out like nothing. "Just merely curious."

"I smell bullshit again." I do my damnedest not to growl as I go past frustration into anger.

Ignoring me, which makes my statement all the more true, "Since you've yet to tell me what the Playroom actually is, I'm going by Mayor Ross's comments," Clover mumbles as she gives a shiver of trepidation. "It's like a sex den or something, isn't it?"

Two can play her '*I'm not upset*' game. I have a hard time judging Clover's reactions when she's freezing me out, so I go with the truth. "Yes, the Playroom is about sexual expression: a place to be free to be who you are without societal oppression. You've called me a pervert for my images. But that's the height of my perversions. You don't know hedonism until you see Auggie in all of his glory. He brings an entirely new definition to the word."

Eyes glazing over, body tensing, worry crossing her expression, "That frightens me, because, you know..." Clover trails off, no doubt thinking of Willow.

Thankful I don't have to lie to the stressed out mother, "Auggie didn't show Willow that side of himself, not really. I promise."

"So why do people go to the Playroom?" She asks, trying to get away from the landmine of a conversation known as Mr. Kline and his Good Girl.

I reach out to tangle my fingers with Clover's. I'm not sure how she's going to take what I have to say. I hope to ease her fears for our future. Deep inside, Clover is living out every bad thing Sam ever said to her. Her self-worth is tied to the lies of a dead man. Clover demeans herself, disrespects herself, and degrades herself in her thoughts. Clover is worthy of so much. I hate how she thinks so little of me, how she thinks I'd truly believe this isn't her business. And if I truly thought that, I hate how she thinks so little of herself to put up with the disrespect. In a way, it's what Sam taught her.

"The Playroom means something different for everyone. The Playroom for me was about reclaiming my manhood," I answer in all honesty.

"Because being a man is about sex?" If Clover didn't sound confused, I'd be insulted.

"No, it's not– not even close," I slowly enunciate, hoping she understands. "I was filled with a ton of self-loathing over what happened to Camille and the boys. It wasn't my fault, but it felt like my manhood shrunk because I didn't take care of them. I was starved for attention, affection, and intimacy, but was left feeling emasculated. I was so starved for attention and touch that I ached for it constantly. I felt hollow… numb… dead."

Clover's fingers clench around mine. A fat teardrop plots to her cheek, and the sight of it kills a part of me. "You needed to survive," she says after a moment, finally getting the gravity of the situation. "The Playroom means different things to everyone. But for you, it was somewhere you could express the emotions you suppressed every day."

"Yes," I say softly. "My dad made me think I was a freak. He made me feel ashamed about how much I loved to hug and cuddle and touch. It's why I said he created what he feared most. Now, I find myself drawn to a place he would loathe. A place he would reign in."

"I won't take that away from you," Clover breathes. "I won't make you feel ashamed."

"I know," I breathe back. "You'd just sit back and allow me to do anything I wanted, even if it was killing you on the inside. You're very transparent, Clover. I can see that you're extremely upset with me right now, and I know you'll never tell me why. You'd let me cheat on you, you'd let me go to the Playroom without you, and you'd never complain about it. While this says how little you think of yourself, it screams how very little you think of me."

"I–"

"Don't deny it," I demand angrily. "I'm a real man, and real men are loyal, faithful, and they do and say what they mean. Got it? If I say I'm going to do something, I always follow through with it. If I tell you how I feel, I mean it. Everything we do, we will do together or not at all from now on. We are a team," I declare as I squeeze her fingers. "Understood?"

Eyelashes lowered, shuttering her true emotions, Clover says, "I do," and I can't be certain she does understand me, not so soon anyway. It may take years, but she will eventually learn that I consistently follow through, no matter what.

"I… I have to tell you something else, because I fear if you hear it from someone else, you'll hate me. I was enticed to the Playroom because my tactile fixation was screaming, and I found relief there. So when my sons showed signs of deep-seated issues, I remembered my father's words. How a semblance of control will carry through to your entire life."

"You didn't?" Clover gasps, a mix of shock and disappointment crossing her face. Within one heartbeat to the next, I promise myself that I'll never tell her about Willow. It will kill her.

"I did," I sigh, gripping Clover's hands tightly in my own, fearing she'll pull away from me. "Kieren started having sex at thirteen, and Devon was a young man who acted like girls were the antichrist. One night they finally admitted why."

"Oh, Malcolm," Clover cries out, tears falling again. I'm thankful that I found someone who knew all of my history. I couldn't have explained the details to her– ever. I'm thankful that Sam actually told Clover the truth– it makes my life easier now.

"Both boys were skittish of the sounds of sex. A groan when you stubbed your toe put them into panic mode. When they were of age, I took them to the Playroom. I wanted them to see and hear consensual sex. It was a controlled environment where I knew everyone. From the outside looking in, I look like a fucking pervert. But the only thing they've seen me do is sit in a chair and that's all I've seen of them. Years of therapy didn't work– nothing did. Was I right or wrong? I'll never know. Did it contribute to Devon's addiction? Possibly, but I think the lifetime he spent watching his mom's lunacy and her violation is the cause, not the hours watching people play and laugh."

Lying on the hotel room's bed, with a slice of daylight pouring from the crack between the draperies, the silence is calming. I watch thoughts flash across Clover's face. Her eyes are knitted together in concentration as she processes every word I've spoken. We don't move or speak, but we don't look away from each other either.

I feel it to the marrow of my bones that our union is right, the correct path in life– for once. But I doubt Clover's had the realization yet. She's well on her way, and when she gets the epiphany, I'll be here to catch her when she falls. Until then, I will bare more of my soul, and I hope to God Clover likes what she sees.

"So the Playroom is a happy place?" Clover looks relieved. "Everyone is expressing themselves, no one is judging, no one is taunting or making fun? You wouldn't have to worry if you were pretty enough or buxom enough? It's not a bunch of guys picking from young girls like they are stock, is it? Big girls and older women don't get heckled, do they?"

The question seems to hold weight. Is Clover debating a visit? "No," I reply, stunned shitless that she might actually consider going to the Playroom with me, even once. I huff a surprised laugh, followed by a snort. "Making fun? We have people from age twenty-one to nursing home. Ross is a randy old fool. It's all good-natured. We're all there for different reasons. What I do is in private, but I like to sit on the sofa and watch their antics."

Getting more inquisitive by the second, "So you don't have to participate? At all?" I reach up and smooth the lines forming between her eyebrows.

My lips twist in a grin. "Well, if I was a thinking man, I'd think you were debating something in this mind of yours," I tease, tapping a fingertip to the center of her forehead. "With a guy like Auggie, you could have him doing something with the rest of us enjoying the show. You'd be surprised at how many people just go there to hold a conversation with their fellow deviants. It's about community and belonging. The whole point of the Playroom is self-expression. If you're a quiet sort, then be quiet.

If you're a watcher, then watch. If you're an exhibitionist, then preen like a peacock."

"Auggie's the peacock, right?" Clover laughs when I shake my head no.

"He's built like a peacock, but I was speaking of your brother, actually. Rob thrives in the Playroom. The Playroom is Rob's big playpen."

"I can't go then," Clover quickly says, looking extremely disappointed and uncomfortable. She gazes at the ceiling, trying to avoid my accurate read on her emotions. It's Clover– I don't need to see her eyes to know what she's thinking, because it's written across her entire body.

"Sure you can," I coax. I grab Clover's upper arms and give a little shake– shaking some sense into her. "The Playroom will be at the Spook House as soon as we have the go-ahead. For the past five years, I've managed to never catch my sister in a compromising position with Rob. Isis usually sits next to me, teasing me. It's our odd bonding time. If you decide you want to check it out, let me know, and I'll make arrangements for your comfort."

"Can I think about it?"

"Absolutely. No pressure. I won't be going without you, nor will I be upset or happy depending on either way you choose. My wife's happiness and comfort comes before my own. It's not like I won't be getting my needs met. I went to the Playroom because I was starving. But you, my silly rabbit, are a delectable buffet," I purr, rolling my words in time with my hips. "This man will never be hungry again."

Wanton little thing, so easily aroused, Clover sways above me, breathlessly panting. Her blue eyes glow with a lust-filled fever. An aroused flush covers her breasts and belly. The sheet between us is drenched with her juices, to the point that moisture beads on my cock and drizzles down my sack. Its tickling presence sliding down the crack of my ass has my eyes fluttering shut. My little bitch likes the fantasy of the sensual side of the Playroom.

Like brother, like sister. If Rob thrives in the Playroom, Clover will flourish.

Heated words flow freely from my lips without forethought, "My fantasy is of you lying on that table with countless hand touching you, drawing out your pleasure. Cocks and fingers and tongues, impaling your sweet pussy, while mouths latch on to your suckable nipples, and your mouth is filled with sex. I want to watch you writhe in torturous ecstasy for hours upon hours as we milk your release from you one finger, tongue, and cock at a time."

"Malcolm," Clover screams the release my words tore painfully from her. She bucks against my hips. One… two… three… inches of my spasming, sheet-covered cock slides into her clenching pussy.

Clover falls to my chest, body quivering as she shamelessly grinds her clit against my abs to extend her climax. "Huh? Imagine that," I breathlessly pant. "Clover wants to visit the Playroom." Clover's resulting giggle will ring in my ears for the rest of my days.

"Good God, woman, I love you," I whisper so quietly she can't hear it while in the throes of her orgasmic high. I believe in the words I told Kieren, never tell a woman you love her during sex, and I stand by those words. I can think it, and I can say it, just not to her. Not yet, anyway.

Head popping up abruptly, Clover looks me in the eyes. Face flushed a beautiful pink, hair a total mussed up disaster, making her the most stunning creature I've ever laid eyes upon. Winking so fast I think I imagined it, she leans forward to brush a kiss to my lips. "Thank you," she mouths against my lips. But a second later my mind fully engages, and I realize she actually mouthed, "me too."

I choke on an emotion I haven't felt in decades. Happiness? No. Being in love? Yes! I have a feeling I'm going to be in this state of madness for the rest of my life.

Clover rocks my world, "I'm going to touch you now… and then you're going to make love to me. We have a few hours of daylight left to burn, and we shouldn't waste this perfectly good hotel room."

Our lips seal the vow. I kiss Clover like my life depends on it. As if she is the last breath of oxygen. The first sustenance after a famine. She fuses her tiny body to my chest and melts into me. I drink her hungry whimpers like the finest wine. She takes everything I have to give and gives back more than I ever hoped to receive.

Clover is my woman, and she makes me a man.

CHAPTER TWENTY-NINE

The Widow

I do the one thing I've never allowed myself to do in the past– I explore. I've never explored what makes me tick. My best friend likes girls, so that cancels out most of the hot guy chat, but the mechanics of sex don't really change. When asked certain questions, all adults have an answer, except for me. Malcolm has asked these very personal questions in text form on many occasions, where I would act offended because I didn't know how to answer.

Where are your sweet spots, Clover? If I kiss your inner thigh, will you moan for me? If I pull your hair, will you scream out my name? If I spank your ass, will you hit me back or come for me?

What's your favorite position, Silly Rabbit? Do you want me to bend you over the Mayor's desk and fuck you raw? How about I hide beneath your desk and feast between your thighs while you conduct your day-to-day business?

What are your deepest, darkest desires? What fantasies do you visit when you touch yourself? What image is superimposed in your mind when you orgasm? Do you call out when you come, or do you seek your release in divine silence?

Does it turn you on to suckle at the flesh between a man's legs like a kitten after a hot bowl of cream? Do you crave the taste of man? Does the thought draw wetness between your legs like an overflowing pool?

Shall I kiss, lick, suck, or bite your clit? Or do I commit a heroic feat and do a combination of all four simultaneously?

Malcolm's words always made me hot, but on the heels of the rapid lust was pain and sadness. I wanted to be able to answer him, but I didn't know how.

How can you know what you've never experienced?

"Just bear with me, okay?" My voice comes out thready, fracturing under the weight of insecurity and inexperience. I may not know the answers to questions about myself, but I do know a thing or two about pleasing a man. My only fear, what if all men are different? I was taught to please Sam, and what if Malcolm doesn't enjoy it. The only solace I have is in the mechanics of the act. We all have the same parts– the rest is in the exploration.

Dark blue eyes narrowing, "You confuse me. You realize this, right?"

"Just keeping you on your toes," I say with a grin, and I actually mean it. "I'm going to touch you now, and I want you to be passive. This is about you, Malcolm. Your life's been rough lately and I want to ease you. But mostly, I need to learn you."

"What if I want to learn you instead?" The words sound teasing, but the intent is nothing but serious.

Stilling, panic slams into me. I can't allow Malcolm to explore me before I prove to him that I can please him. What if he doesn't like how I am? If I show him what he'd be giving up, maybe he could deal with my brokenness. But if he finds my brokenness first, he could cut his losses and go back to his friends at the Playroom, who have satisfied his needs for well over five years. Malcolm and I have no history. We're trying to build a foundation right now, and if Malcolm realizes just how broken I truly am, it will topple down around me.

"You've had a year to learn me, Malcolm," I try to sound reasonable. "I haven't. Yes, I remember every word you've said, but it's not the same. So just lie back and relax, and let me take care of you. Okay?"

Patient but leery, Malcolm gazes up at me, contemplating his next move, I'm sure. "This is undiscovered territory for me, Clover. I might have learned your personality, but when I asked you about sex, you threw up a brick wall, calling me a pervert."

"You're not a pervert," I say instead of the truth. I can't admit why I was hesitant to answer his questions. I can't say I didn't have an answer to the questions he asked. Malcolm wants a grown woman, with grown woman needs and experiences. I may be thirty-five, but I know no more about myself than I did at sixteen.

Sighing, Malcolm relaxes back against the mattress, tucking a pillow beneath his head. "I relent. Arguing about who goes first defeats the purpose, don't you think? If I pride myself in giving you what you want, but argue over what you want, then I fail. If you want to touch me, so be it."

"Don't act like it's a chore to lie here and be serviced, Chief Mason," I tease, drawing a fingertip down his chest. I expected him to smile up at me, not scowl and looked pissed. "Landmine?" I ask, hoping to God I'm correct.

"Serviced?" Malcolm breathes out, sounding furious but trying to hide it. "Clover, answer me this: why do you want to touch me?"

"Because I want to…" I stop myself from telling the whole truth, but something inside me overpowers my mind and spills it in a torrent, "because I want to know what makes you tick, because it would please me to know I please you. I want to find your sweet spots so I can exploit them later. I want to hear you moan my name when I turn you on. I… touching you makes me feel like a real woman instead of a widowed mother whose only role in life is serving my family. I just want to be free to touch you without fear."

Running his fingertips up and down my spine, Malcolm's voice is as intimate as his touch. "Fear of what?"

I lean forward, unable to say the word while he's looking at me. I know how very transparent I can be. I rest my cheek against his and whisper near his ear, "Rejection. Just let me touch you, all right? You'll know when to touch me back… you always seem to know."

"Right answer," he whispers back, and I can hear the smile in his voice. "Nice try, Clover. But even if I can't see your face to read it, the rest of your body is touching mine, and your voice is more expressive than your face. I'm a trained police officer, woman. I might not know exactly what you're thinking, but I'll have a pretty good idea on what you're feeling," he warns.

"Ah," is my only responds. As odd as it sounds, it's freeing to know I can't hide from Malcolm.

I slide from Malcolm's body to sit by his side. I rest with my legs folded beneath me, heels tucked to my ass. Uncomfortable being exposed as I am, I feel silly wearing only a pair of stockings and a bra. Whatever floats Malcolm's boat, I guess.

I start with Malcolm's right hand. First massaging it with the pads of my fingertips, and then I lean forward to place gentle kisses on the tenderized skin. Seeing Malcolm wiggle around the mattress, trying to contain his reaction, releases my insecurities.

I'm a pane of window glass– Malcolm can see right through to my very core. There is no hiding. If I long to be Malcolm's undoing, then I have to allow him to be mine.

"I don't have a favorite position," I begin. I pause to nip the skin of Malcolm's wrist, causing him to arc off the mattress. Smiling against his wrist, I murmur my words, allowing my breath to warm and tickle his skin. "For me, sex was like war. You either won or you surrendered. Either way, it was incredible. It was the in between that I didn't care much for."

I lick a wet path from his wrist, along his forearm to his inner elbow. I get waylaid in my journey when I find a sweet spot. Malcolm's hips thrust forward, spilling the sheet from his waist. "Mmm… do you like your elbow bitten, Chief Mason?"

"I didn't until now." He grunts when I sharply nip him with my front teeth.

"To win the war, I had to overpower myself. I had to shut the worthless bitch up who was incessant with her self-hatred. That tiny voice that screams the loudest was my worst enemy. When the perfect woman quieted, the dirty girl arose, and with her, sex was unforgettable. When I won, I was in charge, and I rode away from battle," I end with my voice dipping deep, tinged with a husky tone.

"Jesus Christ," Malcolm hisses, voice thick with hunger. I lick a path from his well-tended elbow to his muscular shoulder, briefly stopping to explore along my way. As my mouth works his flesh, my fingertips imprint the landscape of his chest into memory. I want to know my husband in the light of day as well as in the dark of night.

"Surrender: to give in to one's fears and release them. Surrender is just another type of win if you look at it from a certain perspective. There is freedom within knowing when to back down and regroup. Sexual surrender meant I was passive, but not merely the passenger of the *in between*."

I run the edge of my front teeth along Malcolm's whisker-stubbled jaw, as if they were the sharp blade of a razor. "Oh, God," Malcolm's voice quivers as he writhes on the bed. "This is you winning, isn't it? Holy fuck," he breathes, and the sound seems to further empower me.

"Sexual surrender was just as rewarding," I breathe into Malcolm's ear. "Those were the times I fully let go. I wasn't perfect, nor was I dirty, and I wasn't merely a passenger in my marital bed." My lips enclose around his earlobe, softly suckling it into my mouth. Tugging, I release a growl-like sound that has Malcolm unable to contain himself. "I was a wife," I purr.

"You're going to be *my* wife," Malcolm stresses in a strained voice. I roll my lips along his cheek until they come in contact with his mouth. I linger, slowly lapping at his lips with my tongue, tugging him open with my teeth, and then plunging deeply inside. Tasting of one hundred percent male, I groan in bliss. Accidentally, I find another sweet spot when the tip of my tongue slides along his soft palate.

"Behave," I growl when Malcolm reaches to roll me beneath him. "Naughty Mason." Taking my time, I work back down his neck, feasting and exploring. I make my way to the hollow of his throat, softly lapping with my tongue.

"There is no such thing as winning or surrendering when you have no partner," I admit sadly. "I had to adapt by using fantasies taken from books. Many readers fall into the story, becoming one with the character as if the events were happening to them in reality."

My suspicions are proven correct when I roughly bite into Malcolm's nipple, sucking it into my mouth as far as I can manage. "Automatic arouser," I tease. "I think your nipples are more sensitive than mine."

"Let's find out," Malcolm drawls out slowly in a sluggish lust-induced voice.

"Let's not and say we did," I taunt, nipping him with each word. Malcolm's palm flies out to slap my ass, his fingers brushing my exposed pussy. "Behave," I breathe while placing his hand back on the mattress where it belongs. "

"I'm not an ordinary reader. That angry, bitter voice wouldn't shut up since she no longer had a combatant. Instead of placing myself in the shoes of the heroine, pretending she was me, I became her or him. Whichever character I related to the most, I became. Clover Webster no longer existed in fantasy, just as she didn't in reality, not the real her anyway."

Malcolm avidly listens to me speak, even as I torture him with my slow seduction. I'd worry that he was more intrigued with my mind than my body, but I'm perfectly fine with that. My mind will always be with me, while my tits will sag and my ass will flatten at the same rate my belly will bulge. Beauty is fleeting, and I plan on keeping Malcolm engrossed for the rest of my life.

I glorify in Malcolm: his tangy masculine scent. The ridges along his narrow torso, peppered with wiry hairs. The grove of his hip as it tapers down to his proud cock. Licking, I catalog his flavor, how it strengthens the further south I follow. Malcolm's arms were salty. His neck was sweet. But the father south I travel, the more musky he becomes, until the bitter scent of aroused male floods my nostrils.

Strongest trigger point found– biting hard, I attack the juncture where Malcolm's leg joins his groin. "Fuck me!" Malcolm shouts to the ceiling, back arching but not nearly as much as his cock. Quivering beside me, I'm enthralled of the sight of his dick jerking as if coming but no ejaculate pours forth.

I speak to quiet Malcolm's intense need for release, because I'm nowhere near ready for the finale. "I couldn't see myself as a sexual being. I had one purpose, and one purpose only– motherhood. So in my fantasies, I was someone else. I was far removed from the scenario. Lying in bed, with my hand between my legs, it wasn't me being touched. It wasn't me who came."

Skating a fingertip down the length of Malcolm's arousal, I marvel at how something so hard can feel so incredibly soft to the touch. Unbidden, a giggle slips from my parted lips when I trail my finger in the air just above Malcolm's cock and it jerks to reach out and touch me.

"I think he likes me," I mutter wryly, earning me a snort from Malcolm's throat. "It could be the magic trick I'm performing." I watch in fascination as his cock tries to touch me when I get within jerking distance. "Or it could be this big pool of future-Mason-juice filling your belly button," I tease, leaning forward to lap at the pre-cum drooling out the tip of his cock.

"Jesus Christ, this is definitely you winning," Malcolm garbles out incoherently. When the head of his penis slips between my lips, he releases a ragged grunt. Then we groan together for two very opposite reasons, which are parallel in nature. Me: Malcolm's intoxicating taste combined with the torturous absence of not performing this act since I was a young wife in my twenties. Malcolm: the first taste of oral sex since he was a husband.

I allow myself time to briefly explore Malcolm's length and the potent, heavy twin weights that dangle beneath. But the absence has been too difficult for Malcolm to bear, and he comes dangerously close to release on my first hardy suck.

I grip the base of Malcolm's cock in my fist, propping it up until it's vertical. I roll my eyes up to connect with his. "Malcolm," I breathe his name in warning, and he doesn't even as much as blink. "This is me winning," I say the words as I lunge forward, straddling his hips to plunge deeply onto his raised cock.

"C-l-o-v-e-r!" Malcolm screams, alerting the entire hotel floor of his release… and I ride away from battle victoriously.

Rocking my hips, sliding the hard, spasming cock in and out of my pussy, I become empowered. Panting, eyes wide with wonder, Malcolm comes undone beneath me, within me. A wash of hot fluid fills my body as Malcolm gasps and groans, twitches and writhes, nearly throwing me off with the force of his climax. I can do nothing but experience: the painful stretch of my body accommodating Malcolm after so many years of being empty, the disbelief that this is actually happening, and the odd twinge in my heart as unheard emotions begin to speak within me.

Jackknifing against the mattress, Malcolm slams his hips up into me. His fingertips bite into the flesh of my hips, bruising me with their intensity. "Don't stop. I'm still hard. Take what you need from me. Please. God, please," he begs, but it sounds more of a prayer to a God he doesn't believe in.

Who knew, sex makes Malcolm Mason a believer.

"I don't want to wear you out, old man," I tease, trying to ignore the feelings clamoring to escape– they rattle their chains, trying to open the locks on the door in the back of my mind.

I allow Malcolm to calm as I sit astride him. Finding him utterly fascinating, my fingertips continue to caress anything that strikes their fancy. "I've always loved a man's forehead," I mutter, blushing as I outline the shape of his brow. "I sound like an idiot, but it's sexy– manly."

"Clover?" Malcolm rasps out my name, voice thready. His fingers twitch on my hips, but otherwise he remains motionless.

"Hmm?" Too engrossed in my exploration, I don't take notice of the calculating look in Malcolm's dark blue eyes.

"My turn," he announces a split-second before I'm picked up. Becoming airborne, I squeak and flail as my back hits the mattress with great force. Fisting a hank of my hair, wrapping the strands around his hand, controlling me, "I wasn't through," Malcolm growls, eyes shining with a deviant light. "Now, *I'm* going to have my way with *you*."

Spreading my thighs wider by nudging me with his hips, Malcolm settles between my legs. With a powerful thrust, it's my turn to jackknife off the mattress, shouting out in surprise. I shudder at the sensation of his hard cock slicing through my body, using his own release to ease the way. Eyes wide open, staring up at my future husband, I surrender.

Flushed and blushing, "I'm not some young buck, but by God, you turn me into one. No way will either of us settle for a one-pump-chump on our first time. By some saving's grace, I'm still hard, and we're going to use it to our advantage." Eyelashes fluttering, shuttering his thoughts, a lazy smile slowly twists his lips. "You better hold on, bunny," he warns. "I'm in the mood for hard and fast."

It's my turn to release a benediction. "Christ," is torn from my throat as Malcolm makes good on his word, proving yet again that he is a man of consistency. One hand fisting my hair, the other firmly planted on the mattress near my head, clutching the sheets, Malcolm gains the leverage he needs to shift my reality.

Hips pistoning at a frantic pace, Malcolm is an erotic sight to behold. Glistening long, lean muscles bunch and release as they perform their satisfying task. Once again, I find myself marveling over the fact that this man wants me, and I believe to the center of my being that it is the truth. Fierce, as demanding as it is coaxing, Malcolm's onslaught changes me. I release the perfect, broken woman and the chaotic, dirty girl, and finally rediscover the Clover I've spent a lifetime trying to locate, but she was always just out of reach. In the arms of the man, I become Malcolm Mason's wife.

Fascinated, enthralled, raptured, Malcolm becomes the center of my world. The locks give way, the chains disappear, and the sensation of every emotion I've long denied nearly suffocates me. Tears spring to my eyes as Malcolm reawakens me.

Breath sawing in my ear, interspersed with sharp grunts from the force of his thrusts, Malcolm dominates every single sense in my body. His taste is coating my tongue as I pant against his cheek. His musky scent tickles my nostrils. The sensation of his body sliding inside mine, against mine, over mine, is as comforting as it is arousing. The sounds of his exquisite ecstasy ring in my ears. Lastly, the intense look of adoration and captivation he bores into me while connecting us in the most primal of ways.

Spreading myself wide, my hands grip Malcolm's ass, fingernails biting into the strong muscular flesh. Refusing to win, to surrender, or to lie passively in the in between, I counterthrust, meeting Malcolm as an equal.

"Malcolm," his name rolls off my tongue, a mix of lust and love. Insanely close to coming, all I can do is moan. His sex twitches inside me, informing me with his body language, not his words, that he's right on the edge with me.

Every muscle in my body goes taut at once, clenching, and they don't relax until the deep moan pours from my throat. With my arms, legs, my sex, I hold Malcolm in an endless embrace as we fly off the precipice together.

Malcolm says he loves me for a third time: once implied, twice whispered. I don't return the sentiment, but not because I don't feel it too. I bite my tongue against laughing out as Malcolm berates himself for breaking some unknown code of sexual conduct.

Silently laughing, I finally feel at home in my skin. "I won't ask," I tease. "But you should know, while I might be easy to read, you speak the words aloud you are thinking in your mind. Right now, is, by far, the worst time to say Ren and Willow's names. But something tells me you know something I don't know."

Flustered, Malcolm raises his head. His cheeks are a brilliant shade of red from embarrassment and sexual satisfaction. "I… um…" He huffs a happy sounding laugh. "I told Ren to never say… um… I love you during sex. It seems I can't stop myself, and I was wondering if he was faring any better."

"Ah," I breathe out, as I slowly slide out from beneath Malcolm. His arms try to stay me, but nature is calling with a vengeance. After a playful struggle, I extract myself. "I'll have to ask Willow sometime– maybe," I add. "But let's never say their names when we're connected in a bed. Eh?"

"I have no boundaries," Malcolm says as if he's telling me something I didn't already know. He rolls to his side to face me, pulling the sheet over his cooling skin. I stand before him wearing only a bra and stockings, shivering in the air-conditioned coolness. "I'm not a pervert, though. It's just…" He sighs, combing his fingers through his hair in a nervous gesture. "I made them. I want to know every single detail about them. They are my children– they are what makes me a man, and they utterly fascinate me. I'm proud of the intriguing creatures I produced. It comforts me when they are happy– even if it's a naughty sort of happiness."

"I know. I understand," and I do. "I wish we could stay here forever, but reality is calling us back home," I say over my shoulder as I make my way to the bathroom, picking up my scattered clothing along the way. "As is nature."

Cleansed, relieved, redressed, with my hair finger-combed, I stare into the mirror expecting the bitter, old me to gaze back. The tap water is running in the sink, the rushing sound a comfort. I stare into my blue eyes and a stranger stares back. I like this stranger, though. She is confident, proud, relaxed, and happy in her own skin. She isn't a woman operating out of fear and insecurity. I look forward to fully embracing the woman gazing back at me.

My heart is at peace, but my mind is a stew of utter chaos. I can't shut the door– the chains and locks no longer exist. No matter how hard I try to grasp the hectic emotions and shove them away, to not be subjected to their piercing pain, there is no longer a door to hide behind. I'm blown wide open: wounded, raw, exposed.

Sam.

The small thread of Sam I saved all these years resided behind that barricaded door. The piece I refused to release, to mourn. He was always with me, silently judging me, tainting not only my view of him and myself, but the world as a whole.

You don't have the pleasure of releasing your deceased loved ones, they leave you. You can live in denial, unable to deal with the pain and mourn in a healthy fashion, but it won't bring them back. You will be the walking dead, an empty husk of who you should be. You do your loved ones a disservice by living in the past. They are gone, never to return, leaving behind the only tangible piece– your memories of them. Sometimes it's easier to hold onto the anger, the bitterness, to feel betrayed by their passing, than to just let them go.

Looking in the mirror, softly sobbing from deep within my chest as tears streak down my cheeks, not only do I say goodbye to the old me, the wounded girl who was left behind, I finally let Sam go to live in peace.

Redressed, pacing the hotel room, "Are you okay?" Malcolm asks as soon as he takes one look at me as I exit the bathroom.

"I think so." I don't elaborate because Malcolm is sorting out his own pain. We look at each other, no need to explain as we experience the same rush of emotions. "You?"

Stopping in front of me, Malcolm smiles. "Yeah," he sounds surprised. "I thought I'd feel guilty. I feared Camille's ghost would haunt me while we were together. But it just felt... right."

My hand raises on its own accord to cup Malcolm's whisker-stubbled cheek. He softly nuzzles my palm, smiling with tears glistening in his eyes. "Me too," is all I have to say, because no one will ever get it– get me –like Malcolm Mason, and no one will ever get Malcolm Mason like I will.

CHAPTER THIRTY

The Widower

"Dude, where the hell have you been all day?" Auggie catches me in the driveway as I exit my SUV.

"Stress relieving," I reply, smirking like I have the naughtiest secret.

Eyes bulging out of his skull, "Holy hell, you got laid, and judging by that perma-smile pasted on your ugly mug, it was damn good, too." Yanking me into a half-hug, Auggie smacks my back a few times.

I grip Auggie tightly, not letting him get away. I whisper to him, "Keep this between us, will ya? Clover and I got engaged, but we're waiting to tell everyone."

Slowly pulling away, Auggie mutters, "Why? I'd think you'd be shouting it from the rooftops."

I turn away, needing to get my stuff from my vehicle. "I want to, but we have some unfinished business first," I reply as I gather up my shit.

"What business?" Auggie asks, taking my jacket and belt from me so I have both hands to pull the clip from my gun and empty the chamber. If my kids are home, I never enter the house with a loaded weapon. Not after our shared nightmare.

"Willow," I say in answer. "Clover's going to tell her, but it's only hours since Devon stepped on Arizona soil. It's a bit too much for the girl to handle all at once."

"Oh," Auggie sounds disappointed, and then an evil grin twists his lips. "I can razz Willow, right? Tease her about you and Clover?"

"You're like a giant child," I say with a laugh. "Sure, knock yourself out. The tiny brat deserves whatever you do to her. Willow's been overworking Clover for months. Somehow sending her messages for more treats– treats I never got to eat."

"Willow, you say?" Auggie arches his furry, red eyebrow. "From your cell? You sure it wasn't Ren sending it for her?"

"Motherfuck!" I take my front steps two at a time. "I'm sure Willow had help. Her ass is growing, did you notice that?" Auggie's snicker is answer enough. "God, stop looking at her like that. It's so fucking creepy. I was only noticing because I was gauging if she was eating my food. Willow's getting a little gut on her too. Cake stealer," I growl.

"Sorry," Auggie says, not sounding sorry at all. "I have some very fond memories of that ass... sadly, before its growth spurt."

"And here I thought nobody could pout like Robin," I taunt Auggie's sad expression. "Growth spurt proves just how young she truly is, so leave the girl alone. You've got your own man... and woman. Don't be a glutton."

"Don't go there, man. That conversation is off-limits." Auggie stomps into my house. I pressed the only button Auggie has, and its name is Isis.

We both skid to a halt in the doorway to my kitchen. Ren and Willow are in an intimate embrace, lips feasting at one another, hands groping and gripping. I wince, never wanting to hear Willow's moans of pleasure. I left the Playroom every time Willow was there to '*play*'. But how do you leave your own kitchen, or unhear how the daughter and mother make the same fucking sex-song.

Feeling nauseous, I clear my throat to gain their attention. "About fucking time," Auggie's voice booms throughout the kitchen. Embarrassed, Willow hides her face against Kieren's chest. "I was wondering how much it would take to make a good girl misbehave. I thought if you told a kid not to do something, they would rebel and do it anyway. So much for reverse psychology for this stubborn one. Willow has a horrible propensity to do as she's told."

"Maybe you should have just told Willow to go to Kieren instead of telling her how naughty he was," I deadpan. I'm amused yet not amused with Auggie's past endeavors. Sickened mostly.

"Eh," Auggie grunts out. "I thought she liked naughty. Plus, I wouldn't have known if she was behaving or making her own decision. Tricky business when dealing with Miss Prynne. Don't forget that, Ren."

"You're so full of shit, Auggie," Willow grumbles in her husky voice, and then blushes a brilliant shade of red when we all laugh at her. "I gotta finish fixing dinner. Auggie of all people should know not to distract me when open flame is involved."

"Remind me to always make sure you only have access to an electric stove," Kieren teases Willow as she turns her attention back to our dinner.

"Son? Ya got a minute?" I interrupt his ogling of Willow's expanding ass. "Living room, please," I jerk my chin in that direction. "I'm sure Auggie can supervise Willow's cooking methods."

After a minute, Ren finally joins me in the living room, finding me wearing a path in the carpet with my pacing. "Is Dev not okay?" Ren's voice cracks with worry, stopping me in my tracks.

"Oh, shit! No, everything is fine. I called the center before I made my way home. We can't have contact with Dev for the next month, but they will keep me in the loop. When I called, Dev had only been on the premises for about an hour, just getting checked in." I grab my son's hand, giving his fingers a squeeze. "Listen, I gotta tell you something, but you can't tell your woman. If you don't feel right keeping Willow out of it, then I won't put that pressure on you."

Ren's blond brows knit together in confusion. "Why can't I share it with Willow?"

"She'll find out in a few weeks, after this latest shit-storm clears. Everything is connected, so if you tell Willow, she'll have to know everything else."

The unwanted cop in my son rears its glorious head, "What's everything?"

"No fucking way, Ren. I'm not doing to you what Seth has been going through. Not on your life." I take a deep breath, fearing his response. "So, can I speak my piece or do you want to wait it out with Willow?"

It's Ren's turn to start pacing. I watch him wear a track in our carpet between the sofa and my recliner. I need to tell him for selfish reasons. I want to share my unexpected joy with my son, especially now that Devon isn't with us. I want to feel that bond between father and son. But at the same time, I don't want to put that pressure on him. It's not fair to ask Ren to keep something so important from Willow. It's why I asked his opinion before blurting out the happy news.

Decision made, "Nope," Ren says while shaking his head no. "Don't tell me, because if it's really important, I'll tell her anyway. I won't keep shit from Willow, Dad. Not even for you."

"Right answer," I praise as I pat Kieren's shoulder. "My boy is growing up into a fine man. Now, let's see if Willow needs any help in the kitchen," I say to distract myself from spilling the beans. "Lord knows, that girl needs help." Ren chuckles at the God's honest truth.

With my forearm firmly planted against his chest, I still Ren from barging into the kitchen. Willow's sole concentration centers around the stove and its contents, while Augustus is lurking behind her with a pained expression on his face. His brows are tightly knitted together over his guilty green eyes. His hand moves toward Willow only to fall back to his side. He doesn't know that we silently watch his moment of indecision.

"I just want to watch them. We need to see how they behave when they're unguarded," I whisper to my impatient son. "We need to see if we can trust Auggie to be alone with Willow."

Kieren relaxes under my touch. My hand slides from his strong chest as he steps to the side for a better viewing angle.

Auggie reaches over, and this time his hand softly connects with Willow's ponytail. The chocolate strands slide through his fingers like a flow of water. Willow looks over her shoulder and smiles sweetly at her boss and friend. The naked relief on Auggie's face crushes my heart.

Augustus Kline is lost, set adrift from his natural path. Auggie had stepped into Willow's natural path and was upsetting the balance of their lives. I don't doubt that Auggie loves Willow, but does he love her the way he should? Willow needs room to grow and flourish. Auggie is fighting his need to shrink the space around Willow until the only thing that exists in her world is him. Willow's innocence is intoxicating for a man like Augustus, to both of their detriments.

Willow chatters, pointing at something in the pan on the stove. Auggie's shoulders dip as the tension flees his taut body. I watch for a suspended minute as the sullen climate changes to the easy companionship they once shared.

"Auggie's looking at Willow the right way," Ren says in obvious relief. "Finally."

"Good," I breathe out. "I was very, *very* worried," I stress, knowing Willow wasn't strong enough to dampen Auggie's manipulations if he truly wanted her. I move to enter the kitchen when the backdoor opens. I put my hand out to stop Ren again, needing to see how Auggie reacts to my sister's arrival.

Auggie's head whips around, eyes landing on Isis as if magnetized by her. My sister pays no one any heed as she starts searching around in the kitchen drawer, asking where the screwdriver is located. The guilty big brother expression on Auggie's face is replaced with one of intense longing. He prowls over to Isis, curling over her back, pretending to help her find the missing tool while stroking her arms.

"Did you just call Auggie a tool?" Ren snickers near my ear. "Because he's a fucking tool, all right." Stepping away from my hand, Ren walks across the kitchen to help Willow with something in the oven. Not that Auggie would even notice since he's kissing a trail up the nape of my sister's neck.

I lean against the entryway to the kitchen, arms crossed over my chest, watching my family interact. Willow and Ren work as a team, getting our supper prepared, while Isis pretends to be oblivious to Auggie's affections. In the distance, I can hear Raven and Weston bickering about a mutual school friend named Sage.

If I blink, in a few years, we won't be in *this* kitchen, but hopefully I will be sharing this type of mundane moment with Clover. Most people thrive on drama and excitement, but after the life I've lived, with the intense occupation I hold, I could use a big dose of mundane. With Clover by my side as we watch over these fools, I'll never be bored.

The backdoor swings opens again, bringing in a chilly air, and not from the late May evening. As soon as Essie walks into the kitchen, Willow walks out toward the dining room, Ren close at her heels. Auggie and Isis ignore the poor girl, so I send her a kind smile and a wave to make her feel at home. At Essie's back is Robin, who smiles blindingly when he notices Auggie's preoccupation with Isis, and then makes a beeline for some affection of his own.

Christ, this isn't going to be a mundane evening after all.

CHAPTER THIRTY-ONE

The Widow

I hum the tune I heard on the way home earlier as I make meatloaf, mashed potatoes, and green beans (half Seth's favorite meal, half Violet's). The twins are studying for their algebra final at the kitchen table, with Seth playing the ever-patient tutor.

It's just an ordinary evening at the Webster household, which is inconceivable after the past few days we've lived through.

"I don't get it," Violet says for the billionth time. The girl got her math skills from her father, as in no skills at all. I went to college for business, and now Willow is following in my footsteps. Sam was clever but not patient, making math too tiring for him to sit through. Sam loved to build things with his hands and be outside. His cleverness has transferred to our son's love of science, as well as his need to roam free.

"I'm at a loss," Seth sighs out, clearly frustrated with Violet's ineptitude. "Why aren't we eating with Grandpa and Grandma?" Still skittish after our long rash of fights, Seth is acting squirrelly around me.

After a day of connecting with Malcolm through touch and talk, I'm a bit more affectionate than usual. I lean down and kiss the tops of both of their heads. They still beneath my kiss, but they no longer pull away. Seth was always cuddly with everyone but me, but Violet was always reserved. Now Violet has changed, turning clingy, especially around Willow and me. She turns around and gives me a hug, and then just as quickly she goes back to her studying while wearing an embarrassed blush.

I go back to my station at the kitchen island, and begin slicing up a fresh loaf of multigrain bread. Violet loves to slather it in butter and eat it with her meatloaf.

"Uncle Will and Aunt Ana are moving in a few days, so Mom and Dad went over there to break bread and iron out a few details."

"What details?" Violet ask, way more interested in gossip than mathematical equations.

"Essie," I state plainly. "That's what happens when you move away when you retire– your adult children don't want to tug up their roots and live their parents' lives." I speak from experience, seeing as how I've been living my parents' life since birth.

"Wouldn't Essie just stay home?" Seth gets up from the table to snag some bread. He's a small guy but he eats like he's fueling a body twice his size.

"They sold the house to pay for the new one in Florida. So in less than a week, Essie is homeless. Essie can't afford to live on her own, so she was going to get a new place with Bethany. They were supposed to sign the lease yesterday, but Beth never showed. Bethany ran off with Rory and eloped. So much for that, huh?"

"Holy shit," Violet says underneath her breath. "Essie's really homeless. I thought that only happened on TV."

"Girl, ya gotta stop watching MTV reality shows. Seriously, stop it," I order while pointing a butter knife at her.

"Weston's the worst. We need to stage an intervention," Seth grumbles, apparently still not getting along with his new baby brother. "So what are we going to do?"

"Mom and Dad are thinking about having Essie move in with them. I'm sure Essie's not going to like that, but it's better than living on the streets. None of us can afford to pay half her rent."

"Essie could get a roommate," Violet adds.

"Essie doesn't have any friends." Seth actually sounds sympathetic to Essie's plight. I thought for sure he'd be drawing the battle lines in the sand and taking sides with Willow and Violet. "If Beth won't be her roommate, Essie's shit outta luck."

"Essie can help Grandma dry her weed," Violet says with a straight face, and I want to be angry, but even I can't help but laugh at that.

"Please, for the love of all that is holy, never, ever say that outside of this house. It is illegal, you know." I just shake my head over and over again as I start setting the food on the table. The kids are more than happy to pick up their study materials for the evening.

"This is nice– peaceful," I say as I begin serving the twins. I flash a genuine smile.

"It's weird," Seth grumbles after he takes a big bite of mashed potatoes. "Uncle Robbie, Essie, and Willow are over at the Masons, and here we sit together… with your big rock on your necklace instead of on your finger." He sounds more hurt than angry.

I place my fork tines on the edge of my plate. I finger the ring in question, feeling odd that it's not on my finger. I think before I speak, mulling over how to explain this to Seth. Malcolm and I had a lot to discuss this afternoon. We actually wrote the issues out on paper and came up with a plan for every single one of them.

"Sometimes you have to divide and conquer. Know in your heart, and never have any doubts, we want to be with them, and they want to be with us. But right now, they have to deal with their problems without us in their way."

"Why?" Violet asks, and she's not hurt like her brother—she's pissed.

"Look at this evening as a buffer." I try to put my thoughts into words. "We have a lot of changes coming up. It's the end of the school year, we don't have a house that will fit us all, and we have the older kids to consider. What about Ren? Is he moving in with us? Willow? But there can't be Ren and Willow in the same house with us. Just as Dev and Willow can't be in the same house. In this, Dev must come first."

"Even I will agree that seeing Willow and Ren together would make the guy take drugs," Violet mutters, eyes huge as she imagines the scenarios. She prattles off animatedly, "Willow enters bitch-mode whenever we mention Essie and Devon. I can't imagine how it would be during family dinner with the four of them at the same table. Dang it!" she shouts, hopping her bottom on her chair. "I wish I was over there tonight. No Dev, but Ren managed to get Essie and Willow in the same building. Fireworks, for sure."

Laughing even though it's not funny, "I'm sure Weston or Raven will give you a play-by-play."

Stabbing at her meatloaf but never taking a bite, Violet's mood sours. "It's no fair," she whines, pouting better than Rob ever could. "We're involved too. Half of the warped foursome belongs to us. But we're banished." She drops her fork onto her plate, slumps to the top of the table, and then rests her chin on her folded arms. She gives me Puss 'n Boots eyes, begging me to fix it.

Seth went from mildly hurt straight into betrayed territory. "When? How long do we have to sit in this house and be excluded?" My son has tears swimming in his eyes. "Shit is going down over at the Masons' tonight, and we weren't invited. My uncle, cousin, and sister are over there. Malcolm said he wanted to be my dad. But here I sit, just like the past five years– fatherless."

Swallowing, I force out, "I'm trying my hardest, Seth. We have nine people to consider here, not just one," I stress. "We are taking one month to get our shit in order: buying a bigger house, selling our two, setting boundaries so we know what is expected of each and every single one of us… and lastly, telling Willow the truth."

"Why wait?" Seth presses. Clearly he has his own agenda– I just wish I knew what it was. But right now, Seth is very hurt that he was excluded tonight.

"Jesus, kid," Violet uses the nickname Ren gave the boys, proving girls do mature faster at this age. Violet is like a mini-me. Ridiculous. "Shit takes time. Mom was just our mom last week. Now she's getting married, gonna be a wife and mother to the Masons. Let the lady wrap her head around that, Seth."

I say the only words that will calm Seth down. "I'm doing this for Willow. When the Masons go to Arizona to visit Devon for their family weekend, I'm telling Willow the truth."

"Why wait?" Seth demands again.

Exhausted on a billion levels, I slump to the table like Violet did, only mine isn't for added dramatic effect. "If I yank Willow out of Malcolm's house tonight to tell her the truth, what do you think she would do?"

Knowing Willow, "Run off with Ren and never speak to you again," Seth offers up immediately.

"N-i-c-e," Violet draws out. "You're such a dick."

"Seth's right," I admit. "We all love Willow, but we know how she gets. Violent. Stubborn. Spiteful. With all of the Masons gone, Willow's choices will diminish. Rob promised to keep Auggie away. Actually, Rob promised to force Willow to keep her ass in this house until we work it out. So, Seth, you asked why we had to wait… there you go."

I experience déjà vu. Seth stares at me from across the table, and it's as if Sam is the one sitting across from me. Sam may be gone, but he lives on in his son– good and bad traits.

Brown eyes narrowed, "I can wait, but do we get to add anything to those boundaries?"

"Sure," I say, not truly meaning it unless it's feasible. Kids come up with the damnedest shit. "Write me a list." My eyes flick between both of the twins. "A reasonable list."

"How is this for reasonable? I don't wanna share a bathroom with the boys." Violet wrinkles up her nose. "They stink."

Releasing a derisive snort, "V, did you forget? We already share a bathroom. Your shit stinks just as bad as mine… and you leave long hairs in the shower, and more hair all over the sink. You're disgusting. Never trust someone who bleeds five days a month and doesn't die."

Glaring, Violet volleys back, "And you're trying to repopulate the earth via the shower drain. I have to dump bleach in the tub before I step foot into it."

"Oh, God," I groan. "Somebody fucking save me from these fools."

"Mom?" Seth and Violet say in unison, exhibiting their twin-powers. Seth reminds me, "There's seven of us now." Violet adds, snickering, "And Malcolm."

I hand Violet a fork and Seth a spoon. They stare at me like I've lost my ever-loving mind. "Kill me now," I beg dramatically. "C'mon, put me outta my misery."

Giggling, the kids pretend to stab me to death while I gasp and wiggle around. My text message alert cuts into our playtime. "What now?" I groan, pointing for Seth to check it out.

"Holy shit!" Seth shrieks. "Mom? Ya better make that eight? No, we gotta add Essie now too. Make that nine. You're gonna freak."

CHAPTER THIRTY-TWO

The Widower

I've had just about enough of Willow for the evening. I was in a great mood, all things considering. Then Willow turned into a frigid bitch because Essie was here, as if Willow had a right to choose who I invited into my own home. I thought after I threatened to kick Willow's ass at the dinner table, she'd straighten up. But no such luck.

Yes, Essie hurt Willow's feelings. Yes, Essie fucked up and made some major mistakes. But it wasn't criminal, nor did anybody die. It also hurts me for Ren, because as Willow rails against Essie over Dev, Ren is left with uncertainty. The girl is fighting over her ex-boyfriend, in front of her current boyfriend. I don't care what moral codes Essie broke, Willow's breaking quite a few right now.

Willow is standing in my kitchen, being snide, snotty, and self-righteous to her own cousin. I want to toss out the '*don't throw stones if you live in glass houses*' analogy, but I can't get a word in edgewise as Willow goes off on a tangent. Not only would Clover kick my ass for not protecting her family, Devon would be upset over how something he did is being pushed off onto a defenseless girl.

I just about shit a brick when Willow told Essie to stop adding drama to the stew we're simmering in, saying Essie's attention seeking was stressing us out. Essie's presence in *my* house was not unwelcome. It was Willow's *reaction* to Essie presence in *my* house that was stressful.

It's been an evening of the pot calling the kettle black syndrome.

Auggie, asshole that he is, starts in on the woman with his John Mason bullshit. "A whore is how you see yourself, so that's why men treat you like one. I'm a man telling you how men think, so you should listen. Women like you fill my Playroom. They feel like shit, they act like shit, so men treat them like shit. You tried to give me a blow job six months ago, and I threw you off me. By your definition of a man, I should have let you do it. I give a girl what she wants– disrespect yourself and I'll disrespect you back. Respect yourself and I'll respect you back. Here's a novel idea, don't fuck losers in cars, and then blame the loser. Blame yourself."

"What. The. Fuck? Are you serious? You tried to blow Auggie?" Willow shouts, adding fuel to the already blazing inferno "Why?"

"I was proving my point. Men like Auggie don't respect women like me," Essie tries to defend herself, backing away from everyone in the room. Willow tracks Essie like a hunter seeking wounded prey.

"You just proved *my* point with your circular argument, little girl," Auggie mutters. "How about you respect yourself? I'm not saying you shouldn't have sex at all. I'm talking about throwing yourself at men you don't even want just to prove you're wanted. Value yourself more than that. Your self-worth doesn't hinge upon whether or not a guy's dick gets hard when he looks at you. My dick gets hard while watching a *Taco Bell* commercial, and I don't plan on fucking my taco– unless it's pink –I'm just hungry."

"Pink Taco: it's the fourth meal." Kieren flashes a devious smirk. "I had some for breakfast this morning. But what do I know, I always get hard when I'm thinking about chocolate cake… I like cake."

"Just shut up," I snarl at Kieren, thoroughly disgusted with his version of comic relief. "Not now. Have some class. Auggie, you're not helping matters, either."

"You know who you sound like, right?" Ren taunts me while Essie and Willow continue to verbally spar.

"I wish Clover was here to referee her girls," I mutter, at a complete and total loss on how to stop this. Was it really this morning I was sitting in the airport, shipping Devon off to rehab? Is this moment in time a sick type of repayment for the small bit of happiness I shared with Clover this morning and early afternoon?

Desperate, Essie cries out, "I'm nine weeks pregnant with a drug addict's baby, and goddamn it, I need your fucking help!"

Well, fuck me, and call me Grandpa.

I'd love to say I didn't see this coming… Christ Almighty!

Not getting the help she was seeking from Willow, Essie stands in the middle of my kitchen with all eyes on her. I breathe a deep sigh of relief when Rob comes to the rescue, pulling his cousin into his arms to cradle her while she cries.

Mayhem ensues: Willow starts screaming like a banshee. Ren is shouting at her to shut the fuck up. Auggie is lecturing anyone who will listen. My youngsters are standing in the kitchen doorway, holding up their cellphones, no doubt immortalizing this Kodak moment. Isis just leans against the counter, observing in a calculating manner.

"I knew you were an attention whore. I knew you were a whore-whore. But this is an all-new low, even for you." Willow is furious, and it flips a switch in me. I love the girl, but she's insulting her own beginnings, her mother, her cousin, and my grandchild all in one fell swoop.

"Am I being punished for something in a former life?" I shout, shutting everyone up. "No one deserves so much shit to happen in one single day."

While calling Essie out on making everything about her, Willow manages to do the exact same thing. God, help me. "You're like the fucking plague," Willow sneers at a weeping Essie. "Look what you're putting Malcolm through, just because you had to get some more fucking attention. Couldn't wait a day or two to spill the happy news?"

Just as Willow couldn't wait two minutes for me to finish speaking before she had to spew more vitriol. "Thank goodness Rob didn't inherit the Prynne self-absorption trait," I mutter to myself. "Willow, I've had enough of your shit for the night. You either shut up or get out," I say while pointing at the backdoor.

Ren looks lost as Willow's face falls. She's confused, so blind to her own immaturity. I don't fault Willow for being an eighteen-year-old child. I fault her for smearing everyone else's shit in their faces, all the while not smelling her own.

Auggie's lectures always seemed to get through to Willow. I decide I'm going to be giving my very first one. "You know the saying 'Bros before hos', Willow?"

"Yes," she replies hesitantly, tiny brow knitted together in confusion. I give Willow props for not crying, even though her bottom lip is quivering.

Our attention is caught as Rob ushers Essie out of the kitchen, most likely taking her to my bedroom. Isis is smart enough to shoo Raven and Weston down the hall to their bedrooms. Ren is caught in indecision. He knows Willow was acting abhorrently, but he doesn't like seeing her hurting… and then there is Auggie, glaring my ass down for speaking to his progeny negatively.

"Willow and I need some alone time," I say to Ren and Auggie. "Beat it," I point to the living room. "You," I pointedly look at Willow, "Sit your ass down at the table."

"I'm going to talk turkey with you," I inform Willow as I sit down opposite her at the kitchen table. "You've offended me several times tonight in my own home, Willow."

I can tell Willow wants to ask why. But smartening up, all she says is, "I'm sorry," in raspy voice.

"My son did the wrong thing. Essie did the wrong thing. We are not debating this right now. It happened. We can't change the past. Whether it was a mistake remains to be seen. But you're making fresh mistakes as of now, Willow," I warn.

"What?" Willow sputters out, shocked at my audacity to call her out on her own shit.

"Kieren. You're not in love with Devon, even though you care about him. Your bitter anger comes across as a scorned woman, and a scorned woman only exists if she still has feelings for the guy. But that's not your problem. You just have to fight to be right."

"I am right," is Willow's immediate reply.

"Right for *you*," I stress. "See, Ren doesn't see this as right versus wrong anymore because it's over and done with. As I said, we all know where the blame lies, so what's the sense of dragging it out every five fucking seconds. It would be like every time you go to say something, I point at you, "*Shut up! You used to smoke pot!*" as if what you have to say isn't important because of something you did in the *past*," I stress. "So your obsession to be right probably has Ren wondering if you're still wavering between him and Devon."

Insulted, Willow shouts, "I'm not!"

"I know." Exhausted, I mumble the truth, "But your need to be right is making this all wrong."

I let Willow think on that for a moment.

"Since you love shoving everyone else's faults into their faces, I will now share with you the mistakes you've made just this evening alone. You're in *my* house, as *my* guest, treating *my* other guest like shit. You are the one creating the chaos and drama, and then blaming it on Essie. This. Is. About. Tonight," I punctuation by pounding the table with my palm. "Not what *Devon* and *Essie* did nine weeks ago."

Vein in her forehead throbbing, Willow screams at me from across the table, "But they cheated on me!"

"Listen to yourself. You are so caught up on what they've done to *you*, that you are doing worse to *them* and not even recognizing it. No one has ever said what they did was okay. We acknowledged it and moved on. It was two months ago, and this is tonight, where *you* were the problem. You were the one stirring the shit-pot and amping up the stress."

Still not getting it, Willow grumbles out, "I didn't mean it."

"Willow... Willow... Willow," I sigh. "You are not sinless. None of us are. I'm not a church goer, but you are. So I will use your own faith against you. We are all to forgive your transgressions. But, because you feel right in your thinking over Essie, we are all to shun her. That is mighty Christian of you, girl. Mighty Christian. I'm rusty on religion, but I'm pretty sure the passing judgment and forgiveness portion is left in God's hand. But I guess it only counts when the judgment and forgiveness are aimed at *you*," I point out.

"I've never cheated on anyone," comes haughtily from the child, as if being addicted to pot and alcohol is nothing to sneeze at. How blind this girl is.

Moving on, because Willow is the definition of thick-headed, "Bros before hos: Essie chose Devon over you, but aren't you doing the same damn thing? You took Devon's side against your own cousin, never once asking Essie why. You forgave Devon for cheating on you while putting one hundred percent of the blame on Essie."

"Devon couldn't help himself," Willow says, sounding like a naïve idiot.

"I thought you'd grown up some, girly?" I twist out, pissed the hell off at her. "First: as a God fearing woman, why are you judging Essie? Second: get over yourself and move the fuck on. You're with Ren now, right? So what's it matter? Third: Only Devon controls where he sticks his dick. Blame him for plunging that unfaithful dick into your cousin. Fourth: Get your head out of your ass and grow the fuck up. You've made some pretty shitty mistakes, and we forgave you for them without an apology."

Confusion and hurt war across Willow's face. "So what? Because Essie is pregnant, she's not at fault?"

"No, that's not why, Willow." I smile sadly at the girl, wishing it wouldn't have come down to having this conversation. I know she is too young to learn from this lesson, and what I'm trying to put across is like explaining color to the blind. Willow was hurt, and that's all she sees, and that's too bad because she's missing the rest of the bigger picture.

"Girl, what you don't get is, that there was *no* fault. It's none of your goddamned business, is what it is. Essie is a human being, and she has a right to do as she wishes with *her* life. If you love Essie, support her choices. If you feel those choices will harm her, tell her why. But know, she doesn't have to take your advice. You are an eighteen-year-old young woman who thinks she's a know-it-all, and you are, but only for *yourself.* Only Essie can live Essie's life– let her live it. Willow, live your own."

I get up from the table and leave Willow sitting there. This was a fruitless conversation. She didn't get it. Willow's just sitting here, trying to figure out why she's in trouble because Devon cheated on her. But the cheating is not the issue. We all know Devon did it, and how both Essie and Devon were in the wrong. It's how everyone behaves *after* that is important. Willow doesn't have to like Essie. If Willow can't tolerate Essie during dinner, then Willow should leave, not try to intimidate the girl like she's a fucking rabid dog sitting across the table. While Willow thinks she's being badass, she's just being classless, and I want more from my future daughter.

But right now, I have more important things to do than shower unneeded attention onto the girl who was just shouting *'attention whore'* at the one who is in true need. Someday, Willow will learn, but sadly that day is not today.

Sighing, I lean down to press a kiss to Willow's forehead. "I love you, even as daft as you are," I tease but there is more than a grain of truth to it. "I see your brain spinning. Until you figure it out, just don't instigate any more altercations. Fair?"

"Fair," Willow grumbles, looking ashamed but confused.

Unsurprised, when I turn around, Auggie and Ren are in the doorway to the kitchen, shamelessly eavesdropping. I look to both of them, "See if you can explain what I was trying to say to her, will ya? Willow's not getting it."

Ren bites his tongue. But Auggie goes into lecture-mode, just as I knew he would. "We have a motherfucking triage situation right now, Willow. You've got a paper cut, and Essie has an amputation. The doctor doesn't care about your sins, they are just doing their job…"

I leave the room as Auggie goes off in the oddest direction ever. Maybe nerdy geeks think different than jocks.

"Christ, what is it, coddle the women-folk tonight?" I grumble beneath my breath when I find my sister leaning against the hallway wall with tears glistening in her eyes. I open the first door I come to– Ren's. "Holy hell," I shout, fed the fuck up and close to gagging.

"Disgusting," Isis spits out. "It's like someone put out an air freshener, and its stench is teenage-sex."

"What in the hell did they do all goddamned day?" I shudder as I slam Ren's door shut, but the odor lingers in the air anyway.

"My guess," Isis looks at me as if I'm stupid. "Fuck." Sighing, Isis twists the doorknob to the only room in the house that's guaranteed to be spotless. "Judging on how strong the stench is, they better be using protection, or we will have another Essie situation on our hands."

"This cannot go on. The kids cannot be around this. They can't know what that scent means." Frustrated, I brush my fingers through my hair. "Clover and I have a lot of things to discuss, that's for sure.

Walking into Weston's room, Isis turns to me, "Got a minute? Rob's talking to Essie, even has her not crying anymore."

"Let me guess," I say as I follow Isis into Weston's immaculate bedroom, "They're talking about Willow, not the baby or Devon."

"Give the man a prize," Isis draws out. Running a fingertip along my youngest son's bookshelves, "Man, Weston's a great kid. I ought to hire him to clean my loft."

"We all have to control something when our lives are in utter chaos. The kid cleans. Clover's gonna love it." I pull Weston's desk chair away from his well-stocked desk, contemplating where he gets all of his office supplies. Isis sees me eyeing them and smiles. Must be she's pilfering Rush's stock. I bet Auggie wouldn't approve.

Isis lounges on Weston's bed, purposely mussing up his blankets and pillows. "Just make sure West doesn't do everyone else's chores, or they won't know shit when they leave the nest.

You don't want to have Clover running over to their apartments to cook and clean, with you doing the maintenance."

"Good point." I lean back in the chair, folding my arms over my chest. "I am so exhausted, but I guess I can take on some more. Why were you crying?"

Isis rolls over onto her belly so I can't see her face. "Don't worry about it," she mutters into Weston's pillow. "You're too involved, ya know?"

"You guys are all that I have," I say with complete sincerity. "I will make time for each and every single one of you, no matter what." For the first time ever, I explain why family means so much to me. "Rob gets lost in his work for days at a time. Auggie walks around with a sketchpad in his back pocket. Their art is their passion. You are passionate about your job and your men. The kids watch TV for escape. Clover reads when reality is too much to handle, and cooks to show her love. For me, I'm intrigued by all of you. You're my endless source of entertainment, my inspiration, and my greatest accomplishments. I'm a dad, and that makes me a man."

"Devon's gonna be a man now, too." Isis tries to divert me away from her tear-stained cheeks.

"Devon's child won't make him a man– how he reacts will," I say more to myself than to Isis. "Why were you crying?" I lean forward and tweak my sister's toe to gain her attention. She giggles like she did when she was a girl, warming my heart.

When Isis doesn't answer right away, I enter a landmine field. "Did Essie and Devon's baby make you think of the one you lost?" I ask softly.

Flipping over on the mattress, Isis moves quicker than my eyes can follow. "You know?" sounding surprised, hurt, and confused.

"You heard the soliloquy I just gave on family, correct? Of course I knew." My voice drips with sadness and sympathy. "I comforted Auggie while Rob was comforting you, and then we switched places and I pretended I didn't know why I was holding you. I understood why you didn't want to talk about it."

Sniffling, "It was just the catalyst that derailed our lives," Isis whispers. "Auggie hates me."

I snort, I can't help it. "Auggie hates you?" I grab Isis's ankle, and then pull her toward me. I force her to sit at the foot of Weston's bed and face me. "I was there when Auggie figured out you were a woman instead of a sidekick. You were chasing

Dev and Ren around the yard, and Robin was chasing you. We were sitting on the back steps and the kid was struck stupid, and he's been looking at you like that ever since."

"Not all the time," Isis mutters.

"Just not when you're looking," I add. "Which one of them went after you first?"

"Rob," is her instantaneous reply. "With those two, I learned size is not an indicator on puberty, or whatever you want to call it. Auggie was the size of a grown man, but he didn't find girls until he was what… fourteen? Rob was trying to dry hump me behind the garage at ten." Isis trails a seductive laugh as she relives the memory.

"I picture Robin Prynne as a naughty beagle puppy in this scenario," I say good-naturedly, and then my voice lowers. "The kind you kick for pissing and shitting on the rug."

"They are very different. There is something about Robin that will make him eternally childlike," she pauses. "Not immature, though. He's the most mature out of us I think." I raise an eyebrow at that, ready to argue. "I don't know… being with Auggie was like being with a man. I was innocent with Rob, while Auggie made me feel like a woman."

"Still?"

"Yeah," Isis breathes out. "It's a good thing, though. Like I said, Rob is mature. He just makes me feel young again. Auggie stresses me out."

"Answer me this time: why were you crying?"

Without hesitation, "I put myself in Essie's shoes. She's a few years younger than I was when I found out I was pregnant. I had both Auggie and Rob for support. Essie doesn't have that. When Devon comes back, he will be our sole focus: his health, sobriety, and sanity. Essie's going to need some support, and I don't just mean financially. Being pregnant messes with your head. I may have never had a child, but I remember how scary it was."

Proving herself wrong, Isis is way more mature than both of her idiots. "I think you're the one who needs to speak to Willow if she doesn't straighten up soon." Just now remembering the '*tool*' scene, "What was Auggie whispering to you so fervently?"

"Auggie's pressuring me to move into the Spook House. That's what was going down in the kitchen. If Rob starts in, I'm screwed."

"True," I say, releasing a sardonic laugh. "I don't know how he does it, but Robin Prynne is the most manipulative person I've ever met. Let's hope he lays off you for a while. Do you want to move in there?"

"I can't while Willow's there," Isis says gravely, voice filled with pain. "Auggie doesn't understand. He keeps telling me how they're finished, that he doesn't see Willow that way anymore. Auggie thinks I should see Willow like all of his other playmates. He laughs about how I'm friends with Nina, and she's been sucking his cock since he was fifteen." Isis draws in a lungful of air, and then releases it in a gust.

"I thought Auggie would grow out of that shit. I truly did. I'm sorry, baby sister," I whisper softly as I caress her hand. "Why does Willow's presence in the Spook House upset you?"

Isis nearly chokes on her words. "Willow is different. She's the female Rob. Willow was our replacement. Willow was everything Auggie was looking for in a mate, all rolled into one singular person who could have kids and the town wouldn't frown upon. Willow is who Dad would have chosen for Auggie. I respect her. I even like her a little bit. But when I look at Willow, I hate Auggie's guts."

Isis lunges off of the bed, tears streaming down her face. I've never heard her speak like this. Essie's news must have really gotten to Isis if it's bringing up all of her issues.

Stopping to face me, Isis throws her hands in the air, frustrated. "On my next birthday, I will be thirty years old. I live alone. I'm not married. I'm in love with two men who also love each other, but they aren't my boyfriends, either. I have no children. I feel like I'm in stasis. Stuck, like a fly in a spider web. My nephew is preparing to start a life with Willow, and they are teenagers. I'm ten years older than them and…"

"Stuck?" Auggie says from the doorway. He's leaning on the doorjamb with his arms crossed over his chest and a remote expression on his face. I have a sneaking suspicion he's been there the entire time. "Get unstuck," he orders. "Move into the room Rob and I made just for you. You won't even look at it."

"How is moving into the Spook House, into a separate bedroom from either of you, getting unstuck?" Isis mimics Auggie's eyebrow raise, challenging him. "We'd be glorified roommates. I'd be disrespecting myself when you fuck your way through Fairport. At least living on my own, I don't feel like I'm a kid living with her daddy."

"We can work something out." Auggie unfurls from the doorjamb, and then slowly approaches Isis. "As for separate bedrooms, you know we each need our space or we feel suffocated."

"Willow–"

"Has never stepped foot into your room, nor did she pick out a single thing for it. I'm not going to kick the girl out of her home, Isis. Not only do I not want to, Rob would kill me." Auggie stands in front of Isis, looking into her eyes.

"I can't do it," Isis grits out, frustrated. Auggie tries to touch my sister, but she flings his hands away. Fed up, Auggie grips Isis's upper arms and shakes her.

"I promised Rob, and now I'm promising you: I haven't touched Willow in months, nor do I plan to." Auggie ducks his head until he's eyelevel with Isis. "Willow belongs to Ren now," he says without a single note of regret. "We just helped Rob beat that into Devon, remember?"

"It's too soon," Isis's voice quivers. Looking away, she breathes, "I can't move in."

"You will," Auggie threatens. "Rory can't babysit you twenty-four/seven now that he's married. Isis, I hate you living over Rush." Voice breaking, "It scares the fuck out of me. Every single night I have to go over there to make sure no one has snuck into the loft, and they're hiding out in there, waiting to attack you. The thought haunts me." Begging, "We want you in our house with us."

"With Willow–"

"Stop this fucking circular argument, Ice!" Auggie bellows, which is my cue to leave.

Isis is my sister, has been since she was placed in my arms on her second day of life. But Auggie and Rob have belonged to Isis since forever. I don't have the power to force her to do the things she doesn't want to do. They do.

I exit to the hallway, leaving the sounds of Isis and Auggie battling behind me. I've listened to their song since they were toddlers. Someday they will get their shit together and realize they are fighting for the same side.

Weston peeks at me from the crack in his sister's bedroom door. I hope he's in there cleaning up, because Raven's room looks like a tornado twisted through it. Poor kid probably wants back into his own clean space.

"Sorry," I mouth at Weston. His eyes dart to the boys' bedroom, asking permission. I shake my head no. I wouldn't wish Devon and Kieren's bedroom on anyone until it's aired out. I'm sure the scent is an aphrodisiac to Ren, but it would turn Weston's stomach.

I'd love to lie down and pass the hell out until morning. But my night has just begun. Rob and Essie are next on my list of problems. I walk the down the hall toward my bedroom with dread pooled in my gut.

Manipulative in my eyes, mature in Isis's, Robin Prynne proves he's respectful as well. Sitting on the floor, Rob gives Essie the lone chair in the room. It's a wooden dining room chair that I drape my shit on every night, but it's a better alternative for Essie than sitting on my bed. Rob moves up in my estimation, especially since I just got done watching Isis roll all around on West's bed, which is surely going to piss the kid off.

Dry-eyed and smiling, Essie was chatting with Rob about Bethany's whirlwind romance with Rush's bouncer. She shut up the second I walked into the room, no doubt intimidated by me. I ignore them both, hoping they will restart their conversation. I rut around in my top drawer, picking out some things I will need later.

They do not reengage. "Carry on," I mutter, feeling awkward. "I'll be with you in a second. Just getting my clothes out for my next shift," I lie. I don't plan on sleeping away from Clover for this next month, even if it's only an hour or so before I head to work. I'm searching for a pair of pajamas that wouldn't insult the twins if they caught me unawares.

Rob, being the one who's most comfortable around me of the pair, picks up where the conversation left off. "So you showed up to rent the place out, and Beth didn't show?"

Rob handles Essie well, knowing how to comfort and encourage her to relax. I noticed it on other occasions. Robin might not be Willow or Essie's actual brother, but he's the perfect big bro. Wonder how he'd fare as a dad, or would Isis and Auggie delegate him as the mom? Rob's definitely more maternal, not that that's a bad thing. Sometimes, I'm too emotional to be the dad.

Thank God for Clover. I'll let her be the dad when my emotions get the better of me, and I'll pick up the tab for when she's emotionally closed off. Balance.

Essie laughs, and it's a nice laugh– like a happy song. "So I call Beth up to bitch her out, and Rory answers the phone." Mimicking Rory's deep voice, *"My wife's in the shower, Hester. She'll call you when we get back from Vegas."* She laughs again. "And then the fucker hung up on me."

"Pregnant?" Rob asks what I was too cowardly to ask.

"Nah, Rory's a smooth dude. It took him a few months to get Bethany to go out with him. Once Bethany was caught, Rory had them hitched on the third date." I hate the wistful note in Essie's voice. It makes me want to board a plane to Arizona and beat the shit out of my son myself.

"Rob?" I call out, not realizing I'm holding onto my nicest undershorts. "Shit," I hiss, dropping them like they caught flame.

Chuckling at me, "Yeah?"

"Thanks for defending Essie and Willow's honor with Devon." I reach down to pick up my navy blue bikini briefs, blushing like a bastard. I tuck them into the bag I'm packing, hoping Clover will find them sexy. "Um... sorry about the hand, though."

"I'm a lover, not a fighter," Rob drawls while wearing a naughty smirk. We just stare at him. Me: because he's an idiot. Essie: because she's confused. "I bruised a finger bone," Rob holds his wrapped hand up, all proud like. "I don't recall what the name of it is, but Seth knew right off."

"What'd you do to your hand?" Essie's voice quivers with worry but it quickly twists with anger. "Did you punch Devon? I was in the wrong."

"I don't care if you were wrong or not," Rob states as he stands up. "Everyone was blaming you for what happened. Devon shouldn't have put you into the position to hurt Willow. You've paid enough– it was time he took some responsibility too."

"You shouldn't talk like that in front of Devon's dad," Essie reprimands Rob, and I huff a laugh.

"Don't mind me, girly," I tease. "Rob's done worse in my presence, and he is right. It wouldn't have happened without Devon. *'It takes two to tango'* isn't just a saying." I point down at Essie's budding belly. "My grandchild didn't make itself, and its father is far from a saint."

Essie turns on the female waterworks, so I busy myself by stepping into my bathroom real quick to pick up my toothbrush and deodorant. When I pop back out, Rob is quietly arguing with Essie, who seems intent on defending my son's worthless honor.

"Rob, did you drive Essie here?" I ask as I zip up my duffle bag.

"Yeah, why?" he answers, sounding suspicious of my question.

"I'm headed that way." I bite my lip to stop the shit-eating grin from spreading. "So I'll drop Essie off. It'll give us a chance to chat." Then I stress, "Alone."

"I don't think that is such a good idea," Rob says, noting Essie's nervousness.

"I wasn't asking," comes out before I can stop it. "Besides, Isis and Auggie are going round for round about your future. You might want to–" Rob dashes from the room. "–get to Weston's bedroom."

"ASAP," Essie adds while silently laughing. "I guess I know where I stand with Rob."

"Directly beneath Auggie and Isis, I suspect. Right along with the rest of us," I assure Essie. "It's rather crowded where we stand, don't you think?"

"Extremely," Essie mutters as she follows me down the hall.

I start banging on doors, shouting, "If you live at the Spook House, you sleep at the Spook House. You know who you are," I call out. "This house is a sex-free zone, and no, that does not mean you are free to have sex."

Auggie peeks his head out, "Huh? Since when? This house is responsible for most of the population of Fairport. Several of its current occupants were made in these bedrooms. I ought to know, I was here. Most likely sleeping in this room."

"Eww..." Raven makes a gagging noise from her eavesdropping position (crack of her bedroom door).

"Auggie means you," I tease Rae as I lean in to kiss her cheek. "And you," I say to Weston when I kiss his forehead.

I find the sex fiends in the kitchen, plotting the grand opening of the Playroom of all things. Fiends. "And you," I call out to Ren, and silently say 'and you' at Willow.

"Yeah, I figured you as a missionary on a mattress sort of dude. None of us are badass enough to have been made in the backseat of a car." Ren stops talking abruptly when he notices my shadow. Blushing, Ren clears his throat. "No offense to your baby, Essie." Feeling awkward, the kid reaches for humor, "I bet Stone was conceived on a tour bus. He's rockin' badass."

Never letting it go, "There was no backseat in my car," Willow chimes in, smirking. "So the kid was made in the front seat. But I have it on good authority that it might have been made on the hood of the car. But it's hard to tell since Devon's such a fucking liar nowadays."

Properly baited, Essie rises to the challenge, "Probably the hood," she agrees, nodding her head and smiling sweetly. "That orgasm was the most explosive. But then again, all five were. It's probably why I got knocked up."

I grab the girl by the back of the neck and tow her toward the door before Willow can't beat her ass. "Brave, but not very wise," I murmur. "Oh, hey!" I call back toward the kitchen, where a seething Willow is being restrained by Kieren. "I'm going to work early." I lie. "I meant what I said: no more sex in this house, and no sleeping over here. It sets a bad example for the kids. Got it?"

"Yes, Dad," Ren draws out, and I know he's rolling his eyes like Willow does. "Devon had to go and fuck up all our fun."

"Yeah, that's why, dumbass," I shout back at him as I close the front door behind Essie and me.

The girl remains quiet, pensive, as we get into my SUV. But I'm guessing it's because it's the Chief Mobile. Not many people are comfortable riding around in a cop car. "I have a few questions," I begin. "I'm not trying to be insensitive, but I need honest answers so I know where to go from here."

Essie doesn't answer me, but I didn't expect her to, either. "Does Devon know? I only ask because I'll have to tell his counselors to prepare him for it."

"Yeah, I told Devon just after I found out. He didn't take the news very well," Essie rasps out, voice sounding raw from unshed tears.

"I'm sorry," and I am. I want to reach over and take Essie's hand to comfort her, but I fear she won't take it well. I wait until we are pulled up to the curb outside of her home to ask my next question. "Do you plan on getting married?"

"No," Essie chokes out, like she's holding back a sob or two, or a billion. "It's not an option. Devon's not healthy enough for fatherhood, let alone marriage. I can't do that to him. Plus, he really doesn't like me."

The man in me is shriveling up and dying as I watch this young woman try to keep her shit intact. Essie's struggling and suffering and bottling it up, and doing it all in silence. I finally see the resemblance between all the Prynnes in this moment. They are their strongest at their weakest point, and the most kind when faced with meanness. Unable to help myself, I reach over and squeeze Essie's hand.

"Devon more than likes you, Essie," I say fondly, remembering her sitting on my sofa, playing monopoly for hours with Devon when they were little shits.

Essie turns to me and pins me with petrified eyes filled with shame. "Do you know what Devon said to me when I told him I was pregnant?"

"What?" I breathe out. I'm petrified myself now, since I've never seen such a bleak expression in my entire life, even at a crime scene.

Essie moves to open the passenger door. She slips out to stand on the sidewalk, and then turns to say to me in a tight voice, "Devon told me to get rid of it, because Masons don't marry whores."

I shout, "Essie!" But it's cut off by the slam of the door. Essie runs up the sidewalk and slips into her house before I can even react.

I drive to the handful of blocks to Clover's house in stunned silence. We will figure out what to do, whether Devon is willing and able to help or not. Essie is a Prynne, and that baby is a Mason too. Both Clover and I have a vested interest in its well-being.

All thought of bitchy teenage girls, wayward twenty-somethings, drug addicts, and pregnant unwed mothers, disappear as soon as I stumble into Clover's bedroom. I'd planned on romancing my wife-to-be, but as my head hits the pillow, even sex takes a backseat. I curl up around Clover's back, and then sleep like the dead.

CHAPTER THIRTY-THREE

The Widow

"This place looks like a real shithole," I mutter in disgust while tapping the screen. Essie and I are sharing the loveseat, heads bent together, staring down at the laptop. The twins are watching *The Bachelor* while Essie and I apartment search.

"You know it's gonna be great when they list a ceiling fan as their only enticement, along with a discount for being near the train tracks," Essie says sarcastically.

"Easy commute for Ward Manufacturing workers," I read off the ad. "Seeing as it shares its parking lot with the factory. Great place to raise a family, Essie."

"I'm guessing the train tracks are for Ward's," Seth says absentmindedly, being a snarky ass. "Maybe you should rethink occupations. New apartment, new career path with medical benefits, easy commute."

"Way to think positive, Seth," Essie deadpans, and then starts giggling. "I'm fucked."

"I think that's what got you into this situation in the first place," Violet adds her two cents, and then shushes us. "The Bachelor's about to give out the roses."

"Are you sure about this, Essie?" I ask for the billionth time as we've sat here searching. "Even the one bedrooms are out of your price range, and they are in the scary parts of town."

"I can't live off of Uncle Dave and Aunt Mary, Clover." Essie sigh heavily, falling back to rest her head on the sofa cushion. "They're barely making ends meet as it is. I know they have the room, but feeding me is one thing, having a baby screaming is another."

I offer the only other solution I can think of, "I'd hate to see you leave, but you could always go with your parents."

"I can't do that to them either. I'm just fucked, and not in a good way. My dad deserves his retirement without me mooching off of him. He should get to play golf, and Mom should get to sit on the beach with a book. They shouldn't have to worry about me and my knocked-up-ness."

"Yeah, and I don't see you smuggling a Mason out of the area, even if it's in your gut," Seth says, earning himself another shush from his sister.

"Devon won't give a shit, that's for sure," voice thick with unshed tears. "Kieren talked to me for a couple hours this afternoon. He told me not to worry about anything, but I do worry. I worry about Willow if she finds out Kieren is trying to take responsibility for my baby."

"Responsible how?" I ask, worried myself. My daughter is going to go postal. No amount of trust will stop the imminent storm, not after the cause of the pregnancy in the first place. Ex-boyfriend made the baby while cheating on her. Now the current boyfriend wants to take responsibility for said baby.

Fuck.

"Ren said he will be my baby's father until Devon can handle it, *if* Devon can ever handle it. Ren feels how I feel about my parents. Malcolm shouldn't have to raise Devon's kid. He should get to be the grandpa. But Ren shouldn't have to raise my baby, either." Sighing again, "I'll figure something out."

"Kieren's turned out to be a good boy," I say to myself, completely surprised. "You're right. Ren shouldn't have to take responsibility, but your child will need a father-figure."

Essie drops a bombshell. "I told Ren no. I wouldn't do that to Willow. I told Ren he could be Uncle Kieren, and that's it. My child's father is Devon Mason, and if Devon wants to be a puke, he will suffer the consequences. The baby will be loved, and that's all that matters. Devon will be the one missing out, not the baby."

"Because Devon is a worthless fuckhead," Violet hisses, joining the conversation since it's a commercial break. "Willow can make excuses for him all she wants. But everything Devon does is by his own choice."

"Why are you so broke?" Seth breaks into Violet's outburst. "You've always lived at home."

"I basically work off of tips. If it's a slow day, I pretty much go to work for no reason. I can barely make my student loans. I'm thinking of selling my car and dropping the insurance, but then I'd be going backward instead of forward."

"This isn't fair," Violet whines. "You can't make yourself pregnant."

"It wouldn't have mattered either way, V. Pregnant or not, Mom and Dad are moving to Florida. Beth and I were going to split a one bedroom shithole, and we would have barely made ends meet. No one will want to room with a pregnant woman. Plus, I won't be able to stand around all day at the salon by the time I'm in my eighth month. My roommate would be pissed when I can't pay my fair share, and then I'd pop a screaming, shitting, money-sucking bundle of joy into our shared apartment."

"Shoot me if I ever have kids," Seth mutters to his sister. "Promise me."

"Oh, I'll keep you to that," Violet vows. "Now, shut up. The shows back on, and if he gives that skanky chick a rose, I'm not watching next week."

"He will," Seth says, sounding sure. "He'll keep her around until the final round so he can get some strange on the side."

"O. M. G. Seth, never use that word again," Essie shrieks.

"Strange?" Looking from face to face, I ask anyone who will answer me. "What the fuck is that?" The twins and Essie burst out laughing like I'm the world's daftest person.

"I'm not touching that, and never ask what DTF means, either. Some things parents shouldn't know." Essie turns silent, taking on a green tinge as if she's going to be sick. "Shit," she breathes out, petrified. "I'm going to be one of those parents. I'm going to be a mom."

"Ah, c'mon!" Violet shouts, throwing the remote. "Don't keep that skank around!"

"They're all skanks," Seth says to calm Violet down. "They're on The Bachelor."

"What the–" The front door meets the wall, with a furious petite girl glaring at us from where the door used to be.

"You're in my house." Willow's smoky voice makes her sound even more sinister. "What did I tell you about being in this house, the Spook House, Wreck & Ruin, and Revamped? I told you not to go where I go."

I shut the laptop, setting it on the coffee table. "Willow," I say in warning. I get up to shut my front door, glaring at my unrepentant daughter on my way by. The shit-storm has finally arrived.

Seth turns off the TV, finding this more entertaining. Violet gets up, and gets the hell away, being proactive. It takes Seth about ten second of watching Willow, as she vibrates with fury, before he joins Violet in the doorway to the kitchen– safety.

"It's all right," Essie says to me as she stands from the loveseat. "I think it's time Willow and I cleared the air."

"Going after Kieren now, are we?" Willow accuses, angrier than I've ever seen her. Willow's on a territory defending mission. "Leave Kieren alone. Don't use your baby as a way to get closer to him."

"W-O-W," Essie draws out. "The fact that you even thought I was doing that, shows just how warped you truly are. Ren came to me. We talked like adults. The end. What you're accusing me of is disgusting."

Both girls seem calm, so I make my way to stand in the doorway to the kitchen with the twins. I give them the semblance of privacy, but don't dare leave them alone.

"You fucked Kieren. You tried to give Auggie a blow job. You fucked Devon, and got knocked up with his kid. Now you're working on Kieren again."

"Grow up," Essie mutters, sounding beyond exhausted.

Willow releases a primal scream in Essie's direction. I move to intervene, but Violet stops me by saying, "Mom, I think they better get this out now, instead of when Essie can't fight back."

I shake my head numbly, hating how we have to go through this, all of us. Willow is hurt and scared and jealous. Essie is hurt and alone and petrified. I'm stressed out and worried. The twins are… entertained.

Pointing at the front door, like it's her house, Willow announces, "Cheating whores are not welcome here anymore." Willow continues on with her tirade, "Especially ones who will fuck with their own family."

Finally snapping, proving that no one can fight as viciously as ex-best friends, "It wasn't about you, Goddamn it!" Essie shrieks. "Everything isn't about you, you self-righteous bitch! IT. WAS. NOT. ABOUT. YOU!"

"Then why does it feel like you fucked me over, cunt? Because from where I'm standing, it sure feels like it was about me. You've always been jealous over me."

Thrown for a loop, "What?" Essie sounds extremely confused. "Jealous of you? Why? You are my cousin. We're family. What you have, I have. What I have, you have. When you have something nice, I'm happy for you."

"Like a nice boyfriend," Willow twist out, sounding extremely sarcastic, "so you have to have him too!"

Seething, "Listen here," Essie gets into Willow's face, "and listen good. Everything you just said is so warped, Willow. Nice? Boyfriend? Had to have him too? ALL. WRONG. So fucking dead wrong."

"You've always been jealous of me," Willow repeats.

"Said the girl who loves to dish the woe-is-me, nobody loves me bullshit. If you truly thought so little of yourself, then explain to me why you think so highly of yourself that I'm supposedly jealous of you. Explain that shit, 'cuz I can't wrap my head around it!"

"I... I..." Stammering, Willow throws her hands in the air, giving the point to Essie. "Fuck you. You still cheated on me because you always want what I have. First Kieren, and then Devon. You even tried Auggie."

"I was testing Auggie, you dumb shit! I did it for you!" Essie screams into Willow's shocked face. "You're a kid, and Auggie's a grown man. I didn't want to see you get hurt. Even after..." Essie chokes on her words. "Even after what happened in the past, I was happy when you and Dev got together because he was better for you than some dirty old man. But it still wasn't right– he wasn't who you wanted. Who set you up with Kieren? And who chose to go off with Auggie instead? Quit blaming me for your mistakes!"

"You're knocked up with Devon's kid now, bitch," Willow snarls. "I guess you're getting the attention you were seeking."

Glaring, Essie just stares Willow down, thoroughly disgusted. "I said it wasn't about you. What don't you get about that? You're three years younger than me. You're clean now, but as of seven months ago, your head was so far up your own ass you didn't know shit. You were too busy sucking on a bowl twenty-four hours a damned day to notice anything around you. You might not know all there is to know. I'm a twenty-one-year-old grown woman, and you're an eighteen-year-old child. When you're in my situation, then, and only then, can you judge me."

"I'm almost nineteen!"

"The fact that you just shouted that, five months before your next birthday, screams how young you truly are. It's why no matter what you scream or yell at me, no matter how often you hit me, I give you a pass for acting like a spoiled brat."

"Said the girl who told me I was no fun anymore because all I did was work, study, and no longer partied."

"I was testing you, you stupid fuck. I was testing to see if you'd take the bait, and if you had, I was going to beat your ass. I was also pissed at you and hurt, because we were at the twins' birthday party after you missed mine. We're family, but you seem to keep forgetting that. I'm your only cousin on this planet, and I'm the only one you're ever going to get. I have no siblings. I only have Clover, Rob, you, Violet, and Seth. That's it. And you are who I've called my baby sister since the day she was born. Yet you think I don't have your back."

Torn from Willow's throat in a torrent of bitterness, "You. Fucked. My. Boyfriend!"

"Goddamn you!" Essie snaps. "It wasn't about you, goddamn it!" Jumping up and down in pure frustration, Essie releases a silent scream. "I. Dated. Devon. All. Through. Junior. High. Devon was my first boyfriend, my first love, and he broke up with me when I grew big tits, saying that was a mark of a whore. So I screwed Ren to get back at Devon, to prove to myself I was that whore, and it was… awful."

"What?" Willow breathes, stunned.

"I wanted you to look up to me, Willow. I wanted to be your big sister. I was ashamed. Devon's mom died, and it changed him. He was nasty to me. I tried to forget about him, so I did something with Ren in the back of my car for all of three minutes. It wasn't about you. It wasn't about me. It wasn't about Ren. It was about Devon, and the word whore he drilled into me. Ren freaked out and I broke down bawling. If Ren hasn't told you that detail, it's because I begged him not to tell anyone."

Arrogant and haughty, Willow smirks. "Yeah, Kieren told me it was nothing special. You were so lame he couldn't even get off."

"Priceless," Essie mouths, tears glistening in her eyes. "And you call me the jealous one. Willow, I never wanted your first time to be like mine. So I never told you who, or how, or why. I was ashamed of myself, and none of that had to do with your crush on Ren. It's not like he didn't screw the rest of the school. Ren couldn't go through with it with me, but he had no problem with the rest of the population."

"Fine!" Willow shouts, pointing at Essie's chest. "Ren's a non-issue now. But Devon, you knew he was my boyfriend. You knew I was in love with him."

"Oh, right… I'll give you this on the jealousy. Here is *my* best friend, going around telling everyone Devon Mason is her new BFF, leaving me in the dust. Completely ignoring me. Never texting or calling me back. Forgetting my fucking birthday after spending the previous eighteen of them with me. My best friend, blood relative, didn't show up to my birthday party because she was grouting tile. My *twenty-first* birthday party was a real rager, too– just me and the fam, minus *my* best friend. It's not why I cheated with Devon, but don't fucking insult me. You are not innocent in this shit."

Proving teenage girls are the most thickheaded creatures on the planet, "I missed your birthday so you cheated with my boyfriend? Does that seem even-stevens to you?"

"Nice," Essie draws out while shaking her head sadly. "Not even going to acknowledge the no-show. Figures," she sneers. "Your boyfriend?" Essie sounds incredulous. "If Dev had waited a day, you would've broken up with him anyway. He knew it, I knew it, and you knew it."

Refusing to hear reason, refusing to see anything besides her point of view, Willow glares Essie down. "It doesn't matter. We weren't broken up yet!"

"Why do I hear Rachel and Ross right now? *We were on a break,*" Violet whispers into my ear, causing both of us to giggle. Seth looks at us like we've lost our ever-loving minds.

"This is better than our reality shows," Seth says, grinning evilly.

"Because it is reality," Violet responds with fiendish delight.

"You guys are wicked sadistic," I whisper back, concerned over their sanity.

Tuning back in to our regularly scheduled program, we find Essie throwing gasoline on a volcano. "In what? Three months' time? You were messing around with Auggie, and then Devon, and then Ren, so don't throw whore-stones, Willow."

"I've been with three guys, and you're calling me a whore?" Willow mutters in disbelief. "You've been with like a hundred guys!"

"Huh?" Essie grunts out. "Bet you don't think twice about kissing your boyfriend. I bet you don't call Ren a whore," she says pointedly. "Funny thing about being pretty with big tits, everyone assumes you're a whore. But a guy with a big, over-sucked dick is looked at in awe."

Ignoring the Auggie jab, which was sickeningly accurate on how we celebrate men while defaming women for the same act, Willow goes on the attack. "It's not the size of your tits, Essie– it's how many dicks you stick into your body."

"Well, some dude has to stick that body to make her a whore, right? Why is the guy not bullied after the fact? Why do women care about how many guys we've been with, when men are proud to be with the most?" Essie asks, knowing Willow won't answer. "I've been with four guys– one more than you. Give yourself some time, cousin. You may add a few more to your total by the time you're my age. Maybe, maybe not. But since we're no longer BFFs, it's none of my business. Just as my sex-total is none of yours."

Furious and frustrated, Willow shrieks, "It is if two of them were my boyfriends!"

"Boy hoarder, are ya now?" Essie teases in the face of Willow's fury. "Technically, you were with Devon and Ren *after* me. From where I stand, you're the one who is going after the men I've been with. Funny thing about perception, little girl. It changes depending on where you stand when you're looking at it."

"You didn't have Devon *before* me," Willow stresses, as if having sex with a guy changes whether or not you can say you dated him.

"You love Devon, I'll give you that. But less than nine weeks later, you were camped out in his baby brother's bed, telling everyone Ren is the love of your life. Mind you, not saying Ren's your BFF. That is telling, isn't it? How quickly you moved on. Like, maybe, just maybe, you were never *in* love with Dev, 'cuz you were always *in* love with Ren. Like maybe, your two best friends hooked up in your car, not your cousin and your boyfriend. Just maybe, that is the real truth you're refusing to acknowledge."

Hurt, frustrated, Willow stomps her feet. "It doesn't matter how I felt about Devon at the time, or how I feel about him now, you still fucked Devon while he was officially my boyfriend."

"Do you honestly think I don't fucking regret it?" Essie screams– the sound pulsing with misery. "I wanted my boyfriend back, and in his place I got a fucking monster. Now, instead of commiserating with me, my best friend is raking my ass over the coals. You forgave Devon and shunned me. Now I'm pregnant with a monster's child, and I need my best friend back."

"Everything you got, you deserved. You acted like the big-titted whore Devon called you," Willow sneers, causing Essie's hand to snap out, slapping Willow sharply across the face.

Eyes darkening with fury, Willow rushes Essie with her cousin's death in mind. Willow takes Essie to the floor, repeatedly pummeling the girl in the face. Willow, sitting on Essie's thighs, beats the ever-loving hell out of Essie. All Essie can do is shield her face with her upraised forearms.

"Upstairs, now!" I shout at Seth and Violet. "Adult shit is going down. Listen at the top of the stairs like normal kids." I step over to the writhing ball of teenage fury and wrap my hand around her long ponytail. With a sharp yank, I pull my daughter off of our cousin.

"Girl, you've crossed a line now," I say in a calm, deadly voice. I pull Willow a few feet from Essie, and drop her unceremoniously to the floor. I walk back over to Essie to make sure she's okay. Face bruising in several places, I make sure her belly is okay. "Are you alright?"

It takes several tries, but she finally forces out, "Yeah, I think so. Just a bit stunned."

"Go into the kitchen and get a drink. Don't come back in here until I'm finished with Willow."

My daughter is lying on the floor, panting. She stares up at me, frightened. I straddle her legs and sit down. I press my palm to the center of her chest until she's lying flat on her back. "How about I beat your ass now? Hmm? You deserve it."

Stunned speechless, Willow just stares back up at me, not moving like a startled bunny rabbit. It wouldn't be the first time I've pounded the little bitch out of her. But I promised myself I'd never raise a hand to her once she became an adult. Most willful child on the planet. At eighteen, Willow's still acting like a spiteful four-year-old.

"You and I are going to have an attitude adjustment, and your behavior will dictate how this goes down. So lie here and listen, or act like a child and I will treat you like a child. In other words, act like an adult and I won't hit you like a little bitch. Got it?"

"Yes," Willow breathes, more ashamed of her atrocious behavior than afraid of my fists. "My God," I say in wonder as I gaze down into the brown eyes of my daughter. "It's like looking in a mirror." All of Sam's bad personality traits are gazing up at me from his eyes, and the rest is all me. That bitch attitude is all mine.

I state unequivocally, "Essie is correct. This isn't about you anymore."

"You're taking her side over mine?" Willow grits out, heartbroken.

"You might not have heard a word Essie said because you were too locked in to how hurt you are, but you're going to hear me," I threaten. "There are no sides with family. You've hurt me, wounded me deeply. But did I ever throw it into your face? Never. You'd call me a bitch, and I still loved you. Mind you, I may not have liked you at the time, but I never stopped loving you. I've never made you apologize, nor have I expected one, because there is nothing to forgive. Family is unconditional."

"Essie hurt me," Willow cries out, tears rapidly sliding down her cheeks. Instead of being upset that she is hurt, I'm glad. It means she's digesting my words.

"I get that, I do… and you've hurt her, too," I sympathize. "I could let you up right now, and you could go do something horrendous, and I'd still let you back into my house. I'd still offer you food and shelter and love. I would never turn you away," I say earnestly. "And I'm not about to turn Essie away. What kind of human being would that make me?"

"Essie's fine. She can take care of herself. You're supposed to be on my side… Clover." Willow stumbles over what to call me, and I know she knows but she's waiting for me to tell her the truth. Soon, very soon. But now is definitely not the time. Essie's coming first for once.

"Right now, your feelings are hurt, that's it. You have a huge support system that rallies around you at all times. What does Essie have? Her parents are moving away. She's homeless and pregnant. If you were pregnant, you'd have the father's unconditional support."

"Essie shouldn't have fucked Devon then, if he's such a piece of shit," Willow bites out.

"Well, that could have been you, ya know? Don't blame Essie for the exact same thing you did, but only she had the misfortune of the consequences instead. You just got lucky, is all." I let that hit home for a minute. I just stare down at my daughter as she computes the parallels.

"The father of Essie's baby can't even take care of himself, let alone Essie or the baby. She has no parents to come to for support. Her best friend hates her guts right now. She has no siblings to lean on. So… should I kick Essie out because you're having a tantrum, or should I be a good human being and take care of our family? What would your boyfriend's family think if I kicked a Mason to the curb?"

"I… I don't like her," Willow mutters, looking thoroughly guilt-ridden.

"Doesn't stop you from loving her, though, does it?" I whisper the sad truth. "That's why it hurts so much. That's why you forgave Devon in a heartbeat, but not Essie."

Pouting like a child, Willow grumbles, "Essie shouldn't have done what she did."

"Granted, but you don't get it, Willow. I've been in her position. I know how in the heat of the moment you can't think about anything but *him*. You totally check out, and I'm sure you've been there with Ren before."

"It doesn't make it right. Essie's getting what she deserves–"

Anger slams into me. "I was sixteen, having sex with a guy whose name I didn't even know. Sam was a grown man. He could have been married with kids for all I knew, and I didn't even think about it until afterward. Essie wasn't thinking of you at the time, and neither was Devon. It's the sad truth. They were in the moment, and it was selfishly all about them."

Willow silently cries, staring up at me in horror.

"I'm happy about that. I'm happy that the newest addition to our family was created because its parents were so into one another for a few stolen moments that they forgot the world. I believe that's how the greatest beings are created. Look at us Prynnes– we're fabulous," I tease. "Mom and Dad have only ever had eyes for each other. When Sam and I made a connection, we could be intense. When we disconnected, we were just as toxically intense. I'm sorry Devon didn't have that with you, Willow. But be happy he felt that, even once, and be proud it was with a Prynne."

"I can't… I can't forgive her," Willow whines.

"Be the adult. Prove it to yourself. Don't be selfish. Don't be jealous. You have a faithful, loving boyfriend who adores you. You have a family that would raze the world to the ground for you. You should be thankful for that, and you should love Essie enough to want the same for her. She has a few bad years ahead of her, and whether you like it or not, I'm going to get her through them. It's up to you on whether or not you stand at my side like a Prynne should."

I rise to stand, leaving my daughter sprawled on the floor, silently crying. I look down at her, and warn, "If I ever hear you call any woman on this planet a whore again, and I don't care what they've done to you, I will strangle you. A woman's self-worth is not centered between her legs. Shit happens, we fuck up and make mistakes, and then we take responsibility for it. Don't allow a guy to get away with the same shit while pushing the blame on the woman. We already have too many crosses to bear to have to worry about what the people who should have our backs are saying behind our backs. Be a real woman, Willow."

"I did that, didn't I?" Willow asks, finally starting to get it.

"Yeah, you did. You defamed Essie for a mistake she made, not only behind her back but to her face. Worse, you said it to Essie's family, both behind her back and to her face. In my eyes, what you were doing is far worse than anything she's ever done to you. It doesn't make you a badassed bitch– it just makes you a bitch," I hammer home.

"I was standing up for myself," Willow sounds so confused that I want to hold her and make everything better, but she has to learn this lesson now.

"There is a difference between standing up for yourself and lowering yourself. Know when to let it go by putting yourself in the other person's shoes, and if you can't do that, shut the fuck up."

"I'm not like Mom and Dad– I can't do that selfless shit," Willow says as if the very thought leaves a bad taste in her mouth.

I can't help it, a grin twists my lips. God, Willow is just like me. It's surreal. "Me too," I say wryly. "Try anyway. If your family can't forgive you, then your family is the worthless one. Willow, don't make us worthless. Got it?"

"Yes, Mom," Willow says, and it isn't even snide, and she doesn't even realize she said it, and it draws tears to my eyes instantly.

"I was a teenage-unwed mother, and I take personal offense to anyone who trashes someone like me. There is no token term for a teenage-unwed father, because the consequences fall onto the girl's shoulders. I'm not ashamed. I'm a good human being and a damn fine mother, just as Essie will be… just as you will be. Now, go into the kitchen and apologize."

Scrambling to her feet, "No, why should I?"

I grab Willow's wrist, and tug her into my arms. I squeeze her tightly as I press my lips to her ear. "Forgive the past, but never forget it. Love Essie, but don't like or trust her until she proves she understands the ramifications her actions had on you." I squeeze Willow as tightly as I can, until she can't breathe. My voice dips low with anger, "But never, ever, put your goddamned hands on a pregnant woman," I fiercely bite out, pushing her toward the kitchen. "Go! Apologize, and mean it!"

CHAPTER THIRTY-FOUR

The Widow

I needed a caffeine jolt after the week I've had, not some sad excuse that looks like it was filtered through a jockstrap. I'm pretty sure all of the coffee in the Courthouse is decaf for Mayor Ross, or he wouldn't spend the majority of the day napping. I should send Mrs. Ross hate mail. I could always trudge down to the basement for the strong stuff, but Malcolm would probably toss me into a jail cell and molest me. Between the coffee and the molestation, I'd never want to leave the Batcave.

If I could tolerate coffee that tasted like dishwater, I'd never step foot into this despicable place again. Hell equals Fairport's bakery, simply called '*The Bakery*'. Other than their semi-decent coffee and terrible baked goods, there is some entertainment value to coming to The Bakery. Their baker is the worst known to man. I snap a few pictures with my cell to upload to *cakewrecks.com*.

The idiots in this bakery are quite literal. '***Congradulations Jane in bold red leters***' is sprawled across a cake that looks like a car wreck. No punctuation, misspellings, and I'm pretty sure they meant the font was to be bold red.

Memorial Day is celebrated on the majority of the confections. Too bad our flag has fifty stars, not the thirty-two on one cake and nineteen on another. Uncle Sam is sporting a dick-shaped nose, and if you tilt your head to the side, his eyes look like cancerous testicles. The firework sugar cookies are the consistency of hardtack, and when placed next to Uncle Sam's nasal passages, an explosion of ejaculate.

What I wouldn't do to bake for a living, while these ingrates take it for granted, never giving their customers what they requested as they hand over their hard-earned money for shit.

Decision made: I'm sneaking a pod coffee maker into the office and hiding it under my desk. No more dishwater piss from the break room or walking two blocks to this shithole. They don't deserve my money. They should pay me to drink this swill.

A young mother and her son are in line in front of me, staring into the display case with great indecision. "I want a chocolate chip cookie," the cherub-cheeked toddler begs his mommy, tugging on her shirt sleeve.

"No, Jake, you chipped your tooth last time. Um...." Flustered, she breathes '*shit*' under her breath. "They're all bad. The banana nut muffin had walnut shells in it last time. Grandma cut her tongue."

With a sigh, I pull a snack baggie from my purse. I hand the little boy an oatmeal, chocolate chunk cookie. I offer the mother one, too. Both are so young and naïve. Don't they know they shouldn't accept food from strangers? Well, this is Fairport, and I don't exactly look like a criminal in my pencil skirt and bun.

"Oh, my God," she moans, biting it in half. Chocolate smears across her mouth as she chews with her eyes closed. "It's real. Do you have any more?" She wipes the chocolate off with the back of her hand.

I dig around in the bottom of my trunk-sized shoulder bag. I retrieve the last of my snacks. A plastic container of fudge the kids and I made a few nights ago. "Here ya go. Um... If you like it, just call Mayor Ross's office. I can hook you up with some more." I speak low, like I'm a drug dealer in a rival gang's territory.

I'm the powdered sugar pusher.

"Hey," she calls after me as I walk away, "What's your name?"

"Clover," I reply with a wave and a smile as I walk away. I did a naughty. I can't possibly buy my coffee here after scabbing two of their paying customers. I'll try the gas station with the motor oil substance that's supposedly high octane coffee.

Hiking my bag up my shoulder to find its comfortable spot, I don't notice a few ladies until I careen into them. "Shoot," I yelp. "Ran right into ya." I smile as I walk away.

"You're Rob's sister, right?" A woman stops me with a hand to my forearm. Annoyed, I back up until her hand falls away. My eyes narrow at the forty-something woman. Five pounds of mascara are caking her lashes and her concealer should be fired for accentuating her crow's feet. She's trying too hard to look young. I want to tell this woman she'd look younger if she didn't try. It's sad and desperate.

"Yes?" I say with polite suspicion, but it ends up sounding like a question.

A nasty sneer covers the woman's face as she inspects every inch of my body. I feel violated by her eyes as they rove over my features. A scoff is grunted from her throat. I guess she doesn't like what she sees. I don't give a damn what this woman thinks. She looks rode hard and put away sopping wet, and then left in the desert sun to bake to a leathery brittleness.

"Nina, don't," a soft voice admonishes. I look at Nina's friend. What's a lovely lady like this woman doing with the likes of Nina? She towers over us at six feet, dressed in a pair of medical scrubs with happy puppies printed on the fabric. Her blonde hair is smoothed back slickly against her head.

Nina is wearing a magenta tube top as a skirt, plastic hoop earrings, and her brown hair is pulled up on top of her head, secured with a scrunchie. If Nina washed her face, put on clothing that teenagers from her time didn't wear, and removed the sneer from her pouty lips, she'd look fifteen years younger. Do men really fall for this kind of desperation?

"Willow's your brat, isn't she?" I cringe at the way Nina talks of my daughter. I wonder how everyone knows the maternity of my eldest child but the kid has yet to confront me over it.

Furious, perfect Clover vanishes in an instant, and the girl who gave Willow her attitude and propensity for violence erupts. "Yeah… Willow is," I snap. "Brat? Who the fuck are you?" I eyeball Nina as she did me. Her sneer has nothing on the look of disgust that flashes across my face.

Smirking, like Nina's enjoying my assessment of her trashiness, "For Malcolm's sake, I hope you're like your daughter. I see you have her foul mouth."

"Willow has *my* mouth, attitude, and need to defend herself… Explain," I clip out.

Stepping in between me and the goading Nina, "Hi, I'm Opal," the pretty blonde offers her hand. I gingerly shake it while she says, "It's nice to meet you."

"Charmed, I'm sure… Clover," I give my name as I pull my hand free of her gentle hand. Opal has that no-nonsense, trustworthy air about her like most nurses.

"Sorry to a... accost you. I hope we meet again sometime. Nina-free, of course. We should go now." Opal smiles and tries to pull her feisty friend away.

"Will you be joining Malcolm at the Playroom?" A vicious light filters into Nina's gaze. "It was weird enough with Rob watching Willow get fucked. It'd take a real pervert to watch their kid take The Beast."

Eye bulging from my skull, heart in my throat, "What?" I shout.

"Yeah, Willow's new daddy watched while she lost her v-card. We all did," Nina taunts, a twisted smirk and a wicked gleam in her eye makes her look like an arrogant two-dollar-whore. "Willow loves to suck big cock."

"Enough!" Opal barks and makes a grab for her friend, fingers circling around the back of Nina's neck. I flinch from the intensity of Opal's anger, but I don't feel bad about the bruises that will necklace Nina's bitchy throat.

"I... You must be mistaken," the words get garbled as I swallow past the bile rising in my throat. Things Willow said have lit up in my mind. "Malcolm wouldn't do that. Goddamnit! Rob wouldn't do that."

"Don't listen to Nina," Opal tries to ease me with lies. "She's acting out of jealousy. Nina has a thing for Auggie, and is pissed because he ignored her while he was... dating Willow."

"Bitch, plleeeaassseee," Nina draws the please out for an eternity. "Jealousy or not, it's the fucking truth. A woman should know the type of man she's marrying."

"The Playroom," I swallow thickly as I hear Malcolm telling me about his past. Horrified, I fear this vile creature has been one of Malcolm's lovers for the past five years. "Malcolm touches you, Nina?"

"No," Opal fiercely bites out. "NO!" she doesn't shout, but it's forceful and powerful and makes me shiver in fear. Noticing my reaction, Opal says in a calm voice, "Yes, Willow did some things in front of people–" Nina's sharp snort interrupts. "But Malcolm never witnessed it, and Rob stayed for Willow's comfort and safety. You need to talk to Malcolm about this."

"No shit," I snarl, and then turn snide. "Ya think?"

"Willow gave Auggie a blowjob, fucked the guy with Devon's help, and then she helped Auggie fuck Bethany. Your little girl is quite the budding whore," Nina takes great amusement in destroying my world view.

A few nights ago, my daughter was tearing into Essie, and if this is true, I'm going to be tearing into Willow, Rob, Devon, and Malcolm. Shaking, furious, stomach revolting, I stand numbly as one woman gloats and the other frowns.

"Nina," Opal cautions and shakes her head in disgust, hand dropping from her friend's throat. "It's your funeral. You know the rules. The second I leave here, you're fucked, and not in the way you want."

Ignoring the warning, "The Spook House's attic is a den of iniquity. Your brother and baby girl live in a house that smells like sex. They're Auggie's pets. I'd feared Willow would pussy-whip Auggie like Isis tried to do, but he still fucks constantly," Nina says with pride.

How could Auggie touch my child and then touch this woman. Nina is a vile creature, just looking at her makes me want to bathe in a vat of lye. Adult or not, I'm dragging Willow to the clinic for testing in the morning. I'm being tested, too. I close my eyes in shame. Did he… did Malcolm touch me after he touched Nina?

"Clover," my name from Opal's lips is full of pity. I flick my eyes to her unflinching stare. "It's not how it sounds. Nina's taking it out of context to make it worse."

"I don't know… The thought of him touching that," I point at Nina, "Makes me want to vomit, and then take a course of antibiotics."

"Malcolm has never touched Nina," Opal states emphatically. "Ever. I promise."

"Augustus did, and then he touched my child." I groan, "I think I'm going to be sick." I grip my sides and swallow back my lunch.

Opal doesn't have to confirm my accusation since Nina is glowing like a crack pipe. "Tell Malcolm that I have a wedding gift for him." She grins and makes a derogatory gesture with her mouth and hand.

CHAPTER THIRTY-FIVE

The Widower

I stand outside of my future home, wondering what it looks like on the inside. Sight unseen, I made an offer because I was pressed for time. Buying a home while trying to sell three others is going to be difficult. Might as well do it all at once.

Visiting Auggie and Rob over the past few months, I've looked at this house from the outside. Directly across the street from the Spook House, it's a huge old Victorian– one of the original homes in Fairport. If it was spruced up, I bet the Historical Society would like it on its roster. No such luck. I don't want any unwanted visitors.

Willow tried to get the Spook House added to the Historical Society's Fairport tour, but several of the members are Playroomers. She was shot down– fast.

"Ugh, I've hated looking at this color for the past eight months. Promise you'll repaint." Ren makes a gagging noise in the back of his throat. "Welcome to the Pink Taco Hut," Kieren taunts as he comes to stand beside me on the front walk.

Turning to face my son, "I thought I'd name it the Pussy House." I chuckle to myself. "For once, we will have an equal ratio of estrogen to testosterone. Why are you here? Did you see me from the Spook House? I thought Willow was at Revamped? Better yet, why aren't you at work?"

"You're in interrogator mode, I see," Ren drawls, picking on me for asking a string of questions without waiting for an answer. "I'm meeting Aunt Ginny, too."

"Oh," I say brightly. I clasp my son on the shoulder, pleased that he wanted to share this moment with me. "We're speeding up the closing. I had to pay a few grand over market value to get the sellers to put a rush on it. It's a good thing I've been contemplating the move for a while, or else the paperwork at the bank would have slowed the process down."

"Yeah," Ren snorts out, looking amused and proud for some reason. "So I'm finding out." The finger combing through his blond hair is a good indication that he has something to tell me I'm not going to like. "I'm not here over the Pussy House, Dad. Aunt Ginny's showing me a few houses this afternoon. I just spent my morning at the bank filling out paperwork."

"What?" I breathe out, shocked. "Why? You're still a kid."

"Dad," Ren sounds exasperated. "You were a husband, father, and homeowner at my age. I'm nineteen. If I can own a business and run it... half-assed okay... then I shouldn't be living with my daddy anymore."

I reach out to my son, wanting to keep him with me forever. "I want you with me." I hate the desperation in my tone.

"I'm not moving far, Dad," Kieren chuckles. "I'd be petrified to leave you fools alone for too long. Aunt Ginny is showing me houses around a four block radius from here. I want to be close to the Pink Taco Hut and the Spook House."

"Why would anyone want to be near that place?" I point across the street at Auggie's den of hedonism. "You're not going to start using the Playroom, are you?"

"Um..." Ren hesitates, blushing. "No, not my bag. It's just time for me to grow up, Dad."

"You don't have to do this now," I plead.

"Yeah. Yeah, I do. You have a lot going on right now. You walk around asking yourself what John Mason would do. The thing is, I do the same thing. Only I ask myself what Malcolm Mason would do."

Using humor to lessen the emotional toll Ren's words had on me, "Kieren, please don't think like me." I chuckle. "That's a scary fucking thought."

We grin at one another, because no matter how much Ren looks like his mother, his personality is all mine. "It's helpful when figuring out what you're up to. I'm taking some of the stress off of you right now, so you can concentrate on Clover and the kids. You guys needs to make sure Rae, West, Kid, and Princess don't turn out like Dev, and you can't do that if you're spread thin worrying about us."

Choking up from the sincerity in my son's voice, "Us?"

"Me. Willow. Devon. Essie. The baby. I'm fixing everyone's shit with one purchase. This house solves a lot of problems. I want to marry Willow, Dad. I want her with me." The tone in Ren's voice catches the air in my lungs. My son talks of

Willow like I do my kids, as if it physically hurts to be apart from her.

"When Devon comes home, he's coming to our house. No one can watch him as closely as I can. No one will spot the cravings as quickly as Willow can. I don't care if Essie and the baby stress him out. He is going to be a father whether he likes it or not. No excuses, he's going to father that baby."

"What about Willow and Essie?" I look at my son like he's lost his mind. "Willow tried to kill Essie a few days ago, remember?"

"Willow will get over it and grow up, or she's not who I thought she was," Ren says gravely. "Essie shouldn't be homeless, sleeping in Willow's old bedroom, worrying about her and her baby's future."

"I'm proud of you, son." I tug Ren in to give him a half-hug. I try to hide my sniffles, hating how I turn into a girl while my son is exhibiting how strong he is as a man. Ren gives me an amused expression when I pull away, seeing right through my bullshit.

"I heard Aunt Isis crying while you were talking to her. I… Willow stayed in the kitchen while I checked on everyone, so she didn't hear. Last night, I talked to Aunt Isis. I get why she feels as she does, and I want my aunt to love my future wife. I don't want her to resent Willow over something that is Auggie's fault. So I'm fixing that, too, by getting Willow out of the Spook House."

"You're a genius," I utter in awe. "But Willow isn't going to leave that house without a fight."

"I know." Worry crosses Ren's expression. "That's why I'm going to go to her with a couple of housing choices, let her pick which one, put her on the deed with me, and let her renovate it until she's happy. If giving Willow a house of her own doesn't appease her, then she's not who I thought she was."

"How are you paying for all of this? Do you need help with a down payment? What about closing costs and taxes and Ginny's fee? Your aunt has to eat too."

"Good God, Dad!" Ren knocks me in the shoulder. "Shut that shit down. I've got it covered. We have four working adults buying this house, and we are splitting it four ways."

"I get that, but where is the down payment coming from?" I point out, and then feel like shit because I can't help my son. "I'm taxed until the houses sell. We hold no mortgages, but we still have to keep up the bills until they sell. That's a lot of extra shit to pay for."

"Devon's being docked for being a drug-taking bastard, for treating us all like shit, and leaving us to clean up his mess." Ren's good mood fizzles, turning to pure anger. "The down payment is coming out of his savings account. You should have taken the cost of rehab outta him instead of your own pocket. I'd rather you bought Rae a car on her birthday than fund Dev's fuck-up camp."

I admit the truth, even though I shouldn't, because I know it will fuel further resentment between my sons. I just have to tell someone. We were doing okay for money, enough for me to buy this house outright since I've never held a mortgage or paid rent in my life. Dad's house was owned outright when he died. Now, I have to sell my father's house to pay down the mortgage I signed yesterday so I won't be eighty-years-old and still paying for this house every month.

"Devon can afford a down payment on a house, or to buy a shitty car, but his *'fuck-up camp'* cost as much as this house," I admit, wishing I didn't have to. "I wasn't going to live like Auggie. One rehab. Once. For life. It's a price I gladly paid to save my son's life– one I'd pay for each and every single one of you. If Devon starts using again, I'll kill him," I threaten, and I mean it.

"Jesus," Ren hisses, fingers going back to his hair, tugging in frustration.

"Reverend Braxton had to refinance and cash out his retirement savings. Mrs. Elsberry had to drain her future inheritance from her parents. Both of them will be working until the day they die. You'd be amazed what a parent is willing to do to make sure their child is healthy and happy… what we'd do to make sure our children survive."

Kieren holds my gaze and makes a vow, "Devon will be the best investment you've ever made, even if I physically have to beat him every single day for the rest of his life."

"Our family. This town. We all will be watching out for Devon. We're all invested in him. I just hope at some point he can learn to appreciate it."

"If Dev can't," Ginny says, joining us on the sidewalk, "Then he's going to be more miserable than he ever thought he was. I hope Dev enjoys a town filled with his personal babysitters."

"Hey," I call out, smiling. I walk over to Ginny to pull her into a hug. I give her a good squeeze. "You smell good." I sniff her hair delicately. "Like marshmallow."

"Clover's gonna make you as fat as I am," Ginny teases us both. "I tried not to overhear, but are you going to afford this place okay? The price was steep, even for Fairport."

"Yeah," I mutter, nodding my head as I speak. "It will be tight until my house sells." I pause. "Ren, can you get me a bottle of water out of the back of the Chief Mobile?"

"Sure," Ren responds, raising an eyebrow. "I'll pretend to get the water until you're through saying what I'm not to hear." Snickering, the kid stalks over to the back of my SUV and leans on the fender.

I answer Ginny's quizzical expression. "Ren didn't want me to share the happy news with him until I could share it with Willow. So Ren and Willow are in the dark on all of this shit. Obviously, Ren knows Clover and I are together, but he doesn't know the details."

"Willow fucked up and called Clover '*Mom*' during the blowout with Essie. The girl knows. One of them has to get off their ass and tell the other, and it should be Clover."

"Clover's waiting until I get Ren out of the area, and Isis is going to detain Auggie while Rob runs interference. We have to wait."

"I get it. I don't like it, but I get it." Ginny sighs heavily. "So about your financial situation?"

"It will be tight while we wait for the house to sell. Clover can do with the proceeds from her house as she wishes. She can pay off our mortgage, or fix the house up, or make Seth a college fund because the kid's gonna need a lot of schooling. It's up to Clover. But we will be fine no matter what she chooses to do."

"You're a good man, Malcolm Mason," Ginny drawls out, teasing me.

"Tell me something I don't already know." I sound so arrogant that I burst out laughing. "Truth: I won't feel like a real man if Sam ends up paying for part of the house I'm buying for my family. I'd rather it went to Seth and Violet. Maybe start a wedding fund for the girl."

"Such high expectations for your new stepdaughter," Ginny says wryly.

"That's not it," I growl. "I'm being realistic. Seth wants to be a doctor, and that is something to be proud over. But I'm no less proud if Violet wants to grow up to be a good mom. Regardless, we know Violet's a diva. As the father of the bride, I'll be drained dry by her demands. So it's better if Sam's house pays for it in part, right?"

Ginning at me, Ginny looks so much like Camille that it makes my heart constrict. "I'm not touching that one. Word of advice: never, ever, say what you just said to me to Clover. Let her believe you think Violet has it in her to be the first female president."

I just look at Ginny.

Laughing, "Okay, so that's never gonna happen."

"Obviously. I'm being realistic here, Gin. I can't stroke egos all day or I'd never get anything done."

"Why am I selling Dave and Mary's house? Better yet, why aren't I allowed to tell Clover about it? I just got off the phone after a lengthy conversation with Dave."

"I'm crossing all my *T*s and dotting all my *I*s. Dave was retired, but had to go back to work when Sam died. It stresses Clover out, and a stressed Clover equals a stressed Malcolm. The woman can barely go ten minutes without checking in with them. So I'm retiring Dave by selling his house."

Looking incredulous, Ginny asks, "How is this going to work?"

"I've been busy." I smirk. "Essie's plight brought it home for me. I'm forcing Rob to step up. So during the summer months when Prynne Renovations is in full force, Dave and Mary will live with us while Dave oversees his foreman. During the winter, Dave and Mary will stay with his brother in Florida, in the room that was meant for Essie. They will love it."

"And Rob?" Ginny sounds confused on what the guy has to do with any of this.

"Will have to work for the first time in his fucking life," I spit out, bitter resentment spewing. I love the fool, but Robin and I do not have the same code of ethics. "Rob's going to be overseeing the foreman in the winter months, after Dave shows him the ropes all summer. Instead of throwing his money at the problem, it's time Rob actually fixed the problem."

"And just how long does Clover have until she's chained in this kitchen?" Ginny points at the house, but she's not joking. She knows me too well.

"Two and a half weeks," I say without remorse. "I have a plan put into place that will be enacted by Mayor Ross while I'm in Arizona."

"Even across the country, Clover's gonna kill you when she loses her job."

"Clover's going to have a new job when I get back from visiting Devon." Taken out of context, the words sound arrogant, misogynistic, but I am giving Clover her dream job.

"Oh, yeah... what's that? Malcolm Mason's devoted wife?" Ginny says stiffly, getting angry with me.

"My wife, our children's mother, the mistress of this house. Those aren't demeaning things to a woman who longs for them. I can understand why you wouldn't enjoy it, Ginny. But everyone is different. I'm not saying Clover can't earn a living. I'm saying she doesn't have to work to survive. If she wants to do something she is passionate about, I will support her one hundred percent."

"God, you're a dying breed," Ginny says in awe. "Too bad I can't find a woman who thinks like you. I'd scoop her up in a heartbeat." Ginny reaches into her jacket pocket, and then places my new house keys in my awaiting palm. "I stand by my word: you are a good man, Malcolm Mason."

Leaning forward, I kiss Ginny's cheek. "I love you, too," I breathe against her skin. I pull away smiling. "Now, go get my kids some affordable housing, preferably a few houses from here. I want my kids shoved so far up my ass," I announce so loudly that Ren can hear me. "They'll be coming out my mouth."

"Kill me!" Ren says dramatically as he walks toward us. "Ready, Aunt Gin? I'm eager to check out some places. The loan officer gave me a cap on pricing, so that will narrow our search."

In a daze, I head up the sidewalk toward my soon-to-be new home, key in hand. "Hey, Dad!" Kieren calls. "Heads up!" A water bottle is lobbed at my face, and I catch it just in time.

"Thanks," I growl at my kid.

"Not sure why you never played ball, Dad," Ren says in appreciation. "You've got the reflexes for it. I'm good, but Weston's going to be a star."

"Good thing." I snicker in disgust. "'Cuz I just spent Weston's college fund on sixty days in the Arizona desert for your brother. I hope your sister never plans on marrying."

"Let's hope West goes pro, then we won't have a financial worry again," Ren's voice flows as he follows his aunt down the street to a house two doors down.

"I hope you're right," I say to myself, not counting on it. "And I hope you don't buy that piece of shit," still muttering to myself as I unlock the front door to my new house.

I step over the threshold with a goofy grin plastered across my face. A real sense of pride overwhelms me. This is *our* home– the house Clover and I will make our home until the day we die. Generations of Masons will bless these walls.

The house my children and I share was *his* house– John Mason's. I've lived there since I was born. It holds horrible memories. My past made me strive to be a better father and husband, not that Dad set the bar very high. I've burnt that damned house in my mind countless times, just as I've burnt the furniture in actuality. I've painted and repainted after every torment. Layer upon layer of pain is sealed into those walls by coats of happy colors.

I envision the warmth of my first real home. The home I bought to protect my family. I'm putting the roof over their heads while Clover fills their bellies with food created from her soul. Their warm laughter will infuse the house with happiness. Their fights will put a smile on my face. The chaos, the mess, the unpredictable nature of unique individuals will entertain me for a lifetime.

A mirage of Clover wavers over the focal point I gaze upon unseeingly. The kitchen: I don't see the torn linoleum or ancient cupboards. I see Clover fluttering around with a satisfied smile on her face as she cooks and bakes. A few of the kids pester to help. Clover turns on her teacher-mode in less than a second, instructing the children on how to take care of themselves in the future.

Christmas, birthdays, holidays, celebrations... births and deaths. Our future is in this house. My entire life I've strived to obtain my ideal on what a real man should be, do, and need: A strong, compassionate wife at my side. A job I respect. Children and grandchildren to complete us. A home that I provided. A firm, yet gentle hand to hold in pain and pleasure, happiness and sadness. It is the measure of a real man.

It almost took me forty years to become a man.

My cellphone vibrates in my pocket. I pull it out while smiling, running my fingertip over the front to unlock it. I press it to my ear. "Hello," I answer, sounding chipper.

"Malcolm, it's Opal," mumbles through the phone.

"What's up, Opal?"

"Nina and I were at The Bakery for lunch. We ran into Clover," she says in a panic.

"Is Clover alright?" My voice wavers in fear. My feet move me through the house to the front door before I even get a chance to look around. My body beads with sweat as my heart beats out of my chest. "She's not at the clinic, is she?"

"No, Clover's physically fine," Opal says in an odd way.

"Then what's the problem?" It takes all of my patience not to bark out demands. Opal's a good woman. I draw in a breath to avoid being disrespectful and ruining our long friendship.

"You know how Nina is when she's jealous. We heard through the grapevine that you're marrying Rob's sister. It pissed Nina off. Something about how Willow and her mom take all the good men. She… she…"

"Opal, spit it out," I demand, fingers testing the tensile strength of my phone. "If Nina touched Clover, I'll break her hands."

I reach my SUV just as Opal finally gets to the point. "Nina told Clover." Opal cries– actually cries. Her sniffles shock me for a second. Women should never cry, especially not a woman as strong as Opal.

"Told Clover what?" My voice strains with fear. *Motherfucking-Cocksucking-shit-cunt-damn-taylorswift-assholes-bastard-hell-whore-justinbeiber…* I mentally swear a litany of curse words until my vocabulary runs dry. Where's Willow? That pirate knows all the good curses.

"Everything." Opal pauses, and I want to reach through the phone and choke the shit out of her. "The Playroom. Nina told Clover about Willow and Auggie in the Playroom. How Robin watched. Only she made it sound like you watched, too. Nina bragged about how she's still fucking Auggie, and then she offered to suck you off as a wedding gift."

"I'll take care of it," I utter in a deadly calm voice, feeling anything but calm. Then I cut Opal's reply off with the press of a finger.

"Houston, we have an irreversible problem. I knew I should have told Clover sooner. I was going to tonight. I was softening the blow." I pace back and forth in front of my SUV, unsure how to proceed.

"FUCK!" I bellow. My shaking fingers instantly seek my hair. I yank on it out of pure frustration. "No more stress. No more drama. This is our home, and Clover is my wife," I give myself a pep talk as I stomp around the street. "I'm not giving my man status back, Goddamn it!" I growl.

Decision made.

"Isis," I bark into my phone. "Call a meeting. I need everyone who is a member of the Playroom at the Spook House by ten p.m. tonight. Not the kids. They are officially ex-Playroomers. They can be naughty with their own friends."

"Why?" Isis languorously purrs, obviously still lying in bed.

I blurt out, "My wife has to have a meet and greet."

"Holy shit!" That wakes my night owl sister up. "Why would you do that?"

"Nina collared Clover at The Bakery and told her everything. I'm not losing my future wife over this. Clover needs to see firsthand what the Playroom is about, and she needs to meet the members. The members also need to know what Nina did, so they know their secrets are no longer safe as well. So I want everyone at the Spook House tonight. If they don't show up, they're no longer a member."

"Isn't that Auggie's call?" Isis sounds like she's bored and could give a shit less, which tells me she's been fighting with the fool again. I imagine Isis picking at her long fingernails while lying in her bed. The girl usually doesn't crawl out of her hole until well after two p.m.

"Augustus is off his rocker. Are you going to get him in hand after all the shit he's pulled lately?" My question is laced with demand.

"I suppose," Isis sighs.

"Ten p.m.– the Spook House," I repeat, and then hang up.

"If I were Clover, what would I do first?" I muse. "Kill me," I mutter as I get into my SUV. "But first she'd have to locate me."

CHAPTER THIRTY-SIX

The Widower

A quick call to dispatch has my wayward wife located in a nanosecond. Clover walked to The Bakery, which meant she had to walk back to the Courthouse to get into her car. Colin intercepted her, and told her I'd meet her at her house. Clover was furious, to the point that she didn't even speak to Colin. She sped off, committing a few moving violations in front of no less than three police officers.

We both reach Clover's house at the exact same time, with a squeal of tires, nearly careening head-on since we arrived in opposite directions. Clover's out of her car like a speeding bullet. She pivots on her heel and glares at me. Her unflinching stare strips me raw: betrayal, pain, disappointment, regret, sadness. The glistening wetness on her eyelashes weakens my knees. If Clover cries, I'll fall to my knees and crawl to her, begging for forgiveness.

"We need to talk," spills from my lips without thought as I exit my vehicle. Clover's car door slams shut, alerting the watching crones from across the street. My eyes flick in their direction, annoyed that they are witnessing our first fight, and enjoying it.

"No shit," Clover growls. She meets my eyes, and doesn't so much as even blink. This tiny, traditional woman, who so desperately needs to be taken care of, cherished, and treated like a prized possession, challenges me. Clover takes on a six foot tall burly man in a police uniform and doesn't even blink.

I thought I was already in love with Clover. I was wrong, because the sensation flowing in my veins suspiciously feels like possession. Clover is going to listen, and she's going to forgive me. I will accept nothing less. I understand why Sam did the dumb shit he pulled. Clover can render a man insane.

Clover's right hand reaches into her shirt, and I charge toward her like a crazed animal. "No!" I shout, pointing at her to drive my point home. "You made a promise to us. You accepted the responsibility. It's not just about your hurt feelings. It's an eight-to-one vote if you're trying to bow out. Majority rules. Hell, it's not just the kids and us. It's your parents, our siblings, our friends. It's the whole fucking town. You're mine!" I bellow so loudly the words ring in my ears, and its range reaches across the street.

Shaking, my fingers gingerly hold Clover's slender wrist, so she doesn't think I'm bullying her. Clover's so pissed right now that I know she's imagining killing me. I can see the menacing thoughts running across her face like a tickertape during a news crisis. It's a good thing I left my gun in my safety-box inside the SUV, because I'm pretty sure Clover is shooting my nuts off in her mind at the moment.

I unhook the necklace from around Clover's pretty neck and retrieve our engagement ring. I slide our ring back on Clover's finger and twist until the ball of gems is where it should rest. Clover's stiff and resisting beneath my touch, but at least she isn't screaming and hitting me. Maybe that is a bad sign, not a good one, though.

"No taking this off, Clover. If you're bathing or cleaning, it's fine. But you're doing neither at the moment." I kiss Clover's ring finger while she glares at me. She doesn't relax so I keep kissing her fingers, one at a time.

Clover's dainty fingers are so soft and smell so good, and make my cock look huge when they're wrapped around it. I love the way our engagement ring feels stroking along my skin. "Shit," I hiss, pulling away. I will my cock to deflate, but the fucker likes her angry. Clover isn't cute when she's angry– she's hotter than hell. Her chest is pumping up and down as she breathes heavily, pushing her tits into her blouse. Her luscious nipples are peaked against the light pink fabric.

"The vote doesn't count when only one person knows the truth." Clover's angry words push the lust-fog from my brain. My cock doesn't give a shit, though. He's tweaking out in my trousers just from the throaty sound of her voice.

"Every adult with the exception of you knew the truth. I was going to explain tonight," I speak without breaking Clover's gaze, trying to drill the truth into her brain. "Please, believe me." My voice leaks desperation like a sieve.

"I'm going to go take a shower," she growls and tries to pull away.

"No, you're not!" I growl right back. "I'm going to be on your skin while we have this conversation. I haven't spent the last two weeks scenting you up to have you wash it down the drain."

"I'm dirty," Clover says in a prissy voice.

"Well, too fucking bad," my ire rises. How dare Clover remove me from her skin! I wrap my fingers around Clover's thin wrist, and start marching toward the house, towing Clover behind me.

I preach while I drag Clover through her house toward her bedroom. "I'm going to explain what went down, *after* I fuck the hell out of you. Tonight, we're going to eat as a family— us and our four youngest. Then the kids are going to bed while the adults are at the Spook House for a meeting. You don't have to like it, but you'll damned well do it."

"I don't have to do anything," Clover mutters defiantly, sounding so much like Willow that I snort.

"Don't make me smack your ass, little bitch. If you don't know what I mean, you can ask your daughter about that later. Her nickname ain't Spanky for no reason. You don't get to just run off without listening to my side of shit. This won't work if you aren't rational. I have to be the man in this relationship."

"I don't think man is the correct term," Clover snarls. I toss her to the bed we've shared for the past week and a half. "Tyrannical, lying, faithless, perverted, controlling bastard is more like it."

"Keep talking dirty like that," I warn. I grab the obvious bulge of my arousal and squeeze until my eyes roll back. "Look," I purr salaciously, "You're already on a bed and everything."

Wide-eyed, Clover shuffles backward until her ass meets the headboard. She starts to tuck her knees to her breasts, but mid-action she thinks better of it. Pity— I saw a flash of panties and my cock twitched for some attention.

"I'm going to fuck the aggression right out of you, so you'll be calm and able to listen. Because if I tried to talk to you right now, you'd act like a spoiled little bitch."

"Would not," Clover mutters, sounding like a petulant child.

"You will not hide from your husband behind that attitude," I warn. "You will never freeze me out. If you are mad at me, I want you to hit me, fuck me, punch me, or scream into my face.

But I will never allow you to internalize it and destroy our relationship like you did with Sam."

"I didn't destroy my relationship with Sam!" Clover screams at me like a banshee, exactly what I wanted her to do. "You're right. I am fucking furious right now." Getting to her knees in the center of the mattress, Clover shrieks at me. "A sleazy woman just told me about my daughter being fucked in public by a man who's been a big brother to her!"

"And that made you mad, didn't it?" I coax Clover to let it out, not to bottle it up inside and let it numb her. I challenge her, "What are you going to do about it?"

"Kick Auggie's ass," Clover snarls, looking wild and unbridled. Her blue eyes are glowing with anticipation, her lungs are heaving, making her breasts rise and fall, and her hair is falling out of its bun. Clover's a fucking wreck, and I've never loved her more.

"Good God, I want you," I breathe underneath my breath. "I don't think that's a wise decision. After you calm down, I'd suggest you talk to me, and then your daughter," I say in a reasonable tone that doesn't compute with Clover. "Auggie would brush you off like a gnat."

"I'm so…" Clover releases a silent scream. "Pissed!"

"Take it out on me," I beg. My hand lashes out to latch around Clover's ankle without thought. I yank her growling form across the mattress, and then flip her over until her ass is in the air. Flicking Clover's skirt up over her waist, "You're never wearing pants," I purrs when her panty-covered ass is revealed. "But I'll make an exception on skin-tight yoga pants."

Face pressed into the mattress, resting on her knees with her ass in the air, Clover is vibrating with fury beneath my touch. She's too angry to speak. Years of bottling up her emotions have left her without a voice, a way to release how she feels. I'm going to fuck her until she's relaxed.

"Come to me for anything, Lucky, and I will fix it," I whisper in a hypnotic tone as I run my fingertips along the crevice of her ass, gliding down along the slit of her pussy. I press the fabric of her panties against her lips, watching the spread of moisture wick into the cotton. Clover's as turned on as the cock trying to tear its way out of my trousers.

"Hmm… so pretty," I purr as I move the seat of Clover's panties to the side, exposing her pink, swollen, glistening lips.

"You don't actually want to wash me off your skin, do you? You were just being spiteful because you're pissed at me."

We're in surrender-mode. Clover's going to make me earn her response. "Silly Rabbit," I mutter calmly, but a second later I wrap my fist around her bun, and then yank her hair until her head is upright. "Answer the question, wife," I demand in deep voice. "Were you being a spiteful brat? Or did you want me to toss this fine ass into the bathtub?"

"No shower," Clover barely breathes the words.

"Hmm… I think I will refuel your pussy with a fresh batch," I murmur as I slowly unzip my trousers. Clover quivers, the sensation running along the column of her neck, and up into her hair. Making her wait, I unpin her hair instead of unleashing my cock.

"You're insane," is said in a throaty voice. "I haven't gone a few hours in the past ten days without your cum in me at all times. Every night, I take a bath, and then you're on me in a heartbeat, and doing the same when I get up in the morning. You're a maniac. What are you trying to prove here?"

Spreading Clover's beautiful blonde hair across her shoulders and down her back, I watch the silky stands slide through my fingertips like a cascade of water. I make her wait for her answer as she made me wait a few minutes ago. I pop the button of my trousers, releasing my throbbing cock.

Recognizing the sound of my pants opening, and craving the outcome, "Malcolm," Clover moans, sounding pained. No longer furious or frustrated or irrational, my future bride only has me on her mind, as is always the case when I touch her.

"I doubt I've ever seen such a gorgeous sight in my entire life." My voice is filled with wonder. I fist my shaft and begin gliding my cockhead along her glistening folds, slowly pressing in. I shudder, spine tensing from the intense pleasure. I tease Clover's clit, running the head of my dick over the swollen nub in the circular pattern that is guaranteed to get her off. "I find so much pride in seeing our bodies joined."

"Please," Clover begs, delirious with want. Not only has Clover surrendered, she's now begging me for it. Her tiny fingers twist in the comforter as she wiggles her curvy behind like flashing red at a bull.

"You asked what I was trying to prove here," I remind Clover. With the flex of my hips, I impale her sweet pussy, tearing a grunt of surprise from her throat and my own. Pressed to the hilt, I curve around Clover's back to whisper near her ear. Lips fluttering against her earlobe, "I'm proving I'm the man."

A deep moan and the swivel of her hips is Clover's only answer. When in the throes of passion, Clover communicates with her body, not her words. Slowly pulling out, I watch my cock slide out of her wet pussy, leaving my cock slicked with our combined passions. It's my turn to groan, a mixture of relief and pleasure.

"I belong to you now, Clover," I inform her as I start to quicken my pace. "And you belong to me. Next time, run to me, not away from me."

Clearing her throat, it takes Clover several tries to speak since I don't let up on my onslaught. Gripping her hips, I thrust at a rapid pace, causing her words to be fragmented. "I wasn't running from you," She gasps out, fingers clenching the comforter. Her pussy begins to spasm around my cock. "I was looking for you, ready to kick your teeth in."

Chuckling, "Well, now, this is so much more fun and productive, don't you think?"

"Asshole," comes grabbled into the mattress. I give Clover a punishing thrust of my cock, followed by a good dozen more. The derogatory nickname changes to words of adoration as I prove my worth.

Pounding Clover from behind while laughing deeply from my chest, "Refill time," I sing. "Gotta fill your cunt with my baby batter. I'll get a good dozen kids out of you by menopause at this rate, and I doubt I'll ever tire of your pussy. We'll get one kid out of the batch to pay for our retirements."

"Kill me," Clover weeps, closing in on her release.

Sharply thrusting, meeting her cervix with the head of my cock, I ask innocently, "What'd you say?"

Screwing Clover harder than I ever have before, I fuck the attitude right out of her. I put my own twist on the term attitude adjustment. Our bodies are swaying and lunging in tandem, slicked with sweat. Our breath comes out in rough gasps and pants as my hips pound into Clover's fleshy ass. My fingertips bite into her skin, bruisingly so.

Moaning in a continual sound, her pussy going insane around my cock, Clover forces out, "I said... I said I was going to come."

"That's what I thought you said," I tease, and a second later I'm joining her. Grunting, jerking, I shoot deep inside her. Gasping for breath, still coming, I muse, "If we make a kid right now, will it be angry like you were when we first started, or relaxed as you are now?"

"Kill me... just kill me," Clover moans again.

"I'll kill you with love." I smother the woman with my body, lips attacking any exposed skin within my reach. "C'mon, now... you don't fool me. You love my kids and we didn't even make them together. Imagine how you'd feel for this one?" I rub her tummy, praying, suddenly finding God.

"That would be... indescribable," Clover breathes out, sounding awed and scared shitless. I squeeze the muscles at the base of my cock, managing to give her a few drops more, causing her to giggle uncontrollably. "You're certifiably insane."

"Certifiable and clinically insane, you mean." I laugh with her. "Perhaps criminally, too."

Cleaned up and redressed for our kids' imminent arrival home from school, Clover wears her conservative persona: perfectly pressed skirt and blouse, with her hair pulled tightly back to the nape of her neck into a bun. Clover has the sexy librarian gig down– kids would be terrified of her, but the dads' tongues would be lolling out of their mouths. You'd never guess that this woman sitting near the head of the bed was the same one from twenty minutes ago, who was begging me to fuck her.

God, I love my wife.

I love knowing that I'm one of the few who will ever see Clover completely unhinge. She is so connected to me while we make love that all else ceases to exist but me. It's a heady, dangerous feeling. I'd kill to keep it, because I've dubbed the sensation '*man*.' Clover makes me a man.

Just finishing up my clean up session, I decide it's time for our landmine of a conversation. "If I could take back some of the things I've done, I would." I stalk forward into the bedroom, need propelling me to touch Clover, as if I could ever stop touching her. "In my defense, Willow was a legal adult, and I had no rights over her. I went to Robin, but talking to him is like bashing my head into a brick wall. But you know all about that, because you and Willow are the same way."

Ignoring my veiled insult, "Did you watch my daughter have sex like Nina said you did?" Clover asks, and I can hear the denial in her voice. But the thread of worry is a punch to the gut.

"Clover, I'm going to be your husband. You need to put some faith in me. Think about what you just said, and ask yourself if you truly believe I'd do that shit?"

I see the change in Clover. Earlier she wouldn't have heard a word I said as her mind spun in anger. Right this second, is the first time she's calmed enough to truly think about it. I keep talking now that she's able to listen. "Rob tried to help by making rules, which Auggie only pretended to follow. Robin moved into the Spook House to watch over Willow, and my boys tried to get her attention."

Clover's face softens a bit, telling me that I'm going the correct route. I haven't had much experience with females outside of Isis and Raven. I tend to treat them like wild animals. Anything can set them off for any reason, like a loaded gun in a toddler's hands. My practice with Isis will come in handy with Clover. I just have to bite my tongue against what really wants to be said and always tell a sweeter version of the truth.

"The first time Willow showed up at the Playroom, it was in the storeroom at Rush. I wasn't there until after Robin and Isis kicked Willow and Essie out. I was there to unclog the shower drain in the loft. It was Willow's eighteenth birthday, and she was on a date with Ren at Rush. Essie and Willow were giving my son the slip because of Auggie's influence. Augustus Kline was just too much of a draw for the girl."

"Willow's birthday?" whispering, Clover looks shell-shocked.

"Yeah." I sit on the edge of our bed, trying to avoid touching Clover in any manner. She's always closed off after the high of sex has worn off, and I respect that. "It was that night that I knew it was too late. I feared Auggie would run his game and destroy her, but I had faith in your kid. Willow's parents were smart and strong, so I knew she could resist Auggie once she grew up some."

Devastated, Clover asks in a thready voice, "How many times?"

"Go to the Playroom?" Unable to speak, Clover nods her head yes. "Three times. Willow only entered the Playroom three times that I know of. The first I wasn't present. The second was the night…" my fingers seek my hair and tear out a chunk. "Shit,"

I hiss. "Auggie broke Willow in that night. It's the only way to describe it. I tried to stop it, but when I couldn't, I left and took Ren with me. When it got more than she could bear, Isis left too. Rob and Devon stayed to protect Willow, and everything she did was of her own volition. She was an adult, and I had no authority over her. My hands were tied."

"You said three times," Clover prompts me, voice cold and distant. She's freezing me out, protecting herself from the pain of my betrayal.

"I won't lie to you, Clover, because I don't want our marriage's foundation to be built on deception. The only reason you found out about Willow in the Playroom like you did is because I was going to tell you tonight. I haven't had the time in the past few weeks for this conversation. I've been a bit busy with a billion other more important things," desperation fills my voice.

"I will concede that there wasn't time and I believe that you were going to tell me. You may sit closer to me, if you wish." Clover says primly as she points to a spot on the bed I'm not allow to cross.

I try to get more comfortable on the corner of the bed, preparing for a long conversation, when all I want to do it prove my loyalty to Clover by using my body, not my words. My leg keeps sliding off the silky comforter, so I tuck it under my ass hoping it'll stay put. I want to give Clover the space she so desperately seeks, but I can't do this without touching her. My fingers turn to claws and grip my thighs. The need– the craving is so intense that I start to sweat.

"May I touch you while we talk," I breathe to Clover, "Just your foot?" Her scent infuses the bedding, the room, or maybe it's just wafting from her. The hit of sugar and almonds fogs my head and arouses my body. The scent causes me to breathe heavily, dragging more and more of the intoxicating fragrance into my system.

Clover reluctantly slides her foot toward me along the purple bedding, but balls up the rest of her body so she's not within arm's reach. I gently encompass her delicate ankle with my fingers, my grip overlapping. When she doesn't protest, I slowly remove her beige high-heeled shoe. A deep, satisfied sound bubbles up from my chest when I see her tiny pink toenails, so feminine and womanly. I bite my lip against the need to kiss each and every one of them, run my tongue in their crevices, and nibble the tips.

I press my thumb into Clover's arch and she groans, back arching a bit. I worry that I'm pushing her after the way I used her body earlier, but her eyes are filled with fire. "I'll just rub your foot while we talk. I'll behave," I promise.

"Okay," Clover mutters. She relaxes a bit, but she's far too emotionally controlled for my liking. She's still freezing me out, and I hate it.

Absentmindedly, I rub Clover's foot while I speak. "I was only going to tell you that Willow was a member of the Playroom, and that you have to ask her for the details yourself. What she did or didn't do, is up to her to discuss with you. It's her private business. While I know the details from other sources, I won't share them with you."

Voice stiff with disappointment, "Did you, at any time, see my daughter in a compromising position?"

"No," I vow. "I've only ever seen Willow kiss Ren, and that was less than two weeks ago in my kitchen. I told you, I'm not a pervert. The only time I've seen my own sister was when I walked in on her in my living room when she was a teenager." I huff an uncomfortable laugh, remembering the look on Robin's face. "We have mutual respect for one another as adults. With that saying, I've seen your brother do just about everything you could imagine." I shrug it off. "But Robin's not my brother."

"Does Willow still go?" voice wavering, but I can't determine why.

"The last Prynne family game night was at the same time as the opening of the Playroom in the Spook House's attic. Willow was the hostess since she and Robin built the room. It took her less than ten minutes to determine she wasn't ready for such a place, that maybe she never would be."

"Willow showed up with Ren and the kids and their friend Langdon Stone," Clover muses, remembering that night. "I would have never guessed she was in a place like that beforehand. It just proves how we never know what our children are up to."

I shake my head sadly, thinking of Devon. "Depends on the kid. I don't judge those in the Playroom, nor do I fault Willow for being there. But I was proud when she left, as you should be. Willow recognized it wasn't healthy for her and left, and hasn't been back since."

"Thank you for being honest with me, and I'm sorry I jumped to conclusions," Clover breathes out, reaching over to touch my hand. At some point, I had pulled Clover's other foot to me as I spoke. Two perfect, pink-toenailed feet rest in my lap. My fingers curl possessively around them, digging into the tender spots and tickling the not-so tender spots. I lean forward and place a kiss to each of her toes. She makes a pleased sound in the back of her throat that warms my heart. Clover craves my touch as much as I crave touching her– even when she's trying her damnedest to stay closed off to me.

"You only thought what Nina wanted you to think. Please, just trust me– trust who I am –before you jump to conclusions. Come to me and ask, and then you have the right to feel whatever you feel afterward. But don't ever just assume I did what someone said. Not all people have good intentions."

Clover's quiet, pensive. "Nina isn't very nice."

It's like I blinked, only to find myself in an entirely different location– teleportation. I'm now at the headboard with Clover's cheek resting on my thigh. My fingers thread through her hair in a gentle rhythm, grounding me to the here and now.

"Sorry," I whisper, and Clover snorts at me. The ease I feel with her in my arms and the frankness of her sarcastic sound pleases me to no end. Clover is as real with me as I'm trying to be with her.

"Your eyes were glazed over. I could tell you weren't here with me anymore," Clover says quietly. Her breath warms me through the fabric of my trousers. I look on in amazement as her fingers stroke my knee– her engagement ring glittering in the light.

"Nina was my father's whore, and I mean that in the true sense of the word. There were monetary incentives for the girl. She's not much older than I am– maybe six or seven years. Nina's always freaked my ass out. After my father died, she tried to get with me, but I turned her down. She waited until Auggie was fifteen before she crept in, and she's been his kept woman ever since. Auggie is John Mason's greatest creation."

"Why'd Nina pull that shit today?" Clover snarls, and it's reminds me of a ferocious kitten. I laugh, the total opposite reaction Clover was expecting out of me.

"Nina stuck around, thinking Auggie would make an honest woman out of her sometime. But it's never going to happen.

Auggie believes a man treats you how you want to be treated. Act like a whore, he'll treat you like a whore. If you want Auggie to respect you, make him respect you by respecting yourself. As the years rolled by, Auggie treated Nina like shit. Since she didn't leave, he kept doing it."

"That's awful," Clover says against my knee, no doubt putting herself in Nina's position.

"Nina is only suffering what she allows. If she didn't like it, she's the only one who can stop it. So that is why Nina accosted you at The Bakery today. She was stirring shit because that's all she has left to get Auggie's attention."

Clover looks relaxed, like I'm telling her a story at bedtime, not my family's dirty history. I pull her farther into my lap and tuck her head beneath my chin. I let my hands wander all over her back and sides, allowing the contact to soothe me. Satisfaction coils deep inside my heart when Clover's fingers unbutton my shirt, making an opening for her to rest her cheek on my bared chest.

This is what I want– exactly what I want.

"I'm taking you to the Spook House tonight. We're discussing what Nina did first, but then I want to take you up to the attic. Just us. I'll have Auggie send everyone else home."

"Will you show me what you've done for the past five years? With your lovers?" Clover hesitantly asks, rocking the world beneath my feet.

I gasp out, "You want to see that? Won't you see that as cheating?" I'm at a complete and total loss.

"I can't stop thinking about it," Clover whispers against my chest. "It's haunting me. I need to see if it was more than what we have together. I need to know what fulfills you."

"Clover," I sigh her name. "Please don't doubt us– *me*," I stress.

"I'm not," is her immediate reply.

"You do realize I will be touching other people, having them touch me back in a sexual manner, correct?" I say as if I'm speaking to a small child and they are being obtuse.

"That's the point, Malcolm. I need to see it. I've thought about it so much since you've told me, that I've spun it around until it's graphic and perverse– scary. But I've also twisted it until I see it as something you can't live without. I can't handle the shit in my head. Make it stop," she begs, which makes me surrender.

"Okay," I agree, wishing I wasn't. "Promise me this, if at any time you are uncomfortable, just tell me to stop and I will instantly stop. I'm not losing you over this, Clover. I bought us a house today. I put our houses on the market. I've begun building our futures. I won't allow the Playroom or anything else to rip that future away from us and our family."

"I promise to say stop if I get upset," Clover vows. She cups my cheek tenderly, gaining my undivided attention. "I was so fucking pissed after Nina said what she said. But not once did I think about leaving you. All I could think of was that bitch touching you, and how I wanted to murder her for it. I have to see with my own two eyes, that what you had with your lovers is nothing like we have now."

"It's not," I promise. "Just know, you can't unsee this like you can something you envision. Nothing will be able to rewrite it in your memories. Clover, it is nothing like what you and I have."

"I believe you," Clover whispers, eyelashes slowly lowering to shutter her eyes. "It's different because I'm in love with you, and now I need to see if they are, too. And if they are, I'll tear their fucking hearts out."

"Holy Christ," I hiss, stunned stupid. Not only did Clover say it first, she said it with violence. "I love you, too. More than you'll ever know."

"And you didn't even have to say it during sex," Clover deadpans, and a second later she's giggling like a little girl.

"Silly Rabbit." I reach out to swat her ass. "I'll be fucking the violence outta you after I prove a massage is a poor excuse for sex. Mark my words, Lucky Clover– you'll be screaming I love you in the throes of passion tonight. You'll surrender."

CHAPTER THIRTY-SEVEN

The Widow

Leaning against the wall of the Spook House's living room, my mind is a muddled up mess– a sieve that holds no true thought. The past few weeks have pushed me to the brink of my understanding. Malcolm is wearing his heart on his sleeve– the good and the bad. I owe him the chance to fully reveal himself.

While the meeting is the main reason everyone is here, it's not why I'm here. I'm here for *after*. I'm petrified over what I will feel when I see Malcolm with his lovers, whomever they may be. I've never been good with emotions, never truly owning what I feel. I tend to bury the feelings, placing myself in the other person's shoes. While it's a selfless way of thinking, it's disrespectful to disregard your own feelings as not being valid, especially when the other person isn't thinking twice about yours.

In this, I need to see that Malcolm will be thinking of nothing but me. I know we reach a wavelength where everything else ceases to exist when we are in our bed together. It's what I was trying to explain to Willow. If you find that plane of existence with another human being, cherish it. Deep inside, the thought of Malcolm having that type of connection with his lovers for the past few years is plaguing me.

"Is that Beth standing over there?" I whisper to Malcolm, voice filled with surprise. "Is it? Is that big guy her new husband? Daaamn," I draw out in appreciation. Rory is a bad girl's version of the boy next door.

Malcolm's eyes flick over to where I'm looking, and then instantly light right back on mine. "Yeah, Bethany has been with us for a year or so. She's a nice girl. Bubbly but not obnoxious. She plays with Opal, and fucks Auggie from time to time."

My lips twist up in disgust when I hear Auggie's name. Malcolm may have calmed me down with sex and a talk, but Auggie's still on my shit-list.

Malcolm gazes back over at the newlyweds. "Well, I'm sure Bethany's extracurricular activities are past tense now because of her new husband. I don't see Rory putting up with Auggie's shit. He already doesn't see Auggie as a boss. Rory only minds Isis."

"You said that all so nonchalantly, like it isn't a huge fucking deal." I'm confused beyond belief. I keep gazing around, imaging these people engaged in sexual deviancy, and I just can't wrap my mind around it.

Making a gesture of *'what are you gonna do'*, Malcolm plainly states, "It's just the truth. Everyone here has a story of their own telling. Who am I to judge?"

"I'm not judging. I'm just shocked, I guess. I was never free with my body, so it's hard for me to empathize," I grumble more to myself than to Malcolm.

The past half hour has been a test of my understanding. Even if it takes a lifetime, I'm not sure I'll ever be able to process the emotions that have assaulted me.

Overwhelmed

The room my daughter has called her living room for the past six months is packed with bodies. People from every walk of life and background. The majority are people who I interact with on a daily basis, whether within my own family or my job. I've seen them all walking the streets of our town. I've chatted with them, ate lunch with them, and babysat their children. In Mayor Ross's case, worked for them for over a decade.

One emotion throbs like a sore nerve as I stand here looking around.

Betrayal

These people watched my child's violation at the hands of the man who sits before me like a king of his castle. No one stepped up and tried to help the impressionable girl. I logically understand that Willow was an adult and it wasn't their place to interfere. Nevertheless, the maternal instinct in me wants to roar its vengeance and bleed them dry.

Twenty-four hours.

What changes a child in twenty-four hours? Willow was the same girl, whether her internal clock clicked over to eighteen or not. Augustus Kline was twenty-four hours from being a predator behind iron bars.

This sense of betrayal flavors my feelings toward the Playroom. I try to distance myself, take Willow out of the equation. But how can I, when all I envision is the way these people ogled my child?

I do my damnedest not to gaze at my brother with judgment and disgust. Robin watched my child's violation. (I must stop thinking of it as such, because obviously Willow doesn't see it as a violation) Robin watches me surreptitiously from the corner of his vision as he sits next to the asshole with the shit-eating grin and my future vixen-in-law.

"Attention," Auggie's booming voice echoes around the room. The man takes charge from his post on the antique sofa like he's a dictator of a small, deviant country. "Today, Robin's sister was accosted at The Bakery by one of our own. Clover Webster is not a member of the Playroom, so anything spoken was in clear violation with our code of conduct."

A wave of furious whispering rolls through the crowd as all eyes flick in my direction. Embarrassed, I sidestep to stand behind Malcolm, which isn't an easy task since he was leaning against the wall. Being small has its advantages. Leaning back against me like I'm a life-sized pillow, Malcolm's amused chuckle vibrates against my chest. When I rest my hands on his hips, the chuckle turns to a satisfied growl.

"Clover Webster was not only told about what you all witnessed within the Playroom, she was told *my* personal business. Chatting amongst friends is one thing, chatting about *me* is another fucking issue all together. What I do with whomever I choose is only *my* business. If you witness it, it is for your pleasure and entertainment, and it shouldn't be taken lightly. I personally chose every single one of you bastards in this room. It is my responsibility to make sure your play is safe, consensual, fun, and kept private."

Isis interjects when Auggie's anger gets the best of him, rendering him unable to speak without shouting. "My nephew was named. Yes, the entire town thinks Devon's a bad seed now, but let's not add fuel to the fire with sexual deviancy. There is a reason we created this group: Fairport's residents wouldn't understand our needs. We'd be ostracized."

"With this new development," Auggie takes back over. "I've decided to close the Playroom—"

Cries of outrage and shock pour throughout the room. Their bodies vibrate with barely contained violence and bitter disappointment. The majority react as if they are in disbelief.

Even Malcolm freezes in front of me. "Holy Christ," he hisses, impressed. "Not in a million years did I ever think I'd hear Auggie say that."

"This is not up for debate. When you are in my care, you are my responsibility. A select few will still have access to my attic, and the rest of you are on your own. Take what I've taught you and play amongst yourselves. I will not be held responsible when your lives turn to shit because some jealous bitch you banged decides to tell your boss you like your ass tickled with a feather or how you love to fuck your sixty-year-old wife when she's dressed as a young girl. That's on your heads now."

"Who narked? Who ruined the Playroom for everyone?" A young woman demands.

"Nina," Auggie says clearly, inciting a storm of rapid-fire questions. "I wouldn't trust Nina to join you wherever you may land after this. She'll be the one telling your boss, your wife, your children, what you like to do behind closed doors. But it's your ass on the line, not mine."

"How can you do this?" Nina shouts above the crowd.

Standing from the center seat on the small sofa, Auggie bellows, "You trash-talked my family. You confronted Robin's sister in a public place where people overheard you, calling us all by name: Me, Malcolm, Robin, Devon, and Willow. You told a young woman's relative about how I took her virginity. That was for Willow to discuss with Clover when she felt it was time. Now you stand in my living room wondering how I can do this to you," Auggie sounds incredulous. "How. Can. You. Do. This. To. ME?" Auggie screams like a madman, radiating violence and fury. "Get the fuck out of my house and never come back."

"You're shutting this down because I ratted out your little bitch? The Playroom hasn't even been open for two fucking weeks. You sure about that, Auggie? Rumor has it that Isis has been pressuring you for months to stop playing. Are you finally going weak?"

"Whether or not I'm doing this for Willow, or for Isis, or because my cock won't rise, is none of your goddamned business, Nina. Don't disrespect my family, in my home, to my face, and think you can get away with it. I'd leave if I were you, because I'm this," Auggie presses his fingers together in example, "close to snapping your neck with the flick of my wrist. Get. Out." Auggie points to the front door.

"I've been with you since you were fifteen years old, and this is how you treat me," Nina screams, voice filled with misery.

"Exactly," is all Auggie says as he retakes his seat.

"What's that supposed to mean?" Nina mumbles, confused.

Rob, silent since I walked into his living room, finally speaks. "Exactly is Auggie's point. He was a child you molested. Auggie wasn't even interested in girls yet. If he was, he would've touched Isis sooner. You were what? Thirty-something? You were an adult going after a boy, and now you want him to respect you for it. You used Auggie, so he's been using you back. If you wanted something different from Auggie, maybe you should have treated him with respect first."

"Don't even," Isis snarls when Nina tries to respond. "I've waited fourteen years for Auggie to finally stand up to you. Rory, toss the bitch out on her head– make it hurt."

"Wait!" Auggie calls out when Rory makes his way through the crowd. "Word of advice to you, Nina, and to every single woman in this room: if you want a man to respect you, don't act like all you have to offer is your pussy. You used to laugh, saying how all men thought with their dicks. No, that's not the case. All you saw was my dick if you thought you could trap me with your over-fucked pussy and mouth. You treated yourself like a whore while you made me feel like one. I kept you around because you were loyal. What you did today made you a disloyal whore, and they are expendable."

Auggie gets up from his seat, and I fear he's going to be violent. All he does is look out over Fairport's most deviant citizens, glare actually. "If I spoke to you before the meeting, you know what to do. If I didn't, please leave," and with that Auggie leaves the room, Isis and Robin in his wake.

"Way to clean house," I mutter in awe, still pissed at Auggie but equally impressed.

Turning to me, Malcolm is radiating pride. "I've been waiting a long while for Auggie to finally do this. I thought the weeding out would happen before he allowed these people into his home, but when that wasn't the case, I thought the Playroom would grow exponentially over time. When Auggie started the Playroom, it was just his friends, and then it snowballed. It became a 'friend of a friend of a friend of a friend', and how can you trust that? Play is about trust and intimacy, not strangers compiling your secrets for later extortion."

"No. Fucking. Way," I articulate slowly as I imagine this roomful of people knowing my deepest, darkest desires. It's no wonder Malcolm sat on the sofa and observed.

Slyly grinning, Malcolm declares, "Yes, fucking way. Up we go," he says playfully while taking my hand. Eyes darting to the side to connect with mine, "Unless you've changed your mind."

"Just you and–" I shrug, not knowing who the hell Malcolm plays with. "No voyeurs?"

"Just us." He squeezes my hand. "Promise."

I watch as a crowd of Fairport residents leave the Spook House on a bitter wave of disappointment. Mayor and Mrs. Ross flash me wide-toothed smiles and wave happily on their way by. I assume they are still in Auggie's inner circle of hedonism. If you can't trust the mayor of your town, who can you trust? Especially when you are collecting the mayor's dirty secrets too.

You can definitely tell the outcasts from Auggie's favorites. The outcasts rush by, snarling to one another about how they are going to flay Nina alive. The rest linger, chatting with one another, pairing off to go elsewhere for some sexual satisfaction.

Auggie wanders back into the living room, with a beer in each hand. Not to be outdone, Rob follows Auggie while hugging a six-pack to his chest like a teddy bear. Isis is nursing a bottle of wine– with no glass. The Spook House is usually a dry house. Must be they feel safe getting their drink on since Willow is at Wreck & Ruin helping Langdon with their accounts.

"Playroom's all yours," Auggie says conversationally as he slumps down to sit on the sofa. But all I hear is, *"Feel free to go fuck in my attic."*

"I'm sorry about Nina," pops out before I can stop it. "I feel responsible for what happened today for some reason." I stare at my feet, wondering what the fuck is wrong with my head. I'm supposed to be pissed at this big, virginity-stealing oaf, but all I see is a sad little boy licking his wounds.

"I suspect you want to murder the three of us." Gesturing to himself, Isis, and my brother, Auggie looks guilty and sounds even guiltier. "If I could, I'd kick my own ass." He drains an entire bottle of beer, and then reaches over to grab one from Rob's six-pack. "No harm, no foul. Willow is sober, educated, happy, and in love, right? A good girl who will make her mother proud. Now, me, I'm neither good nor bad, and I've surely never made my mother proud."

"Auggie," Malcolm huffs out as he crosses the room. "Don't wallow," he orders mid-stride. "Dad would kick your ass for it."

"Thanks for the pep-talk, brother." Auggie drains another beer in one long swallow. "Don't take this as an insult." Auggie points across the room at two lurking figures hiding in the shadows. "Now, go get good and fucked."

"Isis?" is all Malcolm says, and all Isis does in reply is tilt her chin in his direction.

While one pair of siblings has an entire conversation with one word and one body movement, another is glaring at each other– that would be Rob and me, and the conversation goes something along the lines of this.

We are going to have a talk.
No shit!
I want to kill you with my bare hands.
And I'll let you.
Don't you feel ashamed of yourself?
What do you think?

Malcolm stands in front of me, cutting off mine and Rob's silent conversation. "Well, don't get too shit-faced, I guess. We have enough problems with two substance abusers in the family."

"Yes, Dad," Auggie says belligerently while reaching for another bottle. "This is the entirety of our stash. I'll have it gone in half an hour and sobered up by the time the baby alchie gets home from her second job. Promise."

"I doubt that's all of your stash," I mutter to myself while looking pointedly at my brother. Rob's ears tint pink, but he somehow controls his blush otherwise. The corner of Rob's lips lift a fraction because we both know there is some of Mary Prynne's finest hidden somewhere in this house. Not that Auggie could ever find it.

Realization dawns: Rob's the one who's truly in control of Augustus Kline and Isis Mason– they just don't realize it. Robin manipulates them into doing as he wishes, and they believe it was on their own volition. If I were a betting girl, I'd bet Robin somehow made Nina do what she did today, knowing Auggie would react just as he did this evening.

My thoughts broadcast across my expression, causing Robin's mouth to split into the biggest fucking smirk on the planet. He could power Fairport and its surrounding counties with that high-wattage grin.

"Sociopath," I mouth, stunned senseless.

"Determined," Rob mouths back.

Blocking my view again, "I want to show you the Playroom, will you join me?" Malcolm whispers into my ear. I shiver from the closeness, not only from the chill his warm breath created, but the panic that tries to claw its way out of my throat.

I step away, fearing Malcolm will take it as rejection. But in this environment, Malcolm's touch is too much– too intense on my raw nerves. Malcolm gazes at me with endless understanding and patience that loosens the tautness from my shoulders. A shuddering breath falls from my constricted lungs.

"I'm ready." I'm ready to get away from a belligerent Auggie, an ever-watchful Isis, and a silently plotting Rob. They are freaking my ass out more so than what's to come in the Playroom.

"What I do is more sensual than sexual. But I will warn you now, release is involved. So if you can't handle it, this is your last chance to say you want to go home and never come back."

"Malcolm, I'm a rip the Band-Aid off kind of girl," I say dryly. I turn the tables on the man, "I need to see you do this. If you are the one who is uncomfortable, say stop and we'll leave."

A trio of snorts comes from the direction of the sofa. "You guys need to stop hanging out with Willow," Malcolm grumbles. "Come–" he gently takes my elbow. "I'll explain as I show you."

"The house is gorgeous," I murmur, distracting myself from the two forms that broke free of the shadows. It took all of my concentration not to gasp at Malcolm's choices. I would have never guessed in a million years. But now that I know, I realize how perfectly they balance one another.

"You should be proud. Willow did the majority of the work– and Robin. Willow's going to be heartbroken when she finds out Ren's buying them a house. But she will be excited to make it her own. I might ask her advice on some stuff in our house. But then again, I can just ask Dave."

"No weird shit in the attic," I growl, and Malcolm chuckles that deep, intoxicating sound.

"Already have plans for that. A real playroom– it's for the kids. I'm sure Weston will dump his entire savings account into that room. I picture a huge TV, a comfortable sofa, a DVR, Blu-ray player, an Xbox, and superfast Wi-Fi. They will never leave the attic. It'll keep the rest of the house quiet for our sanity," Malcolm says in a tone that bleeds pure happiness.

Malcolm is a man that looks forward to the chaos of so many lives crammed into one space. I can see clearly the man Malcolm longs to be: he wants a huge family surrounding him in a home that is his own. It makes sense after the loneliness of Malcolm's childhood– the absence of his childhood.

"Robin and Willow designed everything in the attic. You should be very proud. They did an exceptional job," Malcolm compliments as we traverse a narrow set of back steps from the kitchen to the attic. The tightness is lung-constricting. The walls close in the farther we ascend. I'm glad the entirety of the members of the Playroom aren't trailing us. I would've freaked the fuck out.

"The Playroom," I whisper, fingertips gliding over the words on the plaque. "I'd recognize Robin's brushstrokes anywhere," I say in a dreamy tone as my brother's work of art draws emotions from my numb mind. Rob truly is a creative genius, which makes his recent machinations that much more diabolical.

"Then you'll love the murals… that is if they don't freak you out," Malcolm teases as a warning. We ascend another set of steps, steps that are far narrower than the last set. As we enter the Playroom, our companions give us privacy by silently ghosting to a settee in the center of the space.

"Whoa," I draw out to hide the small gasp that was torn from my chest. "Not what I expected… not what I expected at all."

I'd expected a cold industrial feel: frightening, clinical, and impersonal. The Playroom embraces me in soft comfort. The attic is warm: dark colors, hardwood, and cushioned antique furnishings. No doubt, the rough-cut throne, which is highlighted by a spotlight, belongs to the arrogant bastard of the house. Classical music drifts down from the speakers above. Malcolm is standing behind a curved bar, fiddling with a stereo system. The music dims in its intensity until it's merely background noise.

"Would you like to look around on your own, or do you want me to guide you?" Malcolm asks, his voice and demeanor are ultra-helpful to cover his nervousness. I'm getting better at reading him.

"No need to show me things you're not involved with," I mutter underneath my breath. Bashfulness hits me out of nowhere. This room: the warmth, the colors and furnishings, the music– is too intimate after years of isolating coldness. If it was just Malcolm and me, I might be more comfortable. But we're not alone.

"How can you know what you like if you don't experience a small taste?" Malcolm's voice is a purr, a rumbling sound deep from his chest. Our environment and the eventuality of his play have heated him, aroused him in a manner I've never witnessed before. Watching Malcolm get hot is turning me on in response. His tongue snakes out to dab at his lower lip, wetting his mouth.

Swallowing, I try to reply, "I have no idea," but it comes out a jumbled up mess of incoherency.

"Those images and videos I sent to you had a purpose," Malcolm states pointedly, eyes seeking mine in the dim of the attic. "I wanted you to look at them." Malcolm ducks his head to my height, eyes tracking mine until I meet his steady gaze. "I wanted you to feel something. If it disgusted you, then it wasn't for you. But, if a spark lit inside you," he says lightly, but then his voice deepens to a husky growl, "I wanted you to explore it."

"Why?" I mumble, eyes wide with unveiled curiosity.

Seeming ten feet fall, Malcolm turns into a sexual creature. He prowls predatorily, hips rolling as he glides across the floor toward me. A feral grin enhances his expression. His presence is massive. The powerful aura that halos his body sucks all the air from my lungs. I freeze in his sights. I become the stunned prey he loves to call me– Malcolm Mason's personal bunny rabbit.

"You never got a chance to figure out what made you tick," Malcolm pops the *K* on tick as he surrounds me. Malcolm maneuvers me around, until my back is pressed to his chest, with his arms gliding up and down my sides. His luscious mouth is pressed to the hollow beneath my ear. The unyielding arousal at his front is aligned with my hip, igniting sparks of lust inside my core that could raze this house to the ground.

"It wasn't very traditional of me to understand how my sister's needs fed into Auggie's and Robin's. It wasn't very traditional of me to push my kids to experiment, but I want them to be happy. It's not very traditional of me to show my future wife the limits of my perversion, nor is it traditional that I long for you to find your own."

"I… ugh… Umm…" I ramble a bunch of nonsensical words, unable to form a coherent sentence with Malcolm surrounding me. He's possessively curled around my body. His love has invaded my heart and soul. His heated words ring in my ear. His masculine scent intoxicates my senses. Malcolm Mason has seeped so far into the recesses of my mind that he's all that I know.

"I want you to be happy, Clover," Malcolm murmurs close to my ear. The sensation creates goosebumps to explode on my skin. "Experiment," he growls, its vibrations striking my spine like lightning– every muscle pulses for Malcolm's attention.

My body lights up like a power-grid. I lick my lips and swallow when my mouth suddenly runs dry, because all of the moisture in my body wicks to pool between my clenched thighs. "Most of the images were nice," shyly leaves my parted lips.

"Nice... that's one way of putting it," Malcolm teases flirtatiously. Warmth instantly gone, he leaves me standing in stunned silence as he walks away to join his companions.

Malcolm's seductive laugh trails behind me as I wander. I wander to distance myself from the need Malcolm elicited within me, and he knows this. He gives me the space to center myself– to adapt to my environment.

A dog house?

What. The. Fuck?

Does someone actually lap at that bowl? Do they get on their hands and knees and crawl, tongue dipping into the water dish and returning wet. What kind of mind needs that activity to feel free?

A lot of scary shit greets me as I snoop. Some things I wish I could unsee. The majority of the objects pique my interests. The softer objects send a thrill of excitement through me, while the mean and nasty objects annoy me more than frighten. I don't see why someone would associate pleasure with pain. That thought alone tells me I don't want to go near that kind of thing. I don't really have any hang-ups, unless you call being inexperienced and cold a hang-up. I can see the appeal of the Playroom. It's a place to let your inhibitions run wild.

Malcolm leaves me to wander and explore while he and his *'friends'* assemble a folding table. Their soft conversation blends into the background music. The happy, companionable murmur is relaxing. I'm sure if the whole of the membership was up here, I'd have freaked out and ran, or judged. But as it is now, it's cozy and comforting. Malcolm trusts these two people, I can tell by how they relate to one another. Seeing them together, I'm not all that surprised by his choice of companions.

A torture device gains my undivided attention. The construction is flawless– I'd recognize Dave Prynne's carpentry expertise anywhere. I can't believe that Dad was in here. Willow would never use this contraption, and only one other person would have the balls to ask my father for help– Robin. I try to picture my brother with his trussed up arms and legs stretched to their agonizing limits by the pulley-system, with the leather straps holding him immobile while he suffers in pain.

Perhaps this is Rob's machine, and he's its operator. Maybe he straps someone down and does despicable acts. No. No, Robin may be manipulative and deceptive, but he is too mild-mannered to raise a hand in violence.

Isis.

I can see my brother in this rack of torture with Isis's fatal touch on his skin. What would make Rob crave such a thing?

This… this… no, never will I touch this. Panic settles within me, skin crawling, at just the thought of being strapped down and harmed.

A mural above the device is a depiction of the rack of torture. A brown-haired man is writhing, whether in pain or pleasure is the viewer's perception, while a creature of the night attacks him with a metal implement clutched in her palm. The painting is magnificent. Robin's utter devotion for the act and for Isis reverently screams through his brushstrokes. I won't judge my brother because you cannot deny the emotions that he feels for this machine or the woman. I don't have the stomach to witness such an act performed on my gentle brother… even if I am angry at him at the moment.

A soft moan resonates around the room, drawing my attention. A gasp jolts me to my core… and I realize it emanated from my chest.

I've never experienced any sexual contact outside of marital congress, and with only Sam and Malcolm. The dirty girl who resides within me is clawing her way out. She is frustrated after nearly twenty years of being pushed down, silenced, suffocated, and stifled.

Opening my mind, pushing down the fear of rejection, believing in the trust Malcolm and I have built over the past year, I finally let the real Clover out.

For weeks, my mind has spun fantasies and nightmares over Malcolm in the Playroom. It haunted me to think about all possible scenarios. This, this is nothing I would've expected to see in my lifetime. I don't know if I like it, or if I'm simply intrigued to see how others look when engaged in sex.

Opal's lithe form is bare to my vision: tall, lean, and almost masculine, with small breasts and a perfectly rounded ass. Her blonde hair is slicked back flat against her skull to keep it clean as she pours oil from a glass container. Rivulets of colorless liquid flood Opal's high, tight breasts, creating an appealing sheen on her skin. The oil flows like a river of silk down Opal's flat belly to mingle in the hair at the apex of her thighs.

A hard swallow sticks in my throat as a nude Colin uses his upper-body to spread the oil on Opal's skin. My eyes bulge in wonder as the pair performs a sensual, choreographed dance: soft breasts sliding against a very hard chest, with hips, thighs, arms, and legs tangling in a passionate writhing motion. Their faces glow in a drug-like bliss: mouths parted, eyes glazed and heavily hooded, and necks arched until they look as if they're praying to the heavens. Opal's tall, lean body against Colin's stocky, defined form is striking in its contrast.

I'd wondered more than a time or two what the cop looked like beneath his skin-tight uniform as he flirted relentlessly with me. Colin is a feast for the eyes. Striated muscles cut mouth-watering, deep grooves along his torso and sides. My mouth falls open when he turns around and I see his rear. *Holy Mary, mother of God, that ass is tight.* I shake my head against the vision of nails gripping it tightly and drawing him deeper. *'Those are not my nails'* I scream in denial inside my private thoughts.

Eyes intently staring, burning into my flesh, draw my gaze. Malcolm lies completely nude on a folding table. His flushed lips are parted in aroused amusement. His midnight blue eyes capture mine in their intensity. I am stripped bare, raw– revealed to my core. Malcolm sees me, he reads me. He doesn't watch his companions' dance– no doubt he's witnessed the glorious act countless times. No, he watches me in curious examination. I blush and look to the floor, feeling as if Malcolm's waiting for me to do a rare trick, or grow a second head, or maybe he thinks I'll attack his friends in a lust-filled craze.

At the first touch, Malcolm releases a long-suffering sigh that flashes heat to every cell in my body. This is what he needs– his skin hunger well fed. The reverent expression of relief is a testament to how much he constantly suffers through his cravings.

Malcolm said it would be sensual, not sexual. Hunger: a starvation of touch, intimacy, affection, and sex. Lust and need permeate the air, because nothing Malcolm ever does will be without sexual connotations. Whereas, Colin seized the breath within my lungs, Malcolm stops my heart. Shining golden skin flexes and releases with every touch. Raw sexuality pours off of Malcolm like a scent in the air.

Feminine and masculine hands rub, massage, tickle, and tease every inch of my husband-to-be's flesh. Soft, firm, gentle, and even a whisper's breath: their touches vary, creating a different reaction out of their friend.

Firm hands glide up the column of Malcolm's neck, thumbs resting over straining tendons. Malcolm arches his back, mouth parted, eyes glazed in erotic ecstasy. A low moan begins in his chest and slowly rumbles up his throat before fleeing out his parted lips.

Malcolm eyes are rapt as he gazes at Colin and Opal's hands as they glide along his oil-slickened skin. Opal's fingers dig into Malcolm's upper-thighs, with her arms gently brushing the twin-weights that rest heavily against his leg. His arousal juts forward with every touch, screaming for what will no doubt be the finale.

Colin's fingertips flutter over Malcolm's face, leaving no flesh untouched. Eyelids, cheeks, nose, and lips: Colin's fingertips skate in a rhythmic pattern that has Malcolm undulating his hips in the air, in a motion that is begging for sexual release. Malcolm moans in a long rush as male fingers encircle his erect nipples and twist. His back rears off the table with a grunt of misery.

Malcolm's legs spread in invitation for questing hands. All I can do it watch in rapt fascination. I can't look away and I can't process thought. I'm not upset by the people who touch Malcolm so intimately. Their claim on his skin is evident. I've touched Malcolm for the past few weeks. But I can sense the countless times they have eased him, and for that I am eternally thankful.

Opal and Colin are no threat to me because Malcolm invited me to watch– wanted me to watch. Even in the throes of ecstasy, he keeps partial attention on me at all times to gauge my comfort level.

Malcolm's and my relationship is so new that any semblance of ownership is absent. I don't feel as if I own Malcolm, or that he owns me. We are equal entities in a partnership, and who am I to tell my equal yes or no?

Control doesn't make a good spouse– it makes a parent.

My only right is to voice how what Malcolm does or doesn't do affects me personally. Malcolm keeps telling me to express my emotions, to not bottle them up inside. He wants me to own my emotions. In the here and now, I make good with the fact that watching Malcolm receive an erotic massage by a man and a woman doesn't harm our relationship. It doesn't lessen our connection. It doesn't bruise my ego. It doesn't make me feel rejected. All I feel is happy that Malcolm's needs arc bcing mct in a way that pleases him.

Enthralled, I find myself standing near Malcolm's feet. I had moved across the room without realization. Malcolm gazes at my face, no doubt cataloging my every response to determine whether or not I find this titillating or horrifying.

I have no need to see my reflection. My skin is tight and prickling as the blood rises to the surface in anticipation. My eyes are glazed with lust. The tips of my breasts ache from the soft contact of my blouse against the lace of my bra. A heavy ache in my lower belly is as painful as it is pleasurable.

I am hungry.

Malcolm lies on the table with a companion on each side of him. Their hands touch him with an intimacy that feels private in nature. I want to ask Malcolm questions as my curiosity overrides my discomfort. He gives me a lazy smile, as if silently saying *later.* I wouldn't interrupt his experience even if I could. Since I can't formulate thoughts at the moment, let alone speech, it's not an issue.

A sharp gasp draws me from my lust-filled fog– my own. The sight of Malcolm's hands skating up the backs of his companions' thighs, causes the ache in my lower belly to bloom. I prepare for a sexual invasion: my body opens, moisture flows, and my nerves turn into a live wire.

As if on a silent cue, Opal and Colin touch Malcolm's sex as his hands seek theirs. My jaw drops as a pair of hands cup Malcolm's hard, slippery length. They stroke in tandem: hands moving up and down, twisting, and repeating the gesture, increasing Malcolm's rapturous pleasure.

Never have I seen the act of a male touching a male. Never have I seen any of this before. Malcolm's hand strokes Colin's eager length as his other hand disappears between Opal's quivering thighs. Inside Opal, Malcolm's fingers disappear and reemerge, glistening with her arousal.

Thunderstruck, I stare at their hands with an astounded expression on my face. Oil-slickened fingers grasp and yank on male flesh, while nimble fingers impale feminine folds. Malcolm's abdominal muscles bunch and relax... bunch and relax... bunch and relax... with every stroke of their hands.

A symphony of sounds flood my ears: sharp grunts, rasping breath, and whimpering moans and groans. The music of sex I've never experienced. The sound of their pleasure arouses and hurts me simultaneously. I love the deep cadence of need, but I remember a lifetime ago. I've always stilted my responses because it drew Sam's attentions back to me. It was always best to be as quiet as possible, to never move. I was always quiet because it was demanded of me. Hearing the three of them makes me jealous, but not in the way that is expected. I'm jealous of their unbridled freedom to express themselves in the way they feel.

Watching this trio is like nothing I've ever witnessed. It makes me sad that I missed out on a large portion of my life because I let fear drive me. But, and at the same time, I am humbled that they are allowing me to witness it.

The hairs on the nape of my neck rise in anticipation as I draw their attention. I'd been deep inside my thoughts, no longer seeing the act before me. Eyes: dark, stormy blue, honey-brown, and green the exact shade of grass, bore into my face and strip me raw under their intelligent evaluation. They scent my inadequacies as if I'd spoken them aloud. Three predators have me in their sights, and I am their trapped bunny rabbit.

Another nonverbal cue has Malcolm arching off the table, a silent moan spilling from his lips. His fingers tighten on Colin and move erratically within Opal, bringing on their releases as he finds his own.

A beautiful display of the sensual nature of sex is enacted before me. The sounds, scents, and the emotions render me mindless. Moans and the rasping of breath, the wet suction of crazed hands, and the movement of writhing bodies is intoxicating. The smell of sex hangs heavily in the air as they complete their act.

I stare in wonder as Malcolm ejaculates up his chest and doesn't anger when Colin spurts his contribution on the same flesh. Malcolm's eyelashes flutter from the heavy weight of completion. Gorged on intimate affection, Malcolm's skin-hunger is satisfied for the time being.

As a unit, Colin and Opal clean Malcolm. Colin swabs down the semen spattered chest with a damp cloth, and Opal washes the sex covered hands with warm water from a porcelain bowl. They care for Malcolm with a level of deference that steals my breath.

"Malcolm, Clover," Colin says quietly in parting as he gathers his clothing and walks to the end of the attic to disappear behind a door. Opal walks in the opposite direction, and disappears behind another door.

Bathrooms?

"Where did you go?" Malcolm asks as he sits up, bending his legs and resting his forearms across his knees. He sits before me, completely comfortable in our awkward silence. His nudity is a glorious sight. No way would I ever be this comfortable being nude.

"That was beautiful," I whisper hoarsely, ignoring his question.

"Thank you," Malcolm murmurs in reply, eyes tracking over my face, reading me. "Why are you sad? Are you disappointed in me?"

"No," I sputter abruptly. "No, you're very lucky to have people you can touch like that– people who want to touch you in return. People you're comfortable doing that with…"

"Did you like watching?" Malcolm's voice is soft, as if worried his normal, deep tone will spook me.

"I did," I admit reluctantly while looking to the floor with my cheeks blushing profusely.

"No shame in that," Malcolm growls, "I want you to enjoy looking at me."

"No worries on that," I reply flippantly, because all of the sudden I feel extremely self-conscious.

Malcolm's responding laugh warms the ice-queen right out of me. I shiver as his deep rumble hits my ears. I can't imagine the sensation of having that amount of power over someone– a sexual power that affects every cell in their body. It thrills me that Malcolm's laugh ignites my fire, but it also saddens me that I'm incapable of doing the same to anyone.

"You went bye-bye again," Malcolm teases to soften the worry lacing his voice. "Where did you go?"

"What's it like?" I ask abruptly before my mind registers the words my tongue released. I had to get the words out before I regretted them.

"What's what like?" Malcolm leans forward to sits cross-legged on the massage table. His expression is open and honest. It makes me comfortable to ask the things that are guaranteed to make my cheeks blaze red.

"The pow–" a cellphone ringing cuts off my question.

"Sorry," Malcolm apologizes, biting his bottom lip as he hops from the table to answer his phone. A flash of his naked rear widens my eyes and catches my breath.

Holy Mary, mother of God, that's the finest ass I've ever seen.

Shit! I think I'm drooling from the sight of those firm butt cheeks... drooling between my thighs.

Hopping back up onto the table, Malcolm smirks arrogantly at me, no doubt reading my expression as if it were flashing *Horny! Horny! Horny!* in brightly lit neon.

"Hello." Malcolm pauses to listen. "Yeah... um-hmm... that's great. Hey!" His dark blue eyes light up in wonder, as if kicking himself for never thinking of something before. "Can you meet someone instead of me? I'm kinda busy at the moment. Ginny," he growls.

Gaining my undivided attention by that name alone, my eyes narrow in suspicion.

"Just do it for me," Malcolm begs, and then presses to end the call. "Opal!" he shouts, and the bathroom door opens almost immediately. Malcolm tosses his cellphone down onto the pile of his clothing.

A fully-clothed Opal walks out without a shred of embarrassment. Once the play was over, we are back to business as usual. "Yeah?" she asks with a nod of her head in my direction.

"I don't want to bail on my wife, 'cuz this is kinda important, don't ya think? My realtor is waiting for me at The No-Name with some paperwork I need to sign. Can you go get it for me and drop it off downstairs?" Malcolm asks Opal, and then he turns to me with the largest grin I've ever seen. "The seller has agreed to my terms. The house is ours, and the closing date is early next week."

"Holy shit," I shriek, completely shocked that this is my new reality. "Whoa..."

"I'll leave it downstairs," Opal stresses, "And lock the door behind me."

Finding Opal's comment odd, I watch as she crosses the attic. After exiting the door, her hand juts back in to flip the lock before shutting the door behind her.

"Ohhh…" I draw out, and then my eyes widen. "OH?"

Tugging me against him, Malcolm's words scare the hell out of me. "You asked what it was like. I'm more of a show-er than a talker."

CHAPTER THIRTY-EIGHT

The Widow

Whispering into my ear, lips fluttering, "Take your clothing off, Silly Rabbit. Or do you want me to strip you?" A shiver rolls down my spine from his promise-filled words.

Defying him, I could walk out of the Playroom and Malcolm wouldn't be upset. The only person who would live with the regret is me. I once told Malcolm how I regret the things I haven't done, not the things I've done that ended up being mistakes. Those mistakes form us into who we were meant to become. To live in fear, to never truly live life, that is the biggest mistake one can make.

I've been filling my princess journal with entries of my deepest regrets. "You've been snooping," I accuse, but my voice holds no real weight, and my furious blush takes the sting out of my words as well. Words rolling off my tongue in a salacious manner, "You're a naughty, naughty boy, Chief Mason."

Dark blue eyes twinkling with mischief, Malcolm grins down at me. He pulls me closer to the table, widening his thighs so he can cradle me between them. "I'm not used to sleeping seven hours straight. Sometimes I wake for a little light reading. But your historical romances are too misogynistic for my tastes."

Snorting, I interrupt Malcolm. "Most ironic statement ever."

"Your regrets are much more interesting than a Duke, Baron, Lord, Viscount, Prince, what have you, getting snagged up by the household's governess. Their use of dowries has me sweating about saving enough money for two princesses' weddings. The use of sexual congress makes me think of a bunch of shriveled up old men sitting around an oval-shaped amphitheater. Compromising a woman to force her to marry you plots, had me rutting on you long before our wedding night."

"You've been reading my books, too," I sputter, laughing, slapping Malcolm's chest with my palms.

Blushing, embarrassed, "In a few weeks, when we move into the new house, I'm stacking a few police procedurals or mysteries on the nightstand."

I sniff the air delicately, mocking something Malcolm did to me in weeks' past. "What's that smell? Why do I smell bullshit?" Sliding my arms up Malcolm's shoulders to rest against his neck, I sober up. "You, my future husband, are a hopeless romantic, and I believe those novels are exactly what you'd read, even if I wasn't filling the nightstand with them."

"I will admit nor deny anything," Malcolm says, putting on the air of an historical romance hero. "Enough distracting me, Silly Rabbit." Malcolm pops the top button on my blouse. "Naked, oily, sensual massage time."

I step away from Malcolm, enjoying the flash of displeasure that rolls over his face. I allow him to believe that I'm going to leave the Playroom. I stand a few feet from him, so he cannot reach out and distract me.

"Malcolm?" I call to gain his attention since he's staring at his empty hands with a lost expression on his face and his lips in a perfect pout. "Malcolm Mason, you are a dying breed." Eyes flicking up to look at me, my words earned his undivided attention. "You are a modern day hero. A super-tough cop, who is sensitive, flawed, and romantic, just like the men in my favorite books… and for that, I feel proud, like the luckiest Clover on the planet."

Taking a deep breath, living a life without regret, my fingers make quick work of the buttons on my blouse. I toss my blouse to land on the pile with Malcolm's clothing. I close my eyes, unable to look at Malcolm as I lower the hidden zipper that runs up the side of my skirt. With another deep breath, heart hammering out of my chest, I step from my skirt while still wearing my bra, panties, thigh-highs, and beige pumps.

"Hair up or down?" I ask without opening my eyes. I step out of my shoes, and then bend down to roll my stockings down my legs, one at a time.

Roughly clearing his throat, Malcolm's voice is thick and deep. "Up, because of the oil. But I prefer it down."

Skin flushing, whether from timidness or arousal is anyone's guess, I reach behind me to unhook my bra. My breasts are small, barely a B-cup. When I was a young woman, I hated their size. Now that I'm older, I'm happy they are small. While not perfectly shaped, or as full as I wished they were, they do not sag.

I stand before Malcolm as he sits on the massage table. My hands are cupped over the front of my bra, holding it into place while I shore up my nerve to drop it.

Malcolm and I have done every sexual act known to man in the past few weeks. Malcolm Mason is all man– a man with a voracious sexual appetite that feeds into my own. It's been a veritable non-stop sex-fest, with mutual masturbation, oral sex, regular sex in every position imaginable, and even a few awkward experiments with anal sex. The shadowy jail cell notwithstanding, it has always been in a bedroom situation, with dull lighting or pitch-black darkness.

Here, in the Playroom, I am out of my element and completely exposed.

A feral growl is released, reverberating around the room to run along my nerves, igniting sparks of anticipation. Malcolm is getting impatient with me for two reasons: I won't look at him, and I won't drop the bra.

I drop the bra, breasts bouncing without the support, nipples tightening from their exposure to the chilly air of the Playroom. Still unable to look at Malcolm, and not for the reason he believes, my fingertips hook into the sides of my panties. Drawing the silk scrap down my thighs, my eyes flick up to meet the reason I'm avoiding eye-contact.

Colin McGregor.

Colin rejoined us just as I stepped away from Malcolm. I never forgot Colin. I knew his reappearance was inevitable since Opal locked him in here with us. My mind has been spinning between my lists of mistakes versus regrets. Will this be a mistake, one I should walk away from, or if I walk away, will I regret not living my life to the fullest?

Taking a life lesson from Malcolm's '*what would John Mason do*', I asked myself what Clover Webster would do. She would think this was a mistake. But I was never Clover Webster. I was born a Prynne, with its rebellious blood flowing in my veins. So I asked the Prynne in me what she would do.

Clover Prynne is messy, chaotic, a fuck-up, and she makes mistakes that she'll never regret.

In a fantasy world: I would sashay across the floor, ass and tits swaying in a seductive rhythm. My head would be held high while I wore a sinful tilt to my lips. I'd be confident, empowered– almost arrogant in the knowledge that the two men in this room were enthralled by my presence. I would roll my hips while I purred every naughty detail I longed for them to perform.

But this isn't fantasy.

In reality: I'm a nervous wreck. My fingers are shaking. My eyes are held wide. I slowly approach the massage table with my heart thumping in my throat. While I'm not a complete troll, or stumbling over my feet in a clumsy display, I'm not an erotic vixen, either.

Judging by the gobstopped expressions on Malcolm and Colin's faces, they are okay with the small-titted, big-assed, awkward woman standing before them.

Hopping off the edge of the table, Malcolm pats the vinyl padded cover. "Up you go," rasps from his throat. He leans forward, placing a gentle, reassuring kiss to my throat.

I crawl up on top of the massage table, completely naked, while two naked and aroused men watch me fumble. Malcolm Mason doesn't want a vixen. He doesn't want a woman who needs to be in charge. Malcolm needs to be the man, while I need to be the woman, and that is a comfort for me. I don't need to be omniscient, and neither does Malcolm. We don't need to know what to do instantly, because Malcolm will teach me as I teach him.

Equal parts of the whole, Malcolm takes charge as I surrender. In other parts of our lives, the roles will reverse as we work as a cohesive team.

Laying down on the massage table, staring up at the paneled ceiling, I mutter anxiously, "Well, this is awkward." I release a shaky laugh tinged with nervousness.

Malcolm's face comes into view as he leans over me. Flashing me a smirk, "This is supposed to relax you, not make you uptight. Relax," he purrs. Pressing his lips to mine, I fall into his kiss, forgetting everything besides Malcolm.

Fingertips twined in Malcolm's unruly black hair, I hold him, trying to tug him onto the table with me. Intoxicating laughter spills from his throat, vibrating my lips. "Dirty Girly, not yet. This is about a slow building fire that will explode into an inferno. This is a thing of beauty, not meant to be rushed."

"Someday, I want a woman to look at me the way Clover looks at you." Colin's thick accent causes me to shiver. "You're a lucky fuck, Mal," he praises, slapping Malcolm on the shoulder. They're just two buddies, as if they didn't share an intimate moment no more than half an hour ago.

"I… I…" Fuck it, I let the words spill. "Colin, what's up with you? Why are you here with us, with Malcolm and Opal for the past few years? I've seen you with girls on your arm. You could have ten women look at you like I look at Malcolm."

Handsome face transforming from amused to tortured, "I'm buried in the same shit as your families. The woman I'm in love with is incapable of loving herself, let alone me. I'm just biding my time. Either she grows up and heals herself, or I've wasted the last five years of my life."

"Who?" I breathe out, intrigued yet saddened. Malcolm walks away, offering Colin and me some privacy while we talk. No doubt he and Colin have had this same conversation ten times over. Malcolm busies himself with the bottle of massage oil as Colin puts a voice to his emotions.

A self-deprecating smile twists Colin's lips. "One night, I ran into young woman attempting a mugging, and fell in love with a train wreck. The lawman and the drug addict: a story of misery-ever-after."

Eyes gone wide with shock, I breathe, "Tina?"

"Sadly, yes," Colin admits without shame, but he's filled with a wealth of grief and guilt. "Do I date? Occasionally. Do I allow my dates to connect with me? No. The arrangement between Malcolm, Opal, and me is unconventional because none of us are attracted to the others. It's odd, guilt-free, yet very satisfying." Turning from somber to sinful, Colin's Irish Brogue deepens, thickens, as he speaks. "You're about to find out just how satisfying."

"Lie back on the table," Malcolm orders as his hands push at my shoulders. I do as I am told, settling down until I find a comfortable position. In a soft, soothing voice, Malcolm coaxes me, "Now, I need you to close your eyes and regulate your breathing. We are here to relax and nothing more."

With a deep breath, I close my eyes. Darkness filtered by my eyelids, I fight the need to open my eyes. With great effort, I find a slow breathing rhythm and escape into the abyss.

"This will not be satisfying if you do not leave everything else behind. You are not Clover Webster: mother, daughter, sister, and employee." Voice turning wry, "You do not have bills to pay, food to cook, or laundry to wash. You are flesh and bone."

"Ah!" I grunt when warm oil is poured over my breasts, the force focused on my nipples. The silken fluid flows down the valley between my breasts, heating me, heightening my sensitivity. Rivulets tickle my sides, my tummy, before pooling on the massage table and filling my belly button.

Back arching off the table, my body tries to meet Colin's hands as he massages my taut shoulder muscles. His fingertips dig in, pulsing, loosening the stress I've been carrying for far too long. Within one second to the next, panic descends. A man's hands are touching me, and they do not belong to my husband. Panting, heart hammering, I freak out.

"Clover," Malcolm says in a soothing manner while rubbing my forearms. "I trust you. You trust me. I trust Colin. Which in turn means you trust Colin. He will not harm you. He is here to help you relax, to express yourself, to find release. This is not scary, nor is it a betrayal to me or yourself. You called what you saw between Opal, Colin, and me as beautiful. You are beautiful—allow us to prove it."

Unable to speak, I show them with my body that I am compliant. I relax into the table, with my body surging up into their touch as their hands roam my flesh. A low moan is pulled from me when Colin's fingers find the sensitive, sore spots along the column of my neck. His fingers sneak beneath my hair, massaging my scalp. My body beads with gooseflesh, skin tightening and quivering.

Malcolm begins at my fingertips, using both hands to massage all the way up to my shoulders, where he meets Colin's touch. The men massage me in tandem, drawing whimpers from me at the decadent pleasure of the act.

"Keep your eyes closed, your breathing even, and clear your mind of everything but your flesh. Focus on the sensation of our fingers releasing your stress. Allow your nerves to reawaken, becoming receptive to every minute difference. Concentrate, and you will even feel the ridges of our fingerprints as they skate over your skin. Sense the fine hairs on our arms as they brush against the sides of your breast. Closing everything else out and opening yourself up to pure sensation, you will even feel our breath on the air from feet away."

Not only do I fall into the sensation of their touch, I fall into Malcolm's deep voice as he continues to speak softly. His words are of encouragement, reassurance, and support. Never in my wildest imaginings did I think touch could draw such emotions from a soul.

I find peace, and on the heels of that peace is pure lust. The contradiction doesn't confuse me, because I just accept it for what it is: me. I accept the fact that Colin's hands massaging my breasts feels incredible, how it causes my legs to widen in silent insistence.

Eyes closed, I have no idea what reaction Malcolm is suffering over the fact that another man is touching his future wife. But that is the point of keeping my eyes closed. This exercise is about two things: trust, and me.

It shouldn't matter what Malcolm thinks, not when it comes to owning *my* personal emotions and desires. They are mine, and mine alone. Malcolm's thoughts on *my* feelings will not change them. The trust is in speaking your voice and believing your partner will hear you. Malcolm spoke by placing me in a situation with Colin in the first place, and I voiced my opinion by staying.

That is why my eyes stay closed with ease now, because it doesn't matter what expression Malcolm is wearing. I must believe in him and myself enough to know we will voice our pleasure and grievances without fail.

Skin heightened with sensitivity, I swallow a gasp when fingers slip inside me, finding no resistance. All I can do is experience as my mind goes from thinking about a billion tasks I've yet to perform to the staticky white noise of nothingness. It is a plane of existence I've never entered before.

I cease to be by turning into a singular throbbing nerve, which only finds relief through touch. Moaning, thighs widening, I encourage the fingers manipulating my sex. A forefinger and thumb massage my nether lips, tugging, pinching, pulling, and caressing, until pleading words bleed from my lips.

A demanding pair of lips suckles at my nipple, drawing hard, as if they can find sustenance in the act. Sensitive, a sharp bite has the opposite effect as usual. I moan, parting my legs farther in reaction. My heels dig into the padded cushion, gaining leverage to split myself wide open, begging for more.

Questing fingers sink deep inside me, curling to find a spot that has long lain dormant. Amazed, blissed out, my eyes pop open wide, only to fall shut again under the drain of immense pleasure. The owner of the fingertips leans down to kiss my clit, lapping at the bundle of nerves before sealing his lips around my flesh and firmly sucking me into a frenzied state of being.

Head rocking back and forth, thighs quivering, body writhing, Malcolm brings me to climax as Colin worships at my breasts. Not only do I surrender, I beg, plead– demand, "More… more… more…" I whimper and moan until he gives me more.

Mid-climax, Malcolm gives me more by pressing into me, sliding inside to fill me until I feel complete. Limp from the relief of having my cravings met, I lay passively while Malcolm thrusts into me in a languid pace. Receptive instead of zoned out, not only do I enjoy the hard press of Malcolm's cock, but I can sense the velvety feel and the ridged strength. I'm so sensitive, I can feel the friction as the veins in his shaft rub against my clenching flesh.

My *mores* change to a frantic, "harder… harder… harder…" and I'm not communicating with Malcolm any longer. Colin manipulates my breasts: twisting, pulling, torturing my nipples with his lips, tongue, and teeth. I hiss, "Yeesssss," when Colin bites me so hard my cunt spasms.

Passive, completely at their mercy, I become their passenger. Rocking into me in a loving, soothing, coaxing rhythm, Malcolm makes it a true coupling. Everything we do, we do it together. Fingers lacing with mine, Malcolm wraps our hands around Colin's engorged shaft, mimicking the pacing of his thrust to the pump of our hands.

Hot breath billowing out on a moan, Colin sears the flesh around my nipple. Continuing to suckle at me while we stroke him to release, Colin's fingertips seek out the apex of our joining, not only caressing my clit, but Malcolm's shaft and sac too.

My journal's regrets disappear from their pages, along with all the acts I never knew I would miss out on by living a life built on the fear of rejection. Malcolm proves to me that we are more together than we are apart. Malcolm makes me believe that I will never regret again.

We become three entities of flesh and bone, beings whose only need revolves around release. I lie beneath two men: Malcolm between my thighs, thrusting inside of me, with Colin fused to my chest, sucking my nipples in time with his fingers thrusting alongside Malcolm's cock.

Orgasm pushing us into madness: I lose myself as Malcolm fires hot and deep inside of me, while my cunt eagerly milks at his cock. Colin erupts into our entwined fingers, covering my hip in a wash of hot release.

Head thrown back in ecstasy, Malcolm laughs to the ceiling. "Sweet Jesus, what a difference it makes to have a woman who loves cock." Tilting his head back to earth, Malcolm's eyes are glittering with bliss.

Colin chuckles against the side of my breast, too weak to move. "Well, we were playing with a lesbian, and they tend to not want to play with cocks."

"Ah, my silly rabbit loves cocks like they're carrots the color of your hair," Malcolm teases.

"Please," Colin groans out, extracting himself from the tangle of body parts. "No gingy jokes." Talking over his shoulder as he makes his way back to the bathroom again, "Just for that, next time, one of you is sucking my carrot, and hopefully it's the cock lover."

"Hmm…" Malcolm purrs as the door to the bathroom closes behind Colin's gorgeous behind. Gazing deep into my eyes, Malcolm makes sure I'm doing okay. "I guess I'll find out about that suggestion some night when I can't sleep. Maybe when I'm doing a little light reading."

"You mean the answer is written in one of my historical romances? I don't recall much ménage in them," I mutter dryly, hiding my smirk.

"I'll write you one, and Robin and Auggie can illustrate it. We'll call it '*Adventures in the Playroom,*' and we'll make it a period piece set with the age of the Spook House."

"And this novel will read as my journal does, won't it? Insight into the desires of Malcolm Mason."

Malcolm ignores my question, because he knows, I know, all I have to do is ask and he will tell me his dirtiest wishes. "This time, I'm saying it after sex. Hot, sweaty, Playroom sex." Smile disappearing, sobering, Malcolm declares, "I love you, Clover."

Simply, because there is nothing else I could say, "And I, you."

CHAPTER THIRTY-NINE

The Widow

"Good morning!" Willow shouts as she skips through the living room into the kitchen, where I'm making lemon bars and brownies. "Mmm… smells good. I love peanut butter frosting."

With a hop, Willow is sitting on the countertop next to my prep area. Knowing the lemon bars aren't for her, "Are you selling these?"

"Yeah." I blush from all the attention my cookie pushing has gained me. The next day, when I came into work, I had several messages waiting for me, all requests for decent baked goods. I bake a few things every night to deliver in the morning when I arrive at work. It's a relaxing alternative to missing Malcolm when he's at the new house, with his kids, or bossing his minions around town.

Fairport's natives are restless, complaining how my work at the Courthouse is getting in the way of their treats. I don't make a lot of money off it, not wanting to tax anyone. I just take a few dollars for my time over the cost of the supplies.

"These are for Mayor Ross. Mrs. Ross is having her ladies over after church tomorrow. I also have to make her two dozen shortbread cookies and miniature lemon poppy seed muffins. My Saturday morning and afternoon will be spent standing right here." Leaning into Willow, I whisper like it's a secret, "I charge the mayor a bit more over cost, since his wife is so demanding."

"HA! Rumor has it, Mrs. Ross is trying to get the mayor to fire you. Half of the town is shouting nepotism, and the other half thinks it's because answering Mayor Ross's phone is cutting into your kitchen time. Bets are being placed."

"I know," I say, smirking. "No doubt you've placed a bet."

Feigning innocence, "Who? Me?" Willow's face is lit with happiness and contentment, skin rosy and eyes twinkling.

"You're in a good mood this morning." Willow's been grumpy for the past few weeks, a combination of missing Devon while being pissed at him, being pissed at Essie while feeling sympathetic toward her (not that Willow will admit it), missing Kieren's undivided attention as he's spread thin through the family, working her ass off, and not buying a lick of my shit.

In less than forty-eight hours, I will be able to breathe easier with the truth out in the open, not that Willow doesn't suspect or know outright. Hints are made, looks are exchanged, heads are butted, but we're both holding our ground. If there were two people on this earth as similar in nature as my daughter and me, I'd be surprised, and our nature isn't very pleasant. By Monday, I'll be handling a raging eighteen-year-old angsty monster in the aftermath of my confession.

Willow's been trying to trap me in my lies, and no doubt she's doing the same bit with everyone in our lives. With Malcolm packing up his house, the kids' excitement, and my distancing routine, Willow is getting more insistent with her needling, not that I blame her. It's not as if I don't feel insanely guilty when I look into my daughter's eyes and lie... again and again.

The wait is for Willow's benefit– an intervention of sorts. The intervention is for my family. With the Masons out of town, Willow will have no one to lean on but us. She can't run off and hide. Willow will have to face me, and I her. Rob will be staying with us for the duration of the Masons' visit in Arizona, as we try to fix the shit that's been plaguing us for eighteen years.

Help has come from two unexpected sources, both caring about Willow's well-being. Auggie's apology was with action, not words. Without saying a word to any of us, Auggie has displayed an incessant need to keep Willow busy and out of our hair, giving us time to get our shit ironed out. I'm not entirely sure how Malcolm pulled it off without Ren finding out, but he recruited Langdon Stone to help. Let's just say, Revamped and Wreck & Ruin are inventoried down to their last comic book and lugnut.

Willow will be devastated to learn that we've all been conspiring against her, not that she doesn't already suspect. Her trust will be broken, and I will not blame her for whatever hatred she throws my way. But for everyone else, they are doing this because they love Willow, and I hope someday she comes to realize this.

Not as innocent as she pretends, Willow has been scheming on her own. Malcolm no longer makes requests for desserts because he's with me when he's not at work, eating whatever I put in front of him. Yet the nonstop secret admirer demands keep coming, and they're coming from my naughty, meddling daughter's widening ass.

"I know brownies with peanut butter frosting are your favorite. Mmm… especially with the crushed up peanuts on top." I sprinkle the nuts as I speak, knowing good and well this batch of brownies is going straight to the Spook House, up into Willow's bedroom, and down into hers and Ren's bellies. Even Ren is getting a gut on him– gluttons.

"I wish I could have one." Testing me, Willow licks her lips while eyeing the dessert. If I hand them to her, admitting I knew they were for her all along, she wins. If I ignore Willow, it's my surrender. But if I outmaneuver my daughter, I win. There is never a middle ground with a Prynne– the middle is a numb existence. Our entire lives are built around winning and surrendering.

Just as my daughter plays, I play to win.

"I made you something earlier," I say sweetly, pulling another batch of brownies down from the top cupboard. "When I had to make this batch, I thought of you the whole time. I even made sure the nuts were honey-roasted."

Clover: 1

Willow: 0

Speechless, Willow just stares at me with a dumbfounded expression crossing her face. I cut her a square of brownie, placing it on a paper towel, and then I set it in her limp hand. "Thank you." Pouting like a Prynne, Willow tastes defeat, and it tastes like brownies with peanut butter frosting and nuts.

I've mulled over how to approach this conversation for the past two weeks, even going as far as to ask Auggie, Robin, and Isis for advice. Only Auggie seemed to know how my daughter ticked, because his response was this, "Pretend you're talking to yourself." While excellent advice, it skeeved me out to think that Auggie knew how I ticked as well.

"Um…" I distract myself by cleaning up the counters, placing the dirty dishes in the sink, and fiddling with the mise en place for my next project. "The Playroom?" I just let the word hang out there in space, not truly asking a question.

Freezing beside me with the brownie raised to her face for a big bite, Willow pulls the stunned rabbit routine. "My God!" I laugh, and it's filled with irony, amusement, and pride. "Pretend you're talking to yourself," I mutter, finally seeing what Auggie was getting at. At the same time, I finally figure out why Malcolm calls me every derivative of rabbit: silly rabbit, bunny, once he even called me bunnikins.

"I don't know what you're talking about," Willow mutters, chewing the last of her treat. She hops off the counter to cross the kitchen, where she ruts around in the fridge for the gallon of milk.

"I know, Willow," I say softly, so softly she barely hears. "I don't know any details. I just know you did things with Auggie in the Playroom when it was at Rush."

Betrayal marring her young face, Willow grits out between clenched teeth, "Who told you?" I can tell she thinks it was Malcolm.

"Truth?"

"That would be a first from you," Willow spits out as she angrily pops the lid off of the milk. She reaches for a glass, and still angry, the milk sloshes everywhere.

"I will preface this by saying I don't judge you. I understand why you would want to go there, how the thought of pleasing Auggie must have been intoxicating." Her tiny shoulders loosen and slope as I talk to her back. "I am only asking because I need to know if you were coerced or manipulated. I need to know that you are okay with what happened. I need to know if I should hate Auggie for you because you don't have the ability to blame him yourself. I know I am a deceitful, lying bitch, but whatever lies I tell, they are with your welfare in mind."

"I know that," Willow whispers. "If I didn't believe that, I wouldn't be here right now, visiting you." I rest my palm against the center of Willow's back as she hides her face from me.

"As an adult, looking back at the past, I wish someone had loved me enough to fight for me. At the very least, someone should have asked me if I was alright, asked me if I wanted them to ignore it or press charges. I will never regret my life with Sam, but what he did was wrong. A grown man should never touch a child. There is no consent in the act because the child is easily deluded and manipulated."

Speaking into her milk glass, "I was eighteen."

"By a few hours," I remind Willow. "But the legality is not the issue. Auggie can't be held criminally liable, but he can be held to a higher standard. If you regret, if you feel shame, if you have doubts, I can blame Auggie for you. I'm giving you the option no one gave me: say the word, and I'll fight for you."

Adamantly shaking her head, refusing to turn around to look at me, I know Willow is composing herself as she cries. I touch my daughter with a familiarity we've never possessed. I rest my forehead between her shoulders while rubbing her back. I wait Willow out, because that is what I would need if our roles were reversed.

Moments pass, but Willow eventually answers me. "I love Auggie. I respect him, and he's done so much for me. Do I wish I had given my virginity to Kieren? Yes and no. Do I regret allowing Auggie to touch me that way? Yes and no. If I could go back and change anything, would I? No, not when it comes to those men."

I'm amazed that Willow is letting me in, even with this big secret between us left unvoiced. "Why?"

Turning around to face me, Willow's face is so open, honest, and earnest, that tears spring to my eyes. "Don't be angry with Auggie. I was the one who always had a choice. Auggie... Auggie not only taught me to love Ren, he taught me to love myself. He's tough love and brutal, but I'm not the easiest student."

Smirking, "I know, and neither am I."

Smirking back, "I know." Stepping away because the intimacy of our conversation is too much if we are physically close, Willow distances herself by putting the milk away.

"I would change what I've done with Devon," she says after great length. "Most of the anger I direct at Essie should be focused inward. I regret it for many reasons. I love Devon like a brother. The sex was horrific, and the aftermath was worse. But right now, I'm angry at Essie for not trusting me. If she would have told me how she felt about Devon from day one, none of that would have happened."

"But what if, by not being with Devon, your life with Kieren would've never happened?" I ask, knowing how everything interconnects.

"Devon had nothing to do with Kieren. Looking back, I realize, if Augustus Kline couldn't stop our mutual attraction, then nothing could. But this thing with Devon, it's going to be a wedge between the brothers, between me and Ren, between me and Essie, between Essie and Devon... forever."

"That's a good life lesson on communication and trust, one teenagers don't even realize." Barking a sharp laugh, "Hell, most adults. Sometimes everything could be solved by a simple conversation."

Brown eyes staring me down, Willow says pointedly, "Yes, it can." No doubt speaking of our upcoming family intervention.

"And it will," I answer Willow's unspoken question, and then quickly change the subject. "Before you go on a rampage, screaming betrayal, you need to know that it was Nina who spilled your secrets."

Furious but not surprised, "Nina? So that is why Auggie shut the Playroom down. We only have like ten members now, and the Spook House feels so empty. I heard rumors that it was because Nina was breaking the only rule we have, but I didn't know it was because of me."

I take the look of guilt from my daughter's face. "It's not your fault. Nina was angry about something else, and she was trying to hurt Auggie by hurting you."

"By hurting *you*," Willow stresses, somehow understanding how much it killed me to think Willow was hurting.

The clang of the screen door has us both jumping out of our skin. "What are you doing here?" Seth asks, stopping in his tracks with his posse right behind him.

"If I didn't know any better," Willow drawls out, smirking at all the kids. "I'd think you didn't want me in this house, or next door, or at the Mason's. Every time I try to make my way to one of those locations, someone intercepts me. If I were the suspicious type..." she trails off.

Standing in the middle of the kitchen, looking at his big sister, Seth is a ball of guilt, to the point that he looks like he wants to cry. I feel so badly that the words are on the tip of my tongue.

Somehow sensing the storm brewing, Willow crosses the room to pull Seth into a hug. "I haven't had my cuddles yet, Mr. Chipmunk Cheeks." Arms squeezing tightly around her baby brother, Willow looks up at me. "It's okay. I was only teasing ya. You're a good kid."

Someone coughs into their hand, Weston, and it suspiciously sounds like the word *bullshit*. After the cough clears, we all stand around in strained silence. This is why Willow hasn't been around. It's killing us to lie to her.

Stepping back from Seth, Willow points at Weston like he's a naughty boy. "Well, I've got to book it. I'm setting up a website for Wreck & Ruin. At this rate, I won't have to sign up for next semester, not that I'll have the time. Instead of learning in a classroom how to do these jobs, I'm getting hands-on experience in the *'fuck it up until you get it right'* way."

"Don't burn yourself out," I warn. "You're still a kid, act like one."

"Never thought I'd hear that come outta your mouth." Willow laughs, causing all of us to smile. She tugs Violet's ponytail and waves to Rae. "Well, catch ya later, munchkins," Willow says over her shoulder as she leave the kitchen.

"I can't be your munchkin, since I'm foot taller than you, Spanky," Weston teases, adopting Ren's nickname for Willow.

Flowing from the living room, "Eh, tis just a young'un."

"Don't tell me Willow's been hanging out with Colin again." I shudder from the thought. The girl has the worst Irish accent and she pulls it on at the most embarrassing times.

"Ren's obsessed with Ladder Ball right now." Rae explains the lame accent as she finds her workstation spot on the countertop.

"Any good?" I ask anyone willing to answer.

Snorting, Violet answers. "Ren sucks. He got so frustrated over Ladder Ball defeating his athletic greatness, he managed to toss the bola hard enough to break a window out of Malcolm's garage."

"We just sit back and watch as Ren throws himself." The stoic behavior Seth has exhibited lately is replaced with the big-cheeked, bright-eyed boy I've had for the past fourteen years. Willow's hug and *'good boy'* erased Seth's prick attitude in a nanosecond.

Getting down to business, "Rae and Seth are on muffin duty. West and Violet are on the shortbread cookies. We have a young woman coming in about half an hour for a cooking lesson. Any volunteers willing to teach her how to read a recipe? If she tips, you can keep it."

"Just her, right?" Rae asks, uneasy around strangers. While Raven has a huge family, she tends to linger on the fringes. Strangers have her running off to hide.

"Yeah, Renee's… I don't know, maybe twenty-five. She just got married, and her husband was surprised to learn his new wife couldn't even boil water. The husband, Kyle, he works with your dad. So we'll be teaching her for a while."

"I'll do it, but I get dibs on the biggest bedroom tonight," Rae tries to negotiate.

Laughing, I pull Raven into my side, squeezing her. "Good try, girl. But that's your daddy's call."

CHAPTER FORTY

The Widower

I don't even dare blink, longing to imprint every minute detail of this momentous occasion into my memories. I'm one step closer to becoming what I believe makes a man a man.

Brother of Isis.

Stepbrother of Augustus.

Father to Devon, Kieren, Raven, and Weston.

Soon-to-be grandfather of Devon and Essie's baby.

Soon-to-be husband of Clover.

Soon-to-be stepfather of Willow, Violet, and Seth.

At last, today, I finally become a homeowner of a house I bought with *my* money, not left to me by mortal circumstance. This huge building of four walls and a roof, will be filled with loving chaos for generations to come. Standing in the nexus of our home– the kitchen –Clover and I are hand-in-hand while the kids run around, giddy with excitement, and I've never felt prouder in my entire life.

"Daddy!" Raven shouts animatedly, breaking into my reverie. Grabbing my arms, tugging me while jumping, Raven makes me laugh. "Daddy! Daddy! Can I have the biggest room? Can I? Can I? Can I? Please. Please. Please."

"You're like a puppy dog's tail, girl. I've never seen you so…" I try to find a word to describe my daughter, and fail. "Happy. Sorry to upset you, sweetheart. But you and Violet have to share a bedroom."

Pouting, "Why?" Rae looks devastated, while Violet's strong reaction would make a sailor blush. I don't even know half of what that profanity means, but hearing it out of a fourteen-year-old girly girl makes it cuter for some reason.

"There are seven bedrooms in this house," Seth enters his analytical mode. "You and Mom have the master. Grandpa and Grandma get the one on the first floor. That leaves five bedrooms and only four of us, so why are we bunking together?"

"I didn't say you were bunking together," I say to get Seth off my ass, because once he gets going, he's like a dog with a bone. Sam was aggressive with what he wanted, but added with the Prynne stubbornness, my new stepkids could make a person tear their hair out.

Huge, dark blue eyes watering on command, a heart-shaped face looking so sad, and pouting lips giving a perfect quiver, my baby girl turns into her Aunt Isis. "Why don't you love me, Daddy? Why do you love the boys more? Who will be in those two other rooms?" Staring intently at my face, Raven figures out her manipulations have no effect on me. Turning petulant, "I'll sleep on the couch, then!" Stomping off, rattling the floorboards as if she weighs three hundred pounds, Rae acts just as I expect.

Trying hard not to laugh, I say what I'd expected I'd have to say. "Violet, you can pick out your room. If Rae has an issue with it, then she can sleep on the couch."

"Cool," Violet chirps, thrilled to be in charge. Sounding suspiciously like Ginny, "I'll make sure to find a room with west-facing windows."

Eyebrows knitted together, Clover is confused by her daughter's response. "Why?"

Looking mildly offended, even though none of us have any idea what the girl is getting at, Violet says, "I can be nice... sometimes. Since Rae doesn't want to help pick out our room, I'll make sure the sun doesn't wake her bratty, introverted ass up too early."

"Nice?" Weston taunts. "I call it self-preservation. Rae is like a barracuda if she wakes before ten on the weekends. I'm going room hunting. Y'all coming?"

Clover and I stand in the kitchen, staring up at the ceiling, as the kids race upstairs. West's footsteps are light, Seth's are clumsy, and Violet's are trailing them.

We find out this old house is not soundproof. "I want the room farthest away from our parents," Seth calls out, trying to catch up with Weston.

"Gross!" Violet shouts, gaining on the boys. "I don't know what those two empty rooms are for, but let's use them as a buffer!"

"Smart thinking, twin," Seth praises his sister. "Help me out, will ya?" Less than a second later, is a shocked yelp, followed by a loud thump– the twins felling my youngest born, working as a team to get Seth that private room.

"Scared yet?" Clover asks me in a sarcastic tone.

I simply answer while wearing a grin, "Ecstatic."

Looking confused and mildly amused, "Why are the girls sharing a bedroom?"

Tugging on her hand, I pull Clover into the walk-in pantry. Arms spread wide, I present one of Clover's prerequisites. "This is your room, woman," I tease, gaining myself a girlish giggle from Clover.

"I believe I hold equal share in the master bedroom, with its en suite bath featuring that two-person bathtub my father installed last week. But I do believe this room will be my second favorite place."

"Along with the back porch for your reading pleasure, minus any snooping crones." The ecstatic feeling overpowers me the more real this becomes.

Clover is just as giddy as the kids. Leaning up on her tippy-toes, smile never wavering, Clover pecks a kiss to my lips.

I finally answer Clover's earlier question about that girls. "It's two-fold: the girls need to bond, and Raven would never leave her room otherwise. Now, she'll never hole up in there if Violet's in there. It means we are guaranteed equal time with the girls, instead of never seeing either one of them again."

"Proactive *and* handsome." Clover looks beyond pleased with me, earning me another peck. Almost five weeks of constant affection has turned Clover into a cuddler, but only with me. She has warmed up to all the kids, touching them occasionally. She no longer exudes cold practicality, and everyone in contact with her has noticed the profound change.

Half inspecting the shelves of her new pantry and half paying attention to me, Clover asks, "Then why aren't you making the boys room together, too?"

I blurt out, never saying it before in my life, "Weston likes boys."

Shrugging as if it's no big deal, "I know." A secret smile pulls at Clover's lips when she spies several drawers perfect for organizing spices. "I'm sure Seth doesn't care."

"Well, I wouldn't allow a boy and a girl to bunk together, so it's not right to allow this either. I'm not saying because West likes boys that he's a girl. I'm saying, I wouldn't allow any kid under my roof to share a room with someone they have the potential to find as a temptation. Basically, I don't want Weston to feel awkward rooming with Seth."

Leaning against the shelves, Clover looks so naïve. "Awkward, how?"

Chuckling, "Do you know nothing of men? From the time we get our first hard-on until our deaths, we are the most perverse creatures. We know no shame. On any given day, our hands are hard at work, taking care of business. The teenage members of our race are the worst. I didn't want to make Weston feel awkward around Seth, because boys are known to do that while in the same room."

Twisting a face, "They do that? Ewww…"

"I'm the father of three sons, soon-to-be four. I am a man who has played handsy with his buddy for five years. I'm an active member of masturbaters anonymous, lest you forgot the images I often text you, especially the ones involving donuts. Straight, gay, or bisexual, our first sexual experiences are sitting around whacking off together, usually timed and to see who had the biggest load."

"You're kidding me, right?" Clover's voice holds a pleading tone, so I lie to her.

"I'm just kidding," I say with a smile.

I'm not kidding.

Appearing a bit green around the gills, "Okay, it doesn't matter whether boys do that or not. It's a good idea they don't share a room then. But why the two extra rooms?"

My palm tenderly cups Clover's belly, rubbing a soothing circle of hope. I stare deeply into her blue eyes and say nothing. "Ahhh…" Clover breathes out, body quivering from fear and anticipation.

"If you keep wearing dresses like this one," I pluck the thin string holding up Clover's dress, "we'll need more than two extra bedrooms."

Rolling her eyes, Clover mutters, "Just once in my life I'd love to get married before a man knocks my ass up. Just saying."

"Hmm…" I purr near Clover's ear. "If the past five weeks are any indication, your chances are very slim on reaching that goal, Silly Rabbit. But just to be sure, we should give it another go."

Voice quivering, "Malcolm."

"You really shouldn't wear this dress again." I smooth my hands from Clover's hips, up her sides, to cup her braless tits.

The thin cotton is a poor barrier against the responsive peaks of her breasts.

"It's a summer dress, and it's summer." The pout is thick in Clover's voice.

Running my nose along the column of Clover's throat, I inhale her cookie scent. "Mmm... I'll have to buy you one in every color, then. Just know, you'll drive me insane when you're wearing it."

"Behave," Clover admonishes me when my knee finds its way between her thighs, slowly raising the hem of her dress. "The kids are in the house."

Lust-fogged, I inch her dress up with my fingertips. "The kids will always be in the house with us, bunny."

As I nudge the fabric of her dress to the side with my nose, exposing her tit, Clover's head falls back against the shelving. She releases a heady moan as my mouth latches around her nipple. Breathless, "But we won't be doing this in the pantry, in an empty house devoid of distraction."

Mouth unlatching, "True," I blurt out, and then descend again, sucking harder this time. Clover loves her nipples punished. With the bite of my front teeth, Clover forgets about anything but me.

Head popping up again, "What's that? Did you hear that?"

Groggy, "What?" she drawls out, fingers twining in my hair to press my face back to her breast. "It's probably the kids."

"Wait," I pull away from Clover's pressing hands. "It's beneath us. I can hear the kids laughing in Seth's new bedroom. Hey, there it is again. In the basement."

"Hey!" Clover's disappointment trails me as I make my way out of the pantry, through the kitchen, to the entryway. I grab my Maglite from my belt where it rests near the front door. Just in case, I grab my cuffs, too.

"Stay up here," I command a snoopy Clover, who's peering down the basement steps, toward where the clanking sound is emanating. "Go upstairs and check on the kids just to be sure."

Goddamned woman.

Ignoring me, Clover tries to creep down the steps to the basement. Frustrated, I grab Clover's arm to yank her behind me. "Fine, if you're going to pull a *too stupid to live–* or in horror film terms, *the first to die –*just walk behind me then."

"Don't be the dumbassed hero, who gets taken out while trying to save his family," Clover hisses fiercely back at me. "Because, if you go down, who's going to protect us, hmm? Besides, He-Man is upstairs with the evil genius and the princesses, living in blissful ignorance. So don't be a fuckhead, be reasonable, and let the woman watch your back."

Growling, "Fine," I cautiously head down the stairs toward the sound, with Clover at my back. "It sounds like the plumbing. What. The. Fuck?"

Scared, Clover pulls out the sarcasm. "I highly doubt our plumbing is having a party on a Saturday night. My guess, some fool thinks this house is still vacant, and didn't hear us up here."

Looking back over my shoulder, I flash Clover the snidest look I can muster. "And why, exactly, would they be in our basement?"

Lips twisting into a superior smile, Clover seems pleased to know something I don't. "Scrapping. This is an ancient house, with original plumbing. I bet some jackass motherfucker is stealing our copper. You get a pretty penny at the salvage yard per pound."

Arching an eyebrow, "And how do you know this? Are you moonlighting as a thief?" Clover's only reply is an eye roll. "Of course, I know what scrapping means, Silly Rabbit. I'm the poor idiot who has to arrest these fools."

"Prynne Renovations, ya *idiot*," Clover taunts me. "It's called recycling, and Dad uses the profits as the workers' bonuses. Ya know, the non-illegal scrappers."

"Oh," I huff, feeling like an idiot. "I doubt that's what's going on. But just in case, go back upstairs."

Snorting, "All two of the stairs we've went down so far, right?" Shoving me, "Get moving, ya pansy ass. Let's catch us a thief."

"You're enjoying this. It's exciting for you." I chuckle at Clover's enthusiasm as she tries to push me down a step. "You were meant to be a cop's wife."

I creep down part way, peering into the darkness. Our new house is massive, larger than the Spook House by a few hundred square feet. The basement is a place I doubt the kids will ever enter. It surprises me that Clover is willing to charge into the spider-infested, damp basement.

On the opposite side of the basement from the stairs, a slight glow from a flashlight illuminates a figure who is wrenching on our copper piping.

The wife was right. I'll have to remember that in the future.

"I have an idea," Clover breathes into my ear. "You go outside, and go around the house to the Bilco door. I'll wait a minute for you to get into position, and then I will yell at the guy. He will run the opposite direction of my voice, to the outside entrance to the basement, where you'll be waiting to arrest him."

"Dumb idea," I mutter.

No, it's not.

I just don't want Clover to get harmed. "Give me two minutes, and I'll fetch Weston to have your back and take Violet with me."

Exasperated, "Violet, really? Over Seth?"

"Her nickname is Violent Violet, so really," I whisper to Clover as I shove her back up the steps. "If you walk down these stairs and get hurt, I'll kill you myself," I issue as a warning as I ghost away.

With Weston, Seth, and Clover's faces peering down the staircase, I find myself outside of our new home with both ferocious girls. Who just so happen to be holding hands and shivering. So much for the nickname.

Maglite raised at the ready as a weapon, with the hapless help at my back, I stare down into the basement. "Hey, dirtbag?" Clover calls, sounding ridiculously cute, and not at all as badass as she thinks. The guy pauses in his thievery, only to resume at a faster clip. "You're in Chief Mason's house," works better than abracadabra for a magician.

Scurrying across the floor, the thief runs headlong into me before he realizes his error. "Fuck!" the guy shouts, spinning in a circle, looking for a different way out. Just as he decides to use the staircase to the first floor, where the mocking woman's voice emanated, Weston's huge form comes into view at the foot of the steps. The choice is running upstairs into the house itself or charging me with the freedom of the outdoors at my back. Decision made, the burglar charges me.

As he emerges from the basement, I lunge to grab the man around his middle to ride him to the ground. But he's lean and strong, flipping over to slide out of my arms. The wiry bastard flat-out runs toward my daughter, who is standing entranced.

Veering to the side, the guy runs around Raven instead of over her. All Rae does is turn her head and watch the guy run by.

"Are you checking the perp out?" I shout at my daughter, disgusted. "If you're gonna act like a dude, the least you could do is fucking help."

A deep grunt fills the air, proving the nickname holds true. Violet trips the thief, and then tries to grabs onto his leg. When he tries to run off, Violet crawls up his back, dragging him down to the ground. Laughing, cussing, Violet is having a field day playing rodeo with the struggling fellow. No doubt terrified, I swear the guy is laughing.

"Now, that, right there, is all Sam," I say in appreciation as I toss Violet the cuffs. "Your dad would be wicked proud."

Entering an alternate universe, where criminals lie passively on the ground, giggling like little boys, while being handcuffed by violent teenage girls. All I can do is snort and ask myself, '*What. The. Fuck?*'

Raven finally moves, to get closer to the thief. The rest of the family rejoins us. All of them are bright-eyed, flushed, and feeling the high my kind gets off on. "Definitely a cop's family," I mutter to myself. "Any other family would be hiding, crying, and be on a cellphone to 911. But, not mine... no, they help apprehend the suspect."

Kneeling by the guy's head, I grab a hank of his thick hair and lift so I can have a look at his face. "Jesus, you're a kid," I breathe.

Please, be eighteen, so I don't have to feel guilty arresting your ass, and so if my daughter doesn't stop gazing at you like a rockstar, I can arrest you when she tries to tempt you.

Please, be eighteen.

"What's your name, kid?" I issue in a gruff voice, causing Weston to snicker.

Not intimidated in the least, "Can you get this crazy chick off my back? Her boney knees are bruising my ass."

"Tell Chief Mason your name," Violet orders, and judging by the grimace that crosses the kid's face, she dug her knee in deeper.

I don't intimidate him, but Violet does. "Anything to make her stop. She's scary crazy." Intense brown eyes stare up at me, as if it's paining him to tell me the truth. "Ozzy. Oliver Zephyr. Just arrest me, take me to jail. I deserve it after being this fucking stupid. Breaking into the Chief's house? Fucking stupid."

"I guess, I don't need to lecture you," I drawl out. "How old are you?"

Please, say eighteen.

Arms wrenched behind his back, "Seventeen," Oliver grunts out as Violet forces him to answer.

Shit.

Raven creeps closer. With a glare, I snarl out, "Traitor."

"Ozzy was in my gym class last year," Rae finally speaks. "I remember when they pulled him out of class when his grandma died… and he never came back."

I breathe, "Fuck," in defeat.

CHAPTER FORTY-ONE

The Widower

Sitting on the edge of my desk, eating a fresh donut, "What are we doing with this kid, anyway?" Colin asks. "He can't live down here. I mean... well, technically he could, but someone is bound to start asking some questions."

"Ah..." tugging at my hair. "Christ, if I know." It's now Sunday morning, after I spent the entire night babysitting a seventeen-year-old criminal. The only highlight was the food delivery brought by Raven and Weston: two western omelets with sides of fresh fruit, and two dozen donuts. The omelets were for me and the kid, the donuts were for my guys, but Colin confiscated them in lieu of raiding the vending machine for breakfast.

Oliver slept on a cot last night, had a good breakfast, and is now reading one of the books I keep in my desk. His afternoon will be spent filing my dreaded paperwork. I thought he'd throw a fit, but he's quiet, respectful, and equally cowed. I'm not arresting Oliver, but I'm making him work off the damage he cost me. Oliver is going to work with Dave, fixing the plumbing, and then at Prynne Renovations until his tab is paid in full. Depending on his aptitude, and whether or not he's an honest kid, I might send him Ren's way. If the kid needs money that badly, he can work at Wreck & Ruin doing odd jobs.

"I see you've been busy," Colin eyes the report I've amassed on the kid over the past few hours. My options were to either stress out or get to work. I got to work.

The words get stuck in my throat, feeling an odd sort of kinship with the kid. "Oliver Zephyr is an orphan. Poor kid has had a rough start. His mom was a teenager, knocked up by some lowlife who eventually died in a prison fight. Oliver lived with his grandmother because his mother ran off to Boston, and then Mom was tossed in jail just like dear ol' dad. Her initial crime was for prostitution and possession with the intent to sell. Mom was released but deemed unfit to raise the child, and judging by length of her rap sheet, I'd say it was a good call. Grandma died of a stroke last year, leaving the kid in the Foster Care System."

Colin grabs for another donut, and I have no idea why he doesn't weigh four hundred pounds. "Why isn't Oliver with his foster parents?"

"I called them about an hour ago. I got the distinct impression they are in it for the money from the state," I say in disgust, grimacing. "It wasn't a pleasant phone conversation. I got ahold of Oliver's case worker, and she said this time he will be sent to a group home until he ages out of the system."

"Age out of one system, only to age into ours," Colin says in a stiff voice filled with sadness. Knowing me better than just about anyone, "I ask again: what are you doing with the kid?"

"Good God," I growl, tugging at my hair again. "I'm trying my damnedest to find something on Oliver that makes him a bad kid. I even accessed his school records. He's smart. All of his teachers commented on how quiet and conscientious he was in class. Somehow he managed to amass enough credits to start senior year in the fall."

Colin, getting frustrated at how slow I am with the flow of information, "Again, I ask: if Oliver's such a good kid, why isn't he with his foster parents?"

"Oliver was kicked out of his foster home because they wanted him to pay rent, and he was working to save up for a place of his own when he aged out. They took all of the money he had hidden in his room, and then kicked him out."

Raising a brow at that, "They wanted rent above what the state already gives them? Daaaammmmnnn," Colin draws out. "What pieces of shits, they are."

"I already reported them to the case worker," I mutter, sickened. "I sent Peter over to arrest them for theft if they didn't give the kid's money back."

Softly chuckling to himself, "Peter, eh? So he will return with more money than was taken, I take it?"

"Fuck yeah! The money from the state was for Oliver's care, and they weren't taking care of him. If they were, Oliver wouldn't have been stealing my pipes to pay for a hotel room after his buddy's mother kicked Oliver off her couch."

With a quick look over his shoulder to make sure the kid can't overhear us, since Oliver's camped out at Kyle's desk, "I know you, Mal," Colin whispers, voice dipping low. "Oliver

Zephyr isn't going to that group home, but he can't live in Fairport's police station until he's of age, either. So what are you really going to do?"

"I can't let a rough start fuck up that kid's life." My voice is filled with conviction and determination. "My son had a few bad times, but his life was stable, filled with love and anything he could ever need, and look where that got him. Oliver hasn't had that, so the odds are stacked against him. I'd be a horrible human being, and less than a man, if I allowed Oliver to slip into crime to survive. He just needs a leg up so he can graduate high school."

"Are you sure Dave and Mary aren't rubbing off on you? That suspiciously sounds like their tree-hugger bullshit." Colin tries to sound serious, but he's taunting me.

"I think it suspiciously sounds like John Mason, actually. Lisa and Auggie were strays he took in. Nina was a stray he took in. But I'd rather be like Dave and Mary, where I really help someone instead of pushing them into the whore-role. The kid needs eleven months of stability until graduation, and then he will have a chance of living a good life."

"What does Clover think about this? I thought those two spare rooms were for the babies you're trying your damnedest to make? She's already dealing with adult children and four teenagers."

"Clover's a mother, pure and simple." I smile fondly to myself. "After we uncuffed Oliver last night, Clover took him to her house to feed him and let him take a shower. Oliver's not as big as Weston, but bigger than Seth, so she called Rob to bring some of his clothes over. Clover was in fix-it, mother-hen-mode."

Colin looks back over his shoulder, noticing we have Oliver's avid attention. "Does he know?"

"Oliver knows he's staying with Dave and Mary until I get back from Arizona, so he can help fix the plumbing and work off his debt. But I'm pretty sure he knows the rest now." I chuckle to myself. The kid looks terrified that he will be in the custody of Fairport's Chief of Police, or maybe it's because he will be under the same roof with Violent Violet. Violet's reputation precedes her, and Oliver heard about her at school, even though she was in junior high. Cute but wrong, Violet kept taunting the kid last night.

Embarrassed and ashamed, Oliver approaches us, jaw clenched to stop himself from saying something. Lean and lanky, a bit under six foot, with a huge head of brown curls and deep brown eyes, Oliver's a good looking kid.

"You wanted me to file stuff?" Oliver asks sheepishly. "I might as well do it right now since I'm just sitting on my ass." A lot of pride in this kid– good.

"Well, I guess I better get off *my* ass." Colin slips off the edge of my desk, trying his damnedest not to laugh, and failing miserably.

We don't work much down here. All of us are lazy, waiting on the excitement of some real crime. We fight over who actually gets to do the traffic stops and patrol the neighborhoods. Sitting at a desk sucks ass. As the Chief, my ass is always at my desk.

"I have evidence to log in." Reaching back, Colin grabs a donut. Thinking the better of it, he grabs two more.

"Glutton," I grunt out, pissed that Colin is eating my share. "It's no wonder your new BFF is Willow. You guys are hogs."

"I've been depressed since I learned the secret admirer gig is nearly up. I'll miss my half of Willow's share of the treats."

Disbelieving, "You're shittin' me, right?"

In answer, Colin jogs off to pretend to put in an honest day's labor– the bastard.

There's a lone donut left, and the kid is eyeballing it, practically drooling. "Here," I press the box in Oliver's hands. "I'm getting a gut on me, anyway."

Donut raised to his lips, Oliver proves Violet isn't the only one with a reputation. "Willow Prynne? The pothead chick who was always reading a comic book? What's that old man doing with her? Yuck."

With so many things wrong with Oliver's comment, all I can do is shake my head, at a total loss. "Old man? McGregor is almost ten years younger than me, dammit! As for Willow, she's my stepdaughter. Willow's no longer a pothead, but she's still a huge geek." Agreeing their friendship is odd, "Colin and Willow are highly competitive. They always seek each other out at functions as game partners, kicking everyone's asses."

Shoving the donut into his mouth, alongside his foot, Oliver blushes and looks around awkwardly. "Filing?"

"That stack right there," I point to the pile on the floor near my desk. "That filing cabinet over there," I point at the cabinet on the opposite side of the office. "I guess I better get to work myself."

"'*The*' doesn't count, right? Like The No-name Diner? Man, you guys order food and charge it to the town? Damn," Oliver proves himself more ethical than the idiots who tried to write-off their lunch. "And you go by the last name, right?"

"Yeah, ignore the '*The*' and file by the last name." Groaning, "Anything food-related, toss back on my desk so I can kick some ass."

Hefting the stack of folders, "Looks like that's most of these," Oliver warns me. "I hope you have more busy work for me– this will only take about ten minutes, at the most."

"There's plenty of scrubbing to do," I mutter, which seems to slow Oliver's pace to turtle-speed.

Sorting through yesterday's mail, a manila envelope catches my attention. **DNA Diagnostic Center. ATT: Chief Malcolm Mason.**

Heart pounding out of my chest, I reach for my letter opener. Patrick came through with his end of the bargain. Tina's in rehab, and we all get our answers. Lisa always feigns ignorance when it comes to the paternity of her children. No matter how many times Auggie, Tina, Patrick, or I have asked, Lisa always mumbles, "*I don't know*," like a delusional idiot.

Tina's, Auggie's, and my DNA was sent off for testing. Not totally trusting my father when it came to his dick, I had to make sure neither of Lisa's children were related to me. For obvious reasons, I don't want inbred nieces and nephews.

Feeling sick to my stomach, it's all written out in plain English and admissible in court. According to their DNA, Auggie and Tina are full-blooded siblings, not the half-siblings we all thought. Heart beating in my throat, I read my own findings, ready to pass the fuck out.

Malcolm Mason is a 0% match in reference to Augustus Kline and Tina Kline.

"Thank fuck," I breathe out, head falling back to rest against my seatback. Less than a heartbeat later, I'm sitting up again, reading the document just to be sure I'm not seeing shit.

Footnote: With the close genetic match, combined with common alleles, it is my conclusion that Augustus and Tina Kline's parents are closely related: parent to child, siblings, or aunt/uncle to nephew/niece.

I'm shocked, but not shocked. Lisa was fourteen when she had Auggie: pregnant at thirteen, a runaway drug addict turned John Mason's whore, and pregnant again at twenty-one. No matter what we did, Lisa would never answer who Auggie and Tina's father was. When we would ask, Lisa would run off and get high.

"Jesus Christ," I pray as I reach for my phone, fingers dialing Auggie without thought.

"Yello," Auggie answers, sounding chipper. "What do ya need, Mal?"

"Your mother has some serious explaining to do," I say without preamble. "I don't know how to tell you this, Auggie." I quickly blurt out, "the DNA test came back. Thankfully, neither of you are related to me by blood. A big motherfucking surprise, Tina's your full-blooded sister. But there's more…"

CHAPTER FORTY-TWO

The Widow

"Why are you doing this to me?" I snarl at my mother. In the summer months, the Prynnes break bread after church outside instead of at the dining room table. Whether indoors or outdoors, it's never uneventful. "You know I can't be set up on a date. For Christ's sake, I just moved some of your shit into my new house."

Feigning ignorance, "I have no idea what you're talking about, daughter. I simply invited the new pastor over for lunch. It's customary, you know."

"Don't play innocent. You keep thrusting the man at me, gloating over my virtues as a woman. You told him to ask for my number." Growling, impatient, I want to scream at my mother. "Hell, he's a baby in his twenties."

"Cody is adorable, and he's a God-fearing man." Blue eyes twinkling with mischief. "And he's available, which I found out when he asked if you were."

"And you told him no, correct?" I prompt.

"Oh, you're no longer single?" My mother is acting more addled than ever, but that crafty tone in her voice means she's fucking with me.

"You're booking yourself an early one-way ticket to elderly housing, Mother," I snarl. "Robin's lazy, so expect no help from him. What the fuck are you pulling, here?"

Blinking at me, I can tell Mary Prynne is doing her damnedest not to laugh. "If you want people to know you and Malcolm are marrying next week, then maybe you should tell them. Until then, I am under no obligation to stop matchmaking."

Rotating in a circle, I look around my yard for a hidden camera. Arms spread wide, I mutter in awe, "Are you punking me?"

My yard and my parents' yard are fenced together, shared for events like these. I expected a smaller turn-out than usual since Uncle Will and Aunt Ana moved to Florida, but today is the biggest turn-out to date. The usual suspects are in attendance: Dave and Mary. Peggy. Seth, Violet, and me. Willow. Essie. Young Pastor Cody is an anomaly. Then there are those who are here to see what I do, as if this fiasco was planned. Rob hardly ever shows, but he did today, and he brought guests: Isis and Auggie. My children invited their counterparts as well: Kieren, Weston, and Raven. Even Ginny made a rare appearance. My mother-in-law invited the Dobsons as an extra-special form of torture.

Scattered across our yard: my father and Auggie are pretending to clean the grill with Robin's and Mr. Dobson's supervision. Isis is roving from group-to-group, soaking up their secrets, with Pastor Cody staring at her ass. The kids are still trying their damnedest to show Kieren how to play Ladder Ball. The women are in lawn chairs, not bothering to pretend they're not gossiping. Our yard is in total chaos, and all eyes are on me as I argue with my lunatic mother.

"Why?" Voice quivering, betrayal thick. "Why are you doing this to me? In less than a week, we will be sharing a house, yet you're pushing the pastor of our church at me. Why?"

Giggling behind her palm, my mother looks insane. She leans into me, whispering in my ear, "Willow says match-point." Eyes wide, I stare at my mother in horror as she laughs at me. "Revenge for the brownies, I suspect."

"Tomorrow can't come fast enough," I mutter to myself. "I'm starting to not feel bad over this. Willow had me up until three a.m. baking her secret admirer requests. I've created a monster."

Leaving my mother to her own devices, the traitor, I make my way toward the gossip circle. Three feet from my destination, Cody traps me near the food table. "Clover, these are delicious," he praises my fruit tarts. "Maybe we could cook together some time."

Mom's right. The *kid* is adorable. Everything about Cody screams goodness and kindness and wholesomeness. I change my assessment on his age. I bet Cody just graduated from seminary school. He's closer to my daughter's age than mine.

As if reading my mind, "I know there is a big age gap between us, but I have a difficult time having an involved conversation with a young woman. Their minds are not where mine is."

"*Pastor* Cody," I sigh, at a loss. Ending this torture, "Piece of advice: I am not the woman you think I am. While mature, my mind is too mature for yours. You won't like where my mind is at. I would wreck you."

Jaw hanging open, stunned by my brazen rudeness, Cody stammers without saying a word.

"You need to find a sweet, young thing who hasn't been around the block. Hell, you need one who hasn't left their driveway yet."

Willow, Kieren, Auggie, Isis, and Rob: Team Willow is bent over at their waists, holding their sides, laughing as if they are dying. The kids are glaring at the adults, as if envisioning what it would feel like to kick their asses for embarrassing their mother.

I slip into my lawn chair next to Ginny, pretending my face isn't the shade of a beet. "There will be no Sunday dinner next week," I announce.

Of course, Peggy is the one to ask. "Why's that, dear?"

"I'm busy," I grunt out, earning me a snort from Ginny. Next Sunday is the day before my wedding, the day Malcolm and the kids get back from Arizona. I plan on spending it with my family, not my ex-family and their snoopy friends.

"You were very rude to that young man," Peggy chastises me. "Sam would have put you in your place for speaking that way. How you've turned bad since you've been hanging out with that Mason man. Don't think for a second that I don't see Malcolm sneaking in and out of my son's house at all times of the night."

Not one to put up with Peggy's shit, "Excuse me." Ginny clears her throat. "*That* Mason man is my brother-in-law, and his children and sister are playing in this yard as we speak. Talk about rude," she draws out.

Meeting Ginny head-to-head, "I don't fault your sister for marrying Malcolm and creating those four children," Peggy says with distaste. "Camille was mentally unstable, after all. However, I thought Clover was entirely sane. But perhaps not."

Insulted, Ginny doesn't even flinch. "I cannot fathom how my mother was best friends with you, Peggy. Maybe it was *her* mental instability. I used to ask God why I was born gay, but I'll never doubt his decision ever again. I was born a lesbian so I would never be forced to marry Sam. God knew with you as my mother-in-law, I would have committed murder."

Huffing, sputtering, acting totally put out, Peggy is rendered speechless for the first time in her life. "C'mon, let's blow this joint," Ginny says to me as she stands up. "They set you up, so now they can entertain themselves."

It takes me half a second to agree, acting like a Prynne for the first time in my life: stubborn, bratty, spiteful, grudge-holding, mischievous, as well as selfless, charitable, and forgiving. "The little ones are innocent," I remind Ginny as I move to stand.

"Good. We'll take them with us." Smoothing her hands down over her hips, Ginny points out, "I could use some more ice cream. These hips don't maintain their shape without a healthy dose of Mint-Ting-A-Ling with crushed Oreos on top."

"Just shout '*ice cream*' and the kids will follow you anywhere," I say, laughing, as I walk across the yard toward my backdoor.

"ICE CREAM," Ginny shouts, gaining everyone's attention. Young and old alike start moving like a herd of cattle. "But only if you're sixteen and under," she adds, gaining a collective groan of disappointment. "Consider that punishment for being mean to Clover."

CHAPTER FORTY-THREE

The Widower

Another sleepless night plagues me. Knowing I had limited time to spend with Clover, I couldn't sleep. The past five weeks have been some of the best of my life. In a few hours, I board a plane to Arizona for the next week. When I get back, the following morning, Clover and I will be husband and wife. It's surreal, and I doubt I will sleep until our wedding night. The next week will be one of the hardest of my life, on so many fronts.

On sleepless nights, I have to read to stop myself from molesting Clover. On the nights I fail at this, neither of us gets any sleep. I found out the hard way Clover gets grumpy when she's tired… and she serves the basics for dinner.

Busy with tying up all the loose ends, the little, pink princess journal has no new entries, so I've had to read the latest paperbacks at my disposal. Damn you, Lisa Kleypas and Eloisa James, your naughty sister Anne Stuart, and your even naughtier sister Kate Pearce, for turning me into a huge historical romance addict. What started out as a joke became an obsession. Clover doesn't realize, but I've '*borrowed*' her latest book for my trip, and since I devour them like cake, I hope I can find the next in the series at the airport bookstore.

"I've got to go, bunny," I breathe against Clover's cheek. She's curled up into a tiny ball, rasping in her wheezy sort of way. Exhausted, she doesn't even stir. I debate waking Clover, but then think the better of it. Saying goodbye will be hard on both of us. "I love you," I whisper. After a soft kiss to her lips, I slip out of bed to go fetch the rest of my family.

I will be thrilled when this shuffling routine is finally over. Every night, I can't stay away even though I promise myself I will. After my youngest kids fall asleep, and Ren sneaks back in from the Spook House, I slip out to sleep here with Clover. I come back around five a.m. to wash up, get a quick nap in, and then wake and feed the kids. Ren always leaves again to wake

Willow up in a way I don't want to acknowledge, same way I usually wake Clover in the middle of the night. Somehow my son and I developed this routine without any communication, and it works. But I'm thankful that this morning will be the last time.

I'm shocked to find Seth lurking in the kitchen five hours before he usually wakes. Sitting at the kitchen table, nibbling on a cookie and reading a chemistry text book (during summer vacation, and two years ahead of his school year). He looks up when I enter the room.

Flashing Seth a fond smile, "Hey, kid. Why are you up so early?"

Angry eyes glaring at me, Seth shuts his book and rises to his feet slowly. "Don't do that anymore. Don't have sex with my mom in this house."

Shocked, "Excuse me," flows sharply from my tongue. "What did you just say to me?"

"I thought you were sneaking in here at night, but I wasn't sure. So I finally came to investigate," Seth admits through gritted teeth.

Flabbergasted, "You were listening to your mother and me—intimately?"

"Hear me out, okay?" Seth takes my arm, tugging me into the living room. "If you want to do that with my mom, make her your wife. Because right now, you're in my father's house, in my father's bed, making love to my father's wife. It's not right."

Drawing in a deep breath, I apologize. "I'm sorry, Seth. I can't promise it won't happen again. Isis and Auggie are moving the rest of our stuff while we're gone, so we'll have to sleep here the night we get back from Arizona. After a week apart… I meant no disrespect. I truly didn't even think of you and your sister when I was sneaking in here at night. I only had one thing on my mind."

Snorting, "No shit."

"Not that," I spit out, exasperated. "Being near your mother was on my mind. I miss her when we're apart." Confused as to why Seth is speaking to me like this, I never thought I'd have to ask this question. "Don't you want me to marry your mother?"

"Yes, damn it!" Seth shouts, frustrated. "I want you to be my dad, and I need to know what to call you: Chief Mason? Malcolm? Dad?"

"What did you call your father?" I tread lightly, not realizing how deeply Seth is wounded. He is upset with me, for sure. But it's not because I was touching his mother. Seth's confused about his place in my life.

Closing his eyes, Seth is in obvious pain. "I was only nine when he died, so I still called him Daddy. Even in my head, I call him Daddy. It's stupid at my age to still think like that. But–" shrugging. "Since I lost Daddy when I was little, when I think of him, I'm still little."

"Holy hell," I breathe out, voice shuddering. I have the most profound urge to cry at this very moment. We all lost Sam. But as a man who lost his father when he was still a young man, no one lost Sam as much as Seth.

"So, what do I call you?" Seth asks again, sounding eager for an answer.

Knowing Seth wouldn't have put it on the list if he didn't want to use it, "I would be honored if you would call me Dad, but I will understand if you call me Malcolm. The choice will be up to you, as it is up to Violet. My children may call your mom Mom, but the decision is theirs. Okay?"

Seth cheeks puff up as he smiles through his tears. "Good," he says in obvious relief. "Now, I will be able to answer people's questions, and they won't flinch anymore."

"Flinch?"

"Yeah, like at school. A teacher, or a parent, or a kid will ask me about my dad. Like, '*What does your dad do? What do you and your dad do for fun?*' So I tell them my father is dead, and they look like I punched them in the gut." Seth twists his face up, as if reliving one of these '*punch to the gut*' moments.

"They get this uncomfortable look on their faces, like, do they say they're sorry? But they can't be sorry because they never knew my dad. It's not like they killed him. So, then they always ask how old I was. I say nine, and then it gets really uncomfortable. This isn't going to change when I move away for college. It'll haunt me everywhere I go."

"I am sorry, Seth," I mutter, at a loss. "If there was one person I could bring back to life, it would be your father. I'd bring Sam back over my own father and wife, even knowing he'd take Clover and you kids away from me. Sam deserved to live, and I'll miss him every day for the rest of my life, as will you and your sisters, and especially your mother."

"I know that," Seth grits out, trying his damnedest not to sob. "I love my dad. I don't really remember him, though. Half of my life I haven't had a dad, ya know?"

"I do know." My head nods in agreement with my words. "I still think of my father constantly. I lost him almost twenty-two years ago, and John Mason still dominates my thoughts."

"I wish I was older, like Willow, so I could remember him better." The kid shrugs and sniffles at the same time. "You're the answer to my problem. When people ask me about my dad, I can say, *'my stepdad's a cop. He likes to hang out with us kids and watch my mom cook.'* Then there wouldn't be any more uncomfortable pauses. They'd just ask me more about you and Mom."

Suffocating, choking on the agony of loss and the happiness of Seth longing to call me Dad, "I want that, too," I barely whisper.

Face glowing with tears rolling down his chubby cheeks, Seth speaks to me with his father's smoky voice in a childlike tone. "Yeah… and then, maybe when you've been my stepdad for eight years, I can drop the step. Say, *'my dad's a cop. He likes to hang out with us kids and watch my mom cook.'* Because, by then, Sampson Webster will always be my father, but he's just a memory. Malcolm Mason will be my dad."

"Kid," I sob out, yanking the little shit into my arms. I squeeze him tightly, promising never to let him go.

"So, no more doing what you were doing in that bed. Don't disrespect my father like that. If you want Mom to be Clover Mason, if you want to touch her like she's your wife, marry her. We're still my father's family. If you want us to be yours, hurry the hell up. Because eight years from next year, or next month, or even tomorrow, sounds like a lot longer than eight years starting today."

"Eight years starting next Monday morning," I promise Seth. Guilt-ridden, I make another promise. "When I get back, I'm burning that bed."

CHAPTER FORTY-FOUR

The Widow

Almost nineteen years of lying have culminated into this very moment. Heart beating in my throat, the plan is set, and there is no turning back now. I'd love to say the plan will go off without a hitch, but that isn't going to happen. The hitch is Willow, and she's never reacted rationally to anything. But how could she? Willow's still a teenage girl, no matter how hard she tries to pretend she's a grown up.

Willow knows something big is going down, so I'm playing into her hands to get her to play into mine. With Willow picking up the '*secret admirer*' gauntlet, she'll be curious as to how I received a message she didn't send. Momma rabbit is trying to capture her baby bunny in an inescapable rabbit snare. All I have to do is get Willow to take the bait.

Our newly recruited Ozzy just delivered my package for authenticity. I crack my front door open and peer out the gap. Like a criminal, my eyes dart to and fro, looking for watching eyes, mainly my mother-in-law and her partner in gossip. I creep out onto the porch on my tippy-toes, like if I don't make a sound it will change my fate.

A compact wooden box is sitting in the usual spot– next to the front door, directly beneath the mailbox. It's always just out of reach from the doorway. I actually have to go onto the porch so I can retrieve it.

I struggle to carry it in– it's rather heavy. After dozens of these deliveries, I walk straight into the kitchen on autopilot. No doubt, Malcolm provided everything we will need to satisfy his request.

The box is big, but only a single, round cake pan is nestled at the bottom. My subconscious remembers how it used to feel when these boxes would arrive– how it felt when I would read the notes. I feel as I did back then, even knowing what is in the box and why.

Perhaps it's a knee-jerk reaction to what's in the note, knowing there is no turning back now, and fearing the aftermath. My breathing and heart rate accelerate. My body beads with sweat. My fingers shake as I reach in for the single sheet of paper. With a shuttering breath, I unfold the paper and read. My heart is beating erratically, causing its drumbeat to fill my ears with a deafening *da-dum… da-dum…*

Lucky Clover,

The lemon meringue pie was delicious. Everyone says your donuts are the best they've ever eaten. I agree, and I've had a lot of donuts in my lifetime. My newest request: This evening by six p.m. I need your famous seven-layers-of-sin chocolate cake. I've heard a lot about this decadent dessert. In fact, someone very dear to my heart said it wasn't sinful at all, but pure heaven. You must teach Willow to make the cake. She is to make it all on her own, and her love is to infuse the sweet treat. Thank you for being so reasonable, Clover– I wouldn't want to miss out because you're being naughty again, or do you want me to send video to Ross next time?

P.S. No donuts until you receive your next gift ☺

P.S. Willow, I believe it's time you asked Clover what Violet so innocently interrupted months ago. I'll know if you didn't!

P.S. Clover, if she doesn't ask, you better borrow some of Willow's balls and tell her yourself!

Hugs, & thanks for the cake, my little ladies! Your secret admirer, Papa Bear

Resigned to my fate, and thinking Malcolm is a lunatic, I call Willow as planned.

"Clover?" Willow mumbles from her cell. I understand her confusion. I never call her. "Is everybody alright?"

I find the strength to force myself to breathe normally and for my voice to sound somewhat level. "I'm sorry to startle you. Everything is fine. Would you like another cooking lesson, just you and me this time?" I try to keep the desperation from my tone, but it rings as loud and clear as an angry bell.

"Sure, I guess. But we usually do this on Saturdays. Aren't you supposed to be at work still? It's only three o'clock on a Monday." Willow sounds so suspicious that it calms my nerves and makes me smile.

"My secret admirer got me sent home. I don't know who the hell this bastard is, but he just sent Ross some very explicit images. Ross was so upset, he told me to leave. Can you believe that shit?"

"Uh… what?" Willow, knowing full and well Malcolm is too busy getting the kids ready for their trip, doesn't buy it.

I spring the trap. "And then when I walked onto the porch, there was a box waiting for me." I let my voice waver for added effect. Too bad I am that nervous– nervous over Willow's reaction. "I'm still getting the text message requests for sweets, but this is the first package in months. Do you want to know what the note said?"

"Yes," Willow gasps. "What the fuck?"

"It said I had to get you over here to bake a cake. Will you come? I don't want to lose my job."

"Oh." Willow chuckles in her deep voice, and it cuts me to my soul. Willow has Sam's voice. My baby boy is developing that same raspy-smoker's voice. "This I have to see. This I really, *really* have to see. I'll be there in two minutes."

"Good," I breathe, relieved and scared shitless.

"See ya in two," Willow hangs up.

I lean against the center island in my kitchen, staring into the living room at the front door. I've never wondered how death-row inmates felt just before execution until now. Nearly suffocating on past regret, guilt, and shame, I'm petrified.

I stare at the door, refusing to blink.

"You okay down there, sis? I can hear you gasping for air all the way up here," Robin calls down from the top of the staircase. "Do you need your inhaler?"

"I won't be okay until this is finally over. Strike that. I'll never be okay, Rob. I'm a horrible human being. Even if I spend the rest of my life raising children, fostering orphans, and volunteering at charities, it will never be enough. Because none of that has a cocksucking thing to do with how I've hurt Willow, of how I shortchanged my daughter and her father of a true relationship."

Appearing in my line of sight, Rob looks devastated and strung out, as if he hasn't slept well for days either. "If Sam were here, he'd have to take the blame for his relationship with Willow. The only relationship you are responsible for with Willow is your own. Don't forget that," Rob stresses as he ghosts out of sight.

"I'll try not to," I mutter to myself as Willow's small frame comes into sight on the front porch.

"Ma!" Willow shouts from the front door, the screen door smashing the frame in her wake. Just once I'd love to hear Willow call me Mom and mean it in the real sense of the word, not the snarky, nearly snide way she always calls me Ma or Mom to get my goad up. I don't ever want Willow to know the searing pain I feel when she calls me the name I haven't earned yet.

"Ready to bake a cake?" I pull my mask firmly into place. A pleasant yet cautious and emotionless expression covers my pain, guilt, and worry.

"Cake?" Willow smirks, her round cheeks dimpling at the corners. I can't help but smile back. Willow and Seth have identical smiles, as did Sam. It's a comfort that Sam lives on. But it's a constant reminder of what I've lost, and what more I could still lose. No doubt this was Sam's diabolical plan. He haunts me from the grave.

"Chocolate cake," I murmur, gathering the ingredients and placing them in order for the steps in the recipe.

"Chocolate cake?" Arching an eyebrow like Auggie, Willow knows I've trapped her into coming here. I can tell she's as resigned to get this over with as I am. "Out of all the recipes in the world, you thought I'd need this," sounding incredulous. "Over say… mac 'n cheese?"

What feels like a lifetime, is actually less than two hours. Neither of us speaks of anything that isn't cake related. I try to imprint this into memory, scared it's the last good memory I will have with my daughter. While not important in the long run, Willow will never bake a cake without thinking of me, even if she hates me.

"Clover," Willow breaks into my reverie, surprising me. My heart starts beating into hyper-drive, knowing this is it.

It's time.

Finally.

"I've been thinking a lot about what you told me. In fact, it never leaves my thoughts," Willow admits reluctantly.

I think I'm going to be sick. I can't do this. I grab at my stomach, bile rising into my throat. I have to lean against the counter, scared I'll drop to the floor. All I can do is stare at the side of my daughter's face as she decorates the cake. I'm thankful Willow doesn't look at me as she speaks, since she's putting all of her concentration into Devon's birthday cake.

Sounding curious, "You said it was an open adoption?" Pensive, Willow swirls the last of the chocolate rosettes around the outside of the cake. She groans when she licks the chocolate ganache off her fingertip. "Divine," she purrs. "Utterly sinful."

If I feed Willow enough, maybe she won't kill me.

"Yes, it was an open adoption," I repeat.

Extremely open.

Feeling close to fainting, I distract myself by cautiously bundling the finished cake into the sturdy box it will need for its flight to Arizona. I'm glad we made the cake first, because I feared Devon would be without a cake if we spoke first. I also feared it would taste of bitter resentment if we made it *after*.

"I'll be right back. I have to put this on the porch. Watch." I smirk, feeling slightly evil that I've enjoyed playing secret admirer with my child for the past few weeks, even if it exhausted me. I felt closer to Willow because of it. This is the last act of this stage in our lives. It saddens me as much as it enlivens me. If only I had a snowballs chance in hell of earning Willow's forgiveness.

"It will be gone in under a minute. I don't know how they do it. I can watch and nothing happens, then I blink and it's gone. Usually the kids pester me and I miss the pickup."

I take Willow's laughter as a good sign as I put the box on the porch. But she's sobered up by the time I return. Back against the island with her arms crossed over her chest, she speaks as soon as I reenter the kitchen.

"Reason I'm asking, is that it's driving me crazy. I walk down the street looking for someone my age. I look for your blue eyes or Sam's chipmunk cheeks. I don't ever find them. I need to know if it was a boy or a girl. I need to know who it is, Clover. What if one of us hooks up with them? That would be incest!"

Plucking my heartstrings. Kicking me in the gut or nuts. Punching me in the teeth. Whatever you want to call it, nothing would hurt as much as this. Willow knows. She has to know. Is she in denial, or is she trying to get me to say it outright?

"No need to worry over that, Sapling. It will never happen." Stress bringing on the early warning signs of an asthma attack, I draw in a deep breath and hold it until I relax enough to breathe normally. "A girl: a lovely, brave, bullheaded child that looks just like Sam, but has my body."

Crying, weak-kneed, every muscle shaking, I feel like I'm either going to fall to my ass and pass out, or throw up, or my airways will constrict until I suffocate. Either way, I'm going to die.

The rational part of my brain supplies what's wrong with me: a panic attack. While the rest of my brain is going insane, fighting for survival, trying to fend off the on-coming broken heart–Willow's.

Gawking at me, Willow looks mortified at how upset I am, which, in turn, only makes me more upset. "You don't have to say any more. I can see how difficult this is for you to talk about."

I look to Willow, trying to center myself by imprinting my daughter into memory. When I'm able to speak, I tell Willow what I love the most about her. "She has Sam's chipmunk cheeks. She has his hair and eyes. His gravelly voice, too. She has his unflinching honesty. Her words sometimes feel like a suckerpunch to the gut."

"She sounds like she could be my best friend," Willow jokes to lighten the tension, no doubt trying to be ironic.

Willow may have her father's features, but she's all me. I smile at the similarities. If Willow rushes out of here when this is all said and done, she'll never escape me when she looks into the mirror or speaks with words I'd use. Willow's gestures, her mannerisms, her attitude… they all came from me.

"Undoubtedly," I reply, loving how after months of trying so very hard, Willow loves herself now. Willow is most definitely her own best friend. "Sam made me promise on his deathbed that I wouldn't keep the secret. Thousands of times I've tried, but the words would get caught in my throat. When she was little, Sam told her the truth. She was too young to understand, but it made him feel better."

I close my eyes and utter the God's honest truth. "I wasn't lying when I'd said Sam never forgave me. He wasn't being harsh. This secret hung heavily over our marriage."

Willow immediately begs to know why I never told her the truth, because we both know we're talking about her, there's no denying it. "Why didn't you tell the truth? Why couldn't you do it for Sam?" A slight edge of accusation and fury laces Willow's voice.

"I love our daughter more than I loved Sam. Sam was an excellent father, but I made a deal and I stuck to it. Responsibility is difficult because you have to do what is right even when you don't want to. I was one week from my seventeenth birthday when I had her. I couldn't take care of her. Hell, I couldn't take care of myself. I would've been a selfish piece of shit to take her from her parents, from her siblings, when she was three and I was ready to be a mom. I tried to take care of her the best I could. I failed more often than I succeeded."

"Who knows?" She asks warily, sounding betrayed.

"Everyone who is older than you." I freeze as if struck, waiting for Willow's explosive reaction. There, I said it.

"Mom and Dad know? Robbie knows?" I have no need to say anything, Willow knows the truth. But the betrayal is demanding I acknowledge every single person who lied to Willow for almost nineteen years. "Auggie?" I just nod my head yes to every single person Willow throws out at me. "The Masons?" Willow practically screams.

Swallowing down the need to vomit, I tell Willow a version of the truth– the version she can handle. I won't sacrifice the kids. If they want Willow to know they knew for the past few months, then they can tell her themselves. I won't choose, because by being loyal to Willow, I'd be disloyal to the rest of the children.

"Malcolm and Isis know, but none of the kids do. Essie doesn't know, either. Essie was too young, but she's came right out and asked me before. She suspects the truth… Violet knows," I whisper. No doubt Willow suspected that because of Violet's rapid personality lobotomy after that night. "She figured it out three months ago."

"Who? I need to know the truth! I need to hear you say it out loud!" Willow screams at me. Her sweet face transforms into pure agony, gutting me where I stand. I grip the edge of the countertop as darkness creeps into my vision. I force myself to breathe.

"Sam was right not to forgive you," Willow growls out harshly. Her words have more impact than an oncoming train. I stumble back, hip hitting the bottom cupboard. "Say it, Clover," she spits out, furious and devastated.

I say the words that release me from nineteen years of secrets and lies. I say the words that will destroy our family as much as set us free. I did this. This is all on me. Even if Willow finds it in her heart to forgive me, I can never forgive myself.

"Willow, she's you. You're my daughter. I'd give anything to hear you call me Mom, and not have it be a snide comment."

"I can forgive you for this." Willow's relief shocks me more than her words. "What I can't forgive you for, is that I never got to call Sam Daddy to his face. I never got to be a daddy's girl. For Sam, I would have been a good girl, Mom."

The ache in Willow's voice drops me to my knees. She called me Mom without a trace of sarcasm. Willow called me Mom the way I call my mom Mom. Sliding down to sit on my ass, I stare up at *my* daughter. Willow finally knows I'm her mother, that Sam was her father. I finally said it.

I set us free with the truth.

Willow cries silent tears, staring down at me in abject horror. Worried this will harm as much as heal, I say the words anyway. "You did," I whimper in pain. "You used to call Sam Daddy when you were little. Your father had Seth make you do it when you grew confused. I also know you called Sam Daddy when no one was listening, when it was just the two of you alone. You were a Daddy's girl, even if you never admitted it to yourself. That's why it hurt you the most when we lost Sam."

Crumpled to the floor, I cover my head with my arms. Heavy sobs wrack my body as I rock back and forth. I always anticipated sharing the moment with Sam. If Sam had lived, we would have done this years ago. To be doing this alone, raising my children by myself, taking all the blame. It forces me to come to terms with the morbid reality that Sam is truly gone, and he's never coming back.

Nothing will ever bring Sam back.

Somewhere in the back of my mind, Sam still lived, even though he's been long dead. "Sam," I call out, wishing he was still with me, knowing he was the only one who could ever make Willow understand.

I thought I'd mourned while Sam was dying and the years that followed his death. I thought Sam had let me go when I pledged myself to Malcolm. I had been wrong. Our secret about Willow was a living, breathing entity between Sam and me. The act of telling Willow alone, severs the last tie that was binding us together. Until this moment, this soul-cleanse, the secret kept Sam very much alive for me. I could blame Sam instead of myself.

I could beg and plead and pray, but Sam will never hear my apology. Sam will never hear me say "*I love you.*" Sam will never hear my goodbye. I imagine Sam finally forgiving me, and I pretend that it wasn't too little, too late.

I can't stop the torrent, the flood of tears, as sobs build in my chest. The agony is breath-stealing. I can't get my lungs to function properly. My lungs burn and protest as I try to draw air without avail.

"Put your head between your knees and try to breathe," Robin's voice filters into my ears above the glug-glug sound of my rapidly beating heart. I do as he says. What's wrong with me? This isn't an asthma attack, at least not like one I've ever had.

"You're having a panic attack and hyperventilating, Clover. Shh… you'll be okay," my brother tries to soothe and reassure me as he answers the question I didn't think I'd spoken aloud. Rob's reassurances mean nothing. Nothing will be right with the world again if my first born hates me.

"Is she going to be okay?" Willow yelps in a panic. I reach for her hand and squeeze, refusing to let my daughter leave me. "You're going to be okay." The tears in Willow's voice cause me to hyperventilate more. "You're going to be okay, Mom."

CHAPTER FORTY-FIVE

The Widower

I'm at ease to finally be in the air. Calm in the knowledge that Rob will take care of Clover and the kids while Auggie and Isis take care of packing up the houses. I move on to the task at hand, telling Kieren the truth, and after, we will solely concentrate on Devon.

Needing both Weston and Raven to sleep through this private conversation, "Weston, hold your sister." They're sitting in the seats in front of Kieren and me. I pinch the bridge of my nose, trying to remove the drilling pain that's boring a hole into my skull from the inside.

"Dad," West whines, forever thinking girls have cooties. "Gross!"

"It's not gross to comfort your sister," I mumble, leaning forward to speak with Weston between the airline seats. "I hold Isis all the time."

"It's unfathomable to imagine Aunt Isis as the cuddly sort," Kieren's snark flows from next to me. "It'd be like hugging a pit-viper."

"Isis can be very cuddly," I say, offended for Isis. It hurts me that no one understands my sister. "If your brother won't hold you, who will?"

"I don't know," Kieren drawls while rolls his eyes. That blasted brat has taught Ren all of her worst habits. "I'm pretty sure Tweety does a lot more than hold her," he taunts.

"Don't be crude," I chastise Ren. "Isis loves Robin." Leaning forward again, "Weston, Raven doesn't like to fly. You know Rae hates being trapped in confined spaces with strangers. Comfort her so she can sleep soundly. It's a long flight."

"Are you sure we shouldn't be calling you *Mom*?" Ren taunts me, annoyed when I get clingy because I'm anxious.

Weston reluctantly does as I bid, tucking his sister's head to his broadening chest and wrapping an arm around her shoulders.

Rae snuggles in deep with a contented sigh. A proud smile spreads my lips. Men should protect their women. All of my boys are going to learn that, even if it kills me.

Feeling raw, not knowing what is happening with Clover and Willow, and not knowing what to expect when we land, my anxiety level reaches an all-time high. I lean forward and make sure my baby girl is cocooned in her hoodie. I brush Rae's hair from her forehead as I smile. Raven will forever be my little birdy– my baby girl with bite. I'll never fear her weakness. She's as strong and intelligent as the bird she was named for– the Raven. Not at all like that weak-assed Robin my sister dreams of marrying. I scoff and lean back in my seat, but not without mussing up Weston's hair first. I'm a tactile creature. I have to touch them constantly. I fear they will poof with the pop of a gun.

I reach over to hold Kieren's hand. He doesn't squirm or pull away after nineteen years of my constant affection. Kieren gives me a squeeze or two as I settle as comfortably as I can in these foul smelling seats. I hate this stale, recycled air blowing in my face. It makes me want to hold my breath and panic.

Rae's snoring," Weston growls, his voice breaking slightly. "She snores like a drunk, three hundred pound man with raging allergies."

"Why do you think I have a headache," I chuckle, and Kieren smirks at me.

When I shift around one too many times, "Dude, stop fidgeting," Kieren grumbles from beside me.

"*Dude*, really?" I arch an eyebrow at the idiot. "I'm going to beat that brat when I get home. Willow's a bad influence."

"Oh, my God. Dad, are you shitting me? We're on a plane to visit your shot-tossing, pot-smoking, heroin-shooting, unprotected-sexed, criminal-minded law enforcement son at rehab, and Spanky is a bad influence?" The tone of Kieren's voice is pure incredulousness as he glares daggers at me. He tries to wrench his hand from mine, but I hold on.

"I'm not even comparing the two, Ren. I'm just trying to say you shouldn't emulate Willow." I can feel Kieren gearing up. "Don't even think of rolling your eyes," I hiss. "It's disrespectful to whomever is speaking with you."

"Sorry," Kieren mumbles, properly cowed. "Don't blame Willow for my behavior. I've been rolling my eyes for years, you just didn't know it."

"Don't be a piss-pot," I warn. "It's unbecoming of an adult." Kieren flinches as if I struck him. I give his hand a squeeze as a silent apology. "I'm sorry. I'm on edge, and I'm taking it out on you. I hate flying. I hate how instead of a family vacation, we're visiting Devon at rehab. I'm also worried about those we left at home."

Accepting my apology before I even uttered it, Ren forgives and forgets. "What was in the box we picked up off of Clover's porch, anyway?"

"Devon's birthday cake. Clover made Willow bake and decorate it. It's a way for both of them to show Dev he's in their thoughts, even though they can't be there with him."

"Is that a good idea?" Ren glares at me, his possessive streak showing. "Dev already has delusions about Willow. I don't want him pining away at rehab for her."

"I did it for Clover," comes out before I can stop it. "I wanted the ladies to have a bonding experience before they talked."

Flashing an arrogant grin, "You say how transparent Willow and Clover are, but we could see through your shit for the past month."

"We, who?" My voice breaks, fearing my son already knows what's going on back in Fairport.

"We, as in Willow and me. We know you and Clover are together, as in screwing like bunnies, creeping into bedrooms at night and creeping back out in the morning, and in possession of an engagement ring."

Confused, I blurt out, "Why didn't you say anything?"

Kieren shakes his head at me like I'm a moron. "We figured it was making you old fuckers feel young again to be sneaky like you're teenagers in heat."

"Old fuckers?" I sputter out, insulted.

"Plus, I assumed that's what you wanted to tell me anyway. Then you bought a house big enough fit all the Masons and Websters combined. When Willow was stopped from visiting her family, I checked it out myself. Dave and Mary's shit is in that new house of yours. It didn't take a genius. For a cop, you make a pretty shitty sneak."

"Well, now that you've insulted your father a dozen times, I should tell you what was really going on. It wasn't so much as hiding the fact that we are getting married, as much as it was about Clover being Willow's mother," I reveal, knowing Ren must already know.

Face as white as a sheet, eyes bulging out, looking in need of an airsickness bag, Kieren didn't already know.

I close my eyes in defeat. "Shit, I'm so sorry, Kieren. I really thought you knew. I take it Willow didn't share her suspicions with you? We couldn't blend our families with this secret hanging over our head like a guillotine."

"Willow knows?" Ren breathes out, looking devastated.

"She does now," I say with absolute certainty. "Clover and Willow are having a mother/daughter talk as we speak."

Eyes flicking around the cabin of the plane, Ren looks like he's trying to figure out how to jump off and find his way back to Fairport. This was exactly what Clover and I were trying to avoid.

"Goddamn you," Ren snarls, fingernails biting into my hand. He yanks his hand from mine, glaring at me like he could kill me with one look. "You trapped me on this cocksucking airplane so I couldn't be there for Willow. This is what she meant by that countdown bullshit. I thought she meant when you guys were going to tell us you were getting married."

Ren seethes, vibrating with anger and frustration. Tears glisten in his eyes. I'd do anything I could to take his pain away, but there is nothing I can do. "Willow needs me," he starts to panic, eyes flicking everywhere. His hands clench on the armrests, nails biting into the plastic.

Taking a deep breath, I tell Kieren the truth. "If anyone knows how you feel right now, it's me. Do you honestly think, I don't want to be with Clover right now? I wish I was holding her hand, the four of us sitting in the Webster's living room, discussing this. You must understand that this isn't about you or me. It isn't about the relationship I have with Clover or the one you have with Willow. This is about a mother and a daughter who need to draw together without using us as a buffer or distraction."

Still angry with me, Kieren calms down enough to stop radiating fury. Ren's not looking at me, he's not speaking to me, but at least he's not gripping the armrest like he's contemplating tearing it off the seat and bashing my skull in with it.

I zone out for a few minutes, using my daughter's heavy snoring as a metronome. Kieren keeps moving around, like there are nails, broken glass, poisonous insects, and hot lava in his seat. I ignore it for as long as possible. But when he nearly elbows me in the face during his struggle to get comfortable, I've had enough.

"Dude, stop fidgeting," I mock him. "Got a woman on your mind?"

"Sorry," Kieren mumbles, and then brightens instantly as if he thought of something incredible. "Yeah, I... I tease Spanky all the time about apologizing too much."

"Christ," I hiss. "You just saw Willow a few hours ago, kid. We'll be gone for a few days, and everything will be back to normal when we get home. They will survive without us. So ya better buck up, son."

"It's not like that," Kieren whines, meaning it's exactly like that. "How did Willow happen? Ya know, how is she Clover's kid?"

"Well, long story short: Aunt Ginny and Clover were new friends, who met at FCC. Ginny brought Clover to my academy graduation picnic. Your brother was a little over a year old, and your mom was pregnant with you. It was magnetic. Sam and Clover hit it right off– in the room that's Raven's. Uh... Willow was conceived in our house," I quickly say, laughing over the absurdness.

Face twisting up in disgust, "I... thank God, we're moving. It's creepy, too creepy that Willow was made in the same house we were. It's borderline incestuous. Nasty with a capital N."

"I thought it was rather fitting that my future-daughter-in-law/stepdaughter was conceived in your little sister's bedroom. As for incestuous, you plan on marrying your stepsister, Ren." My restrained laughter is obvious. I bark a laugh, startling nearby passengers. Weston gazes at me from between the crack of his and Raven's seats. His blue eyes are huge from shock. His mouth a perfect O. *Shit!* I laugh again. West wasn't supposed to hear that part.

"I'm never going into that room again," Weston mutters slowly, mortified. "I've never been in your room because it's... it's grody," Weston sputters out. My son, the germaphobe, clean freak.

Ignoring his brother, "Why didn't Clover raise Willow like she did the twins?" Kieren's voice is tight with suppressed anger, deflating my elated mood.

"Clover was only sixteen, that's why," I defend, feeling a sense of possessiveness out of nowhere. "When Clover talks about why she gave Willow up for adoption, we see her as a thirty-five-year-old grown woman with a set of twins. We forget that she was no older than Raven. Imagine some twenty-one-year-old guy touching Raven right now. We all see Clover as she is now, but she was just a girl when this happened."

"I would kill any man who touched my sister like that," Ren snarls.

The thought of anyone touching my daughter enrages me. Unable to suffer this conversation anymore, I shut it down. "I'm taking a nap until we land." I roll away from Kieren and face the window.

Talking about Sam brings him to the forefront of my mind. The apparition of Sam is burned into my memories, while his son is the living, breathing, walking version of his father. "Willow and one of my sons. It's what Sam wanted," I whisper so softly Kieren doesn't hear me. My breath fogs up the tiny airplane window as immense sadness washes over me.

I thought Sam was delusional when he brought it up that one day he'd love to see our kids marry and make us grandfathers. Sam said that nothing would be better than two best friends' kids mating up because the in-laws already loved one another. There would be no power struggle over who spent what holidays with whom, because we'd genuinely want to be around one another anyway.

Symmetry– it only took a few generations to accomplish it. Peggy and her best friend, Carol Jamison, wanted Sam and Ginny to marry. Instead, Sam married Clover, and Ginny's sister married me. The product of those two unions will eventually marry and create children of their own. It only took several generations, but Peggy and her best friend's DNA will comingle and live on in their great grandchildren. Sam managed to give his mother what she longed for, even from the grave. If there is a heaven, Sam most likely had help from Carol and Camille.

I swipe a tear away, hoping to hide it from Kieren. What would my best friend think of me making his entire family mine? I swipe a few more of those betraying bastards leaking down my cheeks.

Sam won't be here to see it, but I'll do my damnedest to make sure his wife and kids are happy.

I always found it odd how Sam requested both Clover and me to be at his side during his final moments. Not his mother. Not his children. Not his family. Sam specifically had Clover and me sit with him. Just before Sam died, he told me to watch over his family. I'm just now realizing that this is what he had had in mind all along. Sam wanted me to make his family mine, because he could no longer take care of them himself, and I was in need of a family to call my own. The knowledge that we would all be safe and happy must have been a comfort to Sam in his last moments.

I can practically feel Sam smiling his big-cheeked smile at me.

I wonder if I'm closer to Sam being in an airplane…

"I love you, Dad," Kieren whispers to comfort me, and then he settles his cheek between my shoulder blades. "You're doing the right thing."

Scrunched against the airplane window, I worry about whether or not I am doing the right thing for all of us. My house will be like animal kingdom with all those conflicting personalities under one roof.

I fall asleep to the rhythm of my three children's sounds of peaceful sleep: Raven's loud chainsaw snores, Weston's strange hitch, and Kieren's warm breath on my neck. I've never missed Devon's soft snore as much as I do in this very moment. I thank and pray to God that my boy will be the son I love and respect, not that addict freak who flew out here less than five weeks ago.

CHAPTER FORTY-SIX

The Widow

"What's wrong with her, Robin? Why's she like this?" Willow's panicked voice only makes the tightness in my chest compress more. Drawing in air becomes impossible. Burning suffocation increases my terror. Rapidly sucking in air through my nose and mouth in huge gulps, the airways to my lungs constrict until it's like breathing though a clogged cocktail straw.

Rob's arms slide beneath my knees and around my shoulders, lifting me from the kitchen floor where I had slumped. In three paces, I'm set on the sofa, head pressed between my knees.

"Do you have her inhaler?" Willow's voice comes from in front of me, but I can't see because my eyes are clenched shut against the strain of trying to breathe. "We need to make her use it."

"It won't help." Rob's voice comes from far away. "Clover's having a panic attack. Once she calms down, she'll be okay."

Voice wavering in fear, Willow kneels down beside me. "How do you know that? How can you be so calm about this?"

Standing above me, "This isn't the first time, Willow." A damp cloth is draped across the nape of my neck. "It's the third time. Just sit with your mother until she calms down."

The '*your mother*' causes Willow to sob, which in turn, causes me to hyperventilate even more. "Why aren't you giving her a paper bag?"

Sighing, Rob sits next to me on the sofa while Willow rests on the floor at my feet. I feel stupid, and helpless, and over-emotional, and ridiculous. Try as I might, I can't pull myself together. I'm terrified of losing Willow as I lost Sam.

"Worst thing you can do for an asthmatic is to give them a paper bag." Rob's palm presses up on my jaw, closing my mouth with enough force that I can't reopen it. "Calm yourself, relax, and breathe through your nose. Willow is still here, and she's not going anywhere. Are you, Willow? Maybe you should talk to your mother, let her know everything is going to be okay."

Even through my difficulties, it doesn't escape me that Robin is desensitizing us both by using '*your mother*' over and over again. Willow doesn't sob this time when he says it. "Why is she so upset?"

"Gee, Willow, I don't know," Rob says snidely. "It's only been nineteen years of secrets and lies– more than half of her life. Add on top of that all the guilt she's felt these past few weeks for lying to you."

"I knew Clover was lying to me, sneaking around with Malcolm. Mom and Dad's house is nearly empty, and I saw all of their stuff being brought into the house across from the Spook House. Really? My bedroom faces Malcolm's new home. Like I wouldn't see that shit and recognize it. I'm so angry with Clover I could scream at her, but I don't want her this upset. Why didn't she tell me a few weeks ago? Why?"

A gurgling sound comes from my throat as I try to answer my daughter. My breathing is labored but slowed, thanks to the fact that I can't suck air into my mouth. All I can do is rest my forehead on my knees and try to relearn how to breathe again.

Palm falling away from my mouth, I try to stop myself from dragging in a deep breath, which would only exacerbate the problem. "Shhh… Clover, it's okay. I know the answers to any questions Willow will ask. You just calm yourself," Rob reassures me, rubbing my back.

"We were scared you would run off with Kieren and not stick around long enough to listen. We needed you to be present long enough to get the gravity of the situation. Malcolm waited to tell Ren until they were on the airplane, so Ren couldn't come rushing back here or call incessantly."

"Goddamnit, Rob!" Willow's shout is eclipsed by a dull thump. Rob's grunt says the messenger was punched. "Give me more credit than that shit! Sure, the old me would have flew off the handle, but that's not who I am anymore."

"Not flying off the handle anymore, are you? You just punched me," Rob sounds pained. "Besides, I didn't say it was about you. Ren would have interrupted. Being a thousand feet above land is the only thing that would keep him from you. Clover hated having to lie on top of all the other lies. I'm sorry you feel betrayed, but I don't regret it. Ten times outta ten, I'd do it again. We didn't like lying, but it was necessary."

"Yeah," Willow concedes. "Ren would have been over here, championing for me, starting a war in our family. He would mean well, though. I really am different," Willow defends herself. "I could understand Clover not being able to come to me with this before. I would have spit in her face, and then kicked her when she was down. I will acknowledge that. So, don't worry, I'm not going anywhere until I get my answers."

"Good," Rob says, sounding thoughtful. "Willow, I've seen your mother like this only twice before. I don't want you upset, thinking Clover is this way because of you."

"No," I groan, reaching out for Willow's hand. I wrap my fingers around hers as tightly as possible. "Don't leave me."

"I'm not going anywhere," Willow says softly. "Why is she like this? I've never... I never thought I'd see Clover like this."

"Sam. The first time Clover had a panic attack was the night before she married your father. It was bad, worse than this. She was barely conscious, and I was scared about the twins. She wasn't ready to get married."

"You didn't love Sam?" Willow sounds heartbroken as she speaks to me. I try to tell her that's not the case, but I can barely breathe, let alone talk.

"Willow, Clover was only five months older than you are now, preparing to have two children at once. She was petrified. To answer your question on whether or not Clover ever loved your father, the last time she had a panic attack was the worst. It was the night Sam told Clover he had weeks to live, asking her to prepare you kids because he wasn't going to see you guys grow up. I found Clover in the backyard, hyperventilating, and nearly catatonic. I had to take her to the hospital."

"I... I never knew that. I would have been thirteen," Willow quickly sputters out. "Why didn't I know that?"

"Willow," Rob says softly, as if frightened to tell her the truth. "Your mother broke down both times because she realized she had to be stronger than she was, that she had to put everyone else above her own needs. It's difficult to imagine having to pretend your emotions don't matter. How you can't be upset, cry, or mourn, because you have to put on brave face for everyone else. For Clover, it's like, '*I hurt. But so what, when my child is hurting as well.*' She's doing this again right now for you. Willow, you have to tell your mother her emotions are important, too."

"I'm sorry," I mutter, getting myself under control enough to speak. "I didn't want to give you to my parents. You have to believe me. I tried to stay away, but it's like you were calling out to me." A sob is torn from my throat, searing my tender flesh. "Sam finally got me to come home, and I could never leave again. I doubt your remember, but you slept in our bed when you were little. It wasn't until the twins were born that I feared disturbing you every time I had to get up to feed them. I tried to be your mother, even if it was from afar."

"Afar?" Willow snorts. "I lived next door, but I was over here more than over there. I looked at this as my home. My bedroom was literally three feet from Seth's. On a subconscious level, I think I always knew. I used to joke, saying Seth and I were the twins, but our similarities were all Sam."

"I want you to know your father loved you more than anything, more than anyone. He didn't want to leave you. Christ, I can't do this." Wracked with sobs, I tuck my head between my knees and rock back and forth. Hearing my daughter cry makes it worse, so much worse.

Rob fills in the pain-filled silence. "Clover won't say it out loud, but we all know she blames herself for whatever was going on between her and Sam. I think why she is so upset right now, has a lot more to do with Sam, than it has to do with you."

Sniffling, Willow asks, "Why? It's been years. Knowing I never had this conversation with Sam is killing me right now. But it doesn't change anything, though. If Sam wanted me to know he was my father, it was up to him to tell me. Just as it was up to Clover to tell me she was my mother. So why is she so upset over Sam right now?"

"No one is that stupid," Rob sounds exhausted. "Clover and Malcolm are getting married next week. Put yourself in Clover's shoes for a moment. She's not going to admit it, but she's feeling guilty because she's moving on, like she's leaving Sam behind. This right here was the last thread that was keeping Sam alive for her."

"My father's dead," comes straight from Willow's gut, sounding painfully hollow. "Being miserable for the rest of your life wouldn't make Sam happy."

Hysterical laughter bubbles up my throat. "I wouldn't be so sure about that," I mutter. Disgusted with myself, I explain. "Sam and I were toxic together. Looking back, I realize I've villainized Sam in my mind as a way to cope. The good memories were so painful that I couldn't deal with them, so I highlighted the bad. If Sam was a bad person, I didn't need to mourn him. But when I thought about how much I loved him, missed him, I felt like he betrayed me by leaving. So I betrayed Sam's memory in turn."

"Don't you love Malcolm now?" Willow asks, sounding confused. "You're marrying him next week, there is no room for indecision."

"Malcolm and Sam are not the same person. Ask yourself who you love more: Devon or Kieren? Or even Auggie. You will say all of them, that your love is different."

"Don't ask me," Rob mutters, "Because I definitely could never pick between the two people I love. I'd rather be miserable and fighting with them than be without them. Auggie and Isis are too different to be compared."

"No shit," Willow grumbles.

"I will never compare my husbands. I have never felt as sure about anything in my entire life, as I am about marrying Malcolm. But I am petrified, because I don't think I could survive losing Malcolm. I would rather be a selfish bitch, than suffer this torture again. I just pray none of you ever have to find out how horrific it is to be the one left behind."

Facial expression twisting in agony, "I can't... I can't talk anymore." Willow sobs. "I need to be alone."

"Don't go!" I cry out at the same time Rob demands the same thing.

Hugging me, Willow says the most comforting thing I've ever heard. "I'm angry with you. I feel betrayed, lied to, and cheated out of my real parents. I'm frustrated and hurt. But I understand as much as I can, since I've never been in your position."

"Will you ever be able to forgive me?" I plead.

"There is nothing to forgive," Willow declares. "It will take a while before I can trust you again. I can't go straight from being your sister to your daughter."

"I don't expect that, Willow. I just want you to know, I will be here for you no matter what. I'll take you any way I can get you. If you need a mother, a sister, or a woman to talk to, please come to me."

"I'll try," Willow says stiffly. "But I make no promises. I know a lot of big changes are coming up, so I'm going to act like my mother and put everyone else's needs first. I've been your daughter for almost nineteen years, whether I knew it or not. So throwing a tantrum over it changes nothing. Your marriage should be about you and Malcolm, not tainted with all the shit-fits the old me would have thrown. I will behave, just don't push me," she warns.

Standing up, pulling away from me, the absence of Willow breaks a vital piece of me. "I know Rob is here to hold me captive, but I need some time *not* here," she stresses. "To prove my willingness, I will go spend time with my... *brother, sister,* and *grandfather,* and with the new kid, Ozzy. I spied them at the new house on my way over here, carrying a bunch of plumbing into the basement. I need to work so I can think."

I don't want to let Willow go, but I can't be that selfish. All I can do is nod my head '*okay*' and try my damnedest not to start crying again, or hyperventilating.

"Be back here for supper," Rob commands. "Mom and Dad, Isis and Auggie, Ozzy, Essie, and we will be in attendance. With the Masons gone, and with what just happened, we need to bond together, not pull apart. Whether you even interact with your mother is up to you, but you will be here for the rest of the family. Understood?"

"Good God, Robin," Willow drawls out, "Don't let Isis hear you talking all manly." Chuckling to herself, Willow announces, "I'll be back in two hours with a group of people in tow. Make sure the food is fatty, salty, and sweet. We'll need some comfort food."

I jump a foot when the screen door slams shut– Willow's trademark entrance and exit sound. "Willow's definitely my daughter. She uses manual labor to clear her mind. Join me in the kitchen, brother?"

Yanking me to his chest, Rob snarls his final warning into my ear, "If you ever have another panic attack again in your life, I will kill you myself. Don't think I won't be telling Malcolm your horrific reaction. I will not lie for a third time. I will never lie again for you, sister." Holding me at arm's length, "let's go cook."

CHAPTER FORTY-SEVEN

The Widower

I was not prepared for what I found upon my arrival in Arizona. The moment we landed, I rushed to the rehabilitation center, eager to see my son. I was stopped at the door, given a long list of *DOs&DON'Ts,* and was told to come back alone.

I checked us into the hotel, leaving my children to their own devices: swimming for Weston, hot tub for Raven, and poolside cellphone fusion for Kieren. Up to that point, I had absolutely no contact with Clover since I left her sleeping in her bed. I only knew Clover was still breathing by the fact that the cellphone to Kieren's ear gave him a smile instead of a frown. I handed my children twenty bucks for the vending machines, and then told them not to leave the hotel.

Stressed out: mentally, physically, and emotionally exhausted, with the three hour time difference playing tricks on my system, I made my way back to the rehab center. Where my hopes were crushed again because I was not allowed to see my son.

I was ushered into a private room, containing only a conference table and a good dozen chairs. I waited until it was eleven p.m. *my* time, while they rounded up the necessary personnel. I was then subjected to three hours of information being slung at me: reports listing every bite of food Devon had consumed since he was rendered into their custody, plus the times of intake and outtake– yes, even when and what time he used the bathroom. I spoke to Devon's counselors, nutritionists, mental and physical therapists, physicians, and even clergy of different denominations. I was given a list of what books and magazines he's read, what movies and shows he's watched, and even who he has interacted with.

After several hours of reporting every single shit, shower, and morsel of food, I was told what I could and couldn't say to my son when we visited during the half hour per day in the gardens. They tried to restrict our visit to just Kieren and myself, stating Raven and Weston were minors, and that was the first time I put my foot down.

After the reports and negotiations, we really got down to business. I sat with three counselors, who advised me on everything I would need to prepare for Devon's arrival back home. They had done their homework on me and my situation as well, gaining names from Devon's sessions. There were dossiers on every person in our lives. They even knew the date I applied for my marriage license and how much my new mortgage was per month.

The negotiations really heated up when they told me they didn't feel Devon should come home to Fairport. They stated it might be best if perhaps Devon started his life over in a new town without any ghosts that could trigger a relapse. The only point I made was that no person could survive without a support system, especially when that support system is made up of every person who has ever loved them since birth. No one on this planet wants Devon to heal and succeed as much as we do.

No matter how old your child is, I found out the hard way that once you put your child into the arms of another, you lose all control over them. While I agree with the rehabilitation center's practices, I could see how this could be more detrimental to a person if done in the wrong way. The program tears a person down to their core, and then rebuilds them from the foundation up. If in the wrong hands, your loved one could be destroyed, brainwashed, and reshaped into a person you would never recognize.

Five hours into my schooling with the counselors, I was terrified of who or what I would find come the next afternoon. I was wracked with a guilt so strong I could barely talk. Guilt over the fact that I sent my child here, and if they ruined Devon, it was my fault. If the only choices were a drug addict or a reprogrammed robot, I don't know which I would choose.

When the segment of the torture turned to Essie and the baby, they asked how far along she was. When I informed them Essie had just reached her second trimester, they were disappointed. If it had been sooner, they were prepared to inform me an abortion was in Devon's best interests, fearing the stress of a newborn would be too much for him to handle.

Narcissistic. Devon's best interests, not Essie's or the baby's.

I shouted, *"I didn't hear you saying that shit when you paraded a Catholic priest all the way to a Wiccan priestess in here. That is my grandchild you are trying to murder!"*

I stormed out at four a.m. *my* time with a '*fuck you*' on my tongue. I refuse to engage any of their staff for the duration of Devon's stay. I will take back every curse I thought if Devon comes out of this ordeal still human.

A countdown began to play in my head. Five weeks down, one week during our stay, and two more when we get home. The days, hours, minutes, and seconds ticked down in my mind.

I returned to the hotel room to find Kieren in one bed and Raven in the other, with Weston shrunk down on the small couch. I could tell they had fought over the sleeping arrangements, even after I told them to just share a bed. I spent five hours in the bathroom, speaking on my cellphone, and then bawling my frustrations out.

I called Clover, not caring that it was so early for her. She put on a good front, pretending she was fine, saying everything went better than expected. I then poured out all of worries to her. Clover soothed me by saying this program was the best in the country, and to stop worrying until I saw Devon with my own two eyes.

Knowing Clover was lying about her own emotional state, I woke Rob up, who told me Clover had a severe panic attack. We discussed the why and how of it, and then I debated for a good hour on calling Clover back and tearing her a new asshole.

Finally, after more than twenty-four hours since I left Fairport, I'm going to see my son.

"God, what is in this cake, anyway? Lead?" Ren complains for the fifth time on our trek across the massive '*garden*' at the facility.

It's a hundred degrees in the shade, that is if you could find any. This feels like a torturous mile long walk in the desert, not a few hundred yards from the parking lot. There is no such thing as grass and trees and shade around here. It's rocks and spiky plants and cacti. It's incredible, but this New England man wants his humidity back. I miss feeling the thick moisture in the air when I breathe.

"Seven different kinds of chocolate, I suspect," I mutter absentmindedly about the heavy contents of the cake.

Sounding awed, Raven says with grudging appreciation, "This place is like a gorgeous Hell on earth. I just burnt my toe on the ground when my flip flop shifted. It's like trying to breathe while sitting in a preheated oven." Raven complains, again, about the heat of the sun on her pale skin.

"I saw a lizard!" West shrieks. My six foot tall baby boy looks like he's about to jump out of his skin, eyes darting for tiny assassins. Calming down, he murmurs in awe, "I just saw a fucking lizard. I didn't know they existed outside of the reptile house at the zoo. Seth would freak."

Chuckling and shaking my head, "It was the size of a mouse. The first time you saw a black bear, you didn't scream like a little girl. The lizard was probably more scared of you than you were of it."

Glowering yet still actively searching the landscape, "Well, I can see a black bear coming. There are scorpions out here, too. Anything resembling a spider is some serious shit, and I want nothing to do with it." Eyes peeled in front of him, Weston watches where he places his feet.

"I can't believe they took our cellphones away or they wouldn't allow us on the property." Grinning at her younger brother, Raven turns snarky. "How will we call if Weston gets nibbled on by a lizard? And how in the hell are we supposed to serve this honking cake with only plastic spoons?"

"I'm sure if you really hated this place enough to kill yourself, you could do it with the spoon, somehow," Weston adds. "Just break the spoon part off and jab it into your neck. Or capture a lizard, and let it eat you or inject you or whatever its evil defenses are."

"At least they allowed us to bring the paper plates," I sound grateful, but I'm not. "I expected them to force us to eat the cake with our bare hands– just tear a chunk off, chew it, and then swallow it, like it's bitter medicine for ruining Devon enough to land his ass in rehab."

"I thought they wouldn't allow us to have the cake in the first place," Weston says, sounding surprised. "They didn't let us bring the presents."

"Well, Devon will just have to enjoy his new shit when he gets home," I grumble, pissed the fuck off. "If Devon manages to live to be one hundred, this will forever be the birthday with no presents."

"At least we have cake!" Ren sings sarcastically. "Ugh, could you have found a fucking heavier goddamned box."

"Don't let the religious fanatics hear you taking their lord's name in vain. We just passed some guru bitch," I snarl. "Ya better talk fast when we get to Devon. They're probably timing us with a stopwatch: twenty-nine minutes and fifty-nine seconds, I bet."

"Last night, we wrote down what we wanted to say, so we each had our time. Then we broke it up over our five visits. We're good," Ren informs me.

"Yeah, well, you forgot about me," I grumble. "I'm the dad. I get the bulk of the time. Plus, Devon might want to speak instead of having shit fired off at him. As per the *'suggestion'* from the demon counselors this morning."

Grinning, Ren channels Willow. "My first question for Devon: does he know how to do the downward dog? And is anyone standing behind him while he does it."

"Huh?" I grunt out while my children laugh at me, with Weston laughing the loudest. Laughter dying on all of their lips, Devon comes into view. Sitting at a picnic table beneath some manmade shade, he waits for us.

Walking the distance between us, I stare at my son, eyes tracking over every inch of his flesh. I so badly want to hop over the table separating us and tackle him, press him tightly to my chest, and drink in his presence. But the God awful bitchy counselors said no– some lame horseshit about too much stimulation.

Devon stares as intently at me as I stare at him– each of us noting the difference only absence can make. Devon looks healthy, albeit spooked and ashamed. Unlike when I last saw him, his skin is a healthy, young, and darkly tanned. Devon is no longer emaciated, as I knew he wouldn't be after all the food eaten listed in his report. Devon's body is stronger, fuller, from hours of exercise.

Devon is a strong, virile, healthy young man with darkness lurking in the depths of his stormy blue eyes.

I physically ache for my son's touch, hands shaking with need. Even when Devon was at the police academy, I visited him several time a week. Not since Devon was a small child have I been a part from him this long. It's killing me.

A tableau forms: Devon sitting on one side of the table, looking ashamed of himself, with the rest of my children and me standing by the other side. Ren plunks the heavy wooden crate on the table, causing us all to jump.

"I want to apologize for acting like Mom," Devon says softly, voice filled with guilt, grief, and shame. Devon drops his eyes to his folded hands, refusing to look at us.

It takes all of my control not to go off at the mouth, but the counselor's words seep in. I learn a valuable lesson in an instant. We are to be quiet, to allow Devon's words to seep into our brains, because we might say something potentially detrimental to his recovery while in a fit of emotion.

What I wanted to say in greeting was: *Happy twenty-first birthday, son.* But something tells me that reminding Devon of the birthday everyone celebrates by getting rip-roaring drunk wouldn't be a good idea.

What I actually say in greeting is, "Apology accepted." I manage to swallow without gagging on my words. I close my eyes and speak the truth as I see it. "Yes, your destructive behavior was like your mother. But you are not her, son. You are Devon, and I will accept nothing less from you."

Devon looks up to me, tears glistening in his eyes. My knees weaken when his bottom lip quivers like he's trying not to cry. "May I hug you now?" I ask, feeling like I'm a dog begging for a cookie after pulling a neat trick.

Devon meets me halfway in an instant. I've never seen him move so fast in his entire life. I think we may have frightened the kids by our sudden movements, because they back out of our way. My first born and I stand chest-to-chest, breathing heavily, but not touching. Devon is several inches shorter than me, with his eyes a soft blue like his mother's. I begin to understand Devon more in this instant. When he looks in the mirror, all he sees is his mother looking back, haunting him.

I grab a thick hank of Devon's too long, wavy black hair. I shudder at the softness, my tactile fix fed for a moment. I pull until Devon looks me directly in the eyes. I try to broadcast how nothing will ever take my love away, no act or deed can ruin our relationship.

Willow's words ring in my mind: *"You have to love your family, you just don't have to like them."* The thought makes me smile, and Devon gives me a perplexed look.

"Now you bastards have me thinking of her, too," I chuckle heartily. Rambling out of discomfort, "Willow baked you a cake.

Why haven't you gotten a haircut? And I'm positive everything I just said is on the counselor's no-no list of triggers."

"Willow must hate me," Devon murmurs dejectedly underneath his breath, eyes darting away from mine.

I yank Devon's hair, firmly twisting the silky strands around my fingers, controlling his gaze. "Devon," I reprimand. "No one could ever hate you. I was thinking of how nothing could ever take my love away, and Willow popped into my head. She called you family, remember?" I prompt Devon, and his lips lift at the corners.

"Oh, fuck," he groans in defeat, and then falls against my chest. My arms immediately encircle my son. I embrace Devon tightly as he borrows his face against my shoulder. I've missed this. No one gives hugs as good as Devon. I don't care if the kid is ninety, when he's in my arms, he's a little boy again. My hands flutter over the crown of his head, down his back, and up again in a continual circuit.

Mumbling against my neck, Devon says wryly, "I haven't gotten a haircut because I didn't want to cheat on my stylist. How ironic is that shit?" Good humor still intact, Devon pulls away from our hug with a self-deprecating smile on his face.

Kieren's on us in a second, yanking Devon away from me and engulfing him into a tight embrace. Ren's large arms hook underneath his brother's armpits, allowing no escape. Ren tucks his face into the crook of Devon's neck and shoulder, no doubt hiding his tears. The kid has been pacing like a caged animal for the past five weeks.

"Bro, damn, I've missed you," Kieren's gravelly tone melts Devon. "Dude! You've gained weight!" Ren shouts in delight, pushing his brother back to arm's length. Proving Masons have no boundaries, Ren lifts up Devon's t-shirt. "I see abs. Not a six-pack like mine, but there's some definition. Nice," he praises.

"I've missed you, too, Ren," Devon whimpers, clearly overwhelmed by Kieren. Devon's eyes are glazed over in shock, but he has a goofy grin on his face. "I wasn't sure if you were going to hug me, or hold me down so someone could punch me like last time."

Kieren doesn't give a shit. He pats his brother's stomach, making happy sounds in the back of his throat. The idiot even lifts up his own shirt for comparison. I close my eyes and sigh at the dumbass. "By the time you come home, you'll look like me,"

Ren say happily, no doubt looking forward to an exercise partner. Willow won't touch exercise for nothing.

"Don't start in on your regimen, or Kieren will never shut up," I tease in amusement, dragging Ren away from Devon. "Let the little ones say hello."

"Devon looks really good," Kieren says giddily, nodding his head up and down, as he stands at my side.

I want to ask Kieren what he means by that, but then I remember how he saw Devon at his worst, how he thought his brother was dead. I swallow the panic that threatens to rise. I push back the fear that someday I will find my son gaunt with a deathly pallor. I've already seen six dead people up close and personal: three by my own hand, one by her own hand, and two nature stole too soon. No more. I couldn't survive seeing my child dead and gone.

Raven and Weston give Devon small half-hugs, as if they're scared of him. Devon's behavior before he left made them skittish, and his absence has made them bashful.

"You do look bigger," Weston says in awe. "You'll fill out your uniform better."

Devon is in a surprising good mood, but I can tell he's trying his hardest. "West, did you grow another few inches? Again? How tall do you plan on getting? I haven't been gone that long."

"Dad says Grandpa was six-four." Wearing a self-satisfying smirk, "I think I lucked out."

"Yeah, well…" Devon drawls out. "I'm happy I'm normal-sized. I wouldn't want to be a foot or more taller than my girl."

"I won't be having any need of a girl," Weston stresses. "So I'm good. I wouldn't want to be shorter than my guy."

Tan skin blushing, Devon laughs and shakes his head at how much more confident Weston has grown in the past few months. While Devon has only been gone five weeks, he's been absent in our everyday lives for nearly six months. Weston's last growth spurt, where he grew almost four inches, was over three months ago.

I see Raven's wheels turning in her head, wanting to ask Devon which girl he was talking about. Both Willow and Essie barely hit five foot. I give a small nod of my head to tell Raven to keep her comments to herself. She bites her glossed bottom lip and smirks. "Must be the food here is better than what Ren cooks for us," she says instead of the obvious Willow/Essie comment that was on the tip of her tongue.

"Rae," Kieren growls, "I've been cooking your meals since I could reach the stove. You're sixteen. I'd shut up if I were you, or you'll be cooking three squares a day for all of us."

Raven's soft, feminine snort is so like Isis's that I cough into my hand. "We're closer than ever to getting gourmet meals. I'm not worried," she taunts. "Clover may let us help her cook, but she won't allow us to cook all by ourselves."

Moving to sit on his side of the picnic table, Devon asks, "Are you married yet?" Kieren joins Devon, with Raven and Weston flanking me on the other side of the table. I push the box in Ren's direction, telling him to ready the cake.

"Next Monday morning at the Courthouse," I explain. I clear my throat a few times, voice thick with repressed emotions. "I wish you could be there with us, but we wanted everything settled for when you came home. No big surprises. No uproar. As stress-free as we could possibly make it."

"I understand," Devon says absentmindedly, staring down at his watch. "Listen, we only have seventeen minutes left, and I need some questions answered. I can't sleep another night without knowing. It's driving me insane, and they refuse to tell me a goddamned thing in here. No contact from the outside world. They wouldn't even let me see Tommy or Taryn."

"Okay, spit 'em out," I say to Devon, but my attention is diverted to Rae, who is cutting the cake up with the part of the spoon you hold onto.

Smiling, all proud of herself, "It's pointier than the scoop part."

"I cannot wait to hold a knife again. They cut our food up before we get it, saying there is no need for a knife… or a fork. They watch us eat, and we have to eat everything on the plate. I hope you'll leave the cake behind, 'cuz if I have to eat one more goddamned vegetable… no salt or pepper, no butter. Fish. Fish. Fish. Tofu. Tofu. Tofu sauced up to look like fish. I douse everything in balsamic just to cover the pasty, flavorless taste."

Leaning across the table, Devon grabs a hunk right off the cake. "I would kill for a cheeseburger, even one from the No-Name Diner. Tell me about everyone while I gorge myself for the next fifteen minutes." Shoving cake into his mouth, Devon talks as he chews with a blissed out expression plastered across his face. "Watch these assfucks make me take a laxative to cleanse and flush my system. Goddamned torturers."

If I were Devon, I'd want to know about my child. But Devon's not me. I start there anyway. "So Essie was going to move in with Beth, but Beth eloped in Las Vegas with Rory, leaving Essie homeless. So Essie's been living with Dave and Mary– *was*. Clover's been taking Essie to the baby doctor appointments, buying her books to read, and giving her advice. So don't worry about them. We're taking good care of them."

Cake halfway raised to his lips, Devon looks like he's going to be sick. "Is the baby okay? Ya know... I didn't harm it with my drugged-up sperm or anything?" Devon breathes so quietly we barely hear him, "I was afraid I ruined our child– birth defects or killed it. In here, they wouldn't even tell me if the baby still existed."

Trying to comfort and reassure him, "Essie's last appointment was a few days ago. The baby's heartbeat was strong. Everything is on schedule. The ultra-sound is in a few weeks. You'll be home if you want to go with Essie. If not, Clover will go."

Putting his cake down, Devon sighs out, "Thank God. I thought for sure I messed it up by being high. I didn't want to harm the baby for life with some fucked up birth defect. What did you mean by *was*?"

I just look at Ren, not knowing how to answer that. Swallowing hard, Ren begins, "You and I are the proud new owners of a house. The closing is a few days after you get back home. I couldn't do it without your signature. When we get back, everyone is moving into Dad's new house, leaving Essie and me stranded. So we'll be staying at the Spook House while we wait for the closing on our house. You included."

"Homeowner? Who's living in it?" Confused, Devon looks between me and his brothers and sister. We all look to our uneaten cake, waiting for Ren to answer.

"Ahhh... None of us made enough money to live on our own. I didn't want to live apart from you, not until you're ready. I wanted to be able to take care of your child until you were completely able to, but I wanted you to be with him or her. I didn't want to be without Willow, and I thought she would understand your cravings and be able to help Essie out."

"Spit it out, Ren." Devon snarls, the first true emotion erupting from him: rage. "You're putting me in a goddamned house with Willow, while you fuck her? Shoving what Essie and I did to Willow in her face? And not only are you doing that, you're making us legally bound together… and what makes you think this was a good fucking idea?"

Spoon splintering in his hand, Devon doesn't even realize a shard stabbed him, because he is so focused on glaring at Kieren.

"I stand by my decision, Devon," Ren says calmly. "Dad can't fix all of our shit anymore. He needs to create a life for himself and Clover, and take care of their kids."

Plucking the shard from his palm, Devon is calmer than ever. It's as if he is doing some kind of mental exercise to control himself. "I won't burden our father with my problems," Devon promises. "But this will be too much for Willow."

"Willow understands your cravings. I will physically stop you, if need be. Essie needs the support, and you need to bond with your child. It was for the best. Willow understood when I told her. As for your misguided love for Willow, you'll figure out that it's love, but not the marrying kind."

"We'll see about that," Devon utters slowly, as if he's saying something else entirely. "Our time is up. Heather is jogging over here to yank me into some kind of group therapy hell." Rising from his seat, Devon stares down at the cake, wishing he could take it with him.

"You're still coming tomorrow, right? Even though I threw a fit, I didn't mean it. I won't say I couldn't help it." Shuddering, Devon blurts out, "It just felt so fucking good to feel something for once."

"We'll be back," I promise. "And we'll bring you a cheeseburger."

"If we can sneak it passed the douchebags," Raven adds. Weston is silent, scared shitless at the '*exorcist*' Devon just pulled.

Looking over his shoulder at his counselor, Devon speaks. "Thank you for sharing my birthday with me. I've missed you all. I'm sorrier than you'll ever know, for everything I've put you through." When Heather's within shouting distance, "Ren, I will do whatever you want, because anything is better than this fucking prison. If I had to live in an actual prison, I'd have more freedom… I'll see you tomorrow." Devon walks away, meeting his counselor halfway.

"Well, that went better than expected," Weston sighs out, relieved to be away from Devon's angry storm cloud of misery.

"That's what Clover said this morning. Now you have me worried about what's actually happening back in Fairport."

CHAPTER FORTY-EIGHT

The Widow

Phone ringing. Hand reaching. "Mayor's office. Clover speaking. How may I assist you?" I answer the call on autopilot.

"Um… I… do I have the right number?" A young woman's voice comes through loud and clear, although a bit shaky. "Lucky Clover's? I need a baby shower cake?"

Lucky Clover's? What. The. Fuck?

Pinning the phone between my ear and shoulder, "Yeah. Yeah… that is me. Let's me grab my appointment book. When do you need the cake?"

"Oh! Great," the woman sounds relieved. "I need it for July eleventh. It's for a baby boy," she gushes.

"Well, let's set up a time to meet, where you can look at a few design options and we can discuss the payment and delivery. Here's my cell phone number," I rattle off the digits. "I'll take your number down and call you back in a few hours."

After relaying her phone number, "Thanks! You're a godsend."

"Clover?" Mayor Ross takes a seat on the edge of my desk, catching me in the act of writing in my personal appointment book, which suspiciously looks exactly like his, pilfered from the supply closet. "I'm going to have to let you go, darling."

Mortified. Shocked. Stunned. My face pales. "Why?" I whimper. Guilt thick in my voice, "Is it because I was taking down an appointment for myself?"

Smiling kindly, Mayor Ross just shakes his head no. Voice breaking, on the edge of tears, "Did… Malcolm didn't send any more artistic images to you to share with Mrs. Ross, did he?"

"We wish," Ross chuckles. "We miss those dirty shots. Plus, Malcolm's been a bit too busy to send us pornography." Ross shifts on the edge of my desk, amusement disappearing as he sobers. "Clover, I'm doing this for your own good, and the good of your family."

"It's fine. Everything is going according to plan." Suspicion slamming into me, "Hey, wait a minute. Malcolm didn't put you up to this, did he? It would be just like Malcolm to wait until he was in Arizona to spring this on me."

"Clover," Ross says as if I'm testing his patience. "I can't in good conscience have you working for me when you have several houses to pack up and move. You'll have five minors, three adult children, a pregnant cousin, and your parents to keep track of. Not to mention the strain the relationship with your oldest must be under. You're getting married in a few days. I want you to go home and get your shit straight."

"I have it all under control. Please don't do this," I beg, reaching out for my elderly boss's hand. "I need this job."

Smiling, Ross gives my hand a squeeze before placing it back on my blotter. "No, you don't. You have a job. You're going to be a wife and mother. If you need more money..." Ross taps my appointment book. "Do what you love. Your family and the community needs you more than I do."

"Don't do this," I plead, trying my damnedest not to cry. "I've worked for you for almost fourteen years."

"I was angry with Sam when you started working here in the first place," Ross grumbles. "The twins were still in diapers and you should have been at home with them." Face twisting with remorse, "Sorry if I sound sexist. I'm an eighty-year-old man. I'm older than old school– older than dirt. So don't worry yourself– we'll do fine without you. My great niece Ashley will be taking your position in the morning."

Head in my hands, I'm stunned beyond belief. I try to hide my sniffles, but they are obvious. A warm palm settles between my shoulders, trying to comfort me. I try to freeze my muscles from moving while I silently cry, but my boss... *ex*-boss... must feel the quiver.

"I have a parting gift, because I'd hate to have our tax collector after you, and then your husband would be forced to arrest your tiny behind. Here," Ross says as a file folder is slapped down in front of my face. "Open it."

"What?" I sit up, sniffling and wiping at my cheeks. "What is it?" I reach to open the folder.

"It's a business license. It just came through this morning, which solidified your termination." Standing from my desk, Mayor Ross smiles down at me. "Go home and get your houses packed and unpacked. I don't want to see you again until I'm marrying your ass down in the vestibule."

"Thanking you is the polite thing to do. I was raised to say thank you even when I was getting screwed over. So... thank you, boss," I say, sounding unsure if I'm thankful or not.

"Give it a few weeks. When you see how everything worked out as it should, how happy you are, and how less stressful your life is, you'll be kissing my ass in thanks." Winking, Mayor Ross goes back into his office for his afternoon nap.

Still sniffling, heart hammering out of control, I'm as heartbroken as I am exhilarated. Change and Clover Webster are not the best of friends. I flick back the cover on the file folder. With a sharp bark of laughter that echoes around the office, I take in the name of my new business.

"You wily old bastard, Ross!" I shout in the direction of his office door.

Lucky Clover's.

"I've never been more exhausted in my entire life." Rob groans as he falls backward to land on my mattress. "Five straight days of moving shit is not good on a lazy body. I think I actually have muscles in my belly, judging on how badly they ache."

All I can do is snort. "Ya sure you don't have a hernia? You better call Isis in here to cup ya while you cough."

Groaning, rolling around my mattress in misery, "Nah, it's an ab. Instead of a six-pack, I'm finally gaining a pair of shot glasses."

"Again, are you sure it's not your balls pushed up into your gut?" I tease. "I'm pretty sure in the battle of the refrigerator versus Robin Basil Prynne, it was fridge: 1 and Rob: 0."

Since my termination, I've gone balls to the wall on the move, determined to have everything ready for Malcolm's return. The last thing to pack up is my bedroom since the kids and I were sleeping in here while we moved everything else. My parents and Ozzy have been sleeping cozy in the new house for the past few nights, with Essie camped out at the Spook House.

With three households, it was difficult to determine what to keep and what to toss because of duplicates. I gave Isis and Auggie the total authority over Malcolm's belongings– I'd rather have their asses kicked versus mine. Auggie tackled the boys' rooms, boxing Devon and Ren's stuff up, and moving Weston's to the new house. Isis packed and moved Raven's things. Being the mother of two daughters, there was nothing in this world that would've had me touching Rae's things. I could hear a screaming raven-haired beauty ringing in my head, "*How dare you? I feel violated! You touched my stuff!*"

Mom and Dad picked a few things to ship to Florida for their room at Uncle Will and Aunt Ana's, and the rest of the stuff was scavenged. One of those PODS containers is sitting out front of the new house, loaded with anything the kids would need to start a household. With what was left, all of the kids organized a yard sale while Rob, Auggie, Isis, and I unpacked.

It's early Sunday afternoon, with Malcolm and the kids arriving from the airport at eight o'clock tonight. The yard sale is winding down. After which, Willow is taking anything worth anything back to Revamped for resale, with the rest getting shoved into the PODs container. Within a few hours, we will be completely finished.

Our past life is over, with another life newly beginning.

My parents' house has been empty for nearly a week, and Malcolm's for several days, with everything put in its place. Since we packed quickly, drove across town, walked the items to their new locations, and then put them away, we are nearly finished. The only thing left in the Webster household is the mattress Rob's body is holding down and my dresser.

I didn't think it was possible to feel so many choking emotions at one time: despair, guilt, sadness, mourning, mixed with happiness, excitement, anticipation, and a healthy dose of fright. What I'm not feeling, as I did the night before I married Sam, is regret. I regret nothing where it comes to Malcolm Mason.

Life changes, and you either change with it or get swallowed up in its miseries. I had to make a conscious choice to think positively versus negatively. I am leaving the home I built with my dead husband, feeling as if I'm leaving Sam behind with the house. I've been here for fifteen years, and grew up next door since my birth.

If my parents are able to leave the home they had built together for almost forty years, then I can leave without looking back as well.

It's difficult to balance the happy memories with the sadness of never experiencing any more with a specific person or in a certain location. Sam will never call my name or play with the kids. Sam is but a memory. I will never cook in this kitchen again, or sleep on this bed, or have Sunday dinner at the Prynne's dining room table. The memories will always bring life to Sam and to these homes. While we are leaving them behind, they will never be forgotten.

It's a new stage in our lives. We will make new memories that will either make us smile or cry in the future. To live in the past is to stunt the present and to silence the future. It is in our nature to always move forward while looking back.

"You're naughtier than I expected, sister." Rob's voice is muffled since he's lying on his newly acquired stomach muscles. The lazy bum isn't helping me pack up a thing. He will help me load it into Auggie's truck, but that's it.

"How so?" Not giving a shit about being orderly, I just dump the contents of my dresser drawers into several boxes. It's not like I don't have to refold it when I put it away later. To do it twice would be a major timewaster.

Propped up on his elbow, Rob looks at me. "Sleeping in your marital bed the night before your wedding. I thought there were rules against that. No seeing the bride before the wedding or some superstitious shit like that. Or is it no sleeping together before the wedding?"

"I haven't seen Malcolm in a week. If you honestly think either one of us is going to buy into superstitions, you've lost your goddamned mind." Laughing, I toss the last of my belongings into a box. "With that saying, we won't sleep in our new bed until our wedding night. I set a tent up in the backyard for tonight."

Grinning, "See? Naughty, naughty Clover. Outdoor adventures without a dozen ears listening to your happy reunion."

"Oh, shit," I hiss, realization dawning. "Our house will be packed to the rafters when we're consummating." Shuddering in revolution, "I can't do that."

"Consider this a gift from the residents of the Spook House." Rob crawls off the mattress, groaning exaggeratedly. "We're having several family game nights in a row, truckloads of pizza, and sleepovers. Leaving just you and Malcolm in that big, new house for a few days to explore your marital bliss."

"Seriously?" I shriek, excited. "I've missed Malcolm like crazy. The thought of not having to share him with a dozen people is…" I murmur dreamily, "Orgasmic."

"Ugh, don't make me gag," Rob groans out, but he's smirking. "Hey, what's that taped on the back of your drawer?" Pulling the drawer closer to him, Rob tugs an envelope free. Face paling, Rob looks like he's about to pass out. "You might want to sit down for this, Clover."

Voice wavering, I rapidly ask. "What? Why? What is it?"

Sounding grave, "Ghosts of the past, coming to haunt you." Rob presses an envelope into my palm.

Dropping it like I've been burned, I leap as far away from the haunting envelope as possible, back hitting the wall with a loud thump. "I can't," my voice breaks, dropping down into the pits of Hell. "You read it first. If there is anything I didn't already know, then you can tell me."

Picking it up, holding it gingerly between his fingertips, Rob turns emotional. "Are you sure, Clover? This is important."

"Right now, it's not!" I scream, voice cracking from the force. "Right now, it's not even on my radar. How dare Sam do this to me? I'm moving forward, Goddamnit! To read this is moving backward. So unless there is something in there I don't already know, it's not important tonight. I'll read it when I'm ready, or I will give it to our children. But by God, I'm not fucking reading a letter from my dead husband on the eve of my marriage to another man!"

I turn around, refusing to look at Rob as he holds a letter from Sam to me. I pack up the rest of my things in silence. Silence until Rob tears into the envelope. Shivering, I shove my clothing into a box, taking my time. Minutes feel like hours as Rob reads the note.

Rob startles me when he comes to stand at my side. Smashing the letter to my chest, he demands, "Read it, now." Stunned, I just stand there with the note clasped to my chest. Rob picks up my box, and then leaves the room.

With shaking fingers, I smooth out the single-page letter. Before Sam's death, we divided his things. Sam's way of passing them out to the people he wished to have them. I often wondered if he did this because he knew a constant reminder of him within our home would intensify the loss I felt. I haven't seen Sam's precise yet slightly slanted handwriting in almost six years.

Clover,

I'm writing this the night I finally told you my prognosis. I don't have the nerve to give you this letter, so I hope you find it well after my death. Knowing your anal cleaning habits, I suspect it will be sooner rather than later.

I've known for a few weeks, getting my affairs in order, spending time with the kids while I was still strong enough to leave positive memories. You've commented several times in the past few weeks, "Why are you being kind to me?" and "Why are you paying attention to me?" Now you know.

I want Willow to forever remember our last Revolutionary Road concert. Seth and Violet will forever cherish our spur-of-the-moment drive to the ocean. Last night, while I was making love to you, and you were open with me, seeing me clearly instead of the monster I've created, I meant every single word I spoke.

I write this with a happy heart. This will be the oddest confession ever. I heard your breakdown in the lawn. Weak, unable to help you, I called your brother to support you. While worried, it was the ultimate of tests– a test of your love and devotion. I've doubted in the past, just as you've doubted me. Your pain proved your love for me more than any words could ever express. In the end of my life, it's a comfort to know our love is strong enough to wreck the strongest person I know.

I'm selfish, insensitive, insecure, and a bold-faced liar. I have treated you poorly because I felt safe knowing you would never leave me. I've lashed out and tore you down because I felt beneath you. In the end of our lives, we all reevaluate our choices and the reasons behind them. I have been a poor excuse as a man, and an even worse husband. Looking back, I regret that I always acted out of fear. Not afraid in the face of death, I wonder what our life together would have been like if I treated you differently– treated us differently.

We have three months left together at the most, every day worse for both of us than the day before. I wish I was brave enough to end the pain, and I don't mean my own. I don't want you, or our children, or my mother, watching me deteriorate. But I know none of you would ever forgive me if I left you without a proper goodbye. You know me better than anyone, not that you will ever admit, so you know I will be unable to give this goodbye face-to-face.

The thought of seeing no emotion as I speak from the heart, or worse, utter devastation written across your face, would kill me more surely than cancer.

Don't remember me as I am– the shrunken husk consumed by cancer. Don't remember me as I was– the malicious, patronizing piece of shit who tried to break you. Remember me as the young, horny man you first met: enchanted, magnetized, hopelessly lost in you.

In my final days, I hope you see that Sam again. Because in my final hours, I will remember you as you were, as you still are– the tiny sprite of a girl with the mouth of a sailor and the responsive body of a courtesan. The girl I've loved since I set eyes upon her.

In my goodbye, I should apologize. I should tell you how every angry word I've ever said to you was directed at myself. I should tell you how I've never blamed you about Willow. I said I'd never forgive you, but that was because there was never anything to forgive. I should tell you how much I love you, and how much it hurts to know I'll be leaving you and our children behind. I should tell you on the list of importance you have always come first, whether I showed this through action or not. But instead of goodbye, I will simply tell you what I want for you.

I want you to be happy. It's as simple as that. I want you to be happy, Clover.

Don't forget me (I'm narcissistic enough to haunt you)
Your asshole of a husband, but nonetheless loving,
-Sam.

CHAPTER FORTY-NINE

The Widower

Mrs. Mason: *Where– oh, where, are you?*

Clover's Mister: *The kids changed your name in my cellphone to Mrs. Mason. I think they're trying to tell me something, don't you? Lmfao! We're about two minutes from Fairport's border. Where are you?*

Mrs. Mason: *You better not be texting and driving, Chief Mason!!! Well, my tricky kids changed your name in my cellphone, too. You're now Clover's Mister. <3 I have a surprise for you, so come by the new house.*

Clover's Mister: *No worries. Fairport's Chief of Police isn't committing a text&drive. Ren's driving because he's more skilled at eating fast food with one hand. I didn't want to be wearing my Quarter Pounder when I saw you. We've been eating cheeseburgers in honor of Devon's newest cravings. The boy's gonna get fat, let me tell you. See you in thirty seconds.*

"Drive to the new house, I guess. Clover says she has a surprise for us," I tell Ren where to navigate. I don't miss the upturn of his lips. "What's up? You know something, don't you? You were only off the phone with Willow when we were visiting Devon."

"See for yourself," Ren says as he pulls up to the curb in front of our new house.

The first thing I notice is how our big pink monstrosity is lit up like Christmas. The second thing I notice is how there is a PODS container parked in front of us. The next thing I notice is how half the town is scattered between the Spook House and our new home. More than fifty people are milling around.

I'm out of my SUV in a heartbeat, eye searching the crowd for my woman. "Ugh," is wrenched from my chest from the force of a tiny body slamming into mine. I'd check to see who it is, but only one person I know smells like butter and sugar. My arms automatically yank Clover closer to my chest.

"Surprise!" Clover whisper-shouts in my ear. "I didn't want this," she grumbles. "I wanted some fucking privacy… you can blame everyone but me."

"Gimme a kiss," I demand, not giving a shit about all the people invading our house like a small army. With Clover on her tippy-toes and me bending down, our kiss is the sweetest thing I've known after the absence of a week. I was spoiled after weeks on end of endless affection. The stress and worry over seeing Devon just melts away on the supple lips of my bride.

Breaking her lips from mine on a sigh, Clover wraps her arms around my neck and pulls herself up my body until her legs are wrapped around my waist. Like a cuddly koala bear, Clover squeezes me tightly, as if I'm her favorite person in the whole wide world.

My smile couldn't get any bigger. Is this the Clover I started courting? No. She was Mrs. Webster back then. This free creature is a mix of Clover Prynne and Mrs. Mason.

"I've missed you so fucking much," Clover whispers fiercely with conviction. "Next time you have to go somewhere, or I have to go somewhere, I want us to go together. I think this time apart was perfect, though."

Curious as to how this insane ache was somehow perfect, "Oh, yeah? Why's that?"

"Missing you, longing to talk to you, to see your face, to be in your arms… it was the perfect way for me to commit to you. You gave me a taste, and then you went away so I'd know what I'd be missing without you in my life. It was horrible, and very enlightening."

"Exactly," is all I can say in response.

Clover slides down my body, driving me insane with want. I imagine taking her on our front lawn and not giving a shit who witnesses it, which is exactly what my son is currently doing.

"Get a room, dumbass." I kick Ren in the ass for pressing Willow up against my SUV, practically mounting her. The idiots are lip-locked in front of their parents, all of their relatives, and the whole entire town.

Pulling away with kiss-swollen lips and mussed up hair, "You're right, Dad. I'm suddenly very tired." Ren mock-yawns into his palm dramatically. "Good to be home, Mom. Love what you've done with the place. Well, I've had a very long trip. I better go to bed now." Ren tugs Willow toward the Spook House to '*not*' sleep in their bed.

"You're on Arizona time, dumbass," I remind him. It took us three days to acclimate, but now we're three hours off again. I think that's the meaning of jetlag. "And it's barely eight o'clock, which makes it only five o'clock for us!"

Laughing, Ren says over his shoulder, "I know. We need a few hours to… chat… before bed." Gesturing around the block, "I bet you wish these people weren't here so you could go… chat, too!"

"Little bastard," I snarl, suddenly feeling jealous that Ren can just walk off and do whatever he wants. Turning back to Clover, "Why are all of these people here, anyway?"

After the excitement of our arrival, I finally notice how exhausted Clover looks with dark purple bags under her eyes, and she appears to have been crying earlier. Not waiting for Clover to answer, I pull her back to me, tucking her shoulders underneath my arm.

"Who do we beat up for this?" I ask lightheartedly. "We can tag-team 'em."

Drawing in a deep draw of air, Clover releases it in a rush of words. "Actually, I have no idea. It was like a flash mob. I was sitting on the front porch waiting for you to come home, and then the street was filled with all the people we know. It was an insane flood."

"Wow, that would have driven Rae insane." Speaking of which, I gaze around for my introvert daughter. I find her hiding out near the side of the house, behind the shelter of Weston's back as he talks to Seth, Violet, and Langdon. When Oliver makes his way toward their group, Rae reappears from behind her brother's back. I groan in disgust.

Fucking teenage hormones.

"So they brought food and drinks and music, and then more people started showing up. This excuse to party on a Sunday night is for our combined engagement, bachelor, and bachelorette party mixed with our wedding reception. But no matter how many times I say we aren't married yet, they don't listen."

"Let me guess, you asked everyone you spoke to who planned this and they didn't know?"

"Damn straight," Clover bites out, angry and tired. "I tried so hard, I really did. I used the time Mayor Ross gave me," she twists out as if '*gave*' isn't the word she wanted to use, "To get everything finished. I just put the last of our things away, everything is in its place. So I was on the porch waiting for you to come home." Gesturing around our yard, "And they hit like a plague of locusts!"

Pulling Clover away from me, I squeak out in shock, "The house is done? Everything is done? You mean no more going from one house to the next, no more sneaking in bedrooms and getting chewed out by Seth, done?"

Looking extremely proud, albeit exhausted, "exactly," she mocks the word I used earlier. "But I didn't want us sleeping in our new bed– and it is new. I didn't want our marital bed to be one either of us used with someone else or one we slept on during mourning. I had Seth set up our tent in the backyard for tonight, so our first night in our bedroom will be on our wedding night."

Touched, I sigh, "Oh, Clover… and now the lawn is packed with assholes." My eyes rove the people, wishing I could fry them with my glare where they stand. "They won't miss us, you know? I think they are here to spend time together. We could sneak off to our tent?"

Biting her lip, eyes gazing around, "We could," she agrees. "We could say… tell the kids where we're going, and my parents so they will watch the kids, and then go… *chat*."

"I love your naughty mind, woman," I purr in a deep tone. "Let's go do just that."

… Two hours later, after being waylaid by every member of the community and putting our family to bed, the lawn is finally empty. I unzip the tent, allowing a very exhausted, and softly groaning in pain, Clover to go in ahead of me.

Smirking at the primitive setup, "Prynne camping? I remember how Rob always teased Isis and Auggie for being too prissy when it came to camping out." The tent is so small that I bet my feet will stick out the door once I'm inside. There will be no zipping up the door once I manage to crawl in there

"Not quite Prynne camping." Clover lands belly first on the air mattress with a loud groan. "After the hard week I've had, I couldn't do without the air mattress. Mom and Dad taught us that all we needed was a sleeping bag. We didn't even own a tent."

"Must have been all those walks on Washington," I muse.

"We're camping in class tonight: a tent, an air mattress, and a battery-operated lantern. My parents will be so disappointed in us."

"Eh, those loons are upstairs, sleeping on a king-sized mattress, with Egyptian cotton sheets that were probably made in a sweat shop," I grumble as I crawl in to the tent, trying to bend my big body to fit inside. "They can bite me with their hypocritical bullshit."

After some awkward yet comedic maneuvering, we're lying on our sides, with the little spoon facing the big spoon, so I can rub Clover's back while holding her. No '*chatting*' tonight, for sure. The tent is too small and Clover is way too exhausted.

"How's Devon, really?" Clover murmurs softly as we get reacquainted with one another. Our hands can't seem to find enough contact with each other's flesh. Gripping, squeezing, massaging one another, I'm in pure bliss. I feel like a bird settling its feathers after a long flight, so happy to finally be in its nest.

Sighing, I have no idea how to put it into words. "Devon's better than he was health-wise, but I fear he's worse off mentally. He's been diagnosed with bipolar disorder and PTSD. We located a good psychiatrist a few towns over, who Devon will meet with once a week, and webchat with in case of emergencies. We also found the drug and alcohol counselor who runs the AA/NA program at the Presbyterian Church to be Devon's sponsor. We're doing all we can do, and Devon is doing all he can do… so I guess that's the best we can do."

"And that is more than anyone could hope for," Clover sees the positive side even though I want to stew in the negative.

"You are my perfect counterbalance, Mrs. Mason," I say with a smile. "How'd it really go with Willow? Is she what had you upset enough to cry earlier?"

"You noticed?" Clover sounds surprised. "No, that wasn't about Willow. She's… she's acting like her mother." Clover releases a self-deprecating laugh that turns into a quiet sob. "It will take a while before Willow comes to terms with the truth. Nothing has changed between her and the twins because she saw them as her siblings anyway. My parents never parented Willow, either. They assumed the grandparent role since Willow's birth. Same with Rob. He was always older, not brotherly, more uncleish anyway. But with me… I doubt we will ever get to a place where we are mother and daughter."

"Are you okay with that, Clover?" I squeeze her tightly, wanting to remove her pain. "I can't imagine how difficult that is for you."

Clover finally speaks after a few moments of tear-filled silence. "It's not too bad. Willow and I came to an understanding. Whether she ever sees me as her mom won't matter, as long as we see each other as women. Woman-to-woman, where we respect, love, and trust one another. If we can reach that, I won't give a fuck if she calls me Mom or not."

"Willow's just stubborn like her mom. Give it some time, and she'll be calling you Mom so much your ears will bleed," I tease, praying my words will come true. "So why were you crying?"

Clover pulls away from me, reaching for something. The small tent is illuminated when she flicks on the lantern. Sniffling, her voice sounds hollow, "Rob found this. I… nothing will ever get me to talk about it. So if you'd like to know why I was crying, I'd prefer it if you'd just read it."

"What is it?" I ask too soon, because before the words are out of my mouth I recognize the handwriting on the envelope. "Oh, Clover," I cry out, not wanting to read something so personal.

Clover turns her back to me, unable to watch me read the note from her dead husband. I can't imagine how confused and devastated she must be feeling right this second. I try to pretend Camille wrote to me, and I found it the day before I was to marry Clover. I can't even reason out how that would make me feel.

So choked up I can barely speak, I finish the letter with a heavy heart. Not only do I feel agony for Clover, I also fear she sees *us* in a different light. I need to put my thoughts into words, but I just can't.

Somehow sensing my emotional annihilation, Clover reaches back for my hand, pulling me to spoon her on the air mattress. She flicks the lantern off, acting as this is just an ordinary night of camping in the backyard.

"Malcolm, I'd love to say this changes nothing," Clover begins, forcing my heart to beat into hyper-drive. "I will always love Sam, and I know you understand that. Sam and Camille were our first loves, the ones who we made our children with. But loving Sam was difficult, like swimming upstream against the current. It was a test of my endurance."

Still unable to speak, I just squeeze Clover to my chest tightly, refusing to let her go, no matter if she asks me to or not. I bury my face into the side of Clover's neck, wanting to ask what this letter changed for her, but too scared to find out.

"Loving you is so easy. It's as easy as breathing. I barely survived Sam's death. It's an open wound– the pain is raw and unrelenting. People in my life may take the ache away, but it's ever-present. The thing is, I survived the loss of Sam. But I can't survive without breathing."

CHAPTER FIFTY

The Widow

"Wow, you sure do know how to throw a wedding," Violet mutters, sounding disappointed. "Wearing a sundress while standing in the center of your old job while your ex-boss hitches ya. Yay," she mock-cheers lamely.

Rolling my eyes, "Seeing as I'm a thirty-five-year-old mother of seven and a foster kid, embarking on her second marriage, I didn't think we should spend your college fund and/or future wedding fund on a dress I'd wear once, a shitty venue, and catered food I could cook better. What do you think, daughter?"

Violet turns a brilliant shade of red for the burn her mother threw down. Giggles and snickers erupt from all the females who wouldn't give me any breathing room: Willow, Raven, Essie, Mom, Ginny, Isis, and Opal.

"You're right," Violet suddenly agrees. "You should save your pennies for my wedding."

What about MEs? erupt from Willow and Raven's throats.

"There is a limited amount of money being set aside for each kid," I reluctantly admit. "We're taking a half of the sales from our houses to pay off most of the mortgage on the new house, and the rest will be divided by seven."

Hardly ever showing excitement, Rae lights up like Christmas. "We can do whatever we want with it? Can we? Can we? Can we?" I've learned from our interactions over the past few months, an excited Raven Mason says everything in threes.

"Within reason," I stress. "College tuition. A down payment on a house. Waste it on a wedding dress. Buy a car." Glancing at Essie, "Pay for your illegitimate kids. If by twenty-one you don't use it, we'll hand it over to you. Until then, it's sitting in an interest-bearing account."

"I think your dress is beautiful," Ginny pipes in, or else we would be discussing financials until the kids found out the bank account numbers. Teenagers are money-grubbing leeches.

Glowering "You would," Isis grumbles, sounding jealous. "Since you got to pick it out." Folding her arms across her chest, Isis glares at Ginny. "It's my turn to be the sister-in-law. I should have gotten to be the maid of honor." Ginny just ignores Isis, smiling sweetly while looking at my lavender sundress with appreciation.

"You can be my maid of honor," Raven says to appease her aunt.

"Bullshit," Isis snarls. Pointing at the girls, "You're sisters now. Violet will be yours and you'll be Violet's." Pointing at Willow, "That idiot will forgive Essie and stand up with her. You mark my words."

"Best friends stand up with their best friends," Opal becomes the voice of reason. "So, you can stand up with me."

Still pouting, but no longer mad, "You'll never get married, and neither will I."

Blushing, Opal murmurs, "Ya never know."

A sharp knock on the door proceeds its opening, followed by Rob's giant grin shining at us. "It's time. That is if the hen-party has concluded." Smile dimming, "You're not still pissed over not being Clover's witness, are you? I told you, with all those girls, it would have been a bloodbath."

"I suppose you're right," Isis relents, moving to leave the room. "Just as it wouldn't have been fair for Mal to choose between the boys."

"I get how you're feeling, though." Rob's high-wattage smile twists into a grimace. "Fucking Auggie always gets preferential treatment. As their siblings, you should have stood up with Malcolm with me beside Clover."

Both Rob and Isis leave the room, bickering over the injustice of being made to watch instead of participate. "I'll never get to say '*forever a bridesmaid but never a bride.*' Because I'll never be a bridesmaid or a bride."

"Isis is fucking batshit cray-cray," Violet spits out belligerently, like a drunk at last call. "This isn't a real wedding with an aisle to walk down and bridesmaid dresses. All they're doing is signing the license. No offense," Violet tacks on after the fact for insulting Isis to her family's faces. But then she insults Isis more, "I've heard of bridezilla, but I don't know what you call that woman."

Snorting, Willow says, "Jealous. Let's go wiggle into a spot out in the crowd. Weston and Ren said they'd shove people around to make room. But I thought it would be more fun if you and I made our own space," Willow directs at Violet. A violent light fills both of my daughters' eyes as they skip out of the room to go brawl with Fairport's residents.

After a kiss from my mom, a hug from Essie, and a shoulder squeeze from Opal, everyone files out until it's just my best friend and me. "You sure you're ready for this? Last time, I had to stand by you to keep you from running, literally. Something tells me that's not the case this time."

"I'm more than ready," I admit without hesitation. "I was ready last month. Not being married to Malcolm is what feels odd."

"Isis is wrong," Ginny murmurs while drawing me into a hug. "I deserve to be the one to stand up with you. There is a symmetry to me being the only maid of honor at all three weddings. I was Camille's maid of honor when she married Malcolm. I was yours when you married Sam. Now, I am standing up with you as you marry Malcolm. It seems fitting."

Sniffling, getting choked up, "I never even thought of anyone else. It just wouldn't feel right to stand beside anyone else."

"None of that," Ginny chastises me while dabbing underneath my eyes with a tissue. "Let's go get you hitched."

The Courthouse's large, stately vestibule is packed with the residents of Fairport. It's wall-to-wall people. The only reason I know where to go is after fourteen years of walking in here five days a week, I could do it in the dark. Malcolm and Auggie's heads are visible above the crowd, and I eagerly head in their direction.

My wedding to Sam wasn't a huge affair, but I did have a wedding with all the fixings. I was too frightened, too young, and too withdrawn to enjoy a moment of it. It felt as if people were staring at me, as if they were only there out of obligation. It felt as if they ate our food, enjoyed our drink, and danced as a way to party. It had absolutely nothing to do with the union between Sam and myself, and everything to do with their entertainment.

Violet made fun of this simple wedding ceremony, but it's perfect. I'm a conservative girl, no matter what my parents bred into me. To spend thousands of dollars on a few hours is a waste, when I'd rather give it to my children or use it for my future. I'm going to be selfish for Malcolm and myself for once, and make this all about us, as it should be.

Mayor Ross means something to me. I've known Ross for as long as I can remember, and I worked for him for nearly fourteen years. Mayor and Mrs. Ross have been married for fifty-seven years, so I look at Ross officiating as an omen of good luck.

Fairport's Courthouse is not a sunny, sandy beach or a large institution of religion, but it holds a deep affection for both Malcolm and myself. Chief Malcolm Mason holds a position in this town, and they hold him in high regard.

While not in an exotic locale, with thousands of dollars spent on clothing, decorations, and food and drink, my free wedding is perfect because there are no incentives for our guests to attend.

This moment is one hundred percent about our union.

Malcolm and I spot each other at the same time, sharing similar expressions of relief. Just one look at Malcolm Mason, and I know he's where I was meant to be. Malcolm is my future, and I can't wait to spend every day of the rest of my life at this man's side.

I smile over the differences a lifetime can make. As a mature woman, I am in the now. I am not bogged down by fear, or regret, or insecurity. I am wise enough to know my own mind, to judge people on their actions, not their words, and to place trust in those who've earned it.

On a Monday morning in mid-June, surrounded by half of the townspeople and all of our family minus Devon, Mayor Ross pronounces me Mrs. Malcolm Mason, making me the luckiest Clover in all the world.

CHAPTER FIFTY-ONE

The Widower

"Mrs. Mason!" I shout as I charge into the backdoor, mind reeling in utter disbelief over what I found behind my garage. "What is my profession?"

Smiling privately to herself, my wife is at the marble-topped center island, rolling out pie crusts. "Gee, I don't know. Remind me again." Tiny face alight with amusement, her snicker turns to snorts. Like mother, like daughter– their reactions.

Pointing at my chest, "I'm a cop. I'm known as Chief Mason around these parts."

"Tell me something I don't already know," Clover murmurs. She leans over to toss something into the trash. "Motherfuck!" she shouts. "Dad! Dad! Dad!" Clover turns into Raven.

"What?" Dave yells from the living room, not bothering to get off the sofa, where he is entertaining Peggy and the Dobsons.

"Goddamn it, old man. I'm gonna put your ass in a home the next time you take out the trash and forget to put a bag in. This is the third time this week that I'll have to scrub out the can after I dumped egg yolks in it."

"Sorry," comes Dave's muffled reply, not sounding sorry at all.

"If you touch another trash can in this house," Clover warns. "Cut-rate elderly housing. Got it?"

"Clover?" Peggy's voice flows in from the living room, causing my wife to growl. The sound is more sexy than scary, and I almost forget what pissed me off in the first place. "Respect your elders."

Dave's laughter echoes around the house. Clover snarls while replacing the garbage bag. Plotting evil, "I'm changing all the coffee in this house to decaf, see how Dad likes that. He'll be too tired, napping all the time, to touch my garbage cans."

"Devon comes home in two days," I remind Clover.

"Yeah," she grunts out, washing her hands. "I think we all have the Jeopardy theme song playing in our heads at this point. We all know the exact minute Devon's flight lands."

Sighing heavily, trying not to laugh because it's so fucking outrageous. "So, Devon can't be around drugs and alcohol."

Clover gives me attitude, seriously begging for a thorough fucking. "No shit? Gee, I hadn't realized that. Huh?" she grunts out, looking lost and confused. For a split-second, I want to bend Clover over the kitchen island and fuck the bitch attitude right out of her, but I have more pressing issues.

"So, as the GODDAMNED CHIEF OF POLICE IN THE TOWN OF FAIRPORT, WHY ARE THERE COCKSUCKING FIVE FOOT TALL MARIJUANA PLANTS GROWING BEHIND MY GARAGE?" I bellow like an insane person.

"M-O-T-H-E-R!!!" Clover screams louder than I did.

I chase after my furious wife, as she hunts down her batshit crazy, drug grower mother. Rooms blur by as I follow my wife: Living room, with a hysterically laughing Dave, Peggy, and Mr. and Mrs. Dobson. Upstairs. The bathrooms. We catch Raven bleaching her mustache, and receive a death-glare and a door slam. Violet is in the attic, playing video games when she swears she hates them, while Ozzy is looking at a motorcycle magazine. Back through the house to the backdoor, we go, so we can look at Mary's prolific garden.

On the back screened-in porch, "What the–" I grunt out when I run into Clover's back.

"Don't ever make me defend you again," Seth is standing over Weston with his fists clenched, and my son is ass-planted on the ground with a fat lip. "You fucking idiot, what did you think you were doing?"

Scrambling to his feet, Weston towers over Seth. "It's none of your business what I do."

"I'm the big brother, how am I supposed to protect you from this shit? Kissing Sage at the park? Are you insane? Everyone saw you. You being gay will be all over school in the fall."

Backing up, trying to back *me* up, Clover turns around and breathes so quietly I have to read her lips, "We should go."

"No fucking way," I breathe back. "How else are we going to learn this shit, and then ground them?"

Nodding in agreement, Clover turns around to watch the boys. She leans into me, seeking comfort. More than happy to comply, I pull my wife's back to my chest and watch our boys make fools of themselves.

"I kissed Sage on the *cheek*," West stresses. "It's not like I was sucking his dick in the courtyard. Protect me? Puhleeeese… I can protect myself."

Frustrated, Seth is seething. Pointing at himself, and then Weston, "I'm the big brother. It's my job to protect *you* from the assholes."

"I get that. I do." Weston acquires one of my bad habits: the frustrated, exhausted, hair yank. "I'm a big guy– I can protect myself. I'm the biggest guy in the entire school, teachers included. Hell, I've got a few inches on Coach Dixon."

"Yeah, well, what are you gonna do when more than one gay basher gangs up on you? I don't want to get my ass kicked while trying to protect your idiot ass."

Sounding reasonable, Weston tries to calm Seth down. The boys have never looked *and* acted more like their fathers, with Seth a young version of Sam, and Weston a lighter version of me.

"Just don't get into a fight you can't win. That's motherfucking idiotic. They aren't going to do shit to me over this. The teachers, my coach, and the rest of the team will back my ass up. I'm their only chance at State. I'm the best player they've had since Ren– better even. I'm a freshman starting on the varsity team. They won't want to harm their golden boy. As for the rest of the other fucks, with Mom's cooking, I'm closing in on a hundred and ninety pounds. They won't dare touch my ass."

"That's not the point!" Seth shouts, stomping his foot. "Kissing Sage on the cheek, a kid who is out of the closet, it's like coming out of the closet yourself."

"Closet?" Weston scoffs. "That's not me, in or out of the fucking thing. I don't give a shit what people think."

"Well, maybe you should," Seth sounds confused.

"Why? Why should I?" Weston demands. "I don't feel the need to explain myself. I'm not making a big deal out of it. I'm just being myself. You don't go around screaming at the top of your lungs how you want girls, so why should I have to tell every single person I meet that I'm gay? People will figure it out anyway when I never have a girlfriend."

"No, you'll just parade Sage around by his dick," Seth snarls.

"Idiot," he scoffs. "I was letting Sage down easy with a kiss to the cheek. I just told him I wasn't interested. Just because I like guys doesn't mean I want every guy who might be gay. You've had girls ask you out– it didn't mean you had to say yes."

"You don't get it. It doesn't matter why you kissed Sage. It's that you *kissed* him. Your teammates won't want to be in the locker room with you."

"I. Don't. Care." Weston repeats slowly. "If they have a problem with *my* sexuality, it's *their* problem, not mine. If they want to win, they will just have to freak the fuck out as I take a shower after practice. You like girls, doesn't mean you want to fuck very single one of them because they have a pussy. Same goes with a gay dude. I'm not jonesing for them just because they have a dick."

"I don't know why you'd put yourself through this shit," Seth bites out, sounding frustrated.

"I'm not gonna hide who I am, Seth. Deal with it. Are you embarrassed to be around me?" The question visibly hurts my son to ask. "You've known since we became friends. You asked me if I was related to Isis. I said yes. I asked you if you were related to Rob. You said yes. I told you Rob helped me deal with my shit, and you seemed fine with it."

Calming down, getting emotional, Seth sighs out, "I was fine with it. I still am. I just don't want to see you get hurt. Kissing Sage was stupid."

"Sage isn't the first guy I've kissed." Weston puffs up like a peacock. "I made out with Maddox."

"Maddox is a fucking senior!" Seth blows up.

Clover and I freeze, hearing what will get Weston grounded for a good long time, after a lecture on breaking the law, and then Maddox is gonna have a chat with Chief Mason on how statutory rape doesn't care if you're gay. Eighteen and fourteen is illegal in every state in the union.

Shocked, so I missed how Weston replied, Seth is now shouting at Weston. "Just 'cuz you can't get pregnant doesn't mean you can turn into a slut!"

"Nah, I ain't screwing anybody. I didn't want Maddox, either. He's hot and all, but not my type."

Sputtering, "Dude, you're gay, what other way is there to swing?"

Weston snorts, amused. "First of all, there are three gay guys at FAHS. Maddox and Sage, and me, who isn't interested in Sage or Maddox. Slut? I'll be spending my time in the bathroom doing the handy-jay action because I'm not that desperate. I'm my father's son. Gay or not, I won't do casual."

"God, I'm so fucking happy I'm straight, it ain't even funny." Seth releases a manic laugh. "I'm so glad I don't have your problems. Only two dudes to pick from, and you don't like either of 'em. Tragic."

Grinning, Weston replies. "Eventually I'll go to college and find someone who fits me." Doing the hair yank maneuver again, "I don't know. I want someone who is built like me. But I want to be the *man* in the relationship, equal with another man. No stereotypes, no rainbow waving, I just want to live a normal life without having to explain myself or advocate tolerance. I won't be used as an example, gay or straight. I'm Weston Mason, and I won't explain myself to anyone for any reason."

"I...I... what?"

"You love big girls, Seth. Your tongue falls out of your mouth for a big girl. I don't see anyone making fun of you over it, or you having to explain it."

Blushing beet red, Seth looks stunned that anyone figured that out. The kid has been a chubby chaser since he could walk. It amused Sam to no end. "Yeah, they do– I get made fun of all the time. But that's not why I was tongue-tied. What the fuck is a twink?"

Clover turns her face against my chest, muffling her fit of laughter. I do my damnedest not to join her. We're hidden inside the screened-in porch, watching our sons like our teenagers watch reality TV. Violet and Raven are missing out on all the action. Lots of juicy stuff. Lots of reasons to ground their asses.

"Twink? You want to know what a twink is, Seth?" West bites his bottom lip, trying to stop himself from laughing for the same reason we are.

"Yeah," Seth sounds so confused it makes it funnier. Clover's palm presses against her mouth, stifling her snickers.

"If you were gay... you." Weston laughs outright, tipping his head back and releasing a sound from deep within his chest. "A small, girly looking gay guy. I'd keep my adorable ass away from Maddox, if I were you, Seth."

"Not cool, cocksucker," Seth snarls, charging directly for us. Clover and I press ourselves against the porch wall. Seth is so angry he doesn't even see us as he rushes by, going into the house.

Mary Prynne and her gardening is long forgotten by the time Weston reaches the porch. I grab the front of Weston's shirt, stopping him dead in his tracks. "This Maddox kid. I need his full name, address, telephone number, and age… and I want it now," I growl. "If Maddox is anywhere near eighteen, he won't be meeting dear ol' dad. Chief Mason will be paying Maddox a visit."

CHAPTER FIFTY-TWO

The Widow

Making a day of it, Violet, Rae, Essie, and I have appointments at the local clinic, followed by a mani-pedi. It's a ritual I started with Willow and Violet when I first took them to get their birth control shots. Who enjoys going to the doctor? So I made it more of a bonding experience and threw in a reward to follow.

"God, I thought morning sickness sucked." Essie groans, putting her hand out for Violet to pull her up from the sofa. "I'm not very big. I just feel so bloated, like my skin is gonna burst. It makes bending impossible."

"That right there," Rae grumbles, pointing at Essie's swollen midsection, "is the best birth control on the planet."

"I can't believe Dad is letting you get on the shot," Violet says, sounding amazed. "Now, I can't tease you about how great it was not to have to worry about starting my period in gym class and staining my white shorts."

"Ahahahaa…" Essie draws out sarcastically. "Remind me never to share in girl talk with you, ya little narc. Most mortifying moment of my life. I was only twelve."

"I told Daddy that it wasn't about sex," Rae answers Violet. "Seeing as how you'll be a fifty-year-old virgin with a herd of cats."

"Bitch," Violet blurts out, but she's smirking. "You so did not say that to him."

Rae's grinning back, when she's usually reluctant to smile. "Nah, I told him the truth. I didn't bleach my moustache for the last two weeks, and then I cried, telling Daddy it was his horrible genetics that were making me a sideshow freak. I bartered for birth control, hoping for laser treatments."

Violet finishes Rae's sentences as if Rae is her twin. "But Dad's more worried about your new fascination with Ozzy, so that was a no-go. F-A-I-L!"

"I know, right? Sucks. I really wanted those laser treatments," Rae grumbles. She's the first teenage girl who didn't want birth control over all else. "If it gets bad enough, I'll trade in my '*whatever fund*' for them."

"Clover," Essie gains my attention, and then takes the words right out of my mouth. "I'm only twenty-one, but when in the fuck did this shit change? Five, six years ago, this was not on my mind."

"Maybe Mom should've taken you on girls' day before now. You coulda used the protection," Violet so bluntly puts it. "Now, instead of the shot, you're gonna have a doctor listen to your baby's heartbeat. The shit just got real, cousin."

"No shit," Willow says from the doorway, startling me.

"I'm going to install a screen door for you to smash into the wall so I'll hear you coming. This ghostly routine freaks my ass out," I say to my grinning daughter. Willow's proud and happy to have caught us unawares.

"Girls' day? Little late for that, Essie." Willow starts snickering, but stops when I glare at her. "Sorry," she mutters, coughing into her hand.

"Are you coming with us, too?" Violet skips over to her sister, tugging on her hand. "It sucked last time, just me and Mom. I didn't have anyone to grin and bear it while I got stuck."

Going as white as the ghost I just called her, Willow breathes out, "Last time?"

"Yeah, you didn't go with us. I was sad that you were so grown up you were going by yourself. I felt abandoned." Violet issues the patented Prynne pout.

One look from my oldest daughter's panicked face has my ass planting on the sofa. Willow's, "Mom?" draws tears to my eyes. "What… what happens if you miss a course? Aren't you supposed to start your period?"

Eyes closed, swallowing, with a deep breath, I release, "You'll share my appointment with me. Essie can go with the girls for their shots." Rising from the sofa, I walk across my living room as if treading through quicksand. "C'mon girls. Let's start our girls' day," I say, sounding chipper yet strained.

"What's wrong, Mom? Willow?" Violet sounds petrified.

"All's good," Essie steps in because Willow and I are incapable.

"Sure," Rae mutters, not sounding convinced. "I wouldn't call it '*good*'. More like a catastrophe. Fuck those laser treatments. I'm buying a hysterectomy. That will even protect me against immaculate conception."

...Forty-five horrific minutes later.

"Mom, this is not fucking funny!" Willow snarls at me.

Turning to face my daughter, laughter still spilling from my lips, as well as a stream of tears from my eyes, "Don't you know hysterical when you hear it? I. Am. Not. Amused."

Sitting next to me in Dr. Gilmore's office, Willow is surprisingly numb. "I never understood the definition of irony. I was always using it wrong. But now I know."

"But now you know." Laughing harder. "Now, I bet you wished you hadn't called Essie an irresponsible whore. Not that you are a whore. Just that you thought Essie being pregnant made her one."

"I'm not pregnant," Willow denies, voice breaking. "What do you find so funny?"

Still laughing manically. "I've got a joke for you. Ready?" I pause heavily. "A mother and daughter are sitting in their doctor's office, waiting for their piss to be tested. One could be a new mother and a grandmother at the age of fucking thirty-five. That, my daughter, is the definition of irony."

"I don't see why that is ironic," Willow mumbles, confused.

"Because I worked my entire life to give you a different life than the one I led." Gesturing around the doctor's office, "And yet, look where we are. Ironic."

"Like mother, like daughter," Willow whispers. Her tears finally make an appearance. "This isn't fair," she whimpers.

Agreeing with Willow, I reach over to take her hand, squeezing. "It's life. It's not fair. Life is in the driver's seat—we're merely its passengers."

"Mrs. Mason? Ms. Prynne?" Dr. Gilmore announces her arrival while staring at a sheet of paper within a folder. Willow and I share a terrified look as the doctor says, "I have your test results."

Thank you for reading **WIDOW**. Don't miss out on what's to come...

GOOD GIRL, Willow's coming-of-age tale.

WILDLY WEDDED WIFE, Rory & Bethany's novella.

WIDOW, Malcolm & Clover's journey.

WANTON, Opal & Ginny's tasty treat.

WARPED, Devon, Essie, Kieren, & Willow's future.

COMING SOON.

WOVEN, a novellas with surprising narrators.

WICKED, a novella showcasing Auggie & Tina's parents.

WAYWARD, Auggie, Isis, and Robin's angsty emotional roller coaster ride.

...and many more to come.

ACKNOWLEDGEMENTS

A lot of work goes into writing a novel, and it isn't just by the writer herself. **My parents:** for their unconditional support. **My readers**: thank you for reading my twisted words and spreading my books to the masses. For without you, no one would've ever heard of my stories. My readers are my lifeblood. A shout out to the members of the **M&M of Restraint Group on Facebook**: thanks for the endless entertainment and inspiration. **Wicked Reads**: (in all its incarnations) **Angela G.**, thank you for taking over and making Wicked Reads better than I could have done by myself. & thank you for helping promote my work and the work of other authors. Angela? Have I told you lately how much I appreciate you? A huge thank you to the **Wicked Writer's Betas** for keeping me grounded and encouraging me to keep trudging along when I get frustrated. Your thoughts and observations are invaluable. ((Hugs)) Beta readers: **Kris | Suz | Darcy | Sandy | Di | Angela | Diane | Jacki | Linsey | Alexis | Billie Jo | Tassie | Caroline | Judith | Jodi Lynn | Jodi |** Someday, I'd love to meet you all in real life– it would be the experience of a lifetime.

ABOUT THE AUTHOR

Erica Chilson does not write in the 3rd person, wanting her readers to *be* her characters. Therefore, writing a bio about herself, is uncomfortable in the extreme.

Born, raised, and here to stay, the Wicked Writer is a stump-jumper, a ridge-runner. Hailing from North Central Pennsylvania, directly on the New York State border; she loves the changes in seasons, the humid air, all the mountainous forest, and the gloomy atmosphere.

Introverted, but not socially awkward, Erica prides herself on thinking first and filtering her speech. There are days she doesn't speak at all. If it wasn't for the fact that she lives with her parents, giving her a sense of reality, she would be a hermit, where the delivery man finds her months after expiration.

Reading was an escape, a way to leave a not-so pleasant reality behind. Reading lent Erica the courage she gathered from the characters between the pages to long for a different life. Writing was an instrument of change, evolving Erica into the woman she is today– a better, more mature, more at peace thinker.

Erica has a wicked mind, one she pours out into her creations. Her filter doesn't allow all of it to erupt, much to her relief. Sarcastic, with a very dark, perverse sense of humor, Erica puts a bit of herself into every character she writes.

I love hearing from readers. If you would like more information on release dates, works in progress, teaser chapters, and random bits of madness, please visit my Facebook Fan Page: https://www.facebook.com/thewickedwriter my website: ericachilson.com or please contact me via email: wickedwriter.ericachilson@gmail.com
DEVIANTS ONLY, if you'd like to join Erica Chilson's closed Facebook group, M&M of Restraint: https://www.facebook.com/groups/MistressandMaster/